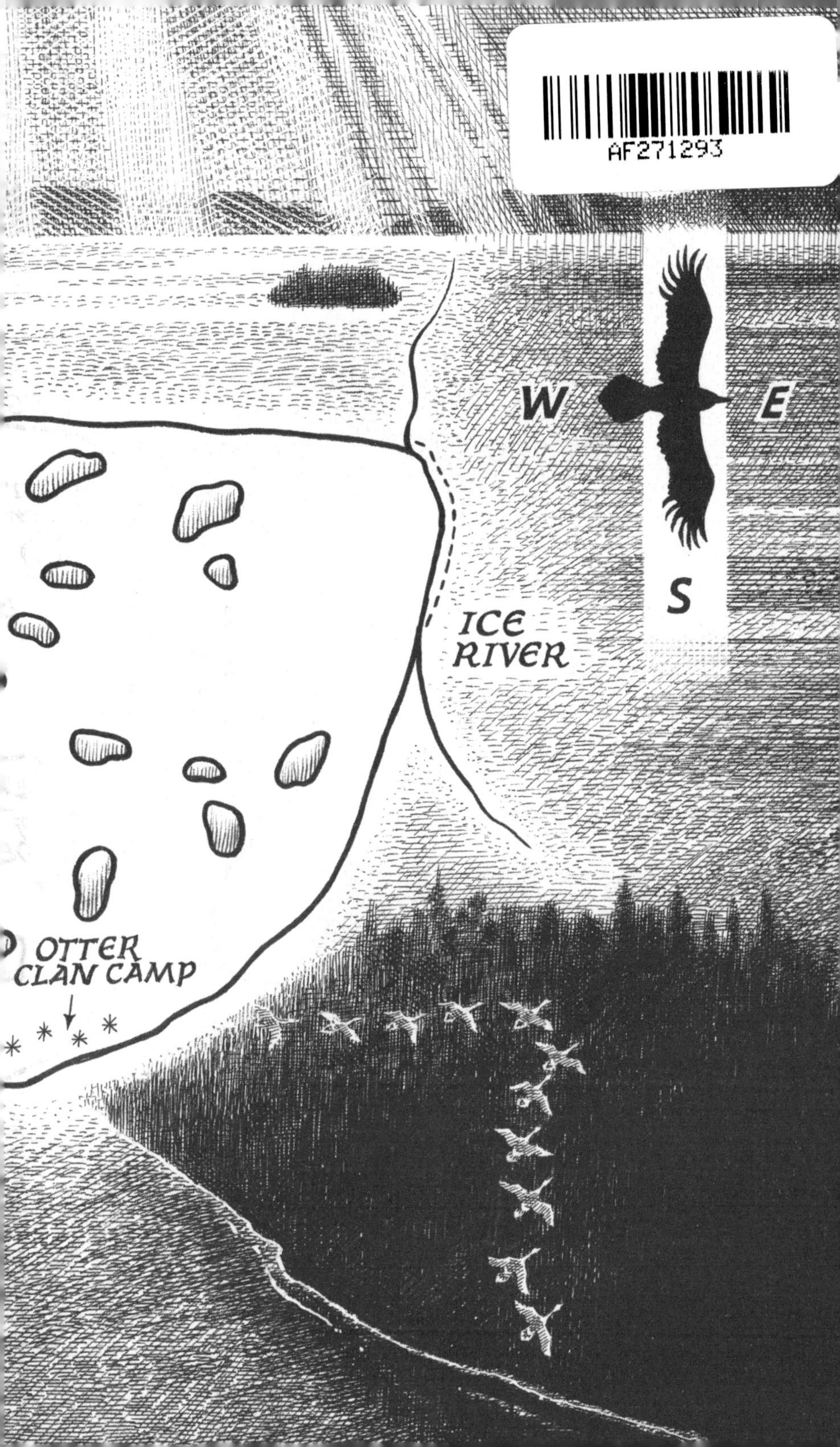

AF271293
W
E
S
ICE
RIVER
OTTER
CLAN CAMP

CHRONICLES of ANCIENT DARKNESS

OMNIBUS

3 books in 1

OUTCAST ✠ OATH BREAKER ✠ GHOST HUNTER

'His (Torak's) adventures in the *Chronicles of Ancient Darkness* series have been thrilling from the first page, and he has become a great hero for the new generation' *The Times*

'another triumph for Paver, a former London lawyer who has meticulously researched natural and ancient history to create this enthralling saga . . . It outclasses *Call of the Wild* and *The Jungle Book* in the pace of its plot, its sympathetically imagined characters . . . Paver's writing is richly sensual.' *Independent*

'stunning 6th and final episode, brings the bestselling 'The Chronicles of Ancient Darkness', which began so dramatically with *Wolf Brother* to a close. Now it is Torak's last adventure; he must travel up into the mountains and find the Mountain of Ghosts . . . Along with Wolf and Renn, Torak faces chilling danger on their journey as they fulfill their destiny.'
Julia Eccleshare, *lovereading4kids.com*

Also by Michelle Paver

Wolf Brother
Spirit Walker
Soul Eater

Dark Matter

Visit Michelle Paver's website at
www.michellepaver.com

and meet other readers of the
Chronicles of Ancient Darkness series
at the official worldwide fan site, www.torak.info

CHRONICLES of ANCIENT DARKNESS

OMNIBUS

OUTCAST ╪ OATH BREAKER ╪ GHOST HUNTER

MICHELLE PAVER

Orion
Children's Books

This omnibus edition first published in Great Britain in 2011
by Orion Children's Books
a division of the Orion Publishing Group Ltd
Orion House
5 Upper St Martin's Lane
London WC2H 9EA
An Hachette UK Company

1 3 5 7 9 10 8 6 4 2

Originally published in three separate volumes:
Outcast
First published in Great Britain in 2007
Oath Breaker
First published in Great Britain in 2008
Ghost Hunter
First published in Great Britain in 2009
All by Orion Children's Books

The Orion Publishing Group's policy is to use papers that are natural,
renewable and recyclable products and made from wood grown in
sustainable forests. The logging and manufacturing processes are expected
to conform to the environmental regulations of the country of origin.

A catalogue record for this book is available from the British Library

Printed in Great Britain by Clays Ltd, St Ives plc

ISBN 978 1 4440 0472 4

www.orionbooks.co.uk

CONTENTS

OUTCAST

ONE

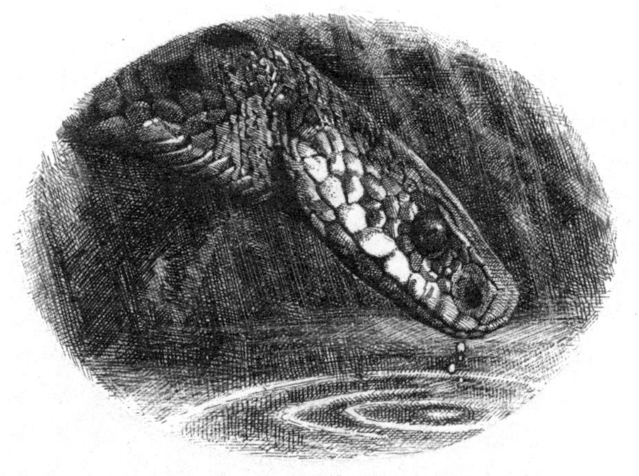

The viper glided down the riverbank and placed its sleek head on the water, and Torak stopped a few paces away to let it drink.

His arms ached from carrying the red deer antlers, so he set them aside and crouched in the bracken to watch. Snakes are wise, and know many secrets. Maybe this one would help him deal with his.

The viper drank with unhurried sips. Raising its head, it regarded Torak, flicking out its tongue to taste his scent. Then it coiled neatly back on itself and vanished into the ferns.

It had given him no sign.

But you don't *need* a sign, he told himself wearily. You know what to do. Just tell them. Soon as you get back to camp. Just say, 'Renn. Fin-Kedinn. Two moons ago, something happened. They held me down, they put a mark on my chest. And now . . .'

No. That wasn't any good. He could picture Renn's face. 'I'm your best friend – and you've been lying to me for *two whole moons!*'

He put his head in his hands.

After a while he heard rustling, and glanced up to see a reindeer on the opposite bank. It was standing on three legs, furiously scratching its budding antlers with one hind hoof. Sensing that Torak wasn't hunting, it went on scratching. The antlers were bleeding: the itch must be so bad that the only relief was to make them hurt.

That's what I should do, thought Torak. Cut it out. Make it hurt. In secret. Then no-one need ever know.

The trouble was, even if he could bring himself to do it, it wouldn't work. To get rid of the tattoo, he'd have to perform the proper rite. He'd learnt that from Renn, whom he'd approached in a roundabout way, using the zigzag tattoos on her wrists as an excuse.

'If you don't do the rite,' she'd told him, 'the marks just come back.'

'*They come back?*' Torak had been horrified.

'Of course. You can't see them, they're deep in the marrow. But they're still there.'

So that was the end of that, unless he could get her to tell him about the rite without revealing why he needed to know.

The reindeer gave an irritable shake and trotted off into the Forest; and Torak picked up the antlers and started back for camp. They were a lucky find, big enough for everyone in the clan to get a piece, and perfect for making fish-hooks and hammers for knapping flint. Fin-Kedinn would be pleased. Torak tried to fix his mind on that.

It didn't work. Until now, he hadn't understood how much a secret can set you apart. He thought about it all the time, even when he was hunting with Renn and Wolf.

It was early in the Moon of the Salmon Run, and a sharp east wind carried a strong smell of fish. As Torak made his way beneath the pines, his boots crunched on flakes of bark scattered by woodpeckers. To his left, the Green River chattered after its long imprisonment under the ice, while to his right, a rockface rose towards Broken Ridge. In places it was scarred, where the clans had hacked out the red slate which brings hunting luck. He heard the clink of stone on stone. Someone was quarrying.

That should be me, Torak told himself. I should be making a new axe. I should be doing things. 'This can't go on,' he said out loud.

'You're right,' said a voice. 'It can't.'

They were crouching on a ledge ten paces above him: four boys and two girls, glaring down. The Boar Clan wore their brown hair cut to shoulder length, with a fringe; tusks at their necks, stiff hide mantles across their shoulders. The Willows had wovenbark strips sewn in spirals on their jerkins, and three black leaves tattooed on their brows in a permanent frown. All were older than Torak. The boys had wispy beards, and beneath the girls' clan-tattoos, a short red bar showed that they'd had their first moon bleed.

They'd been quarrying: Torak saw stone dust on their buckskins. Just ahead of him, he spotted a tree-trunk ladder notched with footholds, which they'd propped against the rockface, to climb up to the ledge. But they were no longer interested in slate.

Torak stared back, hoping he didn't look scared. 'What do you want?' he said.

Aki, the Boar Clan Leader's son, jerked his head at the antlers. 'Those are mine. Put them down.'

'No they're not,' said Torak. 'I found them.' To remind them he had weapons, he hoisted his bow on his shoulder and touched the blue slate knife at his hip.

Aki wasn't impressed. 'They're mine.'

'Which means *you* stole them,' said a Willow girl.

'If that was true,' Torak told Aki, 'you'd have put your mark on them and I'd have left them alone.'

'I did. On the base. You rubbed it off.'

'Of course I didn't,' said Torak in disgust.

Then he saw what he should have seen before: a smudge of earthblood at the base of one antler, where a boar tusk had been drawn on. His ears burned. 'I didn't see it. And I didn't rub it off.'

'Then put them down and get out of here,' said a boy called Raut, who'd always struck Torak as fairer than most. Unlike Aki, who was spoiling for a fight.

Torak didn't feel like giving him one. 'All right,' he said briskly, 'I made a mistake. Didn't see the mark. They're yours.'

'What makes you think it's that easy?' said Aki.

Torak sighed. He'd come across Aki before. A bully: unsure if he was a leader, and desperate to prove it with his fists.

'You think you're special,' sneered Aki. 'Because Fin-Kedinn took you in, and you can talk to wolves and you're a spirit walker.' He raked his fingernails over the scant hairs on his chin, as if checking they were still there. 'Truth is, you only live with the Ravens because your own clan's never come near you. And Fin-Kedinn doesn't trust you enough to make you his foster son.'

Torak set his teeth.

Covertly, he looked about. The river was too cold to swim; besides, they had dugouts on the bank. That meant there was no point running upriver, either – or back the way he'd come, he'd be trapped in the fork where the Green River merged with the Axehandle. And no help within reach. Renn was at the Raven camp on the north bank, half a daywalk to the east; and Wolf had gone hunting in the night.

He set down the antlers. 'I said you can have them,' he told Aki. He started up the trail.

'Coward,' taunted Aki.

Torak ignored him.

A stone struck his temple. He turned on them. 'Now who's the coward? What's brave about six against one?'

Beneath his fringe, Aki's square face darkened. 'Then let's make it even: just you and me.' He whipped off his jerkin to reveal a meaty chest covered in reddish fuzz.

Torak froze.

'What's the matter?' sniggered a Boar girl. 'Scared?'

'No,' said Torak. But he was. He'd forgotten the Boar Clan custom of stripping to the waist for a fight. He couldn't do that, or they'd see the mark.

'Get ready to fight,' snarled Aki, making his way down the ladder.

'No,' said Torak.

Another stone whistled towards him. He caught it and threw it back, and the Boar girl yelped and clutched a bleeding shin.

Aki had nearly reached the bottom of the ladder, his friends swarming after him like ants on a honey trail.

Grabbing one of the antlers, Torak ducked behind a pine, hooked the tines in the nearest branch, and swung into the tree.

'We've got him!' shouted Aki.

No you haven't, thought Torak. He'd chosen this tree because it grew nearest the rockface, and now he crawled along a branch and onto the ledge they'd just left. It was littered with quartz saws and grindstones, a small fire, and an elkhide pail of pine-pitch, planted in hot ash to keep it runny. Above him the slope was less steep, with enough juniper scrub to make it climbable.

Throwing stones and dodging theirs, he raced to the ladder and gave it a push. It didn't budge. It was lashed to the ledge with rawhide ropes, no time to cut it free. He did the only thing he could to stop them coming after him. He seized the pail and emptied it down the ladder.

There was an outraged roar – and Torak dropped the pail in astonishment. Aki was faster than he looked – he'd nearly reached the ledge. Without meaning to, Torak had just dumped hot pine-pitch all over him.

Bellowing like a stuck boar, Aki slid down the ladder.

Torak clawed at juniper bushes and hauled himself towards the ridge.

He ran north-east through the trees, and their cries faded. He *hated* running away. But better be called a coward than get found out.

After a while the slope became gentler, and he was able to skitter down it and make his way to the river again, keeping off the clan trail and sticking to the wolf trails which he could find almost without thinking. Once he reached the ford, he could get across and double back to the Raven camp. There'd be trouble, but Fin-Kedinn would be on his side.

In a willow thicket on the bank, he came to a halt, the breath sawing in his chest. Around him the trees were still waking from their long winter sleep. Bees bumped about among the catkins, and a squirrel dozed in a patch of sunlight, its tail wrapped around the branch. In the shallows, a jay was taking a bath. No-one was coming. The Forest would have warned him.

Shaky with relief, he leaned against a tree-trunk.

His hand moved to the neck of his jerkin and touched the tattoo on his breastbone. The Viper Mage hissed in his mind. *'This mark will be like the harpoon head beneath the skin of the seal. One twitch, and it will draw you, no matter how hard you struggle. For now you are one of us . . .'*

'I'm not one of you,' muttered Torak. 'I'm *not*!'

But as he'd lain awake through the storm-tossed nights of winter, he'd felt the mark burning his skin. He dreaded to think what evil it might do. What evil it might make *him* do.

Somewhere to the south, Wolf howled. He'd caught a hare, and was singing his happiness to the Forest, his pack-brother and anyone else who was listening.

Hearing Wolf's voice lightened Torak's spirits. Wolf didn't seem to mind his tattoo. Nor did the Forest. It knew, but it hadn't cast him out.

The jay flew up, scattering droplets, and for a moment, Torak followed its flight. Then he pushed himself off the tree and began to run. He left the thicket – and Aki head-butted him in the chest and sent him sprawling.

The Boar Clan boy was almost unrecognisable. His reddened eyes glared from a skull that was black and slimy with pitch, and he stank of pine-blood and rage. 'You made a fool of me!' he shouted. 'In front of everyone, you made a fool of me!'

Struggling to his feet, Torak scrambled backwards. 'I didn't do it on purpose! I didn't know you were there!'

'Liar!' Aki swung his axe at Torak's shins.

Torak jumped out of the way, then side-stepped and kicked Aki's axe-hand. Aki dropped the axe. He drew his knife. Torak drew his too, and they circled one another.

Torak's heart hammered against his ribs as he tried to remember every fighting trick Fa and Fin-Kedinn had taught him.

Without warning, Aki lunged. He mistimed it by a heartbeat. Torak kicked him in the belly, then punched him hard in the throat. Choking, Aki went down, grabbing at Torak's jerkin. The throat-lacing ripped – and Aki saw it. The mark on Torak's chest.

Time stretched.

Aki released him and staggered back.

Torak's legs wouldn't move.

Aki glanced from the mark to Torak's face. Beneath the pine-pitch, his features were blank with shock.

He recovered fast. He pointed one finger at Torak, aiming straight between the eyes. He made a sideways cut of the hand: a sign Torak had never seen before.

Then he turned and ran.

Aki must have regained his dugout and paddled faster than a leaping salmon, because when Torak finally reached the Raven camp by mid-afternoon, the Boar Clan boy had got there first. Torak knew at once from the stillness of the Ravens as he ran into the clearing.

The only sounds were the creak of the drying racks and the murmur of the river. Thull and his mate Luta, whose shelter Torak shared, stared at him as if he were a stranger. Only their son Dari, seven summers old and Torak's devoted follower, rushed to greet him. He was yanked back by his father.

Renn burst from a reindeer-hide shelter, her dark-red hair flying, her face flushed with indignation. 'Torak, at last! It's all a mistake! I've told them it isn't true!'

Behind her, Aki emerged with his father, the Boar Clan Leader, and Fin-Kedinn. The Raven Leader's face was grim, and he leaned on his staff as he crossed the clearing; but when he spoke it was in the same quiet voice as always. 'I've vouched for you, Torak. I've told them this can't be so.'

They had such such faith in him. He couldn't bear it.

The Boar Clan Leader glared at Fin-Kedinn. 'Are you calling my son a liar?' He was a bigger version of Aki: the same square face and ready fists.

'Not a liar,' replied Fin-Kedinn. 'Simply mistaken.'

The Boar Clan Leader bridled.

'I've told you,' said Fin-Kedinn, 'the boy is no Soul-Eater. And he can prove it. Torak, take off your jerkin.'

'*What?*' Renn turned on her uncle. 'But you can't even *think* –'

Fin-Kedinn silenced her with a glance. Then to Torak, 'Quickly now, let's clear this up.'

Torak looked at the faces around him. These people had taken him in when his father was killed. He'd lived with them for nearly two summers. They had begun to accept him. Now he was going to end that.

Slowly he took off his quiver and bow and laid them on the ground. He untied his belt. There was a ringing in his ears. His fingers belonged to someone else.

He said a prayer to the Forest – and pulled his jerkin over his head.

Renn's mouth opened, but no sound came.

Fin-Kedinn's hand tightened on his staff.

'I told you,' cried Aki. 'The three-pronged fork, I *told* you! He's a Soul-Eater!'

Two

'Why didn't you tell me?' said Fin-Kedinn in the voice that made grown men blench.

'I wanted to,' said Torak. 'But I . . .'

'But you what?'

Torak hung his head.

They were alone in the clearing. The Boar Clan Leader and his son had left to gather their people, and messengers had been sent to clans camped within reach. Fin-Kedinn – who'd been scraping a reindeer skin before Aki burst in – had returned to his work: a sign to the others to get on with theirs and leave Torak to him. Some had gone hunting, or to spear fish upriver. There was no sign of Renn.

The Raven camp was eerily calm. Torak saw a deerhide canoe drawn up on the bank; a wovenbark net draped over a juniper bush. Around him the birch trees were a brilliant green, the undergrowth bright with blue anemones, yellow celandine and silver fish-scales. Nothing to show that a storm had broken over his head.

He watched Fin-Kedinn fling the hide over a log and stretch it taut. The veins on the Raven Leader's forearms bulged, and his movements – usually so measured – were savage. 'If you'd told me. We could have found a way.'

'I thought I could get rid of it without you knowing.' Torak realized how that sounded: covering one lie with another.

Fin-Kedinn took a deer's rib-bone and started scraping fat from the hide with short, vicious strokes. 'You brought that evil mark into my clan.'

'I didn't mean to! Fin-Kedinn, you've got to believe me! I tried to fight, but they were too many!'

The Raven Leader flung down the scraper. 'But *you* sought them out! *You* got too close!'

'I had to! They'd taken Wolf!'

'Ah, there's always a reason!' The force of his anger made Torak step back. 'You're just like your father! I warned him not to join them, but he wouldn't listen. He said they meant to do good, he went on calling them the Healers even after they'd turned evil.' He broke off. 'In the end it killed him. And it killed your mother.'

Torak saw the deep lines at the sides of his mouth, the pain in the fierce blue eyes. This was his fault. He had hurt this man whom he'd come to love.

The Raven Leader went back to work. Torak smelt the stink of dead reindeer, and watched the bloody fat bubbling over the edge of the rib-bone. He pictured a knife slicing into his own flesh to rid it of the Soul-Eater tattoo. 'I'll cut it out,' he said. 'Renn says there's a rite.'

'Which can only be done when the moon is full. We're in the moon's dark. You've run out of time.'

A gust of wind brought the smell of rain, and Torak shivered. 'Fin-Kedinn. I'm not a Soul-Eater. You know this.'

The scraper stilled. 'But how will you prove it?' He met Torak's eyes, and his own were filled with a sorrow that was even more frightening than his anger. 'Don't you understand, Torak? It doesn't matter what *I* believe. It's everyone else you've got to convince. This is out of my hands. Only your own clan can vouch for you now.'

Torak's heart sank. He was Wolf Clan, but his father had kept him apart from them, and he'd never even seen the rest of his clan. Few had. The Wolf Clan had been deeply ashamed when its Mage – Torak's father – turned Soul-Eater. Since then, it had stayed hidden, becoming as shadowy and elusive as its clan-creature.

Torak touched the tattered scrap of wolf fur sewn to his jerkin. Fa had prepared it for him, so it was precious. It was also his only link with his clan. 'How do I find them?' he said.

'You don't,' said Fin-Kedinn. 'Not if they don't want to be found.'

'But what if they don't come? If they don't vouch for me –'

'Then I'll have no choice. I'll have to obey clan law and cast you out.'

The wind strengthened, and the birch trees lifted their branches – as if Torak was already outcast, and they feared to touch him.

'Do you understand what it means,' said Fin-Kedinn, 'to be outcast?'

Torak shook his head.

'It means you would be as one dead. Cut off from everyone. Hunted like prey. No-one could help you. Not me. Not Renn. We couldn't talk to you, give you food. If we did, we'd be outcast too. If we saw you in the Forest, we'd have to kill you.'

Torak went cold. 'But I didn't *do* anything!'

'It's the law,' said Fin-Kedinn. 'Many winters ago, after the great fire which scattered the Soul-Eaters, the clan elders made this law to stop them coming back. To stop others joining them.'

The first spots of rain pattered onto the reindeer hide. 'Go to your shelter,' said the Raven Leader without looking up.

'But Fin-Kedinn – '

'Go. The clans will gather. The elders will decide.'

Torak swallowed. 'What about Thull and Luta and Dari? It's their shelter too.'

'They'll build another. From now on, don't talk to anyone. Stay in the shelter. Wait for the clans to decide.'

'How long will that be?'

'As long as it takes. And Torak . . . Don't try to escape. You'll only make it worse.'

Torak stared at him. 'How could it be worse?'

'It can always get worse,' said the Raven Leader.

ᚳᚠ

Torak learned the truth of that two days later, when Renn finally came to see him.

Until then, he hadn't caught a glimpse of her. His shelter faced away from camp, so he couldn't see much except by peering through gaps in the hides, or when he went to the midden. The rest of the time he sat and watched the small fire before the opening, and listened to the clans gather.

Late on the second day, Renn stalked up to the shelter. Her face was pale, the blue-black bars of her clan-tattoos livid on her cheekbones. 'You should have told me,' she said stonily.

'I know.'

'You should've *told* me!' She kicked the doorpost, and the shelter shook.

'I thought I could get rid of it in secret.'

Squatting by the fire, she glowered at the embers. 'You lied to me for two whole moons. And don't tell me that keeping silent isn't lying, because it is!'

'I know. I'm sorry.'

She didn't reply. Over the winter, she'd developed a tiny freckle at the corner of her mouth, and he'd teased her, asking if it was a birch seed and why didn't she wipe it off. He couldn't imagine teasing her now. He'd never felt so bad.

'Renn,' he said. 'You've got to believe me. I'm not a Soul-Eater.'

'Well of course you're not!'

He drew a breath. 'So – can you forgive me?'

She picked at a scab on her elbow. Then she gave a curt nod.

Relief flooded through him. 'I didn't think you would.'

She went on picking at the scab. 'We've all got secrets, Torak.'

'Not like this.'

'No,' she said in an odd voice. 'Not like this.'

Then she surprised him by asking which of the Soul-Eaters had put the mark on his chest.

' – It was Seshru. Why?'

She ripped off the scab and dug her fingernail into the rawness underneath. 'Where were the others?'

He swallowed. 'Thiazzi held me down. The Bat Mage watched. Eostra . . .' He shuddered as he recalled the ghastly wooden mask of the Eagle Owl Mage. 'I didn't see her. But there was an owl, watching from an ice hill . . .'

Suddenly he was back in the freezing dark of the Far North. He felt the powerful grip of the Oak Mage. He saw the hunched bulk of the Bat Mage standing guard, and caught the orange glare of the greatest of owls. Then Seshru the Viper Mage was blotting out the stars, and he was staring up into eyes the deep blue of the sky before middle-night. He watched her perfect mouth pronouncing his fate as she drove the bone needle again and again into his skin and smeared him with the blood of murdered hunters. *This mark will be like the harpoon head beneath the skin of the seal. One twitch and it will draw you . . .*

'Torak?' said Renn.

He was back in the shelter.

'What are you going to do?'

'What I should have done in the beginning. I'm going to cut it out. Tell me how to do the rite.'

'No,' she said without hesitation.

'Renn. You've got to.'

'No! You couldn't do it on your own, you don't know Magecraft.'

'I've got to try.'

'Yes, and I'll help you.'

'No. If you helped me, you'd be outcast too.'

'I don't care.'

'Well I do.'

Renn pressed her lips together. She could be incredibly stubborn.

So could he. 'Renn. Listen to me. Not long ago, they took Wolf – because of me. He was nearly killed – because of me. That's why I haven't howled for him now, because he'd only try to help, and get hurt. If you got hurt because of me . . . ' He stopped. 'You've got to swear – swear on your bow and your three souls – that if they cast me out, you won't try to help.'

A noise in the clearing. Torak saw the bent figure of the Raven Mage hobbling towards them.

'Renn!' he said in an urgent whisper. 'Do this for me! Swear!'

Renn raised her head, and in her dark eyes, two tiny flames leapt. 'No,' she said.

'The clans have gathered,' said Saeunn in her raven's croak. 'The elders have decided. Renn. Leave.'

Renn lifted her chin.

'Leave.'

Defiantly, Renn turned to Torak. 'I meant what I said.' Then she was gone.

The Raven Mage told Torak to gather his things, and waited at the mouth of the shelter, clutching her staff in one shrivelled claw. Her sunken eyes watched him without pity. A life spent peering into the world of the spirits had detached her from the feelings of the living.

'Not the sleeping-sack,' she rasped.

'Why not?' said Torak.

'The outcast shall be as one dead.'

Torak's belly turned over. Until now, he'd clung to a faint hope that Fin-Kedinn might be able to save him.

The rain came, pattering onto the hide roof and making the fire smoke. He picked up the last of his gear and glanced around. Often, he'd hated this shelter. He'd never got used to the Raven way of staying in the same camp for three or four moons, instead of moving on every few days, as he'd done with Fa. Now he couldn't imagine leaving it and never coming back.

'It is time,' said Saeunn.

He followed her into the clearing.

The clans were gathered about a huge long-fire. It was still light, but the rain clouds turned it to dusk. Torak was glad of the rain. People would think he was shivering with cold, not fear.

The crowd parted to let them through, and he took in a blur of firelit faces. Raven. Willow. Viper. Boar. But no Mountain or Ice clans, and none from the Deep Forest or the Sea. This was a matter for the Open Forest. He wondered when his kinsman in the Seal Clan would get to hear of what had happened. What would Bale think?

Aki had planted himself at the front of the throng. He'd scrubbed his skin clean of pine-pitch, but it had gone a blotchy red, and he'd had to cut his hair short, like boar bristles. He wore two throwing-axes in his belt, a birch-bark horn at his hip, and a triumphant expression. Clearly he would lose no time in hunting the outcast.

Rain hissed on the fire and dripped off the trees that watched at the edge of the clearing. Rain trickled down Renn's cheeks like tears. But it couldn't be tears, because Renn never cried.

Fin-Kedinn was waiting by the fire with the other clan elders. His face was impassive. He didn't look at Torak.

Saeunn hobbled to Fin-Kedinn's side, and addressed the clans. 'I am the oldest of the clans of the Open Forest,' she declared. 'I speak for them all.' She paused. 'The boy bears the mark of the Soul-Eater. The law is clear. He must be cast out.'

'Ah.' A sigh rose from the crowd.

Torak's knees sagged.

'Wait!' A man's voice called from the edge of the clearing.

All heads turned.

Torak saw a tall figure step into the firelight. Rain plastered his long dark hair to his skull, except for two shaven strips at the temples. His eyes had an odd yellow gleam, but his high-boned face seemed strangely familiar.

Then Torak saw the clan-tattoos, and the back of his neck prickled. Two dotted lines on the cheekbones. A strip of sodden grey fur on the left side of his parka.

Aki had seen it too. 'No!' he cried. 'You can't stop it now, the elders have spoken!'

The tall man stared at Aki – and the Boar Clan boy drew back, abashed.

'Who are you?' said Torak.

The tall man turned and fixed his gaze on him. 'I am Maheegun. Leader of the Wolf Clan.'

THREE

T hey emerged from the trees as soundlessly as a wolf pack.

Women, men and children: plainly clad in reindeer hide to blend into the Forest. An amulet of raw amber gleamed at every throat, and like Maheegun, their temples were shaven and stained with red ochre. As they moved into the firelight, Torak saw that the whites of their eyes were yellow. Like wolves.

The Leader seemed to recognize Fin-Kedinn, as he gave a distant nod; but he neither smiled, nor placed his fists on his breast in friendship. Torak was reminded of a lead wolf loftily assessing a stranger.

The rest of the Wolf Clan gave the same remote half-bow, except for a woman who smiled at Fin-Kedinn in a way that briefly made her young again. For answer, the

Raven Leader put his hand on his heart and bowed to her. Torak recalled that long ago, Fin-Kedinn had been fostered with the Wolf Clan.

'Your message stone was found,' Maheegun told the Raven Leader. 'Why did you summon us? And to such a gathering.'

'I needed you to come,' Fin-Kedinn calmly replied.

Maheegun drew himself up to his full height and they stared at each other. The Wolf Leader was the first to look away. His yellow gaze flicked to Torak's clan-creature skin, then back to Fin-Kedinn. 'Who is this?'

'The son of the Wolf Mage.'

The Wolves gasped. Some grasped their amulets, others made the sign of the hand at Torak, as if warding off evil.

'The one you speak of,' said Maheegun, 'was the greatest Mage we ever had. He alone – for a few heartbeats – managed to become wolf. But he turned Soul-Eater.' He touched his temple. 'Because of him, we bear the mark of shame.'

This was too much for Torak. 'What shame?' he cried. 'My father shattered the fire-opal! He broke up the Soul-Eaters! Wasn't that enough to make amends?'

Maheegun ignored him. 'Again, Fin-Kedinn, I say: why did you summon us?'

Swiftly, Fin-Kedinn told how Torak had come to live with the Ravens, and why he needed his clan to vouch for him now. As proof of Torak's identity, he held up Torak's mother's medicine horn and the blue slate knife which had belonged to his father.

The Wolf Leader listened in silence; but when Fin-Kedinn offered him the objects, he recoiled. 'Keep them away, they're unclean!'

'No they're not!' said Torak. 'Fa gave them to me when he was dying!'

'Torak, enough,' warned Fin-Kedinn.

The woman who'd smiled came forwards. 'Maheegun,' she said, 'we don't need proof. You have only to look at the boy's face. He is the son of the Wolf Mage.'

A shiver ran through her clan. At the corner of his vision, Torak saw Renn raise her fist in triumph.

'Yes,' said Maheegun. 'And yet – I cannot vouch for him.'

Torak's jaw dropped.

Even Fin-Kedinn seemed shaken. 'But you must. He's your kinsman.' When the Wolf Leader did not reply, he said, 'Maheegun, I know this boy. He was marked against his will, he's no Soul-Eater.'

Maheegun frowned. 'You misunderstand, this is not my choice. Did I say that I *will* not vouch for him? No. I said I *can* not. This boy is the son of the Wolf Mage, yes. But he is *not* Wolf Clan!'

For a moment, nobody spoke.

'Of course I'm Wolf Clan!' shouted Torak. 'My mother named my clan when I was born, just like everybody else. And Fa gave me my clan-tattoos when I was seven!'

'No,' said Maheegun.

Drawing close to Torak, he put out his hand and touched Torak's cheek with his forefinger.

Torak flinched. He caught the Leader's musty smell of wet reindeer hide. He felt the calloused finger trace the old scar that cut across the clan-tattoo on his left cheek.

'Not Wolf Clan,' murmured Maheegun, and his yellow eyes pierced Torak's. '*Clanless . . .*'

There was a stunned silence. Then everyone spoke at once.

'What are you talking about?' cried Torak. 'I'm Wolf Clan! I've been Wolf Clan since the night I was born!'

'It's only a scar,' protested Fin-Kedinn, 'it means nothing.'

'How could he be clanless?' exclaimed Renn. 'Nobody's clanless! It isn't possible!'

'Maheegun is right,' rasped Saeunn.

All heads turned to her.

'The scar is no accident,' she declared. 'The boy's father made it on purpose, to show that he is not truly Wolf.'

'That's not true!' Torak burst out. 'Besides, how could you even know?'

'He told me,' said the Raven Mage. 'He sought me out at the clan meet by the Sea.' Her flinty gaze caught his. 'You know this. You were there.'

'It isn't true,' whispered Torak. But in that instant, he knew it was.

He was seven summers old, and Fa had left him with a gaggle of jeering children while he went off to speak to someone, he wouldn't say who. Torak had never seen so many people. He'd been frightened and excited and proud of his new clan-tattoos, although it was annoying that Fa had covered them up with bearberry juice, saying they needed a disguise, making a game of it.

The rain had stopped, and the trees dripped sadly. *Clanless*, they murmured.

'How could this be?' said Fin-Kedinn.

'Only his mother knew the answer,' Saeunn replied. 'She declared him clanless before she died.' Suddenly, she struck the earth with her staff. 'But this is of no concern to us! It alters nothing! The boy has no clan to vouch for him. By law, he must be cast out.'

'*No!*' shouted Renn. 'I don't *care* if he's clanless! This isn't *fair!*'

She ran into the middle of the clearing. Her wet hair clung to her neck in little red snakes, and her face was fierce. Torak thought she looked older than her thirteen summers, and beautiful.

Saeunn opened her mouth to silence her, but Fin-Kedinn raised his palm to let her speak.

'You all know Torak,' began Renn, fixing them with her gaze. 'You do, Thull. And you, Luta, and Sialot and Poi and Etan . . . ' One by one, she named the Ravens. Then she named those in the other clans whom Torak had met over the past two summers. 'You all know what he's done for us. He destroyed the bear. He rid the Forest of the sickness. This winter we would have been overrun by demons if it hadn't been for him.'

She paused to make them think about that. 'Yes, he did wrong. He hid the Soul-Eater tattoo when he should have told us. But he doesn't deserve to be cast out! How can you stand by and let this happen? Where's the *justice* in it?'

Fin-Kedinn ran his hand over his dark-red beard. Doubt crept into the faces of some of the watchers. But there was no swaying Saeunn. Again she struck the earth with her staff. 'Clan law *must* be upheld! The wrongdoer *must* be cast out!' She rounded on Renn. 'And let there be no doubt, if anyone dares help him, they too will be cast out!'

Renn glared at Saeunn in silent rebellion, but Torak caught her eye and shook his head. *Don't. You'll only make it worse.*

Afterwards, he could never remember much of the rite of casting out, except for fragments, like flashes of lightning in a storm.

Renn looking on with her fists clenched and her shoulders up around her ears.

Aki stroking his axe.

Luta swallowing tears as she offered the basket of river clay, for all to mark their cheeks in mourning.

'*The outcast shall be as one dead*,' intoned Saeunn.

One by one, each of the Ravens took a piece of Torak's gear and destroyed it, then purified their hands with a spruce bough, which they threw on the fire – just as they would have done if he'd actually died.

Thull took Torak's fishing spear and buried it under the trees.

Luta laid his cooking-skin on the fire.

Dari did the same with his auroch-horn spoon.

Etan stamped on his birch-bark drinking cup.

Sialot and Poi took his arrows and snapped them in two.

Others took his waterskin and his seal-hide winter clothing – which he'd outgrown and had been saving for bedding – and burnt it.

Finally, Renn laid his medicine pouch gently on the embers. She was the only one to look him in the eye. Torak knew she would have said sorry if she could.

As the clearing filled with the bitter stink of burning hide, Saeunn made Torak lie on his back, and tattooed his forehead with the mark of the outcast: a small black ring, like a Death Mark.

At last he stood alone, with nothing but his bow, three arrows, his knife, medicine horn and tinder pouch. All had been daubed with red ochre. As one who is dead.

So far, Fin-Kedinn had taken no part in the rite, but now he walked towards Torak. His hand shook slightly as he took his knife from its sheath.

Torak braced himself.

It hurt more than he could have imagined. Without a word, the Raven Leader cut the clan-creature skin from Torak's jerkin, and placed the tattered wolf fur on the fire.

Torak bit his lower lip as he watched the fur blacken and smoke.

'The outcast has until dawn to get away,' said Fin-Kedinn. His voice was steady, but the glitter in his eyes betrayed what this was costing him. 'Until then, he may pass freely in the Forest. After that, anyone who sees him must kill him.' He paused. Then he made the sideways cut of the palm, which meant outcast. 'It is done.'

Torak stared at the fire, where the last trace of the boy he had been – Torak of the Wolf Clan – blazed, collapsed in a heap of glowing ash, and was blown to nothingness by the wind.

Behind him, a murmur ran through the crowd. He turned, and was startled to see the watchers parting to let someone through. He saw Maheegun place a hand on his breast and bow low to the newcomer. He saw the rest of the Wolf Clan do the same.

Then he realized why.

A great grey wolf padded into the clearing. Raindrops beaded his silver fur, and his eyes were amber, like sunlight in clear water.

Dogs fled. People drew back. All except Renn, who gave Torak a defiant nod.

Torak knelt as Wolf padded towards him.

There were times when Wolf would have leapt at Torak and given him an ecstatic welcome, waggling his paws and grunt-whining as he licked his nose and smothered him in wolf kisses. This wasn't one of them. Tonight Wolf was the guide, his eyes alight with the mysterious certainty which came to him at times.

They touched noses, and Torak's gaze briefly grazed Wolf's in greeting. *Pack-brother*, he said in wolf talk.

He saw Maheegun stiffen. *Yes*, he told the Wolf Leader

silently. *I may not be Wolf Clan, but I can do what you cannot. I can talk wolf.*

He rose to his feet, and together, he and Wolf passed through the crowd to the edge of the clearing. Then Torak turned for one last look at the people who had cast him out.

'I may be outcast,' he told them, 'and clanless, but I'm no Soul-Eater. And I will find a way to prove it!'

It was a dank, chill night, and Torak ran through the Forest with Wolf running tirelessly beside him. They didn't stop to rest: without a sleeping-sack, Torak would have frozen. Better to keep going. That way, too, it was harder to think.

The sky was beginning to turn grey when Wolf halted: ears pricked, hackles raised. 'Uff!' he barked softly. *Danger!*

Soon afterwards, Torak heard it too. Birch-bark horns in the distance. The baying of dogs.

His hand tightened on the hilt of his knife.

Aki hadn't wasted any time.

FOUR

Wolf heard the dogs baying, and flicked one ear in scorn. They couldn't catch him!

But they might catch Tall Tailless.

As always, his pack-brother ran on his hind legs, which made him piteously slow: Wolf had to keep stopping to let him catch up. And because he couldn't smell or hear very much, he would never get away from the dogs if it weren't for Wolf.

But he made up for it by being so clever. Sometimes he was even cleverer than a normal wolf. Earlier, he'd hidden his scent by swimming through a Fast Wet. Then he'd woken a Bright Beast-that-Bites Hot and smeared ash on his face, paws and overpelt. Wolf didn't like that because it made him sneeze, but he understood why it had to be done.

He just wished Tall Tailless were faster.

With the wind behind them, they wound through the trees, following the trails which wolves made long ago when the Forest was young. The baying faded, and Wolf raised his tail to tell his pack-brother that the pursuers were far behind.

They kept going.

The ground became stony. They climbed a rise where watchful pines whispered encouragement. Tall Tailless slipped, scattering pebbles which hit Wolf on the nose. Wolf moved past him – then realized he'd gone too far and fell behind, because Tall Tailless was the lead wolf.

Tall Tailless pulled off his beaver-hide overpaws and climbed on in his bare pads. Wolf had often seen him do this, but he still found it disturbing. And Tall Tailless had such strange paws! The toes of his hindpaws were stubby and useless, while his front toes were very long and good at gripping. Wolf watched in admiration as his pack-brother used them to grab juniper branches and haul himself up the slope.

Suddenly, Tall Tailless disappeared.

Wolf's pelt tightened with alarm.

Then he saw that his pack-brother had found a Den. It was hidden behind the junipers, and it smelt of pine marten and hawk. Wolf gave a disapproving bark. *Not here!* During the Great Cold, he'd been trapped by the bad taillesses in a Den like this one.

Tall Tailless stayed on all fours, panting. If he'd had a tail, it would have drooped. If only he didn't need so many rests!

Then Wolf remembered when he was a cub, and needed lots of rests himself, and Tall Tailless had carried him in his forepaws.

Feeling bad, Wolf rubbed against his pack-brother and licked his ear. Tall Tailless was shaking. Wolf smelt pain and anger, chewed up with loneliness and fear.

Why was this happening? Wolf didn't understand. Many lopes away, the dogs were angry because they couldn't find the scent. *Where! Where!* they yapped. The wind carried the smell of their anger, and that of the young male tailless from the pack which smelt of boar. But *why* were they hunting Tall Tailless? And why had he left the raven pack? Sometimes a young wolf leaves his pack to start one of his own, but this didn't feel like that. This felt wrong.

The lead wolf of the raven pack had spoken harshly in tailless talk. He'd taken his great claw and torn the wolf fur from Tall Tailless' overpelt: the wolf fur that had been part of Tall Tailless since Wolf first knew him. The lead wolf had done this terrible thing – but underneath, Wolf had sensed his biting sorrow.

The pack-sister puzzled Wolf even more. She hadn't tried to stop the pack leader, and she hadn't come with Tall Tailless.

What did it mean?

Down in the valley, the dogs were casting for the scent. His pack-brother couldn't hear them yet, but Wolf's fur prickled.

What is it? Tall Tailless asked with his eyes.

Wolf glanced at the beloved, furless face. Tall Tailless couldn't lope much further. Wolf had to make sure that the dogs didn't find him.

Grunt-whining softly, he nudged his pack-brother under the chin. *I'm sorry, I must leave. Don't follow.* Then he was out of the Den, racing down the slope.

He flew over the rocks and splashed through the Fast

Wet, thrusting it aside with his big paws. Scrambling up the bank, he shook himself dry and set off again. It was good to run freely, without waiting for Tall Tailless, and he felt no fear of the dogs. Compared to a wolf, dogs are like cubs.

As he ran, he noticed things in the Forest which troubled him. A viper gliding up-Wet with her head held high. An owl feather caught in bracken. An oak tree whispering secrets to its vast and ancient pack. It reminded him of the bad taillesses who'd kept him tied up in the tiny stone Den.

'*Where! Where!*' yelped the dogs.

Wolf forgot the bad taillesses and slowed to a walk.

He reached the valley bottom, and a tangle of scent trails. Through the trees, he saw the young male from the boar pack, clutching a great claw in his forepaw and stinking of blood-hunger. In the other paw he held a scrap of silver hide which smelt of fish-dog and Tall Tailless. Wolf recognized this as a scrap of Tall Tailless' old overpelt.

One of the dogs sniffed the silver pelt to remind herself of the scent.

Now Wolf understood. The pelt was helping the dogs find his pack-brother. He must take it. Then they would chase him, and he would lead them away from Tall Tailless.

Wolf's claws tightened with excitement. He felt the power in his shoulders and haunches, and knew with a fierce joy that he could lope faster than the fastest dog.

Placing his pads with care, he crept forwards.

FIVE

Asmell of earth and decay clogged Torak's nostrils. The cramped little cave reminded him of the Raven bone-grounds.

Don't think about that. Think about staying alive.

The clamour of dogs had faded. Whatever Wolf had done, it seemed to have worked, but Torak wished he would return. He told himself that Wolf would find him when he was ready.

Forcing his stiff legs to move, he crawled out and started up the slope. The rocks were slippery with rain. He kept his boots off till his feet grew numb.

His plan had been to set a false trail north from the Raven camp, then double back and make for the valleys to the south, where he'd lived with Fa. Instead, Aki had forced him into a huge loop up and down the Green River.

He was now somewhere on Broken Ridge, not far from where he'd found the red deer antlers.

His sides ached, and on his forehead the new tattoo throbbed. He found a willow tree, muttered a quick apology, and peeled off a slip of bast. Having chewed it, he smeared the stinging pulp on the wound; then cut a strip of buckskin from his jerkin and tied it round as a headband. It would keep the medicine in place, and hide the outcast tattoo.

With a jolt, he remembered that he'd used the same medicine on the night Fa was killed. For a moment, it seemed as if everything that had happened since – finding Wolf, meeting Renn and Fin-Kedinn – as if none of that had been real. Here he was alone again, and on the run.

Before him the ground fell away into dense woods of oak, beech and pine. He caught the distant glint of the Axehandle. Many canoes plied its course, especially during the salmon run. He must stay well back from its banks.

Keeping to deep cover, he began the descent through willowherb and waist-high bracken. He was light-headed with hunger, but he had no food, no axe, and only three arrows. Somehow he had to eat before he got too weak to run. Somehow he had to find a hidden valley where he could survive on his own. Somehow he had to get rid of the mark of the Soul-Eater and force the clans to take him back . . .

The task was too huge. He'd never do it.

Then he remembered something Fin-Kedinn had said the previous moon, when they were gathering bark to make a fishing net. It had been a bitter day like this one, and Torak had stared at the slimy willow wands piled at his feet, wondering how he was ever going to turn them into a net.

'Don't think about the net,' Fin-Kedinn had told him. 'Take a single willow wand and strip it. You can do that, can't you?'

'Of course.' He'd learnt how to strip a stick before he was old enough to hold a knife.

'Then do it,' said the Raven Leader. 'Step by step. One branch at a time. Don't think about the net.'

Now, as Torak felt the rain soaking his buckskins, he nodded. Step by step. Food. Shelter. Yes. Leave the rest till tomorrow.

He found an elk trail which stayed concealed as it wound east along the valley flank. The rain stopped. The sun came out.

As he went, he became aware that although the Ravens were lost to him, the Forest was not. 'Forest,' he said softly. 'I've always honoured you. Help me survive.'

The Forest shook the raindrops from its boughs, and told him to look around.

By the trail he saw a sturdy birch tree with leaves still pleated from the bud. It would give him a quick, strengthening drink. Why hadn't he thought of that before?

Asking the tree's permission, he used his knife to cut a shallow hole in the bark at the base of the trunk. Tree-blood oozed. He stuck a hollow elder stem in the wound to funnel the drips, and tied on a birch-bark cone with honeysuckle, to catch them.

While the cone was filling, he found a digging stick and dug up some crow garlic. Sticking one bulb in a fork of the birch for the clan guardian, he ate the rest. They made his eyes water, but they warmed him up a bit.

After that he found some comfrey roots – very acrid and sticky – and, in a boggy hollow, the best of all: a clump of spotted orchid. The roots were so starchy it was like eating glue, but they were the most nourishing food in the Forest, if you couldn't get meat.

By now, the cone was brimming. After thanking the tree's spirit and pressing the bark over the wound to heal it, he drained the cone. The birch-blood tasted cool and dizzyingly sweet. The strength of the Forest became his.

Food made him feel a little better.

I can do this, he told himself. I can make dogwood arrows and harden the tips in a fire. I can make willowherb snares, and catch fish with bramble-thorn hooks. The Forest will help me.

Mid-afternoon was wearing on as he neared the valley bottom, where he had to wade through piles of last autumn's leaves. His confidence waned. His legs wouldn't carry him much further.

With no axe, building a shelter would be hard; but again, the Forest helped. He found a storm-toppled beech which had fallen onto a boulder. It gave him the perfect frame. All he had to do was pile branches on either side and leafmould on top of that. It was well placed, too: on the edge of a willow thicket where he could hide if he had to.

The air was turning sharp, but he couldn't risk a fire, so for warmth, he stuffed grass down his jerkin, boots and leggings. It was scratchy, and it tickled when beetles and spiders scuttled out, but it would stop him freezing.

Like a badger, he dragged armfuls of leaves into the shelter and snuggled under them, relishing the woody tang. After a prayer of thanks to the Forest, he shut his eyes. He was exhausted.

He was also wide awake.

Thoughts he'd been avoiding for a night and a day took hold. Like a burr in a wolf's fur, they wouldn't let go.

Outcast. Clanless.

How could he be clanless?

He thought of the garlic he'd put in the tree as an offering for the clan guardian. But if he had no clan, he had no guardian. No guardian. That made him feel breathless. How could anyone survive without a guardian?

His fingers touched the scar that cut through his 'clan-tattoo'. He couldn't remember getting it; scars weren't something you bothered about, everyone had them. He had one on his forearm from the night the bear attacked, and another on his calf from the boar's tusk. Renn had one on her hand from a tokoroth bite, and on her foot from stamping on a flint shard when she was three. Fin-Kedinn had lots from hunting accidents and fights when he was young, and the big, puckered scar on his thigh from the bear.

Scowling, Torak burrowed deeper into the leaves. *Don't think about the Ravens. Think about Fa, and why he never told you. Think about your mother, and why she declared you clanless.*

A gust of wind stirred the willows, and they moaned. In the distance, Torak heard the tuneless bellowing of an abandoned elk. In early summer, the Forest rang with their miserable cries. Their mothers, unable to look after last summer's young as well as a newborn calf, abruptly rejected the older ones, driving them away with savage kicks. For a moon or so, the young elk blundered about, seeking comfort from any large creature they met, until they were killed by hunters, or learned to fend for themselves.

I want my mother, bellowed the elk.

Torak squeezed his eyes shut.

He knew so little about his mother, and yet the thought of her had always been with him: a kernel of warmth, even through the bleakest times. He had loved her almost without thinking. He had believed that she had loved him. But to have declared him clanless . . .

It felt as if she'd abandoned him.

Where do I go now? he thought. Where do I belong?

Another gust, and the willows replied. *You belong here. In the Forest.*

Listening to them, he fell into sleep.

With a jolt, he fell out of it.

Voices. Above him on the slope.

He lay rigid, heart pounding.

Then he thought, if they were hunting, they wouldn't be talking.

Crawling out as quietly as he could, he shouldered his quiver and bow and dismantled his shelter, sweeping the area around it with crushed garlic leaves to mask his scent. He crept into the willows. Shadows were lengthening, but the first stars weren't yet out. He hadn't slept long.

The voices came nearer, then stopped fifty paces above him. Through the branches, he spotted a Viper hunting party on the elk trail he'd used earlier. No dogs. That was something. And he'd swept the trail clear of tracks. Hadn't he?

It wasn't only Viper Clan. A party of Ravens seemed to have met them on the trail. He saw Thull, Sialot, Fin-Kedinn. Renn.

It gave him a sick feeling to be peering at them like a stranger; to be unable to go to them.

He watched the younger Viper men wait respectfully for Fin-Kedinn to speak, then preen themselves as he admired their roe buck kill. He saw two Viper children shyly eyeing Renn, who pretended not to notice as she polished her bow with a handful of crushed hazelnuts.

Their voices reached him. They were talking about Aki.

'His wretched dogs nearly ruined our hunt!' complained a Viper man. 'If this goes on . . .'

'It won't,' said Fin-Kedinn. 'Aki won't catch Torak.'

'Still,' said the Viper. 'Those dogs are frightening the prey. The sooner the outcast is out of our range, the better.'

'Oh, he'll be long gone by now,' said Fin-Kedinn, his voice carrying in the still evening air. 'He wouldn't be such a fool as to stay around here, not with the clan meet coming up.'

The clan meet. Torak had forgotten all about the great gathering of the clans which took place every three summers, and which this summer would be held at the mouth of the Whitewater, not two daywalks from where he hid.

The hunters said their farewells and parted, the Vipers heading south for their camp on the Widewater, the Ravens west.

Don't go, Torak silently begged Fin-Kedinn. He felt hollow as he watched the broad-shouldered figure moving off into the trees with Renn. He watched till his eyes ached.

Long after they'd gone, he remained in the willows, while night deepened around him.

A twig cracked.

He froze.

Another twig. Loud. Deliberate.

'It's me!' whispered Renn. 'Where are you?'

Torak shut his eyes. He couldn't answer her. He'd only put her in danger.

'*Torak!*' Now she sounded angry as well as scared. 'I *know* you're in there! You left a scrap of chewed bast on the trail. It was all I could do to pick it up before the others spotted it!'

He *hated* staying silent.

'Oh, all right then!' she breathed. 'Maybe this will change your mind!' More rustling. 'I've brought what you'll need for getting rid of the Soul-Eater tattoo. That's why I'm here, to tell you how to do it.' Another pause. 'If you don't come out *right now*, I won't!'

SIX

'What do you think you're *doing?*' whispered Torak as he yanked Renn into the thicket. 'If anyone saw you!'

'They didn't,' she replied with more confidence than she felt. 'I've brought you some food and a sleeping-sack, but I didn't manage to steal an axe, so you'll – '

'Renn. No. You can't get mixed up in this!'

'I already am. Have a salmon cake.'

When he didn't move, she added, 'Well if you don't want it, I'll have to leave it for anyone to find!'

That worked, and he snatched it from her, demolishing it with fierce concentration. As she crouched beside him in the sour-smelling gloom, she wondered when he'd last eaten.

'There's lots more salmon cakes,' she told him. 'And

blood sausage and dried auroch tongue, and a bag of hazelnuts. Should be enough for half a moon, if you're careful.'

She was talking too much, she knew that. But he looked so different. That headband made him seem older; and there was a tautness in his face. He kept glancing about, as if at any moment a hunter might leap from the shadows.

This, she thought, is what it is to be prey.

Out loud, she asked where Wolf was, and Torak told her that he'd gone to lure Aki off the scent. Then he asked how she'd got away from Fin-Kedinn, and she told him about turning back to "check some snares", then picking up the supplies she'd hidden earlier, along with a woodpigeon which she would take to camp as proof of the "snares". She didn't mention the tightness in her chest as she'd deceived Fin-Kedinn, or the pain in his eyes when he'd realized what she was doing.

'He guessed I was here, didn't he?' said Torak. 'What he said about the clan meet. He was warning me.'

'I think so. Maybe.'

She passed him another salmon cake, and ate a couple of hazelnuts to keep him company. Then she said, 'I've been trying to understand how all this happened. Those red deer antlers, with Aki's mark rubbed out. Someone did that. Someone wanted you cast out.'

He glanced at her. 'The Soul-Eaters.'

She nodded. 'They'll have come south by now. And they know you're a spirit walker. They want your power.'

'They want the last piece of the fire-opal, too.'

'Wherever that is.'

In the deep blue night, young owls called to each other as they glided between the trees, and bats flitted over the bracken with a swift, light crackling of wings.

Torak wiped his mouth on the back of his hand. 'Renn,' he said. 'I'm sorry.'

'For what?'

'For all this. For not telling you about the mark. If only I'd told you. It just – it never seemed the right time.'

Her throat closed. 'I know how that can be. It's never easy to tell things. Secrets, I mean.'

'Well. I'm sorry.'

They finished eating, then Torak strapped the sleeping-sack to his back and shouldered his quiver and bow, and Renn re-packed the food pouch and placed a morsel of salmon cake in a willow for the clan guardian. As soon as she'd done it, she wished she'd waited till later, so that Torak hadn't seen. He told her he didn't mind, but she could see that he did.

'It's strange,' he said. 'All my life I've been doing that. And I haven't got a guardian.'

'It's still an offering. For the Forest.'

'I suppose.' He paused. 'But how is it possible, Renn? How can I not have a clan?'

'I don't know.'

'I've got a clan-soul, I can tell right from wrong. So how?'

She shook her head. 'Saeunn says no-one's ever been clanless before.'

He looked appalled – and she was furious with herself. Oh, very clever, Renn, that's really made him feel better. 'Anyway,' she went on quickly, 'I don't think I'd want to be part of that Wolf Clan. Those yellow eyes . . . ' She shuddered. 'I asked their Mage how they do it, and she said she puts something in the water. Once she got it wrong, and they turned pink instead.' She chewed her lip. 'I made that bit up. A joke.'

Torak forced a smile. She felt achingly sorry for him.

'But if I'm not Wolf Clan,' he said, 'what am I?'

She drew a breath. 'You're Wolf's pack-brother. You're my friend. And *that's* never going to change.'

Torak blinked. He rubbed a hand over his face and shouldered the food pouch, and coughed. 'Fin-Kedinn will be wondering where you are. You said you know how to do the rite?'

'– Yes,' said Renn.

He caught something in her tone. 'Are you sure?'

'Yes,' she repeated. In fact, she'd had to piece it together in snatches gleaned from Saeunn, so she wasn't *entirely* sure. But it wouldn't help Torak to know that.

The rite didn't take long to describe, but when Renn came to the part about cutting out the tattoo, they both felt sick.

'Here,' she said shakily, untying her swansfoot medicine pouch from her belt. 'It's got most of what you'll need.'

Torak took it and stared at it.

'You must wait till the moon is full,' she went on. 'Until then, you'll have to find somewhere safe to hide.'

'*Safe?*'

'Well. Safer. We'd better decide where to meet.'

'What do you mean?'

'At the full moon. For the rite.'

'Oh, no. No.' To her dismay, he wore his stubborn look: the one that reminded her of Wolf refusing to get into a skinboat.

'Torak,' she said, 'You can't do this on your own. I only told you what's involved so that you can prepare yourself, but I'll be there to help.'

'No.'

'Yes.'

'But you hate Magecraft.'

'That doesn't matter! At least I know how to do it!'

He stood up. 'Listen, Renn. This isn't like those other times, when you ran off and Fin-Kedinn was angry for a while and then forgave you. This could get you killed.'

'I do know the risks, but –'

'No. Coming here tonight was incredibly brave, but you cannot – you *must not* – do any more!'

Renn stood up. 'What I do or don't do is not for you to decide.' She turned to untangle her bow from a branch. 'And in case you've forgotten, on all those "other times", as you call them, I did actually . . . Torak? Torak!'

But he was gone, melting in the night as soundlessly as a ghost.

SEVEN

The full moon was riding high in the dark-blue sky, but Torak still wasn't ready. He'd put off gathering the rowan boughs for as long as he could, dreading the moment when he would have to begin the rite.

For half a moon he'd lain low, surviving on Renn's supplies and any hares, squirrels and birds he could catch. Day had merged into day: scrabbling for food, hiding in thickets; muttering to himself, just to hear the sound of a voice.

Aki and his dogs hadn't come again. The clans were labouring to get in the last of the salmon, and the Boar Leader worked his son hard.

'Find a place that feels as if it has power,' Renn had said as they'd huddled in the thicket. 'Do it there.'

Torak had found such a place – but it probably wasn't

what she'd had in mind. He stood on the south slope of the steep valley which the clans call the Twin Rivers, where the Axehandle and Green Rivers collide in a thunderous battle to make the Whitewater. A desolate place, perpetually misted in spray, where birch and rowan clung to life amid huge, tumbled boulders.

And dangerously close to people. From here the Whitewater crashed down to the Sea – where, not half a daywalk to the west, the clan meet was gathering. Torak was far too close – but that was the plan. No-one would look for him here. And the rapids would mask his cries if the pain got too bad.

Pushing the thought aside, he cut another rowan bough, and wished for the hundredth time that he had an axe.

Behind him, a branch snapped.

He spun round.

A shadow emerged from the trees.

He stumbled backwards.

The shadow lumbered into him – and elk and boy sprang apart with startled bellows.

'You again!' cried Torak. 'Go *away*! I told you, I'm not your mother!'

The elk put down its head and nuzzled him, and he felt the hot, fuzzy nubs where its antlers would grow. The elk was enormous, but it moved with awkward humility, as if apologizing for being so big. Torak saw the wound on its flank where its mother had kicked it, and felt a twinge of sympathy.

The elk didn't understand why its mother had rejected it. It didn't even know enough to be afraid of Wolf, who only left it alone because the hunting was good. Twice it had blundered into Torak and he'd chased it away. He couldn't kill it because he would take days to make use of the carcass, and he couldn't let it follow him, as then it would never learn to fear hunters. Now it seemed to think they were friends.

'Shoo!' he said, waving his arms.

The elk gazed at him with confused brown eyes.

'Go away!' He punched it on the nose.

The elk swung round and wandered off into the trees – and Torak was alone again. Dread flooded back. Now nothing stood between him and the rite.

The thought of cutting out the tattoo turned him sick with terror. The thought of what he might become if he didn't was worse. Over the past few days, the mark had begun to burn. He could feel it eating into his flesh.

The place he'd chosen was twenty paces above the river: a great, hunched boulder guarded by rowans. Moonlight gleamed faintly on the stone. Torak wished the dark were deeper than this eerie twilight; but in summer the sun never slept for long.

Leaving sleeping-sack, quiver and bow at the foot of the rock, he climbed. Moss crumbled beneath his boots, releasing a whiff of decay. The granite felt cold under his fingers. As he reached the top, the roar of the rapids pounded through him, drowning out the sounds of the Forest. To the west, red knife-pricks of campfires mocked his loneliness.

Wolf returned from the hunt, his muzzle black with blood. Rising effortlessly on his hind legs, he placed his forepaws on the rock, ready to leap up and join Torak.

No, Torak told him in wolf talk. *Stay down.*

Wolf sat on his haunches and gazed at him, puzzled.

Torak forced himself to ignore him. Wolf wouldn't understand what he was about to do, and there was no way of telling him.

For the first time in his life, he was going to do Magecraft. He was going to meddle with the forces that Mages use to see the future, heal the sick and find prey: forces he didn't understand and couldn't control.

'It's a way of getting deeper,' Renn had told him, trying to explain what came as naturally to her as tracking did to him. 'A way of touching the Nanuak itself. But you've got to be careful. It's like dipping your foot in a fast river. If you go too deep, you'll be swept away.'

The Nanuak.

Torak felt it inside him: the raw power which pulses through all living things – river, rock, tree, hunter, prey – which links them with the World Spirit itself.

Wiping the spray from his face, he untied the swansfoot pouch from his belt. The claws felt sharp, the hide scaly. Opening the pouch, he laid out the things Renn had given him.

'There are five kinds of Magecraft,' she had said. 'Sending. Summoning. Cleansing. Binding. Severing. The one for this rite will be cleansing. And – severing.' She'd swallowed. 'You'll need something from each of the four quarters of the clans: Forest, Ice, Mountain, Sea. For the Forest, your mother's medicine horn. Take earthblood from it and mix it with fat – any creature's will do, as long as it's not a water creature – then draw a line round the tattoo. That shows you where to – to cut.' She drew a breath. 'For Ice, the swansfoot pouch. It belonged to the White Fox Mage, so it's full of good power.'

'For the Mountain?' said Torak, feeling cold.

From the pouch she drew a wristband of dried rowan berries threaded on a willowherb cord. 'I met some Rowan Clan, they were going early to the clan meet to get the best camping spot. I swapped this for an arrow.'

'Won't they notice if you're not wearing it?'

'I thought of that, split it in two.' She held up her hand to show an identical band. Then she tied the other one round his wrist. She scowled, but he guessed that, like him, she felt better for sharing this between them.

'When the time comes,' she said, 'you must make a special drink to purify yourself. Root of hedge mustard, ground with alder bark, betony and elder leaves, steeped in strong water. Use Axehandle water, that's important, because it gets its power from the ice river in the Mountains. And leave it to stand in the moonlight for as long as you can.'

He'd prepared the drink at dusk, mixing it in a cup he'd made of squirrel rawhide, and leaving it on the rock to catch the first rays of the moon while he went off to gather rowan branches.

'I don't think there's anything in it that'll cause your souls to walk,' Renn had said, 'but you'd better mark your face with the sign of the hand and pass rowan leaves over yourself. And of course, I'll be with you, in case – anything happens.'

'What do I use for the Sea?'

'Your father's knife. It's Sea slate. And Torak – grind it *sharp*. It'll hurt less.'

In horror, he watched her take out a little horn needle-case, a coil of sinew thread and a slender bone fishing-hook.

'What's the hook for?' he asked.

Renn didn't meet his eyes. 'You mustn't cut too deep, or you'll cut into the muscle.'

Torak put his hand to his chest.

'I'll show you.' With her knife she scratched a cross on the knee of her legging. 'This is the tattoo. You – you cut round it in a sort of – willow-leaf shape. Then you – you hook the skin in the middle and lift.' Beads of sweat stood out on her forehead as she hooked the mark, tenting the buckskin. 'That way you can – c-cut under your skin, and lift off the tattoo. Then press the sides of the wound together and s-stitch it shut.'

They had both been shaking by the time she'd finished.

Spray from the Twin Rivers was icy on Torak's face as he knelt and drank the bitter herb drink. He purified himself with rowan, marked his face with the sign of the hand. Set out the needles and the hook. He felt as if he was going to be sick.

Below him, Wolf leapt to his feet: muzzle lifted, tail raised. He'd caught a scent.

What is it? Torak asked in wolf talk.

Other.

Other what?

Other. Wolf padded in circles, then gazed up at Torak, his eyes an alien silver in the moonlight.

Whatever Wolf meant, Torak couldn't let it distract him. If he didn't start now, he'd never have the courage.

He pulled his jerkin over his head. Spray chilled his skin. His teeth chattered. Shakily, he daubed an earthblood line around the three-pronged fork of the Soul-Eater.

He drew his knife. Fa's knife. The Sea slate felt icy, the hilt heavy and warm.

Wolf gave a low growl.

Torak warned him to stay down – and prepared to make the first cut.

It was nearly dawn, and he lay in the shadow of the rock, shivering uncontrollably in his sleeping-sack. It hurt to breathe. It hurt to *be*. Nothing existed except this blazing pain in his chest.

A sob escaped him. He clenched his teeth. Fa did this too, he told himself. Fa cut out the mark, he got through this. So can you.

The voice of the Twin Rivers boomed in his head, like the throbbing in his chest.

But Fa had his mate to help him. Not like you. You're all alone.

Snarling, he pressed his face into the reindeer hide.

Something tickled his nose. It was one of Renn's long red hairs, left behind in what had been her sleeping-sack. He clutched it in his fist. Not alone, he told himself.

Some time later, he woke to the click of claws on stone. A cold nose nudged his cheek, and Wolf settled against him with a 'humph'!

'Not alone,' whispered Torak, sinking his fingers into his pack-brother's fur. *Don't ever leave me*, he said in wolf talk.

Wolf gave him another nose-nudge and a reassuring lick.

Clutching his scruff, Torak slid into evil dreams.

He dreamt that an elk was attacking Renn. Not the young elk which wanted to make friends with him, but a full-grown male.

Torak tried to move, but the dream dragged at his limbs, and he could only watch as Renn backed against the stump of an oak tree, looking about wildly for something to climb. Nothing: the river behind her, knee-high willows in front.

The elk gave a bellow that shook the earth, then put down its head to charge. One kick from those enormous hooves would brain a boar, or snap a wolf's spine in two. Renn didn't stand a chance.

The elk crashed towards her, and Torak felt the ground tremble; he smelt its musky rage. Suddenly he felt a jolting pain in his belly – a pain that was horribly familiar . . .

. . . and now it was *his* rage which powered the great body forwards, *his* antlers thrusting aside the branches as he thundered towards Renn.

This isn't a dream, he thought. *This is really happening!*

EIGHT

The elk burst from the thicket, and Renn flung herself behind the oak. With terrifying agility the elk spun on one hoof. Renn dodged – and dodged again. The elk gallopped off, then swung round for another attack.

Breathless, sweating, she crouched behind the stump. Nothing climbable within reach – this slope had been cleared for a camp two summers before – and although the river was ten paces away, she'd never make it. Besides, elk can swim.

A root was digging into her knee, and as she shifted position, she nearly fell down a hole. Some kind of burrow. Muttering thanks to her guardian, she hugged her weapons and wriggled in backwards. The elk couldn't reach her down here, the hole was too narrow for those antlers. And elk didn't dig. At least, not normal ones.

But this was nothing like a normal elk.

She'd had no warning, nothing at all. After a sleepless night, she'd crawled blearily from the shelter and set off upriver. If anyone asked, she would tell them she was hunting, but the truth was, she was worried about Torak. She wanted to find some trace of him, even though he was probably long gone.

Then the elk had emerged from the waterlogged thicket.

Renn had been startled, but not alarmed. The elk had probably been browsing on sedge, or diving for water lily roots. She would give it space to show that she wasn't hunting, and it would wander off.

Then everything changed.

Earth trickled onto her face, and she shook it off. Peering up at a grey disc of sky, her hunter's eye spotted a few black and white hairs snagged on the edge. She hoped the badger whose sett she'd invaded was fast asleep and a lot further inside. Caught between a mad elk and an outraged badger. Not much of a choice.

What to do now? Her bow and arrows were mercifully unharmed, her axe still in her hand. She could either wait till help came along, or fight her way out.

Fighting would get her killed. The elk was so tall that she could have run under its belly without ducking, and its antlers were wider than her outstretched arms; one swipe would gut her like a fish. And those hooves . . . Once, she'd seen a cow elk kill a bear with just two kicks: one on the jaw to stun, and then – rearing on its hind legs – both front hooves hammering down to split the skull.

But this elk wasn't a cow protecting her calf. It was a bull; and the rut, when bulls become lethal, was four moons away.

So why had it attacked? Sickness? A wound gone bad? She'd seen no sign of either. Demons? No. It didn't feel like that. And yet – there was something.

More earth trickled onto her face, and she spat out gritty crumbs. With infinite care, she pushed herself up and peered over the edge.

Early sunlight speared the bracken. A breeze woke the willows. The river murmured on its way to the Sea. So peaceful . . .

There. Beside that clump of burdock: the edge of a huge, splayed hoof; a fetlock dark with sweat.

The blood roared in her ears.

The elk lowered its head and its long tongue curled out, moistening its nose to sharpen its sense of smell. Its large ears tilted towards her.

She froze.

It knew she was there. One eye was blind red jelly, punctured by a rival's antler the previous rut. The other was fixed on hers.

She caught her breath. She sensed the spirit behind that stare.

'It can't be,' she whispered.

The elk pawed the burdock.

It's an elk, she told herself. Nothing to do with Torak.

And yet, she knew – with the certainty which came to her at times and which Saeunn called her inner eye – she *knew* that Torak's souls were in that elk. He was spirit walking. He was attacking *her*.

'This can't be,' she whispered again. 'Why would he attack me?'

Feeling dizzy and sick, she gripped the handle of her axe. There was no way out. Whatever happened next, one of them would die.

Wolf stood guard while Tall Tailless huddled in the reindeer pelt, twitching and moaning in his sleep.

The scent of the Otherness which Wolf had caught in the Dark was gone, but he sensed that it hadn't gone far. It was a new smell, but it reminded him of something. Something bad.

Ordinarily he would have raced off to find it, but Tall Tailless had said never to leave him. This puzzled Wolf a lot. He left Tall Tailless all the time. To hunt, to roll in scat, to gobble up delicious rotten carcasses which his pack-brother unaccountably disliked. But it didn't matter how long Wolf was away, because he always came back.

Wolf hated not understanding. But he couldn't get his jaws around the answer.

Then he heard howling.

Wolves. Many lopes off, although he couldn't tell exactly where, because they were howling with their muzzles all pointing different ways. Wolf understood this. It was the time when the Lights get longer, eating up the Darks: the time when wolf cubs are born. This pack had cubs. It didn't want others to find its Den. The pack that Wolf had run with on the Mountain had used the same trick.

Wait! He sprang to his feet. This *was* the Mountain pack! He knew the leader's howl!

Lashing his tail, he howled an answer. *I'm here! Here!* In his head he saw the pack standing close together, muzzles lifted to the Up, eyes slitted in the joy of the howl. He was seized with longing to go to them.

The pack fell silent.

Wolf's tail stilled.

He wished Tall Tailless would wake up. But he went on twitching and moaning in his sleep.

A little later, Wolf heard a frantic yip-and-yowling in tailless talk. It was the pack-sister. He didn't understand what she was saying, but he could hear that she was in trouble.

Wolf pawed Tall Tailless to wake him.

His pack-brother didn't stir.

Wolf snapped at his overpelt and tugged at the long dark fur on his head. When that didn't work, he barked in his ears. That never failed.

It did now.

Wolf's pelt tightened as he realized that what lay here, curled in the reindeer hide, was only the *meat* of Tall Tailless. The bit inside – the breath that walked – was gone.

Wolf knew because it had happened before. Sometimes he would see the walking breath leave his pack-brother's body. It was the same size and shape and smell as Tall Tailless, but Wolf knew not to get too close.

Wolf ran in circles. The scent trail told him that the walking breath of Tall Tailless had gone to find the pack-sister. That was what Wolf must do, too.

He flew through the Forest. He startled a mare and her foals, and nearly trod on a sleeping piglet, annoying its mother, but he was gone before she'd lumbered to her feet. Weaving between the alders at the edge of the Fast Wet, he loped towards the pack-sister's howls. He smelt her fierce resolve. He smelt fresh blood and angry elk.

In mid-yowl, the pack-sister's voice broke off.

Wolf quickened his pace.

Suddenly the wind swung round, carrying a new scent to his nose: the scent of Otherness.

Wolf slewed to a halt. The Otherness was heading for Tall Tailless' defenceless body.

Wolf hesitated.

What should he do?

NINE

Torak woke with a struggle, as if fighting his way up from the bottom of a lake. Something had happened in the night – something terrible – but he couldn't remember what.

He was lying in his sleeping-sack with the early sun in his eyes. His mouth tasted as if he'd been eating ash, and the wound in his chest hurt savagely.

Then he saw the strand of dark-red hair in his hand, and everything flooded back. Bracken whipping past his antlers, mud squelching beneath his hooves. Flint flashing, red hair flying. Then – nothing.

What had he done?

In a heartbeat he was out of the sleeping-sack, startling Wolf.

The pack-sister! Torak said in wolf talk. *Is she all right?*

Don't know, came the reply. A lick on the muzzle. *Are you?*

Torak didn't answer. He never spirit walked in his sleep. And it couldn't have been the drink he'd made for the rite, Renn had told him it wouldn't make his souls wander. Besides, he'd daubed the sign of the hand on his cheek, like she'd said. With his fingers he searched his face, but the earthblood was gone. He must have rubbed it off while he slept.

How could this have happened? He glanced at the crusted scab on his chest. The mark was gone – but the power of the Soul-Eaters was great. Maybe while he slept, they had forced him to do this: to attack the person he cared about most.

It took him the whole morning to reach the clearing. He had some idea of where it lay, having noticed the badger sett and the stump on previous hunts; and Wolf helped, too. But when they got there, Torak didn't recognize it. The bracken and willowherb had been flattened as if by a hailstorm, the oak kicked to splinters. Here and there he saw scarlet spatters on green leaves.

The world tilted. He tasted bile. He fought to stay calm, to piece together what had happened.

In the churned mud near the stump he found a print of Renn's boot; a red hair snagged at one of the entrances to the sett. On the riverbank he found drag-marks where canoes had been drawn up. A mess of men's footprints, deeper on their way back to the boats. They'd been carrying something heavy.

Maybe they had arrived in time, killed the elk and taken it with them in the boats.

Maybe it was Renn they'd carried away.

Torak's mind refused to work. His tracker's skill deserted him.

I did this, he thought. There is something inside me that I can't control.

Wolf nudged his thigh, asking when they were going. Torak asked him if he'd tried to help the pack-sister, and Wolf replied that he'd wanted to, but then he'd smelt "Other".

What do you mean? said Torak, but Wolf's answer was unclear. Wolves don't only talk with grunts and whines and howls, but with subtle movements of the body: a tilt of the head, a flick of the ears or tail, the fluffing up or sleeking down of fur. Not even Torak knew every sign. All he could gather was that Wolf had caught a bad scent making for his pack-brother, and raced to his defence, but whatever it was had gone by the time he'd arrived.

Torak stared at the desolation around him. He should get under cover; at any moment a canoe might slide into view. He didn't care. He had to go to the clan meet and find out what had happened to Renn.

Dusk was coming on by the time he reached the river mouth where the clans were gathered. At this time of summer, the night wouldn't get any darker. Which made what he was doing even more dangerous.

Apart from the headband, he hadn't stopped to disguise himself, simply smearing wood-ash on his skin to put off the dogs. For the rest, he would rely on his hunter's ability to stay out of sight, and the fact that he'd persuaded Wolf – with some difficulty – not to come too.

He found a stand of juniper and pine well back from the camp, hid his sleeping-sack in some brambles to retrieve later, and crouched down to plot his next move.

Around the mouth of the Whitewater, fires glowed orange

in the deep blue dusk. Before them, black figures reached stick-limbs towards the sky, like paintings on a rock. So many people! For a moment Torak was small again, just short of his eighth birthnight, and proud to be going with Fa to the clan meet by the Sea.

The Mountain Hare Clan had built their reindeer-hide shelters on the rocks above the shore, perhaps because this reminded them of home. The Rowan Clan's turf domes squatted in the meadows, while the Salmon Clan had pitched their fish-skin tents on the foreshore, and the Sea-eagles, who didn't seem to care, had made their untidy stick piles wherever they'd found space. The Open Forest clans had camped nearest the trees, but Torak couldn't see the Ravens' open-fronted shelters.

'They say the Wolf Clan's headed south,' said a man's voice, startlingly close.

Torak froze.

'Good riddance,' snorted another man. 'I never feel easy with them around.'

A muffled curse as one of them tripped over a root.

'Still, they should've stayed,' said the first man. 'It's a clan meet, that's what it's for.'

'What about the Deep Forest clans?' said his companion. 'No sign of them, either.'

'I hear there's trouble between the Aurochs and the Forest Horses . . .'

Their voices faded as they headed towards the river — and Torak breathed again.

It was some time before he dared move. Keeping to the edge of the Forest, he came to a pine-ringed hollow where a throng of people crowded round a large fire. Smells of baked salmon and roasting meat mingled with the music of voice, pipe and drum.

The fire was made of three pine logs burning along their length. A Raven long-fire. He'd found them.

Dry-mouthed, he hid in a clump of yews beyond the light.

He saw Fin-Kedinn deep in talk with the Salmon Clan Leader as they cut hunks off a glistening side of red deer and filled peoples' bowls.

He saw Saeunn and two other Mages a little way off, by a smaller blaze which gave off a heady scent of juniper. One Mage cast handfuls of bones and watched how they fell, while a second read the smoke snaking into the sky. Saeunn rocked back and forth, spitting spells.

Above Torak's head, a branch creaked – and a raven peered down at him with bright, unforgiving eyes. He begged it not to betray him.

The guardian spread its wings and flew, swooping low over the Mages' fire. Saeunn raised her head to follow it. Then she turned and looked straight at Torak.

She can't see you, he told himself. But in the firelight, the stare of the Raven Mage was red with secret knowledge. Who knew what she could see?

Just when Torak couldn't bear it any longer, Saeunn turned back to her spells.

Shaky with relief, he scanned the firelit faces. He saw the Boar Clan Leader jabbing his finger at the Whale Leader to emphasize a point, Aki sitting nearby, watching his father with an odd mix of fear and longing.

Then Torak saw her.

Renn sat cross-legged at the front of the throng, scowling into the flames. She was pale, and her right forearm was bound in soft buckskin, but apart from that, she appeared unhurt.

The tightness in his chest loosened as if a rawhide strap had snapped.

She's all right.

A dog padded over to him; luckily, one he knew. He shooed it away.

Next time, he might not be so lucky. He had to get away before they found him.

He stayed where he was.

Maybe it was seeing Renn again. Maybe it was the wild hope that with the mark of the Soul-Eater cut out, he could simply step into the light, and everyone would welcome him back.

He stayed.

And that changed everything.

The moon made its way across the sky, and still Torak watched.

He saw men, women and children dipping beakers in pails of brewed birch-blood. He saw them stepping into the space around the long-fire to offer a story, a song.

A Willow man sang of the salmon run to the music of deer-hoof rattles and duck-bone pipes.

A Rowan woman created a prowling shadow bear by moving her hands behind a firelit hide.

So it went on through the brief summer night. Torak found himself drawn into the stories: the ancient memories which the clans had told on nights such as this since the Beginning.

It was a while before he noticed that Renn had gone as white as chalk.

Two masked figures were now dancing round the fire: a midge with a long, pointed wooden beak, and an irascible elk. The midge – with a Viper woman behind the mask –

zoomed about, whining and poking with her beak, to delighted squeals from children and laughter from their parents. But Renn had eyes only for the elk. Her mouth was a tense line as she watched it sweep the shadows with its antlers. Torak could see that she was re-living the attack.

By chance, the elk moved to the other side of the fire, and it was the midge who now targeted her. Distractedly she batted it away, but it came whining back, as midges do.

Leave her alone, urged Torak.

Just as the midge zoomed in for another attack, a young man rose, grasped the midge's beak lightly in one hand, and pretended to swat it with the other. He did it with such good humour that the Viper woman played along with him, buzzing away with an aggrieved whine which made everybody laugh.

Renn threw the young man a grateful glance, and he shrugged and sat down again. Then Torak noticed the wavy blue tattoos on his arms: the mark of the Seal Clan. He nearly cried out.

It was Bale. His kinsman.

Bale had put on muscle since the previous summer, and firelight glinted in the beginnings of a beard, but apart from that he hadn't changed. The same long fair hair beaded with shells and capelin bones, the same intelligent face. The same blue eyes that seemed to hold the light of sun on Sea.

The last time they'd seen each other, they'd talked about hunting together, and Torak had made a joke about a Seal in a Forest. It hurt to think of that now.

Suddenly, a horn boomed into the night.

Ravens exploded from the trees.

Dancers, watchers, all went still.

Leaning on her staff, Saeunn hobbled into the light. 'A Soul-Eater!' she cried. 'A Soul-Eater is come among us!'

Fear rippled through the throng.

'I read it in the bones,' croaked the Raven Mage, circling the fire, searching their faces. 'I see it in the smoke. A Soul-Eater is among us – a Soul-Eater to the marrow!'

People clutched their children and gripped amulets and weapons. Fin-Kedinn's features never moved as he watched his Mage seek the evil one.

As Torak hid in the dark beneath the yews, the meaning of what Saeunn had sensed crashed upon him. A Soul-Eater to the marrow . . .

He had carried the mark on his chest for too long. It had gnawed its way into his bones, and he was one of them. He would never be free.

The rite hadn't worked.

TEN

There was uproar around the long-fire. Dogs barking, a hornet buzz of voices. Mouths turned ugly with fear, eyes became shadowy hollows.

Fin-Kedinn called for calm – and the uproar diminished.

'But we've got to go after him now!' shouted Aki. 'If we don't –'

'If you go now,' said the Raven Leader, 'you'll be setting off blind. Remember, it's not just an outcast out there. What about the Oak Mage? The Viper Mage. The Eagle Owl Mage. Three Soul-Eaters of enormous power – and they could be anywhere. Are you strong enough to fight them alone, Aki? Are any of you?'

Aki made to reply, but his father snarled at him, and Aki cringed as if to ward off a blow.

Torak had seen enough. He fled. What a fool he'd been

to believe they would take him back. They would never take him back.

As he ran, the scab on his chest cracked open. He gasped in pain. *One twitch and it will draw you*, hissed the Viper Mage.

Having retrieved his sleeping-sack, he took a different path to disperse his scent, and now through the trees he glimpsed the Ravens' shelters. They were deserted.

With every moment the danger grew – and yet he couldn't drag himself away. He was leaving them for ever, he knew that now, but he had to be close to them one last time. He had to say goodbye.

He found the Raven Leader's shelter and peered in. There was Fin-Kedinn's axe propped against the doorpost; his bow, his fishing spear. But nothing of Renn's, which was odd.

His axe.

It was beautiful, a blade of polished greenstone mounted on a sturdy ash handle. It fitted Torak's grip perfectly. As his fingers closed around it, he felt the Raven Leader's strength, his force of will. Torak had lost his own axe in the Far North; Fin-Kedinn had been going to help him make a new one. There was much that Fin-Kedinn had been going to teach him.

His grip tightened. To steal a man's axe is one of the worst things you can do. To steal Fin-Kedinnn's . . .

But he needed it.

Scarcely believing what he was doing, he stuck the axe in his belt and moved on, seeking the shelter where Renn slept. It was madness to stay any longer, but he couldn't leave till he'd found it.

He was astonished to discover that she was now sharing a shelter with Saeunn: he recognized it by its stale, old-woman smell. How Renn would hate that.

It hurt to see her gear, piled untidily in the corner. Her beloved bow hung from a cross-beam. As he touched it, he seemed to hear her voice: mocking, kind. The first day they'd met, when the Ravens were enemies and he had to fight for his life, she had given him a beaker of elderberry juice. *'It's only fair,'* she'd said.

On her willow-branch mat lay a new medicine pouch he hadn't seen before; she must have made it when she'd given him hers. He upended it, and among the dried mushrooms and tangles of hair, he was surprised to see the white pebble on which he'd daubed his clan-tattoo last summer. She had kept it all this time.

His hand closed over it. This would tell her better than anything that he was never coming back.

He ran fast and low, heading upstream, keeping to the thickets by the river. He hadn't gone far when he heard slight, furtive sounds of pursuit.

It couldn't be Aki, he would've made more noise. And whoever it was, they were good, moving almost noiselessly, and staying in the shadows.

They were good, but he was better.

The river flowed deep and slow between half-drowned alders. Torak took off his boots and tied them round his neck. Then, balancing quiver, bow and sleeping-sack roll on his head, he waded in. The cold took his breath away, but he gritted his teeth and kept going till he was up to his chest.

Bracing his legs against the current, he waited. He heard the slap and suck of water around the trees. Then stealthy footsteps.

From the bank, someone softly called his name.

He tensed.

'Torak!' Renn whispered again. 'Where are you?'

He made no answer.

Then another voice. 'Kinsman, it's me!'

Torak flinched.

'We're alone, I swear it!' Bale said in a hoarse whisper. 'Come out! I mean you no harm! Renn's told me everything. I know you're outcast, but we're still kin! I want to help!'

Torak clenched his jaw. Renn had already risked her life to help him, and it had come to nothing. He couldn't put her or Bale in any more danger.

Like all hunters, Renn and Bale knew how to wait. So did Torak.

At last, he heard Bale sigh. 'Let's go,' he told Renn.

'No!' she protested. Torak heard a stirring of branches as she moved closer – and suddenly there she was at the water's edge.

'Torak!' Her voice was recklessly loud. 'I know you're there, I can feel you listening! Please. *Please*! You've got to let us help you!'

Not answering Bale had been hard, but ignoring Renn was one of the hardest things Torak had ever done. The urge to cry out – to give some sign that only she would understand – was almost overwhelming. Go back to camp, he begged her. I can't bear it.

Bale put his hand on Renn's shoulder. 'Come on. Either he's not here, or he doesn't want to be found.'

Angrily, she shook him off. But when he started for camp, she followed.

Torak waited till he was sure they were gone, then waded back to dry ground. Frozen, numb, he pulled on his boots. The scab on his chest was open, he felt warmth seeping out. Good. Let it bleed.

He followed the river upstream, running punishingly fast so that he wouldn't have to think, but at last he had to stop. He slumped against a whitebeam tree at the edge of a clearing. It would be dawn soon. Far in the distance, he heard dogs.

He found that he was still clutching the pebble he'd taken from Renn's medicine pouch. He stared at the dotted lines which he'd used to think were his clan-tattoo, but were now meaningless smudges.

That's the old Torak, he thought.

He realized that for the past half-moon, he'd merely been playing at being outcast, finding any excuse to stay near the Ravens. He'd been like that young elk, bleating for its mother. If it didn't learn to survive on its own, it would get killed. He wasn't going to make the same mistake.

His fist closed over the pebble. Leave it. Leave it all behind.

He tucked the pebble in a cleft of the whitebeam tree and ran.

Mist beaded the bracken and lent the leaves of the whitebeam a frosty glitter. Torak's pebble nestled safe in its smooth brown arms.

A roe buck entered the clearing and began to browse. A robin started to sing. A blackbird awoke. The rising sun burned off the mist.

Suddenly the buck jerked up its head and fled. Robin and blackbird flew off with shrill calls of alarm.

A shadow fell across the whitebeam.

The Forest held its breath.

A green hand reached out and took the pebble from the tree.

ELEVEN

'He's here,' said Aki. 'I can feel it.'

'Well I can't,' panted the Willow girl, battling the current to keep abreast of him. 'Won't he have headed south instead of east? That's where he came from.'

'Which is why the others have gone south to cut him off,' growled Aki.

'We're too far upstream,' Raut said uneasily. 'We should go back.'

'No,' snapped Aki.

'Then let's put in for a rest,' protested another boy. 'If I paddle much longer, my arms will fall off!'

'Me too,' puffed the girl. 'There was an inlet back there. Let's go.'

A murmur of assent – to which Aki grudgingly agreed – and they brought their dugouts about.

Perched in a willow, Torak breathed out. When he was sure it wasn't a bluff, he slipped into the water and waded for the bank.

Wolf was waiting. He watched with interest as Torak stuffed his boots with grass to warm up his feet; then they headed upstream.

All day the hunters had tracked them: east of Twin Rivers and up the Axehandle. Whenever Torak tried heading south, the second group of hunters drove him back. It was only by staying in the thickets near the river that he'd kept them off the scent.

He was cold, wet, and he hadn't slept since the night before last. He was beginning to miss things. A while back, he'd almost tripped over a boar enjoying a wallow. Why hadn't he seen its tracks? A child of five summers would have spotted them.

Because of Aki, he'd given up all thought of going south. His only hope was to cross the Axehandle and make for the gullies leading off it to the north. It was rough country without much prey, and few people ventured in except for the odd lonely wanderer. That was the point.

The river turned angrier, and he caught the distant roar of rapids. Around mid-morning, Wolf tensed. Then Torak heard it too: paddles slicing the water; dogs panting, keeping level with the dugouts. Aki and his friends hadn't rested for long.

Torak made his way across the willow bog, squelching through hare-grass, avoiding the pale-green moss which was so delicate that a footprint would remain stamped on it for days. Wolf managed better, his big, slightly webbed paws letting him run lightly over the surface.

To his dismay, Torak saw that his pursuers weren't continuing upriver, but crossing it, as if they'd guessed his plan. In their dugouts they made it with ease. He watched them hoist the boats on their shoulders and climb the bank. They meant to carry them round the rapids and lie in wait for him above.

He had no choice but to go on.

The river turned rougher, crashing over rocks and soaking him in spray. As he clambered past the rapids, he watched for his pursuers on the other side. From memory, he guessed he was nearing the place where – on the opposite bank – two gullies led off from the Axehandle valley. The autumn before last, he and Renn had found a fallen oak and used it to get across. Maybe . . .

The oak was gone, washed away by floods.

For a moment, Torak didn't know what to do. His head felt tight. A buzzing in his ears made it hard to think. There had to be some way of crossing.

There was. Ahead, the valley narrowed, drowned thickets giving way to boulders and straggling trees. A pine had fallen and now spanned the river, ten paces above it. As a walkway, it wasn't promising: the bark was slimy, branches stuck out, and when Torak put his hand on the trunk, it wobbled.

Good enough, he told himself.

Part of him knew this was a mistake – but strangely, he kept going.

Wolf raced lightly along the trunk, leaping the branches. When he reached the other side, he turned to Torak, wagging his tail. *Easy!*

No it's not, Torak wanted to say. Not on your hands and knees in slippery wet buckskin, with a sleeping-sack, bow and quiver on your back – and no claws.

He was nearly across when he heard voices. He glanced down – and nearly fell off in alarm.

Blue water and white foam swirled around moss-green boulders. On one, directly beneath him, stood Aki and Raut.

Torak held his breath. If one of them looked up . . .

'I've had enough,' said Raut. 'I'm going back.'

'Well I'm not!' snarled Aki.

Torak tried to move forwards, but Renn's rowanberry wristband snagged on a branch. He tried to unsnag it. The tree shook.

'The others have gone back,' said Raut, 'and so should we. We're out of our range.'

Again Torak tugged the wristband. It snapped. Rowanberries bounced onto the rocks.

Luckily, Aki was too incensed to notice. 'If you go now, you'll be going on foot! I'm keeping the boat!'

'You do that!' retorted Raut. Then more quietly, 'Aki, this isn't right! Why do you hate him so much?'

'I don't,' snapped Aki.

'Then why all this?'

'I said I'd get him! I told Fa. I can't go back if I fail.'

'Well you'll have to do it without me. We'll split the provisions, then you're on your own!'

Weak with relief, Torak watched them head off downstream.

He'd just begun to move when Aki's voice rang out. 'I know you're out there, Soul-Eater! I'll find you, I swear it on my souls! I'll find you and I'll hunt you down!'

Wolf was waiting for him on the other side, but Torak barely greeted him. Huddled in his wet clothes, he thought about Aki's threat. Such determination.

He glanced at Wolf. Every moment they spent together put him at risk. Clan law forbids the killing of a hunter, *except* in self-defence. What if it came to a fight and Wolf tried to defend his pack-brother and Aki shot him?

A moment of pure panic. He couldn't be without Wolf.
It's the only way, he told himself. And it isn't for ever.
Split up, Torak told his pack-brother in wolf talk.

Wolf threw him a puzzled glance.

Impossible to get across that this wasn't for good, but only while Aki was close. With an effort, Torak hardened his heart and repeated the command. *Split up!*

Wolf looked offended. Then he shook himself and trotted off into the bracken.

Torak hadn't heard Aki or his dogs for a while, or seen any sign of Wolf.

The buzzing in his ears came and went, and the wound in his chest throbbed. Belatedly, he'd smeared it with chewed willow bast, but it refused to heal. The pain was a constant reminder that it wasn't only Aki who hunted him. The Soul-Eaters had hooked him with an unseen harpoon, and were drawing him in.

The ground became stonier. From where he stood, the riverbank dropped steeply to the Axehandle. He'd passed the rapids some time ago, but their thunder still filled his ears.

Leaning against a birch tree, he gulped the last of Renn's blood sausage. He didn't bother with an offering; he needed it all for himself.

He was thirsty, but it was a tough climb down to the river, so instead he slashed the birch trunk and drank. He left the bark oozing tree-blood and stumbled on. He knew that was wrong, but he did it anyway. Something was getting between him and the Forest. He was too tired to fight it.

Below him the river ran swift and deep. Should he stay this close, or get under cover? He decided to stay close.

Wrong choice. The boulders were treacherous with moss and he fell, bumping and rolling down the slope.

He ended up sprawled on a rock by the water's edge. The trees grew sparsely here, and as he struggled to his feet he got a clear view downstream – and saw a dugout nosing round the bend.

Aki saw him, and yelled in triumph.

Desperately, Torak looked about. No time to climb the slope. Up ahead, a rockfall blocked his way. He was trapped.

And Aki had a quiverful of arrows.

TWELVE

Torak threw off his gear and jumped in the river.

The cold was a punch in the chest, and the current tugged off his boots and blinded him with his hair. Spluttering, he surfaced among willows. He clung to one. It didn't give much cover. He took a deep breath and pulled himself under.

The river was murky, eager to carry him to Aki. His numb fingers lost their grip, and as the current spun him, he caught a flash of the log he was about to crash into.

He tried to dive, couldn't get deep enough, took a blow on the temple. Kicking water, he burst free – to a blaze of sunlight and a fishing spear aimed at his chest. It wasn't a log he'd crashed into, it was Aki's dugout.

Frantically, Torak twisted, then dived under the boat. He bobbed up on the other side. Aki was waiting. Again the spear jabbed. Again Torak dived beneath the boat.

His legs were stone, his chest bursting. An image flared in his mind of the elder-branch pipe he'd used for tapping birch-blood. Should've kept it, should've thought . . .

Once more he surfaced – but this time as Aki lunged, Torak grabbed the spear-shaft and yanked with all his might. Aki howled and pitched over the side.

Locked together, they fought, each battling to wrench the spear from the other. Aki jerked the shaft beneath Torak's chin and slammed him against the boat. Choking, Torak drove his knee into Aki's groin. Aki roared and let go of the spear. Torak went for it, but the river carried it away.

That lunge nearly cost him his life. As he reached for the spear, Aki seized his hair and pushed him under. Flailing, Torak clutched Aki's jerkin, leggings – anything. Couldn't catch hold of the slippery buckskin, couldn't claw loose from the grip on his hair. His sight darkened, his mouth gaped to scream – and the river took the bubbles of his breath. In the last moment he twisted round and sank his teeth into Aki's thigh.

A muffled bellow, and Aki released him. Torak exploded from the water, gulping air like a landed salmon.

Forcing himself under again, he surfaced in a clump of alders, upstream of the dugout. Aki was downstream, his bristly scalp just visible as he clung to a tree and fought for breath. The boat was between them, wedged among willows. That gave Torak an idea.

Sinking beneath the surface, he let the river carry him, emerging without a ripple closer to the dugout, but still upstream. He heard Aki's laboured breathing on the other side of the boat, but couldn't see him. The Boar Clan boy sounded spent, and Torak hesitated. Then a hardness like a splinter of bone seemed to enter his heart.

Bracing his shoulders against a willow, he kicked the dugout with both feet. It bucked like a forest horse. He kicked again – it jolted loose – and the river took hold.

The moment before the dugout struck Aki, Torak grabbed a tree and pulled himself high enough to see. He saw the boy's head jerk up, his eyes widen in fear. He saw the heavy oak smack into him and bear him down, down towards the rapids. Aki didn't even have time to scream.

Grimly, Torak clung to the tree. The lapping water was gentle. From downstream came no sound except the roar of the rapids.

Torak turned and swam upriver to where he'd left his gear. He hauled himself out and collapsed. The muddy taste of the river was in his mouth, the sour smell of moss in his nostrils. The wound in his chest ached.

Retrieving his things, he spotted a way up the rocks which he hadn't noticed before, and started to climb. Granite scratched his bare feet, and he remembered that the river had taken his boots. He shrugged.

When he reached the top, he retraced his steps till the rapids were in sight. To make sure.

The dugout had slammed into a boulder above them. Between boulder and boat, Torak glimpsed a hand. It wasn't moving. Maybe Aki was unconscious and drowning. Maybe he was already dead. Torak couldn't bring himself to care.

Drawing his knife, he cut a switch from an elder tree and trimmed it to make a breathing tube. Then he jammed it in his belt and started upstream, leaving Aki to his fate.

There was something wrong with Tall Tailless.

Wolf had sensed this in his pack-brother for a while. Tall

Tailless no longer listened to Wolf, or even to the Forest, and he was beginning to do bad things.

It was getting worse. A badness was gnawing him on the inside, like the badness that had gnawed the tip of Wolf's tail in the Great Cold.

Anxiously, Wolf followed his pack-brother, staying out of sight because Tall Tailless had told him to go away, but watching nevertheless.

Wolf kept level with him now as they followed the Fast Wet towards the Mountains. As he wove between the trees, Wolf smelt otter and beaver, and a whiff of the Otherness which hid its true scent. He didn't know what to do about that, so he chewed a juniper branch, that made him feel better.

Suddenly, he smelt wolf.

The scent drove all else from his mind. Yes, fresh wolf scat, and the strong, sweet scent-markings of the lead wolf.

His heart gave a bound. He *knew* this scent! The Mountain pack!

Wild with joy, Wolf gave two short barks: *Where are you?*

The wind carried an answering howl – and Wolf flew towards it. Now he could be among wolves again, *and* help Tall Tailless! This was what Tall Tailless needed: to be among his own kind, to be among wolves!

It didn't take long to find them, because they'd paused to wash the blood from their muzzles at a little Fast Wet. As Wolf sped towards them, he took in everything in a snap. The hunt had been good: he smelt deer blood on their fur, saw their bellies sagging with meat they were carrying back to the Den.

The lead pair were the same, but there had been changes, as there always are in a wolf pack. The old wolf was gone, and the one who loved digging for mice was lame and had become underwolf, while the cubs who'd played with Wolf on the Mountain were young full-growns like himself, although smaller.

One of these was a beautiful, dark-furred female who'd been extremely good at hunt-the-lemming. She caught Wolf's scent and gave an excited twitch of her tail – but she didn't come to greet him, because it was up to the leaders to decide if he was allowed back.

Skittering to a halt, Wolf approached the lead male in the proper way for a young full-grown to greet his elder. Sleeking back his ears, Wolf belly-crawled towards him, apologizing for being gone so long.

The leader looked proudly away. With fearsome speed, he grabbed Wolf's muzzle in his jaws, threw him onto his back, and stood over him, growling.

Wolf thumped his tail and whined.

The pack watched.

The leader released Wolf and raised his head, narrowing his eyes. Wolf took the hint and licked the leader's muzzle, whining respectfully and waggling his hindquarters to thank him for being allowed back.

Now the lead female shouldered her mate aside to get her share of the greeting, and after that, everyone followed in a frenzy of nibble-greeting and rubbing of flanks.

Darkfur playfully pawed Wolf's shoulder, but was body-slammed away by a male with a black ear: the leader of the young full-growns. Blackear tried to muzzle-grab Wolf, but Wolf wriggled out of Blackear's grip, muzzle-grabbed him back and flipped him onto his flank, straddling him and growling till Blackear thumped his tail in apology. Wolf released him and licked his nose to show that this was accepted. *So. Now I am above you in the pack.* And that was decided.

At the same time, Wolf was breathing in the wonderful, sweet smell of cubs on everyone's fur. The fierce love of wolf cubs flared in his chest. Oh, to race to the Den and meet them! To snuffle them and let them clamber over him!

Why did you leave? Darkfur asked with a glance and a twitch of her tail.

Why did you leave the Mountain? Wolf replied.

The others crowded round, and he got as many answers as there were wolves. *Thunderer. Great Soft Cold. Cubs. Ancient Den. Big Wet. Wrong Smell. Needed. Sent . . .*

Suddenly, the lead female raised her muzzle and tasted the air. Then she flicked an ear at Wolf. *You hunt with us now.*

Wolf wagged his tail. *I bring my pack-brother.*

A ripple of tension ran through her. *You are of this pack. No other.*

Anxiously, Wolf dipped his head. *He is my pack-brother. He is – he has no tail. He runs on hind legs.*

The lead male gave an irritable twitch. *He is not-wolf!*

Wolf whined and dropped his ears to show – as politely as he could – that this wasn't so.

A glance passed between the lead pair. Darkfur threw Wolf a puzzled look.

The lead male moved off, then turned his grizzled head. *A wolf cannot be of two packs.*

Wolf's tail drooped.

The Up darkened, and the Wet began to fall.

Wolf stood in the Wet and watched the Mountain pack trotting away into the trees.

THIRTEEN

It was raining, and Torak was chilled to the bone, but he was too scared to wake up a fire. The rockfall had crushed his shelter. He'd only just escaped.

For half a moon he'd survived in the gulley off the Axehandle. At least, he *thought* it was half a moon, although he was losing track of time, as he was losing his skill at tracking prey. When Wolf was with him, things were better; but then he would start worrying that Wolf was in danger, and send him away again – and things would turn bad.

Now the rocks had forced him from the gully. Or maybe it was the Hidden People. They were everywhere: in tree and rock and stream. Maybe they were watching him right now.

Shouldering his bow, he headed off. 'Step by step,' he muttered, 'that's the way.'

He twitched. Fin-Kedinn had told him that. But Fin-Kedinn had cast him out. Thinking of him hurt.

It hurt to think about Renn, too. She had Bale now. He'd seen that. She didn't need him any more.

At the Axehandle he stooped to drink, and his name-soul stared back. He recoiled. He looked like the Walker. Filthy. Mad. Was that how he was going to end up?

He stumbled upriver, talking to himself, fingering the wound on his chest. He'd yanked out the stitches, but it still refused to heal.

He walked for a long time, till he reached the very edge of the Forest. He found himself on a hillside, with the east wind cold on his face, like icy breath. Before him, stretching all the way to the High Mountains, lay a vast inland sea: an endless expanse of misty, shimmering grey. Lake, mist, rain. He couldn't tell where one ended and the other began. The world had turned to water.

Lake Axehead, he thought muzzily. This must be Lake Axehead.

A strange, shivering cry split the air.

Torak gave a start.

The cry fell away. Its echo lingered in his mind.

'Lake Axehead is – different,' Renn had told him once. 'So are the Otters.' Torak had seen some at last winter's feast, but he didn't know what kind of people they were; except that the Walker had been Otter Clan, and they'd cast him out.

Below him, the Axehandle seeped from the Lake through a marshy bed of reeds. To the south, needle-pricks of watery green light glimmered in the haze. That must be the Otters' camp. He remembered hearing that they only camped on the south shore. He didn't know why.

Better avoid the south shore, then, and keep to the north.

Wolf appeared and gave him a subdued greeting, rubbing his wet flank against Torak's thigh. Together they descended the slope.

The ground turned boggy. They leapt from tussock to tussock, sending up silver darts of water. The reeds – which had appeared knee-high – now loomed taller than the tallest man.

Torak hated them. He hated the murky, rotten-smelling water lapping their stems; their menacing, knife-sharp leaves; their bent brown heads that slyly watched him pass.

He came to a tussock like a hunched man about to rise. Beyond it, a walkway disappeared into the reeds. It was only logs lashed together with wovenbark rope, but Torak felt its power, and caught a faint hum at the edge of hearing.

Nothing would make him go in there.

With the reed-bed on his right, he squelched north. To his relief, Wolf found firmer ground: an elk trail skirting the shore. But shortly afterwards, the mist closed in, and his spirits sank.

Wolf, too, seemed cowed as he padded forwards. Then the mist swallowed him, leaving Torak on his own. He didn't dare howl. He dreaded to think what might answer. Putting out his hands, he groped forwards.

Suddenly, Wolf hurtled towards him, eyes bulging with terror. He sped past Torak and vanished the way they'd come. At the same moment, Torak's fingers sank into a clammy, stinking softness. With a gasp he sprang back. Something red flapped wetly in his face. He tore it off. The mist thinned. His heart jerked. The trail was barred:

strung across with a nightmare tangle of fleshy, glistening coils. He breathed the stench of blood, saw plump, wriggling maggots. He'd stumbled into a web. A web of entrails.

Whimpering, he fled, rubbing his face where the web had touched it. Splashing back into the marsh, he sank to his knees, and the reeds rippled with laughter.

He was back at the walkway.

'No,' he whispered. 'Not in there.'

He ran south. The marshy Axehandle was easily crossed, and Wolf joined him, his big paws scarcely sinking.

They hadn't gone far when they heard voices; saw lights bobbing up and down. Otter Clan hunters.

Then there they were: small, lithe people with spears and fierce green faces, paddling swift craft of yellow reeds.

'There!' shouted one. 'Near the reeds!'

Reeds to his left. To his right, a hillside of crowberry scrub, giving no cover. He barked a command to Wolf to split up – Wolf obeyed – Torak waded into the reeds.

Grimacing as his feet sank into slime, he forced himself deeper, up to his neck. They wouldn't find him here.

The mist parted, and ahead there were no more reeds. He'd reached open water.

He spotted a floating beech bough, probably ripped off in a storm. He ducked behind it.

Something slithered over his foot. He cried out.

More shouts from the Otters – they'd heard him. Now they were coming through the mist: three reed boats curved at prow and stern, like water birds. Two hunters in each, one with a paddle, the other a rushlight and a greenstone fishing spear.

Dipping behind the branch, Torak peered through the leaves.

Somewhere behind him rose the eerie, shivering cry he'd heard before.

The Otters froze. Then the woman in the middle boat dug in her paddle and slid forwards, coming to a smooth halt not two paces from Torak's branch.

He didn't dare duck, in case the movement caught her eye.

As she steadied the craft, her companion scanned the reeds, unaware that the quarry lay under his nose.

Like his mate, he wore a sleeveless tunic of golden wovengrass. His long brown hair flowed free, except for a band of silver fish skin at his brow, and another that braided his beard into a fish tail. His earlobes were pierced by bone fish-hooks, carved to look like leaping trout, and from one hung a tuft of dark-brown otter fur. The man's face was covered in green clay – Torak saw the fine cracks around his eyes and mouth – and his clan-tattoos were blue-green waves undulating up his throat, so that his head resembled an outlandish pod emerging from reeds.

A pod with eyes. Restless with waterlight, they flickered past Torak's branch – then returned for another look.

In the distance, a wolf howled.

The Otter man hissed, and his mate touched her clan-creature fur.

More howls. Torak knew it was Wolf, but he couldn't understand what he was saying. He could only hear the urgency.

The howling unnerved the Otters. The woman steered her craft away from the branch, and Torak sent Wolf silent thanks.

There was a splash behind him, and he turned to see a large grey bird staring at him with a vivid scarlet eye. It flew off, swooping over the Otters.

The woman followed its flight, and nodded as if it had spoken. Raising her hand, she made an undulating signal to her companions in the other boats, and Torak saw them spreading out.

If he left the shelter of the branch, they would see him. If he stayed, they would surround him.

Unless . . .

He still had that elder-stem pipe. It was less than a forearm long, and he couldn't remember checking if it was hollow all the way through. He'd soon find out.

Taking one end between his lips, he sank.

Water filled his nostrils, but he forced himself to breathe through his mouth, praying they wouldn't hear him. Slowly he swam sideways into the reeds, hoping to slip past their cordon.

Staying at the right depth was harder than he'd expected. His gear weighed him down, and to keep the stem upright, he had to tread water and tilt his head back. With aching neck, he stared through a forest of reeds. Above him the skin of the Lake was bright and hard as ice, flecked with drifting constellations of dust.

He heard the nibbles of feeding fish, caught a red flash as a shoal of char sped past. Glancing down, he saw that the bottom of the Lake was within reach. Bars of light slid over boulders and tree-trunks furred with weeds. His feet sank into mud which eddied like green smoke. His free hand touched a lattice of reeds which sagged, then sprang back.

It wasn't reeds, it was a net, a wovenbark net, hanging from wooden floats and weighted with stones: too tough to cut, and so big that he couldn't see the ends.

Whipping round, he glimpsed another. The Otters were surrounding him.

He threw away the elder stem and dived.

Shouts above: they'd spotted him.

He swam deeper, under the nets, dreading the stab of a fishing spear between his shoulder blades.

Lights flashed in his head, and the shouts faded to a dull boom as he swam down.

Suddenly he became aware of a distant shrilling. Faster than thought it sped towards him, louder and louder, a needle of ice piercing his mind.

A dizzying trail of bubbles swept past him. Then another criss-crossed the first, and another. He caught a flicker of fins, a ripple of watery laughter. Dread seized him. He'd heard it before, when he'd been swept over the Thunder Falls. The Hidden People of the Lake had come for him.

They swarmed around him, boneless fingers trailing over his eyes and mouth. *You are for us, they gurgled, boy with the drifting souls! Give us the silver bubbles of your breath, and we will draw you into the deep!*

His chest was caught in a rib-crushing grip. Darkness bled across his sight. Wriggling like an eel, he shrugged off his sleeping-sack, and the Hidden People whirled it away.

His bow went next, but his quiver-strap snagged in his belt. He drew his knife and cut it; felt the tug of hands dragging it into the murk. Grabbing his chance, he kicked for the glimmer of the world above.

Heedless of spears and hunters, he burst from the surface.

The reeds were all around him; silent and still. Then he recognized the humped tussock. He was back at the walkway. Narrow as a hand, it beckoned him into the dripping green tunnel.

In the distance, he heard voices. Hushed, frightened.

'Arrin found a bow,' said a man. 'A little west of south.'

'The Hidden Ones have taken him,' said a woman.

'Or the Lake,' put in another man, older than the first.

'Quiet, they'll hear!' said the younger man. 'Let's go, or they'll take us too!'

'If we go now,' said the woman, 'we go empty-handed. The bow of a drowned outcast isn't what Ananda sent us to fetch.'

'If Ananda wants healing water,' growled the older man, 'she can fetch it herself. I'm not going near that spring now.'

Their voices became less distinct as they paddled away. '. . . keep watch here, in case he tries to come south . . .'

Wretchedly, Torak hauled himself onto firmer ground and stared at the walkway. To the south were the Otters. To the north that terrible, stinking web. He had no choice.

Wolf emerged from the mist and stood beside him. He didn't seem frightened – but then, it was getting harder to read his moods.

Torak knew now that it was to this place that he'd been driven ever since he'd been cast out. East, always east – till he'd ended up here.

The wound in his chest throbbed. Through the hissing of the reeds, he seemed to hear the voice of Seshru the Viper Mage. '. . . *like the harpoon head beneath the skin of the seal. One twitch and it will draw you, no matter how hard you struggle . . .*'

He no longer had the will to resist. He stumbled past Wolf and onto the walkway.

High above the north shore of the Lake, on a stony headland which rose clear of the mist, a stream bubbled.

Beside the stream burned a ring of green fire.

Within the ring of fire lay a pebble marked with the tattoo of the Wolf Clan.

Upon the pebble lay the shrivelled scrap of Torak's skin which bore the mark of the Soul-Eater.

Around pebble and skin wound the coils of a green clay serpent.

Slowly, the clay dried. Inexorably, the serpent tightened its grip upon skin and stone.

A green hand passed over the pebble: once, twice, three times.

A voice began to murmur, mingling with the hissing of the flames, like a demon slipping in and out of evil dreams.

When reed quakes, when storm breaks, remember me
When thunder growls, when wind howls, remember me
I am the reed and the storm, the thunder and the wind
I summon you, I bind your souls to mine
You can never be free
You belong to me

FOURTEEN

The walkway lurched, nearly tipping Torak into the Lake. He dropped to all fours and clung on with both hands.

Behind him Wolf stood, his claws digging into the wood. He hated this.

There was no room for Torak to turn, so he cast an encouraging glance over his shoulder. Wolf dropped his ears and gave an unhappy twitch of his tail.

The walkway stopped rocking, and Torak rose. The logs were treacherous, the reeds so thick he had to push them aside. He shrank from the touch of their long, clammy fingers.

The mist closed in. The walkway dwindled to a line of single logs lashed end to end, secured by posts sunk in the reedbed. There were so many turns that Torak lost his bearings. He didn't know if he was heading out into the Lake, or skirting the shore.

At times, sour brown water slopped over his feet. At others, he found himself crossing a stinking swamp. And the reeds kept changing: from ashen spears with feathery purple plumes, to creaking canes with brown club heads that tapped him furtively on the shoulder. They didn't want him here. If he fell in, they would hold him under till he drowned, or the Hidden People dragged him into the slime.

He'd seen it happen. Once, he and Fa had found a red deer stag trapped up to its neck in a swamp. It was half dead of exhaustion, but they couldn't end its misery. It's bad luck to interfere with those the Hidden People have claimed. Instead, Fa had knelt and stroked its cheek, murmuring a prayer to help it on its way. Afterwards, Torak had been haunted by the look in those dull brown eyes. He'd wondered how long the stag had taken to die.

Wolf's warning 'uff' dragged him back to the present.

Ahead, something crouched on the walkway.

Torak's hand went to his shoulder – but of course he had no clan-creature skin. Nothing to protect him from demon or tokoroth.

As he drew nearer, he saw that it wasn't a creature but a post, planted by the walkway and rising to chest height. It had been limed a sickly grey, and painted with a dizzying fish-bone pattern of tiny green dots. It was topped by a small, misshapen head of green clay into which were pressed two white snail-shell eyes.

The shimmering dots made Torak giddy, but he couldn't look away. The power of the thing filled his mind, like the silent boom after thunder.

Wolf felt it too, and set back his ears. Even the reeds leaned away, fearing to touch.

Torak remembered that he still had Renn's swansfoot pouch, with his medicine horn inside, and the strand of her hair. What would she have done?

The mark of the hand. Maybe that would help.

The ochre in the horn was clogged with damp, and he had to spit in it to make it runny; nothing would have made him use Lake water. Pouring the red liquid into his palm, he daubed the mark on his cheek. He tried to do the same for Wolf – on his forehead, so he couldn't lick it off – but only managed a crude smear. As he finished, the humming in his head grew worse. Someone didn't like him using earthblood.

Holding his breath, he edged past the post. Wolf followed, hackles raised. As they passed it, the reeds stirred angrily, and the humming grew stronger.

Torak reached a turn in the walkway – and there, guarded by club-headed reeds, stood *three* posts, their white eyes staring from mouthless faces of green clay.

Something slithered across his cheek. He dashed it away, and the walkway rocked wildly. Too late, he saw that its far end had been untied and was floating free. He lurched – righted himself – and backed into Wolf, who yelped and nearly fell in.

Trembling, they stood together, while around them the reeds rustled.

'What do you want?' cried Torak.

The reeds fell silent. That was worse. He shouldn't have shouted.

He made to go on – and caught his breath.

The posts were gone.

The reeds were different, too. Those surrounding the posts had had brown club heads, but these were a feathery purple.

With a shiver, Torak realized what this meant. It wasn't the posts which had moved, it was the walkway. While he'd been fighting for balance, someone had rearranged the logs.

For the first time since entering the reed-bed, it occurred to him to turn back. But he couldn't, and that frightened him more than anything. His thoughts were no longer his own. The mist had seeped inside his head. Here, in this nebulous half-world which was neither land nor lake, he was losing his very self.

Wolf nose-nudged his thigh and gave an anxious whine. Torak glanced down – and frowned. Wolf was trying to tell him something, but he couldn't understand. He, Torak, who had learned wolf talk as a baby – *he couldn't understand.*

He stumbled on, with Wolf padding after him.

They hadn't gone far when the walkway forked. Both ways were marked by a post. The left-hand post had been beheaded; the right-hand one bore a green clay head, but the eyes had been plucked out, leaving blind hollows. Tied around the brow was a viper's shed skin. Skewered to it by a bone needle was a tiny, shrivelled heart.

Seshru the Viper Mage.

Torak wiped icy sweat from his face.

Behind him he caught a flash of movement vanishing into the reeds. There, among the leaves. White eyes.

'Who's there?' he said.

The eyes blinked – then reappeared on the other side of the walkway: blue-white, flickering like flame.

'Who's there?' Torak whispered.

Eyes glowed all around him. The humming rose to an ear-splitting whine.

Whimpering, Torak ran for the nearest walkway, the one with the viper skin. The log shuddered – tipped – and threw him off. The murky waters of the Lake closed over his head.

Down he went, groping for reeds, walkway, anything. Couldn't find it, couldn't tell up from down.

A splash and a flurry of bubbles as Wolf leapt in after him. Desperately Torak swam for the flailing paws – but Wolf had disappeared.

Wolf! he screamed in his mind. But his pack-brother was gone.

Frantically, he swam through a slippery mass of reeds.

Suddenly there were no more reeds and the water was freezing and he was swimming over bottomless dark.

FIFTEEN

Torak was woken by something slithering over his face.

With a shudder he started up – and glimpsed a scaly tail vanishing into the undergrowth.

He was lying on a pile of rotting pine-needles at the edge of a silent forest. Below him, a beach of charcoal-coloured pebbles sloped down to the flinty waters of the Lake.

How had he got here? He couldn't remember.

The east wind whistled over the stones, making him shiver. His clothes felt gritty and damp, and there was a humming in his ears. He was hungry and he missed Wolf, but he didn't dare howl. He wasn't even sure if he could.

The mist had cleared, but an ashen haze robbed the sun of warmth. At the south end of the beach, the reeds stood sentinel. Below him the Lake stretched to the edge of sight, opaque and forbidding.

He got to his feet. The pine-needles were strewn along the shore in broad swathes, as if washed up by a great flood. And the trees, he noticed uneasily, leaned back from the Lake.

He ran into the Forest.

There was no birdsong, and the trees watched him sullenly. He found a stream of muddy water and drank; spotted a few shrivelled lingonberries left over from last autumn, and gobbled them up. In the mud he saw tracks: webbed, with a tail drag. He scowled. He knew this creature, but he couldn't bring it to mind. That frightened him. Once, he had known every sign of every creature in the Forest.

He wondered how he was going to survive. He had no sleeping-sack, no bow, no arrows, no food. Only an axe, a knife, a half-empty medicine horn and a pouch of sodden tinder. And he'd forgotten how to hunt.

The ground climbed, and he reached a small, windy lake where the sun stabbed his eyes and the clamour of frogs hurt his head. He stumbled back into the trees, but they tripped him and scratched his face. Even the Forest had turned against him.

The trees ended. He was back at the reed-bed. He staggered north along the edge of the Forest, till he came to a place where the reeds narrowed to a stretch an arrowshot across.

Beyond them rose a granite rockface. It looked strangely enticing. Rowans and juniper clung to cracks, while ferns and orchids trembled in the spray from a waterfall. Above it swallows swooped and ravens wheeled, and on either side, Torak saw carvings of fish, elk, people:

hammer-etched into the rock and painted green. He guessed that the water flowed from the Otters' healing spring. If only he could reach it.

The reeds rattled, warning him back.

The sun began to sink, the trail veered south, and he found himself by the Lake, wading through pine-needles on a charcoal-coloured beach.

He halted. He recognized this beach. He was back where he'd started.

A horrible thought occurred to him.

To test it, he headed back into the Forest and re-traced his steps till he reached the reed-bed – except this time he turned south instead of north. Dusk was coming on when he finally stumbled onto the beach. Same beach. Same tracks. His own.

An island. The Lake had spewed him onto an island, where even the Otters feared to come. He was trapped: his escape cut off by the Lake to the east, the reeds to the west.

The wind stirred the trees. He stared at them. What were their names? 'Pine,' he said haltingly. 'Birch. Juniper?'

Listen to what the Forest is telling you, Fa used to say. But the Forest no longer spoke to him.

Gathering sticks and tinder, he blundered onto the beach and laid them in the lee of a boulder, so the Otters wouldn't see. At first his strike-fire refused to make sparks, but at last he managed it. Muttering, he hunched over the fire.

On the Lake, a lonely cry echoed. The red-eyed bird that had betrayed him in the reeds.

More voices joined in. Not birds. Wolves.

Leaping to his feet, Torak drew his knife. He'd always loved wolf song. But it struck terror in him now.

Another wolf called to the pack. Torak knew that howl. It was Wolf, his Wolf – and yet he couldn't make out what Wolf was saying. The familiar voice had become as incomprehensible as the yowl of a lynx.

'Wolf!' cried Torak. 'Come back!'

But Wolf didn't come.

Wolf had forsaken him.

Torak's fists clenched at his sides. So be it.

Wolf raced through the Forest. *Where was Tall Tailless?*

One moment they'd been together, fighting the Big Wet, and then he was gone! Wolf had tried to howl, but the Wet had come roaring into his gullet and he'd panicked. He'd forgotten Tall Tailless, forgotten everything except lashing out with his paws – until at last he'd struck land.

Now he ran this way and that, snuffing for scents. He smelt bracken and beaver, otter and lingonberry; he heard the taillesses on their floating reeds, and the Hidden Ones slithering in and out of the Wet. Worry gnawed him. Maybe Tall Tailless had become Not-Breath.

A cry rang through the trees: a desperate tailless yowl.

Wolf halted, swivelling his ears, lifting his muzzle. He caught the scent. Tall Tailless!

Wolf flew along the scent trail. He wove between trees, leapt over bracken – and there at last was his pack-brother, crouching behind a boulder at the edge of the Big Wet, by a small Bright Beast-that-Bites-Hot.

Wolf burst from the trees, and Tall Tailless turned and stared.

Wolf loped over the black stones and threw himself at

his pack-brother, pawing his chest and snuffle-licking his muzzle.

Tall Tailless pushed him away. Then he waved his great claw at Wolf.

Wolf jumped back.

Again Tall Tailless lashed out, yowling in tailless talk.

Wolf heard the terror in his yowl, he saw it in the beautiful silver eyes. How could this be? Tall Tailless couldn't be *scared* of him?

Bewildered, Wolf sat down. He felt a whine beginning in his chest.

Suddenly, Tall Tailless grabbed a limb of the Bright Beast and lunged at Wolf – *lunged at him with the Bright Beast!* Wolf leapt sideways, but the Bright Beast bit him on the muzzle and he yelped.

Tall Tailless bared his teeth in a snarl and attacked again. Wolf couldn't understand the yowls, but he knew what they meant. *Go away! You're no longer my pack-brother! Go away!*

Wild with pain and terror, Wolf fled.

After Wolf had gone, Torak stayed shivering on the beach.

He was exhausted but he didn't dare sleep. If he slept, they would come for him. The wolves. The Otter Clan. The Hidden People. The Soul-Eaters. All, all were against him.

Clutching axe and knife, he rocked back and forth, staring at the flames. He was hungry. He ought to set snares and fishing lines, but he couldn't remember how.

He began to nod.

Red eyes came at him. He woke with a cry. The eyes were real. Not red, but yellow. Wolf eyes.

Seizing a burning branch, he lashed out, etching the shadows with a glittering trail of sparks.

The wolves drew back. Their eyes were blank and terrible. They made no sound.

Wolf was among them. Wolf who had been his pack-brother, but had forsaken him.

With head lowered and tail lashing, Wolf moved menacingly forwards.

Torak's heart twisted. Wolf had come to taunt him. *See, I have a new pack! I don't need you!*

'Get away from me,' whispered Torak.

Wolf's ears twitched. His tail went still.

'Get back!' snarled Torak. He swung the branch at Wolf, who leapt out of the way.

The wolves watched in unblinking silence. Then, one by one, they trotted into the Forest.

Wolf was the last to go. For a moment he glanced back at Torak. Then he too vanished like mist.

It was very quiet after he'd gone.

A large black bird flew overhead with a scornful cark! Torak tried to remember its name. Raven. Raven Clan . . . Renn. She'd been his friend. Hadn't she? He couldn't remember her face.

He touched the oozing wound on his breastbone. There had been something he had to do . . .

The Soul-Eaters. He'd been going to prove that he wasn't one of them. Make the clans take him back.

It all seemed very long ago.

The sun dipped below the trees, and shadows crept down the beach as he sat by the dying fire. The buzzing in his head got worse. He sensed the Hidden People all around: watching, waiting. Feverishly, he fed the fire.

The faint moon rose in the blue sky, and it occurred to

him that tonight was Midsummer Night. His birthnight.

'Fourteen,' he muttered. His voice sound harsh and unfamiliar. 'You're fourteen summers old. Happy birthnight, Torak.'

He started to laugh.

Once he'd started, he couldn't stop.

SIXTEEN

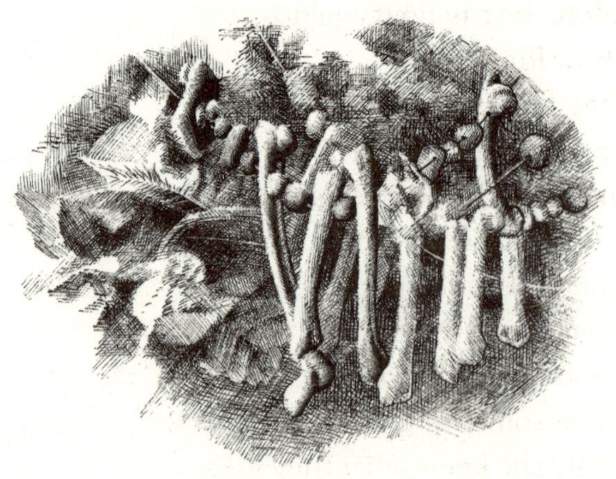

Fin-Kedinn plunged the spear into the fire, and a blizzard of sparks engulfed the antlers mounted on its head.

The Ravens gave a joyful shout and the proud, happy trees rustled approval. It was Midsummer night, the night when the clans honoured the Forest by walking sunwise round the fire, garlanding the trees with necklaces of bone and berries.

All except Renn.

To have taken part would have felt as if she were betraying Torak. Tonight was his birthnight. How could she sit here enjoying salmon-liver stew and flame-blackened boar?

It was nearly a moon since the clan meet; nearly two since he'd been cast out. She missed him all the time. The misery was always with her, like a stone in her chest.

'What if something happens to him?' she'd said to Fin-Kedinn that morning. 'If he fell and broke his leg and couldn't hunt.'

'He's tough,' her uncle had said. 'He's survived on his own before, he can do it again.'

'For how long?'

To that, Fin-Kedinn had no answer.

Since the clan meet, the Ravens had moved east up the Axehandle, and whenever she could, Renn had secretly combed the Forest for any trace of Torak. In vain. Sometimes she woke in the night and thought, what if he never comes back?

She had no idea whether he'd done the rite, but she sensed that something was terribly wrong. The signs were bad. If only she knew what they meant.

She fingered the scar where the elk's antler had gashed her forearm. The wound had healed, but the memory was still raw. If that hunting party hadn't heard her cries . . .

Then, shortly after the clan meet, Aki had gone missing. His friends had found nothing but the remains of his boat. Renn had a dreadful feeling that Torak had been involved.

And nobody seemed to care. Everyone seemed to be pretending he didn't exist.

On the other side of the fire, Bale was twisting bramble twine for more garlands. He'd tied back his hair with a strip of seal hide, and he looked very handsome. Renn resented him. He'd stayed with the Ravens when the rest of his clan had returned to the islands, but instead of trying to find Torak, he'd gone hunting on the coast in his precious skinboat. She was disappointed. She'd expected more of him.

'May the World Spirit walk beneath your boughs,' Fin-

Kedinn told the Forest. 'May you grow strong, and seed many saplings!'

Suddenly, Renn couldn't bear it. Leaping to her feet, she ran from the camp.

The Raven Mage squatted on the riverbank like a toad. She'd left the celebrations to cast the bones. Now she regarded Renn without emotion. 'So. You seek my help at last.'

'No,' said Renn. 'I've never wanted your help.'

'You seek it all the same.'

Renn set her teeth. Throwing herself down in the bracken, she shredded a burdock leaf. 'I've been seeing signs. I don't know what they mean. Teach me how to read them.'

'No,' said Saeunn. 'You're not ready.'

Renn stared at her. 'You're the one who's always forcing me to learn Magecraft!'

'If you tried to read the signs now, you could do great harm.'

'Why,' said Renn.

With her staff, the Raven Mage drew a circle in the mud, and placed within it three dull white pebbles. 'Your talent lies in linking signs to make a pattern. Until now, your dreams have done this for you. To do it at will, in your waking life, you would have to open your mind completely.'

Renn raised her chin. 'I could do that.'

'Fool of a girl!' Saeunn struck the earth with her staff. 'Have you learned nothing? Your first moon bleed has brought a fearsome increase in your power – but it is raw, untried! To open your mind now could be fatal – to you and to others!'

For a moment they glared at each other, the crone and

the girl, linked only by the unforgiving bond of Magecraft.

Renn was the first to look away. 'Why didn't you tell him he was clanless?'

'The time wasn't right.'

'How could you keep that from him?'

'You've kept things from him too.'

Renn flinched.

'He has a destiny,' declared the Raven Mage. 'This is part of it. So is being cast out.'

Renn was about to ask more when Bale came into view on the path. She told him to go away. He ignored her.

'If this is about Torak,' he said to Saeunn, 'I've a right to hear. I'm his kin.'

'Then why don't you act like it,' said Renn, 'and try to help him?'

'Why don't you?' he shot back.

'No-one may help the outcast,' Saeunn reminded them.

'And squabbling won't help anyone,' said Fin-Kedinn, appearing behind Bale.

Saeunn indicated Renn. 'She says she sees signs.'

Renn bridled. She wasn't ready to speak of this to Fin-Kedinn, let alone Bale.

'What signs?' said Fin-Kedinn, sitting on the bank and motioning Bale to do the same.

Renn picked at a hole in the knee of her legging. 'He took your axe. He went into my medicine pouch and took a pebble he'd left me last summer. He spirit walked in the elk and he – he attacked me.'

'I'll never believe that was Torak,' said Bale.

'Well I'm not making it up!' snapped Renn.

'The pebble,' Saeunn cut in. 'Why wasn't I told?'

'Why should I tell you?' muttered Renn.

'Tell me now,' said the Raven Mage.

Renn swallowed. 'He'd put his mark on it. In alder juice.'

'His mark?' said Saeunn. 'His clan-tattoo?'

'Right down to the scar on his cheek.'

'Ah,' breathed the Raven Mage.

Renn felt a prickle of unease. 'I – I kept it safe. But at the clan meet, he took it.' And I know why, she thought miserably. He took it to tell me that he isn't coming back.

'Ah.' Saeunn picked up one of the white stones and turned it in her fingers. 'Now it becomes clear.'

'What does?' said Renn.

The Raven Mage leaned close, and Renn saw the threads of spittle webbing her toothless gums. 'The outcast,' said the Raven Mage, 'has fallen prey to the soul-sickness.'

For a moment there was silence. Then both Renn and Bale spoke at once.

'What's that?' said Bale.

'Is it because of the Soul-Eater tattoo?' said Renn. 'Did he try to cut it out and it didn't work and it made him sick?'

'Tattoos?' Saeunn spat. 'No! Even without tattoos, souls get sick, as well as bodies! They fall prey to demons. Spells.'

From her medicine pouch she shook three small, mottled bones and set them on the black earth. She touched the first with her knotted forefinger. 'If your name-soul falls sick, you forget who you are. You become like a ghost.' She touched the second. 'If the canker attacks your clan-soul, you lose your sense of good and evil. You become as a demon.' Her horny talon moved to the last bone. 'If your world-soul becomes palsied, you lose your link with other living things – hunter, prey, Forest. You become as a Lost One.' Tilting her palm, she dropped the stone, and it struck the world-soul bone, which jumped as if it were alive. 'If his name-pebble fell into the wrong hands . . . '

Renn shut her eyes.

Bale said, 'I don't believe this. Torak isn't sick, he's furious. I would be too, if I'd been cast out for something that wasn't my fault.'

Saeunn bristled like an angry raven, but Fin-Kedinn said, 'I think Saeunn's right, Torak is soul-sick. But who did this to him? Which of the three?'

'You mean the Soul-Eaters,' said Renn.

'Three survived the battle on the ice,' said Fin-Kedinn. 'Thiazzi. Eostra. Seshru. At the clan meet I spoke to people from all over the Forest and beyond, seeking clues as to where they might have gone. No-one's seen any trace of them.' He paused. 'And yet it seems to me that the manner in which Torak's tattoo was revealed, and his spirit walking in the elk – these bear the print of a single mind, working alone.'

Saeunn nodded. 'One mind, but which? For days I've fasted and read the bones. The Oak Mage and the Eagle Owl Mage feel far away. The one who haunts the Forest – who draws the outcast to her – is Seshru the Viper Mage.'

Fin-Kedinn bowed his head.

Renn dug her fingernails into her palms.

Bale was puzzled. 'But – she's only one woman. How much harm can she do?'

'More than you could possibly imagine,' said Fin-Kedinn.

Saeunn turned to Renn. 'You were the last to have seen her. Tell him what she is.'

Renn couldn't speak. She was back in the forest of stone, in the flickering torchlight and the stink of slaughter, watching the snake-haired mask of the Viper Mage whirling, hissing as she sought the Otherworld with dead gutskin eyes . . .

'Renn,' Fin-Kedinn said softly.

She drew a breath. 'She – she does everything sideways, like a snake. She lies all the time. She makes you see things that aren't there. She makes you do things.'

'I don't understand,' said Bale. 'I spoke to some Vipers at the clan meet, and they told me they've never *had* a Mage who turned Soul-Eater. So how can this Seshru be – '

'Like a snake,' said Fin-Kedinn, 'she sheds one self and becomes another.'

Bale was aghast. 'She changed her name? But no-one would do that, it's a kind of death!'

'That's what it means to be a Soul-Eater,' said Renn. 'You sacrifice all that you were. You live only for power.'

Bale stared at her as if seeing her for the first time.

Fin-Kedinn picked up the bones and poured them slowly from palm to palm. 'So now we know. Torak is soul-sick – and at the mercy of the Viper Mage.'

'The Viper Mage has no mercy,' said Saeunn.

Next morning, Renn woke early, and went to see Fin-Kedinn.

She found him fishing for pike in the shallows where a brook flowed into the Axehandle. When he saw her, he drew in his line. The hook was empty.

'What is it, Renn?' His face was grave. He had guessed why she'd come.

'I don't want to lie to you,' she said. 'I don't want to sneak away. But I have to try to find – '

'No, don't say it,' he warned. 'Don't tell me anything you couldn't tell the Leader of any other clan.'

She bit her lip. 'He's out there. Alone. Soul-sick.'

'I know.'

'Then why don't you come with me?'

'I can't be seen to break clan law.' He met her eyes. 'You of all people mustn't do this. What if he's already in her power? A spirit walker in the hands of a Soul-Eater. I can't think of anything more dangerous.'

'He's my friend. I've got to try. You understand, don't you?'

Fin-Kedinn did not reply.

'Fin-Kedinn? You do understand?'

Suddenly he looked tired. 'You're no longer a child, Renn. You're old enough to make your own choices.'

No I'm not! she wanted to say. I need you to help me! Tell me what to do!

That night, Renn sat by a smoky little fire on the banks of the Axehandle, feeling lonely and scared.

Breaking clan law had been even worse than she'd feared. By doing so, she'd cut herself off from her clan and from Fin-Kedinn.

Huddling closer to the flames, she blew on her grouse-bone whistle, but got no answer. Torak and Wolf were far away.

She could feel her power churning inside her; the secrets rising to the surface, like splinters working their way through her flesh. She didn't want to do Magecraft, she hated it, but she had a feeling that to help Torak, she might be forced to try. Because Seshru was out here somewhere.

Hatred flared in her heart, and she perceived the Soul-Eater's plan so clearly that it could have been her own.

Seshru was hunting Torak in the same way that her clan-creature hunted its quarry. The viper sinks its poisoned fangs into its prey, then follows it through the Forest as it wanders, slowly weakening. The viper is patient. It waits till the prey falls. Only then does it feed.

Renn was woken by the sizzle of water on fire.

Bale stood over her, his dripping skinboat balanced on his shoulder.

She sat up, annoyed that he'd caught her dozing. 'I thought you went back to your island,' she said crossly.

He ignored that. 'I was wrong and you were right. Torak is soul-sick. But it's worse than we thought.'

SEVENTEEN

'Aki was barely alive,' said Bale. 'Somehow he'd crawled out of the water and collapsed in a thicket. The Wolf Clan found him a couple of days later.'

'A couple of days?' said Renn. 'He's been missing nearly a moon.'

'No. The Boar Clan just didn't bother to send us word.'

'Typical,' she said in disgust. 'But what were the Wolf Clan doing so far east?'

Bale looked grim. 'Tracking Torak. To "wipe out the dishonour once and for all".'

Renn shook her head. 'Did they say where his trail led?'

'East. They lost him in the reedbeds on Lake Axehead.'

She went cold. 'Lake Axehead? Why?'

Bale brushed that aside. 'Don't you see what this means? Torak left Aki to die!'

'Maybe he didn't know Aki was there.'

'Oh, he knew. Aki says he saw Torak looking down at him from the ridge. Then he turned and walked away.' He rubbed his face. 'I know Aki was hunting him, but to leave him to die . . . That's not Torak!'

Renn stared at the fire. Bale was right. But why Lake Axehead? There was a pattern to this, but she couldn't fathom it. She only knew that of all places, the Lake was the one she was least eager to see. Her father had died on the ice river at its eastern edge. She'd promised herself she would never go back.

Bale set down his skinboat and pulled off his gutskin parka. 'You're trying to find him too, aren't you?'

She didn't reply.

'Why now, when you weren't before?'

'I was.' She told him about her searches in the Forest.

'Me too,' he said, surprising her.

'You? I thought you were hunting with the Sea-eagles.'

He was affronted. 'With Torak an outcast?'

She thought for a moment. Then she said, 'You do know that we're breaking clan law? If you tell *anyone* . . . '

'Of course I know! But that goes for you too.'

Warily they studied each other. Then Bale said, 'I caught a fish. Can I cook it on your fire?'

Renn shrugged.

It was an impressively large bream, and Bale offered her a piece which she refused, then changed her mind when she smelt it cooking. In return she gave him some dried deer meat, and showed him how to spread it with juniper-berry and marrowfat paste.

While they ate, they talked guardedly. Bale told her how he'd prepared his skinboat for its freshwater "ordeal" by coating it with seal blubber and burnt seaweed, and

Renn showed him the seal-hide bow case she'd been given in the Far North. But she didn't mention what she'd guessed of Seshru's plans. Bale was Torak's kin, but she didn't know him very well, and if it came to a battle of wills between her and the Viper Mage, he would get in the way.

On the other hand, he was strong, and he had a skinboat.

She was pondering this when Bale rose to his feet, picked up his pack, and hoisted his boat on his shoulder.

She asked him where he was going.

'Lake Axehead. You go back to your clan. I'll find Torak.'

'What?'

'Well you're not coming in my skinboat.'

'I wouldn't want to,' she lied.

'And if you went overland, you'd never keep up.' Seeing her expression, he sighed. 'Where I come from, women stay on land. The men do the hunting and the fighting.'

Renn snorted. 'Not in the Forest.'

'Maybe. But I'm Seal Clan and that's my way. Go back to camp, Renn. You're not coming with me.'

In disbelief she watched him make for the shallows. 'Even if you do reach the Lake,' she called after him, 'what are you going to do? You don't know anything about it, or the Otters!'

'I'll take my chances,' he replied.

'Fine! But I'll tell you this. You're not going to beat the Soul-Eaters by being good with a paddle!'

'We'll see about that!'

'We shall indeed,' snarled Renn as she battled through the brambles.

There was no trail along this part of the Axehandle – at least, not that she could find – and she was hot, scratched and furious. It didn't help that she kept picturing Bale speeding serenely upriver.

Above the rapids she rested, then struggled through a stand of soggy alders. The river here formed pools where many clans came to fish. Renn noticed that someone had set lines and fish traps in several of the pools. She was wondering who it was when she caught a flash of fair hair by the water's edge.

Bale hadn't seen her. He was kneeling by his overturned skinboat, patching a small tear in its hull.

'Having problems?' she called.

'Snagged on a fish trap,' he said without looking round.

'Oh dear,' said Renn unfeelingly.

'It's not right!' he burst out. 'Leaving them there for anyone to run into! They should've put some kind of marker!'

'They did. Those strips of willow bark tied to the branches? That's what Forest people leave as a warning when they're fishing.'

Bale set his jaw.

'Well, good luck,' said Renn with a cheery smile. 'Hope it doesn't slow you down too much!'

Bale threw her a thunderous look.

She was still grinning as she left the pools.

Her grin didn't last. Across the river, she saw the mouth of the gully where she and Torak had first encountered the Walker, the autumn before last. Wolf had been a cub. When his pads got sore, Torak had carried him in his arms.

A fierce longing for them swept over her.

The pines gave way to towering oaks, and the Forest turned watchful. Renn wished Bale would sweep by in his skinboat. Surely it couldn't have taken this long to sew on a patch?

A little further on, two red deer fawns peeped from the bracken, then wobbled towards her on tiny hooves. They were almost within reach before they took fright and fled.

Renn put her hand to her raven feathers. When a creature goes out of its way to attract your attention, it's often a sign. What did this mean?

It was late afternoon when she climbed the ridge the clans call the Hogback, and stood gazing over the Lake.

The low sun turned the water a dazzling gold. She saw islands scattered across it, fragile as leaves, and below her, the great reed-bed which guarded the western shore. Far to the south, she made out the black dots of the Otter camp, and to the east, the cruel white slash of the ice river.

She'd been eight summers old when she last stood here: bewildered, unable to understand why her fa was never coming back. The Otters had found his body, and Fin-Kedinn and Saeunn had gone to rescue his scattered souls. Fin-Kedinn had insisted that Renn should come too. They'd stood on the Hogback, staring at this vast inland Sea.

'Why did he go all that way?' Renn asks her uncle. 'There isn't any prey on the ice river.'

'He wasn't hunting prey,' murmurs Fin-Kedinn.

'Then why?'

'I'll tell you when you're older.' He takes her hand in his warm, strong grip, and she clings on fiercely.

Now she was back on the Hogback; but there was no Fin-Kedinn to cling to.

By the time she had made her way down the ridge, she'd begun to see the hopelessness of her task. She had no idea where Torak had gone, and there was no-one to ask. No trail led along the shore – the Otters didn't need one, they always travelled by water – and even if she reached their camp on foot, what then?

She'd started picking her way south when she heard a stirring in the reeds.

'Bale?' she said uncertainly.

No answer. Only the creak and crunch of reeds, as if something were pushing its way towards her.

She stumbled backwards over the tussocky ground. 'Bale!' she whispered. 'If that's you, come out now, it isn't funny!'

The wind veered round, engulfing her in a stink that made her gag.

The reeds trembled – parted – and a boat slid towards her. From it stared a green man made of mouldy reeds.

Renn sprang back – and collided with something solid.

'What *is* that?' said Bale, behind her.

'What *was* that?' he said again, when they'd retreated a safe distance to a bay at the southern edge of the reeds.

'I think the Otters made it,' said Renn, 'to honour the Lake. They put food in it and leave it to go where it will. It's sacred. We shouldn't even have seen it.'

Bale bit his lip. 'I'm glad I found you. This place. I don't know its ways.'

Renn shrugged. 'Well, I need a boat, so I'm glad you found me, too.' That didn't sound as friendly as she'd intended, so she went on quickly, 'Before we do anything, we must honour the Lake. The Otters ask its permission for everything.'

Bale nodded. 'What do we do?'

Feeling a bit self-conscious, Renn left an offering of salmon cakes near the reeds. Then she made a paste of earthblood and Lake water and daubed a little on her forehead and her bow, asking the Lake to let them go in peace. Bale let her daub some on his forehead, and – after some persuasion – on his skinboat. After that they had a meal of dried deer meat, and he made a fish trap out of willow withes, and set it in the water.

The sun sank lower and the wind dropped. The Lake turned as smooth as polished basalt.

'The Viper Mage,' Bale said quietly. 'She's after Torak because he's a spirit walker. Isn't she?'

' – Yes,' said Renn. She wished he hadn't mentioned Seshru.

'And she's after the fire-opal, too.'

'Yes,' she said again. Lowering her voice, she added, 'It's the last piece left. One piece was lost in the black ice with the Bat Mage. One when the Seal Mage was taken by the Sea.'

'The Seal Mage?' Bale was startled. 'He had a piece of the fire-opal?'

'How else could he have made the tokoroths?'

He frowned. Renn guessed that he was remembering the bad times on his island, when the Seal Mage had created the sickness. Bale's little brother had been one of its victims.

A lonely, wavering cry echoed over the Lake.

Bale sprang to his feet. 'What was that?'

'A diverbird,' said Renn. 'They're the best swimmers in the Lake. The Otters make offerings to them, too.' She paused. 'Fin-Kedinn says the Otters are like their clan-creature. Always leaving little piles of half-chewed fish at the water's edge.'

Somewhere a trout leapt, and they jumped.
Bale shook himself, and went off to check his fish trap.
Renn stayed, brooding, on the shore.
'Renn,' called Bale in an altered voice.
'What?'
'You'd better come and see.'

EIGHTEEN

The big bream wriggled and gasped in the trap. It was a fine catch – except that it had two heads. Mouthless, misshapen, the second bulged like a canker, fighting its twin with horrible vigour.

'What did this?' said Bale with a grimace.

'Kill it,' said Renn.

'No!' ordered a voice behind them. 'Throw it back. Don't touch!'

They turned to face a cluster of sharp green faces and sharper spears.

Bale moved in front of Renn, but she stepped aside. With her fists on her heart, she addressed the woman who – to judge from her armlet of otter fur – was the Leader.

'I'm Raven Clan,' she said, 'my friend is Seal. We mean no harm.'

'No talk!' admonished the woman. Then to the others, 'Return that accursed thing to the Lake. We're taking the strangers to camp.'

'But Ananda, why?' protested a man. 'At a time like this –'

'At a time like this, Yolun,' cut in the Leader, 'we can't let them go free, they'd only make it worse.'

The man called Yolun lapsed into tight-lipped silence, while two others broke up the trap and set the monster free.

After that, things happened fast. Renn and Bale were seized and bundled into a reed boat with Yolun and another man. When they tried to resist, knives were pressed against their spines. They could only watch as their gear was tossed in the skinboat, which was lashed to the stern of another craft and towed.

They headed south. Beside her, Renn felt Bale shaking with rage. She threw him an urgent glance and shook her head. Fighting was useless. The Otters bristled with greenstone spears and arrows tipped with the beaks of diverbirds. Trying to escape would be futile. The only reason they hadn't been tied up was because there was no need.

Renn studied Yolun as he sat hunched in the prow, stabbing the water with his paddle. His fish-skin jerkin was fringed at neck and hem, evoking the reeds. His eyes were outlined with earthblood to imitate the red glare of the diverbird. He kept glancing resentfully over his shoulder; but beneath his hostility, Renn sensed something else.

Bale bent and whispered in her ear. 'Their craft are heavy and slow. If we could reach my skinboat, we could outrun them.'

'And go where?' she whispered back. 'They know the

Lake, we don't. Besides, I don't think they're angry so much as frightened.'

'That makes them even more dangerous.'

He was right.

The reed craft might not have the speed of a skinboat, but the Otters made steady progress, weaving unnerringly between the islands which dotted the Lake. As the light summer night wore on, their camp rose into view.

Like Bale, Renn was seeing it for the first time. Like him, she gasped.

'Why do they live like this?' he murmured.

'To be close to the Lake,' said Yolun. He stopped paddling, and for a moment his austere features glowed with fervour. 'The Lake is Mother and Father to us. From it comes all life. To it all life must return.' The resentment returned. 'We don't expect strangers to understand.'

'I'm no stranger,' said Renn. 'I'm Open Forest, like you.'

'You're not Otter Clan!' he snapped. 'No more talk.'

Wreathed in greenish smoke, the camp of the Otters floated above the Lake, linked to land by a single narrow walkway.

'It's built on stilts,' said Bale, amazed.

A forest of logs had been planted in the Lake, and on these lay wooden platforms bearing many squat reed domes. A bitter tang of smoke wafted towards them, with a powerful smell of fish. They saw smouldering brands mounted on posts; men and women gazing down at them, their eyes wide in their green-painted faces.

Renn was perplexed. The Otters were known as happy, playful people, like their clan-creature. Something had changed.

And all wore the green clay. Until now, Renn had never seen it, although she knew it was sacred to the Otters, who

took it from a secret place on the north shore, and mixed it
with fish oil. But they only ever used it to protect the sick
and the dying. She wondered why the whole clan needed
it now.

Yolun's companion moored the craft to one of the outer
piles, and a hatch opened overhead. A rope ladder dropped
down, and Yolun ordered them to climb.

They emerged into an acrid haze. Renn saw that what
she'd taken for brands were chunks of horsehoof mushroom
– burnt, she guessed, to keep away midges. And still the
Otters stared.

She and Bale were pushed towards the largest shelter: a
smoky hut lit by rushlights. Inside, she was assailed by a
stink of rotting fish. The Otters seemed unconcerned, and
even Bale merely wrinkled his nose. Out of politeness,
Renn pretended not to notice.

When everyone had crawled inside, Ananda called for
food. Seeing Renn's surprise, she said, 'We have a saying
on the Lake. A stranger is my guest until proven my
enemy.'

Yolun snorted, as if he'd had proof enough.

'We're not enemies,' said Bale.

'So you say,' said Ananda. 'Eat.'

There was silence while a boy and a young woman
brought fish-shaped bowls of tight-woven sedge filled
with reed-pollen gruel, and a basket piled with baked reed
stems: charred on the outside, white and starchy when
peeled.

Renn recognized the young woman as a Raven who'd
mated with an Otter the previous summer. 'Dyrati?'

Dyrati avoided her eyes. 'Eat,' she said, ladling a grey
sludge over Renn's gruel. It looked like thick honey, but
the stench of rotten fish made Renn's eyes water.

'Stickleback grease,' said Dyrati. 'Eat!'

'Eat!' commanded Yolun. 'Or do you scorn our food?'

They were all watching her.

She prodded the stinking mess, and felt her gorge rise.

Bale came to her rescue. 'She isn't used to boats, it's turned her stomach.' Emptying her bowl into his, he started eating with every appearence of relish – and the Otters relaxed.

'How *can* you?' whispered Renn.

'I like it,' he mumbled with a shrug. 'We make the same thing in the islands, but with cod.'

'You'll be wondering why we have no fish to give you,' said Ananda. 'Even this grease is from last spring.' She searched their faces. 'Someone is making the Lake sick.'

The Otters began rocking and moaning, and many touched the tufts of clan-creature fur hanging from their ears.

'A while ago,' Ananda went on, 'a child fell ill, and our Mage sent us to fetch the sacred clay. We found the healing spring plundered. A stranger had stolen what only an Otter may touch. That's when the troubles began.' She shuddered. 'People would fall into a death-like sleep and wake screaming, bitten by slithering demons in their dreams. Then the catch failed.'

Yolun shook his head. 'There used to be times when the fish were so plentiful that you could step from your boat and run across their backs, all the way to the shore. But this spring – hardly any. And what we do take is twisted. Cursed.'

'Every spring,' said Ananda, 'the ice river in the east sends much water to the Lake. It's a time of great blessing, when the water rises so high that its voice beneath our shelters laps us to sleep. Not this spring. The Lake sinks lower and lower.'

'Trouble always comes from the west!' cried Yolun, fixing his red-rimmed eyes on the strangers. 'We heard tell of an outcast, heading for the Lake. Then we saw him. *He* stole the sacred clay, *he* brought the troubles! And now these strangers have come to make it worse!'

At the mention of Torak, Renn and Bale stiffened. Neither dared meet the other's glance.

The Leader was on it at once. 'You know the outcast. Who are you?'

'I'm Bale of the Seal Clan,' Bale said proudly.

'And I'm Renn of the Raven Clan. I'm Fin-Kedinn's brother's daughter. Dyrati knows me.'

Dyrati folded her arms and said not a word.

Renn showed them her wrist-guard. 'See this? It's greenstone. Fin-Kedinn made it for me in the Otter way, which he learnt when he lived with your clan.'

An old man lifted rheumy eyes from his bowl. 'I remember. An angry young man, but he honoured the Lake.'

'Even if the girl is who she says,' said Yolun, 'what of the boy? A Seal on the Lake? How can that be right?'

'He has the waterskill,' Renn said quickly. 'And look at the reeds tattooed on his arms.'

Bale's tattoos were of seaweed, but he had the sense to keep quiet.

'None of this matters!' exclaimed Yolun. 'You all saw how they started when I mentioned the outcast!'

The Leader searched Bale's face. 'Do you know the outcast?'

Bale lifted his chin. 'Yes. But that's no crime.'

'Helping him is,' snarled Yolun.

Bale tensed.

'You see that?' cried Yolun. 'They're in league with him,

that makes them outcast too! Ananda, we must kill them, or the troubles will get worse!'

'No!' protested Renn. 'We have nothing to do with your troubles. But – but I do know who's causing them.'

'How can you know? Why are you here?' Ananda leaned closer. She had strange, grey-green eyes which seemed to hold the light of the Lake.

Renn's heart began to race. If she lied, the Leader would know it. If she admitted their purpose . . .

'The evils you speak of,' Renn said carefully, 'the failed catch, the biting demons – these will spread to the Forest if they're not stopped.' She paused. 'There's a Soul-Eater on the Lake. That's why this is happening. That's why we've come.'

There was stillness in the shelter. The only sounds were the sputter of rushlights and the splash of water far below.

'She's lying,' said Yolun. 'A Soul-Eater? Where's the proof?'

The Leader never took her eyes off Renn. 'She speaks the truth,' she said at last. 'But not the whole truth.' She gave a curt nod. 'The Mage will uncover the rest.'

NINETEEN

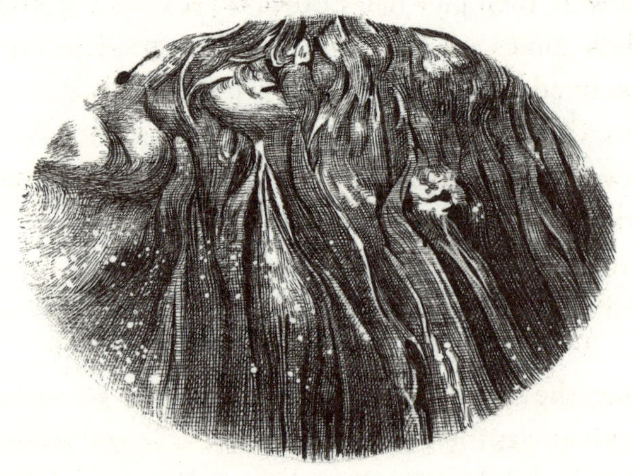

'Say nothing,' Renn whispered to Bale as Yolun pushed them along a walkway wreathed in smoke.

Bale bent his head to hers. 'You heard Ananda. Their Mage will find out the truth. How do we stop him?'

'Keep your thoughts away from Torak,' she replied. 'Fix your mind on the strongest feeling you know. Anger. Hatred. Grief.'

He frowned. 'Those are all bad.'

The smoke parted, and they found themselves on a round platform on which stood a small reed shelter. The doorway was edged with the teeth of an enormous pike. Above it swam an otter, beautifully carved in gleaming alder wood.

Yolun forced them to their knees, and Ananda motioned them to enter. Filled with misgiving, they crawled inside.

Renn caught the dank smell of reeds; the splash and gurgle of the Lake. Through gaps in the floor, its restless glimmer rippled over the walls. She heard Bale's sharp intake of breath. Then she saw why.

Two children sat cross-legged in the gloom. Their heads were bowed, their pale hair pooled on the floor. Both wore sleeveless tunics of silver fish-skin, sewn with strips of green-stained hide in a pattern of waving reeds.

Twins, thought Renn. Dread stole through her. First the twin fawns, then the two-headed fish. Now this. What did it mean?

Ananda and Yolun forced her and Bale lower, then touched their own foreheads to the floor. 'Mage,' they said.

As one, the twins raised their heads.

Their hair was the greenish gold of mildewed reeds, and their skin had the glistening pallor of the newly drowned. The boy's eyes were bright with waterlight, but the girl's were a misty, sightless white.

'She sees the world of the spirit,' said Yolun with reverence.

'How can this be?' said Bale. 'They can't be more than ten summers old.'

The boy's lips drew back from pointed grey teeth. 'Age has no meaning,' he said in a thin, piping voice. 'We are the spirit reborn. We are the Mage.'

Renn felt a shiver run down her spine.

'We were here at the Beginning,' said the boy. 'We saw the Great Flood wash the land clean. We saw the Lake become.'

The blind girl moaned. The boy's face tightened in distress. 'But now evil dishonours the Lake! The terror comes in the night!'

Ananda spoke. 'Mage, these strangers admit to knowing the outcast who took the sacred clay.'

'The outcast didn't take it,' said the boy. 'He caused it to be taken.'

'But Mage,' said Yolun, 'it's the same thing.'

'No,' said the boy.

'Then tell us,' said Ananda. 'Why have they come? What should we do with them?'

The blind girl put her hand on her twin's knee, and he nodded as if she'd spoken. 'We will make them tell.' He gave a sharp grey smile. 'We will ride with the spirits on the voice of diverbird and reed. We will draw out the truth.' Then to Yolun, 'Shut in the dark.'

Yolun untied a rolled-up mat, covering the doorway.

Renn felt trapped. If these weird children discovered that they wanted to help Torak – if they really *could* see her thoughts . . .

In the gloom, she saw the boy take a pouch made from the skin of a whole salmon. From its jaws he drew a segment of reed, which he slit with his thumbnail. Softly he blew through the slit, and the shelter filled with the wavering cry of the diverbird.

Now the girl withdrew a long loop of twisted sedge and wove it between her fingers. Renn saw patterns form: a fishing net, a boat, a tiny Death Platform. Her thoughts began to unravel.

She shook herself awake.

'Soft, soft,' whispered the boy. '*It comes.*'

First they heard it, swooshing and gurgling into the shelter. Then they felt it: water swirling round their legs.

Renn gave a start. Bale shifted in alarm.

'Don't move,' warned the boy.

Now Renn felt the slippery coldness of waterweed

winding about her. She glanced down. The shelter was dry. And yet – *she felt it*: waterweed coiling about her legs, her waist, her arms. She struggled. She couldn't move.

She could only watch as the blind girl reached both hands towards Bale. He tried to pull away, but the unseen waterweed held him fast.

The tips of the girl's fingers were white and puckered, as if they'd been too long in the water. Like minnows they flickered over his face, tracing the line of his jaw, the muscles of his throat.

The blind girl opened her mouth, and her voice was as the rushing of waves drawing back over shingle. 'Your brother is better now,' she murmured. 'Death healed his pain.'

Bale gasped.

The white fingers darted to the nape of his neck – and she drew back with a moan. 'Ah! You must use your time well!'

She released him – and Bale bowed his head, breathing hard.

Renn braced herself as the blind girl turned to her. Shutting her eyes, Renn felt a fluttering on her face, soft and chill as the touch of a frog. She tried to turn her mind from Torak, but the thin fingers reached into her thoughts and pulled him to the surface, so that he was *all* she could think of.

She saw him not as she'd seen him last, huddled in the willow thicket, but on a day in spring when they'd been hunting. He was down on one knee, examining the bitten-off end of a hazel twig. His dark hair flopped in his eyes, and his face wore the rapt expression it always did when he was tracking. He caught her watching, and flashed one of his rare, wolfish grins.

The blind child reached for the image.

With all her strength, Renn thrust the memory down deep.

'Ah,' said the blind girl, 'this one is strong!'

Her fingers flitted to Renn's wrists, lingering on the zigzag tattoos. 'A battle rages within her,' she whispered. 'She must take care, or it will tear her apart.'

Again an image of Torak rose in Renn's mind, but this time he stood on a black shore, and his face was so savage that she hardly knew him.

Again the cold fingers groped for the image.

With a huge effort of will, Renn pushed Torak away and fixed her thoughts on the Viper Mage. She breathed on the spark of hatred which slept in her heart, and it flared into life: a hot, bright flame. She fixed her mind on that.

The blind child sighed.

Renn shuddered and opened her eyes.

Ananda spoke in hushed tones. 'What of the outcast? Are they in league with him?'

'No,' murmured the blind girl. 'But they are bound to him. He by the bone, she by the heart.'

Ananda frowned. 'There's no crime in that. We'll have to send them back to the Forest.'

'No!' cried the twins together. 'The Lake has need of them! The boy's strength, the girl's power! They are needed to fight the terror which comes in the night!'

The girl turned her misty eyes on Renn. 'You know this terror. You have power to fight it, yet you're afraid. Why? Why do you fear your power?'

Yolun stared at Renn. 'Are you a Mage, too?'

She shook her head.

'Tell. Tell,' urged the twins.

For a third time, Renn felt the girl probing her thoughts,

delving even deeper, seeking her most closely guarded secrets.

No! she screamed in her head. She fought, but the waterweed held her fast.

In desperation, she breathed life once again into that tiny flame of hatred. It brightened – engulfed the shelter in fire . . .

The blind girl cried out.

The boy fell back.

Renn felt the waterweed snap and slither away.

Wearily, the boy sat up. 'They may pass freely. Give them clothes and food fit for the Lake and send them east.'

Yolun sprang to his feet. 'No! This can't be!'

'But Mage!' cried Ananda. 'Are you sure?'

'We see them travelling east,' panted the boy. 'East to the ice river. She will use her power. He will help her. They will find what they seek.'

'No!' protested Yolun.

'Let them go,' ordered the boy. 'If they do wrong, the Lake will take them, and you will find their bones rolling in the Bay of Lost Things.'

Yolun looked thunderous; Ananda bewildered.

Trembling, Renn crawled for the mouth of the shelter. Suddenly, the blind girl seized her wrists. Renn tried to pull away, but the bony fingers were strong.

'Beware the cold red fire,' breathed the girl. 'Beware the Lake that kills!'

Renn wrenched herself free and stumbled from the shelter.

TWENTY

'Why are they letting us go?' said Bale. 'It's too easy, I don't like it.'

Renn didn't answer. The encounter with the twins had left her drained, and terrified of what they might have seen in her thoughts.

She and Bale were back in the main shelter, where Ananda had left them. Yolun peered in, and jerked his head at Bale. 'Out,' he growled. 'I'm to give you supplies and Lake-worthy clothes.'

Renn made to follow, but he stopped her. 'Not you! A woman will see to you!'

Renn soon discovered that Yolun wasn't the only one who hated seeing them freed. When Dyrati brought her new clothes, she refused to meet her eyes, and dumped the clothes on the mat. 'You won't be needing your buckskins,' she said sullenly. 'Too heavy when wet, too stiff when dry. Put these on.' She indicated a pair of calf-length leggings of soft elk hide and a sleeveless jerkin of finely woven sedge. 'You'll have to sew on your clan-creature feathers yourself.'

In uncomfortable silence, Renn changed her clothes and cut off her clan-creature feathers to sew on later. When she tried to thank Dyrati, the older girl made for the door.

'Dyrati?' said Renn. 'What have I done?'

Dyrati's mouth tightened. 'As if you didn't know. You might have fooled our Mage, but you can't fool me.'

'What do you mean?'

Dyrati turned on her and made the sign of the hand. 'Stay away! I've told them what you are! I've told them what we used to whisper behind your back. You with your black, black eyes and your dreams that come true! You're bad luck. Everyone knows it. Everyone knows that whoever gets close to you comes to harm!'

Renn felt sick. 'That's not true.'

'You know it is! Your brother. Your father. Torak. Someone should warn that Seal boy before it's too late!' Then she was gone, leaving Renn on her own.

She was shaken. What if Dyrati was right?

Oh, nonsense! she told herself. Dyrati's just a spiteful girl who's never liked you.

The trouble was, nobody did like her much. They tolerated her because she was Fin-Kedinn's bone kin, but they were scared of her talent for Magecraft.

Misery welled up inside her, and she longed for Torak. Only Torak had ever been her friend.

On the walkway she found Bale, who now wore elk-hide leggings and a jerkin of silvery fish-skin. 'Are you all right?' he asked when he saw her face.

'No,' she snapped.

He raised an eyebrow, but made no comment.

Watched by Ananda and a cluster of silent Otters, they made their way towards the hatch, then climbed down the rope ladder and into the skinboat.

'Our gear's all stowed,' said Bale as he untied the moorings and pushed off. 'Let's go before they change their minds.'

The Lake was treacherous with hidden currents, and the skinboat bucked wildly. Several times, Renn nearly fell out.

'It doesn't like fresh water,' said Bale, excusing his beloved craft's poor performance. 'It's my fault. It sits much lower than in the Sea, I'm not used to that.'

Huddled behind him, Renn was soon soaked, despite the beaver-hide mantle she'd found in one of the packs. She felt like a burden. Bale was much stronger and better at skinboating, and when she did try to help, she ended up clashing paddles with his.

Every so often, she made herself feel useful by taking out her grouse-bone whistle and calling for Wolf. But she never got an answer, and that only made things worse.

Dread settled inside her when she thought of what lay ahead. *She will use her power*, the Otter Mage had said. But Renn didn't want to use her power, not ever.

They pitched camp for the night in a sheltered bay. Their Forest food had run out, but the Otters had provisioned them with salmonskins of roasted reed pollen, so they made a cheerless gruel.

Bale seemed preoccupied. When they'd eaten he said,

'What did the Otter Mage mean when she said you're afraid of your power?'

Renn braced herself.

'She meant Magecraft, didn't she?' When she didn't answer, he said, 'If we can't find Torak, it might be the only way. You have the skill. Why not use it?'

'That's easy for you to say,' she muttered.

'But for Torak. You'd do it for Torak?'

She made no reply.

'What are you afraid of?'

'I'm not afraid!'

After that, they didn't speak. Bale upended the skinboat on shoresticks and covered it with pine boughs for a shelter, then rolled himself in his beaver-fur mantle and turned his back on her. It was a long time before Renn got to sleep.

They paddled east throughout the next day, but saw no sign of Torak. Renn had no sense that they were getting closer to him – but they were getting closer to something. The dread inside her grew worse.

As the sun began to sink, they were buffeted by a strong east wind, and Bale had to work hard to keep them moving forwards. Then, as they rounded an island, Renn felt a chill on her face, and there it was: the relentless glare of the ice river.

The dread in her belly hardened to stone. Somewhere out there, her father had found his death.

Bale twisted to face her. 'This doesn't feel right. Why would he go there? There's no prey, nothing!'

'The Otter Mage said we would find what we sought in the east.' But Renn knew better than most that the prophesies of Mages are tricky things, and can have many different meanings.

As they paddled nearer, the chill became a freezing blast, and the ice turned blue. Renn craned her neck at the shining cliffs which towered overhead. She heard the trickle of meltwater, but she couldn't see it. No falls tumbling from the cliffs, just that dazzling blue ice.

'We're too close,' said Bale. 'We'd better turn back, make camp at that bay we passed. We've come as far east as we can.'

In her sleep that night, Renn saw Torak.

He crouched on a beach of black sand, his clothes in tatters, his face wild and hopeless as he lashed out with a flaming brand – *lashed out at Wolf.*

Renn gasped – and woke.

Bale was gone.

Emerging from the shelter, she saw him watching two reed boats putting out from their bay.

'I had a dream,' she told him. 'Torak's worse, he can't last much longer.'

Bale nodded grimly. 'Trouble is, he's a long way away.'

'How do you know?'

He pointed to the boats. 'They've been out here looking for fish for the past five days, so they didn't know who we were. They were helpful. Told me what the others kept from us. Someone found Torak's bow in the reed-bed.'

'The reed-bed?' Renn was aghast.

'Near the Island of the Hidden People. The Otter Mage sent us the wrong way.' He punched his palm. 'Ah, Renn, we were so close! If only we'd known, we might have found him by now!'

'But to send us the wrong way! Why?'

'What does that matter? We're further away than ever. And if you're right, he's running out of time.'

She thought quickly. 'How long will it take us to get there?'

'As the raven flies, maybe a day. By skinboat, with all these islands in between? Two days, maybe three.'

'Let's get going!'

'Not yet.' He pointed east. Above the ice river, purple-grey clouds were massing. The World Spirit was restless.

'But we can still try!' she said desperately.

'If I knew the Lake, yes. But out here, with a storm coming? No. We'd be no use to Torak drowned.'

She ran to the water's edge. Now she saw that everything had conspired to bring her here. Maybe this was why the Otter Mage had sent them east: to force her into doing what she'd resolved she never would.

Turning her back on the ice river, she stared west. Spiky black islands floated on the amber Lake. Somewhere beyond them, Torak was dying of soul-sickness.

'Then I've got no choice.' She faced Bale. 'We'll have to send help from here.'

'What do you mean?'

She took a deep breath. 'I'll have to do Magecraft.'

'Renn, this is madness!' yelled Bale as he fought to keep the skinboat afloat in the teeth of the storm. 'We've got to get back to shore!'

'Not yet!' shouted Renn. 'We have to get past that last island! I *must* have a clear view to the west, or the help won't reach him!'

'But we're taking water!'

'If you care about Torak, *keep going!*'

The sky turned black, the wind screamed in her ears, tugging at her clothes and whipping her hair about her face, churning the Lake to a frenzy of white water. The skinboat reared and plunged, and only Bale's skill kept them from going under.

Somehow, she managed to stay kneeling on the crossbar, gripping the boat with one hand as she thrust the other into her medicine pouch. She'd done all she could on the shore. Only the final charm remained.

As she pulled out what she needed and held it up, she felt a thrill of grim satisfaction. The Viper Mage might have Torak's name-pebble, but she, Renn, possessed something just as potent.

'What's that?' cried Bale.

'His hair,' she shouted. 'Last winter he needed a disguise, and I cut it off and kept it!'

Staggering to her feet, she raised her fist, and Torak's long dark locks streamed in the wind.

Bale grabbed her belt to hold her steady. 'For the last time, we've got to get back to shore! That's hail on the way! If it holes the boat, we're sunk!'

'Not yet!'

Throwing back her head, Renn howled the charm to the storm – she summoned the power of the guardian of all Ravens, who flies over ice and mountain, Forest and Sea – she summoned it and sent it to seek Torak – and the wind wrenched the charm from her lips and bore it west across the Lake.

But in the midst of the charm, as she braced her legs on the frame of the pitching boat and clutched Bale's shoulder to steady herself, she felt a powerful will confronting hers.

I feel your purpose . . . You shall not succeed.

Renn's knees buckled. She nearly went down.

You shall not succeed.

She tried to shut it from her mind – but it was too strong. Stronger than the Otter Mage, stronger even than

Saeunn – it had the awesome power of the Soul-Eater – and it was not to be outdone by the puny spell of some untried girl.

The World Spirit hammered open the clouds, and down came the hail, pummelling their faces with arrows of ice.

Bale swung the skinboat about. 'Rocks! Rocks ahead!'

Renn raised her fist one final time. 'Fly!' she screamed. 'Fly to the aid of the soul-sick!' The wind ripped Torak's hair from her fingers and scattered it over the Lake, and Renn was flung backwards as the skinboat gave a terrific heave and reared out of the water.

'We've hit a rock!' yelled Bale. 'Grab hold of the boat! *Don't let go!*'

The hailstorm thundered west, carrying Renn's charm with it. It swept across the Lake, flattening the reeds, pounding the Island of the Hidden People.

At the edge of the black beach, the pine trees thrashed, and beneath them Torak's miserable shelter shook. Pine cones and branches rained down upon it. Then something heavy dropped out of a tree and thudded onto the roof . . .

. . . and Torak woke up.

TWENTY-ONE

Torak cowered on his scratchy bed of pine-needles, listening to the World Spirit punishing the trees.

He was terrified of the hail, and of whatever had fallen onto the roof. He was terrified of everything: the Lake, the Hidden People, but most of all, the wolves. They were waiting for him in the Forest. Sometimes he glimpsed the big grey one sneaking about just out of stone-shot, waiting to pounce.

Because of the wolves, he hadn't dared go into the Forest. Instead, he eked out an existence on frost-shrivelled berries and blackened mushrooms, with the occasional slimy green hopping thing when he could catch one.

The world no longer made sense. The sky screamed at him, and from the trees, little red scuttling things pelted him with wooden fruit. Darts of green lightning shot past, laughing at him, and slithery brown creatures bobbed about in the water, scolding him. While he slept, a monster came and gnawed his shelter, and when he woke up, he saw branches swimming upstream.

Again something thudded onto the roof. This time, it squawked.

Torak shut his eyes tight.

At last the storm blew over and the hail stopped. Shaking with fear, he grabbed his axe and crawled out.

The ice had flattened undergrowth and ripped off branches; it had covered the beach in hard, translucent pebbles which crunched under his bare feet. In a patch of crushed bracken, something stirred.

No. Two somethings. A pair of big black birds.

Gripping his axe, Torak edged closer.

The larger one gave a terrified squawk and flapped its wings, while the smaller one tucked its head into its shoulders and pretended it wasn't there.

Torak saw the wreck of a nest, high in a tree. The birds must have fallen out, bounced off his shelter, and into the bracken.

He took a step closer – which sent them into a frenzy of wing-flapping and high-pitched squeaks.

He blinked. *They* were frightened of *him*.

He saw that the corners of their mouths were a crinkly pink, and although the span of their wings was almost as wide as his outstretched arms, all that flapping wasn't achieving anything.

'You can't fly,' he said out loud.

That put an end to the flapping. They huddled together and stared up at him, shivering with terror.

His belly tightened. So much meat. And as they couldn't fly, it would be easy.

To his dismay, he couldn't do it. They reminded him of something. Or someone. He didn't remember what.

A rapid 'quork quork quork' split the sky, and he dropped to all fours.

High overhead, another big black bird wheeled – only this one could fly. Alighting on the remains of the nest, it glared down at him. Its head-feathers were fluffed up like ears, its wings spread.

Angrily it snapped off a twig and threw it at him. Then it threw down several of the wooden fruit. 'Quork quork quork'!

'Leave me alone!' he shouted. Greatly daring, he picked up a wooden fruit and threw it back.

The bird hitched itself into the sky and flew away.

When he was sure it wasn't coming back, Torak left the young ones on their own and went to forage on the shore. If he couldn't eat them, they were no use to him.

He found a grubby mushroom which tasted all right, except for the bits that wriggled and crunched because he'd forgotten to shake out the woodlice. Then he caught two of the slimy green hopping things, which he killed with a stone. He ate one raw and tied the other to his belt for later.

Returning to the shelter, he found the young ones where he'd left them. When they saw the green thing at his belt, they flapped their wings and made squeaky begging noises.

'No!' he said. 'It's mine!'

The squeaks became outraged squawks. They didn't stop.

Maybe if he made them a shelter, they'd shut up.

Piling an armful of twigs in the fork of a tree, he grabbed the bigger bird and shoved it on top.

It pecked his sleeve and tugged.

'Let go!' he protested.

The powerful beak was bigger than Torak's middle finger, and it easily ripped off the sleeve. Gripping the buckskin in its formidable talons, the bird settled down to shred it, eyeing Torak as if to say, *I wouldn't have to do this if you'd fed me like I asked.*

In the bracken, the smaller one laughed.

Torak scooped her up and chucked her in the nest. She thanked him by waggling her hindquarters and spurting him with white droppings.

'Hey! Stop it!' he shouted.

'Hey top it!' she croaked.

Torak blinked. Birds didn't talk.

Did they?

If they could talk, maybe he shouldn't let them starve.

Foraging in the undergrowth, he caught some spiders and squashed them in his fist. The birds gobbled them up, and would've started on his fingers if he'd let them.

He fed them a leg of the green thing. And another. He decided enough was enough. The larger bird stared at him reproachfully, then tucked its head into its back feathers and went to sleep. Then the smaller one did the same.

Torak wanted to sleep too, but first he cut a scrap of skin from the green hopping thing and put it on the roof. He had no idea why he did this, but it felt important.

Yawning, he ate the rest of the green hopping thing, then crawled into the shelter and burrowed into the pine-needles.

Just before he slept, he said out loud, '*Frog*. The slimy green hopping thing is a *frog*.'

The young black birds ruled his days.

They were noisy and hungry, and if he didn't feed them often, they got noisier. But they had keen eyes and ears, and they scared off the biting monster which came in the night, and the red scuttling things in the trees.

After a few days, he took to letting them out of the nest. They hopped and waddled after him, and he found himself showing them things, and remembering as he did so.

'This is a pine cone. Hard to eat. And this is lingonberry, very good – ow! And this is willowherb. If you peel it, you can wind it into twine. See?'

The birds watched with their intense black gaze, and prodded everything with their beaks, to see if they could eat it.

Mostly, they could. They ate berries, crickets, frogs, scat, his clothes if he let them. But although they got quite adept with their large beaks, they preferred stealing food to catching it themselves.

They were good at it, too. When Torak caught his first tiny fish with a bramble-thorn hook on a line, he was so proud that he rashly showed it to them. Next day, he found the bigger one pulling in the line with its beak, while the smaller one looked on hopefully.

To deter them, Torak planted his knife by the line; but although they left the line alone, they picked at the sinew binding on the hilt. He swapped his axe for the knife, and that worked better.

Next day, as he emerged from the shelter, the bigger one cawed a greeting from the nest – and flew down to him.

'You flew!' said Torak, amazed.

Startled by its achievement, the bird sat trembling at his feet. Then it spread its wings and flew to the top of a tree –

where it lost courage and begged forlornly to be rescued. Torak eventually tempted it down with a handful of chopped frog and a couple of fish eyes, and from then on, it sat and laughed at its sister, who was still flapping furiously in the nest. It was mid-afternoon by the time she made her first flight.

After that, they learned rapidly, and soon the sky rang with their raucous cries as they wheeled and somersaulted overhead. Their feathers were a glossy black, with beautiful rainbow glints of violet and green, and when they flew, their wings made a strong, dry rustling, like the wind in the reeds. It made Torak wistful, as if he too had once been able to fly, but never would again.

One morning, they lifted into the sky, and didn't come back.

Torak told himself it didn't matter. He set a snare – one of his newly regained skills – and ate a few berries, taking care to leave some on a boulder, as an offering.

But he missed the ravens. He'd got to like them. And they reminded him of something – he couldn't remember what – except that he knew the memory was a good one.

When dusk fell, he checked the snares he'd set the previous night. He was in luck: a water bird. He woke up a fire and roasted it, but didn't have the heart to eat much.

Suddenly he heard a familiar cawing; then strong, rhythmic wingbeats – and down they came, alighting with a thud, one on each shoulder.

He yelped – their claws were sharp – and lifted them off. But he was glad they'd come back.

That night, all three of them had a feast. The ravens – whom he'd named Rip and Rek – ate so much that they got too fat to fly, and he had to carry them to their roost.

After they'd gone to sleep, he sat by the Lake, watching

the young swifts screaming overhead, while a woodpecker flashed past like green lightning, and a red squirrel dangled from one foot to reach an unripe hazelnut on another branch. As the moon rose, a beaver waddled out of the Forest, cast Torak a wary look, and settled down to gnaw on a willow sapling. The tree toppled, the beaver chewed off a branch, then swam upstream, dragging it behind him.

For the first time in many days, Torak felt almost at peace. The wound on his chest seemed finally to be healing, and he was no longer afraid. He knew that a lot was still missing from his memory, but the world was beginning to make sense.

The Lake stilled, and the Forest settled down for the brief summer night.

Torak felt eyes on him, and glanced over his shoulder.

From the trees, an amber gaze met his.

He started to his feet.

A grey shadow turned and disappeared into the trees.

TWENTY-TWO

Awolf cannot be of two packs.

Wolf was tasting the bitterness of this to the full. He couldn't eat or sleep or enjoy a good howl with the others. Since that terrible moment when Tall Tailless had bitten his muzzle with the Bright Beast, misery ran with him wherever he went.

And now, as he made his way through the Forest, jealousy ran with him too. *What was Tall Tailless doing with those ravens?* Wolves and ravens sometimes play together and help each other in the hunt, but they are not pack-brothers.

When Wolf reached the denning place, the rest of the pack had already returned from the kill, and the cubs had fed and gone into the Den to sleep. Wolf ran to touch noses with the lead pair, followed by the others; then everyone padded back to their sleeping places to snooze. Whitepaw, who'd stayed at the Den with the cubs, went off to check that the Forest was clear of lynx and bear and the Otherness which stalked the Big Wet, and Wolf slumped down to guard the cubs.

Tall Tailless no longer wanted him for a pack-brother. He never howled for him or came to seek him in the Forest.

And now those ravens.

The cubs burst from the Den and came racing over to Wolf, barking furiously – and for a while the misery was chased away. Leaping to his feet, he gave the high cub-greeting, and they nudged him with their stubby muzzles, and he lashed his tail as he heaved up the reindeer meat he carried in his belly. The cubs were growing fast, and soon the pack would move from the Den to a place many lopes away, where they would learn to hunt.

As Wolf thought about this, the misery slunk back. Leaving the Den would take him even further from Tall Tailless.

He lay down and put his muzzle between his paws.

As he was cub-watcher, though, he kept one ear on the cubs, and he soon became aware that they were stalking him like prey.

Growler, the cleverest, was innocently pawing a stick, but edging closer all the time; Snap, the smallest but fiercest, was down on her belly, sneaking up on Wolf from behind; and the more timid Digger was waiting to pounce when the others broke cover.

Suddenly, Snap charged – and sank her sharp little teeth into Wolf's flank. Growler sprang at Wolf's muzzle, and Digger attacked his tail. Wolf obligingly lay on his side, and they clambered on top of him. They chewed his ears, so he covered them with his paws, so they chewed his paws instead. And he let them, because they were cubs.

Digger bounded off and dug up a new plaything: the foreleg of a fawn, with the hoof still on. Snap advanced with a snarl – *That's mine, I'm the lead cub!* – and while she was standing over Digger to punish him, Growler sneaked between them and made off with the prize.

As Wolf watched Growler trying to get his jaws around the hoof, he was suddenly a cub again, back with Tall Tailless at their first kill, chewing a hoof that his pack-brother had given him. Misery grabbed him by the throat. The hurt was so bad that he whined.

Darkfur woke, and came to lick his muzzle, careful to avoid the Bright Beast-bitten side. Wolf was grateful, but the hurt didn't go away.

Whitepaw returned and took over watching the cubs, and Wolf went off and tried to sleep. But the thought of those ravens pecking kept him awake.

He sprang up. This was no good. He had to know for sure.

It didn't take long to reach the Den of Tall Tailless. Wolf sank into the bracken and belly-crawled closer.

Before long, Tall Tailless came out, stretching and talking to himself. His voice was deeper and rougher than before, but his scent was the same.

It hurt, being so near, yet unable to greet him. Wolf's tail ached to wag. He longed to feel those blunt claws scratching his flank.

He was wondering whether to risk the faintest of whines, when the matter was taken out of his jaws.

The ravens lit onto the ground, and Tall Tailless greeted them in tailless talk.

Wolf froze.

Tall Tailless squatted and stroked the ravens' wings. Gently, he took the bigger one's beak in his forepaw and gave it an affectionate shake, and the raven gurgled.

Jealousy sank its teeth into Wolf's heart. Tall Tailless used to muzzle-grab *him*, and they would roll together, growling and play-biting.

Now Tall Tailless was walking off along the Big Wet to hunt, and the ravens were with him, wheeling in the Up – just as Wolf used to trot beside him, proud and happy to be his pack-brother.

And still Wolf stayed in the bracken. When he smelt that they were truly gone, he raced into the Den and snuffled about, torturing himself with that beloved, now painful scent.

Suddenly he heard wingbeats – then a rasping 'quork quork quork'! As he left the Den, a pine cone hit him on the nose. The ravens were back. They sat on a branch, *laughing at him*!

Wolf sprang at them – and they lifted into the Up, then swooped low, but just out of reach, *taunting* him.

He waited till they came again – he leapt – snapped a tail feather, tore it to pieces. With furious caws the ravens soared into the Up. Down they came in a flurry of angry wings, diving, pecking. Again and again Wolf leapt – twisting, snapping – until he forced them to seek refuge in a tree, where they sat, cawing and pelting him with sticks. *This is our Den! Go away!*

Wolf's snarls shook him from nose to tail. They didn't dare make another attack.

Bristling with fury, Wolf bit off a willow branch and savaged it to shreds. Then he turned and raced into the Forest. His limbs itched with the blood-urge, his pelt prickled with rage.

So. This was how it ended.

Don't ever leave me, Tall Tailless had said. Then he'd chased Wolf away with the Bright Beast-that-Bites-Hot, and made a new pack – *with ravens*.

Well, let him! Wolf had another pack too.

TWENTY-THREE

When Torak returned to the shelter, he knew at once that something was wrong.

The ravens sat in their pine tree looking ruffled and aggrieved, and the bigger one was missing a tail feather.

'What happened?' he said. But they were too upset to come down.

In the shelter, he found his pine-needle bedding pocked with odd, fist-sized hollows. He sensed that this ought to mean something, but it didn't. His mind was still healing, his tracking powers only slowly coming back; and over the last few days, a fever and a cough had crept up on him, which didn't help.

Outside, he found the remains of a branch, savaged to pieces. A shred of chewed raven feather. A paw-print.

Frowning, he squatted to examine it.

The sun sank below the trees, and the Lake turned a dark wolf grey. Wolf grey . . .

Slowly, Torak rose to his feet. 'Wolf,' he said out loud.

For the first time in days, he saw clearly. He saw Wolf coming to watch over him, as he had done since they'd parted – and finding the ravens. He saw Wolf leaping at them, snapping a feather; taking out his rage and hurt on a branch.

The truth crashed over Torak. It wasn't Wolf who had forsaken him. It was he who had forsaken Wolf. Wolf, his faithful pack-brother, who had hunted by his side and guarded him from danger. And how had he repaid him? He had chased him away with burning brands; he had replaced him with ravens!

The guilt was almost more than he could bear. 'I've got to find him!' he cried. 'I've got to make it all right!'

He hadn't been in the Forest since his madness, and it felt unnervingly dark and still. He wondered if, like Wolf, it was angry with him for having forsaken it.

But trees live longer than people, and are slower to anger. The Forest welcomed him back. It gave him juicy strawberries which soothed his sore throat, and when the midges became annoying, it provided yarrow leaves to rub on his skin. For tinder it offered horsehoof mushroom; and best of all, it showed him Wolf's trail: a hair snagged on brambles, moss scuffed off a log.

The trail led uphill, past the little lake he'd found before, now ablaze with golden water lilies in the evening sun.

The wolves had chosen their denning place well: on a slope just west of the little lake, guarded by watchful pines.

The Den was at the foot of a red boulder almost as tall as Torak, and around it the ground was hard-packed by the padding of many feet, and littered with shards of bone.

But no wolves. And no cubs either, although he saw plenty of tiny paw-prints. Then he realized his mistake. The cubs would be asleep in the Den, and the pack was out hunting, it wouldn't be back before dawn. He had a long wait ahead.

As he breathed in the rich, sweet scent of wolves, he was overcome by longing and remorse. Wolves had saved him when he was a baby; and yet for days, he had feared them as ravening monsters.

With shocking suddenness, a large wolf emerged from behind the boulder. Its muzzle wrinkled in a snarl as it stalked towards him.

Hardly daring to breathe, Torak edged back. The pack had left someone to guard the cubs. He should have thought.

The cub-watcher advanced on him.

Torak averted his gaze and whined distressfully. *Sorry! Don't attack!*

The cub-watcher growled. *Go away!*

Slowly, Torak withdrew to the far side of the water lily lake. To be threatened by a wolf! He was still far from full recovery.

The short summer night descended as he waited. Frogs piped in the reeds. An otter surfaced and stared at him, then flipped under, leaving the lily pads gently rocking.

He nodded off.

His dreams were troubled by strange yowls, and he woke with a start. He felt hot and thick-headed, and his throat was so sore that it hurt to swallow.

The night was unusually quiet.

Too quiet.

Vaguely troubled, he decided to check the Den – even though it wasn't yet dawn, and the pack wouldn't be back.

As before, the denning place seemed deserted, but mindful of the cub-watcher, Torak approached with caution. In the gloom, he made out a birch tree whose bark was badly scratched down one side. Too high for badger, too low for bear.

He felt a prickling between his shoulder blades. He knew that feeling; everyone does, who lives in a Forest. It's the feeling of being watched.

Drawing his knife, he moved as silently as his laboured breathing would allow.

Something lay at the foot of the boulder.

The cub-watcher. Its flank had been ripped open, its throat chewed to pulp. It had put up a desperate fight to save the cubs.

Torak knelt and placed his hand above one white paw. 'Go in peace. May you find the First Tree, and hunt for ever beneath its boughs.'

In the earth around the carcass he found tracks: rounder than a wolf's, their outline blurred by fur.

Lynx.

Rising, Torak looked about him.

Couldn't see anything. He must've scared it away.

But it was odd for a lynx to attack a full-grown wolf. Mostly they take hares and squirrels, and wolf cubs if they can get them. The lynx must have gone after the cubs, and the cub-watcher had leapt to their defence.

A whine from the Den told him that the wolf had done its job well. Sheathing his knife, Torak crawled inside.

The tunnel was just big enough to admit him. As he breathed its earthy wolf tang, he was back in the Den where Fa had put him as a baby. His pack-brothers mewed as they clambered over him, and the breath of the Mother heated his skin as she nose-nudged him to suckle. He snuggled into her furry flank, and her milk tasted rich and warm.

He was through the tunnel and into the birthing place. As his eyes adjusted to the dark, he saw that it was about the size of a Raven shelter, but only high enough for a wolf to stand in. He caught a gleam of eyes. A fluffy huddle shrank from him.

He whined to reassure the cubs, but they were terrified. He was a stranger, and they'd just lost their uncle.

Backing out, he emerged from the Den – to see a large shadow bound away from the slaughtered wolf.

'Be off!' he shouted, waving his arms. His shouts ended in a coughing fit which bent him double.

The lynx leapt into a tree and sat, lashing its tail.

Drawing his knife, Torak took his place by the dead wolf at the foot of the boulder. He would guard the cubs till the pack returned.

It was strange, though, that his arrival hadn't frightened the lynx away. Lynx rarely attack people, and when they hunt, they target the young and the sick.

More coughing seized him. When it was over, he was sweating. His breath sounded like the crisping of dry leaves.

Then it came to him. The lynx knew he was sick. It heard it in his voice and smelt it on his skin.

Like the cubs, he was simply prey.

TWENTY-FOUR

The lynx dropped soundlessly from the branch and began to prowl.

Torak tried howling for Wolf, but only managed a croak.

The night was warm, the stink of the slaughtered cub-watcher thick in his throat. The carcass lay so close that he could touch it.

Too close. He should drag it further off, so the lynx could feed in peace. Let it take the dead, and leave the living.

But while he was doing that, it might come for the cubs. He pictured the small souls padding about, nosing their corpses. He tightened his grip on his knife.

A noise behind him. He spun round. Saw only the boulder. But lynx are superb climbers: they leap on their prey from above.

If only he had his axe. Why had he left it at the shelter? To have left without food, axe or tinder . . .

No tinder.

Fire would have scared it away. He should have taken some of that horsehoof mushroom when he'd the chance. The old Torak – the one before the madness – would never have made that mistake.

Another spasm of coughing gripped. When it was over, his ribs ached, and black spots darted before his eyes.

The lynx crouched in the shadows, just out of reach. He saw its blank silver eyes, smelt its rank cat smell.

Then he saw something which made his belly turn over. At the mouth of the Den, directly behind the lynx, two stubby muzzles were emerging.

Torak barked a warning. *Uff!* Danger!

The muzzles edged back inside.

The lynx caught the movement and turned its head.

'Here! Here!' shouted Torak to distract it. Yelling, throwing stones, he edged away from the Den.

The lynx bared its teeth and hissed at him. But suddenly it twisted, snarling at a bolt of black lighting plummeting from the sky. Rip gave a deafening caw and soared out of reach, as Rek swept in to attack. Now both were mobbing the marauder: wheeling, swooping to peck. The lynx leapt for them – and they took refuge in a pine tree, raucously cawing.

Lashing its tail, the lynx slunk back to the carcass.

Torak stood with legs braced, shaking with fever. The scab on his breastbone had reopened, and warmth seeped down his chest.

He could see no sign of the cubs. But he knew that soon they would be nosing their way out again.

When they did, the lynx would be on them.

Wolf loped through the trees. He recognized those caws! What were the ravens doing at the Den?

The wind turned, carrying scents of lynx and wolf flesh and Tall Tailless. He quickened his pace, and the pack ran with him.

The females were fastest, and reached the Den before him. He saw the lead female leap at the lynx and chase it into the Forest, with Darkfur and the others in pursuit.

Wolf skittered to a halt. He saw Whitepaw lying Not-Breath by the Den. He saw Tall Tailless clutching his great claw in his forepaw. He knew at once what had happened. Anger, joy and sorrow fought within him.

The ravens cawed from the trees, but Wolf ignored them. At the edge of the denning place, he saw the misty shape of a wolf. He cast it a reassuring glance, and what was left of Whitepaw – the breath that walked – lingered for a moment; then, satisfied that the cubs were safe, trotted into the Forest.

Blackear, Prowler and the lead wolf were staring at Tall Tailless, hackles raised.

Wolf trembled with longing to go to him; but it was for the lead wolf to decide if Tall Tailless was a friend of the pack.

The lead wolf went to the meat which had been Whitepaw, then walked stiffly towards Tall Tailless.

Tall Tailless stood quietly, with eyes averted, as a stranger should. Wolf was troubled to see that he swayed.

Still with hackles raised, the lead wolf sniffed Tall Tailless.

The cubs appeared at the jaws of the Den, whining, but

they didn't come out. They were waiting to see what would happen.

The hackles of the lead wolf went down, and he rubbed his flank against Tall Tailless' leg. Then he ran to greet the cubs.

Prowler and Blackear bounded past Tall Tailless to do the same, and he sank to the ground – ignoring the ravens, Wolf noticed happily.

Dropping his ears, Wolf wagged his tail.

Pack-brother, said Tall Tailless.

Wolf gave a whine and raced towards him.

TWENTY-FIVE

Safe with the pack, Torak had his first good sleep in two moons.

He woke in the afternoon, curled up at the edge of the denning place. The wound on his chest hurt, but his cough was almost gone, and he felt much better.

The lead wolf started a howl, and the others joined in. Torak shut his eyes as the wolf-song surged through him. He heard grief for their dead pack-brother and delight in the cubs; gratitude for the friend who had saved them. He gave himself up to the joy of being back with Wolf.

Sensing Torak was awake, Wolf bounded over to him, and they licked muzzles in a playful, everyday way, as if all the bitterness had never happened.

I'm sorry, Torak said in wolf talk – although it was only a tiny part of what he felt.

I know, said Wolf.

And that was that.

The howl ended, and a young female – a beautiful black wolf with eyes like green amber – trotted up to Torak with a rotten fish head in her jaws, and set it before him as a present. He thanked her and they touched noses. Then she and Wolf raced off to play with the cubs.

Once he was sure that Wolf was deep in a game of tag, Torak stuck the fish head in the fork of a birch for Rip and Rek. He'd been careful not to make a fuss of them in front of his pack-brother, and they'd been sulking in a pine tree. Food changed that, and soon they were squabbling over the prize.

It was a hot afternoon and the dead wolf stank, so Torak dragged it into the Forest. Let the ravens peck it undisturbed; and if the lynx returned for its kill, let it feed.

Then he went to find food for himself. After cutting a spear from a hazel tree, he woke up a fire and hardened the tip, then went to try his luck in the water lily lake.

It wasn't long before he speared a pike. Watched by a clutch of curious wolves, he roasted it and ate all except the tail, which he tied to the reeds as an offering. Then he ate a few handfuls of crunchy watercress and some early cloudberries, which burst on his tongue like honey.

Feeling full for the first time in days, he sat under an alder to mend his clothes. Without needles and thread, this was easy. He simply cut off his leggings at the knee, and as his jerkin was already in shreds, he gave up on it and went bare-chested, using the scraps to make a new headband.

When that was done, he leaned back and did nothing at all.

On the lake, a mallard floated on its side, preening its belly feathers. A pair of teal flipped bottoms-up to feed.

An otter taught her cubs to swim, and they paddled furiously, too fluffy to sink.

The ravens were splashing in the shallows, and the cubs were playing hunt-the-cloudberry. In the boggy channels draining the lake, Wolf and three young full-growns were trying unsuccessfully to wade-herd fish.

Torak felt a thrill of pure happiness. Wolves, ravens, otters, trees, rocks, lake: he was at peace with them all. For a moment he felt his world-soul reaching out to the world-soul of every living creature, like threads of golden gossamer floating on the wind. Wolf's amber gaze sought his, and Torak knew that he felt it too: that everything was just *right*.

On the other side of the lake, the reeds parted, as if for an unseen presence, and the lead wolf turned his head to watch. Idly, Torak wondered what he saw.

The leader of the pack was a large slate-grey wolf with a white blaze on his chest. Torak admired the way he asserted his leadership firmly but without bluster, never demeaning himself by bullying, and always watching out for his pack. Like Fin-Kedinn, thought Torak with a twinge of longing.

The young wolves were romping about in the shallows. Wolf bounded over to Torak and went down on his forepaws, lashing his tail. *Come and play!*

Torak pulled off his knife, belt and leggings and jumped in.

After the heat of the afternoon, the water was deliciously cold. Down he swam through spears of sunlight and rippling green weeds. Golden roach flickered past, and blue-black tench. On the underside of a water lily leaf, a bubble hung like a pearl, and he popped it with his finger.

Wolf's paws flashed by, and Torak yanked his tail. Wolf gave a startled yelp – Torak burst into the sunshine in a glitter of droplets – and they wrestled: Wolf play-growling, Torak shouting with laughter.

He was happy. He could live like this for ever.

Wolf gave a great twisting leap and splashed down on Tall Tailless. His pack-brother slipped under the Wet, then burst out again with his yip-and-yowling laugh.

That prompted the lead female to start a howl, and Wolf joined in. The badness in Tall Tailless had been chased away, the ravens knew their place, and he, Wolf, could be with Tall Tailless *and* the pack!

The howl ended. Tall Tailless waded out and threw himself down to dry off, and Wolf trotted up the rise to catch the scents.

He smelt many good smells, but to his dismay, he also caught the scent of the Otherness. It was floating on the Big Wet, much closer than before. It was getting bolder.

The ravens picked up the scent, and lifted into the sky.

Wolf watched them go – but decided not to follow. If there was trouble, they would alert the pack. That was what ravens were for.

Watching Rip and Rek flying east reminded Torak that he had things to do: he needed to build a shelter and set some snares.

Wolf knew before he did that he was heading into the Forest. Wagging his tail to show that he understood, he bounded off to play with the cubs.

Torak pulled on his leggings and started for the spot by the stream where the beavers were busy. He heard the crack of a tail-slam. *Beware! Intruder!* But they weren't really scared, as they knew he would only take the wood which they couldn't use themselves.

He chose three saplings which they'd gnawed through but hadn't been able to drag away, because they'd got stuck halfway down. Back at the denning place, he built a lean-to, filling in the sides with branches and bracken. Then he made his way through the Forest, and at the black beach he dismantled his old shelter and wiped out all trace of his presence.

The wound on his chest was painful and hot, so he dressed it with chewed willow bast and bandaged it with buckskin from his jerkin. By the time he'd finished, he was shaking with fatigue. He'd done too much. He must be weaker than he thought. Curling up at the edge of the trees, he fell asleep.

He dreamed of Renn. He felt her presence, but couldn't see her. He could hear her, though, as plainly as if she stood behind him.

'Better look after that wound, Torak,' she said in her wry, gentle way, 'or it'll go bad.'

'I put some willow leaves on it,' he said.

'It still hurts, doesn't it? Remember that healing spring on the north shore? You go up there and bathe it, right now.'

'If you come too,' he said, desperate to keep her with him.

'Maybe,' she replied, and he heard the smile in her voice. She was getting fainter.

'Come back!' he called. 'Renn, don't go! I miss you!'

'Do you?' She sounded amused. 'Well, I miss you too.'

He didn't want her to go. He was frantic to stay in the dream.

Mewing in distress, he woke up.

Clouds covered the sun, and the beach was desolate. Trudging down to the Lake, Torak stared at his name-soul in the water. He saw the mark of the outcast on his forehead; on his chest, the ragged wound from the Soul-Eater tattoo.

For an afternoon, he had been happy on the island. Ravens, beavers, otters, wolves: all had accepted him. But he missed Fin-Kedinn and he missed Renn.

He wondered if he would ever see them again.

TWENTY-SIX

The morning after the hailstorm, Renn stared at the stony little islet where the Lake had thrown them, and wondered how in the name of the Spirit they were going to get off.

The day before, as she'd huddled on the rocks, she'd simply been glad to be alive. Now she gazed about her in dismay.

There were plenty of trees, so at least they had fire and shelter; but she could have circled the whole islet in less time than it takes to skin a squirrel. And squirrels were doubtless what they'd be eating, because there wasn't room for anything bigger, and all the other islands were too far away to swim to.

She watched Bale walk to the water's edge, scuffing through the pine-needles festooning the rocks. He'd hardly spoken since they'd woken up.

'We've still got our axes and knives,' she said. 'And my quiver and bow.'

'Just as well,' he said without turning round. 'We've lost everything else. Food. The beaver-hide capes. Both paddles.' He couldn't bring himself to mention the skinboat, which lay between them. Its whalebone spine was intact, but the ribs on the left flank were smashed, and the seal-hide covering badly ripped.

'I don't think we can repair it,' said Renn.

'We'll have to,' he snapped.

'There are trees. We could make a dugout.'

He turned on her. 'Do you know how long that would take? To hollow out a tree? Have you ever *made* a dugout?'

She hadn't. The Ravens built their canoes of deer hide and willow, lashed together with spruce root.

'Neither have I,' growled Bale. 'I'm Seal Clan, we take what the Sea Mother gives us. So unless you want to make a raft with a bunch of reeds, we're repairing my boat!'

Renn didn't argue. He hadn't blamed her for the mess they were in, and he could have, because it was her fault.

The worst of it was, she didn't know if her Magecraft had worked. She only knew that she felt more exhausted than ever before in her life. She'd ignored all the warnings, she'd hurled herself against that overpowering will – and achieved what? As much good as a sparrow flying into a rockface.

The wind whispered over the pine-needles, and she seemed to catch a ripple of mocking laughter. How Seshru must be sneering at her!

Bale knelt by his skinboat, stroking its flank as if it were a faithful old dog in need of reassurance.

'Bale,' she said. 'I'm sorry.'

He shrugged. 'It was to help Torak. It was worth it.'

I hope so, thought Renn.

Bale stood up and squared his shoulders. 'Right. I'll make a start on the repairs.'

She nodded. 'I'll build a shelter. And find us something to eat.'

It took them four long days to mend the boat.

Bale had to cut down an ash tree to make the new ribs. Thinning them with an axe would have been impossible, so he had to make an adze, and as there wasn't any flint, he had to fashion one from a lump of granite, chipping and pecking it with a rock. When the ribs were finally shaped, he had to steam them and bend them to fit the hull, then smooth any rough edges which might have pierced the seal hide.

To patch the hide, he and Renn pooled every scrap they could spare: his fish-skin jerkin, her salmonskin tinder pouch, and – with regret – her sealskin bow case. It was barely enough, but when Bale tried to increase their supply by trapping fish, what he caught was too horrifying to use.

Luckily, he still had his repair kit of bone needles and seal-gullet thread, but sewing the stiff hide was painfully slow. 'No, no, you do *double* seams,' he scolded her, 'and don't pierce the outside, it'll leak.' He was much better at it, so she left him to it. But even with his bone thimble, his fingers were raw by the time he'd finished.

While he worked on the boat, Renn built a shelter, tying bundles of reeds with cords of twisted sedge, and lashing these to a bent willow frame. She gathered burdock, mussels and water lily roots to eat – after mistakenly digging up iris, which tasted disgusting.

She also straightened her arrows and shot a goldeneye duck as it flew in to land. That gave much-needed meat, and she used the skin to make a new tinder pouch, and the feathers for fletching. She sneaked a gobbet of fat to oil her bow, although it made her feel guilty, as Bale needed every morsel to waterproof the boat.

For that they heated a paste of pine-blood, charcoal and duck fat in a birchbark pail and daubed it on the hull with sticks wrapped in bark. Renn liked the smell of pine, but Bale wrinkled his nose. 'If only we had seal blubber,' he muttered.

'Surely it's ready now,' she said when they'd finished. She hadn't dreamt of Torak since the storm, but the memory was with her constantly.

'Tomorrow,' said Bale.

Her heart sank. 'Another day?'

'If we don't let it dry completely, we'll sink.'

'But –'

'Renn. I know what I'm talking about. We'll set off in the morning.'

She blew out a long breath. 'It's been so long. Anything could have happened to Torak.'

'I know,' said Bale. 'I do know.'

To work off her frustration, Renn went hunting.

Maybe it was the offerings she'd made to the Lake, or maybe it was the pair of ravens she saw overhead, but her luck was good. Another duck, this time a goosander. She cooked it the way her father had taught her long ago: rolling it in mud and burying it in the embers, then cracking it open to get at the juicy meat.

After they'd eaten, Bale sat on the pine-needles, smoothing one of the new ash paddles with horsetail stems, while Renn set the goosander's innards on the blade of the other paddle and tipped it into the Lake as an offering. It was a warm, still evening, and frogs were piping in the reeds.

From the west came the howling of wolves.

Bale lifted his head. 'There they are again.'

Now and then, they'd heard them; but although Renn thought she recognized Wolf's howl, she couldn't make out Torak's. She felt a stab of worry. How could Torak be without Wolf?

The ravens were back, flying high and turning their heads from side to side to look down at her. She wondered if they were a good sign to set against all the bad ones.

'You're very quiet,' said Bale.

She turned to speak – then froze.

'What is it?' said Bale.

'The first morning, after the storm, you walked from those pine-needles where you are now, down to the water's edge.'

'So?'

'It wasn't far. It only took you about three paces to get to the water. Try it now.'

Puzzled, he did as she asked. Then he did it again, to make sure. He stared at her. 'Five paces. The Lake. It's sinking, just like the Otters said.' His face turned grim. 'Seshru.'

Renn nodded. 'She's getting stronger.'

TWENTY-SEVEN

'Uff!' barked Wolf, warning Torak not to go any further. But Torak couldn't turn back now, and Wolf couldn't come with him.

Torak cast him a reassuring glance and pressed on through the reedbed, jumping from tussock to tussock. The sun was low, but with luck, he would reach the healing spring before dusk.

He couldn't wait till morning. The wound on his chest was burning, and had begun oozing yellow pus. The Soul-Eaters were reasserting their power.

'Uff!' barked Wolf from the edge of the trees.

Go back! Torak said in wolf talk. Through the reeds he saw Wolf running in circles, whining.

The rockface was as he remembered: steep, yet oddly enticing, with its waterfall misting the ferns. It was surprisingly easy to climb, with convenient footholds and bushes; but he was soon soaked in spray.

'Uff!'

Glancing down, Torak saw with a pang that Wolf was coming after him. But the rockface was too much for him. He leapt – clawed granite – and fell back with a yelp. It didn't help that Rip and Rek alighted on a ledge and laughed at him.

Go back! Torak told him. *I'm at the Den in the Light!* He hated not being able to explain that he would be back soon; but in wolf talk there is no future.

When he looked again, Wolf was gone.

Tiring now, Torak climbed on. He passed the creatures he'd seen before, hammer-etched into the rock. He was too close to glimpse more than fragments – an elk's sloping nose, a snake's forked tongue – but he caught their wet clay smell, and made sure not to touch.

At last he heaved himself over the top.

Except it wasn't the top, but a rocky hollow where part of the cliff had fallen away.

Before him lay a pool of luminous green, as bright as beech leaves with the sun shining through. Around it, purple orchids and black crowberries flourished in green clay: the same clay he'd seen on the faces of the Otters. As with the rockface, stone guardians thronged the encircling boulders. Stone elk raised antlered heads; stone waterbirds flew across stone skies, or plunged after stone pike who swam forever out of reach.

Torak couldn't see the spring itself, but he heard its echo and felt its power. It felt neither good nor evil; it had existed long before either.

He was only too well aware that he didn't know the proper rites, and he sensed the Hidden People watching.

Bowing to the pool, he offered what he'd brought with him: the wing of a woodgrouse wrapped in burdock leaves, which he buried under a rock, in case Rip and Rek came back.

Then he knelt, cupped water in his hands, and bathed his chest, asking the spring to heal him. The water was icy. He welcomed its clean, sharp bite on his burning flesh.

Tentatively, he drank. The water tasted flinty. So did the crowberries, which bore an odd greyish bloom.

He thought about smearing some of the green clay on his chest, but decided not to risk it. He'd only seen that clay on the Otters and on the posts among the reeds. It belonged to the Lake. He was of the Forest. It wouldn't feel right.

Rip lit down beside him with a loud 'rap rap rap'! – and he jumped. 'Rap rap rap'! croaked Rek, thudding down beside Rip and fluffing up her feathers in alarm. In the last rays of the sun, the spray on their wings glittered scarlet, like drops of blood.

'What's the matter?' said Torak. 'Do you want some berries?'

To his surprise, they refused to eat, and pecked angrily at the crowberry bushes, scattering twigs. Torak shooed them away before they could do much damage.

In the world below, an elk bellowed, and the wolves started their evening howl.

Torak yawned. His chest went blessedly numb, and an irresistible languor was stealing through him. He curled up in the ferns and shut his eyes.

Moon and stars whirled above him, trailing silver fire across a dark-blue sky. He felt giddy and tired, so tired.

He heard the hiss and spit of embers; the spring gurgling a song which had no end. Then another voice joined in, murmuring words he couldn't understand. It sounded like Renn.

It *was* Renn.

She sat with her back to him, tending the fire. In the gloom he made out her pale arms and her long, loose hair.

To make sure she was real, he put out a clumsy hand and grasped her wrist.

Her bones were light and small. Yes, real.

'I knew you'd find me,' he said. It didn't begin to express what he felt.

Her skin was warm and smooth; he didn't want to let go. *Smooth.*

No zigzag tattoos.

'I knew I'd find you too,' said Seshru the Viper Mage.

TWENTY-EIGHT

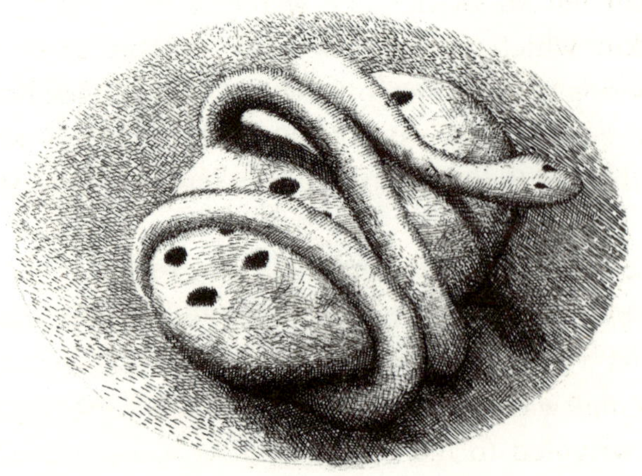

'How you've grown since last we met!' said the Viper Mage with her mocking sideways smile.

Her hair was a mantle of darkness, and the viper tattoo seemed to throb on her high white brow; but her beautiful lips were black.

Torak tried to move, but he couldn't. He wasn't tied up, his limbs simply refused to obey. He said, 'The crowberries. You poisoned them.'

Her eyes glinted. 'But I'm not going to hurt you.'

'Why would I believe that?'

'Because I would have done it by now. I could have cut out your heart and eaten it. Not even your wolves could have reached you up here.' She leaned down and whispered in his ear. 'But I want you alive!'

His heart was thumping so hard that she must be able to hear it. 'Why?' he said.

But she only laughed, and licked her lips with her little pointed black tongue.

As she twisted to tend the fire, her tunic of supple buckskin fell about her like water. It was fringed with snakeskin which caressed her naked arms and calves, shimmering with every move. Torak couldn't take his eyes off her. Fear and revulsion burned in him – this woman was evil, she'd helped kill his father – but he couldn't look away.

He watched her pass her hand over the lid of a basket, evoking a rustle from whatever lived within. He watched her twist a garland of herbs and set it on her brow, and paint long, wavering stripes on her arms: green snakes which wriggled to life on her pale skin. Fascinated and repelled, he watched – and she smiled her knowing smile, enjoying her power.

With a forked stick, she dropped a stone from the fire into a rawhide pot, sending up a hiss of steam.

'What's that?' he said.

Her lip curled. 'Hot water. I was a Healer, remember?'

Wringing out a piece of buckskin, she bathed his chest, then smoothed on a cooling salve. It felt good. The pain was gone.

'It won't fester any more,' she told him. 'I no longer need it to draw you to me. Though it's as well I summoned you when I did.'

I summoned you. The voice he'd heard in his sleep hadn't been Renn, but Seshru.

'What do you want?' he said between his teeth.

Rising to her feet, she went to the edge of the cliff and gazed down. 'All the tiny creatures,' she murmured. 'The wolves, the frightened little Otter people. They belong to me now. They must submit – or I will empty the Lake.'

Torak thought of the pine-needles on the black beach. The Lake was draining away. He tried to stir, but managed only a twitch of his head.

The Viper Mage touched the green clay on her arm. 'This – this has power! When I wear it, those I meet see only a woman masked in green: sick, frightened, like them. Not even your wolf knows my scent.'

As if she'd called to Wolf, a howl rang out from below. *Come down!*

Seshru smiled. 'Now he knows me! I've shed my mask. He knows who has defeated him!'

Torak saw that the garland she wore was nightshade, which on a single stem bore purple flowers, green berries and ripe scarlet ones: a most potent herb, whose every part was deadly, like the Viper Mage herself. She was too strong. For a moment, he despaired.

He heard wings. Rip and Rek alighted on a boulder behind her.

'Ah, but you're strong!' said Seshru, oblivious. Kneeling beside him, she drew off his headband and gently pushed the hair from his forehead. 'To have spirit walked in an ice bear!' She stroked his temple. 'Brave, too. To cut out the mark of the Soul-Eater. Who taught you the rite? It must have been a Mage of great power.'

She was trying to flatter him. She wouldn't succeed. And yet – her touch was gentle. He struggled to keep his thoughts together.

'You – stole the red deer antlers,' he said. 'You poisoned the drink when I did the rite. You made me spirit walk in the elk.'

She smiled her beautiful, maddening smile. 'So strong.

And to fight off soul-sickness!'

His thoughts were darkening, her fingers reaching into his mind. 'The F-Far North,' he stammered. 'How did you get away? Where is the Oak Mage – the Eagle Owl Mage?'

She laughed. 'Ah, we're so alike, you and I! Both outcasts, both unimaginably strong. That's why the clans hunt us. The weak will always fear the strong.'

Rip and Rek flew away. Torak scarcely noticed.

'So alike,' breathed Seshru. 'Why fight it? Why not accept it?'

'No,' he said with an effort. 'We're not alike. You've killed people. You've broken clan law.'

'But that's all it is,' she countered, 'the law of the clans. Only the Soul-Eaters know the law of the World Spirit. That's why it delivered the spirit walker to me.' She paused. 'But why didn't I know you at once for what you are? How did you conceal yourself from me? The answer must lie somewhere.' With a supple movement, she reached for his gear.

The spell of her touch was broken. Torak hated seeing her handle his things.

'Your father's knife,' she said with distaste. 'A traitor's knife. Slate, antler, sinew. Nothing there. The axe, then. Not yours, I think.' Taking his hand, she measured it against the axehead. How clever she was! If the axe had been made for him, its head would have spanned from the heel of his palm to the tip of his middle finger. It was slightly longer.

'It has the Raven mark on the handle,' she mused, 'but the head is greenstone . . . They say that Fin-Kedinn lived with the frog-eaters for a time.'

She read the truth in his face. 'So it *is* his! You stole Fin-Kedinn's axe! *You* broke clan law!'

Next, she took his medicine pouch and drew out his medicine horn. Her lips thinned. 'Your mother's.' She set it down. 'Nothing. The answer lies elsewhere.'

With a shudder of relief, Torak remembered that the strand of Renn's hair was inside the pouch. Seshru hadn't found it. She was not all-powerful. She could make mistakes.

Seshru sensed the change in him, and her features turned colder than wind-carved ice. 'Do not imagine you can hide from me.'

Torak met her stare and held it.

With the speed of a striking snake, she brought her face close to his. 'You cannot defy me! Not while I have this!' In her fingers she held something small, caught in the coils of a green clay serpent.

Torak's belly turned over. The pebble he'd made for Renn.

'Have you any idea of the power this gives me?' she hissed. 'With this I blighted your souls! You have no will of your own. You belong to me!'

Her fist tightened on the pebble – and Torak's heart clenched.

She opened her fist – and he breathed again.

She laughed, and on her breath he smelt the carrion stink of the root which turned her mouth black. How could he have thought her beautiful? Her spirit was hollow, and where her heart used to be there was only a shadow, like the dark stain where a carcass once lay.

Now she was casting off the lid of the basket, and a viper was sliding over the edge. Silently, silently it flowed into her lap. Its zigzag markings were stark down its glistening silver length, and its lidless red eye was fixed on its mistress.

Seshru picked it up and it wound itself about her arm, its black tongue flickering out to meet hers. 'Keep very still,' she told Torak. 'Their bite is worse than any you will encounter in the Forest. Their bite can kill . . .'

A second viper, black as a moonless night, poured from the basket, and Seshru showed it the pebble. As its forked tongue flicked out to taste it, Torak gasped. He had felt that tongue on his skin.

'You wanted this, spirit walker,' breathed the Viper Mage. 'You put yourself in my power. You left the stone for me to find.'

'No,' he whispered.

Her eyes pierced his souls. 'Then why make it?'

'A – a present,' he stammered.

'For whom?'

'– A girl.'

'Why take it back?'

'To tell her I was gone.' He tried to push Renn's image from his mind, but the Viper Mage was faster.

'Her name is Renn,' she said. 'Who is she?'

With a huge effort, he dragged his gaze from hers – only to settle on the greenstone axe.

Seshru was on it in a heartbeat. 'Fin-Kedinn's. She's Fin-Kedinn's child.'

'– His brother's.'

There was a moment of stillness. Then the Viper Mage turned her back on him and sat, staring at the Lake, while the snakes in her lap twined their sleek coils about each other.

'– His brother's child,' she said tonelessly. 'Of course. He would have cared for his brother's child.'

Torak couldn't bear to hear her mention Renn.

But Renn is far away, he told himself. Renn is safe.

'No.' Seshru twisted round again. 'She is here on the Lake. I saw her in a boat with a boy, a tall boy with yellow hair. But they can't help you now.'

Was she telling the truth? Were Renn and Bale looking for him, or was it another of her lies?

'Why do you want me alive?' he said. 'What do you *want*?'

'You know what I want.'

'My power. You want to be the spirit walker.'

'I have that already. I can make you spirit walk whenever I wish. I want more. I want – the fire-opal.'

To hear her name it . . . Her voice breathed life into the image in his mind. He saw its pulsing red heart.

'It – it was lost in the ice,' he said.

'Don't lie to me,' said Seshru. 'I am a Mage, don't you think I have ways of knowing? When your father shattered it, three pieces were left – *three*! One held by the Seal Mage, one taken by the black ice. One remains. Your father must have told you before he died.'

'No.'

'He hid it. He hid it and he told you where, as he lay dying –'

'No –'

'– as he lay in agony, his life bleeding away, his guts ripped out by the demon bear –'

'No!' he screamed.

Clawing the nightshade from her brow, she flung it on the fire. Blue smoke wound about her, pungent, dizzying.

Powerless, Torak watched her open a pouch at her breast and dip in her finger. He tried to resist, but she held his jaw and smeared a stinking black sludge on his lips. Grasping the dark viper in one hand, the silver in the other, she brought them to her mouth and whispered a charm. Then she placed both snakes on his chest.

He didn't dare breathe. He felt their cool softness gliding over him; the tiny contractions as their scales gripped his flesh. He felt their tongues on his skin. Seshru observed his terror with the dispassionate gaze of a serpent watching its prey.

'Your body can't move, but your souls can. Your souls will go wherever I command. Your souls will do whatever I want.'

The black sludge was bitter in his mouth. Lights flashed behind his eyes, sickening spirals of light.

He saw the dark hair of the Viper Mage floating like snakes about her white face. He felt his souls ripped from his marrow. He screamed . . .

. . . silently, his black tongue tasted the air.

The last thing he heard before he became snake was the voice of the Viper Mage, commanding him to find Renn.

TWENTY-NINE

Faster than thought, the snake slithered down the rockface.

It tasted the scent of cricket and fern. It felt the scurrying of ant and shrew. Air, leaf, water, prey, light – it ignored them all. Its mistress had sent it after richer quarry.

The rocks burned with the heat of the vanished sun, and the snake took in that heat as it passed. Noiselessly, it slid off the rocks; the water enfolded it, and it took in the chill of the Lake.

The snake felt this change, but that was *all* it felt. No pleasure or discomfort, eagerness or fear. Those feelings it recognized, because it tasted them on the struggling prey and on the mountains of warm meat which shook the earth – but such feelings were not snake.

This made the souls of the snake very strong: pure

intent, unclouded by emotion. Torak would not have believed such strength could exist in so slender a body. His own souls were weak from the poison; he couldn't turn the snake from its purpose. He could only shiver inside its small, cold brain as it sped through the Lake, deadly as an arrow.

He felt the coolness of weed and water flowing over his coils. His lidless eyes knew the flash and flicker of fish. Then he was out in the heat again, and the scent of pine was thick on his tongue. The sand was rough, he gripped it with his scales. Raising his snake head, he tasted the scent of raven.

The hot bird swooped – its cries muffled by air, then piercingly loud as it thudded to earth. The snake darted into a hole and prepared to strike.

He felt the raven hop towards the hole. It smelt him, but it couldn't reach. Frustrated, it pecked the tree-root which sheltered him. The ground shuddered as it flew away.

When the threat was past, he emerged. He crested the mossy hillside of a log, slithered under bracken taller than trees. At last he caught the scent of slumbering male, and beyond it, the sweeter scent of female.

Torak's souls fought to get free – to turn the snake from its purpose – but it glided on, relentless. And now as he slid under leaf and over stone, he felt waves of heat from sleeping flesh.

Bite, bite. The voice of his mistress wove in and out of his snake mind.

Again the part of him that was Torak tried to turn the creature, but his muscles would not obey.

Bite, bite.

His coils gripped a naked foot, slid up a pale calf; over soft elk hide and rough wovengrass, into a band of warm raven feathers heaving in sleep. His snake head recoiled from the markings on the wrist – so like his, yet different – but beyond, his cloven tongue tasted uprotected flesh.

No! shouted Torak in the cold snake brain. *No! This is Renn!*

The snake stretched its jaws wide – its fangs unfolded from the roof of its mouth and pointed down – they filled with venom, ready to strike . . .

Bite, bite.

ᛒ

Torak woke.

Above him the clouds spun, jolting him on a sea of sickness. Gradually, he became aware of the sound of the spring. At his side the Viper Mage sat motionless, her face as white as bone. The vipers were gone.

'It is done?' she said.

He nodded.

She breathed out. Rising to her feet, she gazed across the Lake. Then she turned, and he could tell that she wasn't seeing him, but was looking through him to the power he could give her.

'Until now, 'she said, 'not even I understood the strength of the spirit walker.' Returning, she knelt, and her long hair brushed his chest as she brought her face close to his. 'Think what I can do with such power! I can learn the darkest secrets. I can bend all, all to my will!'

Torak shut his eyes. That made the churning worse. He tried to sit up – but although movement was returning to his limbs, he remained weak as a fledgling.

Seshru pushed the sweat-soaked hair back from his forehead. '*This* is the will of the World Spirit! *This* is why it sent such a gift to me! With the spirit walker and the fire-opal I shall rule! All creatures, all demons will fear me and obey!'

Sickness engulfed him. Clumsily, he raised himself on his elbow and retched.

With her icy hand, the Viper Mage pressed him to her breast. 'Great power is bought with suffering, I know. But now you understand. You belong to me.'

Exhausted, he slumped against her.

'Say it,' she whispered, and her breath was hot and foetid on his skin. 'Say that you belong to me!'

He gazed up at her, and she was very beautiful. Even her black smile was beautiful.

He said, 'I belong to you.'

THIRTY

Renn was shaken by her dream about the viper.

'What did it mean?' said Bale as they loaded the skinboat.

'I'm not sure. But it was in colour, so it must be true. I think . . .'

'Yes?'

'I think it means she has him now.'

Bale stopped with his paddle in his hands. 'You said the Magecraft had worked.'

'I said I *thought* it had. You can never be certain.'

He considered that. 'Well, I've got more faith in you. And in Torak.'

Renn didn't reply. She hadn't told him about the real viper she'd glimpsed as she'd started awake. What would have happened if those ravens hadn't chased it away?

Oh, Seshru was cunning! She'd cut Torak off from the clans, from his friends, even from Wolf – and now she had him to herself, on this Lake which she was taking for her own. Somewhere, she was laughing at them all.

It was a hot dawn, and with the wind at their backs they made good speed. Their islet turned out to have been much further west than they'd thought, and by mid-afternoon the Island of the Hidden People came into view.

As they bobbed in the shallows, Renn made an offering, asking leave to go ashore; then they landed the skinboat on a black beach backed by a watchful Forest. It had rained recently, and a steamy haze rose from the trees. A smell of decay wafted from a band of reddish pine-needles which reminded Renn of a snake.

'No sign of Torak,' said Bale, returning from a search further up the beach. 'But I found other tracks.'

When Renn saw them, her heart quickened. 'A wolf.' She blew her grouse-bone whistle, but got no answer. Her unease deepened.

As soon as they entered the Forest, the wind dropped and the heat settled on their skin. Clouds of midges whined in their ears. The rasp of crickets was loud, but there was no birdsong, except for the brief warble of a redstart.

Wading through springy lingonberry scrub, they followed a rivulet upstream. They passed man-high nests of wood-ants, and hunched boulders mantled with steaming moss. Over her shoulder, Renn caught the glint of the Lake between the trees; then the pines closed in and she saw it no more. The presence of the Hidden People was strong. She saw Bale touch his seal-rib amulet.

They reached a clearing where the stream had been dammed by branches. Brown pools spread amid gnawed stumps and piles of wood-chips. The air was fresh with the tang of tree-blood.

'Beaver,' they said together.

Bale gave a lopsided smile, and Renn's unease lessened. If the Hidden People allowed beavers on their island, then maybe Torak . . .

Again that redstart.

Renn froze. 'Torak?' she called softly. 'Is that you?'

Bale raised his eyebrows, and she explained that it was a signal they sometimes used.

Once more she called. The Forest tensed. Her heart raced.

'Maybe it's our weapons,' said Bale in a low voice. 'He'll be wary.'

Renn stared at him. 'Not of us!'

'Renn. He's been outcast a long time. Let's set them aside; and we should move into the trees. If it is him, he won't come into the open.'

Propping their weapons against a stump, they left the clearing and re-entered the Forest.

'Torak!' Renn breathed to the watching pines.

'We came to help you,' whispered Bale.

They hadn't gone far when they rounded a boulder and found their weapons neatly laid on a lingonberry bush — except for Renn's bow, which hung from a birch tree.

'Couldn't let it get wet,' said Torak.

There was no time for greetings.

Torak jerked his head at them to follow, and headed into the trees. 'Got to get deeper in, or she'll see us.'

'She's *here?*' cried Renn and Bale together.

'Up on the north cliff,' muttered Torak, 'that's her eyrie. I don't think she'll risk the island because of the wolves.'

Renn's skin prickled. 'You've actually seen her?'

'She lured me there. She thought I was going to help her. I – I got away.'

'How?' said Bale.

Torak's face closed. 'Even the Viper Mage has to sleep.'

'Not for long,' said Renn.

Torak didn't answer. His expression was taut and unsmiling, and he kept turning to listen for sounds of pursuit. There was a bruised look about his eyes that told of broken nights and not enough food. And Renn noticed with a pang that he no longer wore the rowanberry wristband.

She couldn't tell if he was glad to see them. She couldn't tell *what* he was feeling. She tried to overcome the awful sense that he'd become a stranger.

And he looked so different! He'd been a skinny boy when he left, but now he was as tall as Bale, and the veins on his arms stood out like cords. There was a scab on his chest where the mark of the Soul-Eater had been, and some puzzling scratches on his shoulders; and although he still wore the headband, it only reminded her of the outcast tattoo beneath, and of all the dangers he'd survived on his own. Without her.

They found a fallen pine and hid behind it while Bale shared out dried duck meat from his food pouch. Torak ate fast, like a wolf. He didn't say much about the past two moons, just told them briefly about Wolf joining a pack. Bale told how they'd met the Otter Clan and wrecked the boat, but to Renn's relief, he didn't mention her attempt at Magecraft. Throughout, Torak spoke mostly to his kinsman, and avoided looking at her.

Silence fell and she plucked up courage. 'You got rid of the Soul-Eater mark.'

He nodded. 'I did the rite, but I'm not sure it worked. I got sick. A kind of madness.'

'Soul-sickness,' said Bale.

'Is that what it was?' said Torak. 'Well. I got better.'

'How?' said Renn.

'I don't know. I just did.'

There was a whirring of wings, and a raven flew down onto Torak's shoulder. Wincing, he lifted it off. 'I told you not to do that!'

Renn and Bale exchanged startled glances.

Another raven alighted on a juniper bush. Torak gave each bird a scrap, and they flew to a nearby tree, where they eyed the newcomers suspiciously.

Renn was astonished. Ravens are supremely wary birds, but with Torak they behaved with perfect ease.

'Where did they come from?' said Bale.

'There was a hailstorm,' said Torak. 'They fell out of their nest, and I – I had to look after them. It's odd, but after that I got better.'

Bale caught Renn's eye and smiled.

She didn't smile back. She didn't *want* to be good at Magecraft. And she was a bit envious of the ravens.

'I call the bigger one Rip,' said Torak. 'The smaller one's Rek. Watch your gear, because they like to steal, and what they can't steal, they shred. And when Wolf's around, *don't* make a fuss of them. He gets jealous.'

Feeling self-conscious, Renn bowed to the ravens. 'Well met, little grandfathers, and thank you.'

Rek flapped her wings and croaked, 'Well met well met!' and Rip lifted his tail and spattered the ferns with droppings.

Torak glanced at Renn in surprise, but she didn't speak.

Let him think the ravens had come to him by chance.

Bale stood up and said he was going to hide the skinboat, and suddenly Torak and Renn were alone and the awkwardness was worse.

Torak frowned. 'Renn . . .'

'What?'

'That elk. The one that attacked you –'

'I know,' she said quickly.

'Do you?' His frown deepened. 'I was so worried. That's why I went back to camp, to see if you were all right.'

'I know. Torak –'

'She made me do it!' he burst out. 'She made me do terrible things! Attacking you, then Ak – the Boar Clan boy . . .'

'Aki?' Renn snorted. 'He's all right!'

He stared at her. 'He is?'

'Broken arm, but it's on the mend.'

'He's *alive*.'

'Actually, I wish it'd been a bit worse. Bale said that when he left, Aki was trying to get his clan to come after you.'

Torak wasn't listening. He had both hands to his temples, and he looked younger and more vulnerable.

Renn said, 'Maybe you haven't changed as much as I thought.'

He blinked. 'You're the one who's changed.'

'Me?'

He touched his cheek, to show that he'd noticed her moon-bleed tattoo. 'You seem older.'

She was embarassed. 'I *hate* sharing with Saeunn. She grinds her gums in her sleep. First time I heard it, I thought someone was sharpening a knife. But it went on *all night*.'

His lip curled. 'Does she smell?'

'Like a three-day-old carcass.'

He grinned. And suddenly he wasn't a stranger any more.

Bale returned, looking worried. 'I should have hidden the skinboat earlier, she might've spotted it.'

'Whatever you do,' said Torak, 'she'll soon know you're here. She knows everything.'

Renn went cold.

'But what does she *want?*' said Bale.

'She wants to crush the Lake into submission,' said Torak. 'She wants me to help her find the last piece of the fire-opal. She wants to rule.'

'How would she get you to help her?' said Renn, feeling breathless.

Torak hesitated. 'That pebble I made for you? She has it.'

Renn shut her eyes. She'd been dreading this.

'But – I still got away,' he said uncertainly. 'And I fought off the soul-sickness. And when she made me spirit walk in the viper, I fought back.'

No you didn't, thought Renn. The ravens woke me in time. Out loud she said, 'She'll make you do it again, Torak. Or she'll think of something else. She's like a snake. If she meets an obstacle, she slithers around it.'

Torak stood up. 'Then we'll have to find the fire-opal before she does. Come on. We'll be safer with the wolves.'

丰丰

Everything was happening too fast, Torak couldn't take it in.

First his flight from Seshru: scrambling down the rockface, splashing through reeds, crashing into the Forest. Fearing at any moment to feel a viper's fangs sinking into his calf; to come face to face with that all-seeing, all-powerful gaze.

And now suddenly, Renn and Bale.

He should have been elated, but he was too churned up. Renn looked so different! The birch-seed freckle was still there at the corner of her mouth, but the red bar on her clan-tattoo made her seem older, less like his friend. It was a stark reminder that the life of the clans had gone on without him; that he'd been left behind.

It was a shock, too, to see her with Bale. As they moved through the Forest, he saw how easily they fell into step together. He watched Bale hold a branch out of the way of her bow, and felt a twist of jealousy. The Seal boy had taken his place.

Renn, though, didn't seem to notice. She wanted to know everything Seshru had said and done when he'd been with her at the spring, and she listened with the same intense concentration which she brought to hunting.

'She'll find some way to get you,' she said. 'If only we knew what she was doing.'

Bale watched Rip alight in a pine. 'Torak could spirit walk in a raven, and find out.'

'I thought of that,' said Torak, 'but I can't. In the Far North, I promised the wind I'd never fly again.'

'How she'd laugh if she knew that,' Renn said bitterly.

The light was failing as they reached the water lily lake. The denning place was quiet.

Torak gave two short barks. *I am here!*

No answer.

He ran to search the Den.

No cub-watcher. No cubs.

'They've gone,' he said in disbelief. 'The pack is gone.'

Renn stood with her hands on her hips, looking about her. 'Where would they take the cubs?'

Torak thought for a moment. 'When they get big enough,

the pack takes them to a new place, to learn to hunt.' He breathed out. 'Yes, that must be it.'

'Will it be far?' said Bale, his voice strained.

'A day's lope, maybe more.'

'So – it'll be off the island?' said Renn.

'Yes,' said Torak. 'But Wolf will come back for me, or we'll find each other by howling –'

'Torak,' cut in Bale, 'don't you see what this means? If the wolves have left the island, it means –'

'Yes,' said the Viper Mage, 'it does.'

THIRTY-ONE

She sat cross-legged on the boulder above the Den, gazing down at them with her mocking sideways smile. 'The wolves are gone,' she told Torak. 'I sent them all away.'

'Don't listen to her,' said Renn.

'Why, what harm can I do?' said the Viper Mage without taking her eyes off Torak. 'It's three against one, and I have no weapons.' Her voice was as smooth as water that wears away stone, and she made him feel as if she spoke to him alone: as if they were the only ones here in this hot, airless dusk. 'No weapons,' she murmured, 'not even a knife.'

Torak felt the sweat starting out between his shoulder blades. He darted a glance at his friends. Bale stood transfixed, his axe forgotten in his hand. Renn gripped bow and arrow, but did not take aim.

'Not even a knife,' repeated the Viper Mage, drawing his gaze back to her. At her breast the medicine pouch softly rose and fell. In the failing light her eyes were black, unblinking as a snake's. 'You lied to me,' she told him. 'You deceived me and ran away. I thought you were braver than that.'

Torak swayed. 'You can't make me go with you,' he said with an effort.

'Ah, but I can.' She touched the pouch. *You know I can. I have your stone, caught fast in the coils of the green clay serpent. You cannot defy me!*

'Don't listen to her,' snarled Renn again.

'So this is Renn,' said Seshru, leaning back on her hands and regarding her with amusement. 'What a little vixen! It was you who helped him resist me, wasn't it? You must have some small talent for Magecraft.' She paused. 'But of course you do! And we both know why.'

Shakily, Renn nocked an arrow to her bow.

Torak grabbed her arm. 'Renn, no!'

'You can't, she's not armed!' cried Bale.

Seshru laughed, baring her white throat. 'Oh, she won't shoot! She can't. Can you, Renn?'

Trembling from head to foot, Renn lowered her bow.

'I knew she wouldn't,' said the Viper Mage with contempt. She turned her gaze on Bale. 'To kill a weaponless woman . . . who could do such a thing? Could you?'

Her beauty caught him in its web, and his axe slid from his grasp.

'I didn't think so,' she said. 'That would be the mark of a weak man, and you're not weak. You're a Seal Clan hunter. You're strong.'

Bale shook himself and drew a deep breath, as if coming up for air. But his arms hung limp at his sides.

The Viper Mage withdrew her gaze from him, and again Torak felt its force. It was like staring at the sun.

'Don't look at her,' said Renn. 'Don't listen to her!'

Torak gripped his knife-hilt till his knuckles were white. This knife had belonged to Fa. Fa had had the strength to resist the Soul-Eaters. So must he. 'I – won't go with you,' he said at last. 'I won't help you find the fire-opal.'

'Oh, but you will,' said Seshru, and her lips parted in noiseless laughter. 'When you know the truth, you will!'

'No.'

'You see,' she continued as if he hadn't spoken, 'I can make you leave your friends – I can cut you out from your safe little herd – just as easily as snapping my fingers.'

'No,' whispered Torak.

'She's lying,' said Renn in an odd, pleading tone. 'That's what she does, Torak, she lies! She takes credit for things she didn't do; she denies the crimes she did. You can't believe anything she says!'

'Some things you can,' Seshru told Renn, her voice tinged with venom. 'We both know that, don't we, Renn? Although I must say, I'm surprised that you never told him. If he's your friend – if you care for him as much as he cares for you – and he does care, he really does . . . Not to have told him! *Such* a mistake! But then,' she added slyly, 'you already know it was a mistake. Don't you, Renn?'

Torak saw that Renn's face had gone chalk-white. 'Renn?' he said. 'What's wrong?'

Renn's eyes were shadowy hollows, her expression unreadable. 'I was going to tell you,' she said in a strangled voice. 'But I could never . . . It was never the right time.'

He began to feel cold. 'Tell me what?'

'Haven't you guessed?' said Seshru, leaning forwards and watching him with the fixity of a snake closing on its prey.

'Guessed what?' said Torak. 'Renn, what is it?'

Seshru smiled her carrion smile. 'Tell him, Renn. Tell him!'

Renn opened her mouth, but no sound came.

'*What?*' shouted Torak.

The Viper Mage licked her black lips and hissed, '*She is my daughter!*'

THIRTY-TWO

Renn wished Torak would say something – anything – but he just stood there, staring at her. And that was worse.

'I wanted to tell you,' she said. 'It was never the right time.'

He looked as if he'd been kicked in the chest. He looked as if he didn't know who she was.

She said, 'I couldn't tell you in the beginning. You would never have been friends with me.'

'Two summers,' he said quietly. 'You hid this for two whole summers.'

She felt cold: a deep inner cold that went beyond shivering. 'I thought maybe you'd guessed. When you spirit walked in that elk. And the viper. I thought you were angry.'

'No. You hid it too well.'

She flinched. 'You – you hid things too,' she faltered. 'You didn't tell me about the Soul-Eater tattoo. But I got over it. I understood.'

'That was for two moons. Not two summers.' He took a few steps away, then turned and confronted her. The blood had left his face. His lips had a greyish tinge. 'The first time I met you,' he said slowly. 'I felt there was – something. I didn't trust you.' He paused. 'Turns out I was right.'

'How can you say that?' she burst out. 'Of course you can trust me!'

He was shaking his head in disbelief. 'Two whole summers. I was your friend and you lied to me, every single day.'

'You're still my friend!' she cried. 'I'm still Renn! Still the same person!'

Bale stepped between them. 'Torak. She never meant to hurt you.'

'What do you know?' snapped Torak. 'Keep out of this, it's got nothing to do with you!'

'Torak, *please*,' said Renn. 'I *know* I should've told you . . .'

'Get away from me!' His face worked. 'I never want to see you again! Just – get away!'

She turned and fled.

'Renn, come back!' shouted Bale. 'No – Torak – don't you go too! *Renn!* We've got to keep together! This is just what she wants!'

Renn tore through the bracken, not caring where she went. As she ran, she saw that the Viper Mage was gone from the boulder. She had scattered them just as she'd said she would: as easily as snapping her fingers.

4

Torak's only thought was to be on his own. He could hear Bale crashing after him, but the Seal boy was no match for him in a darkened Forest, and he was soon left behind.

At last, Torak reached the shore and had to stop. The reeds stood deathly still, like a thicket of spears. He hardly saw them. It was a hot, still night and the sweat was pouring off him, but he was shaking with cold.

Images from the past flashed before him. Renn's talent for Magecraft. Her reluctance to practise it. Her refusal to explain why.

She and the Viper Mage even looked alike! The same pale skin and high-boned, regular features. Why hadn't he seen it?

But what hit hardest and hurt the most was that she'd kept this from him for so long. That she could be capable of such deception. It turned her into someone else, someone he didn't know. And that was the worst, because it meant that he'd lost her. He was alone again, just like when Fa was killed.

No, he thought, not alone. Never alone, while you've got Wolf.

Wolf never lied to him. Wolf wouldn't know how.

Putting up his head, Torak howled. *Come to me, pack-brother! I need you!* Reckless of the Viper Mage, he shut his eyes and put all his pain and loneliness into his howls.

At first, he heard nothing. Then, very faint, came an answering howl.

At least – Torak *thought* it was Wolf, but it was too far away to make out. Maybe it wasn't Wolf at all, but one of the others. Maybe it was nothing to do with him.

Bereft, he wandered along the shore.

Much later, he found himself sitting at the southern tip of the island, gazing over the Lake. He had no idea how he'd got there. He only knew that he was very, very tired.

Far to the south, he made out the lights of the Otter camp; nearer, to the west, the glimmer of campfires. Distractedly, he wondered what that meant. Maybe the clans were coming after him. He couldn't bring himself to care.

On the Lake, a shadow slid towards him.

He couldn't summon the strength to hide. With his axe in one hand, he rose to his feet.

Whoever it was moved skilfully, nosing towards him as silently as a pike.

'Torak. Get in.' Bale spoke quietly from the gloom.

Torak didn't move.

'Torak! Come *on*, the Viper Mage could be anywhere! And judging from those campfires, half the clans have come after you!'

When Torak still didn't move, Bale sighed. 'I know this is hard, but there's no time! We'll head for the north shore, they won't dare hunt us there; then we'll look for Renn.'

'No,' said Torak. 'You do what you like. I'm going to find Wolf.'

'Wolf will find you, but Renn's out there alone, and that – creature – could be anywhere!'

'I don't care.'

'Yes you do. If anything happened to Renn, you'd never forgive yourself – and neither would I. Now get in!'

The Bright White Eye was shining in the Up as Wolf paced the ridge.

During the Light, he'd told himself that all was well: that once he knew the cubs were safe at their new resting place, he could race back and fetch Tall Tailless. Then, far in the distance, he'd heard his pack-brother's desperate howl.

The other wolves had heard it too, but to his dismay, they'd hardly stirred. The cubs lay in an exhausted heap, and the full-growns – tired from the journey – sprawled, whiffling, in their sleeps. Tall Tailless was their friend, but he wasn't of the pack, as Wolf was of the pack.

This troubled Wolf. He wanted everyone to be together, as they had been on the island.

Trotting down to Darkfur, he snuffle-licked her muzzle. Sleepily, she raised her head and thumped her tail, then slumped back on her side. Soon her paws were twitching in her sleep.

The lead wolf felt Wolf's worry and woke.

Wolf dropped his ears and wagged his tail, apologizing for leaving. Then he started down the ridge.

It helped to be on the move. He would hurry back to the Den and find Tall Tailless. Then he would lead him to the pack, and everything would be all right.

For a while he gave himself up to the whisper of the grey flowers against his fur and the sweet breath of the slumbering trees; but the part of him that was always on watch noted that this Dark, smells and sounds were keener than usual. His pelt was tight, his pads tingled. The Thunderer was restless. There was going to be a storm.

Reaching flatter ground, he slowed. He smelt dogs. Some he knew, many he didn't. Keeping downwind, he crept past the great Dens of the taillesses, which clustered by the Wet like a herd of aurochs. So many taillesses! Here were ones who smelt of boar and raven and even of wolf; but he couldn't stop to explore.

Beyond the Dens, he quickened his pace, weaving through the reeds, following the ancient trails known only to wolves and Hidden Ones. As he loped, he glimpsed them: silent, swaying. He ignored them, and they let him pass.

At last he reached the denning place, and suddenly everything was wrong wrong wrong. It stank of Viper-Tongue!

Wolf smelt that Tall Tailless had been here, and to his surprise, he also caught the scent of the pack-sister who smelt of ravens, and of the pale-pelted male who was their friend. *But they had fought!* Wolf smelt rage and pain and biting sorrow. He smelt Viper-Tongue's dreadful pleasure.

A breeze woke the birch trees, and in the distance, Wolf heard howls. The pack was singing its joy at having found a safe place for the cubs.

Wolf lifted his muzzle to tell them he was coming back – but suddenly, he stopped.

A terrible certainty came to him. It hurt more than strong teeth tearing into his flank. *A wolf cannot be of two packs.*

Wolf saw now that Tall Tailless couldn't be with the pack, because that wasn't what he was for. Fighting bad taillesses was what he was for; just as hunting demons was what Wolf was for.

Pain sank its teeth into Wolf's heart. Not for him to run with the pack and teach the cubs to play hunt-the-lemming. Tall Tailless had rescued him when he was little; and later, he had braved the Great Cold to save him from the bad taillesses. Tall Tailless was his pack-brother. A wolf cannot be of two packs.

Something pecked Wolf's tail.

Wake up! cawed the ravens.

With a half-hearted snap, Wolf chased them away.

The ravens perched on the rock, then flew to earth and stalked him again. Now that they'd found him, they weren't going to leave him alone.

They were right.

Swallowing his sorrow, Wolf cast about, untangling the scent trails. He soon found that of Tall Tailless, and followed it into the Forest.

He hadn't gone far before he reached the Big Wet. He smelt fish-dog and pine-blood and the pale-pelted tailless. He sat on the shore and whined. Tall Tailless had gone with the pale-pelt in the floating hide. Those floating hides were Not-Breath – Wolf knew that because he'd chewed one once – and yet they swam faster than a blackfish. It would be useless to swim after Tall Tailless. He was gone.

Again Wolf cast about for scents. He caught that of the pack-sister. *Yes.* Now he knew what to do!

Once he'd found the pack-sister, he would find his pack-brother. They wouldn't stay apart for long.

THIRTY-THREE

Renn didn't care which way she ran. The dark pines watched her impassively, but the junipers snagged her clothes, telling her to slow down. She ran on.

Torak's voice echoed in her mind. *Get away from me – I never want to see you again!* The look on his face . . . Retreating into himself, like a wolf licking its wounds.

She had done that to him. It was her fault.

The sound of a waterfall broke through to her, and she found herself at a narrow stretch of reeds backed by a looming cliff-face.

Her fists clenched. Somewhere up there was the woman who had ruined her father's life and overshadowed her own; who had burdened her with unwanted powers and robbed her of the only friend she'd ever had.

Leaping from tussock to tussock, she made her way to

the foot of the cliff and stood, craning her neck. She could climb up and confront the Viper Mage; but that might be just what she wanted. She could set some kind of trap and capture her alive – or dead – she didn't care which.

With a cry, she turned and ran.

She found a trail which tracked the north shore. She hadn't gone far before she felt eyes on her and spun round.

'Bale?' she whispered. 'Torak?'

No-one. No-one was coming after her. She was back where she'd been before Torak. Friendless.

At last she reached a little bay that glowed dark-blue in the summer night. Driftwood lay in piles, bleached silver by wind and rain. At the head of the bay, three posts stood guard. They had misshapen clay heads, and their white eyes stared over the Lake. Renn caught the faint, high whine of their power, and clutched her clan-creature feathers. She edged behind them, so as not to be seen.

At the eastern end of the bay, screened from the posts by pines, she found a small deerhide boat tethered in the shallows. Maybe it belonged to the Viper Mage. She didn't care.

Quickly, she unlashed the mooring and jumped in. The boat lurched, but she dug in the paddle and headed off. She had no idea where she was going; she just needed to be on the move.

Something made her glance back.

The Viper Mage stood at the water's edge, watching her.

Terror washed over her. As if caught in an invisible net, she brought the boat about, and they faced each other across the shimmering water.

'What do you want?' Renn said, hating the way her voice shook.

'Nothing you can give,' said the Viper Mage, her face livid in the moonlight.

'Then why are you here?' said Renn. 'Haven't you done enough?'

The black lips parted. 'You disappoint me, daughter. I'd hoped for less passion. More control.'

'I hurt him. I hurt my best friend.'

Seshru tossed her head in scorn. 'What a pity, you have your father's heart! Although – ' her lip curled as she indicated the stolen boat, 'you have your mother's courage.'

'I have *nothing* of yours!' spat Renn.

'Ah, but we both know that isn't true. You have my talent for Magecraft. You did well to help the spirit walker resist me. Perhaps I should be proud of you.'

Renn's chest tightened with hatred.

'He belongs to me, daughter,' warned the Viper Mage. 'He is my reward for the long winters of waiting.'

'He belongs to no-one but himself.'

'Don't fight me. It would be fatal to pit your power against mine.'

'Maybe. But you're not invincible. Saeunn's power was less than yours, and yet she triumphed over you once.' That struck its target. Renn saw the white fists clench.

'Not in Magecraft,' Seshru said thinly. 'She was nothing but a thief. She stole you from me.'

'She saved me!' Renn flung back. 'I was a baby and you were going to sacrifice me!'

'Is that what she told you?' Seshru drew herself up, like a snake recoiling to strike. 'Why would I carry you for nine long moons, if only to kill you? No, you were destined for greater things.' Her black mouth twisted. 'You were to have been my finest creation – you were to have been my tokoroth!'

Renn no longer heard the frogs or the lapping of the Lake.

'I could have done it,' said the Viper Mage. 'The fire-opal would have drawn the mightiest demon – a very elemental – and I would have trapped it in my newborn child! *My* thing, *my* creature! With such power, what could we not have achieved!'

For a moment, she stared past Renn at visions of impossible glory. Then she dragged herself back and regarded her daughter with contempt. 'Instead, the old crone "saved" you. And there you sit: weak, powerless, wondering if you have the courage to kill me.'

'I could,' said Renn between her teeth. 'I could shoot you right now.'

Seshru laughed. 'Never make a threat you can't carry out, daughter! Against me you have no power. You cannot vanquish me and you cannot kill me! Remember that.' Stretching her arm towards the boat, she twisted her wrist so that her palm faced down. Renn jerked back as if she'd been struck, and nearly lost her balance.

When she looked again, the Viper Mage was gone.

Ψ

The stink of Viper-Tongue bit Wolf's nose as he raced along the edge of the Big Wet. But the bad tailless was out of reach on the rocks, so he ran on, following the scent of the pack-sister.

He passed the bay where the Hidden Ones gathered to drag things from the Wet. He loped through a stand of watchful pines and out the other side. As he ran, he caught the distant smell of the Great White Cold. He sensed its restlessness. He heard the Thunderer stirring in the Up.

After many lopes, he found the pack-sister. She was crouching by the Wet, near a floating hide which stank of Viper-Tongue – but to Wolf's astonishment, she didn't seem to care. She had her head in her forepaws and she was shaking and yowling as taillesses do when they are very, very sad.

Cautiously, Wolf padded towards her. Then he sat down and licked her knee.

She raised her head and blinked. Then she said something miserable in tailless talk and flung her forepaws round his neck, and buried her face in his scruff. Wolf didn't like this much, but he let her do it, because he sensed that she was breaking inside.

At last her yowls changed to snufflings, then gulps. To Wolf's relief, she let go of him. Leaning against each other, they sat, looking out over the Wet. This time, when Wolf licked her toes, she gently batted him away, and he knew she was feeling better.

Raising his muzzle, he snuffed the air, but of Tall Tailless he caught no scent. Wolf was puzzled. His plan to find his pack-brother wasn't working.

Renn hadn't cried like that since her father had died. It left her feeling empty and brittle as an eggshell.

Wolf had helped a lot. He'd left as suddenly as he'd come, but she could smell his strong, sweet wolf smell on her clothes and skin, and that was extremely comforting. She wasn't entirely without friends while she had Wolf.

After washing her face in the Lake, she thought about what to do next.

Torak no longer wanted her for a friend, but maybe she

could still find a way to help him. 'So think,' she said out loud. 'What does the Viper Mage want?'

She wanted Torak and the fire-opal. And she'd thought she had him, until the ravens came.

That made Renn feel better. After all, her Magecraft *had* worked. She was the one who'd sent the ravens.

She began to pace the pebbles. The night was breathless and sticky, and a ring around the moon told her that the World Spirit was not at peace. There was a storm on the way. For now, though, the Lake was quiet, except for a pair of diverbirds skimming the water. Thoughtfully, she followed their flight.

All of a sudden, they swerved and headed straight for her.

Startled, she ducked.

They sped overhead, so close that she heard the whisper of wings, and caught the glint of a scarlet eye. With ear-splitting cries they veered and vanished into the reeds.

Renn stayed where she was on the pebbles. This was another sign, she was sure of it. Twin fawns. A two-headed fish. The Otter twins. Two birds. Everything in pairs. For a long time now, the spirits had been trying to tell her something. If only she could see the pattern.

Slowly, Renn got to her feet.

To read the signs, she would have to open her mind completely. No matter what the cost.

The moon had fled across the sky and still Renn sat, grinding the white pebble on the black as Saeunn had taught her. All night she had rocked back and forth, grinding the pebbles, working herself deeper into the trance.

The juniper smoke made her head spin, and the alder juice stung her eyes, forcing them shut. That was part of it. She had to remove herself from the outer world, to see with her inner eye. She had to empty her mind so that the answer would come.

Her muscles ached. The scrape of stone on stone filled her thoughts, drawing her into darkness.

'Spirits of Lake and Mountain,' she breathed, 'spirits of Forest and Ice, I ask for guidance. You've sent me signs and I thank you. Now help me find their meaning.'

Suddenly she felt a strong will buffeting hers. Frightened, she nearly opened her eyes.

Seshru.

Gritting her teeth, Renn went on grinding, retreating behind the shell of sound.

I see you . . . Seshru's mind reached for hers. *I know the limits of your power . . .*

The pebble in her hand was heavy as a boulder, she could hardly lift it. She forced herself to keep going, shutting out the Viper Mage.

I am the reed and the storm, the thunder and the wind . . . You cannot prevail . . .

Her muscles burned, her head swam. She felt Seshru's will surging towards her: stronger than the tempest which fells the mightiest oak.

The grinding of stones grew louder. And now it was a buzzing like bees, many bees, and she was floating on the sound and travelling down, down into the deep of the Lake. Far away in the upper world, a howl of fury faded as she sank deeper.

Cowering at the bottom of the Lake, she felt its pain soughing through her, its unimaginable age.

Now she was hovering above the healing spring, watching the hands of the Viper Mage clawing the sacred clay.

Now she was bobbing on the water at the edge of the ice river, craning her neck at the ice wall glittering in the sun: such a fierce, hard, cruel blue. So *blue* . . .

With a cry, Renn awoke.

Her cramped muscles screamed as she lurched to her feet and staggered to the water's edge.

'I've got it wrong,' she whispered. 'It's not Seshru. It's the *Lake* that kills!'

THIRTY-FOUR

The moon had set when Torak and Bale put in at a bay on the north shore of the Lake.

Three staring posts warded them off, and only the hope of finding some trace of Renn made them risk going ashore – after Bale had first offered a scrap of dried duck meat on his paddle.

Searching the island by night had proved hard even for Torak, and the only sign they'd found had been one of Renn's prints near the reeds, and another on the Lake's northern shore. At the eastern end of the bay, he found more.

It was Renn's, he would know her footprint anywhere, but she hadn't been alone. Another track overlaid hers: slender, high-arched, the same shape as Renn's – but longer. Seshru.

Torak rubbed a hand over his face. Renn had confronted the Viper Mage alone and at night, in this haunted place.

'What happened to her?' said Bale in a low voice. 'Did Seshru –'

'I don't know,' snapped Torak. 'Let me think!'

They'd hardly spoken all night, except for brusque exchanges to determine where to search next, but Torak could feel Bale blaming him. He forced himself to concentrate on the tracks.

The trail of the Viper Mage led back into the Forest, then disappeared. More encouragingly, the upper part of the shore was criss-crossed with paw-prints. From the look of it, Wolf had been casting for scents.

'Wolf was with her,' said Bale. 'That must be a good sign.'

'Maybe,' muttered Torak. He scanned the shore.

Oh, Wolf, where are you?

He didn't dare howl, for fear of drawing Seshru. Her presence hung in the air, like the smell of smoke which lingers after a fire.

'But if Renn was here,' said Bale, 'where did she go?'

Head down, Torak traced her trail from the trees at the eastern end of the bay to where it ended. Then he did it again. Same result. The trail ended in the Lake.

Shutting his mind to the worst, he continued his search.

Over here, something had scraped through the mud into the shallows. Near it he found an alder sapling, its bark slightly worn in a narrow band, as if by rope. 'A boat. She found a boat moored to this tree.'

Bale blew out a long breath. 'That means she could be anywhere.' He flexed his shoulders. 'We need to rest. Start again when it's light. Otherwise, we'll make mistakes.'

I started doing that a while back, thought Torak.

To get away from the guardian posts, they took the

skinboat round a spur of pines and put in at the next bay, then carried the boat a good distance up the wooded slope beyond the shore. Bale shared out a few strips of dried duck meat, and they ate in prickly silence.

Dawn wasn't far off, but the Forest was strangely hushed. No frogs, no crickets. And no birds, thought Torak uneasily. Only Rip and Rek, who were making a nuisance of themselves picking at his gear.

From where he sat, he saw the flicker of campfires on the western shore. He guessed that the Raven Clan would be among them. Fin-Kedinn would have come in search of Renn.

'Torak,' said Bale, cutting across his thoughts.

'What,' he replied.

'I know she should've told you sooner.'

Torak set his teeth. For Bale to mention Renn was like ripping off a scab.

'But the fact that her mother is . . . I mean, it doesn't change that she's your friend.'

'What changes everything,' said Torak, 'is that she didn't tell me.' But inside, he was finding that harder and harder to believe.

'To carry such a secret.' Bale shook his head. 'What a burden.'

Torak picked up a stone and threw it at a tree-trunk. He missed. The ravens raised their heads and gave him reproachful stares.

'Although,' Bale went on, relentless, 'she's tough. Brave, too.'

Torak turned on him. 'All *right*! You've said what you want, now leave me in peace!' Snatching up his things, he moved off a few paces, then threw himself down with his back to Bale.

Wisely, the Seal boy left him alone.

Torak wasn't hungry any more, and although he was exhausted, he knew he wouldn't sleep. To make matters worse, Rip and Rek were being particularly annoying. Rek kept fluttering her wings, pretending to be a fledgling in desperate need of food, and Rip was pecking at his knife-hilt.

'Stop it,' Torak told him. Of course that didn't work.

He tossed Rip a scrap of meat. The raven ignored it and made another attack on the knife.

'*Stop* it!' said Torak in a hoarse whisper.

'What's the matter?' Bale called softly.

Torak didn't reply.

Rip was staring up at him: not asking for food, just staring. His eyes were black as the Beginning, and his raven souls reached out to Torak's.

Torak glanced from Rip to the sinew binding on the hilt of his knife, then back to Rip. He turned his head and stared at Bale. He tried to speak, but no sound came.

The Seal boy saw his expression and came towards him.

Still without speaking, Torak drew the knife from its sheath and picked feverishly at the binding. It was tight – Fa had renewed it the summer before he was killed – and not even raven beaks had made much impression.

Without asking for an explanation, Bale handed him his own knife. 'Cut it,' he said.

Once the sinew was cut, it was easier to unpick. Torak's heart raced as he peeled back the final layer.

The trees stilled.

The Lake held its breath.

Sweat streamed down Torak's sides as he beheld the thing which had lain concealed for so many summers in the hilt of his father's knife. He tilted the knife, and out it fell onto his palm, from the hollow which Fa had cut to hold it. As Torak stared at it – at this thing which was no bigger than a robin's egg, yet possessed the power to enthrall the demons of the Otherworld – the sun crested the ice river and a blazing shaft of light struck deep into the cold red heart of the fire-opal.

Bale drew in his breath with a hiss. 'All this time.'

Torak did not reply. He was twelve summers old again, kneeling beside Fa.

'Torak,' gasped Fa. 'I'm dying. I'll be dead by sunrise.'

Torak saw the pain convulse his father's lean brown face. He saw the tiny scarlet veins in the light-grey eyes, and at their centres, the fathomless dark.

'Swap knives,' Fa told him.

Torak was aghast. 'Not your knife! You'll need it!'

'You'll need it more.'

Torak didn't want to swap knives. That would make it final. But his father was watching him with an intensity that allowed no refusal . . .

'Oh, Fa,' whispered Torak. He felt the fire-opal burning his palm with a searing cold. He stared into its fiery, pulsing heart.

Bale's brown hand covered the stone, shattering the spell. 'Torak! Cover it up!'

Torak blinked.

'She'll see it!' hissed Bale. 'Cover it up!'

Roused from his daze, Torak replaced the fire-opal in its nest, and wound his headband around the hilt to hold it in place. Only when it was safely concealed did they breathe again.

At last Bale said, 'How do we destroy it?'

Torak frowned. How could he think of destroying something so beautiful?

'Torak! How?'

Of course Bale was right. 'You've got to bury it,' Torak said in a cracked voice, 'but only earth or stone will do. And . . . ' he broke off.

'Yes?' said Bale.

'It needs a life buried with it. Or it won't stay dead.'

They didn't meet each other's eyes.

Torak thought about Renn, and how, in the Far North, she had been ready to give her life so that the fire-opal would be destroyed. He wondered if he would ever find the courage to do that.

He thought about all the times she'd risked her life to help him.

Suddenly, Rek gave a loud 'kek kek', and both ravens lifted into the sky with a clatter of wings.

Torak leapt to his feet.

'Listen!' whispered Bale. 'There's something down by the Lake!'

Straining his ears, Torak caught a faint trickling of water. Then a dragging sound, as if something were crawling out of the Lake – then a squelching, stumbling tread.

Clutching their knives, they crept through the trees.

There, twenty paces below them in a shadowy clump of alders, something moved.

Torak felt Bale grip his arm as the thing lurched to its full height. Weeds dripped from its limbs and its streaming hair.

Bale turned to Torak, his lips bloodless. 'What is it?'

Torak glimpsed the pale arms hanging limp at the creature's sides. The band of rowanberries on one wrist. He rose to his feet. 'It's Renn!'

THIRTY-FIVE

Renn saw them running towards her, shouting her name. Her knees buckled and she went down. Bale caught her by the shoulders. Torak took her quiver and bow.

'It's coming!' she gasped. A spasm of coughing seized her and she sicked up swampy Lake water.

'Where've you been?' said Bale.

She tried to reply, but more coughing took hold. No time to tell of that terrible moment when she'd foreseen the disaster which threatened them all; of her frantic dash to warn the clans, while the boat did its best to thwart her: spinning, bucking, finally pitching her overboard. And now Bale was kneeling beside her with no idea of the danger, while Torak was drying her bow with a handful of grass, and avoiding her eyes.

'You're safe now,' said Bale.

'Nobody's safe!' She clutched his arm. 'Listen to me! *The flood is coming!*'

They stared at her.

'The ice river,' she panted. 'All spring it's been keeping back the meltwater! *That's* why the ice wall was so blue, *that's* why the Lake is sinking!' Again she broke off to cough. 'I kept seeing twins. *Two* lakes, do you see? This Lake – and the one *behind the ice!* Seshru stole the sacred clay, she made the Lake sick. And now there's a storm coming, and the World Spirit's going to shatter the ice wall! The flood will take us all!'

She turned to Torak. 'Whatever you think of me, you've got to believe me! You've got to warn the Otters! Get them into the hills, or they'll never stand a chance!'

Still without meeting her eyes, Torak set down her bow. 'It's not just the Otters.'

'What do you mean?' she said.

'Campfires on the western shore,' said Bale. 'We think it's the Boar Clan, after Torak. Maybe other clans too.'

Renn bit her knuckle. 'The Ravens. Fin-Kedinn will have come to find me. They'll be drowned.'

Torak spoke to Bale. 'We'll take the skinboat. It's the quickest way to reach them.'

Bale nodded. 'But not all of us, that'd slow it down; besides Renn couldn't make it.'

'Yes I could!' cried Renn.

'No you couldn't,' said Bale. Then to Torak, 'This slope's not too steep, I can get her up to higher ground, we'll be safe there. You take the boat. You warn them.'

'Me, take your boat? You never let anyone –'

'Torak,' cut in Bale, 'this is your chance to show them you're not a Soul-Eater!'

'If they don't shoot him first,' put in Renn.

Torak ignored her.

Within moments Bale had the boat in the water and Torak was ready, but suddenly he leapt out and ran back to Renn. Untying his knife-sheath, he pressed it into her hands. 'Keep it safe,' he muttered.

'But it's yours, you'll need it!'

'No time to explain. Bale will tell you.' Over his shoulder he added, 'She's after me *and* the fire-opal, she mustn't get both!'

The World Spirit was turning day to dusk as Torak made the skinboat fly across the water. Thunder growled. The air crackled with foreboding. The flood could come at any moment.

In his mind, he saw the creatures of Forest and Lake fleeing for safety. Elk, deer and horses racing for the ridges; beaver and otter scampering up the slopes as best they could; squirrel and marten seeking refuge in the sturdiest oaks. Even the fish would be hiding at the bottom of the Lake.

And the wolves? This must be why they'd fled the island, because they'd sensed what was coming. Torak hoped they'd taken the cubs high enough – and that Wolf was with them.

In the east, the sky was a boiling mass of storm clouds. Soon, lightning would lance the ice river, releasing the awesome fury of the waters behind. Torak pictured the flood engulfing the Lake: devastating islands, washing away the Otter camp and everything in its path.

The wind strengthened, and still he paddled. He was

almost spent when he reached the western shore and put in just south of the Axehandle river. No sign of boats or people. Only the reeds, flattened by the wind.

Leaving the skinboat on the shore, he slipped into a thicket at the foot of the ridge. The trees moaned, warning him back. For all he knew, the whole slope might be crawling with hunters on the lookout for him, and all he had was his axe. Not much use against arrows and spears.

Exhausted, he soon had to stop for breath. He was wondering which way to go when something leapt from the junipers and knocked him to the ground.

At last Wolf had found Tall Tailless!

In a snap, his sadness at leaving the pack was chased away, and he was covering his pack-brother's face in snuffle-licks.

I couldn't leave you! he told Tall Tailless. *I'm back now and I'm never leaving, just like you said!*

But Tall Tailless' greeting was rushed and urgent, and Wolf caught his mood. He smelt Viper-Tongue on his pack-brother. He sensed great worry and danger. *What do I do?* he asked.

Find the ravens, Tall Tailless replied.

That made Wolf cross. *Why them?*

No, said Tall Tailless, *not the birds. Wolves that smell of raven. Find the pack leader!*

Now Wolf understood. Giving his pack-brother a nose-nudge to acknowledge this, he raced off through the trees.

The great denning place of the taillesses wasn't many lopes away, and he was soon in the bracken at its edge. Stealthily, he padded forwards to find the pack leader.

The denning place seethed with anger, and Wolf heard much snarling among the boar, wolf, and raven packs. Then he caught the quiet, strong tones of the raven leader. This tailless never yowled loudly. He didn't need to. He had the respect of all the others.

Placing his paws with care, Wolf crept closer.

The dogs were restless, but on the way, Wolf had rolled in a pile of auroch droppings, so he approached un-smelt. When he'd got as far as he could, he crouched down to wait.

Soon, the raven leader felt his stare and saw him.

Ah, he was cunning! Like a normal wolf, he grazed Wolf's glance with his own, then looked away, so the others wouldn't notice. A little later, he left the denning place: calmly, so as not to awaken suspicions.

When Wolf knew he was following, he headed off to find Tall Tailless.

When Torak glimpsed Fin-Kedinn striding through the willowherb, it didn't occur to him to hide. He rose to his feet and stood in the open. The Raven Leader saw him, and his face lit up. Torak's heart twisted. He'd missed Fin-Kedinn more than he'd realized.

'Torak!' Fin-Kedinn gripped his shoulder. He glanced behind him. 'Come. We're too close to camp, and Aki's nosing around after you.'

With Wolf trotting after them, they moved into a wind-tossed thicket. The Raven Leader's sharp eyes searched Torak's face, and took in the scar on his chest. 'Where's Renn?'

'Safe with Bale on the north shore. Fin-Kedinn, you've

got to listen!' As briefly as he could, he told the Raven Leader of the coming flood. Fin-Kedinn heard it without question or interruption.

'You've got to get the clans to higher ground,' said Torak. 'Right now! The flood could come at any moment!'

The Raven Leader's face was unfathomable as ever, but Torak knew from the glint in his eyes that his thoughts were racing. 'Everyone's in camp,' he said, 'arguing about the best way to hunt you. That'll make them easier to move.'

'I've got a skinboat,' said Torak, 'I'll find the Otter camp and warn them.'

'No. They'd shoot you before you got the chance.'

'But someone's got to.'

'I'll see to it.'

'And the clans?'

'I'll get them up to the Hogback.' He jerked his head at the ridge behind them. 'You get up there too, fast as you can. Try to reach the south side, there'll be fewer people.'

Torak nodded. But as he made to go, Fin-Kedinn held him back. 'Where's the Viper Mage?'

'I don't know. On the north cliff, I think.'

Fin-Kedinn looked grim. 'She hasn't finished with you yet. I know her, Torak. Never underestimate her. Never forget that she might be closer than you think!'

Torak hadn't told him of the fire-opal and he didn't now, but as the Raven Leader turned, he said, 'Fin-Kedinn. You wouldn't be here – in danger – if it weren't for me. I'm sorry.'

A shadow crossed the Raven Leader's face. 'I cast you out. You're not the one who should be sorry.' He touched Torak's arm. 'Get as high as you can. Go!'

The wind screamed in Torak's ears as he scrambled up the slope, while Wolf raced ahead. The Forest was dark as night, and the trees thrashed and groaned.

He was halfway up when he had to stop, bent double, chest heaving. Slumped against a pine, he told Wolf to go on without him.

Wolf hesitated.

Lightning flared. Thunder crashed directly overhead. Rain pattered on the leaves – and swiftly became a downpour.

Torak saw Rip and Rek take cover in an oak tree. Yes. Climb the tree. No time for anything else. Maybe the Forest would protect him, too.

Go! he told Wolf again, and Wolf – sensing what he meant to do – turned and sped to safety.

In the distance, Torak heard a deeper reverberation behind the thunder: an echoing boom that he'd heard before, in the Far North. The boom of breaking ice.

He stumbled for the oak – tripped – and fell headlong in the mud. Lightning flickered on a footprint by his hand. Behind him, a branch snapped. He rolled sideways just as Aki's axe thudded into the root where his head had been.

'Got you at last!' bellowed the Boar Clan boy. With his good arm he tugged at his axe, which he'd buried in the root.

'Aki, are you mad?' shouted Torak against the wind. 'The flood is coming! We've got to get into the trees!'

'I said I'd get you and I will!' yelled Aki.

More lightning, more thunder. The ice river boomed across the Lake.

As he struggled to his feet, Torak saw that Aki wasn't driven by hatred, but by fear of failing his father – and against that there was no reasoning. Leaving him yanking at the axe, Torak raced for the oak and leapt for the lowest branch. Desperation lent him strength, and he was soon ten paces up.

'Aki!' he shouted. 'Leave the axe! Climb!'

Another boom from the ice river – and suddenly Aki let go of the axehandle and ran for the oak. But he was heavier than Torak, he couldn't reach the lowest branch.

'Grab my hand!' Torak leaned down as far as he could.

Not far enough. And Aki couldn't climb with only one arm.

Through the rain, Torak saw the Boar Clan boy's right arm strapped to his chest: the arm that he, Torak, had broken when he'd sent Aki crashing into the rapids.

With a snarl, Torak leapt from the tree and linked his hands to make a step. 'Quick, climb!'

Aki was aghast. Then he put his foot on Torak's hands, and Torak boosted him into the tree with the last of his strength.

The roar came again, but this time it wasn't ice, Torak realized, it was the flood. Far in the distance he saw it: a giant wall of water powering across the Lake – obliterating islands, uprooting trees, coming for him.

Aki was shouting and leaning down to give him his hand, but now it was Torak who couldn't reach. He wasn't going to make it.

In the moment before the flood hit, he saw Wolf racing towards him. Torak staggered to meet him – he flung his arms around his pack-brother's neck . . .

. . . and the wave took them both.

THIRTY-SIX

Torak came to his senses lying on his back, with rain pattering on his face.

A dead fish hung in the birch tree above him. The storm had passed. The flood had thrown him onto a stony hillside strewn with broken saplings. There was no trace of Wolf. Torak prayed that he'd found his way to safety.

He raised himself on one elbow. He was battered and bruised, but otherwise unhurt.

He was also surrounded.

Behind a forest of spears – all pointed at him – he saw a throng of Boar and Wolf and Raven, maybe eighty strong. Some of them he knew – Thull, Raut, Maheegun – but they stared at him as if he were a stranger. To a man, they were filthy, frightened and eager for the kill.

An arrow thudded into the mud by his thigh. He got to

his feet. He was alone and weaponless. The flood had taken his axe.

Then he saw Wolf on the slope behind them, preparing to leap to his aid.

Stay away! Torak barked. *Too many*!

Wolf didn't move.

Agitated murmurs. They didn't like him speaking wolf.

A stone struck his temple. He managed to stay standing. If he went down now, it would be the end.

'No stones.' A familiar voice spoke, and the spears parted to let Fin-Kedinn through. Leaning heavily on his staff, he moved towards Torak, then faced the throng, shielding him with his body.

'Stand aside, Fin-Kedinn,' cried the Boar Clan Leader. 'I found the outcast! To me goes the honour of the kill!'

'No!' Aki pushed forwards. 'You can't do this! He saved my life!'

The Boar Clan Leader turned on his son, and Aki quailed – but stood his ground. 'He could have saved himself, but instead he helped me! Father, you can't kill him, it's not right!'

'Not right?' With his fist, the Boar Clan Leader struck his son a blow which sent him flying. 'He's an outcast! That's the law!'

'How can you say that?' shouted Bale, shouldering his way through. 'Torak saved you all!'

'He warned you of the flood!' panted Renn behind him. She looked bedraggled and furious. 'If it weren't for Torak, you'd have drowned, every last one of you!'

'Don't listen to her!' cried an Otter man, the only one Torak could see. 'All this is his fault! The outcast angered the Lake, *he* caused the flood!'

'No, Yolun,' said Fin-Kedinn. 'Not Torak. The Viper Mage.'

'The Viper Mage!' sneered the Boar Clan Leader. 'So you say, but where is she? *There's* the Soul-Eater!' He jabbed his spear at Torak.

'He's no Soul-Eater,' said Fin-Kedinn. 'He cut out the mark, you can all see the scar.'

But the Boar Clan Leader had the support of the crowd, and it lent him courage. 'He's an outcast! The law says an outcast must die!'

'Then the law must change!' retorted the Raven Leader.

'Why? Because you say so?'

'Because it's right.'

'He's a Soul-Eater and an outcast –'

'He's my foster son!' roared Fin-Kedinn.

Ravens flew up from the trees. People shrank back.

Nervously, the Boar Clan Leader licked his lips. 'Since when?'

'Since now,' snapped the Raven Leader.

'Fin-Kedinn!' called Renn. 'Catch!' She threw him Torak's knife and Fin-Kedinn caught it, then drew the blade across his forearm, raising beads of blood. Grasping Torak's wrist, he did the same to him, and they clasped hands as the Raven Leader spoke the words of fostering. Then he turned on the crowd and his blue eyes blazed. 'If he stays outcast, then so do I! Kill him – and you'll have to kill me too!'

The Boar Clan Leader gripped his spear, but made no move.

No-one stirred.

But Torak sensed that not even the Raven Leader could hold them for long. He saw the violence in their grimy faces; the desperation with which they clutched axes and spears. They'd just survived a disaster, they needed someone to blame. And if Fin-Kedinn stood in their way – or Bale or Renn – they would get themselves killed.

Taking his knife from the Raven Leader, Torak said quietly, 'I don't want your blood on my hands.'

The Boar Clan Leader taunted Torak. 'Hiding behind your foster father?'

'Fin-Kedinn,' urged Torak, 'I've got to face them on my own.'

Reluctantly, the Raven Leader moved aside.

'Where's your courage now, outcast?' jeered the Boar Leader.

'Right here,' said Torak.

It was a strange relief to be confronting them at last. 'No more hiding, I'm sick of it!' he cried as he circled the ring of spears, his arms spread wide. 'Here I am! You can kill me if you want! Who *cares* if I'm the wrong target? Who *cares* if this is what the Soul-Eaters want? The Oak Mage – the Eagle Owl Mage – the Viper Mage – they're still out there! Kill me, and you solve *nothing*!'

'This is a trick,' spat the Boar Clan Leader. 'Don't listen. *He's* the Soul-Eater!'

'I *was* a Soul-Eater,' Torak flung back. 'They made me one against my will.' With his fist he struck his scar. 'I cut out their mark – with this!' Brandishing his knife, he flicked a glance at Renn, and her lips parted as she guessed what he meant to do.

'My father gave me this knife as he lay dying!' Torak told them, 'and here's how I choose to use it: to prove to you – once and for all – that I'm no Soul-Eater!'

There was a ringing in his ears as he unwound the headband which bound the handle. The last layer came away, and he let fall the buckskin and tilted the hilt to drop its dreadful burden into his palm. The cold red light of the fire-opal blazed out.

The Boar Clan Leader gasped.

Fin-Kedinn's hand tightened on his staff.

Terror and awe filled every face.

'The fire-opal,' said Torak, holding it up for all to see. 'The heart of Soul-Eater power. This is the last fragment of the one my father shattered. *My father,*' he glared at Maheegun, 'who defied the Soul-Eaters and broke their power! And now it's *mine!*'

A soft voice spoke. 'Give it me.'

Torak turned.

The Viper Mage stood on the ridge above him, twenty paces beyond the ring of spears. Her face and limbs wore the sacred clay of the Otter Clan, and calmly she gazed down upon them: inhuman, invincible.

A shiver ran through the crowd. *'The Soul-Eater . . . The Viper Mage is come . . .'*

'Stay back,' warned Seshru, stretching out her green hand and sweeping them with her forefinger. 'Death shall come to any who attempt to harm me.'

Such was the power of the Soul-Eaters – such the terror the Viper Mage inspired – that not one of them moved.

'Give it me,' she said to Torak, and her words were a caress meant only for him.

He fought to look away from that perfect green face.

A movement caught his eye. Some distance behind the Viper Mage, Wolf stood watching. Silently, Torak warded him back. The Soul-Eater was too strong even for Wolf.

'Give it me,' repeated Seshru.

Unable to resist, Torak met her gaze. He forgot the spears, he forgot Bale and Renn and Fin-Kedinn and Wolf. Nothing existed on this ruined hillside except the Viper Mage and the fire-opal, hot and heavy in his hand.

'I will,' he said at last. 'I will give it to you.'

Everyone gasped.

Stooping, Torak placed the fire-opal on a boulder between himself and the Viper Mage. 'Take it,' he said. 'It's yours.'

Seshru's black lips parted in a triumphant smile.

Still stooping, Torak snatched a lump of granite in his fist. He raised it high, and the eyes of the Viper Mage widened in horror. As she whipped out her knife and leapt towards him, he shouted, 'Take it! Take the fire-opal!' He saw Renn nock an arrow to her bow and aim at her mother; Bale grab the weapons from her hands and take aim in his turn. He saw Seshru give a terrible scream and fall with an arrow in her breast as he brought the granite crashing down and shattered the fire-opal to fragments.

Silence rang from hill to hill.

The granite fell from Torak's hand as he stared at Bale. The Seal boy stood panting, Renn's bow in his hand.

Still alive, the scarlet fragments of the fire-opal glittered in the mud.

Still alive, the Viper Mage reached for them: writhing like a snake that has been cut in two.

Renn burst through the throng. Clawing the fragments of the fire-opal in a handful of mud, she pressed them into Seshru's palm and clenched the green hand in a fist around them, then tied it shut with Torak's discarded headband. 'There,' she breathed. 'You've got what you wanted! The fire-opal dies with you!'

Seshru gazed at the scarlet light bleeding through her fingers, and bared her teeth. 'This – is not the end,' she hissed. Blood trickled from her mouth. Her eyes glazed. As her souls left her body, the red glow between her fingers flickered and died.

Grimly, Fin-Kedinn raised his staff. 'The Soul-Eater is dead,' he declared. 'Let all bear witness: the outcast shall be outcast *no more*!'

After a moment's hesitation, Maheegun bowed his assent.

Then the Boar Clan Leader.

Then Yolun for the Otters.

Then all the others.

Renn stayed on her knees by the Viper Mage, watching the rain wash away her blood in muddy rivulets.

She's too close to the body, thought Torak. The souls of the Viper Mage must be perilously near.

Quickly, he took Renn's medicine horn and poured earthblood into his palm, then grasped her hand and, making sure that she still wore her finger-guard, dipped her forefinger in the ochre and helped her draw the Death Marks on her mother's forehead, heart and heels. Then he pulled her gently away from the corpse.

The crowd parted to let someone through.

Wolf's hackles were raised, his lips peeled back in a snarl as he walked stiffly towards the corpse, stalking something no-one else could see.

As the rain fell, Torak watched his pack-brother leap – snap the air – and race off into the Forest, chasing the souls of the Viper Mage away from the living.

THIRTY-SEVEN

The pack is leaving without him, and Wolf knows this must be so – but it hurts.

The full-grown wolves tread neatly in the paw-prints of the leader, but the cubs jostle one another, pouncing on interesting bits of moss.

Digger and Snap see that Wolf isn't following, and scamper back to fetch him. *Come on! Don't get left behind!*

Mournfully, Wolf wags his tail.

The lead female gathers the cubs and they trot after her, looking back in puzzlement.

Darkfur is the last to leave. A wistful glance over her shoulder, then she too disappears.

Wolf woke with a jolt. Lying in the mud, he felt sorrow press upon him. The pack was gone.

Through the trees came the sound of the taillesses

beginning to stir. Wolf padded along the rise to sniff the scents.

Since the Big Wet had come roaring through, everything had changed. The Thunderer was gone, and the Big Wet was at peace, although it had grown, and there were fish in the trees, which was odd. The Hidden Ones were quiet, as they had their island to themselves; and the taillesses were no longer hunting Tall Tailless, but had welcomed him back. Wolf didn't understand why.

Tall Tailless had changed, too. Over the past Lights and Darks, his scent had altered and his howls had become deeper. Wolf *did* know the reason for this. Unlike wolf cubs, tailless cubs take an extremely long time to grow up, but even they manage it eventually. Tall Tailless was almost full-grown.

Right now, he was in the Den with the other taillesses, having one of his endless sleeps. Wolf wished he would wake up, and sense that his pack-brother needed him.

But he didn't come.

'Time to go back,' said Fin-Kedinn, and Renn, sitting on a rock above the healing spring, nodded, but didn't move.

Nearby, a group of Otters was returning the sacred clay to the Lake by washing it off their faces. Bale stood at the cliff edge, lost in thought, and Torak was searching the ferns for his name-pebble.

Renn wanted to help, but she couldn't muster the courage. He hadn't really talked to her since he'd found out about her mother. She wasn't sure if they were all right again – or if everything had changed.

The Otters had arrived in their reed boats at dawn. It

turned out that they hadn't needed warnings of the flood, as their Mage had read the signs and led them to safety. That was why Yolun had been sent to the Forest clans' camp: to warn *them*.

Nor had the Otters seemed surprised when Fin-Kedinn told them of the Viper Mage. They'd accepted it as they'd accepted the flood which had destroyed their camp – then quietly taken over the funeral rites.

After bearing the body to a remote bay on the north shore, they'd washed the corpse, laid it on a Death Platform, and covered it in juniper branches so that it wouldn't walk. Then they'd led everyone to the spring, to be purified. They'd gently insisted that Renn should keep a little apart, because, as she'd put the Death Marks on the corpse, she would be unclean for the next three days. She didn't mind. It was a relief. That's what she told herself.

'She left no trace,' said Torak, making her jump.

He stood on a boulder behind her. She couldn't see his face for the sun.

'You didn't find the name-pebble?' she said.

He shook his head. 'What should I do about that?'

She noted that he said I, not we, and wondered if that meant something. Out loud she said, 'We'll ask Saeunn. She'll know.'

The Raven Mage had remained at the new camp on the Hogback, and although Renn would never have admitted it, it was reassuring to know she was there. If Magecraft was needed, Saeunn would do it.

Torak looked over the Lake. 'The only thing I found was her snake basket. Empty.' He paused. 'They didn't feel evil, those snakes. Maybe they'll like being free.'

Renn broke off a fern frond and tore it to bits.

Why can't you just say it, she thought. Torak, I'm sorry I

never told you. But it doesn't change anything, does it? Not really?'

But Torak mumbled something about helping Bale look for the wreckage of the skinboat, and then he was gone, and she'd missed her chance.

Fin-Kedinn came and sat beside her.

Renn said, 'He knows about the Viper Mage. I mean, about me.'

'Yes, he told me.'

'Did he? What did he say?'

'Just that he knows.'

She scrunched up the fern and threw it away.

Fin-Kedinn asked her who else knew, and she said, only Bale. Fin-Kedinn said he thought some of the older Ravens had recognized the Viper Mage despite the green clay, and that Renn should tell them when things had settled down, and she said she would.

Fin-Kedinn said, 'Are you sorry she's dead?'

'No. – I don't know.' She scowled. 'I hated her for so long, and now she's gone. Somehow it feels worse.'

He nodded.

He looked tired. Renn saw the grey hairs flecking his dark-red beard, the lines at the corners of his eyes. With a twist of terror, she realized that he was getting older. People died when they were younger than him. But he was Fin-Kedinn, he couldn't die.

'Why can't things stay the same?' she cried.

Fin-Kedinn followed a damselfly skimming the water. 'Because that's how it is. Everything changes, all the time. Mostly, you don't notice.' He turned to her. 'The thing to remember, Renn, is that not every change is bad.'

She drew a breath that ended in a gulp.

Fin-Kedinn said, 'Torak was outcast. Now he's not.

That's a good change. But it'll take him a while to get used to it.' Using his staff, he rose to his feet. 'We'll go back now. You're exhausted.'

'No I'm not,' she lied.

He snorted. 'When was the last time you had a proper meal?'

That night, the clans held a feast to give thanks for surviving the flood.

The fish had mysteriously returned to the Lake, and although the Otters didn't dare remark on this aloud for fear of chasing away the good luck, there was a lightness in them as they bustled about, directing the preparations.

Like everyone else, Torak and Bale had to help, but Renn, being unclean, wasn't allowed. She hung around the camp, trying not to look spare, then went to find Wolf. She didn't, but she heard him howling. He sounded sad. She guessed that he was missing the pack, and resolved to take him a treat, to cheer him up.

Before the feast could begin, the best of everything was placed in a reed boat and taken to the Lake; then everyone settled down to eat. It was a cool, still night, and they sat around a long-fire: Otter and Boar Clan, Wolf and Raven. All except Renn, who'd been given her own little blaze at the edge of camp.

The food was better than she'd expected, and Fin-Kedinn was right, she was ravenous. There was stewed elk and succulent bream roasted over alderwood fires; toasted trout cheeks and crisp golden cakes of reed pollen with sweet, sticky gobbets of reed gum; and the thickest, smelliest stickleback grease, which the Otters had taken with them when they'd abandoned camp. This Renn avoided, but she saw Torak – who didn't know any better – struggling to compose his features after his first mouthful.

He sat in the place of honour with the clan leaders, looking uncomfortable with the attention. Renn saw him self-consciously touching the outcast tattoo on his forehead; but either he didn't see her, or he was avoiding her. She told herself not to worry.

Not far from Torak sat Bale. He caught Renn's eye, and seemed about to smile, but checked himself. They hadn't yet spoken of what he'd done, and she guessed that he wasn't sure how she felt. She gave him a brief smile, and he looked relieved.

When the eating was over, the Otters collected all the fish bones which were too small to be useful and took them to the Lake, so that they could be born again as new fish. Then the Otter Mage twins stood up and started to sing.

Like a silver stream falling into a pool of clear water, their voices dropped into the listening silence. In her head, Renn saw the dark of the Beginning, when all the world was water. Then a diverbird dived to the bottom and scooped up a speck of mud in its beak, and flew back to the surface – and made the earth.

Now they were singing a new song. This time, Renn saw the viper who stole the sacred clay and made the Lake sick. The Lake sought the aid of the World Spirit, who loosed the waters behind the ice and washed away the evil; and the Forest people would have been swept away too, if they hadn't been warned by the Clanless Wanderer. Then the boy from the Sea killed the viper, and peace returned.

When the song was over, everyone bowed to Torak, and he went red. The Boar Clan Leader's bow was grudging, but Aki's was whole-hearted. Standing up to his father had given him new respect for himself, and he'd relaxed a lot. Maheegun and the Wolf Clan bowed lowest of all.

By now it was nearly dawn. Surely, thought Renn, the feast must be over soon. Food had made her feel braver. She would simply march up to Torak and say what had to be said.

But now the Otter Leader was giving gifts, so once again she had to wait.

Bale was given a diverbird claw as an amulet – so that, like the most skilled of water creatures, he would always stay afloat.

Torak got a wristband made from a pike's lower jaw sheathed in elkhide, so that he would be as skilled a hunter as the pike. And his knife had been repaired; in the hole left by the fire-opal lay a piece of greenstone, precisely cut to fit.

Just when Renn was feeling left out, Yolun came and laid something at her feet. He bowed, murmuring his thanks for the part she'd played in saving his beloved Lake. His gift was a beautiful little beaver-tooth knife with a hilt carved like a fish's tail.

Dawn came, and at last people went off to sleep. Suddenly there was Torak, coming towards her.

Renn stood up, scattering her bowl and spoon, which she'd forgotten were still in her lap.

Torak helped to retrieve them, and gave her an awkward nod. 'Renn . . .'

'Yes?' she said, more sharply than she'd intended.

'Ah, Torak,' said Fin-Kedinn, coming over to them.

For once in her life, Renn was *not* glad to see her uncle.

'Come with me,' said the Raven Leader, unperturbed. 'There's something we need to do.'

Torak opened his mouth, then shut it again.

'Where are we going?' said Renn.

Fin-Kedinn motioned her back. 'No, Renn,' he said gently, 'just Torak. This isn't for you.'

Torak threw her a glance that could have meant anything. Then he followed the Raven Leader into the Forest.

THIRTY-EIGHT

Torak bit back his impatience as he followed Fin-Kedinn.

Now that he was no longer outcast, he'd hoped that he and Renn and Wolf could be together again, but maybe he was wrong. Wolf hadn't come near the camp since the flood, and with Renn there was a great awkwardness of things unsaid.

And now Fin-Kedinn was leading him along an elk trail without even telling him why. He moved fast, leaning on his staff, and he had a rawhide pouch slung over one shoulder.

They hadn't gone far when Fin-Kedinn halted. Setting the pouch under a hazel tree, he told Torak to lie down.

Torak asked why.

'I need to fix your tattoo. You can't live the rest of your life with the mark of the outcast.'

Torak had been wondering about that, but now he was apprehensive. 'Are you going to cut it out?'

'No,' said Fin-Kedinn. 'Lie down.'

Torak lay on his back and watched the Raven Leader take from the pouch a bone needle, a small antler tattooing hammer, a grindstone and a buckskin bundle. This he unwrapped to reveal lumps of earthblood, white gypsum and green tufa stone.

'I've sent Bale to find the woad,' he said, as if that explained anything. 'Now keep still.'

Mounting a needle in the hammer, he stretched the skin of Torak's forehead between finger and thumb, and began the rapid piercings which you need for a good tattoo, pausing occasionally to wipe away the blood.

At first it hurt a lot. Then it simply hurt. To keep his mind off the pain, Torak fixed his eyes on the hazel tree. The nuts were still green, but a squirrel was busily foraging, stopping now and then to churr at the intruders below.

After a while, Torak shifted his gaze to Fin-Kedinn.

His foster father.

He felt honoured and pleased, but also perplexed. 'There's something I don't understand,' he said.

Fin-Kedinn did not reply.

'When I first met you – when you found out who my father was – you were angry. Since then, sometimes I've thought you liked me. Sometimes not.'

Placing the earthblood on the grindstone, Fin-Kedinn crushed it with a piece of granite.

'I know you were angry with my father,' Torak went on carefully. 'But my mother . . . You didn't hate her too?'

Fin-Kedinn carried on grinding. 'No,' he said. 'I was in love with her.'

Birdsong echoed through the Forest. Bees buzzed among the meadowsweet.

'But she loved me as a brother,' the Raven Leader went on. 'Your father she loved as a woman loves her mate.'

Torak swallowed. 'Is that why – why you hated him?'

Fin-Kedinn sighed. 'Growing up can be a kind of soul-sickness, Torak. The name-soul wants to be strongest, so it fights the clan-soul telling it what to do. You've got to find a balance, like a good knife. It took me a while.' Dipping a corner of buckskin in earthblood, he rubbed it into Torak's forehead. 'I stopped being jealous of your father a long time ago. But I went on blaming him for your mother's death. I still do.'

'Why?'

'He joined the Soul-Eaters. When she gave birth to you, she was in hiding, far from her clan. If he hadn't put her in danger, she might still be alive.'

'He didn't mean to put her in danger.'

'Don't ask me to forgive him,' warned Fin-Kedinn. 'For her sake I took you in. For her sake, and yours, I've made you my foster son. Don't ask for more.' Cleaning the grindstone with a clump of moss, he crushed the tufa stone.

Torak studied the features of the man he'd come to love. 'Did you never find a mate?'

Fin-Kedinn's lip curled. 'Of course I did. There was a girl in the Wolf Clan. But after a time she said we should part, because I still thought of your mother. She was right.'

Silence. Then Torak said, 'What was my mother like?'

Fin-Kedinn's face tightened. 'Your father must have spoken of her.'

'No. It made him too sad.'

The Raven Leader was quiet for a long time. Then he said, 'She knew the Forest like nobody else. She loved it. And it loved her.' He met Torak's gaze and his blue eyes glittered. 'You're very like her.'

Torak hadn't expected that. Until now, his mother hadn't been truly real to him: just a shadowy woman of the Red Deer Clan who'd made his medicine horn – and declared him clanless.

Fin-Kedinn stared unseeing at the hazel tree. Then he squared his shoulders and resumed his work. 'In a way, it's because of your mother that you survived as an outcast. Those creatures who helped you. Beaver, raven, wolf. The Forest itself. Maybe they saw her spirit in you.'

'But why did she make me clanless? Why did she *do* that?'

Fin-Kedinn sighed. 'I don't know, Torak. But she loved you, so –'

'But how do you know? You didn't even know that she'd had a son!'

'I knew her,' Fin-Kedinn said quietly. 'She loved you. So she must have done it to help you.'

Torak couldn't see how being clanless was any help at all.

'Maybe,' Fin-Kedinn added, 'the answer lies where she came from. And where you were born.'

'The Deep Forest.'

A breeze stirred the trees, and they nodded agreement.

'When should I go?' said Torak.

'Not for a while,' said the Raven Leader, grinding gypsum. 'There's trouble among the Deep Forest clans, they won't let in outsiders. And it would be foolish to venture in when Thiazzi and Eostra could be anywhere.'

Bale came through the bracken. His face was grave as he handed Fin-Kedinn a small horn cup containing the woad. 'I heard you talking about the Soul-Eaters. I don't think you'll find them in the Deep Forest. I think they're in the islands.'

Torak sat up. '*What?*'

'Something Renn said, a while back. She said the Seal Mage had a fragment of the fire-opal, and it went down with him in the Sea.' He shook his head. 'I don't think it did. He always kept what he needed for spells in a seal-hide pouch. He didn't have it when he was killed. Later, when we burnt his shelter, it wasn't there.'

'That could mean anything,' said Torak uneasily.

'Before you came to the islands,' said Bale, 'when he was simply our Mage, we would sometimes see a red glow on the Crag. We didn't know what it was. I do now.'

'The fire-opal,' said Torak.

'And before I left for the Forest,' Bale went on, 'there were disturbances – in the woods and around our camp. As if someone were searching for something.'

Torak thought of the last words of the Viper Mage. Then he noticed that Fin-Kedinn didn't seem surprised.

'Think about it, Torak,' he said as he applied the woad. 'If the fragment in your father's knife had been the last, why was only the Viper Mage after it? Why not Thiazzi and Eostra, too?'

'So we've achieved nothing!' cried Torak. 'It's all to do again!'

'Not so,' said Fin-Kedinn. 'Step by step. Remember?'

Torak made to reply, but the Raven Leader was gathering his things. 'Time to go back,' he said firmly. 'And Torak – we won't tell Renn of the fire-opal just yet. She's got enough to think about.'

When they reached camp, Renn was waiting for them. She glanced at Torak's forehead and nodded. 'Ah. I see.' Then to Fin-Kedinn, 'Although the white bit isn't really white, is it?'

The Raven Leader shrugged. 'He's too brown. But it'll do.'

'What *is* it?' said Torak. 'What have you done?'

Fin-Kedinn grasped his wrist and raised it high, then spoke to the others who were gathering round. 'Each of you bear witness,' he said in his clear voice. 'This is my foster son: the one who was outcast, but is outcast no more. He's clanless – but from now on, because of this mark he bears, he is for *all* the clans!'

There were smiles and murmurs of assent, and Torak could see that whatever the Raven Leader had done, it had worked.

Bale explained it to him. 'He's divided the circle of the outcast into four: one for each of the four quarters of the clans, then he's filled them in. White for the Ice clans, red for the Mountains, green for the Forest, and blue for the Sea. It looks good.' He grinned. 'Well. Better.'

Torak was still taking that in when Rip and Rek swooped out of nowhere. Rek made a barking noise that drove the camp dogs wild, and Rip – who was carrying something in his beak – dropped it in the mud, narrowly missing Bale. Then they were off, somersaulting over each other with raucous caws.

Bale picked up what Rip had let fall, and his eyebrows rose. 'Here.' He handed it to Torak.

It was his name-pebble. His "clan-tattoo" could still be seen – but every speck of the green clay serpent had been pecked off.

Torak and Bale had gone with Yolun in a reed boat, and when they'd reached the deep part of the Lake, Torak had dropped his name-pebble over the side and watched it disappear into the dark-green water.

Yolun was pleased. 'The Lake will keep it safe for ever.'

Torak thought so too. At first he'd been frightened of the Lake, but he'd come to understand that it was neither good nor bad; just very, very old.

On reaching land again, Bale and Yolun went off to talk about boats, and Torak was finally free to go in search of Renn.

He found her on the shore, oiling her bow. He sat down beside her, but she didn't look up.

After a while she said, 'It's had so many soakings, I think it may be warped.'

He glanced at her. 'If Bale hadn't done it – would you have killed her?'

She rubbed more oil into the wood, which was already gleaming. 'Yes,' she said between her teeth. 'When you smashed the fire-opal, whose life were you going to give it?'

'I don't know,' Torak admitted. 'And I don't know why Fa gave it to me. I suppose he guessed that some day I might need it.'

'But why keep it at all? He could've destroyed it along with the rest.'

Torak had wondered about that too. In his mind, he saw the awful beauty of the fire-opal. Maybe Fa just couldn't bring himself to do it.

He turned to Renn. 'Your mother. Have you always known?'

A flush stole up her neck. 'No. Fin-Kedinn told me after Fa was killed.'

'So you were – seven, eight summers old.'

'Yes.'

'That must have been hard.'

She glared at him, repudiating pity.

He scooped up a handful of sand and poured it from palm to palm. 'How did it happen? I mean, how did she come to . . .'

Renn chewed her lip. Then she told him, staring at the sand between her bare feet, and spitting out the story like poison. 'When she left my father for the Soul-Eaters, she changed her name. People thought she was dead. Not my father. Fin-Kedinn told him to forget her. He couldn't. Then she came back to him in secret. The clan never knew. She needed another child, a baby. My brother was too old for – for her purpose. So she got one. Then she left my father again. She broke his heart. She didn't care. She bore me in secret. Saeunn found her and took me from her, I don't know how. I was very small. I hadn't been named.'

'Why did Saeunn take you?' said Torak. 'It can't have been out of pity.'

Renn smiled mirthlessly. 'It wasn't. She needed to stop the Viper Mage using me . . .' She took a breath. 'Anyway. Saeunn told everyone that Fa had mated with a woman in the Deep Forest, who had died; she said that woman was my mother. They believed her.' Her fists clenched. 'Saeunn saved me. Sometimes I hate her. I owe her everything.'

Torak was silent. Then he said, 'Why did the Viper Mage need a baby?'

Renn hesitated. 'Can I tell you later?'

He nodded, pouring sand from palm to palm. 'Who else knew?'

'Only Fin-Kedinn and Saeunn. He said it would be my secret, to tell when I wanted.' Laying down her bow, she turned to him. 'I *was* going to tell you, I swear! I'm *so* sorry I never did!'

'I know,' he said. 'I'm sorry too, for all those things I said. I didn't mean them. You know that, don't you?'

Renn's face worked. Then she put her elbows on her knees and buried her head in her hands. She didn't make a sound, but Torak could see the tension in her shoulders.

Awkwardly, he put his arm around her. For an instant she resisted; then she relaxed and leaned against him. She felt small and warm and strong.

'I'm not crying,' she muttered.

'I know.'

After a while she straightened up and wiped her nose on the back of her hand, and wriggled out from under his arm. 'You're lucky,' she sniffed. 'You never knew your mother.'

'Well. But I remember my wolf mother.'

Another sniff. 'What was she like?'

'She had soft fur and a tongue like hot sand. Sometimes her breath smelt of rotting meat.'

Renn laughed.

Side by side, they gazed across the Lake. Torak heard the plop of a watervole; the distant tail-slam of a beaver. An otter broke the surface and regarded them, then dived underwater, trailing bubbles.

Watching it, Torak felt his spirits lift. If only Wolf were with them now, he could cope with anything.

As if in answer, a mournful howl rose from the Forest.

Torak turned and gave two short barks. *I am here!*

'Poor Wolf,' said Renn.

'Yes. He misses the pack.'

'I think he misses you, too.'

'Come on, then.' Torak pulled her to her feet. 'Let's go and cheer him up.'

They didn't find Wolf; he found them some time later, under a stand of pines not far from the camp.

Listlessly, he wagged his tail as he padded over to greet Torak. His ears were down and the brightness was gone from his eyes.

Squatting beside him, Torak gently scratched his flank.

Wolf lay down and put his muzzle between his paws. *I miss the pack*, he told Torak.

I know, Torak replied in wolf talk. He thought of Wolf's delight in the cubs and his affection for the black she-wolf. Wolf had given up all that for him.

I am your pack, Torak said.

Wolf thumped his tail. Then he sat up and licked Torak's nose.

Torak licked him back, and blew softly into his scruff. *I never leave you.*

Wolf's tail lashed from side to side, and his eyes gleamed.

Renn ran off, saying she had to fetch something from camp. Soon she was back, carrying a large alderwood bowl with otters carved around its sides. Torak helped her set it in the bracken. It stank. It was full of stickleback grease, speckled with mysterious black lumps.

'Yolun insisted I used this bowl,' said Renn. 'He said wolves are special, because they make strong music. There,' she told Wolf, 'I hope you like it!'

When they'd moved off a polite distance to give Wolf eating space, he went to sniff the bowl. Then he started to eat. He liked it. In a remarkably short time, he was licking the sides clean of the last remaining smears.

'What were the black bits?' said Torak.

'Dried lingonberries,' said Renn.

For a moment, Torak forgot about the Soul-Eaters – and laughed.

OATH BREAKER

N
W
E
S
THE DEEP FOREST
BURNT HILL
JAWS OF THE DEEP FOREST
TO ELK RIVER FORD
1ST AUROCH CAMP
HIGH
2ND AUROCH CAMP
AUROCH MAGE
BLACKWATER
LAKE BLACKWATER
DEEP FOREST CLAN CAMP
BEAVER LAKE
ISLET
RED DEER CAMP
SACRED GROVE
BEAVER LAKE
VALLEY OF THE HORSES
HILLS
WINDRIVER

TAINS

ONE

Sometimes there's no warning. Nothing at all.

Your skinboat is flying like a cormorant over the waves, your paddle sending silver capelin darting through the kelp, and everything's just right: the choppy Sea, the sun in your eyes, the cold wind at your back. Then a rock rears out of the water, bigger than a whale, and you're heading straight for it, you're going to smash . . .

Torak threw himself sideways and stabbed hard with his paddle. His skinboat lurched – nearly flipped over – and hissed past the rock with a finger to spare.

Streaming wet and coughing up seawater, he struggled to regain his balance.

'You all right?' shouted Bale, circling back.

'Didn't see the rock,' muttered Torak, feeling stupid.

Bale grinned. 'Couple of beginners in camp. You want to

265

go and join them?'

'You first!' retorted Torak, slapping the water with his paddle and drenching Bale. 'Race you past the Crag!'

The Seal boy gave a whoop and they were off: freezing, wet, exhilarated. High overhead, Torak spotted two black specks. He whistled, and Rip and Rek hurtled down to fly alongside him, their wingtips nearly touching the waves. Torak swerved to avoid a slab of ice and the ravens swerved with him, sunlight glinting purple and green on their glossy black feathers. They edged ahead. Torak raced to keep up. His muscles burned. Salt stung his cheeks. He laughed aloud. This was almost as good as flying.

Bale – two summers older and the best skinboater in the islands – pulled ahead, disappearing into the shadow of the looming headland called the Crag. The Sea turned rougher as they left the bay, and a wave smacked head-on into Torak's boat, nearly upending him.

When he'd got it under control, he was facing the wrong way. The Bay of Seals looked beautiful in the sun, and for a moment he forgot the race. Spray misted the waterfall at the southern end, and gulls wheeled about the cliffs. On the beach, smoke curled from the Seal Clan's humped shelters, and the long racks of salt-rimed cod glittered like frost. He saw Fin-Kedinn, his dark-red hair a fiery beacon among the fairer Seals; and there was Renn, giving an archery lesson to a gaggle of admiring children. Torak grinned. Seals were better with a harpoon than a bow and arrow, and Renn was not a patient teacher.

Bale yelled at him to catch up, so he turned and applied himself to his paddle.

Once past the Crag, they realized they were famished, and put in at a small bay, where they woke up a fire of driftwood and seaweed. Before eating, Bale threw a morsel of dried cod into the shallows for the Sea Mother and his clan guardian, while Torak, who didn't have a guardian, stuck a chunk of elk-blood sausage in a juniper bush as an offering to the Forest. It felt a bit odd, as the Forest was a day's skinboating to the east, but it would have felt even odder not to have done it.

After that, Bale shared the rest of the dried cod – sweet, chewy and surprisingly un-fishy – and Torak pulled clumps of mussels from the rocks. These they ate raw, prising off a half-shell and using it to scrape out the deliciously rich, slippery orange meat. Then Bale helped finish the elk sausage. Like the rest of his clan, he'd become more relaxed about mixing the Forest with the Sea, which made things easier for everyone.

Still hungry, they decided to make a stew. Torak filled his cooking-skin with water from a stream, hung it from sticks beside the fire, and added pebbles which had been heating in the embers. Bale tossed in handfuls of purple sea moss he'd found in a rockpool, and a pile of shellworms he'd dug from the sand, and Torak threw in a bunch of sea kale, because he wanted something green to remind him of the Forest.

As they waited for it to cook, Torak squatted near the fire, scorching the feeling back into his fingers. Bale made a spoon by wedging half a mussel shell in a piece of kelp stem, and binding it with seal sinew from his sewing pouch.

'Good fishing to you!' called a voice from the Sea, making them jump.

It was a Cormorant fisherman in a skinboat. His walrus-hide net bulged with herring.

'And good fishing to you!' Bale returned the greeting

common among the Sea clans.

As he paddled into the shallows, the man peered at Torak, taking in the fine black tattoos on his cheeks. 'Who's your friend from the Forest?' he asked Bale. 'Are those tattoos – Wolf Clan?'

Torak opened his mouth to reply, but Bale got in first. 'He's my kinsman. Fin-Kedinn's foster son. He hunts with the Ravens.'

'And I'm not Wolf Clan,' said Torak. 'I'm clanless.' His stare told the man to make of that what he would.

The man's hand went to the clan-creature feathers on his shoulder. 'I've heard of you. You're the one they cast out.'

Without thinking, Torak touched his forehead, where his headband concealed the outcast tattoo. Fin-Kedinn had altered the tattoo so it no longer meant outcast, but not even the Raven Leader could alter the memory.

'The clans took him back,' said Bale.

'So they say,' said the man. 'Well. Good fishing, then.' He spoke only to Bale, giving Torak a doubtful glance before paddling away.

'Don't mind him,' said Bale after a moment's silence.

Torak didn't reply.

'Here.' Bale tossed him the spoon. 'You left yours in camp. And cheer up! He's a Cormorant. What do they know?'

Torak's lip curled. 'About as much as a Seal.'

Bale lunged for him and they wrestled, laughing, rolling over the pebbles until Torak got Bale in an armlock and made him beg for mercy.

They ate in silence, spitting out scraps for Rip and Rek. Then Torak lay on his side and roasted, and Bale fed the fire with driftwood. The Seal boy didn't notice Rip approaching from behind at a stiff-legged walk. Both ravens were fascinated by Bale's long fair hair, which he wore threaded with blue slate beads and the tiny bones of capelin.

Rip took one of the bones in his powerful bill and tugged. Bale yelped. Rip let go and cowered with half-spread wings: an innocent raven unjustly accused. Bale laughed and tossed him a piece of shellworm.

Torak smiled. It was good to be with Bale again. He was like a brother; or how Torak imagined a brother would be. They enjoyed the same things, laughed at the same jokes. But they were different. Bale was nearly seventeen summers old, and soon he would find a mate and build his own shelter. As the Seals never moved camp, this meant that apart from trading trips to the Forest, he would live out his days on the narrow beach of the Bay of Seals.

Never to move camp. Even thinking of it made Torak breathless and cramped. And yet – to have such certainty. Your whole life unrolling like a well-tanned seal pelt. Sometimes he wondered how that must feel.

Bale sensed the change in him and asked if he was missing the Forest.

Torak shrugged.

'And Wolf?'

'Always.' Wolf had flatly refused to get in a boat, so they'd been forced to leave him behind. *Soon back*, Torak had told his pack-brother in wolf talk. But he wasn't sure if Wolf had understood.

Thinking of Wolf made him restless. 'It's getting late,' he said. 'We need to be on the Crag by dusk.'

That was why he and Renn and Fin-Kedinn had come. The disturbances on the island had started again after the winter, and they suspected it was the Soul-Eaters, searching for the last piece of the fire-opal which had lain hidden since the death of the Seal Mage. For the past half-moon, they'd taken turns to keep watch. Tonight it was the turn of Torak and Bale.

Bale looked preoccupied as he scoured the cooking-skin with sand. He opened his mouth to say something, then shook his head and frowned.

It wasn't like him to hesitate, so it must be important. Torak twisted a frond of oarweed in his fingers and waited.

'When you go back to the Forest,' said Bale without meeting his eyes, 'I'm going to ask Renn to stay here. With me. I want to know what you think about that.'

Torak went very still.

'Torak?'

Torak placed the oarweed on the fire and watched the flames around it turn purple. He felt as if he'd reached the edge of a cliff without knowing it was there. 'Renn can do what she likes,' he said at last.

'But you. What do you think?'

Torak sprang to his feet. Anger made his skin prickle and his heart bump unpleasantly in his chest. He stared down at Bale, who was handsome, older, and part of a clan. He knew that if he stayed, they would fight, and this time it would be for real. 'I'm off,' he said.

'Back to camp?' said Bale, studiedly calm.

'No.'

'Then where?'

'Just off.'

'What about keeping watch?'

'You do it.'

'Torak. Don't be – '

'I said, *you* do it!'

'Right. Right.' Bale stared at the fire.

Torak turned on his heel and ran to his boat.

He headed up the north coast, away from the Bay of Seals. His anger had gone, leaving a cold, churning confusion. He longed for Wolf. But Wolf was far away.

He found another inlet and put in. He carried the skinboat into the straggling trees on the lower slopes, needing the smell of birch and rowan, even if they were stunted and saltblown compared with those of the Forest. He couldn't return to the Bay of Seals, not tonight. He would stay here.

He had no pack or sleeping-sack, but since being cast out, he always carried what he needed wherever he went: axe, knife, tinder pouch. Propping the skinboat upside-down on shoresticks, he stacked branches and last autumn's bracken against the sides to make a shelter. Then he woke a driftwood fire and piled rocks behind it to throw back the heat. There was plenty of dry bracken and seaweed for bedding, and he'd be warm enough in his reindeer-hide parka and leggings. If not, too bad.

It was a clear night at the end of the Birchblood Moon – the Seals called it the Moon of the Cod Run – and from the shallows came the clink of a lonely little ice floe bumping against the rocks. Beyond the firelight, Rip and Rek slept huddled together in the fork of a rowan, their beaks tucked under their wings.

Torak lay watching the flames. It was nine moons since he'd been outcast, but it still felt strange to be in the open and not hiding his fire.

He should go back.

But he couldn't face Bale. Or Fin-Kedinn. Or Renn.

As he hunched deeper into his parka, something dug into his side. It was Bale's spoon; he must have shoved it into his belt before he left. He turned it in his fingers. It was carefully made, the sinew wound tight, the loose end neatly tucked in.

He blew out a long breath. He would go back in the morning and say sorry. Bale would understand. He was good that way, he never sulked.

Torak slept badly. In his dreams he heard an owl calling, and Renn telling him something he didn't understand.

Some time after middle-night, he woke. It was the time of the moon's dark, when it had been eaten by the sky bear, and only a glimmer of starlight rocked on the quiet Sea. He needed to get going: put in at the Bay of Seals, climb the Crag, find Bale.

Feeling groggy and unrested, he dismantled the shelter and poured water on the fire to put it to sleep. Rip and Rek reluctantly stretched their wings and fluffed up their head-feathers to show their dislike of such an early start; but when Torak carried his boat into the shallows and set off, he heard the strong, steady whisper of raven wings.

In the east, the sun was a scarlet knife-slash between Sea and sky, but the Bay of Seals was in shadow, the Crag looming against the stars. The gulls were roosting, the seal-hide shelters silent. Only the waterfall broke the stillness, and the stealthy lapping of the Sea, and the cod creaking on the racks.

Torak came ashore at the north end of the bay. Shells crunched beneath his boots, and he breathed the bitter tang of banked-up fires. On the racks, the cod watched him with dead, salt-crusted eyes.

Rek gave an eager cark – she'd spotted carrion – and both ravens flew to the rocks at the foot of the Crag.

It was too dark for Torak to see what they'd found, but something made the skin on the back of his neck tighten.

Whatever it was, Rip and Rek approached cautiously, as

ravens do, hopping nearer, then flying away.

Torak told himself it could be anything. But he was running, stumbling through mounds of rotting seaweed. As he drew closer, he caught the sickly-sweet smell that is like no other. He sank to his knees.

No. No.

He must have shouted it, because the ravens flew off with caws of alarm.

No.

He crawled closer. His fingers touched wetness and came away red. He saw shards of white bone and spatters of greasy grey sludge. He saw darkness seeping through the long fair hair that was beaded with blue slate and capelin bones. He saw the familiar face staring sightlessly at the sky.

Sometimes there's no warning. Nothing at all.

Two

This isn't happening, thought Torak.

He wasn't staring at those claw-like fingers; at that blood blackening under the nails. It wasn't real.

A gull screamed on the cliff, and Torak raised his head. High above, at the lip of the Crag, a juniper bush hung down. He pictured Bale on his knees, leaning over too far. His desperate grab at a branch, the sickening jolt as it gave way. The rocks hurtling towards him.

Oh, Bale. Why did you go so close to the edge?

A chill wind stole down his neck, and he shivered. Bale's souls were close, and they were angry. Angry with him. *If you'd been with me, I wouldn't have died.*

Torak shut his eyes.

Death Marks. Yes. The souls must be kept together, or Bale might become a demon or a ghost.

At least I can do this for you, thought Torak.

With clumsy fingers, he untied his medicine pouch and shook it. Out fell the medicine horn which had been his mother's, and the little mussel spoon. He blinked. He hadn't even thanked Bale for it. They had eaten in silence. Then they'd fought. No, he corrected himself. Bale didn't fight. *You* did the quarrelling. The last thing you ever said to him was in anger. Death Marks.

He shoved the spoon back into the pouch. Shaking earthblood into his palm, he tried to spit on it, but his mouth was too dry. He stumbled to a rockpool and made the red ochre into a paste with seawater. On his way back, he wound oarweed round his forefinger, so as not to touch the corpse.

Bale lay on his back. His face was unmarked. It was the back of his skull that had cracked like an eggshell. Numbly, Torak daubed earthblood circles on the forehead, chest and heels. He'd done the same for Fa. The mark on Fa's chest had been the hardest, as he had a scar where he'd cut out the Soul-Eater tattoo. Torak's own chest bore a similar scar, so when his time came, that mark would be difficult, too. Bale's chest was smooth. Flawless.

When it was done, Torak sat on his heels. He knew he was too close to the body, that this was the most dangerous time, when the souls are still close, and might try to possess the living. But he stayed where he was.

Someone was crunching through the seaweed, calling his name.

He turned.

Renn saw his face and stopped.

'Stay back.' His voice was rough, as if it belonged to someone else.

She ran to him. She saw what lay beyond. Her cheeks

drained of colour.

'He fell,' said Torak.

She was shaking her head, her lips soundlessly shaping *No, no*. Torak saw her take in the empty gaze, the spattered brains, the blood under the nails. These things would stay with her for ever, and he could do nothing to protect her.

The blood under the nails.

The meaning of it drenched him like an icy wave. That blood wasn't Bale's. Someone else had been with him on the Crag. Bale didn't fall. He was pushed.

Fin-Kedinn appeared behind Renn. His fingers tightened on his staff and his shoulders sagged, but his face remained unreadable. 'Renn,' he said quietly. 'Go and fetch the Seal Clan Leader.'

He had to repeat it twice before she heard, but for once she didn't argue. Like a sleepwalker she trudged towards camp.

Fin-Kedinn turned to Torak. 'How did it happen?'

'I don't know.'

'Why? Weren't you with him?'

Torak flinched. 'No, I . . . I should have been. I wasn't.' *If I'd been with him, he wouldn't have died. This is my fault. My fault.*

Their eyes met, and in Fin-Kedinn's sharp blue gaze, Torak saw understanding and sorrow: sorrow for *him*.

The Raven Leader raised his head and studied the Crag. 'Go up there,' he said. 'Find out who did this.'

The morning sun glinted on the juniper thorns as Torak climbed the steep path towards the Crag. Bale's bootprints were unmistakeable – Torak knew them as well as he knew

Renn's or Fin-Kedinn's or his own – and they were the only ones on the trail. So whoever had killed him hadn't come this way; not from the Seal camp.

Whoever had killed him. It still wasn't real. Only yesterday they'd been gutting cod together on the foreshore; Rip and Rek sidling closer to the steaming entrails, Bale tossing them scraps now and then. At last the final cod hung by its tail from the rack, and they were free to go skinboating. Asrif had lent Torak his boat, and Detlan and his little sister had come to see them off, Detlan on his crutches, waving so hard he nearly fell over.

Only yesterday.

The neck of the Crag was shaggy with rowan and juniper, but from there it broadened into a huge, flat boat shape jutting over the Sea. Long ago, the surface had been traced with a silvery web of hunters and prey. In the middle squatted a grey granite altar shaped like a fish.

Torak swallowed. Two summers before, the Seal Mage had tied him to that altar and prepared to cut out his heart. He could still feel the granite digging into his shoulder blades; still hear the click of the tokoroths' claws.

From far below came a cry like a creature being torn in two. Torak sucked in his breath. Bale's father had found his son.

Don't think about that. Think about this. Do this for Bale.

The Crag glistened with dew. It was naked rock, except for the odd crust of lichen or stonecrop. Tracking would be hard, but if the killer had left any trace, Torak would find it.

From the neck, he scanned the Crag. Something wasn't right, but he couldn't work out what. Storing that for later, he moved forwards. Fa used to say that to track your quarry, you must think yourself into its spirit. This took on a dreadful meaning now. Torak had to see Bale alive on the Crag. He had to see his faceless killer.

The killer must have been strong to have overcome Bale, but that was all Torak knew. He had to make the Crag tell him the rest.

It wasn't long before he found the first sign. He crouched, squinting sideways in the low morning light. A bootprint, very faint. And there: the suggestion of another. An older man walks on his heels, a young man on his toes. Bale had walked lightly onto the Crag.

Step by step, Torak followed him. He forgot the voice of the Sea and the salt wind in his face. He lost himself in the search.

The sense of being watched brought him back. He stopped. His heart began to pound. What if Bale's killer were still hiding in the rowans?

Whipping out his knife, he spun round.

'Torak, it's me!' cried Renn.

With a harsh exhalation, he lowered his knife. '*Never* do that again!'

'I thought you'd heard me!'

'What are you doing here?'

'Same as you!' She was angry because he'd frightened her, but she recovered fast. 'He didn't fall. His finger-nails . . . ' They stared at one another. Torak wondered if he, too, wore that bleak, stretched look.

'How did it happen?' she said. 'I thought you were with him.'

'No.'

She met his eyes. He glanced away. 'You go first,' she said in an altered voice. 'You're the best tracker.'

With his head down, he resumed his search, and Renn

followed. She rarely spoke when he was tracking; she said he went into a kind of trance which she didn't like to break. He was grateful for that now. Sometimes, she saw too much with those dark eyes; and he couldn't tell her about his quarrel with Bale. He was too ashamed.

He hadn't gone far when he found more signs. A crumb of lichen scraped by a running boot; and behind the altar, a lobe of stonecrop ground to a green smear. Snagged in a crack, a strand of reindeer hair. Torak's skin crawled. Bale wore seal hide. This had belonged to his killer. An image began to take shape, like a hunter emerging from mist. A big, heavy man clad in reindeer hide.

At once a name sprang to mind, but Torak pushed it aside. Don't guess. Keep your mind open. Find proof.

He pictured Bale leaving his hiding-place in the rowans, running towards the figure kneeling by the altar. The killer rose. They circled one another, moving closer and closer to the cliff edge.

At one point, the lip of the Crag was cracked, and in the soil the wind had blown in, a juniper clung to life. It had been half yanked out by the roots, and was still oozing tree-blood. Torak saw Bale desperately clutching a branch, his free hand clawing mud. He had fought so hard to live. And the killer had stamped on his fingers.

A red mist descended over Torak's sight. Sweat broke out on his palms. When he caught the killer, he would . . .

'Whoever it was,' said Renn shakily, 'he must have been hugely strong to have beaten B—' she jammed her knuckle in her mouth. For the next five summers, it would be forbidden to speak Bale's name, or else his spirit might return to haunt the living.

'Look there,' said Torak. He picked up a tiny speck of dried spruce-blood. 'And this.' He drew aside a branch to reveal a handprint.

Renn breathed in with a hiss.

Bale's murderer had leaned on one hand to watch his victim fall. That hand had only three fingers.

Torak shut his eyes. He was back in the caves of the Far North, facing the Soul-Eater. Wolf sprang to his defence, leaping at the attacker, snapping off two fingers.

'So now we know,' said Renn in a cold voice.

They stared at one another, both remembering cruel green eyes in a face as hard as cracked earth.

Torak's fist closed over the spruce-blood. 'Thiazzi,' he said.

THREE

The Oak Mage had made no attempt to cover his tracks. He'd found his way down the steep north flank of the Crag to a small pebble beach, picked up his skinboat, and paddled away.

Torak and Renn tracked him to where the trail ended in the Sea.

'From where I was,' said Torak, 'I might have seen him.'

'Why were you camping out here?' said Renn.

'I – I needed to be alone.'

She gave him a penetrating stare, but didn't ask why. That was worse. Maybe she'd guessed that he'd made a terrible mistake; so terrible that she couldn't bring herself to talk of it.

'He might be anywhere by now,' she said, turning back to the waves. 'He could've made for the Kelp Island, or one of the smaller ones. Or gone back to the Forest.'

'And he's got a head start,' said Torak. 'Let's go.'

To return to the Seal camp, they had to climb all the way to the Crag again. The altar still looked subtly wrong. It was Renn who noticed why. 'The carvings. The tip of the altar is lying across that elk's head. That can't be right.'

'It's been moved.' Torak was appalled that he hadn't seen it sooner. The scrape marks were as plain as a raven on an ice floe. He pictured the Oak Mage – the strongest man in the Forest – putting his shoulder to the altar to shift it, then moving it back, but leaving it just out of true.

Under the tip of the altar, Torak found what Thiazzi had uncovered: a small hollow hacked from the surface of the Crag. It was empty.

'He found what he was after,' said Torak.

Neither of them voiced their fear. But among the rowans on the neck, Torak found proof: the remains of a little pouch of dehaired seal hide. The crumbling hide still bore the faint imprint of something hard, about the size of a sloe, which had nestled inside.

Torak's blood thudded in his ears. Renn's voice reached him from a great distance. 'He found it, Torak. Thiazzi has the fire-opal.'

'Tell no-one,' said Fin-Kedinn. 'Not that he was murdered, or who did it, or why.'

Torak agreed at once, but Renn was aghast. 'Not even his father?'

'No-one,' said the Raven Leader.

They squatted by the stream at the south end of the bay, daubing each other's faces with clay mourning marks. The roar of the waterfall drowned their voices. There was no danger of being overheard by the Seal women downstream who were preparing the funeral feast, or by the men readying Bale's skinboat for the Death Journey. The Seals worked in silence to avoid offending the dead boy's souls. Torak thought they seemed like people in a dream.

All day, they had worked, and he had helped. Now dusk was falling, and every shelter, every skinboat, every last rack of cod had been moved to this end of the bay, furthest from the Crag. To the north, only the shelter Bale had shared with his father remained. It had been doused in seal oil and set ablaze. Torak could see it: a red eye glaring at him in the gathering dark.

'But that's *wrong*,' protested Renn.

'It's necessary.' Her uncle caught her gaze and held it. 'Think, Renn. If his father knew, he'd seek revenge.'

'Yes, and so?' she retorted.

'He wouldn't be alone,' said Fin-Kedinn. 'The whole clan would want to avenge one of their own.'

'So?' repeated Renn.

'I know Thiazzi,' said Fin-Kedinn. 'He won't hide in the islands, he'll head back to the Forest, where his power is greatest. The quickest route takes him past the trading meet on the coast . . .'

'And if the Seals came after him,' put in Torak, 'he'd set them against the other clans and get away.'

The Raven Leader nodded. 'That's why we say nothing. The Sea clans and the Forest clans have never been on easy terms. Thiazzi would use that. That's his strength, he fosters hate. Promise me, both of you. Tell no-one.'

'I promise,' said Torak. He didn't want the Seals going after Thiazzi. Revenge must be his and his alone.

Reluctantly, Renn gave her word. 'But his father's bound to find out,' she said. 'He must have seen what we saw. The – the blood under his nails.'

'No,' said Fin-Kedinn. 'I saw to it.' With the grey bars across his brow and down his cheeks, he looked remote and forbidding. 'Come,' he said, rising to his feet. 'It's time we joined the others.'

On the shore, the Seals had set a ring of kelp torches: a leaping orange beneath the dark-blue sky. Within this, they had laid Bale in his skinboat. Greasy black smoke stung Torak's eyes, and he breathed the stink of burning seal oil. He felt the mourning marks stiffening on his skin.

He thought, Bale's funeral rites. This can't be.

First, Bale's father stepped towards the boat and gently covered the body with his sleeping-sack. He had lost both his sons to the Soul-Eaters, and his face was distant, as if he weren't experiencing any of this. As if, thought Torak, he was at the bottom of the Sea.

After him, every member of the clan added a gift for the Death Journey. Asrif gave a food bowl, Detlan a set of fishing-hooks, while his little sister – who'd been very keen on Bale – managed to keep from crying for long enough to put in a small stone lamp. Others gave clothes, dried whale meat or cod, seal nets, spears, rope. Fin-Kedinn gave a harpoon, Renn her three best arrows. Torak gave his pike-jaw amulet, for hunting luck.

Standing to one side, he watched the men raise the skinboat on their shoulders and carry it down to the shallows. There they lashed two heavy stones to prow and stern, and Bale's father got in his own skinboat and began towing his son out to Sea.

The others trudged back for the silent feast, but Torak remained, watching the skinboats dwindle to specks.

When they were out of sight of land, Bale's father would take his spear and gash the funeral boat, sending his son down to the Sea Mother. The fishes would eat Bale's flesh, as in life he had eaten theirs; and when his shelter was ashes and the ashes had blown away, all trace of him would be gone, like a ripple on the Sea.

But he'll come back, thought Torak. He was born here. This was his home. He'll be lonely at Sea.

Fin-Kedinn was speaking his name. 'Torak. Come. You must join the feast.'

'I can't,' he said without turning round.

'You must.'

'I can't! I have to go after Thiazzi.'

'Torak, it's dark,' said Renn at her uncle's side, 'and there's no moon, you can't leave now. We'll set off first thing in the morning.'

'You must honour your kinsman,' Fin-Kedinn said severely.

Torak turned on him. 'My kinsman? That's what we've got to call him, isn't it? My kinsman. The Seal Clan boy. For five whole summers, till we've forgotten his name.'

'We'll never forget,' said Fin-Kedinn. 'But it's better this way. You know that.'

'Bale,' said Torak, very distinctly. 'His name. Was Bale.'

Renn gasped.

Fin-Kedinn watched him narrowly.

'Bale,' said Torak again. 'Bale. Bale. Bale!'

Shouldering past them, he ran the length of the bay, only stopping when he reached the smouldering ruins of Bale's shelter.

'*Bale!*' he shouted at the cold Sea. And if that summoned Bale's vengeful spirit to haunt him, then let it. It was *his* fault that Bale lay at the bottom of the Sea. If he hadn't

quarrelled, Bale would not have been alone on the Crag.
They would have faced the Oak Mage together, and Bale
would still be alive.

His fault.

'Torak!'

Renn stood on the other side of the fire, her pale face
shimmering in the heat. 'Stop naming him! You'll draw his
spirit!'

'Let it come!' he flung back. 'It's only what I deserve!'

'You didn't kill him, Torak.'

'But it was *my* fault! How do I bear it?'

To that she had no answer.

'Fin-Kedinn's right!' he cried. 'The Seals can't avenge
Bale, that's for *me* to do!'

'Don't keep naming him – '

'Vengeance is *mine!*' he shouted. Drawing his knife and
taking his medicine horn from its pouch, he raised them to
the sky. 'I swear to you, Bale. I swear to you on this knife
and this horn and on my three souls – I will hunt the Oak
Mage and I will kill him. I *will* avenge you!'

FOUR

Wolf stands in the Bright Soft Cold at the foot of the Mountain, gazing up at Darkfur.

She is many lopes above him, gazing down. He catches her scent, he hears the wind whispering through her beautiful black fur. He lashes his tail and whines.

Darkfur wags her tail and whines back. But this is the Thunderer's Mountain. Wolf can't go up, and she can't come down.

All through the Long Cold he has missed her, even when he was hunting with Tall Tailless and the pack-sister, or playing hunt-the-lemming; especially then, because Darkfur is so good at it. Of all the wolves in the Mountain pack, Wolf misses her the most. They are one breath, one bone. He feels this in his fur.

Darkfur goes down on her forepaws and barks. *Come! The*

hunt is good, the pack is strong!

Wolf's tail droops.

Her bark becomes impatient.

I cannot! he tells her.

With a leap, she is bounding down the Mountain. The Bright Soft Cold flies from her paws as she races towards him, and Wolf's heart flies with it. Joyfully he lopes towards her, running so fast that he . . .

Wolf woke up.

He was out of the Now that he went to in his sleeps, and back in the other now, lying at the edge of the Great Wet. Alone. He missed Darkfur. He missed Tall Tailless and the pack-sister. He even missed the ravens, a bit. *Why* did Tall Tailless leave him and go off in the floating hides?

Wolf hated it here. The sharp earth bit his pads, and the fish-birds attacked if he got too close to their nests. For a while, he'd explored the Dens of the taillesses along the Great Wet, and the Fast Wet that ran into it, but now he was bored.

The taillesses didn't hunt, they just stood around yipping and yowling and staring at stones. They seemed to think that some stones mattered more than others, although they all smelt the same to Wolf; and when the taillesses gave each other stones, they quarrelled. When a normal wolf gives a present – a bone or an interesting stick – he does it because he likes the other wolf, not because he's cross.

The Dark came, and the taillesses settled down for their endless sleep. Wolf heaved himself up and went to nose around the Dens. Scornfully evading the dogs, he ate some fishes hanging from sticks, and a delicious hunk of fish-dog fat. Then he found an overpaw outside a Den and ate that too. When the Light came, he trotted into the

Forest, trod down some bracken to make a comfortable sleeping-patch, and had a nap.

The smell woke him instantly.

His claws tightened. His hackles rose. He knew that smell. It made him remember bad things. It made the tip of his tail hurt.

The scent trail was strong, and it led up-Wet. With a growl, Wolf leapt to his feet and raced after it.

'I told you,' said the Sea-eagle hunter, tying up a bundle of roe buck antlers. 'I saw a big man coming ashore. That's it.'

'Where did he go?' said Torak. He was relentless. Renn, cradling a cup of hot birch-blood in her hands, wondered how much more the Sea-eagle would take.

'I don't *know!*' snapped the hunter. 'I was busy, I wanted to trade!'

'I think he went upriver,' said the hunter's mate.

'Upriver,' repeated Torak.

'That could mean anywhere,' said Renn. But already Torak was heading for the Raven camp and the deerhide canoes.

It was the second night after Bale's funeral rites, and after an exhausting crossing, they'd reached the trading meet on the coast. Fog shrouded the camps along the shore and the mouth of the Elk River. Willow, Sea-eagle, Kelp, Raven, Cormorant, Viper: all had come to barter horn and antler for seal hide and flint Sea eggs. Fin-Kedinn had gone to return their borrowed skinboats to the Whale Clan, and the ravens were roosting in a pine tree. There was no sign of Wolf.

Renn ran to catch up with Torak, who was shouldering

through the throng, earning irritable glances, which he ignored. 'Torak, wait!' Glancing round to make sure they weren't overheard, she said in a low voice, 'Have you thought that this could be a trap? The Soul-Eaters have set traps for you before.'

'I don't care,' said Torak.

'But think! Somewhere out there are Thiazzi and Eostra: the two remaining Soul-Eaters, and the most powerful of all.'

'I don't *care!* He killed my kinsman. I'm going to kill him. And *don't* tell me to get some sleep and we'll start in the morning.'

'I wasn't going to,' she replied, nettled. 'I was going to say I'll fetch some supplies.'

'No time. He's already got two days' lead.'

'And it'll be more,' she retorted, 'if we have to keep stopping to hunt!'

When she reached the shelter she shared with Saeunn, the sight of its familiar, lumpy reindeer hides brought her to a halt. Less than a moon ago, she'd left it and run down to the skinboats, eager to have Fin-Kedinn and Torak to herself, and to see Bale again.

She shut her eyes. In disbelief, she had stared at his broken body. The blind blue gaze. The grey sludge on the rocks. Those are his thoughts, she'd told herself. His thoughts soaking into the lichen.

Night and day, she saw it. She didn't know if Torak did too, because if he talked at all, it was about finding Thiazzi. He didn't seem to have anything left for grief.

Fog trickled down her neck, and she shivered. She was tired and stiff from the crossing, and hollow with grief, and *lonely*. She hadn't known she could be so lonely among people she loved.

Around her, hunters appeared and disappeared in the murk. She thought of Thiazzi gloating over the fire-opal. A man who took pleasure in others' pain. Who lived only to rule.

The Raven Mage huddled in her corner beneath a musty elk pelt. Over the winter, she had shrunk in upon herself till she reminded Renn of an empty waterskin. She rarely hobbled further than the midden, and when the clan moved camp, they carried her on a litter. Renn wondered what kept that shrivelled heart beating, and for how much longer. Already, Saeunn's breath carried a whiff of the Raven bone-grounds.

Trying not to wake her, Renn gathered her gear and crammed supplies into auroch-gut bags. Baked hazelnuts, smoked horse meat, meal of pounded silverweed root; dried lingonberries for Wolf.

The elk pelt stirred.

Renn's heart sank.

The speckled pate emerged from the fur, and the flinty eyes of the Raven Mage regarded her. 'So,' said Saeunn in a voice like the rattle of dead leaves. 'You're leaving. You must know where he's gone.'

'No,' said Renn. Saeunn could always place her talon on a weakness.

'But the Forest is vast . . . You must have tried to see where he went.'

She meant Magecraft. Renn's hands tightened on the gutskin. 'No,' she muttered.

'Why?'

'I couldn't.'

'But you have the skill.'

'No. I don't.' Suddenly, she was close to tears. 'I'm supposed to see the future,' she said bitterly, 'but I couldn't foresee his death. What's the *good* of being a Mage if I couldn't foresee that?'

'You might be able to do Magecraft,' rasped Saeunn, 'but you're not yet a Mage.'

Renn blinked.

'You'll know it when you are. Though perhaps your tongue will know before you do.'

Riddles, thought Renn savagely. Why always riddles?

'Yes, riddles,' said Saeunn with a wheeze that was almost a laugh. 'Riddles for you to solve!' She paused to catch her breath. 'I've been casting the bones.'

Torak appeared in the doorway and threw Renn an impatient glance.

She motioned him to silence. 'What did you see?' she asked Saeunn.

The Mage licked her gums with a tongue as grey as mould. 'A scarlet tree. An ash-haired hunter burning inside. Demons. Scrabbling under scorched stones.'

'Did you see where Thiazzi went?' Torak said brusquely.

'Oh, yes . . . I saw.'

Fin-Kedinn appeared beside Torak, his face grim. 'He's heading for the Deep Forest.'

'The Deep Forest,' echoed Saeunn. 'Yes . . .'

'A group of Boar just arrived,' said Fin-Kedinn. 'They came down the Widewater. At the ford, they saw a big man in a dugout, heading up the Blackwater.'

Torak nodded. 'He's Oak Clan, that's Deep Forest. Of course, that's where he'll go.'

'We'll take two canoes,' said Fin-Kedinn. 'I've told the clan they're to stay here while we head upriver.'

'*We?*' Torak said sharply.

'I'm coming with you,' said Fin-Kedinn.

'So am I,' said Renn, but they ignored her.

'Why?' Torak asked Fin-Kedinn. With a pang, Renn saw that he didn't want them. He wanted to do this on his own.

'I know the Deep Forest,' said Fin-Kedinn. 'You don't.'

'No!' Saeunn was fierce. 'Fin-Kedinn. You must not go!'

They stared at her.

'One thing more the bones revealed, and this is *certain*. Fin-Kedinn, you will not reach the Deep Forest.'

Renn's heart clenched. 'Then – we'll go without him. Just Torak and me.'

But her uncle wore the expression she dreaded: the one which told her there was no point in arguing. 'No, Renn,' he said with terrifying calm. 'You can't do this without me.'

'Yes we can,' she insisted.

Fin-Kedinn sighed. 'You know there's been trouble between the Aurochs and the Forest Horses since last summer. They won't let in outsiders. But they know me –'

'No!' cried Renn. 'Saeunn means it. She's never wrong.'

The Raven Mage shook her head and gave another rattling sigh. 'Ah, Fin-Kedinn . . .'

'Torak, tell him!' pleaded Renn. 'Tell him we can do it without him.'

But Torak picked up a bag of supplies and avoided her eyes. 'Come on,' he muttered, 'we're losing time.'

Fin-Kedinn took the other bag from her hands. 'Let's go,' he said.

FIVE

Wolf raced after the scent trail.

Around him the Forest was waking from its long sleep, and the prey was thin from scraping away the Bright Soft Cold to get at its food. Wolf startled an elk nibbling a sycamore's juicy hide. A herd of reindeer sensed he wasn't hunting them, and raised their heads to watch him pass.

The hated scent streamed over his nose. Many Lights and Darks ago, the bad tailless had trapped him in a tiny stone Den and bound his muzzle so that he couldn't howl. The bad tailless had starved him and stamped on his tail, and when Wolf yelped in pain, he'd *laughed*. Then he'd attacked Wolf's pack-brother. Wolf had leapt at the bad tailless, clamping his jaws on one hairy forepaw, crunching bones and rich, juicy flesh.

Wolf loped faster. He didn't know *why* he sought the

Bitten One – wolves do not hunt taillesses, not even bad ones – but he knew that he had to follow.

The scent thickened. Through the voices of wind and birch and bird, Wolf heard the tailless stirring the Wet with a stick. He smelt that the tailless had no dog.

Then he saw him.

The Bitten One was sliding up-Wet on the trunk of an oak. Wolf caught the glint of a great stone claw at his flank. He caught the smell of pine-blood and reindeer hide, and of the strange, terrible Bright Beast-that-Bites-Cold.

Terror seized Wolf in its jaws. The Bitten One sat fearless, relishing his strength. He was very, very strong. Not even the Bright Beast-that-Bites-Hot dared attack him. Wolf knew this because he'd seen the tailless thrust his forepaw *right into the muzzle of the Bright Beast* – and take it out unbitten.

From many lopes away came the high, thin howl of the bird bone that Tall Tailless and the pack-sister used for calling him.

Wolf didn't know what to do. He longed to go to them; but that would mean turning back.

The bird bone went on calling.

The Bitten One went on sliding up-Wet.

Wolf didn't know what to do.

'You let him get away!' shouted Torak, so angry that he forgot to talk wolf. 'He was right there and you let him get away!'

Wolf tucked his tail between his legs and shot behind Fin-Kedinn, who was on his knees, waking a fire.

'Torak, stop it!' cried Renn.

'But he was so close!'

'I know, but it's not his fault. It was me!'

He turned on her.

'*I* called Wolf,' she told him. 'It's my fault he let Thiazzi get away.' She opened her palm, and he saw the little grouse-bone whistle he'd given her two summers before.

'*Why?*' he demanded.

'I was worried about him. And you – you didn't seem to care.'

That made him even angrier. 'Of course I care! How could I not care about Wolf?'

Behind Fin-Kedinn, Wolf dropped his ears and doubtfully wagged his tail.

Remorse broke over Torak. What was wrong with him?

Wolf had bounded so joyfully into camp, proudly telling Torak how he'd left the trail of the Bitten One as soon as he'd heard his call. He'd been bewildered when Torak lost his temper. He had no idea what he'd done wrong.

Torak sank to his knees and grunt-whined. Wolf raced towards him. Torak buried his face in his scruff. *Sorry.* Wolf licked his ear. *I know.*

'What's wrong with me?' murmured Torak.

Fin-Kedinn, who'd ignored his outburst, told him to go and fetch water. Renn simply glared.

Torak grabbed the waterskin and ran to the shallows.

They'd spent the night and next morning heading up the Elk River, pausing only for brief rests, and were now close to the rapids where the Widewater and the Blackwater crashed together. Twice they'd met hunters who'd seen a big man heading upstream.

He's getting away, thought Torak. Slumping onto a log,

he glowered at the river.

It was a blustery day and the Forest was at odds with itself. An abandoned elk bellowed mournfully. In the dead reeds on the other side, two hares battered each other with their forepaws.

Torak caught the scent of woodsmoke and an appetizing sizzle of flatcakes. He was hungry, but he couldn't join the others. He felt cut off from them, as if he were trapped behind a wall: unseen, but tough as midwinter ice. Saeunn's prophesy about his foster father haunted him. What if Renn was right, and Thiazzi was setting a trap? What if he, Torak, were leading Fin-Kedinn to his death?

And yet – he had no choice but to go on.

Wolf padded down the bank and dropped a stick at Torak's feet as a present.

Torak picked it up and turned it in his fingers.

You're sad, said Wolf with a twitch of one ear. *Why?*

The pale-pelt who smells of fish-dog, Torak said in wolf talk. *Not-Breath. Killed by the Bitten One.*

Wolf rubbed his flank against Torak's shoulder, and Torak leaned against him, feeling his solid, furry warmth.

You hunt the Bitten One, said Wolf.

Yes, said Torak.

Because he is bad?

– because he killed my pack-brother.

Wolf watched a damselfly skim the water. *And when the Bitten One is Not-Breath – does the pale-pelt breathe again?*

No, said Torak.

Wolf tilted his head and looked at Torak, his amber eyes puzzled. *Then – why?*

Because, Torak wanted to tell him, I have to avenge Bale. But he didn't know how to say that in wolf talk, and even if he could, he didn't think Wolf would understand. Maybe wolves didn't seek revenge.

Side by side, they sat watching the midges darting over the brown water. Torak caught the flicker of a trout, and followed it deeper.

He'd always known there were differences between him and Wolf; but Wolf couldn't seem to grasp that. At times it made Wolf frustrated, especially when Torak couldn't do everything a real wolf could. Thinking of this made Torak sad, and vaguely uneasy.

He looked round to find that Wolf had gone, and clouds had darkened the sky. Someone stood in the reeds on the other side of the river, staring at him.

It was Bale.

Water ran soundlessly from his jerkin. Seaweed clotted his streaming hair. His face had a greenish underwater pallor, and his eyes were dark as bruises. Angry. Accusing.

Torak tried to cry out. He couldn't. His tongue had stuck to the roof of his mouth.

Bale raised one dripping arm and pointed at him. His lips moved. No sound came, but his meaning was clear. *Your fault.*

'Torak?'

The spell broke. Torak jerked round.

'I've been calling you!' said Renn, standing behind him, looking cross.

Bale was gone. Across the river, dead reeds creaked in the breeze.

'What's wrong?' said Renn.

'N-nothing,' he faltered.

'*Nothing?* You're as grey as ash.'

He shook his head. He couldn't bring himself to tell her. She gave a small, hurt shrug. 'Well. I saved you a flatcake.' She held it out, wrapped in a dock leaf to keep warm. 'You can eat it as we go.'

From the canoe, Renn watched Wolf running between the trees: now lifting his muzzle to catch the scent, now snuffling in the brush.

Too many times, he'd found the places where the Oak Mage had stopped to eat or camp. Thiazzi seemed in no hurry to reach the Deep Forest, and this worried Renn, although she hadn't mentioned it to the others. Fin-Kedinn was preoccupied, while Torak . . .

She wished he would turn and talk to her. He sat in front, his back straight and unyielding as he searched the banks for signs of Thiazzi.

Angrily, she dug in her paddle. He didn't care about anything except finding the Oak Mage. He didn't even care that Fin-Kedinn was in danger.

At last they reached the rapids, and went ashore to carry the canoes around them. Wolf was already trotting purposefully up the Blackwater.

'How far to the Deep Forest?' asked Torak as they set down the second canoe.

'A day,' said the Raven Leader, 'maybe more.'

Torak ground his teeth. 'If he reaches it, we'll never find him.'

'We might,' said Fin-Kedinn. 'He's taking his time.'

'I wish we knew why,' said Renn. 'Maybe it *is* a trap. And even if it isn't, he'll soon know he's being hunted.'

Fin-Kedinn nodded, but did not reply. All day he'd been distant and uncommunicative, and every so often he narrowed his eyes, as if the Blackwater revived memories that cut too deep.

Renn didn't like it, either. She didn't know this river, as Fin-Kedinn had never led the Ravens to camp on its banks, but she thought it was well-named. It was shadowed by dank trees, and so murky that she couldn't see the bottom. When she leaned over, it gave off a sour smell of rotting leaves.

Once they had the canoes in the water again, she insisted on sitting in front. She was sick of staring at Torak's back, wondering what he was thinking. No doubt it was about finding Thiazzi. Although what, she wondered, would he do if he did? Clan law forbade killing a man without warning, so he'd have to challenge the Oak Mage to a fight. Her mind shied away from that. Torak was strong and quite good at fighting, but he wasn't yet fifteen summers old. How could he challenge the strongest man in the Forest?

'Renn?' he said, making her jump.

She twisted round.

'When someone's asleep, can you tell if they're dreaming? I mean, by watching them?'

She stared at him. His mouth was set, and he avoided her gaze. 'If you're dreaming,' she told him, 'your eyes move. That's what Saeunn says.'

He nodded. 'If you see me dreaming, will you wake me up?'

'Why? Torak, what did you see?'

He shook his head. He was like a wolf; if he didn't want to do something, it was impossible to make him.

She tried anyway. 'What *is* it? Why can't you tell me?'

He opened his mouth, and for a moment she thought he would. Then his eyes widened and he grabbed her hood, yanking her down so hard that she bashed her temple on the rim of the canoe.

'Ow!' she yelled. 'What are you –'

'Fin-Kedinn, get down!' shouted Torak at the same time.

As Renn struggled to right herself, something hissed over her head. She saw Fin-Kedinn reach for his knife and slash; she saw Wolf yelp as if stung by a hornet and leap into the air. She saw a line as thin as a thread of gossamer snap and trail harmlessly in the water.

There was a breathless silence. Renn sat up, rubbing her temple. Torak steered the canoe into midstream and caught the end of the line. 'It was taut as a bowstring,' he said.

He didn't need to say more. Canoes powering towards a strong line of sinew stretched between trees on opposite banks. At head height.

Renn's hand went to her neck. If Torak hadn't pulled her down, it would have cut her throat.

'He knows he's being hunted,' said Fin-Kedinn, bringing his canoe alongside theirs.

'But – maybe he doesn't know it's Torak,' said Renn.

'Why do you say that?' said Torak.

'If he knew it was you,' she said, 'would he risk killing you? He wants your power.'

'Maybe, maybe not,' said Fin-Kedinn. 'Thiazzi is arrogant. Above all things, he believes in his own strength. And he has the fire-opal. He may not think he needs the power of the spirit walker. And if that's right,' he added, 'it means he doesn't care who he kills.'

SIX

The sinew had cut across Wolf's foreleg. It was scarcely bleeding and he wasn't in pain, but Torak insisted on rubbing in a salve of yarrow leaves in marrowfat which he made Renn produce from her medicine pouch.

'He'll only lick it off,' she told him, and Wolf immediately did.

Torak didn't care. It made him feel a bit better, even if it didn't do much for Wolf.

He'd nearly missed that sinew. What if he had, and Renn or Fin-Kedinn had suffered for his mistake? The mere thought made his belly turn over. It only takes one mistake, just one, and you've got to live with the consequences for the rest of your life.

Squatting on the bank, he mashed a handful of wet soapwort to a green froth, and washed his hands.

He glanced up to find Fin-Kedinn watching him. They were alone. Wolf was drinking in the shallows, and Renn was already in the canoe.

Fin-Kedinn emptied the waterskin over Torak's hands. 'Don't worry about me,' he said.

'But I do,' said Torak. 'Saeunn meant what she said.'

The Raven Leader shrugged. 'Omens. You can't live your life by what *might* happen.' He shouldered the waterskin. 'Let's go.'

They followed Wolf up the Blackwater until long into the night, then slept under the canoes, and headed off before dawn. As the afternoon wore on, the Forest closed in. Wakeful spruce thronged the banks, dripping with beard-moss, and even the trees not yet in leaf were vigilant. Last autumn's oak leaves rattled in the wind, and ash buds glinted like tiny black spears.

At last, the hills bordering the Deep Forest rose into view. Torak had reached them two summers before, but then he'd been further north. Here they were steeper, stonier: sheer walls of grey rock, hacked and slashed as if by a giant axe. The hammering cries of black grouse echoed like falling stones.

As the light began to fail, Wolf leapt into the river and swam across. Once on the north bank, he gave himself a good shake, and set off. Then he doubled back, snuffing the mud.

They edged into the shallows, and Torak got out to examine the mess of tracks. No wonder Wolf was puzzled: they were almost unreadable, as a boar had recently taken a wallow.

'This isn't only Thiazzi,' said Torak. 'See that heel print? It's not as heavy, and the weight's more to the inside of the foot.'

'So someone was with him?' said Renn.

He chewed his thumbnail. 'No. Thiazzi's tracks are darker, and a beetle crawled over the other's but not over his. Whoever it was, they came before.'

Wolf had smelt something. Leaving the canoes, they went after him, into a gully cut by a stream feeding into the Blackwater.

Twenty paces up, Torak stopped.

The footprint shouted at him from the mud. Bold, mocking. *Here I am*. Thiazzi stamping his mark for all to see.

'The Oak Mage,' said Fin-Kedinn.

It told Torak a lot more than that. A single footprint is a landscape which can tell a whole story if you know how to read it. Torak did. And before leaving the Seal Island, he'd studied Thiazzi's tracks till he knew every detail.

He found more. He made the gully reveal its secrets. 'He left his dugout in the shallows,' he said at last, 'then climbed up here. He was carrying something heavy on his left shoulder, maybe his axe. Then he retraced his steps, got into his dugout, paddled away.' He clenched his fists. 'He's well fed and rested, moving fast. He's enjoying this.'

'But why come here?' said Renn, looking about her.

'I don't like it,' said Fin-Kedinn. 'Remember that sinew. Let's go back to the boats.'

'No,' said Torak. 'I want to know what he was doing.'

Fin-Kedinn sighed. 'Don't get too far ahead.'

Warily, they advanced: Torak and Wolf first, then Renn, with Fin-Kedinn at the rear.

The trees thinned, and Torak clambered between massive, tumbled boulders, while Wolf bounded lightly ahead. The trail veered to the right. The trees ended.

Torak found himself on a huge, desolate hill of bare

rock. A hundred paces above, the crown was streaked black, as if by fire. Before him, the slope was a chaos of fallen trees thrown there by a flood, with boulders jutting through like broken teeth. Below, the Blackwater coiled round the base of the hill and disappeared between two towering rocks that leaned crazily towards each other. Beyond these great stone jaws rose the looming oaks and jagged spruce of the Deep Forest.

Wolf pricked his ears. Uff! he barked softly.

Torak followed his gaze. Under the willows overhanging the river, he saw the flash of a paddle.

Wolf bounded down the slope. Torak ran after him, nearly losing his footing as a tree-trunk shifted under his boot.

'Torak!' Renn whispered behind him.

'Slow down!' warned Fin-Kedinn.

Torak ignored them. He couldn't let his quarry escape now.

Suddenly there he was, not fifty paces away: driving the dugout with long, powerful strokes towards the Deep Forest.

Wobbling and lurching over the fallen trees, Torak pulled an arrow from his quiver and nocked it to his bow. He no longer heard the others. All he heard was the splash of Thiazzi's paddle, all he saw was that long russet hair lifting in the breeze. He forgot clan law, he forgot everything except the need for revenge.

A log rolled beneath him. Something snagged his ankle. He kicked himself free. Behind him, a loud snap. He glanced round. In one frozen heartbeat he took in the trip-line lashed to the trigger log, its end sharpened to a point and smeared with mud to hide the fresh-cut wood.

The hill of logs began to move. *You fool. Another trap.*

Then the logs were crashing towards him and he was yelling a warning to the others and leaping for the nearest boulder, flinging himself into the tiny hollow beneath it; and logs were bouncing over him, smashing into the river, sending up plumes of water. Huddled under his boulder, Torak heard laughter echo from hill to hill. He pictured Thiazzi's dugout sweeping between the great stone jaws, disappearing into the Deep Forest.

Then the whole hillside was giving way, and Fin-Kedinn was shouting, 'Renn! *Renn!*'

SEVEN

Silence boomed in Torak's ears. Dust clogged his throat.
'Renn?' he called.

No answer.

'Fin-Kedinn? Wolf?'

The rocks threw back the sound of his terror.

He was squashed under a tangle of saplings which had fallen on top of his boulder. A surge of panic. He was trapped. Wildly, he struggled. The saplings shifted. He pushed his way out and greedily gulped air.

'Renn!' he shouted. 'Fin-Kedinn!'

Wolf appeared on the crown of the hill and ran down to him, his claws clicking on rock. Torak didn't need to say anything. A terse nose-nudge, and they began to search. Tree-trunks shifted and creaked ominously. Someone was whimpering. 'No no, not them, please not them.' It took

Torak a moment to recognize the voice as his own.

A flurry of wings, and Rek lit onto a branch ten paces away. Wolf raced towards her and barked. Torak wobbled after them.

Through the branches he saw a shock of dark-red hair. 'Renn?'

He tore at the branches, dragged saplings out of the way. Thrusting his arm through a gap, he grabbed her sleeve.

She moaned.

'You all right?'

She coughed. Mumbled something that might have been yes.

'There's a gap, I'll make it bigger. Give me your hand, I'll pull you through.' Being Renn, she pushed her bow through first – then wriggled out. Her eyes were huge, but apart from scratches, she was unhurt.

'Fin-Kedinn,' she said.

'I can't find him.'

The blood drained from her face. 'He saved my life. Threw me out of the way.'

Wolf stood below them in a wreck of dead spruce, looking down between his forepaws. His ears were pricked. Eagerly he glanced at his pack-brother.

The spruce lay on top of a larger beech, itself aslant more spruce. Under the beech lay Fin-Kedinn.

'Fin-Kedinn?' Renn's voice shook. *Fin-Kedinn!*

The Raven Leader's eyes remained closed.

Frantically, they tugged at branches and tree-trunks. There was a creak, and the whole pile shuddered. They didn't speak, for fear of bringing down disaster.

The sun set, and they worked on. At last they cleared a way to the beech. It wouldn't budge. Torak wedged a sapling underneath and pushed with all his might. The beech shifted slightly.

'We'll have to drag him out,' said Renn.

It took both of them to haul him free. Still he didn't move. Renn held her wrist to his lips to feel for breath. Torak saw her throat work.

Half-carrying, half-dragging him, they finally made it to solid rock. On the hill's eastern flank, facing the Deep Forest, Torak found an overhang. The ledge beneath it was big enough to shelter them, although not high enough to stand up in.

Renn knelt beside her uncle, twisting her hands. Rip and Rek flapped their wings and cawed. Wolf sniffed the Raven Leader's temple. Then he whined, so high that Torak could hardly hear. He went on whining.

Fin-Kedinn's eyelids flickered. 'Where's Renn?' he murmured.

By taking the weight of the other trees, the beech had saved his life, but it had crushed the left side of his chest.

Renn set to work, pulling off his parka and cutting the laces on his jerkin. She was as gentle as she could be, but the pain was so bad that he nearly passed out.

'Three ribs broken,' she said as she probed his back with her fingers.

Fin-Kedinn hissed. His eyes were closed, his skin clammy and grey. He was breathing shallowly, and Torak could see that every breath, in and out, was a knife in his side.

'Will he live?' Torak said in a low voice.

Renn glared at him.

'Is he bleeding inside?' he whispered.

'I don't know. If he bleeds from his mouth . . .'

Fin-Kedinn's lips twisted in a wry smile. 'Then it's over. Saeunn was right. I won't reach the Deep Forest.'

'Don't talk,' warned Renn.

'Hurts less than breathing,' said her uncle. 'Where are we?'

Torak told him.

He groaned. 'Ah, not here! Not the hill!'

'We can't move you, not tonight,' said Renn.

'This is a bad place,' muttered Fin-Kedinn. 'Haunted. Evil.'

'No more talk!' admonished Renn, cutting strips from the hem of her jerkin for bandages.

Wolf lay beside her, his muzzle between his paws. Rip and Rek stalked up and down at a stiff raven walk. Torak watched Fin-Kedinn turning his head from side to side. He'd never felt so powerless.

Renn told him to fetch wood for a fire, and he ran off. His hands were shaking and he kept dropping sticks. He thought, if that beech had fallen just a little differently, it would have crushed his breastbone, and we'd be putting on Death Marks. It would be my fault. I could have killed us all.

From where he stood, the hill sloped down to the Blackwater. A deer trail wound along its bank, past one of the stone jaws and into the Deep Forest. He pictured the Oak Mage vanishing into the shadows. He had been so close.

Back at the ledge, Fin-Kedinn had slipped into an uneasy doze, and Renn was on her knees with a handful of birch-bark tinder, grimly trying and failing to get a spark with her strike-fire. 'Well, go on then,' she said without looking up.

'What do you mean?' said Torak.

'Go after him. That's what you want.'

He stared at her. 'I'm not leaving you.'

'But you want to.'

He flinched.

'It'll take days to get Fin-Kedinn back to the clan,' she said, still failing to get a spark. 'And all the time, Thiazzi's getting away. That's what you're thinking, isn't it?'

'Renn –'

'You never wanted us to come!' she burst out. 'Well, here's your chance to be rid of us!'

'Renn!'

They faced each other, white and shaking.

'I won't leave you,' said Torak. 'In the morning I'll bring round the canoes. Then we'll work out what to do.'

Savagely, Renn struck a spark. Her lips trembled as she blew life into it.

Torak went down on his knees and helped feed the fire with kindling, then sticks. When it was fully awake, he took her hand, and she gripped so hard that it hurt.

'He's beaten us,' she said.

'For now,' he replied.

Night deepened, and the sliver of moon fled across the sky. Renn said they should take comfort from it; it would grow stronger, and so would Fin-Kedinn. Torak thought she was trying very hard to persuade herself.

While she tended Fin-Kedinn, he fetched their gear from the canoes, then used branches to turn the ledge into a rough shelter, leaving a gap for the smoke. He'd found a clump of comfrey near the river, and Renn pounded its roots into a poultice, while Torak made the leaves into a strengthening brew in a swiftly fashioned birch-bark bowl. Together, they bandaged Fin-Kedinn's ribs. The binding had to be tight, to help set the broken bones. When it was done, all three of them were sweating and pale.

After that, Renn fed the fire with juniper boughs and wafted some of the smoke into the shelter to drive off the worms of sickness. Torak tucked a slip of dried horse meat in a crack in a boulder to thank the Forest for letting his foster father live. Then, as they were both famished, they shared more meat. Fin-Kedinn did not eat at all.

The moon set, and his restlessness increased. 'Don't let the fire die,' he murmured. 'Renn. Draw lines of power around the shelter.'

Renn gave Torak a worried look. If his wits were wandering, it was a bad sign.

Torak noticed that the ravens hadn't settled to roost, but were hopping warily among the rocks, while Wolf lay at the mouth of the shelter, watching the dark beyond the firelight. Torak had the uneasy sense that they were on guard.

Renn took her medicine pouch and went to draw the lines.

'Don't go far,' warned Fin-Kedinn.

Torak fed the fire another stick. 'You said this was a bad place. What did you mean?'

Fin-Kedinn watched the flames. 'Nothing grows here now. Nothing has since — the demons were forced back into the rocks.' He paused. 'But they're close, Torak. They want to get out.'

Torak dipped a clump of moss in the cup and cooled his foster father's brow. Renn would be angry if he let Fin-Kedinn talk, but he had to know. 'Tell me,' he said.

Fin-Kedinn coughed, and Torak held his shoulders. When it was over, the skin around the Raven Leader's eyes had a bluish tinge. 'Many summers ago,' he said, 'this hill was thick with trees. Birch, rowan, in cracks between the rocks. Holding the demons inside.' He shifted position and winced. 'Souls' Night. Long past. People came to let them out.'

Renn returned and knelt beside him. 'But the demons couldn't get out, could they?' she said. 'I feel them under the rocks, very close.'

'One man stopped them,' said Fin-Kedinn. 'He set a fire on the hill. Banished the demons back into the rocks. But the fire escaped.' He licked his lips. 'Terrible . . . It can leap into a tree faster than a lynx, and when it does – when it gets into the branches – it goes where it likes. You wouldn't believe how fast. It ate the whole valley.'

Torak began to be afraid. 'Was anyone hurt?'

Fin-Kedinn nodded. 'Trapped. Terrible burns. One killed.' He grimaced, as if he smelt charred flesh.

Torak peered into the dark. 'What *is* this place?' he whispered.

'Don't you know?' said Fin-Kedinn.

The hairs on Torak's arms prickled. 'Is this where . . . '

'Yes. This is where your father shattered the fire-opal. Where he broke the power of the Soul-Eaters.'

Out in the night, a vixen screamed. From far away came the deep oo-hu, oo-hu of an owl. Torak and Renn exchanged glances. It was an eagle owl.

Renn said, 'When I was drawing the lines of power, I felt a presence. Not only demons. Something else. Lost. Searching.'

'There are ghosts here,' said Fin-Kedinn. 'The one who died.'

Flames leapt in Renn's dark eyes. 'The seventh Soul-Eater.'

The Raven Leader made no reply.

An ember collapsed in a shower of sparks. Torak jumped. 'Were you here that night?' he said.

'No.' Pain contracted Fin-Kedinn's features. Torak didn't think it was caused by his broken ribs. 'After the great fire,' Fin-Kedinn went on, 'your mother and father sought me. They begged me to help them get away.'

Renn put her hand on his shoulder. 'You need to rest. Don't talk any more.'

'No! I must tell this!' He spoke with startling force, and his burning blue gaze held Torak's. 'I was angry. I wanted revenge against him for – for taking your mother. I turned them away.'

Torak heard the click of raven talons on stone. He looked into the face of his foster father and wanted it not to be true, and knew that it was.

'Next day,' said Fin-Kedinn, 'I relented. I went after them. But they'd gone. Fled to the Deep Forest.' He shut his eyes. 'I never saw them again. If I'd helped them, she might have lived.'

Torak touched his hand. 'You couldn't have known what would happen.'

The Raven Leader's smile was bitter. 'So you tell yourself. Does it help?'

Wolf leapt up with a growl and sped after a quarry only he could sense. An ember dislodged from the fire. Torak nudged it back with his boot. Suddenly, the light seemed a fragile shield against the dark.

'Keep the fire bright,' said Fin-Kedinn. 'And stay awake. Demons. Ghosts. They know we're here.'

The Chosen One watches the unbelievers sleep, and hungers to punish them and set the fire free.

The girl who woke the fire did it wrongly and without respect. She is an unbeliever. She does not follow the True Way.

The boy threw a branch at the fire and kicked it. He too has lost the Way.

The Master shall know of this. The Master honours the fire, and the fire honours him. The Master will punish the unbelievers.

The fire is sacred. It must be honoured, for it is the purity and the truth. The Chosen One loves the fire for its terrible glare and its hunger for the Forest, for its dreadful caress. The Chosen One longs to be one with the fire again.

The wind changes and the Chosen One moves to crouch in the breath of the fire, to drink its sacred bitterness. The Chosen One's hand cups ash. The ash is acrid on the tongue, heavy in the belly. It is the power and the truth.

The injured man moans in painful dreams. The boy's sleep is also troubled, but the girl slumbers as one dead. And over them, wolf and raven keep watch — while the fire sinks untended. Dishonoured.

Anger kindles in the breast of the Chosen One.

The unbelievers are evil.

They must be punished.

EIGHT

Torak woke before dawn. The fire had burned low. The others were still asleep. Renn lay on her side, one arm flung out. Fin-Kedinn was frowning, as if even sleeping hurt. Both looked disturbingly vulnerable.

Quietly, Torak wriggled out of his sleeping-sack and crawled from the shelter.

Below him on the slope, a wolverine rose on its hind legs to snuff his scent, then bounded off. This told Torak that Wolf must have gone hunting. If he'd been near, the wolverine would have stayed away. With a twinge of apprehension, Torak wondered what else might have managed to creep close.

Below him the valley of the Blackwater floated in mist. The Forest rang with birdsong, but the ravens were gone.

On the hill, he could see nothing except naked rock. He climbed to the crown. Nothing. Only an ancient tree stump on the western slope, its roots still clinging to the demon-haunted cracks. He thought of his father, who had sparked the events that had brought him to this place. He was shocked to realize that he could scarcely remember Fa's face.

As light crept into the sky, he spotted a faint dew trail of booted feet. Drawing his knife, he followed it round to the overhang above the shelter. Near the edge, he found a small cone of fine grey ash. He frowned. Someone had poured it with care, like an offering. Someone who had watched them in the night.

He caught a flicker of movement in the mist by the river. His heart contracted.

Someone stood on the bank, staring up at him. The face was indistinct; the hair long, pale. An arm rose. A finger pointed at him. Accusing.

Torak touched the medicine pouch at his hip and felt the shape of the horn within. Sheathing his knife, he started down the hill. He dreaded coming face to face with Bale's ghost. But maybe it would speak to him. Maybe he could say he was sorry.

The birds had stopped singing. On either side of the trail, hemlock floated in vaporous white.

Footsteps heading his way.

A wild-eyed man burst from the mist and blundered into him. 'Help me!' he gasped, clutching Torak's parka and glancing back over his shoulder.

Staggering under his weight, Torak breathed the stink of blood and terror.

'*Help me!*' pleaded the man. 'They – they –'

'Who?' said Torak.

'The Deep Forest!' Blood sprayed Torak's face as the man brandished his stump. *They cut off my hand!*

'You'd be mad to go in there,' snarled the man as Renn finished binding his stump. He'd stopped shaking, but whenever an ember cracked, he cringed.

He said his name was Gaup of the Salmon Clan. His parka and leggings were muddy fish-skin lined with squirrel fur, and one cheek bore the sinuous tattoo of his clan. Around his neck he wore a band of sweat-blackened salmon-skin, and small fish bones were braided into his fair hair, reminding Torak of Bale.

'And it was Deep Forest people who did this?' said Fin-Kedinn. He sat with his back against a rock, haggard, breathing through clenched teeth.

'They swore that if they saw me again, it'd be my head.'

'But they made sure you survived,' said Renn. 'They seared the wound with hot stone so that you wouldn't bleed to death.'

'So I should thank them?' retorted Gaup.

'How about thanking Renn for sewing up your stump?' said Torak.

Gaup glared. He hadn't thanked Torak either, for helping him to the shelter and giving him food and water. And Torak hadn't missed the smear of ash on the heel of his boot.

Out loud, Torak said, 'When you were in the Deep Forest, did you see a man in a dugout? A big man, very strong.'

'What do I care about that?' snapped Gaup. 'I was looking for my child! Four summers old, and they took her!'

Torak glanced at Renn. She'd had the same thought. Soul-Eaters took children as hosts for demons. To make tokoroths.

Fin-Kedinn shifted position. Torak could see that his thoughts were racing. 'To cut off a hand,' he said, 'that's a punishment from the bad times after the Great Wave. The clans forbade it long ago. Who did this to you?'

'The Auroch Clan.'

'*What?*' The Raven Leader was incredulous.

'I thought they were going to help me,' said Gaup. 'They gave me food. Told me to rest by their fire. Then they said I was in league with the Forest Horses. Accused *me* of stealing one of *their* children.'

More stolen children, thought Torak. Thiazzi's flight to the Deep Forest seemed to be turning into something else.

'They said the Forest Horses started it,' Gaup went on. 'The Forest Horses planted a curse stick, and claimed the land between the Blackwater and the Windriver as their range. The Aurochs burnt the curse stick. Then the Forest Horse Mage died of a sickness, and the new Mage found a dart in the corpse. Now all the clans have taken sides. Everyone has to wear a headband: green for Auroch and Lynx, brown for Forest Horse and Bat.' He peered suspiciously at Torak's buckskin headband.

'When you were with the Aurochs,' said Torak, 'was there a big man among them?'

'Why do you keep asking?' said Gaup. Awkwardly, he crawled towards the doorway. 'I've wasted enough time, I'm going to fetch my clan. We'll *make* them give her back!'

'Gaup, wait,' commanded Fin-Kedinn. 'We'll go together. You and me.'

Renn and Torak stared at him. So did Gaup.

'We'll find your clan,' said the Raven Leader, 'and we'll

find mine. We'll get your daughter back – without shedding more blood.'

'How?' demanded Gaup. 'They won't listen, they're not *like* us!'

'Gaup,' Fin-Kedinn said firmly. 'This is what we will do.'

Gaup's shoulders sagged. Suddenly he was just an injured man who needed someone else to make the decisions.

After that, things happened fast. Torak fetched one of the canoes, and he and Renn helped Fin-Kedinn down to the river. Renn made him as comfortable as she could in the canoe, giving him willow bast to chew against fever, and hazelnuts to keep up his strength. Torak could see that she was sick with worry.

'How will you manage?' she asked her uncle when Gaup was out of earshot.

'We're heading downriver,' said Fin-Kedinn. 'The current will take us.'

'And if Gaup gets ill and is too weak to paddle?'

'He'll be all right,' Torak told her. 'You're a better healer than you think.'

'You only say that because you want this,' she retorted. 'Because it leaves you free to hunt Thiazzi.'

Torak did not reply. She was right.

Renn threw him a look and marched up to the canoe. 'I'm coming with you,' she told Fin-Kedinn.

'No,' he said. 'Torak needs you more.'

Torak was astonished. 'You'd let her come with me? After I nearly got you killed when I didn't see that trap?'

'You made a mistake,' said Fin-Kedinn. 'Don't make another.'

'But you can barely walk!' cried Renn. 'What if something happens? What if . . . ' She couldn't bring herself to go on.

'Renn,' said Fin-Kedinn. 'Can't you see that there's more at stake now than me or you or Torak? Thiazzi isn't merely hiding in the Deep Forest, he's up to something. It's Torak's destiny to stop him. He'll need your help.'

He spoke in the tone that brooked no refusal, and Renn didn't argue. But soon afterwards she ran off, unable to watch him leave.

'What will you do?' Torak asked his foster father when she'd gone.

'Try to stop a war,' said Fin-Kedinn.

War. Torak hardly knew what it meant. 'You think it's as bad as that?'

'Don't you? The Deep Forest clans no longer trust the Open, not after the sickness and the demon bear. If the Salmon Clan moves against them, it could be the spark that lights the tinder.' A spasm of pain took hold, and he gripped the side of the canoe. 'Listen to me, Torak. Find the Red Deer Clan. For your mother's sake, they'll help you. If you can't find them, find the Auroch Mage. His clan acted savagely, but I'm certain he didn't sanction it. I know him. He's a good man.'

Gaup returned, impatient to be off, and Torak helped him into the canoe.

'Find your mother's clan,' repeated Fin-Kedinn. 'Till you do, stay hidden. Climb trees if you have to; Deep Forest people are like deer, they seldom look up. And do *not* harm any of the black forest horses. The black ones are sacred. It's forbidden even to touch them.' Then he did something he'd never done before. He grasped Torak's hand.

Torak couldn't speak. Fa had done the same thing as he lay dying.

'Torak . . . ' The blue eyes pierced his. 'You seek

vengeance. But don't let it take over your spirit.'

With his paddle, Gaup pushed the canoe away from the bank, forcing Torak to let go of his foster father's hand.

'Vengeance burns, Torak,' said Fin-Kedinn as the river bore him away. 'It burns your heart. It makes the pain worse. Don't let that happen to you.'

Renn had run up the slope towards the shelter. She couldn't bear to watch the Blackwater take her uncle away.

Then she'd changed her mind and raced down again. She was too late. Fin-Kedinn had gone.

In a daze, she went back to the shelter. She shouldered her sleeping-sack, quiver and bow, and stamped out the fire. She told herself that Gaup would get Fin-Kedinn safely back to the clan. But the truth was anything could happen. Fin-Kedinn might succumb to a fever, or start bleeding inside. Gaup might abandon him. She might never see him again.

When she reached the river, Torak was gone, probably to fetch the other canoe. She couldn't face doing nothing, so she dumped her sleeping-sack and stumbled along the trail that led to the Deep Forest.

She stopped well short of the gaping jaws. The mist had lifted, and the rocks glittered in the sun. To her left, a slope of alders and birch whispered secrets. To her right, the Blackwater snaked slyly past. Twenty paces ahead, the spruce trees of the Deep Forest warded her back. They were taller than their Open Forest sisters, and beneath their mossy arms, shadows shifted ceaselessly.

Torak had once reached the borders of the Deep Forest, but Renn had never been this close. It filled her with dread.

The Deep Forest was different. Its trees were more awake, its clans more suspicious; it was said to shelter creatures which had long since vanished elsewhere. And in summer, the World Spirit stalked its valleys as a tall man with the antlers of a stag.

Out of nowhere, Rip and Rek swooped, startling her. Then they were off, disappearing into the sky with caws of alarm.

Renn couldn't see anything wrong, but just in case, she moved off the trail, behind a juniper bush.

At the edge of the Deep Forest, the shadows beneath the spruce trees coalesced – and became a man. Then another. And another.

Renn held her breath.

The hunters emerged without making a sound. Their wovenbark clothes were mottled brown and green, like leaves on the Forest floor; Renn found it hard to tell where men ended and trees began. Each hunter wore a green headband – she couldn't remember whose side that was – and each head was obscured by a fine green net. These hunters had no faces. They were not human.

One raised his hand, his green-stained fingers flickering in a complex signal that meant nothing to Renn. The others headed up the slope to her left.

A hunter passed within a few paces of where she crouched. She saw his thin slate axe and his long green bow. She smelt tallow and wood-ash, and caught the glint of eyes behind the net. She saw how it sucked in and out where the mouth should be.

From the Deep Forest, another faceless hunter emerged, this one carrying a spear. When he was five paces from Renn, he thrust it into the ground with such force that it quivered.

At head height, the spear-shaft bore a bundle of leaves which Renn recognized as poisonous nightshade. From this dangled something dark, the size of a fist.

The hunter shook the spear to make sure that it was firmly planted, and walked back into the Deep Forest.

Renn's gorge rose.

The thing hanging from the spear *was* a fist. It was Gaup's severed hand.

The meaning of the curse stick was clear. *The way is shut.*

Renn couldn't take her eyes off the hand. She thought about living the rest of her life like Gaup. Unable ever to use her bow again . . .

A movement to her right.

Her heart lurched.

Torak was walking up the trail towards her.

NINE

Sweat slid down Renn's sides.

Torak was walking up the trail, looking for her. He hadn't seen the hunters on the slope, the trees blocked his view, and for the same reason, the hunters hadn't seen him. But they would, in about fifteen paces, when he reached that patch of sunlight where a fallen birch had left a gap.

Quiet as cloudshadow, the hunters spread across the slope, melting into wind-tossed shade and sun-dappled leaves. Renn dared not shout or make the redstart warning call. She couldn't throw a stone at Torak without standing up.

Suddenly, he stopped. He'd seen the curse stick.

Swiftly, he stepped off the trail, and kept moving, getting closer to the gap.

Renn had no choice. She had to warn him, despite the

risk. She whistled the redstart call.

Torak vanished in the bushes.

She felt rather than saw the hunters turn towards her. Like well-aimed spears, their gaze converged on her hiding-place. How had they known it wasn't a real bird? She'd added the uplift at the end which she and Torak used to distinguish it, but no-one else had ever noticed that. They must be unbelievably observant. And suspicious.

The hunters started down the slope towards her.

Her mind darted in panic. Her body ached to run, but she knew that her only hope was not to move. Keep still, wait till they were almost upon her – *then* run like a hare, jump in the river – and pray to the guardian.

They were spreading out to surround her. She tensed to run.

Another redstart whistle, behind them on the slope.

The blank heads turned.

There it was again. It had to be Torak. Renn recognized the uplift at the end. Somehow, he'd found his way behind them.

Holding her breath, she watched them climb towards the sound.

Again the call came, but this time it was in the reeds by the river. How could that be? Torak couldn't have moved that fast.

Suddenly a shadow swept over her, and Rek alighted in an alder near the curse stick, whistling like a redstart.

The hunters paused. Painted fingers flickered in silent speech. They started down, heading for the tree where the raven perched. They passed within three paces of Renn's juniper without sensing her presence. Their ferocious intent blasted her like heat.

Rek gave another perfect imitation of the redstart

signal, and as they drew near, she flew off with a harsh raven laugh.

Silently, the faceless hunters watched her go. Then they headed up the trail and vanished into the Deep Forest.

'Are you all right?' said Torak, grasping her shoulder.

Renn nodded. She was shaking, clenching her teeth to stop them chattering.

'Let's get out of here,' muttered Torak.

They retreated to an alder thicket. 'They'll have found our tracks,' said Renn when she could trust herself to speak. 'They'll know we're here.'

Torak shook his head. 'They'll think we went with Fin-Kedinn.' He told her how he'd left the remaining canoe downstream, judging it too conspicuous to take into the Deep Forest, and had hidden their gear and covered their tracks.

'How did you know they'd come?' said Renn.

'I didn't. Didn't even know they were there till I heard you call. But I got used to covering my tracks when I was outcast. Come on. I'm hungry. Last chance for hot food.'

It hadn't occurred to Renn that once they were in the Deep Forest, they'd have to do without fire. Feeling childish and ignorant, she went off to forage. They ought to save their supplies for the days ahead; at least she'd thought of that.

When she got back, Torak had woken up a fire. He'd set it under a rock facing away from the Deep Forest, and used only small, dry pieces of beech, without the bark, so that it burned almost without smoke.

Renn thought, he learned these things when he was

outcast. It made her feel as if she didn't really know him.

Food steadied her a bit. She made a stew of chickweed, bittercress and bramble shoots, with meaty spring mushrooms, and woodpigeon eggs and snails baked in the embers. The snails were particularly delicious, as they'd been feeding on crow garlic.

While they ate, Rip and Rek took their morning bath in the shallows, flicking water over themselves with their wings, and splashing Wolf, who'd returned from hunting and lay on the bank, pretending not to notice.

Renn gave Rek a peeled egg and whispered her thanks. Then to Torak, 'Who *were* those people?'

'Aurochs, I think. Green headbands, and one had a horn amulet.' He asked her about the spear in the trail, and she told him it was a curse stick. 'If you pass it without the proper charm, you fall sick and die. You can't *see* the curse, but it's there. It draws fever demons like moths to a flame.'

He thought about that. 'Can you get us past?'

The knot in her belly tightened. 'Maybe.' In fact, she doubted it. The Deep Forest had the best mages of all. She would be no match for them. 'But they won't rely on curse sticks,' she added. 'They'll keep watch.'

He didn't reply. Often, when he was working up to say something, he would run his thumb over the scar on his forearm. He was doing it now. 'Renn . . .'

'*Don't* say it,' she broke in.

'What?'

'He wasn't my kin, I don't have to go with you, it's too dangerous, I might get killed.'

He set his jaw. 'It *is* too dangerous. And it's not just them, it's me. Look what happened to Fin-Kedinn. Next time it could be you.'

She began to protest, but he talked over her. 'There's

something else. We were watched in the night. I found a trail and a pile of ash.'

'*Ash?*' She tried to conceal her alarm. 'Do you think it was Gaup?'

'I did at first. Now I'm not sure.'

She realized what he was doing. 'You're trying to put me off. Why must you always do this? Do you think it'll work? Do you think I'll say, Oh, well, in that case I'm going back to my clan?'

'That's what you should do. Yes.'

'Well I won't!'

He glared at her. In the morning light his face looked older. Ruthless. 'Renn. I warn you. I'll do whatever it takes to get Thiazzi.'

'Fine,' she retorted. 'Let's get started. We'll need a disguise. We're on the Aurochs' side of the river, so we'd better try to look like them.'

He gave a curt nod. 'Right,' he said.

'There,' said Renn. 'I defy even an Auroch to spot you now.' She was being very practical and brisk, but Torak wasn't fooled. She was as scared as he was.

Over the winter, Fin-Kedinn had taught them a few tricks about concealment. It had taken all afternoon to put them into practice. Renn turned out to be extremely good at it, which Torak found unnerving. She seemed to have a Mage's skill for making things appear other than what they were.

First, she'd made a greenish-brown stain of lichen and river clay, taking the clay from below the waterline, so that no-one would notice. She'd mixed it with wood-ash and the marrowfat salve, to mask their scent and make it waterproof. Then she'd unpicked her clan-creature feathers and tucked them inside her jerkin, and they'd daubed the stain on each other's faces, throats, hands and clothes, dappling it in blotches: some light, some darkened with charcoal.

They knew from clan meets that Aurochs daubed their scalps with yellow clay to resemble bark, so they tucked their hair inside their parkas and did the same. They didn't have time to make nets for their faces, so they simply stained Torak's headband green and made one for Renn. Next, they padded their quivers with moss to prevent the arrows rattling, and agreed a new warning signal. Finally, Torak cut them hogweed breathing tubes, in case they had to hide underwater.

When it was done, Wolf approached Torak cautiously, gave a tentative sniff, and jerked back in alarm.

It's me, Torak told him in wolf talk.

Wolf flattened his ears and growled.

It's me. Come here.

Warily, Wolf moved closer.

Torak breathed softly on his muzzle, talking in wolf talk and person talk. It took a while before Wolf was reassured.

'He didn't know you,' Renn said in a strained voice.

Torak tried to smile, but his face felt stiff beneath its disguise. 'Do I look so different?'

'You look frightening.'

He met her eyes. 'So do you.' Her smooth green face was disturbingly like her mother's. She even moved differently. Her body, her hands, seemed fraught with mysterious power. He thought that if he touched her, he might burn his fingers.

'Do you think it'll work?' she said.

He cleared his throat. 'At a distance, maybe. Not up

close. The best defence will be – '

'Not getting caught.' She flashed him her sharp-toothed grin, and was Renn again.

Dusk fell, and the half-eaten moon rose above the trees. Moths flitted among glowing white campions. High in a spruce tree, Torak heard the hungry cheeping of woodpecker nestlings.

'Now for the charm,' said Renn.

In the faint moonlight, Gaup's severed hand turned slowly on its cord. It should have been crawling with ants and flies, but there were none. Such was the power of the curse that no creature would touch it.

Torak stood watch with Wolf, while Renn approached the curse stick, keeping to the shadows and placing her feet on dock leaves to obscure her prints. She clutched a bundle of wormwood and rowan twigs, and as she squatted near the stick, she muttered the charm and struck the spear-shaft over and over with the bundle.

The river flowed more quietly. The trees stilled to listen. Torak felt the curse hanging heavy in the air. He worried that Renn was too close; that it might be seeping into her skin.

She broke off with a gasp. 'I can't,' she whispered.

'Yes you can!' he urged.

'I'm not strong enough.'

He waited.

She went on. At last, she heaved a ragged sigh, rose, and threw the bundle in the river.

'Did it work?' said Torak.

'I don't know. We'll soon find out.'

They withdrew, taking care to brush away their tracks. It seemed to Torak that a tension had leached from the darkness.

Wolf padded towards the curse stick and sat gazing up at the bloody hand. Without warning, he seized it in his jaws, worried it to make sure it was dead, and trotted off to eat in peace. Soon afterwards, they heard a flurry in the undergrowth and an irritable growl; then Rip and Rek flew off, each bearing a finger in their beaks.

Torak unclenched his fists. 'I think it worked.'

'Maybe,' said Renn.

They went to fetch their gear.

'We'll go in after moonset,' said Torak.

Renn didn't reply, but he knew what she was thinking. They still had no plan for getting past any watching Aurochs.

Above him in the spruce tree, the woodpecker nestlings called tirelessly for food. Torak saw that their parents had been clever, pecking the hole under a bracket mushroom which made a roof to keep off the rain, and choosing a hollow tree riddled with more holes, so they'd have lots of escape routes if a marten attacked. He remembered Fin-Kedinn's lessons on concealment. *The first rule is to learn from other creatures.*

The male woodpecker flew in with nightmeal for his children, spotted Torak, and sped to another tree some distance away, where he perched, calling loudly, kik-kik-kik! *Not that tree, this one!*

'I think,' said Torak, 'I've got an idea.'

The moon had set, the wind had dropped. The trees stood breathless. Waiting.

Torak knelt beside Wolf and told him in wolf talk that they needed to hide from everyone, but were still hunting the Bitten One. He wasn't sure if he got it across.

Rising to his feet, he nodded at Renn. She nodded back.

Keeping off the trail, they started upriver. They passed the curse stick. They drew level with the great stone jaws.

A squirrel scampered up a tree. A roe buck fled, flashing its white rump.

Good, thought Torak. Maybe the Aurochs aren't so close.

Maybe.

Renn walked beside him, silent as a shadow. Wolf's paws made no sound.

The spruce trees waited for them, their arms dripping with dark clots of moss.

Torak paused. He thought of the Oak Mage. He thought of Bale. He took a breath and entered the Deep Forest.

TEN

olf's hackles rose. Torak glanced at Renn to make
sure that she'd seen. She had.

Bitten One, said Wolf.

Near? said Torak.

Many lopes.

Torak bent close to Renn. 'He's picked up Thiazzi's trail,'
he whispered, 'but he's far away.'

'And still no Aurochs?'

He shook his head.

She was puzzled. So was he. They'd been creeping
between the shadowy trees for ever, following the river
upstream, but staying well back from its banks. So far, no
sign of Aurochs. The trees, though . . . Roots snagged
Torak's boots. Twig fingers brushed his face. It was warmer
in the Deep Forest. The air smelt greener, more alive. Bats

flitted overhead, and the undergrowth stirred with secret rustlings. Moss dripped from every branch and log and boulder – as if, thought Torak, a great green tide had drowned the Forest and then receded. And behind it all, he felt the immense, watching presence of the trees.

Wolf turned aside and ran to an ash tree. Rising on his hind legs, he put both forepaws on the trunk and sniffed a low-hanging branch. *Odd*, he told Torak with a twitch of his whiskers.

Torak touched the branch. His fingers came away slimy, smelling strangely of earth.

Renn pointed to the branch. *What is it?*

He shook his head, wiping his hand on his leggings and wishing he hadn't touched it. Deep Forest clans were known for their skill with poisons.

They reached a grove of murmuring alders. As they entered, the trees fell silent, as if they didn't want to be overheard.

Wolf halted and snuffed the air.

Bitten One. Over the Wet.

Torak was still taking that in when Wolf lowered his head.

Den.

Beyond the alders, Torak glimpsed shadows moving in blackness. Bulky shapes that might be shelters.

'Camp!' Renn breathed in his ear.

'And Wolf says Thiazzi is *across* the river, in Forest Horse territory.'

'We have to go back,' she urged, 'cross downstream.'

That risked confusing Wolf and losing Thiazzi's trail, but they had no choice. They started to backtrack.

At least, they tried, but Torak got the sense that they'd lost their way. The gurgle of the river seemed fainter, and he caught the sharp, unmistakeable scent of crow garlic, which they hadn't encountered on the way in.

He strained to pierce the gloom. A dock leaf skewered on a twig glimmered in starlight. A whisper of air cooled his cheek as an owl or a bat swept past.

That leaf.

He stopped so abruptly that Renn walked into him.

'What is it?'

'Not sure. *Don't* move.'

That twig could not have speared the leaf by chance. It pierced the leaf blade like a needle, straight down its length, to the right of the midrib. It had to be a signal.

To the right of the midrib.

He glanced to his right, saw only a dim lattice of branches.

There.

Ahead, to the right, a sapling had been bent back and secured by a deft arrangement of crossed sticks. Mounted at its tip was a vicious spike. From the crossed sticks, near-invisible, a rope stretched across his path at chest height. Another step and he would have sprung the trap, releasing the sapling and sending the spike plunging into his side.

Torak licked his lips. They tasted chalky from the disguise. He showed Renn the trap. Her hand went to her shoulder, where her clan-creature feathers had been.

They had to push through junipers to get around the trap, which had been cunningly set between the thorny bushes, to drive its victim towards it. When they were through, Renn hissed, 'This isn't the way we came.'

'I know. And it was sheer luck I spotted that trap.' He didn't need to say it: how many more lay in wait?

Wolf turned his head towards the river, and they followed his gaze. Did that shadow just move?

A moment later, starlight glinted on a spearhead.

The Auroch hunter was maybe twenty paces away, walking upstream. Torak and Renn sank into the bracken – slowly, so as not to attract attention by sudden movement. Torak's mind raced. Upriver lay the Auroch camp. Downriver, the way back to the Open Forest, and maybe more lethal traps. On the riverbank, at least one Auroch hunter was keeping watch.

Renn voiced his thoughts. 'We'll have to try your plan right here.'

'Could you make the shots?'

'I think so. If we climb a tree.'

He nodded.

Renn found a tall lime that looked easier to climb than the others, as it had an odd snake of thickened bark rippling down its trunk. 'Lightning-struck,' she murmured, 'but it survived. Maybe that'll bring us luck.'

We'll need it, thought Torak. His plan was simple, and if it worked, their decoys would draw the Aurochs north, away from the Blackwater, allowing them to slip across.

If it worked. He was losing faith fast.

Linking his hands, he boosted Renn into the tree. Then he knelt and told Wolf to stay close, to come back in the Light – and be alert for traps.

Wolf's breath warmed his face as his muzzle brushed his eyelids. *Stay safe, pack-brother*, he told Torak.

He was so trusting. And Torak was leading him into terrible danger.

On impulse, Torak took his medicine horn from its pouch, shook out a little earthblood, and daubed it on Wolf's forehead, where he couldn't lick if off. *Stay safe, pack-brother*, he said. Putting his hand on the lime's rough bark, he begged the Forest to protect Wolf.

The lightning scar was thicker than his wrist, and he climbed it like a rope. He felt the tree sensing their presence. He asked it not to give them away. Below him, Wolf's silver eyes glowed. Then he vanished into the dark.

Huddled in a fork made by three great limbs, Torak and Renn kept their sleeping-sacks rolled, relying on their reindeer-hide clothes to stay warm. 'We'll wait here till morning,' whispered Torak, 'less chance of being seen.' And less chance of escape if they *were* seen, but neither of them mentioned that.

Renn pointed to a tall spruce north of the Aurochs' camp. Its upper branches spiked the stars; they should catch the rising sun. From her quiver she drew one of the arrows she'd prepared.

As she took aim, her face tensed with concentration. Her disguise made her alien: as if, thought Torak, she'd become Deep Forest.

Her bow creaked. She lowered it again. The night was too quiet. The Aurochs might hear the twang.

At last a gust of wind woke the trees. She took aim and let fly. The arrow struck the spruce and its burden swung free on the cord tied to the shaft. Renn nocked another arrow and hit another tree, further east; then another and another, each time waiting for the breeze to cover the sound.

Now they had to wait till dawn, and hope the plan worked.

They didn't have another.

In the darkness, firelight flared.

Renn gripped Torak's arm. The Auroch camp was much

closer than they'd thought.

High in the lime tree, they watched tall figures moving with the silent purposefulness of ants. Several gathered round a tree in the centre of camp, smearing something dark on its lower branches. Two more knelt to waken another fire.

Torak was mystified. Why waken one from scratch when you could take a burning branch from the first? And they weren't using strike-fires. One man spun a stick between his palms, drilling it into a piece of wood on the ground which he held down with one foot, while he kept the drill straight by means of a cross-bar clamped between his teeth. It worked. Smoke curled. The second man fed the flames beard-moss, then kindling. When the fire was fully awake, everyone knelt and touched their foreheads to the ground.

More Aurochs emerged from the Forest. Torak counted five, seven, ten. Each man – and they were all men – bore an axe, a bow, two knives, and a shield: a narrow, arm-length wedge of wood, whose pointed end he thrust into the earth, before drawing off his netting hood to reveal a caked head and bizarrely ridged and furrowed face.

Torak broke out in a cold sweat. Gaup was right. These people were different.

And yet they were setting spits over the fires, and soon he smelt the delicious, familiar smell of roasting woodgrouse, weirdly at odds with the silent camp.

'Why don't they speak?' he whispered.

'I think it's to make them more tree-like,' breathed Renn. 'That's what Deep Forest people want above all: to be like the trees.'

'I can see more shields down there than men.'

She nodded and held up three fingers. Three hunters

still out there, stalking the Forest. They'd been right to climb the lime.

They took turns to stay awake. A thin rain pattered into Torak's dreams, and the Forest became a dark, soughing sea where night birds flitted like fishes. From far away came the oo-hu, oo-hu of an eagle owl.

Renn was shaking his shoulder. 'Dawn soon.'

He blinked, kneading cramp from his calf. The day was blustery, with a dry south wind. Chaffinches and warblers were already in full voice, the woodpigeons just beginning.

'I hope Rip and Rek are still asleep,' muttered Renn. 'The last thing we need is a raven greeting.'

Torak tried to smile. He thought it less and less likely that their plan would work. Even if it did, they'd have only a brief chance to swim the Blackwater; and then they'd be in Forest Horse territory. And all the time, Thiazzi was getting away.

Grey light seeped into camp, and Torak made out humped shelters around the central beech.

He peered at it. It couldn't be. Those lower branches were *red*. It wasn't the morning sun, the branches themselves – bark, twigs, leaves – had been daubed all over with earthblood. Why, he thought, would anyone paint an entire branch red?

No time to wonder. The sun was rising. Soon they must be on the move.

To the north, something glittered in the tall spruce tree. And there, further east. Renn flashed him an edgy grin. So far, the plan was working. The flint flakes they'd tied to her arrowshafts shimmered and clinked in the wind.

The Aurochs had seen them. Men were pointing, running for weapons and shields.

Swiftly, Torak and Renn climbed down to earth. Wolf appeared, his fur wet with dew. They headed for the river.

Willows overhung the Blackwater, holding in the night. There was no sign of Aurochs. Torak prayed that they'd all been drawn by the decoys. Yanking off their boots and tying them to their sleeping-sack rolls, they made their way down the bank and into the reeds, moving cautiously, so as not to startle any water birds into betraying them. The shallows were choked with leafy saplings felled by a flood further upstream.

'Good cover,' murmured Renn.

They risked strained smiles. Maybe this was going to work.

Bracing themselves for the cold, they waded into the river. Torak's feet sank into a freezing slime of dead leaves, and he saw Renn's stained lips tighten in disgust. He grabbed a floating sapling for cover. She did the same. They swam after Wolf, who was already halfway across.

The Blackwater wasn't as sleepy as it looked. It was a struggle to resist its stealthy underwater pull.

Suddenly Wolf veered, and came swimming *towards* them, his ears pinned back in alarm.

'What's *that?*' whispered Renn.

Torak's belly turned over. Those logs in midstream: they were floating *upriver*. And some of them had eyes.

One raised its head. Torak saw a fierce green face tattooed with leaves. A brown headband. Long hair braided with horse tails.

A Forest Horse raiding party. Heading straight for them.

ELEVEN

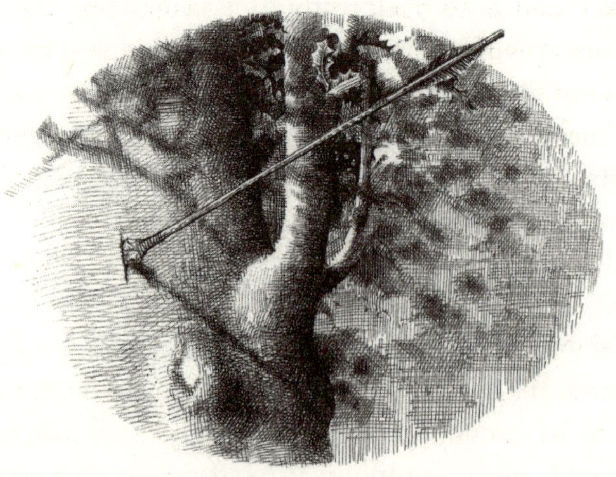

'Get underwater, head back to the bank,' Torak told
Renn just before he dived. He couldn't find the
breathing tube in his belt. Too bad, he'd hold his breath.
He only hoped Renn had heard him.

She had. She surfaced soon after he did in the same
patch of reeds, and they waited, gritting their teeth to stop
them chattering.

The Forest Horses hadn't seen them. The green men lay
on their bellies, paddling silently with their hands, knives
clamped between charcoal-blackened teeth.

Not far from Torak, Wolf hauled himself onto the bank
and shook himself noisily.

Eyes flicked sideways in leaf-tattooed faces, then back
again. A lone wolf was no concern of theirs.

The reeds gave good cover, allowing Torak and Renn to

crawl up the bank and get their bearings. Torak was shocked. The treacherous Blackwater had carried them *nearer* the camp, not further away.

Soaked and shivering, he wondered what to do. Any moment now, the Aurochs would realize they'd been tricked and head back to the river, spreading out to hunt the unknown intruders. He and Renn would be trapped between them and the Forest Horses.

Unless he could steer both sides away from them.

'Head downriver,' he told Renn in a whisper. 'Wait for me past that bend, I'll meet you there.'

Her eyes widened. 'Where are you going?'

'No time to explain! Watch out for traps!'

Telling Wolf to stay with the pack-sister, he started towards the Auroch camp. When he was as close as he dared, he crouched and whipped two arrows from his quiver. Then he took out his medicine horn and quickly smeared the arrowshafts with earthblood. He had no idea what those red branches meant to the Aurochs, but they were easy to spot, which was all that mattered.

Still crouching, he nocked the first arrow to his bow and waited.

He glimpsed a Forest Horse hunter coming ashore: stealthily, keeping upright so that the water ran noiselessly down his body rather than pattering on leaves.

Torak took aim. He wasn't as good a shot as Renn, but he didn't need to be. His arrow thudded into a holly a good distance away.

The tattooed head turned to follow it.

From the corner of his eye, Torak saw an Auroch hunter making for the river. His belly tightened. They were faster than he'd thought. He loosed his second red arrow and hit another tree.

Without waiting to see the response, he fled, running fast and low to where Renn was waiting. If his trick worked, both sides would make for those mysterious red arrows, and then . . .

Shouts behind him, a clash of spears. He felt a spurt of savage joy. The Aurochs were fighting the Forest Horses, leaving him and Renn to cross the river and hunt Thiazzi.

Renn's shadowy figure beckoned from a dense stand of spruce, and he grabbed her hand. Her grasp was hot as ash as she led him through the gloom to the hiding-place she'd found: the hollow ruin of an enormous oak.

Panting, he collapsed against the tree, and as her fingers slipped from his, he gave a shaky laugh. 'That was *too* close!'

No reply. He was alone in the tree.

Twenty paces away, Wolf emerged from a clump of willows, followed by Renn, dripping wet and furious. 'Where,' she whispered, 'in the name of the Spirit have you *been?*'

TWELVE

'Who *was* that?' hissed Torak.

'Who was who?' demanded Renn. His disappearence had shaken her badly, and she was struggling not to show it.

'Someone took my hand. I thought it was you.'

'Well it wasn't.'

He grabbed her hand. 'Yours is cold, the other was hot.'

'Of course I'm cold, I'm soaking wet! Where did you *go*?'

From the Auroch camp came shouts, a scream of pain.

'Tell you later,' said Torak. 'Let's get across while we can.'

Renn was so cold that the Blackwater felt almost warm. The sodden gear on her back weighed her down, and the river was strong. As she reached the midstream, it sucked her under. She kicked to the surface, spluttering and spitting out leaves. Torak and Wolf were ahead and didn't notice.

The south bank was a forbidding tangle of willows, and as she neared it, her spirit quailed. She pictured leaf-faced hunters taking aim. She thought, Out of the cooking-skin and into the fire.

If the others were frightened, they gave no sign. Wolf scrambled up the bank, shook vigorously, and started casting for Thiazzi's scent. Torak waded noiselessly towards the willows.

Watching him scan the trees, Renn shivered. His disguise made him a creature of the Deep Forest: a dark-faced stranger with cold silver eyes.

He flicked her a glance and nodded – *clear* – then vanished into the willows. As she struggled to free her leg from a tangle of waterweed, he reached out and pulled her in.

'There's no-one here,' he said. 'I think they've all crossed to attack the camp.'

Hastily they dried themselves with grass, stuffing more down their boots and inside their clothes, to warm up. Torak cut some horsetail and scrubbed the green stain off their headbands, while Renn tended her poor, soaked bow.

Wolf found the scent and started south, away from the river and into a boggy woodland of alders rising from brown pools. Renn thought of traps and curse sticks and invisible hunters, and said a prayer to the guardian.

It was difficult country. They had to jump from one clump of alders to the next, and edge along fallen tree-trunks squelchy with moss. The water was clogged with frogspawn. Renn fell in and came out beslimed.

She tried to convince herself that this was a forest just like the one where she'd grown up. She saw a spruce tree whose fissured trunk was studded with cones jammed in by woodpeckers, so they could peck at the seeds. Open Forest woodpeckers did that, too. She spotted a pile of leaves near a badger's sett; the badgers had been cleaning up after the winter, and had dragged out their old bedding. All familiar, she told herself.

It didn't work. The trees murmured that she didn't belong. The woodpeckers were black.

Torak had found something.

Beneath an ash tree, the earth had been scraped to make a muddy wallow. It was five paces across, far bigger than even an auroch would make. Wolf snuffed it eagerly. Torak pushed his muzzle aside to examine a huge, round hoof-print. 'Some kind of giant auroch?' he said.

Renn nodded. 'Fin-Kedinn says there are creatures here that survived the Great Cold. I think they're called bison.'

He frowned. 'So they're prey?'

'I think so. But sometimes they charge.'

In the distance, an owl hooted. Oo-hu, oo-hu.

Renn caught her breath. In her mind, she saw the dread wooden face of the Eagle Owl Mage.

Torak was thinking the same thing. 'Could they be working together?' he said in a low voice. 'Thiazzi *and* Eostra?'

Renn hesitated. 'I'm not so sure. He's selfish. He'll want the fire-opal for himself. Besides, Saeunn told me – she can't be certain, but she thinks Eostra is in the Mountains.'

'And yet her owl is in the Deep Forest,' said Torak.

Renn was silent. She watched him rise to his feet and look about. She could see from his expression that whether Eostra was here or not, he was undeterred. He would find Thiazzi.

'Torak,' she said. 'What happened at the Auroch camp?

What did you do?'

Briefly, he told her how he'd set the two clans against each other. It was clever, but his ruthlessness shocked her. 'But – people might have been killed,' she said.

'That might have happened anyway.'

'Maybe. Or maybe the Forest Horses were only scouting, you don't know.'

'I warned you. I said I'd do whatever it takes to get Thiazzi.'

'Starting fights? Getting people killed?'

Wolf glanced doubtfully from one to the other.

Torak ignored him. 'Last spring,' he said, 'everyone was hunting me. This time, *I'm* doing the hunting. I swore an oath, Renn. So yes. I am ruthless. And if you can't take that, don't come with me!'

They went on in silence. Renn resolved not to be the first to speak.

The ground climbed steadily, and black spruce gave way to beech. They waded through waist-high nettles and clambered over rotting tree-trunks blistered with poisonous mushrooms. Renn noticed that the trees were taller than in the Open Forest, which would make them harder to climb; and the wood-ants didn't build their nests only on the south side of the trunks, but all around, which would make it easier to get lost.

No sign of people.

And yet . . .

Behind her a branch swayed, as if someone had edged out of sight.

She put her hand to her knife-hilt.

The branch stilled. If it was Forest Horse hunters, she thought, we'd know it by now.

Torak had gone ahead, and was kneeling to talk to Wolf. She ran to catch up. 'I saw something!' she panted.

'And Wolf smelt something,' said Torak. 'He says it smells like the Bright Beast.'

'That means fire.'

'It also means ash. The one who took my hand . . . it felt hot.'

Their eyes met.

'Whatever grabbed my hand,' said Torak. 'It's followed us across the river.'

As the light began to fail, they decided to pitch camp under a yew tree.

They'd reached a valley where beavers had dammed a stream to make a narrow lake. Renn saw the beavers' lodge in the middle: a sturdy pile of branches, some streaked yellow where they'd gnawed off the bark. She guessed it was still occupied, as a few willows remained along the shore. Fin-Kedinn said that beavers liked to eat all the willows before moving on.

Thinking of Fin-Kedinn hurt. She tried to imagine him safely back with the Ravens, busy with the salmon run, but her mind showed him grey-faced, hunched in the canoe. Maybe the worms of sickness were already eating into his marrow. And no Renn to chase them away.

Torak went scouting with Wolf, so to take her mind off Fin-Kedinn, she left her gear under the yew and went to forage. At least the plants were familiar. She gathered handfuls of succulent saxifrage and sharp-tasting sorrel, and as they couldn't have a fire, she dug up spear thistle and silverweed roots, which they could eat raw.

Rip and Rek flew down, fluttering their wings and making famished gurgles, so she tossed them a couple of roots. Over the winter, she'd persuaded them to come when she called, but they would not yet perch on her shoulders, as they did with Torak.

Feeling slightly better, she went to refill the waterskins. The lake was sheened a dusty yellow with pollen, and around it, the trees leaned over to peer at their name-souls in the water. Renn held the skins down deep, to avoid scooping them up. It had never bothered her before, but here . . .

While the skins filled, she watched the ripples smoothing out, and wished Torak would come back and be Torak again: play tug-the-hide with Wolf, tease her about the freckle at the corner of her mouth. For the first time it struck her that his mother's father had been Oak Clan – which meant he was kin with Thiazzi. She wished she hadn't thought of that.

The waterskins were full. As she pulled them out, her name-soul stared back at her: an inscrutable, clay-headed Auroch.

A figure appeared behind it.

In one nightmare heartbeat, Renn took in clenched fists and a shock of long, pale hair.

With a cry she spun round.

Nothing. Just a stirring of willows, very close.

She whipped out her knife.

A branch creaked. Claws clattered on bark. She thought of tokoroths scurrying down trees, agile as spiders. She left the waterskins and raced back to camp.

Torak hadn't returned, but the ravens perched high in

the yew, cawing in distress. Her gear had been savagely attacked. Her quiver was slashed, its moss padding flung about, and most of her arrows had been snapped. Luckily, she'd hung her bow on the yew, and the attacker had missed it, but her sleeping-sack had been trampled into the dust, her tinder pouch cut to pieces, and her strike-fire smashed under a rock. Malice and rage throbbed in the air like sickness. And over everything lay a scattering of fine grey ash.

Drawing her axe, Renn backed against the yew. 'I'm not scared of you,' she told the shadows. Her voice sounded reedy and unconvincing.

Moments later, Torak and Wolf returned. Wolf raced to snuffle furiously at Renn's things. Torak's jaw dropped.

'I saw something at the lake,' she told him. 'Then this.'

'What did you see?'

'It had pale hair. It looked angry.'

He flinched.

'Do you know what it is?' she said.

'No, I – no.' He started searching for tracks, but the light was almost gone, and he didn't find any. 'Either it knows how to cover its tracks,' he said, 'or it doesn't leave any.'

'What do you mean? Torak, what *is* it?'

He chewed his lip. Then he stood up. 'Whatever it is, we're not sleeping on the ground.'

The yew didn't like being climbed. It choked them in clouds of pollen and tried to evade their grip by shedding bark. Twice, a branch whipped round and tried to throw them off. They were scratched and exhausted by the time they'd settled in its arms.

'The wind's getting up,' said Torak. 'We'd better tie ourselves to the trunk.'

Renn hung their damp, gritty sleeping-sacks to dry, and

peered down into the gloom. She saw Wolf silently pacing. She said, 'Let's hope Wolf and the ravens warn us of danger.'

Wolf ran in circles round the yew, bristling with disapproval. He *hated* it when the taillesses climbed trees. Why did they do this?

Normal wolves do not climb trees. And normal wolves *like* the Dark, it's their best time, when they run about and play. They do not curl up and sleep for ever.

Wolf hated it here. The Forest felt different. The trees were too alert and the smells were all mixed up. Some of the trees smelt of earth, while the taillesses who lived here smelt of trees. They were angry and scared, and although each pack had quite a big range, they fought; Wolf didn't know why. Worse still, Tall Tailless and the pack-sister had changed their overpelts and even their smells, so that Wolf hardly knew them.

His sleeps were troubled by the scratching of demon claws and the cries of eagle owls, and sometimes when he woke up, he caught the nose-biting scent of the tailless who smelt of the Bright Beast. This tailless worried Wolf a lot, because its mind was broken, so he couldn't sense what it wanted.

The scent of the broken-minded tailless was thick in Wolf's nose as he prowled the yew's roots, but he sensed that the tailless itself was gone. Maybe it also climbed trees. Wolf decided to stay close, in case it came back.

In the Up, the Bright White Eye was half-open, sleepily watching over her many little cubs. Wolf stalked a weasel, but it got away. He caught a moth, but it made him sneeze, so he spat it out. And still the taillesses slept.

Suddenly, Wolf pricked his ears. Further down the valley, the ravens were cawing. They'd found a roe deer which was Not-Breath, they wanted Wolf to come and rip it open, so that they could feed.

Wolf wondered what to do. He had to stay and guard the taillesses.

But he was hungry.

THIRTEEN

As night deepened, the other inhabitants of the Forest emerged.

Bats flitted from hollows in the yew. A grey owl settled on the end of Torak's branch, its body swaying, its moonlit eyes fixed on his. He stared back till it flew away.

It was a blustery night and the trees were wide awake.

So was he.

Who – or what – had attacked Renn's gear? Was it Bale's vengeful spirit, or something else? *An ash-haired hunter burning inside.* Saeunn's prophecy could mean anything.

Straining at the rope that bound him to the trunk, he twisted round to see if Renn was awake on the other side. She was curled up like a squirrel, fast asleep.

He ached to be on the move. Somewhere in these secret valleys, Thiazzi was hiding; and the trail was getting cold.

Not even Wolf could follow it much longer.

On the ground, branches rustled as something large pushed its way through. Torak couldn't see anything, but as the creature drew nearer, he heard munching and huffing breath. Then a darkness like a walking boulder passed beneath him. He glimpsed massive, humped shoulders; an enormous head with short, half-moon horns.

Bison.

He watched the creature lean against the yew's trunk and give itself a luxuriant scratching that made the whole tree shiver. Then, with a deep, satisfied grunt, it ambled off.

Soon afterwards, Torak caught the familiar tail-swish of horses. As the herd moved beneath him, he glimpsed a wobbly foal duck beneath its mother's belly to suckle; a young mare nibble-grooming the mane of an older one whose scarred rump showed her to be the survivor of many a hunt. He felt a settling of awe. Unlike the dun-coloured horses of the Open Forest, these were as black as a moonless night.

Renn mumbled in her sleep, and the lead mare jerked up her head. The sacred herd melted into the darkness like a dream.

The Forest felt lonely after they'd gone. Torak wished Wolf and the ravens would return.

The wind strengthened and the trees creaked and moaned. He wondered what they were saying. If he knew their speech, they could tell him where to find Thiazzi.

The thought dropped into his mind like a pebble into a Forest pool. *Become one of them. Spirit walk.*

He wondered if he dared. Trees are the most mysterious of beings. They harbour fire and give life to all, yet eat only sunlight. Alone among creatures, they grow a new limb when one is lost. Some never sleep, while others slumber naked through the cruellest winter. They witness the scurrying lives of hunters and prey, but keep their own thoughts hidden.

Torak wrenched open his medicine pouch and sought the piece of black root he'd kept secret even from Renn. Saeunn had given it to him. *For when you need it*, she'd said.

He chewed fast. Bitterness flooded his mouth. The root was potent. Before he'd swallowed it, a sharp pain pierced his guts. Waves of cramp took hold, and he doubled up, the rope cutting into his midriff. He began to be afraid. He should wake Renn. But the rawhide held him. He couldn't reach.

The cramps were coming faster, a relentless tide sucking at his souls. He opened his mouth to call Renn's name . . .

. . . and his voice was the groaning of bark and the roaring of branches. His twig-fingers knew the chill moonlight and the wind's screaming caress, his boughs the scratch of wasp and the weight of sleeping boy and girl. Deep in the earth, his roots knew the burrowing moles and the soft, blind worms, and all was good, for he was *tree*, and he rejoiced in the wildness of the night.

Lost in the coursing tree-blood, the speck of spirit that was Torak begged it to tell him where to find Thiazzi. The yew gave a sigh and lifted him out into the night.

Helpless as a spark borne by a rushing wind, Torak was carried through the Forest on a soughing sea of voices, from yew to holly, from seedling to sapling to mighty oak, faster than wolf can lope or raven fly. Terror seized him. Too far, he thought, you'll never get back!

When at last he came to rest, his tree-fingers knew the icy winds sweeping down from the High Mountains. He was in the golden tree-blood of another yew, but this one was old beyond imagining, ancient as the Forest itself. His boughs speared stars, his roots split stone and trapped demons in the Otherworld. His limbs sheltered owl and marten, squirrel and bat. To the creatures who dwelt in him, he was the world, but to the Great Yew their lives were as brief as the trembling of a leaf, and long after they were gone, he would endure.

Lost in the vast awareness, Torak felt the prick of tokoroth claws on his bark. He heard demons howling for the fiery stone that was almost within their reach. Flames seared his branches. He sensed the Oak Mage circling, chanting spells.

The Oak Mage raised his arms to the sky. *I am the truth and the Way. I am master of fire. I am ruler of the Forest!*

The wind rose and the voice of the Great Yew rose with it. Torak was drowning in voices, all the trees of the Forest rising, swelling to an obliterating roar, tearing him apart . . .

'Torak!' whispered Renn. 'Torak! Wake up!'

His head turned, but she could see that he didn't know her. His eyes were empty and unseeing, no souls inside.

No souls. He was spirit walking.

He had woken her by wrenching himself free from the rope, and now he knelt on his branch, swaying, muttering. She was terrifed that he would step into nothingness and break his neck.

She edged round to his side of the trunk. He was out of reach. She stayed where she was, afraid of startling him.

At last he spoke, in a hollow voice that was not his own. 'I am the Great Yew,' he told the rushing wind. 'I am older than the Forest. I began amid the roots of the First Tree. I was seedling when the last snows of the Long Cold melted into the earth; sapling at the coming of the Wave. I have never known sleep. But I have known anger . . .'

Renn didn't know what to do. Her Magecraft wasn't strong enough to call back his souls. Praying to the guardian, she stretched out her hand.

Torak rose on his branch and began to walk.

Pain jolted him awake: a raven beak, tugging at his earlobe.

He was dizzy. The wind was blowing in his face, the trees roaring in his head.

'Torak!' Renn's voice came to him from far away. 'Torak, look at me. Only at me. *Don't move!*'

The raven lifted off his shoulder and he staggered. Beneath him, the ground swayed.

Not the ground. *The branch.* He stood on the end of the branch, his hands clawing empty air.

'Look at me,' commanded Renn. She crouched near the bole of the tree, one hand gripping the rope that circled the trunk, the other straining towards him. *'Do not look down.'*

He looked down. A dizzying drop. Far below, on the yew's snake-like roots, something squatted. He saw ashen hair and a pale, upturned face. He swayed.

Renn's voice called him back. 'Torak. Come – to – me.' Her dark eyes drew him.

He sank to his knees and crawled towards her.

'You don't remember *anything?*' said Renn.

Torak shook his head. He was shaking and sick, worse than she'd ever seen him. It had been all she could do to get him down from the tree.

'Not untying the rope or crawling onto the branch? Nothing?'

'Nothing,' he mumbled.

At last she got the waterskin open. 'Here. You'll feel better.'

He didn't respond. He sat with his back against the yew, staring into its branches.

The wind had dropped, and dawn was coming. Rip and Rek perched in the lower boughs, sleeping off the horse meat Renn had given them to say thank you. She doubted if Torak even saw them. There was a strange, shattered light in his eyes, and when she looked closer, she saw that they were no longer a pure light-grey. In their depths were tiny flecks of green.

'I saw him,' he said. 'I saw Thiazzi. He's near the Mountains. Making spells. He thinks he can rule the Forest.' He rolled onto all fours and retched.

When it was over, he collapsed against the tree. 'I thought I'd never get back.'

'What do you mean?'

He shut his eyes. 'When you spirit walk in a raven – or a bear or an elk – you stay in that creature. But the trees – they're not separate. For them, thinking, talking, spirit walking, it's all the same thing. From tree to tree, ash to beech to holly, it passes between them. Faster, further, than you could ever imagine.' He clutched his temples. 'So many *voices!*

Renn could only watch helplessly. What worried her most was that this time, while he was spirit walking, his body had moved. That had never happened before.

She knew that people do sometimes sleepwalk, if their name-soul slips out during a dream. The body wanders, trying to find the errant soul, and usually they get back together before either has left the shelter. But she had no idea what this might mean for Torak.

'Why did you do it, Torak? Why spirit walk now?'

He opened his eyes. 'To find Thiazzi.' He hesitated. 'I see him, Renn. Sometimes it's a flash of fair hair. Sometimes he's right there. Streaming wet. Accusing.'

A chill crawled over her skin. She saw from his face that he meant Bale.

She thought of the day of the death rites, when Torak had stood on the beach and shouted Bale's name to the sky. As if he'd *wanted* to be haunted. 'Why would he be accusing?' she said.

He struck the back of his head against the yew, hard enough to hurt. 'We had a fight. I went off on my own.'

Oh, Torak. 'What – what did you fight about?'

He avoided her gaze. 'He was going to ask you to stay with him.'

Renn felt the heat rising to her face.

'He didn't want to quarrel,' Torak went on. 'It was me. I was the one. I left him to keep watch alone. That's why he was killed.'

Around them, the birds were waking up. Renn saw the dew glistening on fat caterpillar curls of bracken. A bumblebee bumping about among the windflowers.

All this suffering, she thought. Bale dead. His whole clan grieving. Fin-Kedinn hurt. Torak tormented by guilt. All because of Thiazzi. Until now, she hadn't grasped how the evil of the Soul-Eaters spread, like cracks on a frozen lake.

'Torak,' she said at last. 'That doesn't make it your fault. Thiazzi's the killer. Not you.'

The bee settled on Torak's knee, and he watched its unsteady progress. 'Then why is he haunting me? I have to fulfil my oath, Renn. Or he'll be with me for ever.'

She thought about that. 'Maybe you're right. But I'll be with you too. And Wolf. And Rip and Rek.' She paused. 'Only from now on, *don't* tell me to go back to my clan.'

His lip curled. Then he snorted. Easing the bee onto his palm, he placed it on a dock leaf.

Dawn came, and they sat side by side, watching sunlight slanting through the Forest.

After a while, Torak said, 'If he had asked you to stay with him, would you have said yes?'

Renn turned to stare at him. 'How can you ask that?' she said, exasperated.

He was puzzled. 'I'm sorry, I . . . Does that mean no?'

She opened her mouth to reply, but at that moment, Wolf returned, his muzzle dark with blood. Giving them both a carrion-smelling greeting, he licked Torak under the chin, and they exchanged one of their speaking glances.

Renn asked him what Wolf was saying.

'Bright Beast,' he told her. 'And – I'm not sure, something broken. Think? Mind? Broken mind?'

'Mad,' they said together.

They never had time to wonder what it meant.

Wolf broke into an odd, excited little whimper and shot off into the undergrowth. Torak pulled Renn to her feet and moved in front of her. Five silent hunters came out from the trees. In the time it took Renn to draw her knife, they were surrounded. The hunters were clad in plain buckskin and carried no weapons. Somehow, they didn't need them. Renn saw that they wore no headbands. Whose side were they on?

'You will come with us,' said a quiet voice which was used to being obeyed. 'Your search is at an end.'

FOURTEEN

The woman wore a necklet of beechnuts and a remote expression, as if her thoughts were on matters no-one else could understand.

Renn guessed she was the Mage or Leader, or both. Her long brown hair was loose, except for a lock at the temple, matted with earthblood; and from her belt hung an antler tine. The clan-tattoo on her forehead was a small, black, cloven hoof.

'You're Red Deer,' said Renn.

'And you're Raven,' said the woman, calmly seeing through her disguise. 'And you,' she turned to Torak, 'are the spirit walker.'

He gaped. 'How did you know?'

'We felt your souls walk. You can mask it from others, but not from the Red Deer.'

'He doesn't mask it,' said Renn.

'Then someone does it for him,' the woman replied.

Renn wanted to ask what she meant, but Torak said eagerly, 'My mother was Red Deer. Did you know her?'

'Of course.'

He took a breath that ended in a gulp. 'What was she like?'

'Not here,' said the woman. 'We'll take you to our camp.'

There was a gesture of protest from one of her companions, a man whose hair was hidden by a binding of reddish bark. 'But Durrain, they're outsiders! They shouldn't see our camp, especially not the girl!'

'I'm not an outsider,' said Torak, 'I'm kin.'

'What have you got against me?' said Renn.

'We will go to camp,' repeated Durrain. Then to Torak and Renn, 'You may keep your weapons, but you won't need them. While you're with the Red Deer, you'll be quite safe.'

Renn felt that she spoke the truth – after all, Fin-Kedinn had said to seek them out – but she didn't like Durrain. Her thin face was as unfeeling as stone. And she hadn't even asked their names.

Durrain led them east, on a deer trail which kept to the thickets. Twice, Renn spotted Wolf, staying level with them. She wondered what he thought of their turning away from Thiazzi's scent trail, but when she mentioned this to Torak, he brushed it aside. 'Durrain said she'd help us.'

'She said our search was at an end. That might not mean the same thing.'

'They're my bone kin. They *have* to help.'

Pushing through the thickets was hard work, and a handsome young hunter offered to carry Renn's sleeping-sack. She declined, then wished she hadn't. The hunter guessed, and carried it anyway.

She pointed to the man with the bark-bound head, who was walking in front. 'Why doesn't he like me?'

The young man sighed. 'We fostered a Raven once. He helped the Soul-Eater make the demon bear.'

Renn bridled. 'That was my brother. The Soul-Eater tricked him, too.'

The man with the bark-bound head glared at her. 'So *you* say. The bear killed my mate. That's why I don't like Ravens.'

When he was out of earshot, the young hunter apologized. 'He still misses her.'

'Is that why he binds his head?' asked Renn.

'Yes, we place our dead in their chosen tree, then bind our heads in its bark, to remember.'

'But you don't wear headbands. So whose side are you on?'

He drew himself up. 'We take no sides. We never fight.'

Renn raised her eyebrows. 'What do the other clans think of that?'

'They scorn us, but they leave us alone.'

For now, she thought. She glanced at Torak, but he wasn't listening. He was drinking in every detail of his mother's clan, his face full of longing. Renn felt a twist of worry. She hoped these strange, distant people didn't let him down.

They walked for most of the day, and Renn soon lost her bearings. At last they reached a lake with a wooded islet in the middle. She was told it was Lake Blackwater, amid surprise that she didn't already know.

The Red Deer camp lay above the lake, and was so well concealed that she would have passed it if it hadn't been for the fire. A mound of juniper turned out to be the biggest shelter she'd ever seen: she counted seven doorways covered by reindeer-hide flaps stained green. A couple of dogs – the first she'd encountered in the Deep Forest – came to investigate, caught Wolf's scent on her, and fled. Children peered out, then ducked inside.

It was weirdly quiet, but for the first time in days, she felt safe. Nothing could get her here: neither tokoroths, nor Forest Horse hunters, nor the ash-haired menace. The fabled Magecraft of the Red Deer kept them at bay. And yet all she could see were a few tiny bark bundles tied to trees.

The young hunter led Torak to the lake to wash, and a woman beckoned Renn to a secluded bay. After some persuasion, she stripped and stood shivering while the woman used a cake of what appeared to be hard grey mud to scrub off her Deep Forest disguise. It was good to be herself again, but her skin stung. She asked what was in the grey cake.

The woman was surprised she didn't know. 'It's ash. We burn green bracken, then mix it with water and bake it.'

Ash, thought Renn. Always ash.

'Everyone in the Deep Forest uses it,' said the woman. 'It's like soapwort, but better.'

Another woman brought clothes: leggings and jerkin of roe deer buckskin lined with hare fur, neat elkhide boots, and a supple, hooded cape which Renn mistook for wovenbark, but was told was nettlestem. Everything fitted, but she was upset to learn that apart from her clan-creature feathers, her Raven clothes had been burnt.

'But ours are so much better,' protested the women.

Better clothes, better washing, better everything, Renn thought crossly. Maybe we should all give up and imitate them.

To boost her spirits, she pretended she had to go to the midden, and when she was alone, she rolled up one legging, took the beaver-tooth knife the Otter Clan had given her, and tied it to her calf with her spare bowstring. There. Just in case.

When she got back, Torak was sitting by the fire, also in new clothes, and scrubbed of his disguise. It was a relief to see him looking himself again; but they'd taken away his headband, and he kept touching his outcast tattoo.

He made room for her beside him while the rest of the clan settled round the fire. 'Stop scowling,' he whispered, 'they're helping us. And smell that food!'

She snorted. 'It's bound to be *so* much better than ours.'

But she had to admit it was good. A huge wovenroot basket had been hung directly over the embers. It was full of a fragrant stew of chopped auroch meat, mushrooms and bracken tops, which was cooked when the basket was nearly burnt through. There were also delicious flatcakes of crushed hazelnuts and pine pollen, and a big pail of honey to ladle over everything, with steaming spruce-needle tea to wash it all down.

It was wonderful to roast by a fire again, but apart from a brief prayer to the Forest, the Red Deer ate in silence. Renn thought with a pang of the Ravens' noisy nightmeals, with everyone swapping hunting stories.

As soon as they'd finished, Durrain began to question Torak. Surprisingly, she showed no interest in why they had come; she only wanted to know what it was like to spirit walk in a tree.

Torak struggled to explain. 'I – I was a yew. Then I was in tree after tree. Too many voices . . . I couldn't bear it.'

'Ah,' sighed the whole clan.

Even Durrain betrayed a flicker of emotion. 'What you heard was the Voice of the Forest. All the trees that are, or have ever been. It's too vast for men to bear. If you'd heard it for more than a heartbeat, your souls would have been torn apart. And yet – how I envy you.'

Torak swallowed. 'My mother . . . You said you knew her. Tell me about her?'

Durrain dismissed that with a wave of her hand. 'She chose to leave. I can tell you nothing.'

'Nothing?' Torak was aghast.

Renn felt angry for him. 'Surely you tried to find her?'

Durrain gave her a chilly smile.

'But – she and Torak's father were fighting the Soul-Eaters. They needed your help.'

'The Red Deer never fight,' said Durrain. Her eyes were a vivid beechnut brown, and they pierced Renn's souls. 'I see that you have some small skill at Magecraft. In the Deep Forest you're out of your depth. You are no Mage.'

She was right. It was Renn's turn to be crushed.

Beside her, Torak stirred. 'You don't know anything about Renn. Last summer, her visions warned us of the flood. She saved whole clans.'

'Indeed,' said Durrain.

Torak lifted his chin. 'We're wasting time. You said our search is at an end. Do you know where the Oak Mage is?'

'There is no Oak Mage in the Deep Forest,' declared Durrain.

'You're wrong,' said Torak. 'We tracked him here. The trail leads south.'

'If there was a Soul-Eater in the Deep Forest, the Red

Deer would know it.'

'You didn't before,' said Renn. 'The crippled wanderer lived with you for a whole summer and you never knew who he was.'

That drew angry murmurs from the others, and Durrain's lips thinned. 'Your search is at an end. Tonight we will pray. Tomorrow we'll take you back to the Open Forest.'

'No!' cried Renn and Torak together.

'You don't understand what you've blundered into,' said Durrain. 'The Deep Forest is at war!'

'But you never fight,' retorted Renn, 'so why should that affect you?'

'It affects us all,' said Durrain. 'It keeps the World Spirit away, which blights the Forest. Surely even in the Open Forest you know of this?'

'No, we're much too ignorant,' said Renn, 'why don't you enlighten us?'

Durrain flashed her an angry look. 'In winter the World Spirit haunts the fells as a willow-haired woman. In summer it walks the deep woods as a tall man with the antlers of a stag. This much you know?'

Renn made a huge effort to hold onto her temper.

'In spring, at the moment of turning, the Great Oak in the sacred grove bursts into leaf. Not this spring. The buds have been eaten by demons. The Spirit hasn't come.' She paused. 'We've tried everything.'

'The red branches,' said Torak.

Durrain nodded. 'Each clan beseeches the Spirit in its own way. The Aurochs paint branches. Lynx and Bat make sacrifices. The Forest Horses also paint branches, and their new Mage fasts alone in the sacred grove, seeking a sign.'

Renn felt Torak stiffen. 'The Forest Horse Mage,' he

said. 'Is that a man or a woman?'

'A man,' said Durrain.

Renn's heart began to race. 'What does he look like?'

'No-one sees his face. At all times, he wears a mask of wood, to be one with the trees.'

'Where is the sacred grove?' said Torak.

'In the valley of the horses,' said Durrain.

'Where's that?' said Renn.

'We never tell outsiders.'

'In whose range is it?' said Torak, 'Auroch or Forest Horse?'

'The sacred grove is the heart of the Forest,' said Durrain. 'It belongs to no-one. All may go there, though only in greatest need. At least, this was the way until the Forest Horse Mage forbade it.'

Renn took a deep breath. 'What if we told you that the Forest Horse Mage is Thiazzi in disguise?'

Durrain gave her a pitying stare, while the others smiled in disbelief.

'But if we're right,' said Torak, 'you'd help us? You'd help me, your bone kin, fight the Soul-Eater?'

'The Red Deer never fight,' repeated Durrain.

'But you can't do nothing!' cried Renn.

'We pray for the fighting to stop,' retorted Durrain. 'We pray for the World Spirit to come.'

'That's your answer?' said Torak. 'To pray?'

Durrain rose to her feet. 'I'll show you why we do not fight,' she said, spitting out her words like pebbles. Seizing Torak and Renn by the wrist, she dragged them out of camp.

They headed uphill, and soon reached a small glade where the evening sun glowed in drifts of yellow hawkbit. There was no birdsong. The glade was eerily quiet. In the middle, Renn saw a tangle of bleached bones: the skeletons of two red deer stags.

It was horribly easy to guess what had happened. Last autumn's rut, and the stags had fought over females. Renn saw the great heads clashing, the antlers locking. The struggle to untangle themselves. They couldn't. They were trapped.

'*This* is the sign the Spirit sent,' said Durrain. 'See what befell our clan-creatures! They fought. They couldn't get free. They starved to death. *This* is what happens when you fight. *This* is why the Red Deer will have *none* of it!'

FIFTEEN

As Durrain led them back to camp, Torak hung back, and Renn fell into step beside him. 'Are you all right?' she said.

'Fine.'

She touched his hand. 'I know you hoped for more from them.'

He forced a shrug. Because she was Renn, he didn't mind her feeling sorry for him, but to stop her saying anything else he said, 'I think they're wrong about not fighting.'

'Me too.'

'How can you not fight Soul-Eaters? If nobody fought them they'd take over the Forest.'

'Although,' she said, mimicking Durrain's lofty tones, 'who are *we* to question the ways of the Red Deer?'

He grinned. 'Especially not you, you ignorant Raven.'

She jabbed her elbow in his ribs and he yelped, earning a disapproving glance from Durrain.

As they neared the camp, Torak said in a low voice, 'But they have told us something important.'

Renn nodded. 'We need to find the sacred grove.'

Dusk was falling, and most of the Red Deer had gone into the shelter. Durrain was waiting for them. 'We pray till dawn,' she announced. 'You will pray with us.'

Renn tried to look obedient, and Torak bowed, although he had no intention of praying. He wasn't going to be distracted any longer.

A woman emerged from an adjoining trail, spotted Durrain, and dithered, as if wondering where to hide.

Durrain heaved a sigh. 'Where have you been?'

'I – I took an offering to the horses,' stammered the woman.

'You should have told me first.'

'Yes, Mage,' the woman said humbly.

Torak caught Renn's eye. *The horses.*

To give him a chance to tackle the woman, she asked Durrain to explain how the Red Deer went into a trance. The Mage gave her a look, and took her into the shelter.

'We should go in,' bleated the woman. She had flaky skin which reminded Torak of dried reindeer meat, and she kept blinking as if anticipating a blow. Her bark head-binding was filthy and needed replacing.

To set her at ease, he asked whom she mourned.

'M-my child,' she mumbled. 'We should go in.'

'And you make offerings to the horses? In their valley?'

'The Windriver, yes.' She gestured behind her, then clapped her hand to her mouth. 'We should go *in!*'

Simmering with excitement, Torak left his axe and bow

where he could find them, and followed her in. It was almost too easy.

Inside, it was as dim as the Forest at Midsummer. From the cross-beams, thousands of nettle fibres hung to dry: they brushed his face like long green hair. Men and women sat on opposite sides with Durrain in the middle, cradling a pair of deer-hoof rattles. There was no fire. The only warmth was the dank heat of breath.

Torak made out Renn, who gave him a conspiratorial smile. He felt guilty, because she wasn't coming with him. He couldn't have said why; he just knew that when he confronted Thiazzi, she mustn't be there to see it.

Making his way to the men's side, he found a place in front of one of the doorways.

The last Red Deer crawled in and set a bowl and a platter before Durrain. She lifted the bowl and drank. 'Rain from the tracks of the tree-headed guardian,' she intoned. 'Drink the wisdom of the Forest.' She handed on the bowl.

From the platter she took a piece of flatcake. 'Bark of the ever-watchful pine. Eat the wisdom of the Forest.'

When it was Torak's turn, he hid the flatcake up his sleeve and only pretended to sip from the bowl. Surreptitiously, he put out his hand, and felt cool air beneath the hide flap.

Durrain's gaze raked the throng.

He froze.

Durrain began shaking the rattles in a steady, cantering rhythm. 'Forest,' she chanted, 'You see all. You know all. Not a swallow falls, not a bat breathes, but you know it. Hear us.'

'Hear us,' echoed the others.

'End the strife between the clans. Bring the stag-headed Spirit back to your sacred valleys.'

On and on went the chanting and the galloping hooves, and still Durrain watched her people. Middle-night came and went. Torak had almost given up hope, when, without breaking rhythm, she cast her hood over her face – and the others did the same.

As the Red Deer chanted themselves deeper into the trance, Torak backed closer to the flap. The men flanking him were lost in their wovenstem darkness. They didn't see him escape.

Grabbing his weapons, he headed up the trail.

He hadn't gone far when Rip and Rek swooped and gave him a welcoming caw. *Where have you been?*

Wolf appeared like a grey shadow and ran at his side. *Bitten One. Not far.*

The half-eaten moon was setting, dawn was not far off. Torak quickened his pace. The thrill of the chase fizzed in his blood. He felt swift and invincible, a hunter closing on his prey. This was meant to be.

The boy escapes. This was meant to be.

For three days and nights the Chosen One has watched the unbelievers, as the Master willed. The girl drains the power from a curse stick as easily as pouring water from a pail. The boy summons ravens from the sky and speaks with the great grey wolf – and his spirit walks.

The boy believes he is cunning, tracking the Master to the sacred grove. No-one tracks the Master. The Master summons, and others obey. Even the fire obeys the Master.

The will of the Master must be done.

SIXTEEN

Dawn had broken, and neither the Red Deer nor Renn came after him. Torak almost wished they would. Soon, nothing would stand between him and his vengeance.

As the day wore on, he followed the trail up the Windriver, although this swift brown torrent bore scant resemblance to the mighty river it would become in the Open Forest.

Wolf padded at his side with drooping tail and lowered head. Even the ravens had stopped swooping after butterflies. The thrill of the hunt had given way to apprehension.

The valley narrowed to a gorge and the river became a rushing stream. A dry south wind had been blowing all day, but now it dropped to a whisper. Torak felt a tingling in his spine. They were entering the foothills of the High Mountains.

Wolf sniffed a clod of earth that had been kicked up by a horse's hoof. Torak stooped for a long black tail-hair. Above him, the new leaves of beech and birch glowed a brilliant green. Blackthorn blossom glittered like snow. The air was fresh with the scent of spruce, and alive with birdsong: chaffinch, warbler, thrush, wren. Even the speedwell on the trail was a preternatural blue, like flowers in a dream. He had reached the valley of the horses.

Wolf raised his head. *Do we go on?*

I must, Torak told him. *Not you. Dangerous.*

If you must, I must.

They walked on in the flickering shade.

The trail, Torak noticed, had been trodden by many hooves and paws, but no boots. The prey showed no fear of him, and he guessed that here, people were forbidden to hunt. A black woodpecker hopped backwards along a branch, probing for ants. It was so close that Torak glimpsed its long grey tongue. A roe buck munched deadnettle. He could have touched its coarse brown fur. He came upon a boar snuffling for roots; she watched him pass without raising her snout.

The valley narrowed to a gorge, and birch gave way to mossy spruce. The breeze died. The birds fell silent. Torak's footfalls sounded loud. He touched his shoulder, where his clan-creature skin used to be. A knot of dread tightened under his heart.

Ever since Bale's death, his whole purpose had been to find Thiazzi. He hadn't thought about what came after. He did now. He had to kill the strongest man in the Forest.

He had to kill a man.

Perhaps this was why he'd left Renn behind: because he

didn't want her to see him do it. But he missed her.

A murmur of wings behind him and he turned, hoping it was Rip and Rek. It was a sparrowhawk on a stump, plucking the breast of a headless thrush.

Maybe, thought Torak, the ravens have gone because they know what I'm going to do.

But Wolf was still with him. He was gazing at Torak, and his amber eyes held the pure, steady light of the guide. *Do not go on.*

I must, Torak replied.

This is bad.

I know. I must.

The sun sank lower and the trees closed in. The river disappeared, but Torak heard it echoing underground. Finally, its voice fell to nothing.

A stone clattered behind him. When it came to rest, the stillness surged back like something alive.

The trail rounded a bend and the Mountains reared before him, startlingly close. The valley walls leaned in, shutting out the dying light. Ahead, the tallest holly trees he'd ever seen warded him back. Beyond them, he knew, lay the sacred grove: the heart of the Forest.

Some places hold an echo of events; others possess their own spirit. Torak sensed the spirit of this place as a soundless humming in his bones. From his pouch, he drew his mother's medicine horn. He shook earthblood into his palm and daubed some on his cheeks and brow. The horn seemed to vibrate, like the humming in his marrow.

Wolf nosed his hand. His ears were flat against his skull. He was no longer the guide. He was Torak's pack-brother, and frightened.

Torak knelt and blew gently on his muzzle, feeling the tickle of his whiskers and breathing his sweet, clean smell.

He couldn't let Wolf come any further. It was too dangerous. He had to do this alone. Hating the confusion he would cause, he told Wolf to go.

Wolf refused.

Torak repeated the command.

Wolf ran in a circle. *You must not hunt the Bitten One!*

Go, Torak replied.

Wolf pawed his knee. *Danger!* Uff!

Torak hardened his heart. *Go!*

Wolf gave an anxious whimper and raced off into the Forest.

So now you're alone, thought Torak. He felt the chill of the night seeping out of the earth. He rose and walked into the dark beneath the trees.

As Wolf raced up the slope, worry and fear fought within him. This was a terrible place. The holly trees whispered warnings he didn't understand. They were very old, and they didn't want him here.

He reached a ridge above the whispering trees and skittered to a halt. The breeze carried a tangle of scents to his nose. He smelt the Bright Beast-that-Bites-Hot, and the Bitten One, and a whiff of demon. He smelt his pack-brother's fear and his blood-hunger. This was not the hunger of the hunt, it was deeper, fiercer. It was not-wolf. Wolf didn't understand it, but he feared it. And he feared for Tall Tailless, because he felt in his fur that if Tall Tailless attacked the Bitten One, he would be killed.

The Bitten One was stronger than a bear. Not even the Bright Beast dared attack him. What could one wolf do?

Wolf trotted up and down the ridge, mewing in distress.

He felt a faint shudder in the earth. He swivelled his ears. Loping to the top of the ridge, he leapt onto a log. He caught the rich scent of the huge prey that is like auroch – but not.

He smelt that a herd of these not-aurochs was feeding in the next valley. They were enormous creatures, but timid, although they could be extremely bad-tempered, and hated being chased, as Wolf had learnt the previous Dark.

He raced off to find them.

The holly trees smelt of dust and spiders. Their vigilance pressed upon Torak, drawing the breath from his lungs as the wind draws smoke from a shelter.

Eventually, the hollies thinned, and between their straight black trunks he saw the red glimmer of a fire. He drew his knife. As he went closer, he heard the crackle of flames. He caught the stink of charred flesh.

He reached the last tree and edged behind it. The holly's bark felt cold as slate beneath his palm.

The sacred grove was washed in blue moonlight, and shadowed by the broken shoulders of the Mountains. A circle of raked embers smouldered on stony ground. Beyond it, hazed by smoke, two enormous trees stood side by side, their upper branches intertwining like hands.

The Great Oak pushed skywards in eternal struggle. Its mighty trunk was furrowed like an ice river, and in the uncertain light, Torak saw gnarled bark faces glaring at him. No leaves softened the oak's twig fingers: its buds had been gnawed by demons. But from some branches hung small, lumpy shapes. Torak couldn't see what they were. He dreaded finding out.

The Great Yew was ancient beyond imagining. Torak knew, because he had walked in its deep green souls. Its twisted limbs were weathered to a driftwood silver, but underneath, the golden sapwood pulsed. Its ever-wakeful boughs had survived fire and flood, lightning and drought. Its roots were harder than stone, and held down the Mountains. The Great Yew feared nothing, not even demons.

From nowhere, a gust of wind cleared the smoke and breathed life into the fire. Torak saw that a stake had been driven into its heart, and from this hung a slender, blackened carcass.

Torak felt sick. Now he understood what dangled from the Great Oak. Carcasses. Too small to be human, too charred to be recognizable.

To murder a hunter. He remembered the Soul-Eaters' dreadful sacrifices in the caves of the Far North. He remembered Fin-Kedinn telling of the bad times long ago, when the clans had killed hunters, including people.

This, he thought, is evil. He could feel it in the air: a rotten, choking sickness, palsying the heart of the Forest.

His hand on his knife-hilt was slippery with sweat. There was no turning back. He had to leave the shelter of the holly trees and find Thiazzi.

He was about to take the first step when one of the rocks beyond the fire rose, spread its arms and became a man.

SEVENTEEN

The Mage rose from the very roots of the sacred grove. He wore a mantle of flowing horsehide and a long, graven mask crested with a mane of horsetails. Painted eyes glared scarlet, and the gaping mouth was fringed with black feathers that shuddered at every breath.

Spirit breath, Renn had told Torak once. *A mask is a spirit's face. When you put on a mask, you become that spirit. The feathers show that the spirit lives.*

Mask and mantle declared him to be the Forest Horse Mage, but upon his breast he wore a wreath of acorns and mistletoe, the tokens of his true clan, and from it hung a small, heavy pouch. The fire-opal.

Behind the holly tree, Torak clumsily sheathed his knife. It would be useless against such power. He unslung his bow and fumbled in his quiver for an arrow. His heart was pounding so hard that it hurt. He felt like a mouse about to attack an auroch.

Standing before the fire, the Mage began to pant, forcing the air from his chest in harsh exhalations, ugh – ugh – ugh. He stepped closer to the fire. He stepped *into* it. Through the shimmering heat, Torak watched his naked feet tread the living embers. Not possible, he thought.

Panting faster, ugh ugh ugh, the Mage snatched the carcass from the stake and walked back to solid ground.

Torak's head reeled. If not even fire could harm him . . . He couldn't do this. He couldn't do it.

He watched the Mage raise a fallen spruce tree as if it were a twig, and set it against the trunk of the Great Oak. The spruce was notched to make a ladder. The Mage ascended and hung the carcass from a bough. Descending, he took a sack from among the roots of the Great Oak and drew out a hawk.

Torak's belly turned over. The hawk was alive. It fluttered wildly as the Mage tied it by one leg to a stake.

Again the Mage began those harsh, panting breaths. But this time, as he raised the stake, his mantle fell away from his forearms, and Torak saw his three-fingered hand and his Oak Clan tattoo. The skin was scored with angry scabs. Torak thought of Bale, clawing his attacker as he fought for life. His souls hardened. It was time to fulfil his oath.

Wiping his palms on his leggings, he nocked the arrow to his bow. He would move away from the tree, into full view. He would shout the challenge, give Thiazzi a chance to seize his weapons. And then . . .

The Soul-Eater carried his fluttering burden into the fire, planted the stake and walked away.

Torak couldn't bear it. He took aim and let fly. The

hawk hung dead, the arrow quivering in its breast.

Slowly, the Mage took off his mask and placed it on the ground. He turned, and Torak saw him at last. The russet mane, the thicket of beard. The face as hard as sun-cracked earth. The pitiless green eyes.

'So, Spirit Walker. You obeyed my summons.'

Torak stepped out from behind the tree. 'Take up your weapons, Thiazzi. You killed my kinsman. Now I'm going to kill you.'

EIGHTEEN

Torak faced Thiazzi across ten paces of drifting smoke. 'You won't get away from me this time,' he said, nocking another arrow to his bow.

The Oak Mage threw back his head and laughed. '*I*, get away from *you*? You're here because I want you here!' Flicking his mantle behind his shoulders, he brandished a whip in one hand, an axe in the other. The lash was coiled like a viper. The axe was the largest Torak had ever seen.

'I wondered who dared follow me from the islands,' said Thiazzi, slicing the air with deft twists of his wrist, 'so I sent my minion to find out. Since you entered my Forest, I've known every step you've taken, every breath you've drawn. Now it ends.'

'You won't find it that easy,' said Torak, edging sideways round the fire. 'I could have killed you in the Far North.

Remember?'

The whip cracked, wrenching Torak's bow from his hand. 'My power is greater than yours!' spat Thiazzi, tossing the bow in the flames. 'See, even the fire obeys me!'

Smoke wafted across Torak's sight. When it cleared, Thiazzi stood no more than two paces from him.

'But since the World Spirit has delivered you into my hands,' the Oak Mage went on, 'I shall add your power to my own.'

Wrenching his axe from his belt, Torak put the fire between them once more. 'How can the World Spirit be on your side? Killing hunters? How can that please the Spirit?'

'To offer a hunter to the fire is to give it the noblest death of all. It is the Way.'

Again the whip cracked, Torak dodged, and the rawhide struck stone. 'It's not the clans' way,' he panted, 'and it's not your Forest.'

'I am the Master!' boomed Thiazzi. 'I have taken the Deep Forest for my own!' Foam flew from his lips, and his green eyes glittered.

As Torak stared at him, everything fell into place. 'The war between the clans. You started it. You set them against each other.'

Yellow teeth flashed in the russet beard.

'You planted the curse sticks,' said Torak, moving backwards, nearly losing his footing. 'You murdered the Forest Horse Mage and blamed it on the Aurochs. You made them fight.'

'They wanted to fight. They *needed* to fight!'

The whip bit Torak's wrist, and with a cry he dropped his axe. He lunged for it, but Thiazzi was faster, snatching it and throwing it on the fire. 'The clans are *weak*,' he snarled. 'They've forgotten the True Way, but *I* will unite them. That's why the World Spirit gave this land to me: to root out differences, to return the clans to the Way! No more clan guardians, no more clan Mages. One way. One Forest. One Leader!'

Dashing the sweat from his eyes, Torak pulled his knife from its sheath.

Again, Thiazzi's yellow grin flashed. 'I *cannot* be hurt!' He pointed to the mistletoe at his breast. 'The deathless heart of the oak shields me from harm! I am invincible!'

Torak's knife trembled in his hand.

'But come,' taunted the Oak Mage, 'try your luck. Let's see if you can break me. Or shall I break you, as easily as I broke your mother and your father?'

The red mist descended. Torak saw him through a haze of blood.

' . . . As I broke your kinsman,' boasted the Oak Mage. 'As I threw him over the Crag and spattered his brains across the rocks . . .'

Torak roared and launched himself at Thiazzi.

Wolf stalked the not-aurochs upwind, which he would never normally do. But this time, he *wanted* them to smell him.

A cow caught his scent and swung round. Wolf lowered his head to tell her he was hunting. The cow gave a nervous snort and pawed the earth. Wolf came on. She charged. Wolf dodged her nimbly and ran off to worry a bull. The bull rounded on him. Wolf leapt clear of his horns by a whisker and bounded away. He was enjoying this.

Now the whole herd was anxious. It stopped munching willowherb and started lumbering up the slope. Wolf prowled behind a cluster of young cows who were huffing and showing the whites of their eyes. He chose the edgiest and snapped at her fetlock. The cow squealed, jerked up her tail and fled. Panicked, the rest of the herd followed.

Up the ridge they went, with Wolf racing after them, loping this way and that, so they'd think they were hunted by many hungry wolves. Rocks fell and branches snapped as they crashed into the next valley, down towards Tall Tailless and the Bitten One.

The earth shook as Wolf drove them on, and his heart leapt. *This* was what one wolf could do!

NINETEEN

At first, Torak thought it was a rockfall.

The earth shook as if the Mountains were falling. He froze, knife in hand. The thunder swelled to a roar. A bison crashed into the grove. Torak ran for his life.

He reached the hollies, threw himself at the nearest branch, and swung himself up – as the grove was engulfed by a heaving torrent of hoof and horn.

Like a flash flood, the bison swept through, and Torak clung to the shuddering tree. The din pounded through him. It was never going to end.

It did. The silence after it had gone was deafening. A pall of smoke and dust hung in the air, with the musky smell of bison. The Great Oak and the Great Yew towered above it: inviolate, their branches pricking the night sky.

As the dust settled, Torak saw sparks from the trampled

fire scattered like stars over the ground. He dropped to earth and ran to search the grove. Thiazzi was gone.

In disbelief, Torak stumbled about in the gloom, searching the stony slopes. Nothing. The pounding hooves had obliterated all hope of a trail. Thiazzi had vanished like smoke.

'No!' shouted Torak. The echoes died. Pebbles fell like a rattle of stony laughter.

He slumped onto a boulder. He'd lost his chance for vengeance.

Wolf bounded out of the darkness and pounced on him joyously. His fur was full of burrs, and fluffed up with excitement. Torak had no idea why.

Much prey, Torak told Wolf wearily. *Nearly trampled. Good you weren't here.*

To Torak's bemusement, Wolf dropped his ears, gave an embarassed yawn, and rolled onto his back, saying sorry.

Torak asked him if the Bitten One was close.

Gone, was all Wolf would say.

Torak rubbed a hand over his face. He'd achieved nothing. The only thing to do now was make the long trudge back to the Red Deer camp, and try to persuade them that the Forest Horse Mage was indeed Thiazzi. And start all over again.

A great weariness swept over him. He missed Renn. She would be furious with him for leaving her; but whatever she said couldn't be as bad as what he was saying to himself.

By moonset, he'd reached the end of the valley of the horses and could go no further. He found a fallen tree a few paces above the Windriver and made it into an inadequate shelter with branches and mouldy bracken. He'd left his sleeping-sack with the Red Deer, but he was too tired to care, he would drag in more bracken for bedding. After chewing a slip of dried horse meat and tucking the last of it in a birch tree for the Forest, he wrapped his nettlestem mantle about him and fell asleep.

This time, he knows he is dreaming. He is lying on his back in the shelter, but above him the sky is a blizzard of stars. He is in a cold sweat of terror, but he cannot move. A shadow darkens the stars as something leans over him. Wet hair slithers over his face. He hears the soft creak of mouldering seal hide. His flesh shrinks from icy breath.

It's lonely at the bottom of the Sea . . . Fish eat my flesh. The Sea Mother rolls my bones. It's cold. So cold.

Torak tries to speak. His lips won't move.

Why didn't you come to me on the Crag? I was lonely, waiting for you. I'm lonelier now. And so cold . . .

Torak woke with a start.

Dawn had not yet come. He hadn't slept long. Wolf was gone, but Rip and Rek were hopping about outside the shelter, cawing. *Wake up, wake up!*

Torak dug the heels of his hands into his eyes. 'I'm sorry, kinsman. I missed my chance. But I'll find him again, I swear. I will avenge you.'

The ravens would watch over Tall Tailless, and Wolf would not go far. But he couldn't ignore those howls.

He had heard them in his sleep. Darkfur had come down from the Mountain, she was trying to find him! Then he'd woken up, and disappointment had crushed him. She was in the *other* Now, not this one.

But he'd heard her again. Very faint and far away, but it was her. He would know her howl anywhere.

Panting with eagerness, he loped through the Forest. As the Light came, he leapt a little Fast Wet, and splashed through a bigger one. Tall Tailless would be all right with the ravens. And Wolf would not be away for long.

The ravens flew from tree to tree, fluffing up their head-feathers and making stony chuk-chuk warning calls.

Warning of what? wondered Torak.

Dawn was breaking as he left the Windriver and headed north, towards the Red Deer camp. The wind was gusting, the trees moaning. His misgivings grew: a tightness in the chest that made it hard to breathe.

Others felt it too. Birds fled across the sky – jays, magpies, crows. Reindeer cantered past, scarcely swerving to avoid him, as if escaping a greater threat. Torak thought of Renn and quickened his pace.

Ahead, a figure emerged from behind a rowan, and he recognized the Red Deer woman with the bark-bound head. She dithered, then overcame her shyness and ran down to him. 'At last!' she said with a timid smile. 'We've been looking for you everywhere!'

'What's wrong?' he said brusquely. 'Is Renn all right?'

'She's safe with the others, it's you we were worried about. We didn't know where you'd gone.'

They headed up the trail, the woman lagging behind, Torak running ahead. He heard a distant growl of thunder. The first drops of rain pattered on the leaves, and he put up his hood. Something grabbed his ankle and yanked him high into the air.

The earth swung sickeningly. As the dizziness cleared, he realized that he was hanging by one leg from a young rowan tree – which, moments before, had been bent double.

You *fool*, he berated himself. A simple spring trap, and you blunder right into it!

His knife wasn't in its sheath. It lay where it had fallen in a clump of goosefoot, out of reach. Furious, he shouted at the woman to come and cut him down.

She came running up the trail. 'You're caught in a trap,' she said.

'Well, obviously!' he snapped. 'Cut me down!'

Her arms hung limp at her sides.

Were her wits completely gone? Snarling with frustration, Torak made a grab for the rope, which was drawn tight around his left ankle. He fell back with a growl. *'Cut me down!'*

'No,' said the woman.

'What?' The rope creaked. Rain pattered on the leaves.

Only it isn't rain, he realized. It's ash. Flakes of ash, swirling like dirty snow. And that glow in the sky, it's in the wrong place for dawn. Not east, but west. 'Fire,' he said. 'There's a fire in the Forest.'

'Yes,' said the woman in an altered voice.

Upside-down, Torak saw her pull off the bark which covered her head and shake out her long, ash-grey hair.

'The fire has escaped,' she said. 'It is eating the Forest. The Chosen One has set it free.'

TWENTY

Like a fish on a hook, Torak dangled from the tree, while the sky darkened to an angry orange twilight which had nothing to do with the sun. 'You can't leave me here to burn!' he cried.

'You are an unbeliever,' said the woman. 'You are for the fire.'

'Why? What have I done?' Bending double and hauling himself up the rope, he made a grab for the nearest branch. It snapped. He fell back, jarring his leg. 'What have I *done?*'

Squatting on her haunches, the woman peered at him. Her face was blistered and peeling, and in her lashless eyes he saw the cunning behind the madness. 'The Chosen One watches him,' she hissed. 'She sees him wake the fire with stone, she sees him dishonour it. She knows.'

'What do you *want?*'

She licked her cracked lips, and he saw the ash crusting the corners. 'To serve the Master, and through him to know the fire once more. The red so pure it makes all else grey . . .'

'But the Master wants to *rule* the Forest,' he panted. 'He can't want you to destroy it!'

She smiled. 'The Master says to watch the unbeliever, but the Chosen One will do more. She will give him to the fire.'

'Wait,' he said, desperate to keep her with him. 'Was it – was it the Master who made you the Chosen One?'

Her features lit up like embers. 'It was the fire,' she whispered. 'On a clear blue day, the lightning sought her from the sky. No thunder, no warning. Just that blazing brightness, brighter than the sun – and she at its very heart.' She leaned closer, and he smelt her acrid breath. 'In that moment, she sees *everything*. The bones in her flesh, the veins in the leaves, the fire that sleeps in every tree. She sees the truth. *Everything burns.*'

The roar of the fire was getting louder. Smoke was seeping through the trees. 'But you survived,' he said. 'The lightning let you live. You should let me live. Cut me down!'

She was oblivious, lost in her story. 'The fire took her for its own. It turned her hair to ash. It scorched the child from her womb. It *transformed* her . . . ' Her burning fingers stroked his cheek, and her smile was tender and merciless. 'It will transform you, too.'

He thought of Thiazzi's charred sacrifices on the tree. 'You can't leave me here to burn,' he pleaded.

'Listen to it grow!' With raised arms she saluted the fire. 'The more it eats, the greater its hunger! You are honoured. The fire will take you for its own.' Then she was gone.

'Don't leave me!' shouted Torak. 'Don't leave me,' he begged.

A shard of blazing bark struck the ground by his head. Around him the trees thrashed in the fire's searing breath. The sky had deepened to bloody amber. In the west, he saw it coming for him. He remembered what Fin-Kedinn had said. *It can leap into a tree faster than a lynx, and when it does — when it gets into the branches — then it goes where it likes. You wouldn't believe how fast . . .*

The Bright Beast came roaring through the Forest, faster than Wolf thought possible. It was eating everything: trees, hunters, prey. Where was Tall Tailless?

Wolf should never have left him. He hadn't found Darkfur and now he couldn't find his pack-brother.

Desperately, Wolf loped into the bitter breath of the Bright Beast. The panicked prey thundered past, fleeing the other way, and he dodged their trampling hooves. He splashed across a little Fast Wet. He skittered down a gully — and the Bright Beast reared above him, big as a Mountain. His pelt crisped, his eyes stung. He couldn't go any further, couldn't seek his pack-brother in its very jaws. It was eating everything, and if it caught him, it would eat him too.

Spinning round, he raced back up the gully, and the Bright Beast raced after him. It lashed out a glittering claw. Wolf leapt to avoid it. It pounced on a tree and ate it. Another sapling groaned — Wolf sped beneath it just before it crashed — and the Bright Beast's cubs flew through the air and devoured more trees.

Hot stones bit Wolf's pads, he ran as he'd never run

before, and the Bright Beast raced after him. It flew, it leapt from tree to tree, it soared over the Wet. It was eating the Forest. Nothing could escape.

Snarling with effort, Torak pulled himself upright and made another grab at the rowan. His fingers brushed bark, but couldn't grasp it. Yet again he fell back.

He had another try. This time, he caught a branch. He clung on. This had to work. If it didn't, he was finished.

Shaking his boot off his free foot, he slapped his bare sole against the rowan's trunk and half-kicked, half-hauled himself into the fork. He lay gasping, the tree digging into his belly. He was upright at last.

No time to rest. He wriggled and squirmed till he'd got into a crouch in the fork, supported on his right foot. His left leg, tethered to higher up the trunk, stuck out awkwardly.

Chunks of blazing bark thudded like fiery hail as he tugged at the noose around his ankle; but his weight had pulled it savagely tight around his boot, it wouldn't budge. Frantically he worked at the knot. His right calf trembled with the strain of supporting him.

The noose gave slightly. He worked at it. It loosened a little more. It was all he needed. Twisting and tugging, he yanked his foot from his boot, wriggled out of the noose, and jumped to earth.

After a desperate scramble in the undergrowth, he found his knife and staggered to his feet. His eyes were streaming, his skin prickling with heat. Smoke had turned day to night.

A roe buck sped past. He guessed it was heading for

wetlands and ran after it. Cinders stung his feet. He was barefoot. No time to go back for his boots.

As he ran, he glanced over his shoulder. Flames taller than trees were licking at the sky. The noise was like nothing he'd ever heard, it was the thunder of a thousand thousand bison, it seized his heart and squeezed it dry, it sucked the air from his lungs.

He dropped to a crouch and gulped cleaner air, and when he straightened up, the smoke was so thick that he couldn't see his hand in front of his face. He didn't know where he was, but he knew he had to decide now, this instant, which way to run – or he would die.

A loud cark!

He couldn't see the ravens but he heard them calling to him as they flew high above the smoke. Blindly, he followed their cries. Burning branches rained down. He was running in the very breath of the fire, and all around him trees were snapping and groaning.

Again he glanced back. A river of flame slithered up a pine tree, which exploded in a shower of sparks. A woodgrouse flew skywards, then dropped back again, sucked to its death in the burning wind.

Quork! Quork! called Rip and Rek. *Follow!*

Suddenly the ground was gone and Torak was rolling and bumping downhill.

He jolted to a halt and struggled to his knees. Hands and feet sank into mud: cold, wet, blessed mud. The ravens had led him to a lake. He splashed into the shallows – and fell headlong over a rock.

The rock gave a piteous whinny. It was a foal, a small black foal, sunk to its knobbly fetlocks in mud, shaking with terror. It was too frightened to move, but Torak couldn't stop to help. He waded past.

Ahead of him, the murk thinned for a moment, and in the lake he made out the bobbing black heads of horses swimming for their lives, and beyond them a beaver lodge as big as a Raven shelter.

Another anguished whinny from the foal – and in the lake, one of the black heads turned. The mother must have waited as long as she dared, but when her foal wouldn't follow, she'd had to leave. Now she swam reluctantly with the herd, forced to leave her young one to its doom.

That was what Torak should do: swim for the beaver lodge and leave the foal to burn.

With a growl, he turned back, grabbed a handful of its spiky mane, and pulled.

The foal rolled its white-rimmed eyes and refused to budge. 'Come *on!*' yelled Torak. '*Swim!* It's your last chance!' That only made things worse. The foal didn't understand people talk, but what was Torak supposed to do? If he said it in wolf talk, it'd die of fright.

Getting behind the little creature, he shoved his head under its belly and heaved it onto his shoulders. It struggled feebly, so he grabbed its legs to hold it still, and staggered into the lake.

When he was waist-deep, he chucked the foal in the water. 'You're on your own!' he shouted above the clamour of the fire. 'Swim!' He threw himself in and struck out for the beaver lodge.

The fire's name-soul glared at him from the water. Over his shoulder, he saw it claiming the slope down which he'd fallen. He saw the foal swimming bravely behind him.

He was nearly at the beaver lodge, and tiring fast. Billows of black smoke rolled towards him. He couldn't breathe. He'd intended to climb onto the lodge and shelter there till the fire had leapt the lake, but now he realized that if he did, he would choke to death. He had to get inside. Beaver lodges have a sleeping-chamber above water level, which the beavers reach by underwater tunnels. Torak took a deep breath and dived.

Groping at branches, he sought the mouth of a tunnel. His chest was bursting. He couldn't find a tunnel, couldn't see a thing, it was like swimming in mud.

He found an opening. Squeezed through it – burst from the water – and struck his head on a sapling.

He could barely see in the red gloom, but the roar of the fire wasn't quite so deafening. Through the stench of smoke, he caught the musky stink of beaver, but he couldn't see any; maybe the fire had overtaken them on the shore.

They had built their lodge well. The sleeping-platform was littered with wood chips to keep it snug and dry, while above, the branches were loosely packed to make an air vent which reached to the top of the lodge. The sleeping-platform was only beaver high, and Torak didn't want to get stuck, so he decided to stay in the water and wait out the fire.

Gasping for breath, he thanked the beavers and Rip and Rek and the Forest for his shelter.

'Please,' he panted, '*please* keep Wolf and Renn safe.'

His words were lost in the roar of the fire, and he felt in his heart that it was hopeless. The fire was eating the Forest. Nothing could survive.

Not Wolf. Not Renn.

TWENTY-ONE

Renn stumbled about in a world burnt black.

The Forest was gone. It simply wasn't there any more. She wandered between charcoal spikes which had once been trees. She felt their bewildered souls thronging the soot-laden air, but was too devastated to pity them. Even the sun was gone, swallowed up in an unearthly grey half-light. Had the fire taken the whole Forest? The Open Forest as well as the Deep?

The stink made her cough, and the sound echoed eerily. When she stopped, all she could hear was a furtive crackle of embers, the occasional crash of a falling tree.

Death, she thought, death everywhere. Where is Torak? Is he alive? Or is he . . .

No. Don't think it. He's with Wolf. They are both alive, and so is Fin-Kedinn, and Rip and Rek.

Rubbing her face, she felt the grittiness of soot. She was covered in it. She tasted it on her tongue. Her eyes were swollen and sore. She'd swallowed so much smoke she felt sick.

She was thirsty, too, but she had no waterskin. Only her axe and knife and the wovenstem quiver the Red Deer had given her, containing her last three arrows. And of course her bow.

To give herself courage, she unslung it from her shoulder and rubbed the grime from its waist. Golden heartwood gleamed, and she thought of Fin-Kedinn making it for her many summers ago, and felt a little less alone.

But her thirst was becoming pressing, and it was a long time since she'd left the lake. She had no idea which way she'd come. Where *was* she?

She should never have escaped from the Red Deer.

Durrain had sensed the fire almost before the prey, and the whole clan had taken to the lake, seeking refuge in canoes which they'd moored to the islet in the middle. There Renn had done as they did, soaking her cloak, huddling beneath it.

She hadn't been frightened, not then. She'd been too angry with Torak for leaving her. A whole day of patient questioning. *Where did he go? I don't know. Where did he go?* It astonished her that they didn't guess, but they seemed to think it impossible that anyone would brave the sacred grove alone. It would've served him right, she'd thought furiously, if she *had* given him away.

But as she lay in the rocking gloom with the fire roaring towards them, she forgot her anger. A child sobbed. A woman whispered a charm. Renn shut her eyes and prayed for Torak and Wolf. Please, please, let them live.

Then it burst upon them, and the canoe rocked wildly and people shouted prayers.

It had taken Renn a while to realize that the fire had jumped the lake and swept on without devouring them. Then the World Spirit had lanced the clouds and released a torrent of rain, and in the confusion, she'd slipped overboard and swum away.

She *thought* she'd headed south, but in the smoke and the rain it was hard to tell. Now, as a breeze cleared the haze, she saw that she stood in a narrow gully where a stream had once run. Maybe it led to a river.

She hadn't gone far when a branch crashed behind her. She turned. The dead trees looked like hunters stalking her.

One of them moved.

She ran, blundering down the gully. She ran till she had to stop, hands on knees, gasping for breath.

Around her, the gully was quiet. Whatever had moved, hadn't come after her. Maybe it had been a tree, after all.

She stumbled between the smoking spikes. Beyond a spur, she saw green. She blinked. Yes, *green*!

Moaning, she rounded the spur – and the green of the Forest blinded her. Rowan and beech and whitebeam rose before her, their boughs a little sooty, but alive.

Panting with relief, she sank to her knees amid ferns and celandine. By her hand lay a sky-blue shard of thrush's egg, pushed from the nest by the hatchling. On a log she saw a spruce sapling as tall as her thumb, thrusting bravely through the moss. She thought, the Forest is eternal. Nothing can conquer it.

But there was no sign of a river. Straining for sounds of water, she wandered through the trees.

At last she was halted by a grove of tall pines which had

been toppled by a storm. Dead trunks and earthy root discs blocked her way in a criss-crossed tangle. She ought to turn back, that was what you did when you were lost. But she couldn't face returning to the wasteland.

The pines didn't want her in their bone-ground. Their mossy trunks tried to throw her off, their branches jutted like spears. It was a relief to get out the other side, back among living oaks and limes.

But these trees didn't want her, either. Furrowed bark faces glared at her, and twig fingers dragged at her hair. Some of the trunks were hollow. She thought what it would be like to be trapped inside, and hurried on.

The wind strengthened, blowing soot in her face. She coughed and went on coughing, doubled up, leaning against a tree.

Beneath her fingers, she felt eyes.

With a cry she snatched her hand away.

Yes, eyes. A fierce red gaze had been carved in the trunk, and a square mouth, edged with real human teeth.

Renn had never seen such a thing. She guessed it had been done to give voice to the tree's spirit. But who would give a tree teeth?

Uneasily, she scanned her surroundings. Lime trees, nettles, a scattering of boulders.

She went on.

When she glanced back, the trees had moved. They'd been much closer to that boulder, she was sure of it. Now they were more spread out.

She started to run.

A root tripped her and she fell – and came face to face with another trunk mask, its eyes tight shut in its lichen-crusted face.

Panting, she got to her feet.

The eyes opened. Bark limbs detached themselves from the trunk. Bark hands reached to grab her.

Whimpering, she fled.

To her left, another bark creature separated from a trunk. Then another and another. Bark people moved to surround her, reaching for her with ridged hands and blank, fissured faces.

As she ran, her axe banged against her thigh. She wrenched it from her belt, but knew that she'd never dare use it.

Her breath rasped in her throat. With nightmare slowness she waded through piles of crackling leaves. She stumbled down a slope and into another tree bone-ground where she wobbled over fallen trunks, while the bark people ran along them like fire, hunting her in eerie silence.

Something yanked at her shoulder, pulling her back. Her bow had snagged on a branch. She struggled to free it.

Bark hands seized her and dragged her down.

TWENTY-TWO

'Where are you taking me?' said Renn.

The bark men did not reply.

'Please. Why won't you speak? What have I done?'

One of them jabbed at her with his spear. She didn't wait for him to do it again.

All day she had walked in a silent throng of hunters. They'd taken her weapons, but they hadn't touched her again. They seemed to regard her as unclean.

In vain she'd begged them for water. They ignored her. She stumbled through a haze of thirst and a forest of poisoned spears.

She had no idea where she was. The great fire hadn't touched this part of the Forest, but its stench hung in the air, so she guessed that the wasteland wasn't far.

From her captors' green headbands and horn amulets,

she guessed they were Aurochs, but in her mind they were the bark people. Their clothes were yellowish-brown wovenbark, and rolls of bark pierced their earlobes. Their shaven scalps were caked with yellow clay to resemble bark, and the men's beards were clogged with it, like straggly tree-roots. But unlike the Aurochs she'd seen at clan meets, they hadn't stopped there. They had carved their very flesh into bark, disfiguring their hands and faces with rough, ridged scars.

Renn knew a little about such scars. Some of her own clan, including Fin-Kedinn, bore a raised zigzag on each arm, to ward off demons. Creating them was very painful. After slitting the skin with a sliver of flint, a paste of ash and lichen was rubbed in, and the wound bound tight. Renn thought about having her face slashed, and felt sick.

They reached another stream, and again she begged to be allowed to drink. The hunters stared at her, their eyes unresponsive. *No drink.*

The light was failing when they finally reached camp. By then she was dizzy with thirst.

The Auroch camp lay in a hollow guarded by watchful spruce. Smouldering pine knots dispersed a smoky orange light and an eye-stinging tang of tree-blood. Birch-bark shelters squatted round a central pine. Outside each shelter lay a pile of wooden shields like a nest of giant beetles, and a fire ringed with stones. From the trunk of the pine hung an auroch's horned skull.

Beneath it, a group of silent children twisted piles of pounded spruce root into twine. All stared at Renn without expression. Like the adults, their faces were disfigured with ridges, many still crusted with blood.

Renn couldn't see anyone who looked like a Leader or a Mage, but she noticed that not everyone was Auroch.

There was another clan here, too. Dark hair was braided tight, two braids for women, one for men, and faces were unscarred, but dusted red with ground pine bast. In fact, everything was stained red: lips, partings, even fingernails. The women were dressed in plain buckskin, but the men wore splendid belts of black and gold fur. Lynx Clan.

Auroch or Lynx, all gave her the same unfeeling stare. They didn't know what pity was.

As her captors approached the fires, they squatted in the smoke, wafting it over themselves. They pushed Renn in too, as if to cleanse her, then dragged her to the pine tree and forced her to her knees.

Women emerged from the shelters. Like the men, their faces were bark-scarred, but their caked scalps were studded with tiny alder cones, and they wore tunics, not leggings.

One carried a waterskin.

'Please,' mumbled Renn. 'I'm so thirsty.'

The woman glared at her.

Weakly, Renn beat the ground with her fists. 'Please!'

An old man stooped and peered at her. He was the ugliest, hairiest old man she'd ever seen. Although he was Auroch, he hadn't shaved his scalp, but had simply smeared his mane and beard with clay, which hung in clots. Bristles sprouted from his ears and nostrils, and his brows were tangled creepers overhanging the caverns of his eyes.

With a horny finger he prodded her greenstone wrist-guard.

She jerked back.

He spat in disgust and hobbled away.

A younger man emerged from a shelter. His face was a web of scars.

Renn pointed to the waterskin. 'Please,' she begged.

Using hand speech, the man gave a command, and the woman set the waterskin before Renn.

She fell on it and drank greedily. Almost at once, the throbbing in her head eased, and strength flooded back into her limbs. '*Thank* you,' she said.

Another woman brought a large bark bowl which she placed before the hunters. Renn felt a surge of hope. The food smelt good. It made the Aurochs seem a little more human.

The woman scooped some into a smaller bowl and put it in a fork of the pine as an offering. Then she scooped up another helping and laid it before Renn.

It was an appetising stew of nettles and scraps of meat, possibly squirrel, and Renn's belly growled.

The woman bunched her fingers to her mouth and nodded. *Eat.*

The man who'd allowed her to drink cleared his throat. 'You,' he said to Renn in a voice which sounded hoarse from disuse. 'You must rest. And eat.'

Renn looked from him to the bowl, then back again.

They told me to rest, Gaup had said. *They gave me food. Then they cut off my hand.*

TWENTY-THREE

Fear is the loneliest feeling. You can be in a throng of people, but if you're afraid, you're on your own.

Renn felt like an offering being prepared for sacrifice. When she refused to eat, she was taken to a pool and made to wash, while women wiped the soot from her clothes with moss. By hiding in the reeds, she managed to conceal the beaver-tooth knife tied to her calf and the grouse-bone whistle at her neck; but when they gave her back her clothes, her clan-creature feathers were gone.

Back at camp, hunger got the better of her and she forced down some of the stew under the watchful gaze of both clans. Scarred hands flickered in silent speech, and a young man with a mouth like a sliver of flint sharpened an axe and eyed her wrists.

The hairy old man sat cross-legged, straightening a pile

of arrowshafts. Renn watched him drawing each stick through a grooved piece of antler. Her own clan used the same method. Now and then, he slapped one hairy paw with a bunch of nettles to sting away the stiffening sickness. Older Ravens did that, too.

She edged closer to him. 'What will they do to me?' she said in a low voice.

He scowled and bent over his arrows.

She asked if he was the Clan Leader.

He shook his head and pointed an arrowshaft at the man who'd ordered that she be given water.

'Are you the Mage?'

Another shake of the head. 'I make the best bows in the Deep Forest,' he growled.

'Don't talk to her,' warned the young man with the axe. He clapped his hand to his mouth. 'She tricked me into talking! She's a Forest Horse spy!'

'I've never even met a Forest Horse,' protested Renn.

'We *hate* them,' muttered the young man.

'But why?' she said. 'You all follow the Way.'

'We follow it better,' he snapped. 'They use a bow to waken fire. We use sticks. That's proof.'

'Only *we* follow the *True* Way,' said a clay-headed woman. 'That's why we bear the scars. To punish ourselves for ever having left it.'

'All other clans are wicked,' declared the young man, sprinkling sand on his grindstone.

Renn thought that if she could keep them talking, maybe they wouldn't hurt her. She asked him why.

He glared at her. 'The Mountain clans are wicked because they use stone to waken fire, and worship the fire spirit. There *is* no fire spirit, there is only tree! Ice and Sea clans are wicked because they live in terrible lands that *have* no trees, and wake false fire from the fat of fishes. You in the Open Forest are worst, because you *knew* the Way, but turned your backs on it.'

An Auroch woman threw him a reproving glance. 'Don't talk to her, she's evil. She stole my child!'

'No I didn't,' said Renn.

'No more talk!' ordered the Auroch Clan Leader.

After that, they made her crouch among the roots of the pine tree. Men scowled at her. A girl spat in her face. Her hand went to her grouse-bone whistle, but she saw the young man staring, and tucked it back in her jerkin.

The camp had fallen silent again, but hands flickered, weaving hidden meanings. Renn thought of the Raven camp, with its squabbling children and dogs nosing for scraps, and Fin-Kedinn telling stories by the fire. Her heart twisted with longing. Fin-Kedinn, help me. What do I do?

Clear and bright, she remembered a frosty morning many winters ago, when he'd taken her into the Forest to try out her new bow. She hadn't wanted to go. Her fa had just died, and the other children were ganging up on her; she'd wanted to stay in her sleeping-sack and never come out. But there was her uncle, warming his hands at the fire, waiting for her.

Their breath had smoked as they'd crunched through the snow. Fin-Kedinn had found tracks and shown her how to read them. 'When the red deer know that the wolves are hunting them, they trot proudly and lift their hooves high. *See how strong I am*, they're telling the wolves. *Don't attack me, I can fight back!* His blue eyes met hers. He wasn't only talking about the deer.

Renn gripped the pine roots with both hands. Fin-Kedinn was right. She would not sit meekly while others decided her fate. 'What are you saying about me?' she called in a voice which carried across the camp.

Heads turned. Hands stilled.

'If you're deciding what to do with me, tell me. Keeping it from me – that's not justice.'

The Auroch Leader stood up. 'The Aurochs are always just.'

'Then talk to me,' said Renn.

For the first time, the Lynx Leader spoke. 'Who *are* you?'

She rose to her feet. 'I am Renn of the Raven Clan. I am a Mage.' As soon as she said it, she knew it was true.

'Women can't be Mages,' sneered the young man with the axe. 'It's against the Way. I'll show you how much of a Mage she is!' He ran to snatch her grouse-bone whistle.

'Stay away!' she warned. 'This is a Mage's bone for summoning spirits! None may touch it but me!'

He drew back as if she'd burnt him.

Putting the whistle to her lips, she blew. 'None of you can hear its voice,' she said, 'but I can. This bone speaks only to Mages and to spirits.'

Now she had the whole camp's attention. Raising her head, she cawed a raven summons to the stars. Then she held up her hands and showed the zigzag tattoos on her inner wrists. 'See the marks I bear! It's lightning: the spears of the World Spirit, who chases demons into rocks and wakes the fire from trees. Harm shall come to any who attempts to harm me!'

That was an eerie echo of her mother, but she didn't care; whatever else she was, Seshru had been a powerful Mage.

Above the trees, she saw the gibbous moon riding high. It had been dead when Bale was killed, but now it was stronger. So was she.

'If she's a Mage,' said the Lynx Leader, 'she's an Open Forest Mage. The World Spirit doesn't want her here. That's why it stays away.'

A nodding of heads and fluttering of hands.

'She stole my child,' repeated the Auroch woman. 'She took him for a tokoroth!'

'No,' said Renn. 'I hunt the one who did.'

'And who is that?' said the Auroch Leader suspiciously.

'Thiazzi,' she replied. 'Thiazzi the Oak Mage.'

People frowned in disbelief, and the old man looked disappointed, as if he'd caught Renn lying. 'There's no-one left from the Oak Clan,' he said. 'They all died out.'

'The Soul-Eater didn't,' said Renn. 'Take me to your Mage and I'll give him proof.'

'Our Mage keeps to his prayer shelter,' said the Auroch Leader, 'he doesn't see outsiders.'

'If you were really a Mage,' snarled the young man, 'you'd know that.'

People nodded. The throng closed in around her. Scarred faces leered. Red hands gripped poisoned spears. Her knees shook, but she stood her ground. To waver now was to fall.

A harsh caw echoed through the Forest.

All heads turned skywards.

A shadow cut across the stars – and Rip lit onto a pine branch, his black eyes fixed on Renn.

She cawed a greeting and he swooped, landing with a thud on her shoulder. Talons dug into her parka, stiff feathers brushed her cheek. She made a gurgling sound, and Rip raised his bill and half-spread his wings in reply.

People drew back, clutching clan-creature amulets.

At the edge of camp, a wolf appeared.

Relief washed over Renn. If Wolf had survived the fire, maybe Torak had too.

Wolf's amber eyes grazed the camp, then returned to Renn. His hackles bristled. The sinews of his long legs were taut. One sign from her and he would spring to her aid.

He had helped her simply by showing himself. It would be dangerous for him to do more. 'Uff,' she warned.

He tilted his head, puzzled.

'Uff!' she said again.

He turned and vanished into the trees.

The clans breathed out. The young man stood dumbstruck, his axe dangling from his hand.

The old man cleared his throat. 'I think,' he said, 'we'd better not harm her just yet.'

Wolf was frightened and confused. His paws hurt from the hot earth, and he couldn't find Tall Tailless because the Bright Beast had eaten all the scents. And now the pack-sister had howled to him, then told him to go.

He didn't. He stayed near the Den.

The taillesses stank of fear and hatred. They hated the pack-sister, but were too scared to hurt her. The pack-sister was frightened too, but she hid it extremely well. This was something taillesses did much better than normal wolves.

Not far from the Den, Wolf found a small Still Wet, and cooled his sore pads in the mud. He waded deeper and washed the stink of the Bright Beast off his fur.

When he got back to the Den, he scented a change. The

taillesses were getting ready to move. Wolf decided to follow and keep a close nose on the pack-sister.

Then maybe Tall Tailless would come too.

Two Lynx hunters ran into camp, breathless and sweating, and spoke to the Leaders in a flurry of hand speech. Renn tried and failed to follow what was going on.

Wolf had gone, but the ravens were playing in the pine tree, hanging by their talons from the auroch horns, then dropping almost to the ground before soaring and swooping round for another turn.

The young man cast them hostile looks, but the old man shrugged. 'They're ravens, they like games. And trickery.'

Renn wondered if that was meant for her.

'Here,' he said, 'you might as well take this, although I can't let you have any arrows.'

To her astonishment, he held out her bow. It had been cleaned and oiled, the bowstring freshly waxed.

'Thank you,' she said.

He grunted. 'It's a good bow, and you've looked after it. Unlike some.' He shuddered in sympathy for all mistreated bows. 'But the string's frayed. Give me your spare and I'll replace it.'

Renn hesitated. 'This *is* the spare string,' she lied.

He peered at her through the tangle of his brows.

Had he laid a trap for her? Or was he telling her to use what she had? She was about to ask why he'd given it back when the young man ran over to them.

'It's decided,' he told the old man, 'We're breaking camp.'

'Where to?' said Renn.

He ignored her, but the old one gave her a regretful

look. 'I'm sorry,' he muttered as he hobbled away.

Renn barely had time to sling her bow over her shoulder before her wrists were tied and a blindfold was pulled over her eyes.

TWENTY-FOUR

After the darkness of the beaver lodge, daylight blinded Torak.

Blinking, spitting out lake water, he clung to a branch. It was sooty; his hand came away black. The air was hazed with bitter brown smoke.

Scrambling onto the piled branches of the lodge, he cast about. Dimly, he made out charcoal hills jagged with dead trees. Nothing else.

He sank to his knees. Renn. Wolf. How could they have survived?

If there had been a single bird in the sky, he would have broken his promise to the wind and spirit walked to find them. If there had been a single tree left alive on the slopes . . .

Behind him, something sneezed.

The foal lay in a sprawl of spindly legs. It looked as startled as Torak by its sneeze.

Gently, he stroked its mane, and it blinked at him through long lashes. He felt a spark of hope. If a foal could live through the fire, maybe Wolf and Renn had too.

Talking to the foal in an undertone, he untied his belt and looped it over its neck. It wobbled to its feet and swayed. Then it threw down its head and coughed.

After a short struggle, he got it into the water, and together they struck out for the shore.

They'd hardly made it to the shallows when a shrill whinny rang out. The foal gave an answering whinny, startlingly loud, and tugged at the rawhide. Torak released it and it wobbled towards a black shape moving among the trees. Mother and foal nuzzled each other; then the foal ducked under her belly to suckle.

Torak made out more horses. The lead mare turned and gave him a penetrating stare – and in that moment, he knew what to do.

Feverishly, he took the last of Saeunn's root from his medicine pouch and crammed it in his mouth. If Wolf or Renn were anywhere in this devastation, who better to sense them than prey?

The other horses side-stepped and tossed their heads, uneasy at his nearness, but the lead mare stood her ground. Swivelling her ears, she listened to his moans as the cramps took hold. She lowered her head and watched him clutch his belly, falling to the ground in a cloud of ash . . .

. . . and through her horse eyes, Torak stared at the body which lay twitching and frothing at the mouth.

For the first time in his life, he felt the ceaseless vigilance of prey. He twisted one ear to listen to the human kicking at cinders, and flicked back the other to catch the nicker of a mare chivvying her foal. One eye scanned the shore for hunters, the other the slope above, while his horse nose told him the movements of every member of the herd.

The mare's souls were surprisingly strong, but very fearful, and although Torak wanted her to canter up the hill, she refused. She was a wise horse, she knew it was best to avoid anything strange, and since *everything* was strange, she wouldn't budge. Her herd had been through the terrors of the fire, and now they found themselves in this black Forest where there was no grazing and only the water smelt the same, so she would stay near that.

But the alien souls in her marrow were making her restive. She snorted and rolled her eyes, and the worried herd did the same.

In the battle of souls, Torak overcame her. Kicking up his hind hooves, he broke into a canter. With effortless strength his four legs hammered the earth. Such power, such speed! He felt a surge of wild joy as he thundered up the hill, and his herd came thundering after him.

At the top he halted, puffing and blowing. The ashen wind played in his mane, cooling his sweaty neck. He flared his nostrils to catch the scents.

Almost at once, he caught the scent of a wolf.

The mare shivered, remembering sharp fangs biting her flanks. Torak forced her to stay where she was. Then he heard it: a long, wavering howl. *I am seeking you . . .*

It wasn't Wolf.

The disappointment was so great that he lost control of the mare's spirit, and she wheeled and crashed down the slope. Blundering through the bemused herd, she raced back to the safety of the water.

She skittered to a halt in a cloud of ash. She smelt the

meaty breath of humans. She smelt that some bore the skins of bats, others the tails of horses. She was startled, but not frightened. Of all the hunters in the Forest, people never threatened her.

It was Torak who was afraid. He saw his human body lying defenceless on the ground. The hunters saw it too.

He saw them crunch towards him over the brittle earth, their tattooed faces merciless. He saw a Forest Horse hunter prod his body with the butt of his spear. Another kicked him in the ribs. Dimly, he felt the kick.

Now they were crowding round him, kicking, beating. With a jolt, he was back in his body, and pain was opening inside him. He moaned. Something struck his head.

In his last glimmer of awareness, he sent a silent howl to Wolf. Sorry, pack-brother, sorry I couldn't find you.

Sorry, Renn.

TWENTY-FIVE

Renn was jostled and dragged till she lost track of time. Sometimes they carried her, sometimes they tossed her in a dugout. Once they fed her food and water.

She smelt charred corpses, and knew they'd entered the wasteland. It seemed endless, but at last they were back among hooting owls and rustling leaves.

Suddenly, her wrists were untied, the blindfold torn off, and she stood blinking in a glare of firelight.

It was night. She saw torches staked in a vast ring. She caught the tang of pine, the murmur of a river. The Aurochs and Lynx had pitched their camp to one side of the ring of fire. At its centre rose a scarlet tree. Root, trunk, branch, leaf – all had been painted red with earthblood. An entire living tree was being offered, to draw the World Spirit into the Deep Forest.

Someone pushed her forwards, and she found herself beside a sputtering torch. To her amazement, she saw not only Auroch and Lynx gathered here. On the other side of the ring of fire, there was a *second* camp and a shadowy throng, bristling with axes and spears. One of them moved closer to the light, and she saw that his beard and lips were stained green, his face tattooed with leaves. His long green hair was braided with horsetails, and his headband was brown. Renn couldn't believe it. The Forest Horse Clan was camped not an arrowshot away from their deadly enemies.

Among the Forest Horses, others flitted, half-seen in the moonlight. Their mantles were the colour of night; a web of charcoal lines obscured their faces. Renn saw thorny black tattooes on their chins. Bat Clan.

The two sides faced each other across twenty paces of smoky torchlight. Arrows were nocked to bows. Hands flexed on axes and spears.

At the roots of the scarlet tree, Renn made out a huge figure in flowing robes and a glaring mask crested with horsetails. Her skin crawled. Thiazzi.

His long sleeve hid his mutilated hand, but in the other he held a heavy staff incised with burnt spirals. 'See what I bear,' he told the clans in the sonorous tones Renn had last heard in the Far North. 'I, the Forest Horse Mage, bear the speaking-staff of the Auroch Clan.'

The Aurochs stirred in alarm.

'The Auroch Mage,' Thiazzi went on, 'is known for being wise and just. I have talked with him in his prayer shelter. In token of trust, he has given me his staff.'

Doubtful head-shaking among the Aurochs. What trickery was this?

As the Forest Horse Mage approached the Auroch

Leader, they aimed a thicket of spears at his chest. Thiazzi never flinched. 'To honour that trust, I return the staff to his clan.' With a bow, he proferred it to the Leader.

Even Renn had to acknowledge his bravery. If things went wrong, he would fall transfixed by twenty spears.

With a wary bow, the Auroch Leader took the staff, and Thiazzi stepped back. Slowly, the Aurochs lowered their spears.

Renn watched him return to the scarlet tree, where he addressed both sides.

'For a moon,' he told them, 'I have fasted in the sacred grove, and the Auroch Mage has fasted in his prayer shelter. To both of us the same vision has been sent.' He raised his arms. 'We must fight *no longer*! Auroch. Forest Horse. Lynx. Bat. Red Deer. We must *unite*!'

Gasps of amazement. Hands fluttered in urgent speech.

What is he after? wondered Renn. She could understand why a Soul-Eater might wish for strife, but why . . .

'We must unite,' repeated the Mage, 'against a *greater foe*!'

In the hush that followed, one could have heard the wingbeats of a moth. All eyes were on the masked Mage prowling the scarlet tree.

'Many winters ago,' he began, 'the clans turned their backs on the True Way.'

People hung their heads. Some of the Aurochs scratched their faces to reopen their wounds.

'They were punished,' said the Mage. 'Whole clans died out. Roe Deer. Beaver. Oak. Since then, more evils have assailed the people of the Deep Forest. *All* have been caused by outsiders – by unbelievers who spurn the Way.'

That's not right, thought Renn.

'Three winters ago,' said Thiazzi, his voice swelling like the wind in the pines, 'an Open Forest trickster duped the

Red Deer into sheltering him, then repaid them by creating the demon bear.'

People hissed and shook their fists.

'Two summers ago, the people of the Open Forest sent the sickness and the tokoroths . . .'

No we didn't, thought Renn, it was the Soul-Eaters!

' . . . only our vigilance kept them from the True Forest.'

Axes were shaken in triumph, spears beaten on shields. Rapt, painted faces drank it in.

'The winter before last, the Ice clans sent hordes of demons to invade us. Last spring, the Otters tried to drown us in a flood.'

This is all lies! Renn shouted in her head.

'This spring, outsiders stole our children and sent the great fire to destroy us. They failed!'

The shield-rattling intensified.

'Until now, we have only *resisted*! But now . . .' He swept round the ring of torches, 'Now we must *fight*! *All* evils come from outsiders! They seek to destroy us because we follow the Way, but we of the Deep Forest – the *True* Forest – we shall unite! We shall rise and crush the Open Forest!'

The roar that burst from every throat shook the pines and hammered the stars.

'Cast off your headbands!' bellowed the Mage. 'Embrace your Deep Forest brothers and unite against the outsiders!'

In a frenzy, headbands were torn from brows. Auroch ran to embrace Bat, Forest Horse touched foreheads with Lynx. Beneath the scarlet tree, the Mage watched from behind his painted mask.

Suddenly, he raised both arms for silence.

People shrank back behind the torches.

'Never forget,' said Thiazzi in a voice of subtle menace, 'that the malice of outsiders is sleepless.' He paused. 'I bring proof. I bring you the very menace itself: the Open Forest spy who sought to destroy us by releasing the great fire.'

Three men bore a bundle into the ring and threw it at the feet of the Mage.

Renn made out a struggling figure entangled in a net. She bit back a cry.

The figure groaned.

It was Torak.

TWENTY-SIX

The net was wrenched open, and Torak staggered to his feet. He stood with legs braced, hands tied behind his back. Renn saw blood on his face and bruises on his chest. She saw how he swayed.

Raising his head, he looked straight at her. His eyes widened.

She mouthed his name, but he frowned. *Stay out of this.*

'On your knees.' A Forest Horse woman put her spear to his back and forced him down. She had a mistrustful face tattooed with holly leaves, and green lips tight with anger. A horse's tail cascaded over her hair, and Renn guessed she was the Leader. She bowed low to her Mage.

Thiazzi accepted the homage in silence, but Renn caught the glint of eyes behind his mask, and thought, he's enjoying this.

'Mage,' said the Leader. 'Here is the evil one who tried to destroy the True Forest. I've seen him before. Two summers ago, we caught him trying to poison us with the sickness.'

'I was seeking the cure,' said Torak. He sounded spent.

'We should have hung him then,' said the Leader. 'We should make good the mistake.'

People rattled spears on shields in violent assent.

Renn threw herself forward, but two hairy paws held her back. 'Stay silent,' the old Auroch man hissed in her ear. 'You'll only make it worse.'

Releasing her, he took the speaking-staff from his Leader and shambled forwards. 'But if we kill him,' he said, 'we break clan law. *Our* Mage, the Auroch Mage, wouldn't sanction this.'

'To kill an unbeliever is to do good.' Thiazzi's powerful voice filled the clearing. 'And this is no ordinary unbeliever. See the scar on his chest where he tried to conceal his evil nature. See the tattoo on his brow. The mark of the outcast.'

This was too much for Renn. 'He isn't outcast any more!' she cried. 'Fin-Kedinn took him back, all the clans agreed!'

'The Deep Forest never agreed,' replied the painted mask. 'The Raven Leader sought to change clan law. Clan law cannot be changed.'

'Except by you,' said Torak.

'Be silent!' hissed the Forest Horse Leader.

Torak raised his head and glared at Thiazzi. 'You break clan law whenever you want. Don't you, Thiazzi?'

Puzzled faces turned to the Mage.

'Slaughtering hunters,' Torak went on. 'Murdering my father. My bone kin . . . '

'Silence!' shrilled the Forest Horse Leader. 'How dare

you insult our Mage!'

'He's not your Mage,' Torak flung back as he struggled to his feet. 'He's a Soul-Eater.'

Howls of outrage from the crowd, but Thiazzi was triumphant. 'By his own mouth he condemns himself! Here's proof of his wickedness!'

'What's *wrong* with you all?' thundered Torak.

Trees stirred. Torches flickered. Even the Forest Horse Leader stepped back.

With his scarred chest and glittering eyes, Torak looked terrifying — and exactly what Thiazzi had said he was. 'Have you forgotten how to *think?*' he bellowed at the crowd. 'Doesn't it seem odd that your new Mage has suddenly grown so war-like? Can't you *see* that he's not one of you?'

Renn had never seen him so angry. His rage was like the freezing white fury of the ice bear, and it frightened her. It frightened the others, too.

Thiazzi's laugh broke the spell. 'See how desperate he is! He knows he is condemned!'

Relief shuddered through the crowd. The Mage had restored their certainty.

'I've heard enough for judgement,' declared Thiazzi. 'An outcast in the True Forest is an insult to the World Spirit. This is why the Spirit stays away. The outcast must die.'

The wind got up. The red tree sighed.

Renn stood aghast.

Torak stared stonily at Thiazzi.

'Although,' said the old man, still holding the staff, 'if this truce is to stand, the Auroch Mage must also agree.'

That brought his clan to their senses, and they watched to see how the Forest Horse Mage would respond.

Torchlight played on the wooden face. Behind it, Renn

sensed the racing thoughts. He wanted Torak dead, and soon. But if he snubbed the Aurochs, he risked a riot and the ruin of his plans.

'Of course he must agree,' Thiazzi said between his teeth. 'Tonight, the Auroch Mage keeps to his prayer shelter, as I shall keep to the sacred grove. Each clan shall paint a tree with earthblood. When both Mages return, and if we are of one mind, the outcast shall die.'

Torak woke to a raging thirst.

Horsehair ropes constricted his wrists and ankles. His bruises throbbed, his head ached. Drifting in and out of wakefulness, he tried to work out where he was. A cramped shelter. Roots against his cheek . . .

He jolted awake. They had laid him beneath the scarlet tree. Soon they would hang him from it.

He couldn't see how he was going to get out of this. How long did it take to paint a tree red? That was how long he had.

He thought of Renn. She didn't look as if she'd been beaten, so maybe they would let her live. If only she didn't try to help him.

And Wolf? He saw Wolf – if he was still alive – seeking him through the charred Forest. Lost, bewildered, howling for his pack-brother. Never getting an answer.

Helpless, Torak slid into a blazing sea of thirst.

Someone was holding his head, pouring water into his mouth.

He coughed and spluttered. His tongue was swollen, he couldn't swallow. 'Don't stop,' he pleaded. It came out a meaningless mumble.

Birch bark was rough against his lips, and a cool hand supported the back of his head. Water coursed down his throat, soaking into his flesh like a flood drenching sun-cracked earth.

'How do you feel?' whispered Renn.

'Better,' he croaked. It wasn't true, but it would be soon. Shutting his eyes, he felt strength stealing into his limbs, while Renn sawed the ropes at his wrists with her beaver-tooth knife. 'Wolf,' he muttered.

'I saw him yesterday. He's fine.'

'Thank the *Spirit*. What about – '

'The ravens are fine, too. Try to sit up, we've got to be quick.'

'How did you manage this?' he asked as she started on his ankles.

'I didn't,' she said tersely. 'Everyone's asleep, I don't know why. It's as if they've taken a sleeping-potion. It can't last much longer.'

Biting down on the pain, Torak rubbed the feeling back into his wrists, while Renn washed the blood off his face and told him how Thiazzi had declared a truce among the clans. 'He must've tricked the Auroch Mage, and now he's got them all in his power.' She paused. 'Torak, this is much bigger than we thought. He's turning them against the Open Forest.'

He was trying to take that in when they heard a noise outside. A sleepy murmur, horrifyingly close. A rustle of wovenbark that subsided in a snore.

When all was quiet again, Torak breathed out. 'Why didn't they tie you up too?'

Renn strapped her knife to her calf and yanked her legging over it. 'They're scared of me . . . Because I'm a Mage.'

He met her eyes in the red darkness. Her face was sternly beautiful, and a shiver ran down his spine.

Then she was his friend again, reaching behind her and thrusting a pair of buckskin boots at him. 'I stole them from a Lynx. They'd better fit.'

As he pulled them on, she peered from the shelter. 'Can you walk?'

'I'll have to.'

The moon had set and the torches had burned out; both camps were dark and still. Around the shelter, four hunters sprawled asleep beside their weapons. Their breathing was so faint that at first Torak thought they were dead. He grabbed a bow and a quiver, jammed an axe in his belt.

Crossing the open ground to the torches seemed to take for ever. His head throbbed. Pain flared in his bruised limbs at every step. Renn vanished into the shadows, and he thought he'd lost her. She reappeared with her bow and a quiver, and pressed something into his hands. It was his knife.

'How did you –'

'I told you, they're all asleep!'

At last they were past the Auroch camp, huddled behind a clump of junipers. Renn leaned close, her hair tickling his cheek. 'They brought me here blindfold, I don't know where we are. Do you?'

He nodded. 'We came in dugouts. The Blackwater's about twenty paces over there. We'll take a boat and head upriver. Then we leave the boat and cross into the next valley, that's the valley of the horses. From there it's straight to the sacred grove.'

She frowned. 'Let's get to the boats.'

They reached the river without mishap, and found a line of dugouts drawn up on the bank. Quietly, they pushed the end boat into the shallows, and Torak climbed in. The pain of his bruises was gone, numbed by the thrill of the chase. 'The current's not strong,' he said softly. 'If we paddle hard, we might even overtake him.'

Renn stood in the shallows with her boots strung around her neck, but made no move to get in. 'Torak. Turn the boat around.'

'What?' he said impatiently.

'We can't go after Thiazzi. Not now.'

He stared at her.

'If you killed him now,' she whispered, 'you'd be confirming every lie he's told them about the Open Forest.'

'But – Renn. What are you saying?'

'We have to go back to the Open Forest. Find Fin-Kedinn. Warn the clans what's happening.'

'You can't mean this.'

Wading closer, she gripped the dugout with both hands. 'Torak, I've *seen* these people! They do everything he says. Slashing their faces, cutting off hands. They will attack the Open Forest!'

He began to be angry. 'I swore an oath, Renn. I swore to avenge my kinsman.'

'This is bigger than vengeance. Can't you see? If Thiazzi dies, they'll think it's an Open Forest plot.'

'But he's not their Mage! Once he's dead, they'll see that!'

'They won't *care*! Torak, *think*! If you killed him, they'd see it as proof of what he said. They'd attack. The Open Forest would fight back. There'd be no stopping it!'

He wanted to grab her by the shoulders and shake her. 'You said you'd help me. Are you deserting me now?'

She flinched as if he'd struck her. 'If you go after Thiazzi, I'll have to. Someone has to warn the Open

Forest.' In her voice he heard an echo of Fin-Kedinn: the same flinty resolve to do what was right, no matter what the cost.

'Renn,' he said. 'I cannot turn around now. I need you to come with me. Do this for me.'

'Torak – I *can't!*'

He looked at her standing there with the black water swirling round her calves. 'Then that's how it is,' he said. Digging in his paddle, he started upriver.

TWENTY-SEVEN

Renn stood in the freezing shallows, staring blankly into the darkness.

She couldn't believe Torak was really gone. It was a mistake. It had to be. Any moment now and he'd reappear and say sorry. 'You're right. We've got to get back to the Open Forest.' He wouldn't just leave her.

But he had. She faced the long, dangerous journey without him.

And she was quite sure that he would never get near Thiazzi. How could he, when the Oak Mage held the Deep Forest in his fist? Thiazzi would kill him. She would never see Torak again.

A reed tapped her on the shoulder, and the willows murmured a warning. *Better get away from here, fast.*

Biting her lower lip hard, she squelched towards the

nearest dugout. She got behind it and pushed, but the heavy pine didn't budge. Slithering in the mud, she gave it another heave, and the boat jerked loose and splashed into the shallows.

Swiftly she tossed in quiver, bow and boots, and jumped in after them. But as she made the first stab with her paddle, the dugout tipped sharply, nearly throwing her out. She paddled frantically.

Shadowy hunters dragged her back to land.

'You helped the outcast get away,' said the Forest Horse Leader.

'Yes.'

'Where did he go?'

'B-back to the Open Forest.'

'You're in league with him.'

'He's my friend.'

'You're in league with him against the Deep Forest.'

'N-no.' Her teeth were chattering – the chill of the river was seeping into her marrow – but they wouldn't let her ashore. Scarred faces loomed over her, engulfing her in a stink of tallow, wet wovenbark and hate.

'You poisoned us with Magecraft,' said the Forest Horse Leader.

'No.'

'You put a sleeping-draught in our water.'

So she'd guessed rightly. But who had done it, and why?

'You put a spell on us!'

Renn hesitated. Taking credit for others' deeds had been her mother's skill. 'I warned you I was a Mage,' she said coldly. 'None of you was hurt. And none will be – if you take me to the Auroch Mage.'

The air crackled with fear and hatred. Renn prayed that their fear would prove the stronger.

'Why would we do that?' said the Forest Horse Leader.

'The Auroch Mage has the respect of all,' Renn said haughtily. 'I will speak only to him.'

'You're in no position to bargain,' hissed the Leader.

Renn thought fast. 'Is this how the Forest Horses respect the truce?' she said. 'By scorning the Auroch Mage? What do the Aurochs say about that?'

It was the turn of the Forest Horse Leader to hesitate.

The shelter of the Auroch Mage squatted like a toad in the lee of a fallen spruce.

The Aurochs had brought her here blindfold – by river, then overland – and she had no idea where she was, although she knew by the smell that she was close to the burnt lands.

'Our Mage is old and frail,' they'd warned her as they slipped off the blindfold, 'you mustn't tire him. And remember, you're only seeing him because he wishes it.' Then they'd vanished into the Forest, leaving her alone before the shelter.

She stood with her hands tied behind her back, in a tangle of deadnettle still damp with dew. Above her towered the tree's root disc, smelling of earth and rotting wood. It was pitted with the nests of bats and owls, and hung with auroch horns incised with spirals. From these and the encircling pines, slender ropes of red wovenbark trailed into the shelter's smoke-hole. Renn guessed they were spirit ladders, to help the Mage climb to the spirit world.

The shelter itself appeared oddly homely. A fragrant haze curled from the smoke-hole, and the wovenbark cloth across the doorway was decorated with a border of trotting aurochs.

'Come inside,' said a faint voice.

Awkwardly because of her bound hands, Renn got down on her knees, nosed aside the wovenbark, and shuffled in.

The fire was small, but welcoming. Above it, the red tails of the spirit ladders dangled through the smoke-hole, dancing in the heat. On the other side of the fire, Renn saw her bow and the stolen arrows lying beside a mound of leaves.

It shifted. 'I've sent my people away,' wheezed a voice as quiet as a summer breeze in a sapling. 'When two Mages meet, it's best if they're not overheard.'

Renn bowed respectfully. 'Mage.'

As her eyes adjusted to the gloom, she saw that the Mage was entirely covered in leaves. Layer on layer of fresh foliage – holly, birch, spruce, willow – feathered his robe in every shade of green. On his breast hung chunks of grass-coloured amber knotted on a nettlestem string. His hood was drawn low over his face – Renn couldn't see his eyes – but she felt his scrutiny.

'Why do you disturb my prayers?' he murmured, although without reproach.

Renn wondered how to begin. If the Auroch Mage was as fair as people said, and if he hadn't fallen wholly under Thiazzi's spell, she had a chance. If not . . .

'There's a Soul-Eater in the Deep Forest,' she blurted out.

'A *Soul-Eater*?'

'His name is Thiazzi. He set the Aurochs against the Forest Horses and now he's making them attack the Open

Forest.' She gulped. It was a huge relief to get it out.

The green robe rustled as the Mage reached for a stick and prodded the embers. Willow leaves at the hem curled in the heat, and Renn saw a beetle scramble for safety. 'This is grave news,' whispered the Mage. 'Who is this – *Thiazzi?*'

A small amber bead fell from a fold in his robe and rolled to the edge of the fire. Renn wondered if she ought to pick it up. 'He's the Oak Clan Mage,' she said. 'He killed the Forest Horse Mage. He took the place of their new Mage. The Mage you've been speaking to . . . he's not who you think.'

'No?' He sounded bemused. 'And – you've made all this out by yourself?'

'Yes,' Renn lied.

'Who are you?'

'I'm Renn. A Mage of the Raven Clan. I tried to warn the others, but they wouldn't listen.'

'And you came here to defeat the Soul-Eaters.'

'With your help, Mage.'

'Ah,' sighed the Mage, his chest gently heaving with each breath.

In the fire, the amber bead sizzled and flared. Renn caught a familiar tang. That's not amber, she thought. It's spruce-blood.

'To defeat the Soul-Eaters,' said the Mage, who seemed to be growing, filling the shelter. His chest heaved with laughter as he threw back his hood and shook out his russet mane. 'And how,' said Thiazzi, 'do you intend to do that?'

TWENTY-EIGHT

The Oak Mage was in no hurry to kill her.

Reaching into the sleeve of his robe, he brought out a handful of spruce-blood pellets and shook some into his mouth. Renn watched his yellow teeth grinding them to nothing. She saw a golden speck caught in the tangle of his beard. The truth settled upon her like snow. Thiazzi was the Auroch Mage *and* the Forest Horse Mage. He'd killed them both and taken their place, making use of the Forest Horse mask and the Auroch's solitary vigils. Soon one of them would disappear, and the other would rule alone.

Only Renn knew his secret. And he knew that she knew.

The yellow teeth went on grinding. The green eyes watched her lazily.

Kneeling before him with her hands tied behind her

back, she was utterly in his power. He spat a crumb at the fire and smiled to see her cringe. 'I suppose you're going to swear to me that you won't tell anyone.'

She tried not to tremble. 'No point,' she said.

His eyes gleamed. 'And no point pretending you're not terrified.'

She did not reply.

With awesome speed for so huge a man, he crossed to her side of the fire, engulfing her in rustling leaves and a stinging smell of spruce. His hand circled her throat: his three-fingered hand. Rough stumps searched her flesh till they found the vein. He grinned to feel her terror hammering under her skin. He could snap her neck like kindling. One twist, and it was the end.

Her thoughts darted like minnows. Say something. Anything. 'The – the fire-opal,' she gasped.

Out of the corner of her eye, she saw his free hand move to his chest. Had she imagined it, or did a shadow cross his face? But what could the Oak Mage possibly fear?

She took a leap in the dark. 'You haven't told her,' she said.

'Told who?' he replied a shade too quickly.

' – Eostra,' she whispered, and the name turned her voice as cold as the breath of a bone-mound. 'You haven't told her you've got it. But she knows. Oh, yes. The Eagle Owl Mage always knows. She's coming after you.'

His red tongue slid out and licked his lips. 'You can't possibly know that.'

'But I do. I have my mother's gift.'

'Your – mother?'

'Can't you see?' She met his gaze. 'The Viper Mage. I bear her marrow in my bones . . . I know what Eostra intends.'

'How could you know? You're not a Mage!'

'I know that the spirit walker has escaped,' she said, feeding on his unease. 'I know that your plans have gone awry. What's gone wrong? Who's turned against you?'

He threw her from him, and she hit her head on the doorpost. Dazed, she struggled upright. She heard him laugh.

'Yes,' he mused, 'maybe this way is better. Maybe live bait will be more effective than dead.'

From his sleeve he drew a jagged flint knife as long as Renn's forearm. She shrank from him, but he barely noticed. No time for pleasure now, he was intent on his work. Yanking a handful of spirit ladders through the smoke-hole, he severed them and used the rope to bind her ankles, then gagged her with bruising force.

He brought his face close to hers. 'You've got something to do before you die,' he breathed. 'You're going to give me the spirit walker.'

Wildly she shook her head.

'Oh yes. You're going to bring him to me at the sacred grove.'

After a brief, brutal search, he found her beaver-tooth knife and her grouse-bone whistle, cut the medicine pouch from her belt, and tossed all three on the fire. The last thing he did before casting his hood over his face was to take her bow in his hands and snap it in two.

TWENTY-NINE

Torak thought he saw Wolf on the bank, but when he called, he did not appear. Nor did the ravens. It was as if they knew what he'd done, and condemned him for it.

'But I didn't abandon her,' he said. '*She* left *me*.'

A gust of wind ruffled the river, and the alders stirred reproachfully. A gnarled oak scowled at him as he paddled by.

He could not believe that Renn had left him and gone back to the Open Forest. Surely she would change her mind and come after him? But when he listened for the sound of a dugout, all he heard was the gurgle of water and the sighs of slumbering trees.

She'll be all right, thought Torak. She can look after herself.

Oh, of course she can, Torak. Why would she need your help,

hunted by hostile clans in the heart of the Deep Forest, with a Soul-
Eater on the loose?

As dawn broke, he stopped for a rest and something to eat. Everything reminded him of Renn. The early morning sun trembled in a patch of wood strawberries. If she'd been with him, she would have dug up a couple of roots and chewed them to clean her teeth. As he groped in the shallows for reed stems and crunched them raw, he remembered a day last summer when she'd tried to feed one to Wolf, and it had turned into a game of tag. All three of them had ended up in the water, Torak and Renn helpless with laughter, while Wolf splashed about, worrying his prize and play-growling as if it were a lemming.

'*Enough!*' said Torak.

On the opposite bank, an otter raised her sleek head and stared at him, then went back to munching the trout in her forepaws.

Rek flew down, grabbed the otter's tail in her beak, and tugged. The outraged otter spun round, snarling at the intruder, and while her back was turned, Rip swooped and snatched the fish from her paws.

Both ravens alighted near Torak and demolished the fish. Sharing it, he noted, just as he and Renn shared everything. He struck the earth with his fist.

When nothing was left of the trout but bones, Rek flew onto Torak's shoulder and gently tugged his ear. Rip walked towards him and gazed at the medicine pouch at his belt: the swansfoot pouch which had been Renn's until she'd given it to him last spring.

'Not you too,' Torak told the ravens irritably.

Rip waggled his tail and stared at the pouch.

Without knowing why, Torak opened it and took out his

medicine horn. Both ravens tilted their heads, as if listening.

Moodily, Torak turned the horn in his fingers. It was carved with spiky marks which looked like spruce trees. Fin-Kedinn had once told Torak that this had been his mother's sign for the Forest, which was how he'd recognized the horn as hers. Now, Torak saw what he'd forgotten. Twisted round the tip of the horn was the strand of Renn's hair which he'd found in her sleeping-sack when he was outcast.

Slowly, he unwound it. Rip hopped onto his knee, took the hair in his beak, and ran it through his bill as delicately as if he were preening a feather.

Torak heaved a sigh. Renn had sent the ravens to help him last summer when he was soul-sick. And he'd abandoned her.

Just as he'd abandoned Bale.

The thought made him go cold. It was happening again. He'd quarrelled with Bale, and Bale had died. Now Renn . . .

His fist closed over the strand of hair. He would go back and find her. He would *make* her come with him. Vengeance must wait a little longer.

Jumping into the dugout, he turned it around and started downriver.

This time, the ravens flew with him.

Now Wolf was confused as well as worried. What was Tall Tailless doing?

Ever since the Bright Beast had eaten the Forest, Wolf had followed, and not understood. He'd prowled about the great Dens of the taillesses and watched them snarl at each other, then tear the strips of hide from their heads. Then they'd dragged in his pack-brother, and Wolf had been about to leap to his aid when Tall Tailless had snarled at *them*. That terrible, snarling blood-hunger . . . It was not-wolf. Wolf didn't understand it. It frightened him.

Then he'd followed Tall Tailless and the pack-sister to the Fast Wet, where *they* had snarled at each other, and then – *Tall Tailless had abandoned her.* A wolf does not abandon his pack-sister. Was Tall Tailless sick? Was his mind broken?

After that, Wolf had kept to the Dark as he'd followed his pack-brother up-Wet. Tall Tailless had called, but Wolf hadn't gone to him. Wolf *hated* hiding from his pack-brother, but he knew – with the certainty which came to him at times – that he could not go to him.

Although he didn't yet know why.

THIRTY

There must have been a storm in the Mountains, because the Blackwater bore Torak swiftly back to the Deep Forest camp.

Masking the dugout with leafy branches, he lay flat, trusting the reeds to conceal him. He was lucky. Everyone was hard at work, painting trees. He saw women, men and children laboriously smearing on earthblood.

What madness, he wondered, made them blindly follow orders? Couldn't they see that Thiazzi was stealing their freedom, like a fox raiding a carcass?

When the camp had drifted out of sight, he took up his paddle. The afternoon wore on. The west wind carried the stink of the wasteland. And still he found no sign of Renn.

As he rounded a bend, he saw that the north bank was muddied, as if by dugouts. The boats were gone, but something flashed on a willow branch. A lock of dark-red hair.

Landing the dugout, Torak made his way warily up the bank.

A swathe of men's tracks led into the Forest. Among them he found Renn's. She'd been re-captured. Why had they brought her here?

Forcing himself to concentrate, he worked out that the men had returned a short while later and paddled away. Had they taken Renn with them? He didn't think so.

Further in, he found another strand of her hair, tied to a twig. Then another. The tightness inside him unclenched a little. She must have been all right if she'd been able to do that. And she'd wanted him to follow.

Drawing his knife, he headed into the Forest.

Dusk was falling when he reached a small shelter in the lee of a fallen spruce. He saw slender scarlet ropes strung from trees, and auroch horns carved with sacred spirals. He guessed this was the prayer shelter of the Auroch Mage. But it had the peculiar stillness of an abandoned camp.

The doorway was barred by two crossed branches: one oak, one yew. Filled with misgiving, Torak stepped over them and went inside. The fire was dead white embers, crumbly as bones, but something lay across it. His belly turned over. It was the remains of Renn's bow.

In disbelief he took up the black, broken pieces of yew on which she had lavished so much care. He remembered a day last summer when he'd found her grinding hazelnuts to oil it. The sun had blazed in her red hair, and he'd wondered what would it feel like to wind it round his wrist. She'd turned and met his eyes, and his face had flamed. Wolf had nosed past him after the hazelnuts, and Renn had batted his muzzle away, 'No, Wolf, not for you!' But she'd soon relented and given him a handful.

Kneeling in the embers, Torak gripped the remains of the bow. He smelt ash, and the tang of spruce. By his knee, he saw a tiny amber pellet. He picked it up. Yes, spruce-blood. Beside it, a handprint. The hand of a large man. Missing two fingers.

Everything fell into place, and Torak spiralled down, down from a great height. Thiazzi was the Auroch Mage. Thiazzi was the Forest Horse Mage. They were one and the same.

And Thiazzi had Renn.

Lurching to his feet, Torak stumbled from the shelter. Moonlight washed the clearing in icy blue. He thought of Renn being forced to watch Thiazzi snap her bow in two. How the Soul-Eater must have enjoyed that. And he'd wanted Torak to know it. He'd left the bow as a sign, with his three-fingered handprint. *Thiazzi did this.*

It was Thiazzi, not Renn, who had left those strands of her hair on the trail: leading Torak here, making sure that he took the bait. And those crossed branches . . . Proclaiming where he'd taken her.

The sacred grove, where corpses dangled from the oak.

Torak staggered to a tree and retched.

This was his fault. In his hunger for vengeance, he had delivered Renn into the power of the Oak Mage.

Tall Tailless was only a pounce away, but Wolf couldn't go to him. Something was keeping them apart, like a great Fast Wet rushing between them.

Tall Tailless had been holding the pack-sister's Long

Claw-that-Flies in his forepaws, and now he put it carefully in the tree. Wolf sensed his fear, and underneath it, his terrible blood-urge.

It was the blood-urge which stopped Wolf going to him. *I have to kill the Bitten One,* Tall Tailless had once told Wolf. *Not because he is prey or in a fight over ranges, but because he killed the pale-pelted tailless.*

But *why*? This was not what a wolf does. This – this was not-wolf.

Worry clawed at Wolf's belly. He savaged a branch. He ran in circles.

Tall Tailless had heard him. He stooped and whined. *Come to me, pack-brother. I need you!*

Wolf whimpered. He backed away.

He remembered the time in the Great Cold when he'd found the white wolves, and had tried to tell their leader about Tall Tailless. *He has no tail*, Wolf had said, *and he walks on his hind legs, but he is . . .*

Then he is not-wolf, the lead wolf had sternly replied.

Wolf had known the leader was wrong, but he hadn't dared protest.

But now.

Tall Tailless rose on his hind legs and came towards Wolf, his face puzzled. *Why won't you come to me?*

His face . . .

From the beginning, Wolf had loved his pack-brother's flat, furless face; but as he stood in the Dark, staring up at it, he saw how different it was from that of a wolf. The eyes of Tall Tailless didn't throw back the light of the Bright White Eye, as the eyes of wolves do.

Not like a wolf.

It crashed upon Wolf with the force of a falling tree, the knowledge that had been stalking him for many Lights and Darks. Tall Tailless was not-wolf.

A pain such as Wolf had never known bit deep into his heart. Not even when he was a cub on the Mountain and missing Tall Tailless terribly, not even then had he felt such pain.

Tall Tailless was not-wolf.

Not wolf.

Tall Tailless was not wolf.

THIRTY-ONE

I *thought you knew*, said Torak in wolf talk.

Wolf backed away, his amber eyes clouded with misery.

Oh, Wolf. I thought you knew.

Whimpering, Wolf turned tail and fled.

Torak ran after him, crashing through the trees. It was hopeless. Lurching to a halt, he doubled up, gasping for breath. Around him, whitebeams unfurled their silver leaves to cup the light of the full moon. He howled. Wolf did not howl back. Torak's howl sank to a sob. Wolf was gone. Gone for ever?

The trees stirred in the wind, whispering, *Hurry, hurry.* Already, Thiazzi might have reached the sacred grove. He might have woken another fire and sunk a stake into its heart. He might be dragging Renn towards it . . .

Torak ran past the shelter, back to where he'd left the dugout. He jumped in and headed upstream, stabbing the river as if it were Thiazzi. He was in an endless tunnel of dark trees and hopeless thoughts. Because of him, Wolf was in misery. Because of him, Renn was in the power of the Oak Mage.

The Blackwater was implacable. His muscles burned. He deserved it.

Through the trees, he glimpsed the glow of the Deep Forest camp. But the river was barred. A wovenbark net stretched from bank to bank.

Jamming in his paddle, Torak drove the dugout back. When he was out of sight, he put in at a clump of alders and scrambled up the bank. He couldn't go any further by river, he'd have to go on foot. He'd never reach the sacred grove in time.

Suddenly, he froze. Through the soles of his boots, he caught a faint tremor in the earth.

He sank to his knees and placed both palms on the ground. Had he really felt it? Was it heading towards him?

Maybe, after all, there *was* a way.

Wolf felt the earth shudder beneath his paws, but still he loped. He smelt that he was heading towards the Bright Beast-bitten lands. He didn't care.

At last, thirst scratched his throat and he had to stop. He found a little Still Wet and snapped some up. Then he raised his muzzle and howled his misery to the Forest.

Tall Tailless was not wolf.

Tall Tailless was not Wolf's pack-brother.

Wolf no longer *had* a pack-brother.

Wolf was alone.

The shuddering beneath his pads grew stronger. Listlessly, Wolf recognized it as the pounding of many hooves.

To get out of the way, he trotted up a rise, from where he watched the horses gallop past. Their rich smell swirled about his nose, but he was too miserable to be tempted, or to wonder what was making them run.

When they'd gone, he slunk down to the little Still Wet again.

The earth around it had been chewed up by the horses' hooves, and it clung to his paws in cold, soggy lumps. He didn't care. He wondered if Tall Tailless would hear the horses in time to get out of the way. Tall Tailless who could hardly hear or smell at all, and who no longer had a pack-brother to warn him.

As Wolf stood with drooping tail at the edge of the Still Wet, he saw the wolf who lives in the Wet gazing up at him. This was a very odd wolf, who had no scent. That had frightened Wolf when he was a cub, but he'd soon learnt that the odd wolf meant no harm, and always drew back when he did.

Right now, the wolf in the Wet looked almost as miserable as Wolf felt. To cheer him up, Wolf gave a faint wag of his tail, and the wolf in the Wet wagged his tail, too.

Then a very strange thing happened. *Another* wolf appeared in the Wet, standing beside the first one.

Only this wolf was black.

THIRTY-TWO

Darkfur stood very still, waiting to see what Wolf would do.

Wolf, too, kept very still. His claws dug into the mud. His pelt tingled with excitement.

Darkfur twitched her tail.

Wolf lifted his muzzle and sniffed.

Slowly, Darkfur raised her foreleg and pawed his shoulder.

They touched noses.

Wolf seized her scruff in his jaws. She lashed her tail and whined, showing him her belly. He released her, and now they were rolling and tumbling in a muddy blur of fur and fangs. In and out of the Wet they chased each other, Wolf making fast little greeting snaps at her flanks, Darkfur whimpering with delight and snapping him back. She leapt high, her black pelt glittering with Wet, then twisted round and body-slammed him, and he chased her over the rise and down again, snuffing her fierce, strong scent, the most beautiful scent he'd ever smelt.

Now she was pawing some leaves off the Wet and they were snapping it up, then slumping together for a rest. Panting, she told him how she'd missed him, so she'd left the pack to find him. After many Lights and Darks and much sniffing and listening, she'd howled for him and thought he'd howled back, but then the Bright Beast had eaten all the scents.

Wolf shut his eyes and heard the soft wind ruffling her fur. He felt surprised and happy and sad.

Darkfur was clever, and quick to sense what he was feeling. *Why are you sad?* she asked. *Where is the one who has no tail?*

Wolf jumped up and shook himself. *He is not wolf. He is not my pack-brother.*

Darkfur twitched one ear in puzzlement. *But we played together. He was your pack-brother. This can't be.*

Wolf trotted back and forth. He found an interesting stick and dropped it before her as a present.

Darkfur ignored it. She rose and nose-nudged his shoulder. *Do you remember when the cubs tried to eat his overpelt and you stopped them? And I gave him a fish-head?*

The pain was so bad that Wolf whined. Of course he remembered that shining day when he and Tall Tailless had been part of the Mountain pack; when they had swum together and been happy.

Darkfur rubbed her rump against his shoulder and nuzzled his scruff. *I've been chasing horses. There's a juicy little foal. I nearly caught it but its mother kicked. Let's hunt!*

Wolf turned his muzzle into the wind, and the horse

scent flowed over his nose. The herd must have halted as soon as Darkfur stopped chasing. It wasn't far off.

Darkfur bounded into the trees, wagging her tail. *Come!* Then she was loping after the horses, a sleek black wolf flying through the nettles.

Hunger woke up in Wolf's belly. He forgot his pain and raced after her.

Torak felt the tremor of hooves through the earth. The horses were heading his way. Something must have panicked them, maybe a lynx or a bear. Good, he thought. The faster the better.

Now he could hear them. As they came closer, he caught huffing and blowing and the breaking of branches. He moved off the trail, flattening himself against a beech tree.

Moments later, the lead mare burst into view. Her head was up, her tail flying. She sped past and the herd raced after her, a glossy black river of straining necks and powerful haunches.

As soon as they'd passed, Torak gave a piercing whinny.

He heard the slap of horseflesh on horseflesh as they skittered into one another; then an answering whinny.

Torak stepped onto the trail and waited.

Bracken stirred. He heard a snort. A stamp. A sleek black head pushed through.

The lead mare halted twenty paces away from him. Her flanks were heaving, her nostrils flared.

He nickered to reassure her.

She tossed her head.

In a low, gentle tone, he began to talk. 'You've smelt me

before, remember? I helped a foal back to the herd. You know I mean no harm.'

Her ears swivelled to catch his voice, but her head stayed nervously high, and she swung her hindquarters round towards him. *Stay back. I kick!*

Slowly he walked towards her, talking, not taking his gaze from her, but not alarming her with a direct stare.

Steam rose from her flanks. Her great dark eyes were wide, but no longer rimmed with white. For an instant, Torak met her gaze, and a current of knowledge flowed between them. His souls had hidden in her marrow. He had known what it was to be horse. And she knew that he knew.

'I know,' he said, moving nearer. 'I know.'

She side-stepped and swished her tail. No man had ever got this close.

He felt the heat from her flanks. He bent and sniffed her nostrils, as he'd seen horses do in greeting, and she let him, her grassy breath warming his face. Placing his hand lightly on her shoulder, he pinched his thumb and fingers together and scratched the sweaty pelt, mimicking the nibble-greetings of a horse.

A shiver rippled from her withers to her tail, and she gave a snorty blow of pleasure.

'I'm your friend,' he told her. 'You know that, don't you?'

Still finger-nibbling, he worked his way up her neck, and she turned her head and gently nipped his shoulder, returning the greeting.

His hand moved down to her withers, and he grasped a handful of mane.

Then he did what no-one in all the clans had ever done before.

He vaulted onto her back.

THIRTY-THREE

The mare gave an outraged squeal and did her best to buck Torak off. He clung to her mane and hooked his legs in front of her belly.

She reared – maybe *that* would rid her of this infuriating burden – but he flung himself forwards and gripped with his thighs.

She launched into a gallop, nearly wrenching his arms from their sockets. He slithered about on her broad, slippery back, just managing to stay on.

She made for a low-hanging branch. He ducked. Twigs scraped his back. He stayed low in case she tried that again.

They crashed through thickets, and the herd – panicked by her panic – crashed after them. Between the trees, Torak glimpsed the river. The mare was heading upstream towards the valley where she felt safe.

Her hide was rough against his cheek, and as he smelt her horsey sweat and heard her breath sawing in her chest, he felt a pang of guilt. She was his friend and he'd frightened her. Too bad. Nothing mattered except saving Renn.

Without warning, the mare's forequarters rose, her withers smashing into his cheekbone, and for a moment they were flying over a fallen tree. Then the mare thudded to earth, bashing his cheek again.

Seeing spots, he scrambled upright as they sped into the glare of firelight, into the heart of the Deep Forest camp. Trampling pails and cooking-skins, they galloped between the scarlet trees, while around them people scattered, snatching up children and gaping at Torak.

Over his shoulder he shouted, 'Your Mage is a Soul-Eater in disguise! Come to the sacred grove and see for yourselves!' Then the camp was behind them and they were racing uphill towards the ridge.

Only then did Torak realize that no-one had shot at him. No arrows, no poisoned darts. They dared not risk harming the sacred herd. His medicine pouch banged against his thigh, and without knowing why, he thanked his mother's spirit for keeping him safe.

Another fallen tree rushed towards him, and he threw himself against the mare's neck just before she jumped. Mud splattered his face as she landed in a bog, sinking up to her hocks. She struggled to free herself, and he leaned forwards to help her. Her hindquarters gave a tremendous heave and they were out, flushing grouse from the rushes in a gobbling flurry.

The moon was sinking, the shadows leaching from the Forest as they hurtled towards the Windriver. Torak saw that they were further east than the trail he'd taken before; this way was steeper, more overgrown. The wily mare knew a shortcut to her valley.

Branches tore at his hair, blackthorn blossom flew like snow. Suddenly, the mare jolted to a trot, then halted altogether, throwing down her head and nearly pitching him over her withers. Behind her, the herd ran into each other, shook themselves, and began to graze.

'No!' panted Torak, flapping his legs and punching her neck. 'Don't stop, we're not there yet!' It was useless. The mare scarcely felt it. When he went on punching, she stamped and lashed her tail, catching him stingingly on the cheek. She was on her own ground now, and not to be intimidated.

Or not by Torak.

A familiar cark! overhead, and Rip and Rek swooped, their talons almost grazing the mare's rump, before flicking skywards.

Startled, she jerked up her head, and behind her the herd snorted in alarm.

Again the ravens swooped. The mare side-stepped, showing the whites of her eyes. But it wasn't only the ravens, Torak realized. She'd caught a scent she feared.

Once again, she broke into a canter. Once again, they crashed through the willows. The mare was tiring and so was Torak. His limbs ached, and he rode in a blur of black branches and raven wings.

The Windriver vanished underground, and willows gave way to spruce. In the east, Torak saw a red sliver of dawn, livid as a wound.

The mare's hoofbeats sounded loud as they entered the holly trees, and Torak felt the power of Thiazzi swirling around him. The mare didn't like the hollies. But whatever had spooked her still drove her on.

She smelt the fire before he did. Then Torak saw it: black smoke piercing the bloody sky. Dread became a stone in his belly. Was he too late?

He put his hand to the pouch at his belt and felt the medicine horn. He had no breath left to pray out loud, but in his head he prayed to his mother to save Renn. He prayed to the World Spirit. He called upon Wolf.

As Wolf and Darkfur loped after the horses, Wolf sensed that their hunt was changing its purpose, although he didn't know what it was.

He slowed to a trot, and Darkfur slowed with him. He pricked his ears. On the wind he caught a faint, high keening: higher than the highest wolf whine or the sharpest bat-squeak.

Darkfur heard it too, but she didn't recognize it. Wolf did. It was the yowl of the deer bone which Tall Tailless carried at his flank. The deer bone which used to be silent, but had now begun to sing.

With it, Wolf caught another sound, but this was one that Darkfur couldn't hear, as it was inside Wolf's head. It was Tall Tailless howling for him, just as Wolf had howled for Tall Tailless in his head long ago, in that terrible time when the bad taillesses had trapped him in the stone Den. *Pack-brother! Come to me! The pack-sister is in danger!*

A cold nose nudged Wolf's flank. Darkfur was puzzled. *Why do you slow?*

Wolf didn't know what to do. *He is not wolf*, he told her.

Darkfur's gaze turned stern. *You were pack-brothers. A wolf does not abandon his pack-brother.*

Wolf stood miserably on the trail, listening to the howling in his head, while the Great Bright Eye peered above the Mountains, and the scent of the Bright Beast-that-Bites-Hot flew towards him on the wind.

THIRTY-FOUR

The stink of burnt meat sickened Renn.

'Next time it's you,' Thiazzi had told her. She hadn't made a sound, but he'd laughed just the same.

After the nightmare journey in the dugout, he had slung her over his shoulder and strode off through the Forest. She'd swung like a sack, her face banging into his back at every stride.

She'd known at once when they'd reached the sacred grove, because the trees felt intensely aware. They'd watched, but they hadn't helped. To them she was as insignificant as dust.

The Soul-Eater had carried her through a wall of thorns and past the embers of a great round fire. He'd climbed a pine trunk notched with footholds which stood propped against an enormous tree. Renn had seen peeling bark and caught the scent of yew. She'd tried not to think of her bow. Then Thiazzi was thrusting aside branches and throwing her down, and she was falling into the Great Yew's cavernous heart.

Her wrists and ankles throbbed and her shoulders ached from being pinioned for so long. Her mouth hurt from the gag, but she couldn't chew it because Thiazzi had tied it so tight. Worst of all, she'd landed with her left leg twisted under her, and whenever she moved, pain shot through her knee.

All through the endless night she'd huddled in the dark, listening to her panicky breath. To keep up her courage, she'd told herself that somewhere above, the full moon was shining. Then it had occurred to her that soon its strength would wane, when the sky bear caught it and began to feed.

For the first time in her life, she had nothing to wish for. She couldn't wish for Torak to come, because Thiazzi would kill him. But if he didn't come, Thiazzi would kill her.

Around her rose the gaunt flanks of the Great Yew: fissured, flaking, fiercely alive. She shifted to ease her cramped limbs, crunching owl pellets and bones beneath her, some large, some brittle and delicate as frost. She thought, I'm lying on the remains of thousands of winters.

Far above, unreachably far, a patch of sky slowly bled from grey to red, and a last star glimmered. She craned to see it, and by her knee, a spider scuttled for safety. She wished it would come back. She didn't want to be alone.

She ached for her bow. For so many summers it had been part of her, a silent friend who'd never let her down. In her head, she heard again that terrible snap.

Now she had nothing. No knife, no axe, no medicine

horn. No whistle for calling Wolf, no means of summoning Rip and Rek. She was going to die here, alone. Unavenged.

She slumped against the yew, and something dug into her forearm. It was her wrist-guard. At least, she thought, I still have that.

It was polished greenstone, very smooth and beautiful. Fin-Kedinn had made it for her when he'd taught her to shoot. The thought of him was a blaze of light in the darkness. She would *not* die unavenged. Fin-Kedinn would find out, and then Thiazzi had better beware. When the Raven Leader was angry, it was worse than any Soul-Eater. Renn pictured the lines of her uncle's face hardening to carved sandstone; his vivid, blue, freezing stare. She sat straighter.

Fin-Kedinn said that a hunter's most precious possession was not his strike-fire or his weapons, it was the knowledge he carried in his head.

Think, Renn told herself. Think.

The smell of smoke made her head throb. It was hard to order her thoughts.

The smoke.

It wasn't coming from above; that patch of sky was clear. But it had to be coming from somewhere.

After a painful circuit of the yew, she found several cracks: none wider than a finger, but at least she might be able to see what was going on.

This small victory of reason over dread made her feel a little better. Rising awkwardly to her feet and trying to favour her good leg, she hopped to the largest crack and peered through.

She saw the fire with its terrible offering. Behind it, very close, the trunk of an enormous oak. Bark faces leered at her, but the branches were blighted and barren.

Renn's heart jerked. Against the oak stood the pine-trunk ladder. Thiazzi hadn't left it against the yew, as she'd thought. So even if, by some amazing feat, she managed to free her hands and ankles and climb to that patch of sky, she would probably break her neck trying to get down.

And even if she didn't . . . Beyond the oak was the wall of thorns: juniper boughs piled chest-high, encircling the fire and the sacred trees. Thiazzi had closed the ring when he'd carried her in. If anyone came, they wouldn't be able to reach her; and she wouldn't be able to get out.

As she peered through the crack, a shadow cut across it. She recoiled and fell, jolting her knee and squealing in pain.

Thiazzi laughed. 'Not long now.'

Grimly, she struggled back to the crack.

The Oak Mage crossed in and out of sight as he circled the fire. He still wore his mantle of leaves, but his hood was thrown back to let his long hair flow free, and on his chest he wore his clan-creature wreath of acorns and mistletoe. The berries were the misty white of blinded eyes. Nestled among them, Renn saw a small black pouch.

The fire-opal.

She knew that Thiazzi felt her scrutiny and relished it, but she couldn't tear herself away. She watched him feed more branches to the fire. She stared at the charred meat dangling from the stake.

She forced her gaze upwards. The star had been snuffed out. *No help for you here*, taunted the empty sky.

Her mind scuttled like a spider. Where were Rip and Rek? And Wolf? And Torak?

No. *Don't* pray for him to come, that's what Thiazzi

wants. You're the bait. If he comes, you'll have to watch him die.

And Thiazzi would win, she had no doubt of that. He was the strongest man in the Forest, and he had a Mage's cunning.

The throbbing in her head was worse. With a jolt, she realized that she could no longer see her boots. Smoke was seeping through the cracks, pooling about her ankles.

Her eyes began to smart. She tried to cough, but only managed a muffled splutter through the gag.

'Not long now,' repeated Thiazzi.

Again she peered through the crack. The Oak Mage stood with legs braced, tossing a rawhide whip from palm to palm. His harsh features were taut with anticipation. What had he heard that she had not?

The noise in her head grew louder.

It wasn't in her head, it was outside, beyond the ring of thorns.

It was the pounding of horses' hooves.

Nearer came the thundering hooves, and Renn pressed her face against the crack, straining to see.

A shadow at the corner of her eye, then a black horse was soaring over the thorns, with Torak – yes, *Torak* – on its back. In one hand he grasped the horse's mane, in the other his blue slate knife. His dark hair flew, and his face was stern and intent on Thiazzi.

The mare's hooves struck the ground, raising spurts of ash, but Torak clung on, his eyes never leaving the Oak Mage – who stood silent, tapping his whip against his thigh.

The mare snorted and tossed her head. Torak jumped from her back, staggered, but stood firm. The mare flicked up her tail and leapt the thorns again, and her hoofbeats faded to nothing.

Renn heard the crackle of the fire and the settling of ash. She ground her cheek against unyielding wood. *No, Torak, he'll kill you!* she wanted to scream.

With unhurried ease, Thiazzi cast off his mantle. Beneath it he wore the hides of many hunters – fox, lynx, wolverine, bear – and their strength was his strength, and from his belt hung his massive knife, its edge stained dull red from many kills. He was invincible: no longer a creature of leaves and bark, no longer *of* the Forest, but its ruler.

Torak stood glaring at him. 'Where is she?' he shouted.

'Where is she?' panted Torak. He was exhausted. His legs were trembling. It was a struggle to stay on his feet.

The Oak Mage faced him through the smoke: huge, silent, in control. Torak could see no sign of Renn. Only the pine-trunk ladder against the blighted oak, and the horror on the stake.

'This is what you wanted, isn't it?' he demanded. 'You wanted me. Well, here I am! Let her go!'

'And what do *you* want, Spirit Walker?' said Thiazzi. 'Revenge for your dead kinsman? Well, here *I* am. You have only to come and take it, and your oath will be fulfilled.' Baring his yellow teeth, he spread his arms, displaying the awesome might of his shoulders and chest.

Torak hesitated.

'If you so much as scratch my hand, Spirit Walker, the Raven girl dies. But if you give yourself into my power, she goes free.'

The fire hissed. The holly trees, the Great Oak and the Great Yew, all waited to see what Torak would do.

Without taking his gaze from Thiazzi, he unslung his quiver and bow, drew back his arm, and flung them over the thorns. His axe went next. Last of all, he hefted the blue slate knife which had been his father's, and threw it after them.

Weaponless, he faced the Soul-Eater through the shimmering heat. 'I renounce my vengeance,' he said. 'I break my oath. Take me. Let her live.'

THIRTY-SIX

'Let her live,' repeated Torak, but his voice had sunk to a pleading whisper. Dread seized him. Maybe Renn was already dead.

Thiazzi saw it in his face, and his lip curled. 'It's all for nothing, Oathbreaker. You'll never see your girl again.'

For an instant, Torak despaired.

Then, small and bright, he remembered Renn standing in the mouth of the cave, shooting her last arrows at the demon bear. She had known that she couldn't win, but she'd gone on fighting.

He lifted his head. 'I don't believe you.'

The Soul-Eater's whip crackled out, loosing a shower of sparks from the fire. 'It's over, Spirit Walker. Against me you have no power.'

'I'm not dead yet,' said Torak.

Thiazzi drew his knife and moved towards him.

Torak circled to escape.

The Oak Mage laughed. 'I'm going to rip out your spine. I'm going to grind your skull beneath my heel till your eyeballs burst. No more Spirit Walker buzzing round me like a gnat round a bison. I am the Oak Mage! *I* rule the Forest!' Foam flew from his lips. His voice echoed from the rocks.

Somewhere, a wolf howled. Two short howls. *Where – are you?*

Torak howled back. *I'm here! Where is the pack-sister?*

But Wolf didn't know.

Snarling, Thiazzi shook his three-fingered fist. 'Your wolf got a chunk of me once, but not this time!' Sheathing his knife, he snatched a brand from the fire and swept it round the ring of thorns. The juniper caught with a *wssh* – and became a wall of flame. Thiazzi was exultant. 'Even the fire does my will!'

Beyond the blazing wall, Torak heard a rattle of pebbles, then furious snarls and a yelp which ended in a whine. The flames were too high. He barked a warning. *Stay back! You can't help me!*

He put his hand to his medicine pouch – the swansfoot pouch which Renn had given him. 'Renn!' he shouted. 'Renn, where *are* you?'

Torak was shouting her name, but Renn only managed a squeal which ended in a cough. The Great Yew was full of smoke. If she didn't do something soon, it would become her death tree.

And yet – she couldn't tear herself from the crack. She felt that by watching, she was keeping Torak alive; if she looked away, Thiazzi would kill him.

Stupid, stupid! she told herself. But still she watched as Torak circled the fire and Thiazzi came after him: slowly, cracking his whip, playing with his prey as a lynx plays with a lemming. Torak was exhausted. His hair was stringy with sweat and he kept stumbling. He wasn't going to last much longer.

With a huge effort of will, Renn tore her gaze away. Shuffling backwards, her boots scuffed leafmould and bones, useless, crumbling bones. She fell, landing on her hands, hurting her palms. It was hopeless.

Warmth trickled between her fingers. She twisted round, but couldn't get far enough to see.

She'd cut her hand on a bone or a root. If she could find it again . . .

The smoke was too thick. She couldn't breathe, couldn't see. She groped behind her. Where *was* it?

There. A thin, jagged edge. Surely not flint? Whatever it was, it seemed to be wedged immovably in the yew.

Shuffling closer, she began sawing at the bindings round her wrists.

Sounds from outside were muffled and remote. Was that a wolf's yelp? A raven's caw? Through her rasping breath, she caught Thiazzi's mocking tones, but nothing from Torak.

She went on sawing at the rope.

The ravens wheeled and cawed, and for a moment Thiazzi glanced up. Torak seized his chance, grabbed a branch from the fire, and lashed out.

The Oak Mage dodged it easily, and Torak saw that his branch wasn't burning, it was a lifeless grey stump.

'You can't use fire against me,' sneered Thiazzi. 'I am Master of Forest *and* fire!'

As if in answer, a gust of wind stirred the trees, blinding Torak with smoke.

Again Rip swooped. Thiazzi's whip caught his wing, and though Rip soared to safety, a black feather drifted onto the embers.

The smoke made Torak cough. When he stopped, the coughing went on.

Thiazzi saw him falter, and his eyes glittered with malice. 'The fire can't hurt *me*, but it'll only take smoke to kill your girl.'

Wildly, Torak cast about him. Where was the coughing coming from? But the wind was gusting more strongly, he couldn't tell.

Thiazzi darted a glance at the Great Oak.

Of course. The ladder. The oak must be hollow. *Renn was inside the oak.*

Edging round the fire, Torak moved closer – and raced for the ladder.

To his surprise, the Oak Mage simply watched. When Torak was halfway up, he called out. 'Not as clever as you think you are, Spirit Walker. Now I've got you like a squirrel up a tree, while she chokes to death.'

Torak gripped the ladder. Thiazzi had tricked him. The coughing wasn't louder, it was fainter. It wasn't coming from the oak, but from the yew.

Shakily, he wiped the sweat from his face. 'Don't wait too long,' he panted with a desperate show of defiance. 'The clans are on their way . . . And you don't have your mask. They'll see you for what you really are.'

'Then I'll make it quick,' said Thiazzi. Striding to the foot of the ladder, he started to climb.

THIRTY-SEVEN

The wrist-bindings snapped. Renn yanked the gag over her chin, swallowed a chestful of smoke, and coughed till she retched. Frantically, she sawed at the bindings round her ankles, then struggled to her feet and hopped to the crack.

She couldn't see for smoke, couldn't hear Wolf or the ravens – or Torak. Don't think about it. Get out, get out.

Groping through the haze, she sought for footholds, handholds, anything to help her climb. Her fingers found something jutting above her head. It felt like a peg. It couldn't be. It was. She swung herself up, her good foot scrabbling for a hold. She found a dent barely deep enough for her toes. Her free hand clawed wood. *Another* peg. Someone had hammered them in, someone taller than her, she had to stretch to reach; and the yew seemed to be helping, leading her from peg to peg. Or maybe it just wanted her gone.

The top was the hardest, as the pegs ran out and the edge was rotten. Grabbing a branch, she hauled herself over and hung half in, half out. She'd scraped her fingers raw, and a broken branch was digging into her belly, but she was clear of the smoke, gulping the cool green breath of the Forest.

She was dizzyingly high up. No boughs below, and too far to jump. Trying not to jar her knee, she thrust aside branches. They sprang back in her face as if to say, *We helped you once, don't push your luck.* Then she saw Torak.

He was almost level with her, having cleared the top of the ladder and climbed onto one of the oak's outstretched arms. He didn't see her, he was straining to push the ladder away, while Thiazzi, still on it, held firm to both ladder and tree.

It was a battle Torak couldn't win. Renn watched helplessly as Thiazzi pulled himself onto a branch and reached round the bole of the tree. Torak dodged – and caught sight of Renn. His mouth shaped her name as he took in her predicament: trapped, no way to get down. Thiazzi darted round the other side to grab him. Torak dodged, seized the ladder, and heaved. Renn saw the pine trunk tilt towards her and crash into the yew, striking it halfway up the trunk. Torak had given her a way down.

It nearly cost him his life. As he reached for the next branch, Thiazzi lunged. Torak swung himself out of the way an instant too late, and Thiazzi's blade caught his thigh. Snarling in pain, he stamped on Thiazzi's wrist and sent the knife flying.

An empty victory. Renn could see that he didn't have a chance. The Soul-Eater didn't need weapons, he would climb after Torak till he reached the uppermost branch, and then . . .

She tore her gaze away. She couldn't help him from here, she had to get down.

The pine-trunk ladder was too far below, she'd have to jump onto it. Twisting round, she lowered herself over the edge till she was hanging by her hands, and let go. The pine shuddered as she struck it with her good foot, but it held. She didn't bother with the notches, she simply slid, scraping her hands and landing in a blaze of agony on her injured knee. When she looked, Torak was gone.

No – there he was, clinging to the oak's tapering bole. The Soul-Eater was gaining on him. Renn saw Thiazzi stretch to grab Torak's leg. He missed by a finger. Torak was nearly at the crown, where the tree branched for the last time. Renn saw him dark against the stormy sky, turning his head, wondering what to do. She pictured the Oak Mage seizing him by the ankle, hurling him screaming to his death.

Setting her teeth, she crawled towards the fire, dragging her bad leg. She grabbed a pine knot full of tree-blood, fiercely ablaze. She crawled towards the oak.

'Torak!' Her voice came out as a reedy gasp. '*Torak!*' she yelled. '*Catch!*'

His head whipped round.

Kneeling on her good leg, Renn drew back her arm to take aim. This had to be the finest throw of her life.

The burning brand spun through the air in a flurry of sparks – and Torak caught it.

Hanging on with his free hand, he lashed out at Thiazzi.

The Soul-Eater dodged behind the bole of the oak –
reached round – and would have grabbed Torak's foot if
his clan-creature wreath hadn't snagged on a branch,
jerking him back. He tore it off, raining acorns and
mistletoe, but clutching the fire-opal pouch to his breast.

That gave Torak a moment to scramble higher. He
reached the crown and edged onto the sturdiest branch. It
sagged beneath him. He made a swipe with the brand. The
Oak Mage struck it a blow with his fist that nearly broke
Torak's wrist and sent the brand flying. Time stopped as
Torak watched his last chance spin in a trail of sparks and
thud to earth.

Thiazzi was exultant. *I am the Master!* he roared.

But as he bellowed his triumph, the breath of the Forest
blew a spark into the tangle of his hair. Torak saw it catch.
The Oak Mage did not.

Desperately, Torak tried to distract him. 'You'll never be
Master,' he taunted. 'Even if you kill me, you'll never get
what you want!'

'And what's that?' sneered the Oak Mage, climbing
closer.

'What you killed my kinsman for: the fire-opal.'

'But I have it!' Gloating, he brandished the pouch.

A bolt of black feathers shot from the sky and Rek made
a grab for it, but Thiazzi brushed her aside with a sweep of
his arm.

The laughter froze on his lips as a shadow slid over him.
The eagle owl scythed the air with silent wings, swung her
talons forwards, and ripped the pouch from his hand.
Howling in fury, he reached for her, but she was gone,
winging her way towards the High Mountains.

Now Thiazzi's howl became a scream, for the fire had
taken hold, and it was hungry. Clawing at his mane, his

beard, his clothes, he faltered – lost his balance – and fell.

High in the oak, Torak saw the Soul-Eater lying lifeless on the roots. He saw a throng of Deep Forest hunters emerge from the hollies, break through the ring of thorns, and surround the corpse. Then the clouds burst and the rain lashed down, quenching the flames and sending up plumes of bitter smoke; and the Forest gave a vast, shuddering sigh, having purged itself of the evil which had threatened its green heart.

Rain streamed down Torak's face as he climbed to safety, but he scarcely noticed. He was shaking with fatigue, yet strangely numb. He couldn't even feel the wound in his thigh.

Jumping to earth, he staggered to Renn, who was slumped by the ruins of the fire. Kneeling beside her, he gripped her shoulders. 'Are you hurt? Did he hurt you?'

She shook her head, but she was white as bone, and her eyes were shadowed with a darkness Thiazzi had created. She opened her mouth to say something; then her face worked and she twisted away from him. The nape of her neck was smooth and defenceless. He put his arms around her and pulled her close.

As they clung together, the medicine horn at his hip began to hum. Raising his head, he saw Wolf standing between the Great Yew and the Great Oak, his eyes glowing with the amber light of the guide. *Watch*, he told Torak. *It comes* . . .

From nowhere, a fierce wind swept through the sacred grove, whipping branches but making no sound. The sun rent the clouds, the great trees blazed so green that it hurt to look, but Torak could not avert his eyes. The humming of the horn was deep inside him, thrilling through his bones. The world splintered and fell away. He couldn't hear the sizzle of embers or the hiss of rain. He couldn't smell the smoke, or feel Renn in his arms.

In the drifting haze between the oak and the yew stood a tall man. His face was dark against the dazzling sky, and his long hair floated in the voiceless wind. From his head rose the antlers of a stag.

With a cry, Torak covered his eyes with his hand.

When he dared look again, the vision was gone, and there was Wolf, his pack-brother, wagging his tail and bounding towards him through the rain.

THIRTY-EIGHT

When Torak woke up, he didn't know where he was.

He lay beneath a mantle of warm hare fur. Green sunlight shone through a spruce-bough roof. He smelt woodsmoke, and heard the sounds of a camp: the crackle of a fire, the little grinding crunches of someone sharpening a knife.

Then it started coming back. Kneeling with Renn in the sacred grove. The Deep Forest clans crowding round; someone pressing his knife into his hands. The journey to camp, on foot and in a dugout. A woman sewing up the wound in his thigh, another poulticing Renn's knee. A honeyed drink which made him drowsy, then – nothing.

Shutting his eyes, he curled into a ball. There was a faint ache in his chest, as if something were trying to get out, and he had a gnawing feeling of apprehension. Thiazzi was dead; but Eostra had the fire-opal. And he and Renn were at the mercy of the Deep Forest clans.

When he emerged from the shelter, he found a throng of people waiting. They bowed low. He did not bow back. Two days before, they'd been baying for his blood.

To his surprise, he spotted Durrain and the Red Deer among them, with a few Willow and Boar Clan, but no Ravens. Where was Renn? He was about to ask when the Forest Horse Leader made an even deeper bow, and bade him come to the scarlet tree and wait.

Wait for what? he wondered. Around him the Deep Forest clans stared in unnerving silence.

It was a huge relief to see Renn hobbling towards him on crutches. 'Do you know,' she said in an undertone, 'you've slept a whole day and a night? I had to prod you to make sure you were still alive.' Her voice was brisk, but he saw that something was wrong, although she wasn't yet ready to tell him.

'Everyone keeps bowing,' he said under his breath.

'Nothing you can do about that,' she replied. 'You rode the sacred mare and fought the Soul-Eater. *And* the Great Oak is coming into leaf. They're saying you made it happen.'

He didn't want to talk of that, so he asked about her knee, and she shrugged and said it could be worse. He asked why Durrain was here, and Renn told him that the Deep Forest clans had rejected the Way as fiercely as they'd adopted it, and that they no longer scorned the Red Deer, who'd never followed it at all. 'And the Aurochs are so ashamed of having been tricked by a Soul-Eater that they mean to punish themselves with lots more scars. And nobody's going to attack the Open Forest.'

'Is that why the Boars and Willows are here, too?'

Her shoulders rose, and she stabbed the earth with her crutch. 'Fin-Kedinn sent them,' she said in a taut voice. 'He had a struggle preventing Gaup and his clan from attacking, but in the end he persuaded them to send only their Leader: to talk, not fight. The Willows and Boars came with them for support.'

'And Fin-Kedinn?' Torak said quickly.

She chewed her lip. 'Fever. He was too ill to come. That was a few days ago. No-one's heard anything since.'

There was nothing he could say to make that better, but he was about to try when the crowd parted and two Auroch hunters approached, dragging the ash-haired woman between them.

They released her and she stood swaying, peering at Torak with lashless eyes.

The Forest Horse Leader forced her to her knees at the point of her spear, and addressed the throng. 'Here is the sinner we caught near our camp!' she cried. 'She confessed. She was the one who released the great fire.' She bowed to Torak, her horsetail sweeping the ground. 'It's for you to decide punishment.'

'*Me?*' said Torak. 'But – if anyone, it should be Durrain.' He glanced at the Red Deer Mage, but she remained inscrutable.

'Durrain says you must do it,' said the Leader. 'All the clans agree. You saved the Forest. Decide the sinner's fate.'

Torak regarded the prisoner, who was watching him intently. This woman had tried to burn him alive. And yet he felt only pity. 'The Master is dead,' he told her. 'You do know that, don't you?'

'How I envy him,' she said with weary longing. 'He knew the fire at last.' Suddenly, she smiled at Torak, baring her broken teeth. 'But you – you are blessed! The fire let you live! I will submit to your judgement.'

Beside him, Renn stirred. 'It was you,' she said to the woman. 'You put the sleeping-potion in their water.'

The woman twisted her dry red hands. 'The fire let him live! They had no right to kill him.'

Angry murmurs from the crowd, and the Forest Horse Leader shook her spear. 'Speak the word,' she told Torak, 'and she dies.'

Torak looked from the vengeful green face to the ash-haired woman. 'Leave her alone,' he said.

There was a storm of protest.

'But she drugged us!' cried the Forest Horse Leader. 'She released the great fire! She *must* be punished!'

Torak turned on her. 'Are you wiser than the Forest?'

'Of course not! But –'

'Then this is how it will be! The Red Deer will keep watch on her always, and she will swear never to release the fire again.' He met the Leader's gaze and held it, and at last she lowered her spear. 'It shall be as you say,' she muttered.

'Ah,' breathed the crowd.

Durrain stood motionless, observing Torak.

Suddenly he wanted to be rid of them all, these wild-eyed people with their caked heads and scarlet trees.

As he pushed through the crowd, Renn hobbled after him. 'Torak, wait!'

He turned.

'You did the right thing,' she said.

'They don't know that,' he said in disgust. 'They'll let her live because I told them to. Not because it's right.'

'That won't matter to her.'

'Well it matters to me.'

He left her and headed out of camp. He didn't care

where he went, just as long as it was away from the Deep Forest clans.

He hadn't gone far before the wound in his thigh began to hurt, so he flung himself down on the riverbank and watched the Blackwater glide by. The ache in his chest was worse, and he wanted Wolf, but Wolf didn't come, and he didn't have the heart to howl.

He sensed someone behind him, and turned to see Durrain. 'Go away,' he growled.

She came closer and sat down.

He tore off a dock leaf and started shredding it along the veins.

'Your decision was wise,' she said. 'We will watch her well.' She paused. 'We didn't know how far her wits had wandered. We were wrong to give her so much freedom. We – made a mistake.'

Torak wished Renn could have heard that.

'She sinned,' Durrain went on, 'but it's wise to leave vengeance to the Forest.' She turned to Torak, and he felt the force of her gaze. 'You understand this now. It was something your mother always knew.'

Torak went still. 'My mother? But – you said you couldn't tell me anything about her.'

She gave him her thin smile. 'You were bent on revenge. You weren't ready to hear.' Tilting her head, she studied the shifting leaves above her. 'You were born in the Great Yew,' she said. 'When your mother felt her time come, she went to the sacred grove to seek the Forest's protection for her child. She went into the Great Yew. You were born there. She buried your navel-cord in its embrace. Then she and the Wolf Mage fled south. Later, when she knew her death was near, she sent him to find me, so she could tell the things she couldn't tell him.'

She held out her hand, and a spotted moth settled on her palm. 'The night you were born, the World Spirit came to her in a vision. He decreed that you must fight all your life to undo the evil which the Wolf Mage had helped create. She was frightened. She begged the World Spirit to help her child fulfil so hard a destiny. He said he would make you a spirit walker – but that you must then be clanless, for no clan should be so much stronger than the others.' She watched the moth flutter away. 'And he decreed that this gift must cost your mother her life.'

Torak stared at the leaf skeleton in his hands.

'To seal the pact, the World Spirit broke off a tine of his antler and gave it to her. She made it into a medicine horn. The day she finished it, she died.'

A redstart alighted on an alder, wiped its beak on the branch, and flew off.

'Your father,' said Durrain, 'left you in the wolf den and went to build her Death Platform. Three moons later, he brought her bones to the sacred grove and put them to rest in the Great Yew.'

Torak cast the leaf skeleton on the water and watched it carried away. The Great Yew. His birth tree. His mother's death tree.

He thought of his father, setting pegs in its ancient flanks to help his mate climb in when she was ready to give birth; then bringing back her bones and laying them to rest, along with her knife: the knife which, many summers later, had saved Renn's life.

On the other side of the river, a troop of ducklings followed their mother down the bank. Torak saw them without seeing them. He was clanless *because* he was a spirit walker. His mother had chosen to make him so, at the cost of her life.

A painful anger kindled within him. She could have lived, but she'd chosen to die. She had done it for him; but she'd left him behind.

Unsteadily, he got to his feet. 'I never wanted this.'

Durrain made to speak, but he motioned her back. 'I never *wanted* it!' he shouted.

Blindly, he ran through the Forest. He kept running till his thigh hurt too much to go on.

He found himself in a green glade netted with sunlight, where swallows swooped and butterflies flitted over windflowers. Beautiful, he thought.

And his dead would never see it.

As he sank to his knees in the grass, he thought of his mother and his father and Bale. The pain in his chest became as sharp as flint. For so long he had clung to his need for vengeance. Now it was gone, and there was nothing left but grief. A lump seemed to work loose under his breastbone, and he cried out. He went on crying: loud, heaving, jerky sobs. Crying for his dead, who had left him behind.

Renn lay in her sleeping-sack, staring into the dark. Her thoughts went hopelessly round and round. Fin-Kedinn had made her bow. Thiazzi had broken it. Fin-Kedinn was sick. The bow was an omen. Fin-Kedinn was dead.

Eventually, she could bear it no longer. Grabbing her crutches, she hobbled from the shelter.

It was middle-night, and the camp was quiet. She made her way to a fire and lowered herself onto a log, where she sat watching the sparks fly up to die in the sky.

Where was Torak? How could he do this? Running off

without telling her, when she was desperate to get back to the Open Forest.

Some time later, he limped into camp. He saw her and came to sit by her fire. He looked drained, and his eyelashes were spiky, as if he'd been crying. Renn hardened her heart. 'Where have you been?' she said accusingly.

He glowered at the fire. 'I want to get out of here. Back to the Open Forest.'

'Me too! If you hadn't gone off like that, we'd be on our way.'

With a stick he stabbed the embers. 'I hate being a spirit walker. It feels like a curse.'

'You are what you are,' she said unsympathetically. 'Besides, some good comes out of it.'

'What good? Tell me what good ever came out of it?'

She bridled. 'When you were a baby, in the wolf den. It's because you're a spirit walker that you learnt wolf talk. Which let you make friends with Wolf. There. That's good, isn't it?'

He went on glowering. 'But it's not just wolf talk, that's the thing. When you spirit walk – I think it leaves marks on your souls.'

Renn shivered. She'd been wondering about that, too. The rage of the ice bear, the viper's ruthlessness . . . At times, she saw traces of them in Torak. And yet – those green flecks in his eyes. Surely they were good: specks of the Forest's wisdom which had rubbed off on him, like moss off a branch.

But she was too annoyed to tell him about that now, so instead she said, 'Maybe it does leave marks, but not always. You spirit walked in a raven, and it didn't make you any cleverer.'

He laughed.

With her crutches, she pulled herself to her feet. 'Get some sleep. I want to leave as soon as it's light.'

He threw the stick into the fire and stood up. Then he reached behind him and put something into her hands. 'Here. I thought you'd want this.'

It was the pieces of her bow.

'Now you can lay it to rest,' he said. He sounded uncertain, as if he wasn't sure he'd done the right thing.

Renn couldn't trust herself to speak. As her fingers closed about the much-loved wood, she seemed to see Fin-Kedinn carving it. It *was* a sign. It had to be.

'Renn,' Torak said quietly. 'It's not an omen. Fin-Kedinn is strong. He will get better.'

She drew a breath that ended in a gulp. 'How did you know I thought that?'

'Well. I – know you.'

Renn pictured Torak limping through the Forest to retrieve the broken bow. She thought, Maybe spirit walking does leave marks. But this . . . this is simply Torak. 'Thank you,' she said.

'It wasn't much.'

'Not just for this. For what you did. For breaking your oath.' Putting her hand on his shoulder, she rose and kissed his jaw, then hobbled quickly away.

Wolf watched Tall Tailless blinking and swaying after the pack-sister had gone, and sensed that his feelings were as scattered and blown about as a flurry of leaves.

Taillesses were so complicated. Tall Tailless liked the pack-sister and she liked him, but instead of rubbing flanks and licking muzzles, they ran away from each other. It was extremely odd.

Thinking of this, Wolf trotted off to find Darkfur. She joined him, her muzzle still wet from the kill, and after play-biting and rubbing pelts, they ran together up-Wet. Wolf liked the feel of the cool ferns stroking his fur, and the patter of Darkfur's paws behind him. He snuffed the delicious smells of fresh fawn blood and friendly wolf.

The Forest was at peace again, and yet something made Wolf head for the place where Tall Tailless had fought the Bitten One. When they reached it, they slowed to a trot. The Bright White Eye gazed down upon the wakeful trees, and the dread of the Thunderer still floated in the air.

The Thunderer was a great mystery. When Wolf was a cub, the Thunderer had made him leave Tall Tailless and go to the Mountain. Later, when Wolf ran away, the Thunderer had been angry. Then Wolf was forgiven, although he wasn't allowed back on the Mountain. All this was very strange; but then, the Thunderer was male and female, hunter and prey. No wolf could understand such a creature.

Wolf used to *hate* not understanding, but now he knew that some things he just couldn't. The Thunderer was one, and Tall Tailless another. Tall Tailless was not wolf. And yet – he was Wolf's pack-brother. That was how it was.

A faint scent drifted past Wolf's nose, and he sprang alert. Darkfur's eyes gleamed. *Demons.*

Eagerly, Wolf put his muzzle to the ground, taking deep sniffs as he followed the trail. It led past the ancient trees and up the rise.

The Den was nearly blocked by a rock, the gap too narrow for Wolf to get in. He made it bigger by digging the earth with his forepaws, and Darkfur helped. At last,

Wolf squeezed through.

Inside, he caught a whiff of demon, but the scent was old. No demons here. Just a very thin, smelly tailless cub.

Wolf whined softly and licked her nose. She didn't even blink. Something was wrong. Wolf backed out of the Den and raced off to fetch Tall Tailless.

The Light had come when he drew near the Dens of the taillesses, and he saw at once that he would have to wait. On the edge of the Fast Wet, a group of floating hides had drawn up. Wolf watched the leader of the Raven pack climbing the bank, and the pack-sister throwing away her sticks and hopping towards him, and the pack leader laughing and swinging her into his forepaws.

THIRTY-NINE

'How long till we reach the Open Forest?' asked Torak.

Fin-Kedinn, rolling up his sleeping-sack, said, 'We should make it by dusk.'

'At last!' sighed Renn.

She tucked a scrap of dried boar in a birch for the guardian, but Rip promptly stole it. Torak tried to make his offering to the Forest raven-proof by stuffing it down a crack in an ash tree. Then Fin-Kedinn told Renn to put the fire back to sleep, and he and Torak carried the gear down to the canoes.

It was two days since they'd left the Deep Forest camp, and they were taking it slowly, as Fin-Kedinn's ribs were still mending. The Raven Leader had come alone, the rest of the clan being busy with the salmon run. It was good to be just the three of them.

Around him, Torak sensed a great healing. Even among the Deep Forest clans, there had been a coming together, sparked by the need to heal the stolen children. Five had been freed from holes dug into the slopes behind the sacred grove. All were stick-thin, their teeth filed to fangs, their minds scoured white as mistletoe berries. But after peering into their eyes, Renn had declared that Thiazzi hadn't yet trapped demons in their marrow, so they were still children, not tokoroths; and since she had more experience of this than anyone, even Durrain had deferred to her. The last Torak had seen of the Deep Forest clans, they'd been earnestly debating the best rites to aid the recovery.

The Forest, too, was beginning to overgrow its wounds. It had taken a day to paddle through the burnt lands, but in places, Torak had glimpsed patches of green, and a few hardy deer nibbling shoots. On the shores of Blackwater Lake, he'd seen the sacred mare. She'd whinnied at him, and he'd nickered back. It seemed that she'd forgiven him for riding her.

And yet, he thought as he stowed the waterskins in the canoes, some hurts would never heal. The Aurochs' scars would never fade. Gaup was maimed for life. His little girl, who'd been found with the others, was mute. Worst of all, one of the stolen children was lost for good. *Demon*, Wolf had said as he'd followed its trail, before losing it in the foothills of the Mountains. Torak pictured the tokoroth scuttling over the stones towards Eostra's lair.

'Better tie down the gear,' said Fin-Kedinn, making him jump. 'There's white water ahead.'

Torak was surprised; he didn't remember any rapids. Then he realized that he and Renn had made this part of the journey on foot, and south of the river. It was a relief to know that from now on, Fin-Kedinn was in charge.

They got under way, gliding past chattering alders and reed-beds alive with warblers. At last, as the light softened to gold, the Jaws of the Deep Forest loomed into view.

Over his shoulder, Fin-Kedinn asked Torak if he was sorry to be leaving the place where he was born.

'No,' said Torak, though it saddened him to admit it. 'I don't belong here. The Red Deer would've let the Oak Mage take over the Forest, rather than fight. And the others . . . They wanted to kill anyone who didn't follow the Way. Now I think they'd kill anyone who did. How can you trust people like that?'

Fin-Kedinn watched a swallow catch a fly on the wing. 'They need certainty, Torak. Like ivy clinging to an oak.'

'What about you? Do you need it?'

Fin-Kedinn rested his paddle across the boat and turned to face him. 'When I was young, I travelled to the Far North and hunted with the White Fox Clan. One night, we saw the lights in the sky, and I said, Look, there's the First Tree. The White Foxes laughed. They said, It's not a tree, it's the fires which our dead burn to keep warm. Later, when I was on Lake Axehead, the Otter Clan told me the lights are a great reed-bed which shelters the spirits of their ancestors.' He paused. 'Who's right?'

Torak shook his head.

Fin-Kedinn took up his paddle again. 'There is no certainty, Torak. Sooner or later, if you have the courage, you face that.'

Torak thought of the Aurochs and the Forest Horses, painting trees. 'I think some people never face it.'

'That's true. But not everyone in the Deep Forest is like them. Your mother wasn't. She had more courage.'

Torak put his hand to his medicine pouch. He hadn't yet told Fin-Kedinn what he'd learnt about the horn, but he had told Renn – and being Renn, she'd thought of something he hadn't. 'Maybe it's been helping you all the time. I always wondered why the Soul-Eaters never sensed that you're a spirit walker. And that humming noise at the sacred grove? Maybe it did bring the World Spirit. Though I don't think we'll ever know for sure.'

No certainty, thought Torak. The idea blew through him like a clean, cold wind.

As they swept into the shadow of the Jaws, he glanced back. The low sun glowed in the mossy spruce, and it seemed to him that they whispered farewell. He thought of the hidden valley where the Deep Forest clans had taken Thiazzi's corpse for secret funeral rites. He thought of the sacred grove where the great trees stood as they had stood for thousands of summers, watching the creatures of the Forest live out their brief, embattled lives. Did they care that he had broken his oath? Had they already forgotten?

It was not even a moon since Bale was killed, and yet it felt like a whole summer. Torak said to Fin-Kedinn, 'I promised to avenge him. But I couldn't do it.'

The Raven Leader turned and met his eyes. 'You broke your oath to save Renn,' he said. 'Don't you think that if things had been different – if you were the one who'd died, and he'd sworn to avenge you – don't you think he would have done the same?'

Torak opened his mouth, then shut it again. Fin-Kedinn was right. Bale would not have hesitated.

Fin-Kedinn said, 'You did well, Torak. I think his spirit will be at peace.'

Torak swallowed. As he watched his foster father deftly

plying his paddle, he felt a surge of love for him. He wanted to thank him for lifting such a load from his shoulders; for watching out for him; for being Fin-Kedinn. But the Raven Leader was busy steering their canoe around a submerged log and calling a warning to Renn in the other boat. Then they were out of the Jaws and into the Open Forest, and Renn was grinning and punching the air, and soon Torak was, too.

That night, as they camped by the Blackwater, Bale came to him for the last time.

Torak knows that he is dreaming, but he also knows that what's happening is true. He stands on the pebbly shore of the Bay of Seals, watching Bale carry his skinboat down to the Sea. Bale is strong and whole again, and he balances his skinboat on his shoulder with easy grace. When he reaches the shallows, he sets it on the water, jumps in and takes up his paddle.

Torak runs down to him, desperate to catch up, but already Bale is flying like a cormorant over the waves, leaving him behind.

Torak tries to call to him, but only manages a broken whisper. 'Wait!'

Out on the shining Sea, Bale brings his craft about.

'May the guardian swim with you!' cries Torak.

Bale waves his paddle in a glittering arc, and breaks into a grin. 'And run with you, kinsman!' he calls back.

Then he is off, his golden hair streaming behind him as he heads west, to where the sun is going to sleep in the Sea.

'Why *not?*' said Renn three moons later. 'You miss him. I do too. So let's go and find him.'

Torak didn't reply. He wore his stubborn look, and she knew it was no use suggesting that he should simply howl for Wolf. He wouldn't want to risk the disappointment, because these days, Wolf didn't often howl back. From time to time over the summer, he'd come to them, but although he was as affectionate and playful as ever, and had clearly got over his shock at Torak not being a wolf, at times, Renn sensed a distance in him, as if he were somewhere else. Torak didn't talk of it, but she knew that he felt it too, and that in his worst moments, he feared it meant the end of their old closeness.

So why doesn't he go and *find* him? she thought in exasperation. 'Torak,' she said out loud. 'You're the best tracker in the Forest. So. Track!'

She had to admit, though, it did feel odd to be tracking *Wolf*. But then, everything about this summer felt odd. She was still getting used to being a Mage, and although Saeunn remained the Clan Mage, people treated her even more warily than before.

Her gear, too, was unfamiliar: new medicine horn and pouch (this an unexpected gift from Durrain), new strike-fire, new axe, new knife. New bow. She'd laid the remains of her faithful friend in the Raven bone-ground, and the old Auroch man – who turned out to have known Fin-Kedinn in the past and taught him bow-making – had made her a splendid new one. It was of yew wood felled by the light of the waxing moon, and subtly fitted to her left-handed way of shooting. But she couldn't get used to it, and today she'd left it in camp; although she was beginning to worry that it might feel left out, so maybe next time she'd bring it along.

It was the Moon of Green Ashseed, and the willowherb stood shoulder-high. It was so hot that Rip and Rek flew with their beaks open to keep cool. It had been an unusually good summer, with plenty of prey and no-one dangerously ill. If Renn sometimes woke in the night from dreams of eagle owls and tokoroths, she soon went back to sleep.

She watched Torak stoop to examine a furrow where a wolf had scratched the earth after scent-marking. He sighed. 'It's not Wolf.'

Later, he picked a strand of black wolf hair off a juniper bush.

'Wolf has some black in his fur,' Renn said hopefully. 'In his tail and across the shoulders.'

'His hairs are only black at the tips,' said Torak. 'Not like this.'

For a long time after that, he went into what she called his tracking trance, following no sign that she could detect. Then he crouched so abruptly that she nearly fell over him.

By his knee, she made out the faintest shadow of a paw-print. 'Is it Wolf?' she whispered.

He nodded. His face was tense with hope, and Renn felt sorry for him, and cross with Wolf for not sensing that his pack-brother needed him.

But as they went on, she forgot her crossness and gathered some green hazelnuts as a present. The previous summer, Wolf had watched her forage in a hazel bush, then done the same, although he'd ignored the ripe ones and only crunched up the green.

She was thinking of that when a wolf howled in the next valley.

She stared at Torak. 'Wolf?' she mouthed.

He nodded. 'He's asking us to come to him.' He frowned. 'But I've never heard him make that call before.'

They reached the rise above the river, and suddenly Wolf was flattening Torak with a huge wolf welcome mixed up with a fervent apology. *I'm so happy you're here! Sorry, sorry, I missed you too! Happy! Sorry!*

Eventually he jumped off Torak and pounced on Renn to say it all over again, leaving Torak free to look about.

The space around the Den was littered with well-chewed scraps of bone and hide, the earth packed hard by many paws. Torak noticed that Wolf was thinner, probably because he'd had to do so much hunting. He began to smile. 'I should have guessed,' he murmured.

'Me too,' said Renn, pushing Wolf's nose away. Her eyes were shining, and she looked as happy as Torak felt.

A magnificent black she-wolf with green amber eyes emerged from the Den and trotted towards them, wagging her tail and sleeking back her ears in a diffident greeting.

Torak thought, Yes, of course. This is right.

Turning to Renn, he told her that the she-wolf had been part of the pack he'd befriended the previous summer. Together, they watched her lie down on her belly and sweep the earth with her tail, while Wolf disappeared into the Den.

'I think we should move back a bit,' said Torak, suddenly unsure how they should behave. He and Renn retreated a polite distance from the Den mouth, and sat cross-legged on the ground.

They didn't have long to wait. Wolf backed out, carrying a small, wriggling bundle in his jaws. Lashing his tail, he padded to Torak and set it before him.

Torak tried to smile, but his heart was too full.

The cub was about a moon old. It was fat and fluffy and not very steady on its short legs. Its ears were still crumpled, its eyes a slatey, unfocussed blue; but it wobbled eagerly towards Torak, as fearless and inquisitive as its father had been when he was a cub.

Torak whined softly and held out his hand for the cub to sniff, and it yipped and wagged its stubby tail and tried to eat his thumb. He scooped it up and nuzzled its belly. It batted him with small, neat paws, and snagged his hair with claws as fine as bramble thorns. When he set it down, it scampered back to its father.

The she-wolf raised her muzzle and whined, and two more cubs emerged from the Den and bounded towards her, mewing and nuzzling her jaws. One was black, with its mother's greenish eyes, while the other was grey, like Wolf, but with reddish-brown ears. All were trembling with excitement at this amazing new world.

Rip and Rek flew down, and two of the cubs fled, while their sister began to stalk. The ravens walked about, apparently unaware. They let the cubs prowl almost within reach, then flew off with raucous laughs.

Torak watched Renn lying on her side and dragging a stick for the cubs to chase, while – unknown to her – the black one sneaked up and gnawed her boots.

Torak glanced at Wolf, who stood proudly wagging his tail. *Thank you*, he said in wolf talk. Then to Renn, 'Do you realize what this means?'

She grinned. 'Well, I *think* it means Wolf has found a mate.'

He laughed. 'Yes, but it's more than that. This is the cubs' first time ever out of the Den. That's the most important day of all, because it's when they meet the rest of the pack.'

With a wave of his hand, he took in Wolf and his mate and the cubs, and Renn and himself. 'The rest of the pack,' he said again. 'That's us.'

GHOST HUNTER

TO THE OPEN
FOREST
FELLS
REDWA
N
W
E
S
LAKE
CAMP OF THE
MOUNTAIN CLANS
REINDEER
CROSSING-PLACE
REINDEER RIVER
FELLS

THE MOUNTAIN OF GHOSTS
BOULDER -FIELD
GORGE OF THE IDDEN PEOPLE
HILL OF KNIVES
LLS
The High Mountains

ONE

Torak doesn't want to enter the silent camp.

The fire is dead. Fin-Kedinn's axe lies in the ashes. Renn's bow has been trodden into the mud. The only trace of Wolf is a scatter of paw-prints.

Axe, bow and prints are dusted with what looks like dirty snow. As Torak draws closer, grey moths rise in a swarm. Grimacing, he flicks them away. But as he moves off, they settle again to feed.

At the shelter, he halts. The doorpost feels sticky. He catches that sweet, cloying smell. He dare not go in.

It's dark in there, but he glimpses a heaving mass of grey moths – and beneath it, three still forms. His mind rejects what he sees, but his heart already knows.

He backs away. He falls. Darkness closes over him . . .

With a gasp, Torak sat up.

He was in the shelter, huddled in his sleeping-sack. His heart hammered against his ribs. His jaws ached from grinding his teeth. He had not been asleep. His muscles were taut with the strain of constant vigilance. But he had seen those bodies. It was as if Eostra had reached into his mind and twisted his thoughts.

It's what she wants you to see, he told himself. It isn't true. Here is Fin-Kedinn, asleep in the shelter. And Wolf and Darkfur and the cubs are safe at the resting place. And Renn is safe with the Boar Clan. *It isn't true.*

Something crawled along his collarbone. He crushed it with his fist. The grey moth left a powdery smear and a taint of rottenness.

At the back of the shelter, another moth settled on Fin-Kedinn's parted lips.

Torak kicked off his sleeping-sack and crawled to his foster father. The moth rose, circled, and flitted out into the night.

Fin-Kedinn moaned in his sleep. Already, nightmares were seeping into his dreams. But Torak knew not to wake him. If he did, the evil images would haunt the Raven Leader for days.

Torak's own vision clung to him like the moths' unclean dust. Pulling on leggings, jerkin and boots, he left the shelter.

The Blackthorn Moon cast long blue shadows across the clearing. Around it, the breath of the Forest floated among the pines.

A few dogs raised their heads as Torak passed, but the camp was quiet. You had to know the Raven Clan as well as he did to perceive how wrong things were. The shelters clustered like frightened aurochs about the long-fire which burned through the night. Saeunn had ringed the clearing with smoking juniper brands mounted on stakes, in an attempt to ward off the moths.

In the fork of a birch tree, Rip and Rek roosted with their heads tucked under their wings. They slept peacefully. So far, the grey moths had only blighted people.

Ignoring the ravens' gurgling protests, Torak gathered them up and went to sit by the long-fire, his arms full of drowsy, feathered warmth.

In the Forest, a stag roared.

When he was little, Torak loved hearing the red deer bellow on misty autumn nights. Snuggled in his sleeping-sack, he would gaze into the embers and imagine he saw tiny, fiery stags clashing antlers in fiery valleys. He'd felt safe, knowing that Fa would keep the dark and the demons away.

He knew better now. Three autumns ago, on a night such as this, he had crouched in the wreck of a shelter, and watched his father bleed his life away.

The stag fell silent. Trees creaked and groaned in their sleep. Torak wished someone would wake up.

He longed for Wolf; but howling for him would disturb the whole camp. And he couldn't face the long walk to find the pack.

How has it come to this? he wondered. I'm afraid to go into the Forest alone.

'This is how it starts,' Renn had told him half a moon before. 'She sends something small, which comes in the night. Something you can't keep out. And the grey moths are only the beginning. The fear will grow. That's what she feeds on. That's what makes her strong.'

Far away, an eagle owl called: oo-hu, oo-hu.

Torak grabbed a stick and jabbed savagely at the fire. He couldn't take much more of this. He was ready: he had a quiverful of arrows, and his fingertips ached from sewing his winter clothes. He'd ground the edges of his axe and knife so sharp they could split hairs.

If only he knew where to find her. But Eostra had hidden herself in her Mountain lair. Like a spider, she had cast her web across the Forest. Like a spider, she sensed the least tremor in its furthest strand. She knew he would hunt her. She wanted him to try. But not yet.

Scowling, Torak tried to lose himself in the glowing embers.

He woke to a voice calling his name.

The logs had collapsed. The ravens were back in their tree.

He hadn't dreamt that voice. He had heard it. It was familiar – unbearably so. It was also impossible.

Rising to his feet, Torak drew his knife. When he reached the ring of juniper brands that protected the camp, he paused. Then he squared his shoulders and walked past them into the Forest.

The moon was bright. The pines floated in a white sea of mist.

Above him on the slope, something edged out of sight.

Torak's breath came fast and shallow. He dared not follow. But he had to. He climbed, scratching his hands as he pushed through the undergrowth.

Halfway up, he stopped to listen. Nothing but the stealthy drip, drip of mist.

Something tickled his knife-hand.

At the base of his thumb, a grey moth fed on a bead of blood.

'*Torak* . . .' A pleading whisper from the trees.

Dread reached into Torak's chest and squeezed his heart. This wasn't possible.

He climbed higher.

Through the swirling mist, he glimpsed a tall figure standing by a boulder.

'Help me . . .' it breathed.

He blundered towards it.

It melted into the shadows.

It had left no tracks; only a branch, faintly swaying. But behind the boulder, Torak found the remains of a fire. The logs were cold, covered in ash. He stared at them. They'd been laid in a star pattern. This couldn't be. Only he and one other person built their fires that way.

Look behind you, Torak.

He spun round.

Two paces away, an arrow had been thrust into the earth.

Torak recognized the fletching at once. He knew the one who had made this arrow. He wanted desperately to touch it.

He tried to lick his lips, but his mouth was dry.

'Is it you?' he called, his voice rough with fear and longing.

'Is it you? . . . *Fa?'*

Two

'It may not have been him,' said Fin-Kedinn.

'It was Fa,' said Torak, rolling up his sleeping-sack. 'His arrow, his fire, his voice. His spirit.'

Fin-Kedinn prodded the earth in front of the shelter with his staff. 'Voices can be mimicked. Those who knew him remember how he woke his fires. As for that arrow—'

'I know,' Torak cut in, 'anyone could have found it. Because I left him in the Forest. No rowan branches, no chants. Just a botched attempt at Death Marks. No wonder he's not at peace.'

Grabbing strips of dried meat from the cross-beams, he crammed them in his food pouch. *The dried deer meat*, his father had gasped as he lay dying. *Take it all.* But in his haste, Torak had left it behind.

'You were twelve summers old,' Fin-Kedinn said quietly. 'You did your best.'

'It wasn't enough. Now he's begging me for help.'

'Or Eostra wants you to think so.'

Torak stiffened. These days, few dared say that name out loud.

'This is what she does,' said the Raven Leader. 'She steals into thoughts and dreams. She breeds fear.'

'I know.'

'Do you? Do you have any idea how powerful she is? She has tokoroths at her command. She has the fire-opal. All the other Soul-Eaters were afraid of her. And you want to seek her alone.'

Torak paused. The mist had thickened to fog, and in the wakening camp, people loomed and vanished like ghosts. He saw pinched, terrified faces. He wondered if the fog had been sent by Eostra.

Opening his medicine pouch, he found the chunk of black root which he'd begged from Saeunn, in case he needed to spirit walk. But what use was that against the Eagle Owl Mage?

'Maybe you're right,' he said. 'Maybe what I saw last night was her doing. Fa was a Soul-Eater for a time. Maybe she's got some hold over his spirit. But I have to do something.'

'Not yet. It's been only days since the moths came. Not even Saeunn has seen anything like them. I've had word from Durrain of the Red Deer, she agrees with me. We must gather the clans. If we don't – if we give in to fear – we fall into Eostra's hands.'

'I can't wait any longer!' Torak burst out. 'Again and again I've wanted to set off, and you've always said no! The Mountains are vast, you said, you could search your whole life and never find her. But now we're under attack. Who knows what she'll send next? It's my destiny to face her, Fin-Kedinn. Must I wait till she has the whole Forest in her grip?'

'So what would you do, head off for the Mountains and trust to luck?'

'I won't need to! She wants my power. When she's ready, she'll tell me where she is.'

'When she's ready, Torak! When she's got you alone. When it's too late. No. I won't let you go.'

'You can't stop me.'

They faced each other. Fin-Kedinn was broader and stronger, but Torak no longer had to look up to him.

Taking up his medicine pouch, Torak yanked the drawstring tight. 'When Renn gets back, tell her I'm sorry. It's too dangerous for her to come with me. At least that's one decision you'll approve of,' he added with some bitterness. Since he'd turned fifteen – the age at which clan law permits a boy to seek a mate – it had seemed as if Fin-Kedinn were trying to keep them apart.

Casting away his staff, Fin-Kedinn took a few paces, then returned. 'I understand the urge to contact the dead. Believe me I do; when your mother died … But Torak. It must be *resisted*. The living and the dead can't be together. It casts a blight on the living, it drags them down into madness!'

He spoke with startling vehemence, and for a moment, Torak was shaken. Then he shouldered his quiver and bow and took up his axe. 'He's my father,' he said.

'*Your* father. *Your* destiny. But this is not only *your* battle! This threatens us all!'

'That's why I have to leave. I can't do nothing any longer.'

Torak left the Raven camp soon afterwards. The fog oppressed his spirits, but he saw no grey moths, and felt no immediate menace as he headed east.

Around midday, the fog lifted and the sun came out. Beads of moisture sparkled on amber bracken and silver-green beard-moss. The last of the willowherb gleamed purple beneath golden birch and blazing rowan: the Forest's final burst of brilliance before going to sleep for the winter. It had been a good autumn for nuts and berries, and the undergrowth rustled with small creatures enjoying the feast. Jays squabbled over acorns. Squirrels buried hazelnuts in the leafmould.

Rip and Rek flew past, making woodpecker noises and pretending to ignore Torak. They were in a sulk at having to leave the Raven camp, where they'd grown fat on offerings, especially Rip. He'd lost a wing-feather fighting the Oak Mage in the spring, and it had grown back white. This meant he was revered by the clans.

Torak barely noticed the ravens. He hated leaving Renn behind. She would never forgive him. And yet, he knew this had to be. His vision of the slaughtered camp could have been real. When he faced the Eagle Owl Mage, it had to be without Renn.

And without Wolf.

This was why he'd decided on an indirect route towards the Mountains. The quickest way would have been to cross the Ashwater and head south-east, following the Fastwater upstream, then onto the fells. Instead, he headed north-east up the Horseleap, towards the ridge above the river, where Wolf and Darkfur had recently moved the cubs.

To say goodbye.

The resting place was a patch of level ground on top of the cliff, bordered on one side by a fallen ash, and by a bramble patch on the other. It was late afternoon when Torak reached it, and Darkfur and the cubs gave him an ecstatic welcome; but Wolf was away hunting.

Torak was relieved. Now he would have to make a shelter and wait for his pack-brother. He could put off leaving until tomorrow.

As dusk came on, he woke a fire and built a spruce bough lean-to against the ash tree, hanging his gear out of reach of inquisitive muzzles. There were only two cubs to get under his feet. The one with the foxy ears, whom Renn had named Click, had died of a sickness the moon before.

When the shelter was finished, Torak went to pick blackberries, and the cubs came too: Shadow, the black cub with a passion for gnawing boots, and Pebble, who'd been the first to emerge from the Den and greet Torak in the summer.

The blackberries were so ripe that they fell to pieces in his hands, and the cubs snuffled them up from his palm. Shadow placed her forepaws on his knee and rose on her hind legs to give him a sticky wolf kiss, while Pebble, his muzzle stained purple, bounded off to attack the shelter. Seizing a branch in his jaws, he gave a tug that made the whole thing shudder and sent him hurtling back to his mother.

As Torak watched Darkfur licking her cubs, he knew he was doing the right thing. They were only three moons old: too small to make the trek to the Mountains. And Wolf would never leave them behind.

Thinking of this, Torak crawled into his sleeping-sack.

It was a frosty night, and he was glad of his winter clothes: a duckskin jerkin and under-leggings, with a parka and over-leggings of warm reindeer hide, and beaver-hide boots. He hadn't been asleep for long when he was woken by excited whimpering.

Wolf had returned. Darkfur and the cubs were lashing their tails as they gulped the meat he'd sicked up for them, while Rip and Rek sidled about looking for scraps. Darkfur was too clever for them, and the cubs had learnt the hard way about raven thievery, and warded them off with growls and body-slams.

In the moonlight, the resting place was spangled with frost, and the eyes of the pack shone silver. Wolf bounded over to Torak and they rolled together, nose-nudging and licking each other's muzzles. *The hunt is good, the cubs are strong!* said Wolf.

Glancing up, Torak saw that the black sky was spotted with downy white flakes.

It was the cubs' first snow, and they loved it. They chased and snapped and stalked this strange, silent prey, batting it with their paws and licking it off each other's fur. Torak knelt and they clambered over him, butting him with small, cold noses. Wolf and Darkfur joined in, and everyone chased each other up the ridge and round the resting place, skittering so near the edge that they sent pebbles splashing into the Horseleap far below.

At last, Torak squatted by the fire, and the wolves lifted their muzzles and howled to the moon. Torak listened to the cubs' wavering yowls and their parents' strong, sure voices. It didn't seem possible that he could bring himself to leave. And the worst of it was that he couldn't tell Wolf, as that would only force him to make an agonizing choice: either to follow Torak and desert his family, or to stay with them and abandon his pack-brother.

Sensing Torak's unhappiness, Wolf stopped howling and trotted towards him. His thick winter pelt sparkled with snow, but his tongue was warm as he licked Torak's cheek.

You're sad, he said.

No, lied Torak.

Wolf didn't ask again, but leant against him, comforting by his presence.

Safe with the pack, Torak slept without fear of Eostra's grey moths, and woke at dawn. The cubs lay in a snow-sprinkled huddle, with Darkfur and Wolf curled nearby.

Quietly, Torak put the fire to sleep and shouldered his gear.

Wolf's paws twitched in his dreams, but as Torak knelt beside him, he opened his eyes and stirred his tail. *You go to hunt?* he said with a tilt of his ear.

Yes, Torak replied in wolf talk. Burying his face in his pack-brother's scruff, he inhaled deep breaths of the beloved scent. Then he tore himself away.

It was a bitterly cold morning, and the snow-crust crackled under his boots. On the higher ground, the wind had exposed patches of flat bearberry scrub: the startling scarlet of spilt blood. On one patch, Torak found a dead grey moth. He touched it with his boot, and it crumbled to dust.

As he went on, he found more dead moths littering the undergrowth. The frost had put an end to them.

Or maybe, he thought uneasily, Eostra no longer needs them. Maybe they've already done their work.

THREE

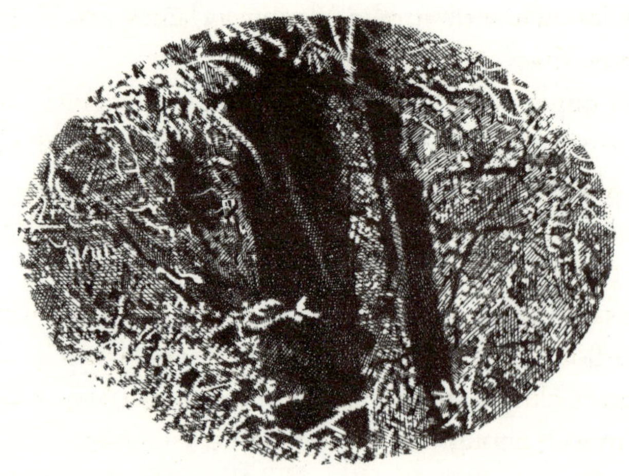

'Can't you hear them?' whispered the sick boy.

'Hear who?' said Renn.

'The demons . . .'

Renn took a brand from the fire and showed him every corner of the Boar Clan shelter. 'Aki, look. There are no demons here.'

'The moths drew them,' he muttered, rocking back and forth. 'They'll never leave me now.'

'But there's nothing—'

Grabbing her arm, he breathed in her ear. *'They're in my shadow!'*

Renn jerked back.

Aki stared about him with haunted eyes. 'I hear them all the time. The clicking of their jaws. Their angry breath. In the morning when my shadow's long, I see them. At midday, when my shadow creeps closer, they're inside me. Under my skin, gnawing my souls. Ai! Get away!' He clawed at his shadow.

Renn wondered what to do. She was exhausted. For days she'd done her best to keep the grey moths from the Boar Clan, while their own Mage was laid low with fever. And now this.

Aki's fingers were bleeding as he clawed the mat. Renn tried to stop him, but he was too strong. She called for help. Aki's father ran in and clasped his son in his arms. A second man, haggard from fever, raised a spiral amulet and made the sign of the hand.

'He says there are demons in his shadow,' Renn told him.

The Boar Mage nodded. 'I've just seen two more with the same sickness, Renn. If it's here, it'll be with the Ravens, too. I'm well enough now. Go back to your clan.'

The Boars had camped on the River Tumblerock, less than a daywalk north of the Ravens, but the fog made Renn's progress slow. As she stumbled through it, she thought of grey moths and Eostra the Masked One. Every falling leaf made her jump. She regretted having declined the Boar Clan Leader's offer to accompany her.

Her tired mind went in circles. How to stop the grey moths? How to fight the shadow sickness? What if Saeunn was too old and weak to cope, and everything came down to her?

And like a dark current beneath it all was the gnawing anxiety about Torak.

For days she'd been reading the embers, and last night she'd placed a dream-stave under her sleeping-sack: a stick of rowan wound with a lock of his hair. Now she wished she hadn't. Everything pointed the same way. She prayed that she'd got it wrong.

The fog was gone by mid-afternoon, and she paused for a salmon cake under a beech tree. She was opening her food pouch when the zigzag tattoos on her wrists began to prickle. Quietly, she closed the pouch and examined the tree.

On the other side, someone had gouged a strange, spiky mark in the trunk. It was about a hand wide, and it had been hacked – not carved but *hacked* – into the smooth silver bark.

Renn had never seen anything like it. It resembled a huge bird with outstretched wings. Or a mountain.

And it was fresh. Tree-blood oozed from the wounds. Whoever had done this had acted from hatred and a desire to inflict pain.

Drawing her knife, Renn scanned the Forest. The light was beginning to fail. Shadows were gathering under the trees.

She knew of only one creature who could treat another with such savagery. A tokoroth. A demon in the body of a child.

She touched the scar on the back of her hand, where one had bitten her two summers before. She pictured filthy, matted hair. Vicious teeth and claws. She fancied she saw branches stir, heard a cackling laugh as the creature leapt from tree to tree.

There's nothing here, she told herself.

But she was running up the slope.

Not far now. Just over the ridge, then I'll be back in the valley of the Ashwater, and it's downhill all the way.

It was a frosty night when she reached the Raven camp. Her clan, hunched round the long-fire, greeted her with subdued nods. Nobody asked why she was frightened.

Fear hung in the air. The Boar Mage was right: things were worse here too.

Two young hunters, Sialot and Poi, had fallen sick; they said there were demons in their shadows. All day they'd been gouging strange, spiky marks on everything: earth, wood, even their own flesh. Fin-Kedinn was at the river, making an offering. And Torak was gone. He'd left for the Mountains that morning.

When she heard this, Renn gave a strangled cry and rushed to her shelter.

Inside, the Raven Mage was reading the embers.

'Why didn't you stop him?' cried Renn.

Saeunn didn't look up. She sat beneath her elkhide mantle, feeding slivers of alder bark to the fire, watching how they twisted, straining to catch the hissing of the spirits. 'The Mountain of Ghosts,' she breathed. 'Ah ... Yes ...'

Renn flung down her gear and scrambled closer. 'The Mountain of Ghosts. Is that the mark I found on the tree?'

'She has made her lair in the Mountain. She seeks power over the dead. Yes ... This was always her desire.'

Renn thought of Torak making his way through the Forest, not knowing what he was heading into. She started cramming salmon cakes into her food pouch.

'You would set off at night?' mocked Saeunn. 'With the moths and the shadow sickness, and tokoroths waiting in the Forest?'

Renn paused. 'Then at first light.'

'You cannot leave. You're a Mage. You must stay and help your clan.'

'You help them,' retorted Renn.

'I am old,' said Saeunn. 'Soon I shall seek my death.'

Alarmed, Renn met her flinty gaze. Even while she'd

been away, the Raven Mage had declined. Beneath her mottled scalp, her skull looked as fragile as a puffball: one touch and it would collapse into dust.

But her mind remained as sharp as a raven's talons. 'When I am dead,' she declared, 'you will be the Raven Mage.'

'No,' said Renn.

'There is no choice.'

'They can find someone else. It happens. People do choose Mages from other clans.'

'Fool of a girl!' spat Saeunn. 'I know why you shirk your duty! But do you think that even if he survived this final battle – if he vanquished the Soul-Eater and lived to tell of it – do you think he'd stay with the Ravens? He's a wanderer, it's in his marrow! You will stay, he will leave. This is how it will be!'

In that moment, Renn hated Saeunn. She wanted to shake those frail shoulders as hard as she could.

Saeunn read her thoughts and barked a laugh. 'You hate me because I tell the truth! But you know it, too. You've read the signs.'

'No,' whispered Renn.

Saeunn grasped her wrist. 'Tell Saeunn what you saw.'

The Mage's claws were as light and cold as a bird's, but Renn couldn't pull away. 'The – the crystal Forest shatters,' she faltered.

'The shadow returns,' added Saeunn.

'The white guardian wheels across the stars—'

'—but cannot save the Listener.'

Renn swallowed. 'The Listener lies cold on the Mountain.'

'Ah . . . ' breathed the Raven Mage. 'The embers never lie.'

'They must be wrong!' cried Renn. 'I'll prove them wrong!'

'The embers never lie. Eostra will take him alone. Without you. Without the wolf.'

'She *won't*!' Renn burst out. 'She can't keep us apart, he won't face her alone!'

'Oh, he will. I've seen it in the embers, I've seen it in the bones, and they tell me – yes, and you know this in your heart – they tell me that the spirit walker will die!'

After a dreadful night, Renn slid into a dreamless sleep. When she woke, she was horrified to find that the morning was half gone.

The first snow had fallen, and the white glare made her blink as she emerged, thick-headed and heavy-limbed. Camp was bustling. The clan was taking down the shelters and using the saplings and reindeer hides to make sleds, while the dogs – who knew what this meant – raced about, eager to get into harness. The Ravens were breaking camp.

Renn found Fin-Kedinn dismantling his shelter. 'Where to?' she said. 'And why now?'

'East, to the hills. The clans will gather there. They'll be safer near the Deep Forest.' He saw her expression and stopped. 'You're going after him.'

'Yes.' She expected him to try to stop her, but he went on with his work. His face was grey. She could see that he hadn't slept.

'Why are you breaking camp now?' she said again.

'I told you. They'll be safer near the Deep Forest.'

'They? But – aren't you going with them?'

'No. Thull will lead them while I'm gone. Saeunn will counsel him when the clans gather.'

'*What?*' Renn stared at him. 'But – they need you more than ever! You can't leave now!'

Fin-Kedinn faced her. 'Do you think I would leave my people if I wasn't convinced it was the only way? I've thought of little else for days. Now I'm sure.'

'Why? Where are you going?'

He hesitated. 'I need to find the one person who can help Torak. Who can help us all.'

'Who's that?'

'I can't tell you, Renn.'

She flinched. 'You can't? Or won't?'

He didn't reply.

With a cry, Renn turned her back on him. Everything was happening too fast. First Torak. Now Fin-Kedinn.

She felt her uncle's hands on her shoulders, gently turning her round. She saw the snow sprinkling the white fur of his parka; the silver hairs threading his dark-red beard.

'Renn. Look at me. *Look at me*. I cannot tell you. Because I swore on my souls, I swore, that I would never tell.'

Ice flowers grew on the banks of the River Horseleap. The trees sparkled with frost. It was too cold for the Blackthorn Moon. It didn't feel right.

Renn guessed that as Torak had decided it was too dangerous for her to go with him, he would also try to leave Wolf behind; which meant that he would go first to the resting place, to say goodbye. To save time, she crossed the river and headed up its gentler south bank. It didn't look as if Torak had done the same. At least, she didn't find any tracks.

She was too worried to be angry with him. He had lived with the burden of his destiny for three winters, and over the last summer, she had watched the dread grow. He never spoke of it, but sometimes, when they were sitting by the fire or playing with the cubs, she saw a tightening around his eyes and mouth, and knew he was thinking of what lay ahead.

If only he didn't feel that he had to do everything alone.

She'd set out so late that she wasn't even near the resting place when she had to start looking for a campsite. She ground her teeth in frustration. Torak had a day's lead on her, and he walked fast.

A day's lead was all it would take.

FOUR

Torak had wasted the whole morning seeking a place to cross the Horseleap. The north bank got steeper and steeper as he'd headed upstream, so at last he'd been forced to double back.

He was exasperated. He'd grown up in these valleys. How could he have forgotten them so quickly?

And already, he was missing Wolf. They'd been apart before, but this felt different. He almost hoped that Wolf would seek him out, and he would see that grey shadow loping towards him through the trees.

Overnight, the Forest had turned white. Torak saw drag-marks where a badger had collected bracken for winter bedding, and patches where reindeer had pawed away the snow to get at the lichen beneath.

The mark on the yew tree shouted at him from ten paces away.

He wasn't sure what it meant – maybe a mountain with a great bird swooping towards it – but he sensed its intention. *I am here*, said the Eagle Owl Mage. *I am waiting*.

Torak bristled with outrage. The sign had been hacked through the bark and into the sapwood. It was as if Eostra were threatening the Forest itself.

On impulse, he shook some earthblood from his mother's medicine horn into his palm, and patted it into the tree's wounds. There. The horn was special, made from the World Spirit's antler; maybe the ochre it contained would help the yew to heal.

It was also a gesture of defiance to the Soul-Eater. *Torak did this*.

As he moved off, he heard Darkfur's distant, questioning barks: *Where – are you?* And far away, Wolf's answering howl: *Here!* They sounded happy. Torak told himself he'd done the right thing in leaving them.

But he still missed Wolf.

Wolf had slept through the Light, but as the Dark came on, he set off to hunt. He left his mate teaching the cubs to avoid auroch horns. She'd found an old one, and was tossing it up and down; the cubs were doing the rest, by leaping for it and getting biffed on the nose.

As Wolf trotted through the Forest, he caught the scents of prey gorging on nuts and mushrooms. At a spruce tree where a reindeer had scratched its head-branches, he rose on his hind legs and chewed the delicious, bloody tatters.

But some things troubled him.

It was so cold that the ground was stone beneath his pads, and even the trees were shivering. This cold felt odd. Dangerous.

And Tall Tailless was hiding something. He'd told Wolf that he was going hunting, but Wolf had sensed that he wasn't after prey. So why hadn't Tall Tailless told him? How could he hide things from his own pack-brother?

Worst of all, the Stone-Faced One had appeared to Wolf in his sleep. Through the hissing Dark she had come, and terror had seized him by the scruff. Her yowl had bitten his ears like splintered bone. Her smell was the smell of Not-Breath. Her terrible face was stiff: her eyes were not eyes but holes, and her muzzle never ever moved. As Wolf cowered before her, she had plunged her forepaw into the Bright Beast-that-Bites-Hot – *and taken it out unbitten*.

When he'd woken up, she was gone. But now, as Wolf followed the scent of a roe buck through the willowherb, he wondered if *this* was why Tall Tailless had left. Was he hunting the Stone-Faced One?

If that were true, he couldn't do it without his pack-brother. And yet – how could Wolf go with him, when he had to look after the cubs?

As Wolf was trying to get his jaws around this, a bad scent hit his nose. He caught the smells of the Stone-Faced One, and a fierce hunger to kill. And the smell of owl.

Wolf's fur stood on end.

He forgot about the roe buck and set off in pursuit.

It was the time when the light begins to turn: the clans call it the demon time.

Rip and Rek had been unsettled for a while, but Torak couldn't work out why. Maybe, like him, they were missing Renn and Wolf. Maybe it was this strange, windless cold.

Hungry, he paused on the cliffs above the river, woke up a small fire, and chewed a slip of dried horse meat. The banks were still too steep to climb down, and he'd had to backtrack almost two-thirds of the way to the resting place. He wasn't proud of himself.

He tossed a few crumbs in the ferns for Rip and Rek, but to his surprise, they ignored them. Instead, they flew to the top of a pine tree and gave long, penetrating calls: rap-rap-rap. *Intruder.*

Torak made a quick search, but found nothing.

With agitated caws, Rip and Rek flew away.

When you have ravens for companions, it's wise to heed their warnings. Drawing his knife, Torak made a second, more careful search.

At the foot of a rocky outcrop a short distance from the fire, he found an owl pellet. It was huge: longer than his hand and three times as thick as his thumb. Peering, but not wanting to touch, he saw that it was made of packed fur and bones, mostly weasel and hare. No wonder the ravens had fled. Like many creatures, they, too, feared the eagle owl.

Torak pictured the great bird alighting with its prey on the rocks above his head: ripping the carcass to shreds and gulping it down, then spewing out the pellet of bones.

Rising to his feet, he scanned the rocks above.

One moment he was gazing at mottled granite; the next, the eagle owl raised its tufted ears and hissed at him.

It was so close that he could have touched it. In one frozen heartbeat, he took in the powerful talons and the cruel, curving beak. He stared into the unblinking orange glare. He recoiled. Its pupils were black pits of nothingness. Nothing except the urge to destroy.

The owl gave a piercing cry, spread its enormous wings, and flew away, forcing Torak to duck.

He watched the owl disappear into the Forest. His palms were clammy with sweat.

Swiftly, he put the fire back to sleep and gathered his gear.

Further on, he found a pine marten's mangled remains. The owl had not eaten. It had killed for pleasure.

He saw one of its wing-feathers, barred with tawny and black, and coated with an unclean dust that smelt of rottenness. He'd found one just like it on the day the Soul-Eaters had taken Wolf.

That was when it hit him.

The owl had flown west.

Towards the resting place.

Towards the cubs.

FIVE

Torak couldn't reach the resting place for the brambles.
He slashed at them with his knife, he tore at them
with his hands. He couldn't see what was happening, but
he heard the ravens' strident caws and the snarls of a
furious wolf. Darkfur was defending the cubs alone. Wolf
was still out hunting.

At last Torak tore free and stumbled into the resting
place. He saw Pebble cowering under a juniper bush at
the edge of the cliff; Shadow lying by the ash tree at the
far end: a crumpled heap of black fur. He saw Rip and Rek
mobbing the eagle owl as it swooped to snatch the fallen
cub. He saw Darkfur springing to the defence.

Yanking his axe from his belt, Torak raced to help her.
The owl tilted its wings and soared out of reach. Torak
caught a blast of foetid air as it swept back towards him.

He flung up his arm. The owl struck him a dizzying blow on the forehead. As he fell to his knees, he saw it swoop with outstretched talons at Pebble's hiding-place.

Dashing the blood from his eyes, Torak struggled to his feet and ran to fend it off. He was almost there when Darkfur made a desperate leap to save her cub. The owl twisted with blinding speed, and the she-wolf's jaws clashed empty air. To Torak's horror, Darkfur landed at the very edge of the cliff. Frantically, she scrabbled. Her claws raked frozen earth. She fell.

Torak saw her hit the water far below. She went under, came up struggling. The river was too strong. She went under again.

The owl was harrying Pebble's juniper bush, the ravens beating it back. Shouting and swinging his axe, Torak threw himself into the attack. At the corner of his eye, he saw Wolf burst from the Forest and leap at the marauder. The owl wheeled, evading axe and fang and claw. It kept coming back. It had killed before and it meant to kill again.

Torak glimpsed Pebble shaking with terror beneath the juniper bush. If he stayed hidden, he had a chance, but in the open . . .

Torak barked a command, *stay*, but at that moment, Pebble's courage broke. He bolted from his hiding-place and made for the brambles. The owl snatched him in its talons and soared into the sky.

Torak threw down his axe and unslung his quiver and bow. His fingers were slippery with blood, he couldn't get the arrow nocked.

With awesome power, the owl rose out of range, Pebble hanging limp in its talons. Mockingly, it circled. Then, in a wide, lazy arc, it turned and headed south.

Rip and Rek sped after it with raucous cries.

Wolf disappeared over the edge of the cliff.

As Torak stood swaying, he saw his pack-brother skitter down the rocks and run along the bank, frantically sniffing for his mate. Then, finding no scent, Wolf raced over a fallen pine that spanned the river, and vanished into the Forest, in a futile effort to save his cub.

SIX

The eagle owl was taunting Wolf.

Dangling the cub from its talons, it flew back to make sure that he was following, then glided out of reach. Wolf's paws scarcely touched the ground as he raced after it.

Up the rise he loped, and down into the valley where he'd had his Beginning. His claws clattered as he sped across the Bright Hard Cold that had once been the Fast Wet.

The owl swept so low that he heard the hiss of its wings. Then it rose over the treetops and disappeared.

Tirelessly Wolf ran, as only a wolf can run. But at last he halted. The wind was at his tail, he couldn't catch the scent, and he couldn't see the Up for the trees. He could no longer hear the caws of the ravens.

Wolf felt in his fur that this time, the owl wasn't coming back.

A great emptiness opened inside him.

Darkfur was gone. The cubs were gone. *This could not be.*

The cubs were part of him. He could no more lose them than he could lose a paw. And he and Darkfur were one breath. As one wolf, they hunted in the Forest. As one wolf, they sensed which cub was planning to stray too far, and which had got stuck in the brambles. When they howled, their voices rose together into the Up.

This could not be.

Wolf lifted his muzzle and howled.

Wolf's howls drifted to Torak as he knelt on the clifftop. Such desolation. Grief without end.

Torak resolved that his pack-brother would not bear it alone. He would go after him and find some way to comfort him.

But as he got to his feet, the resting place went round and round. He touched his forehead. His fingers came away red.

Better do something about that, he thought muzzily. And yet he made no move to open his medicine pouch.

The resting place was a dismal mess of ravaged snow. Shadow lay by the ash tree, as if asleep. There was no blood. The eagle owl must have snatched her up, then dropped her from a great height. The fall had killed her instantly.

Kneeling by the corpse, Torak pictured her small souls padding about, seeking Wolf and Darkfur and her pack-brother. He longed to help her, but he didn't think

wolves had death rites, or Death Marks. He'd asked
Renn about that once, and she'd said that wolves don't
need them. Their ears and noses are so keen that their
souls always stay together, and never become demons.
So instead, Torak simply prayed for the guardian of all
wolves to come and fetch Shadow's spirit soon, before
she got scared.

As for her body, he carried it to the edge of the brambles
and laid it on a bed of ferns. There let it lie, with the moon
and the stars wheeling over it; and in time, like all creatures,
it would become food for the other inhabitants of the
Forest.

It was dark. There was a ring around the moon, which
meant it would get even colder. He couldn't go after
Wolf tonight. He'd have to sleep here and head off at
dawn.

Numbly, he collected his scattered gear and woke up a
fire in front of the shelter he'd left only that morning.
Then he took dried yarrow from his medicine pouch and
pressed it to his forehead, bandaging it with the buckskin
headband he'd worn when he was outcast.

The musty smell of yarrow reminded him of when he'd
hit his head going over the waterfall, and Renn had treated
his wound. He missed her. He wondered if he'd been
wrong to have left the Raven camp without her. At the
time, he'd been convinced he had to be on his own. But
maybe that had been Eostra's trick. She wanted him alone.
And now she'd made brutally sure that he stayed alone, by
sending her creature to slaughter the pack and lure Wolf
away.

From the south came his pack-brother's howls. Torak
did not howl back. He knew the only howls Wolf wanted
to hear were those he never would again.

At dawn, Torak found a precipitous way down the cliff-face and half-climbed, half-fell to the bank below.

Wolf's trail led across the pine trunk that spanned the river, but Torak did not follow it. First, he headed downstream, searching the ground beneath the cliff. Maybe – *maybe* – Darkfur hadn't been killed in the fall. Maybe she'd got ashore, and was lying battered but alive . . .

The snow was untouched, the shallows crusted with unbroken ice.

Torak crossed the Horseleap by the pine trunk, and checked the other bank. Again, nothing. Darkfur was gone.

Gone, gone, echoed Wolf's lonely howls.

Torak started along his pack-brother's trail. When the snow-crust is too hard for paw-prints, a wolf leaves barely any trace – a few flakes of frost brushed off a branch, a frond of bracken bent slightly out of place – but Torak tracked Wolf almost without having to think. His trail headed south, up the side of the valley and down into the next: a rocky, steep-sided gully.

Torak recognized it at once: the valley of the Fastwater. When he was little, he and Fa used to camp there in early summer, to gather lime bark for rope-making.

The river was frozen now, but three summers ago it had been a torrent. Torak recognized the big red rock shaped like a sleeping auroch. Beneath it he had found a pack of drowned wolves lying in the mud. And a small, wet, shivering cub.

Crossing the frozen river, he started to climb.

He went very still.

An arrow had been lashed with a twist of creeper to the trunk of a birch tree about ten paces above the auroch rock. It pointed east, towards the High Mountains.

Holding his breath, Torak climbed closer. He studied the fletching, but didn't dare touch. The arrow had belonged to Fa.

As if his father had spoken aloud, Torak heard his voice in his mind. *Help me. Set my spirit free.*

Maybe Fin-Kedinn was right, maybe Eostra was making use of Fa's arrow. But Torak couldn't forget that lost spirit calling in the night. If Eostra was summoning him to her mountain lair, then so was Fa.

And yet – if he headed east, as Fa's arrow begged him to, he would be abandoning Wolf.

Torak stood irresolute, fists clenched inside his mittens. Should he follow the dead, or seek the living?

He knew what Fin-Kedinn would have done.

Facing the invisible Mountains, he lifted his head. 'You tried to separate me from my pack-brother,' he shouted to the Eagle Owl Mage. 'Well, you won't succeed. I won't let you!'

Turning his back on his father's arrow, he headed south. To find Wolf.

SEVEN

It turned colder and colder as Fin-Kedinn headed
north.

The night before, there had been a ring around the
moon, and the stars had flickered with an intensity he'd
rarely seen. Storm on the way. The clan would have
pitched camp early. He must do the same.

He crossed the Tumblerock at the Boar Clan camp, then
made his way into the valley of the Rushwater. He was
now less than a daywalk from the Windriver, where the
Ravens had camped in the time of the demon bear. He
thought of the day when Renn and her brother had
brought in two captives: a wolf cub squirming in a buckskin
bag, and a bedraggled and furious boy . . .

The Rushwater echoed noisily between its ice-choked
banks, but the Forest had a peculiar, waiting stillness.

Fin-Kedinn realized that he'd seen no birds all day, save for a few last, lonely swans flying south.

And no people. The frosts had killed the grey moths, but the victims of the shadow sickness remained terrified, and their terror infected others. Most people were staying close to camp, only braving the Forest when hunger drove them.

So it was good to encounter a small Viper hunting party: three men and a boy, hurrying west to rejoin their clan. They'd caught two squirrels and three woodpigeon. It wasn't much, but they urged Fin-Kedinn to come with them and share.

'Bad weather on the way,' said one. 'Dangerous to be in the Forest alone.' Out of respect, he didn't ask what the Leader of the Ravens was doing so far from his clan.

Fin-Kedinn declined the offer and ignored the unspoken question. Instead, he told them of the gathering of the clans.

'The Ravens have already set off, and I told the Boar Clan when I passed their camp, they'll have left by now; and Durrain has sent word throughout the Deep Forest. Go back to your people and tell your Leader. If the clans stay together, we will remain strong. Even against Eostra.'

That he dared speak her name aloud gave them courage. But the hunter who had spoken grabbed Fin-Kedinn's arm. 'Come with us, Fin-Kedinn. We need you. You can't leave us now.'

'Others can lead,' said Fin-Kedinn. 'I must seek the one who can bring down the Soul-Eater. The one who knows the dark places under the earth.'

'Who? Where are you going?'

'North,' was all Fin-Kedinn would say.

Before they could ask more, he was on his way. Time was against him. And to find the one he sought, he must rely on knowledge many winters old.

He hadn't gone far when the boy came racing after him. 'My father says to give you this,' he panted, holding out a squirrel.

Fin-Kedinn thanked him and told him to keep it. The boy glanced up at him shyly. 'Can I go with you? I know the land to the north, I could help you find your way.'

The Raven Leader bit back a smile. He'd hunted in this part of the Forest since before this boy was born.

He was about twelve summers old, with loose limbs and a sharp, intelligent face; a little like Torak at that age. 'They say you've journeyed further than anyone,' he ventured. 'To the Far North and the Seal Islands and the High Mountains. Can't I come too?'

'No,' said Fin-Kedinn. 'Go back to your father.'

As he watched the boy plodding off, Fin-Kedinn became suddenly alert. The crunch of the boy's boots had an odd, brittle sound, which rang too sharply through the trees. And the snow looked wrong. It had an almost greenish tinge.

Fin-Kedinn's hand tightened on his staff. No wonder the Forest was bracing itself.

'Tell your father to hurry,' he shouted to the boy. 'Get back to camp, quick as you can!'

The boy turned. 'I know! Snowstorm on the way!'

'No! *Ice storm!* Much worse! Tell your father! Run!'

Fin-Kedinn watched till the boy was safely back with the others. Then he started looking for a place to build a shelter.

As he did so, he prayed to the World Spirit that Torak and Renn – wherever they were – had seen the signs too, and got under cover.

EIGHT

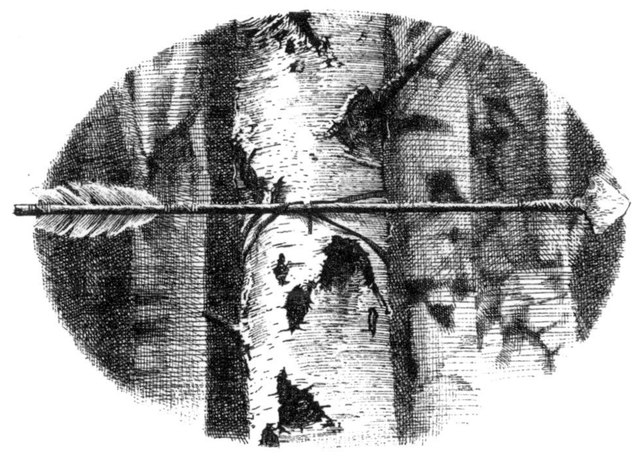

A sense of foreboding had been growing on Renn since she woke up.

It was cold. Too cold for snow. The night before, there'd been a ring around the moon. Tanugeak the White Fox Mage had once told her that this meant the moon was pulling the ruff of her parka closer around her face, because bad weather was coming.

And to make matters worse, Renn had heard Wolf howling in the night. She'd never heard him howl like that before.

The River Horseleap was beginning to freeze, the shallows congealing in fragile, pale-green swirls. In an inlet, Renn found splintered ice and a trace of a paw-print; further on, boot prints, unmistakeably Torak's. She was puzzled. He'd headed *downstream*, then backtracked. Why?

Soon after, she drew level with the resting place on the other side of the river, and craned her neck at the cliff. She howled, but no wolves peered over the edge. She told herself they must have taken the cubs exploring. But her uneasiness grew.

Her spirits rose when she found the pine trunk where Torak had crossed the river. His trail was fresher than she'd dared hope, and he'd been walking with his usual long strides, so he must be all right, which meant that Wolf couldn't have been howling for him.

She followed the trail into the gully of the Fastwater. She didn't know it well, except from Torak's description of where he'd first met Wolf, but halfway up, she spotted an arrow, tied to a birch tree and pointing east. This was baffling. Torak must have put it there as a sign for her. But if he wanted her to follow, why not just wait?

For some reason, she passed the arrow without examining it, and hurried on. But to her dismay, she found no more tracks. Torak *hadn't* come this way.

She went back to the birch tree, and came to a dead stop. The arrow had been tied in place with nightshade: a deadly plant, beloved of the Soul-Eaters – especially Seshru, her mother. Torak would never have used it. This wasn't his sign. It wasn't his arrow.

A gust of wind threw back her hood. She shivered. While she'd been tracking, the wind had got up, and the sky had darkened ominously. Storm coming. She should make camp right now.

But then she would fall even further behind.

Fighting a rising tide of panic, she decided to flout everything she'd ever learnt, and keep going.

As the wind strengthened, she found Torak's trail and followed it into the next valley. She paused for breath under a huge, watchful holly. Her sense of wrongness deepened. It wasn't even mid-afternoon, but as dark as twilight. The snow had an odd, greenish tinge. She hadn't seen a single living creature all day.

Fin-Kedinn would have called a halt long before now. 'The first rule of living,' he'd told her once, 'is *never* leave it too late to build a shelter.'

And this was a good place for a camp: a patch of level ground near the holly tree, even if it was a bit far from the river.

Renn chewed her lip. 'Torak?' she called. 'Torak!'

Angrily, she flung down her gear. *Why* had he left without her? And why hadn't she caught up?

Now that she'd stopped, she realized how little time she had left.

Come on, Renn. You know what to do. First, the fire. Wake it *now*, before you're tired from chopping wood, and build the shelter around it. Plenty of tinder in your pouch, keeping warm inside your jerkin; and you've got a bit of horsehoof mushroom smouldering in a roll of bark, so no messing about with a strike-fire.

Which was just as well. The trees were moaning, and the wind was tugging at her clothes and whipping branches in her face. It was malicious. It wanted her to fail.

Gritting her teeth, she woke the fire, then wrenched her axe from her belt. Now for the shelter. Bend saplings and tie them together with willow withes, leaving a smoke-hole at the top. Build long and low to weather the storm, and cut off the saplings' heads so the wind can't pull them over – sorry, tree-spirits, you'd better find a new home. Fill in the sides with spruce boughs, plug the gaps with bracken, and weigh it down with more saplings, as many as you can.

Despite the cold, sweat ran down her sides. Too much to do, and the trees were thrashing and creaking. They sounded frightened.

Bracing herself against the wind, she wove a rough door from hazel and spruce branches, then crawled inside, dragging in firewood, and more spruce boughs for bedding. The shelter was thick with smoke, it was swirling close to the ground, too scared to leave. Coughing, Renn pulled the door shut. The smoke-hole sucked the haze upwards, and the shelter cleared.

She'd made it just big enough to take two people, in case Torak needed it too. Now she recognized that for the delusion it was. Torak was long gone.

'Water,' she said out loud, trying to banish her fears. The river was too far, so she'd have to melt snow. Yanking her parka and jerkin over her head, she used the jerkin's lacings to tie its neck and sleeves shut, to form a makeshift bag. Then she pulled her parka back on and crawled out into the jaws of the storm.

The wind pelted her with flying branches and stung her face with ice needles. Quickly, she crammed snow into the jerkin, and crawled back inside. With her spare bowstring, she hung the snow sack from a support sapling, and placed a swiftly-made birch-bark pail underneath to catch the drips.

The wind screamed. The shelter shuddered. Suddenly, the World Spirit speared the clouds and sent the hail hammering down. Renn hugged her knees and prayed for Torak and Wolf.

A thud shook the shelter.

She gave a start. That wasn't a branch.

Pulling up her hood, she shifted the door and peered out.

Hail struck her face.

Only it isn't hail, she thought, it's *rain* – and it's turning to ice on everything it strikes.

Screwing up her face against the onslaught, she saw the freezing rain hitting twigs, branches, trees – imprisoning all it struck in a heavy mantle of ice. Boughs bent beneath the weight. Already ice was forming on her clothes.

She groped to find whatever had fallen against the shelter. Her mitten struck a lump which didn't feel like a branch. She squeezed.

The lump squawked.

Rek's wings were clogged with ice, but once Renn got the raven inside and brushed her off, she began steaming gently in the warmth.

Shivering with terror, she cowered on Renn's lap. As Renn gazed into those deep raven eyes, she sensed in them more than terror of the storm. Where had Rek come from? Where was Torak?

A thunderclap split the sky. The Forest roared as Renn had never heard it roar before. She heard deafening cracks and tremendous, splintering crashes.

And then, quite distinctly, she heard a voice in the storm. She strained to listen. Was that – could it be Torak, calling her name?

It would be madness to go out again.

And yet – if there was a chance that Torak needed help.

She grabbed a brand from the fire.

The fury of the storm beat upon her. The Forest was under attack. She saw trees flailing wildly, desperate to break free of their burden of ice. Branches crashed. A pine snapped like kindling. Even the boughs of the great holly bowed so low they threatened to split the tree in half.

'*Torak!*' yelled Renn. The ice storm ripped away his name like a leaf. '*Torak!*'

It was hopeless.

A flash of lightning, and from the holly, a face peered down at her. Icicle hair. Eyes glittering with malice.

Renn screamed.

Thunder boomed.

The tokoroth leapt into the dark.

The holly gave a groan – and tore itself apart.

Renn threw herself out of the way a heartbeat too late. One of the holly's limbs crashed across her calf, pinning her to the ground.

Wildly, she struggled, but the tree held her fast. She'd left her axe in the shelter. With her knife, she hacked at the branch. The wood was like granite, the blade bounced off. Frantically, she dug at the earth beneath her leg. Frozen hard.

Already, ice was weighing her down, sucking the life from her marrow.

'Torak!' she screamed. 'Wolf!'

The wind whipped her voice away into the night.

NINE

The hill below Torak was a precarious jumble of flood-tossed logs.

He'd spent ages searching in vain for some trace of his pack-brother. And now he couldn't even get down. He guessed that Wolf had run lightly over the logs; but if he tried, he'd start a logslide.

'Fool,' he muttered. A while ago, he'd passed a good campsite on some level ground near a big holly tree, but he'd been so intent on finding Wolf that he'd ignored it. The strange thing was, he'd known at the time he was making a mistake, but he'd done it anyway.

The wind tore at his hood and pelted him with branches. The trees roared a warning: *Get under cover, fast!*

Rip thudded onto his shoulder, making him stagger.

Quork! cawed the raven. He looked bedraggled. Torak

wondered how far he and Rek had chased the eagle owl.

The raven lifted off and flew uphill.

That was the way Torak had come. Maybe Rip wanted him to get back to that campsite while he still had the chance.

Quork! Follow!

Torak followed.

The light was so bad that he could hardly see. As he crashed through the undergrowth, he glimpsed Rip's white wing-feather. Then the clouds let loose the hail.

Only it isn't hail, he thought as he ran, *it's freezing rain. Torak, you're caught in an ice storm!*

Bent double, he battled up the slope. He couldn't go much further. He had to find some hollow under a boulder, anything, and wait out the storm.

He would have missed the shelter completely if Rip hadn't perched on top.

A shelter? Torak couldn't believe it. He recognized the patch of level ground, although it looked different: the holly had toppled over. And there had been no shelter here, he was sure of it.

A flash of lightning showed him the wattle door weighted shut with a stone. Thrusting it open, he threw Rip inside and crawled after him.

With the door closed behind them, the wind's screams lessened a little, but the ice hammering the walls was deafening. The shelter was empty, but by the look of the fire, whoever had built it hadn't gone far.

And they had known what they were about. As Torak brushed the ice from his clothes, he saw that the fire had been set on a platform of sticks to keep it off the cold earth, and ringed with stones to stop it escaping. Wood was stacked on one side, while a quiver and bow hung to dry – but not too close to the flames – and a bag of snow, improvised from a jerkin, dripped water into a half-full pail.

Rip was pecking eagerly at the sleeping-sack. It moved. Rek peered out. The ravens greeted each other with much gurgling and holding of beaks. Torak's belly turned over. Why was Rek in here?

That bow. That jerkin.

Renn.

This was her shelter. Her quiver, her arrows. Over there were the crumbs of the salmon cake she'd left for Rek. And being Renn, she'd raven-proofed the rest of her food by weighting her pouch with her axe.

She'd left her weapons, which meant she couldn't have gone far.

Fear trickled down Torak's spine. In winter, you don't *need* to go far to die in a storm. Every clan has its stories of people lost in a blizzard, whose frozen corpses are later found just a few paces from camp.

Beside the wood-pile, Renn had stacked some stubs for use as torches. Torak jammed one in the embers to wake it. Then, leaving his gear and the ravens inside, he seized his axe and threw himself out into the storm.

'Renn!' he yelled.

She could have been right beside him and he wouldn't have heard her.

Branches flew at him as he began to search. Doubled up against the onslaught, he circled the shelter. His torch died. He could hardly see a pace ahead.

He made another round, widening the search. Still nothing.

On his third pass, lightning flickered in the fallen

holly, and through the branches he glimpsed a flash of red.

Dropping to his knees, he tore at the branches. 'Renn!'

TEN

Renn didn't seem to be breathing. Her eyes were shut, her lips tinged blue. It was only when Torak got her into the shelter and felt her throat that he detected a tremor of life.

He shouted her name. She didn't respond. The cold had sent her deep inside herself. It would kill her if he couldn't get her warm.

Her clothes were stiff with ice. Torak pulled her parka over her head, then yanked off his own parka and jerkin. The birdskin was warm from his body, he got her into it fast. Drawing off her outer leggings, he bundled her into her sleeping-sack, checking her face, hands and feet for the waxy flesh of frostbite, but finding none.

With a stick, he rolled a hot stone from the edge of the fire and wrapped it in his empty waterskin. Then he

reached inside her sleeping-sack and placed it on her belly.
After that, he unrolled his own sleeping-sack and put it
round her shoulders, rubbing her back, willing her to wake
up.

Her eyelids flickered. She looked at him without
recognition.

He dropped another hot stone in the water pail, raising
a hiss of steam. Then he emptied his medicine pouch,
scooped up some dried meadowsweet, and tossed it in.
Tipping some of the steaming brew into his drinking cup,
he held Renn's head and trickled a few drops between her
lips. She spluttered. He made her drink more. She started
to shiver. His dread lifted a little. Shivering was good.

The shelter was low and cramped, so he had to sit
hunched, with one arm around her. As he made her drink,
faint colour stole into her cheeks, and her mouth lost that
terrifying blue tinge. Now when she looked at him, she
knew who he was.

'You're going to be all right,' he told her. He needed to
say it out loud. To make it true.

Her gaze took in his bandaged head. 'You found me,'
she mumbled.

'And you built the shelter. Rip led me to it.'

Hearing his name, the raven stretched his neck and
fluffed his chin-feathers.

Torak did his best to scrape the ice off their parkas,
laying Renn's on the other side of the fire to dry, and
pulling on his own, chill and unpleasant against his bare
skin. Then he shared out some salmon cakes.

Renn gave a corner to the ravens and solemnly thanked
Rip for guiding Torak to her. Then she began to eat,
holding her cake in both hands, like a squirrel. She was
sitting up now, with the sleeves of Torak's jerkin flopping

over her hands. Her face was flushed, her hair a mass of fiery tendrils. Torak felt that he could warm himself simply by her nearness.

The fire had burned low. He fed it more wood. Outside, the ice storm battered the Forest. He began to shake. The storm had nearly killed Renn. It had nearly killed Renn.

He told her he was sorry for leaving her, and she gave him an unreadable look. Then she told him how things had been after he left: about the shadow sickness, and Fin-Kedinn going off on a secret journey of his own. When Torak couldn't delay it any longer, he told her about the eagle owl attack, and the deaths of Darkfur, Shadow and Pebble.

Renn took that in appalled silence. 'All three?' she said at last.

He nodded. 'I don't know how Wolf will bear it.'

'All three,' repeated Renn.

But she was not Fin-Kedinn's kin for nothing, and Torak could see that already she was pondering what this meant. 'The owl,' she said. 'There must be something wrong with it.'

'I saw its eyes. They were – empty.'

'Ah. So not a demon.'

'I don't think so.'

'I wonder what Eostra did to it.' Her tone was that of one Mage assessing the craft of another, and Torak admired the speed with which she'd recovered. 'You say it flew south?' she said.

'Yes. It took Pebble, I think to decoy Wolf away. He's out in the storm. If he's still alive.'

Renn met his eyes, and now she was more girl than Mage. 'He's alive,' she said. 'Wolf knows how to look after himself.'

Torak did not reply. In his mind, he heard his pack-brother's howls. Wolf hadn't sounded as if he cared whether he lived or died.

As Torak crouched in the flickering gloom, he fancied that amid the roaring of wind and weather, he heard wild laughter. 'This storm,' he said. 'Eostra sent it. Didn't she?'

Renn's raven eyes gleamed. 'She holds the Forest in a grip of ice.'

Together they listened to the trees fall.

'After you left,' said Renn, 'she sent signs.'

'I think I saw one. Like a spiky bird, gouged in a yew.'

Renn hesitated, and he sensed her deciding what to tell him and what to keep back. She said, 'The sign means that Eostra has made her lair in the Mountain of Ghosts.'

The Mountain of Ghosts. Torak had never heard of it, but the name made him feel cold inside.

'Fin-Kedinn told me it's sacred to the Mountain clans,' Renn went on. 'He says if we can find them, they might help us find the Mountain.'

With part of his mind, Torak heard her voice; but another part was thinking, there will be caves. The knowledge dropped into his heart like a stone. Twice in his life he'd ventured into caves: once in the time of the bear, to find the stone tooth, and once in the Far North, to rescue Wolf. Both times, the Walker had warned him. 'Once you've gone in,' the old man had said, 'you'll never be whole.' The Walker was mad, but now and then, he showed flashes of sanity. His warnings had force. Torak had a sudden presentiment that if he ignored them – if he ventured again into a cave – the jaws of the earth would snap shut on him for ever.

Renn spoke his name, and he was back in the shelter.

'Are you all right?' she said.

'Yes,' he lied.

She took his hand. Her fingers were thin and warm. He drew strength from them.

'Torak,' she said. 'I don't know what Eostra means to do in the Mountain. But I know this. She wants to keep you apart from me and Wolf. She wants you alone. She won't succeed.'

They sat side by side while the ice storm fought the Forest with unabated fury. Presently, Renn slept, but Torak remained awake. For now, he and Renn were safe. Wolf was not. It seemed to Torak that the bond between them was a fragile thread stretching through the night – and that Eostra's icy hand was reaching out to sever it.

ELEVEN

The Bright Hard Cold was savaging the Forest. It was crushing trees and hurling birds from the Up. It was attacking Wolf with freezing claws.

Let it. He didn't care what happened to him.

He'd been running for ever, casting for the scent of the eagle owl, trying to catch the least whimper from his cub. Nothing. The Bright Hard Cold had eaten hope.

He came to a hill of roaring pines where a boulder hid a small Den. Without pausing to sniff for bears, he ran in and slumped onto broken bones and ancient scat.

He knew that Tall Tailless was seeking him, but not even the thought of his pack-brother could rouse him. Darkfur and the cubs were gone. Wolf longed to be with them – but they were Not-Breath. He didn't understand how this could be. Darkfur and the cubs were . . . *not*.

Wolf shut his eyes. He wanted to be *not* too.

Torak was woken by silence.

He was cold – the fire was half-asleep – and the shelter had sagged till it was only just above him. His breath was loud in the stillness, frosty on his face.

The door had frozen shut. He hacked it open, waking Renn, who sat up before he could warn her, and banged her head.

Bracing himself against the cold, Torak crawled out – into a piercing glare and a Forest turned to ice.

The storm had beheaded trees and transformed what remained to glittering spikes. It had flattened entire groves to mounds of twisted crystal. Tree, branch, leaf: all were caught fast in Eostra's prison of ice.

Slowly, Torak got to his feet. He took a few steps. The ice beneath his boots was hard as stone. The cold seared his lungs and crackled in his nose. The glare was a knife in his brain. Everywhere he turned, ruined trees flashed and glinted. The shattered Forest possessed a terrible beauty.

'Can you feel their souls?' Renn said behind him.

He nodded. The air shivered with the spirits of dead trees seeking new homes.

'They can't get into the saplings,' said Renn. 'The ice is keeping them out.'

'What will they do?'

'I don't know. Let's hope the thaw comes soon.'

Torak didn't think it would. A dead, windless cold lay upon the land. The hand of Eostra.

Shading his eyes with his palm, he saw a reindeer calf

on the slope below. It wobbled on spindly legs, frightened by this treacherous new world, while its mother, hungry for lichen, chopped at the ground with her sharp front hooves. She couldn't break through.

Torak thought of lemmings trapped in frozen burrows; of beavers sealed inside their lodges.

He thought of Wolf.

Rip and Rek flew out of the shelter and perched on a bough, loosing a clinking cascade of shards. The echoes took a long time to die.

Renn called Torak's name, her voice shrill with alarm.

She was crouching ten paces away in the lee of a boulder, peering through the tangle of a spruce that had fallen against it. As Torak approached, she warned him back. 'Wait. Don't look—'

He shouldered her aside. Between the branches, he glimpsed a patch of grey fur tipped with black. Wolf fur.

Renn was pulling his arm. He shook her off. He tore at the branches, desperate to reach – to reach what lay entombed beneath the ice.

Renn wriggled past him and got there first.

Torak's world shrank to that grey fur under the rock.

Renn's voice came to him from far away. 'It isn't Wolf.'

She crawled backwards, clutching a band of wolf hide in her mitten.

It was about the width of a hand: rolled up, frozen stiff. 'It was staked in place,' she said. 'We were meant to find it. It's been tanned, the edges pierced for sewing. Looks like what's left of someone's clan-creature fur.'

'It is.' Torak took it from her, and tried to unwind it. The frozen fur cracked, and something fell out. The world tilted as Torak picked up the little seal amulet. He knew the turn of its sleek head. He'd often counted the tiny claws on its flippers. He said, 'It belonged to my father.'

Renn stared at him.

'His mother was Seal Clan, he always wore it.' He swallowed. 'He left it as a sign. He's been begging me for help. And I turned my back on him to find Wolf.'

'You had to,' said Renn. 'Wolf needs you.'

'I turned my back on Fa. That's why he left me this.'

'No.' Her tone was hard. 'This was left by tokoroths.'

'You can't know that!' he cried. 'How can you possibly know that?'

'I don't, not for sure. But I know this. Eostra sent her tokoroths and her owl and the ice storm to separate us – but she *failed*. And she will fail to keep us apart from Wolf.'

'And Fa?' he demanded. 'What about Fa?'

She turned to the ruined Forest, then back to him. 'It might not be him.'

'And if it is? What then?'

'And if it is,' she said, unflinching, 'you were *still* right to follow Wolf. Because Wolf is alive. Your father is dead. You cannot have dealings with the dead.'

Torak glared at her, but she did not back down.

'He's dead, Torak. Nothing can bring him back. Wolf needs you more.'

In prickly silence they returned to the shelter, where they gathered as much firewood as they could carry, and Renn made masks of slit buckskin to shield them from the glare. Torak checked their provisions: a bag of hazelnuts, some salmon cakes, dried horse meat and lingonberries. He wanted to take Fa's clan-creature fur, but Renn shook her head. 'No, Torak. You can't take a dead man's things.'

He gave in to that, but determined to keep the seal amulet. When she saw his face, she did not protest, merely insisting that he wrap it in rowan bast before putting it in his medicine pouch.

He could feel her wanting to make things better between them, but he stayed stubbornly silent. She hadn't heard his father's spirit calling in the night. How could she understand?

The ice storm had obliterated all hope of a trail, but the day before, Wolf had headed south, so that was where they went.

It proved almost impossible. The ice was the snow's evil sister. When they broke through frozen branches, it sent shards flying at their eyes. It made them fall, and punished them when they did. Soon they were covered in bruises.

Now and then, Torak stopped to howl. *I am seeking you, pack-brother!* The Forest threw back his howls unanswered.

At last they reached the frozen river. Torak saw the corpse of a mallard trapped in reeds, its brilliant green head carapaced in ice. He put his hands to his lips and howled.

No reply.

The river was so slippery they had to cross it on hands and knees, but when they reached the opposite bank, they found the way blocked by a stand of fallen beech. They had no choice but to head upstream.

Torak howled till he was hoarse.

'Don't stop,' said Renn. 'He will hear you. He will howl back.'

But Wolf did not howl back, and Torak feared that he never would. This was the valley of the Redwater, where the demon bear had killed his father. Maybe it was where Wolf, too, had met his death.

Around mid-afternoon, the trees thinned and a bitter wind rattled the leaves. It was the wind off the fells. They were nearing the edge of the Forest.

They came to a grove of crushed pines, and a boulder hung with icicles longer than spears.

Beneath the boulder, they found Wolf.

TWELVE

Wolf was alive – but only just.

Ice caked his fur, and his muzzle was white with frozen breath. When Torak swung his axe and sent the icicles clattering from the boulder, Wolf opened his eyes. Renn was shocked. His gaze was dull. It didn't light up when he saw his pack-brother.

Renn watched Torak crawl in beside him, trying to reassure with glance and touch and whine. Wolf's tail barely twitched.

'We've got to get him warm,' said Torak, clawing ice from Wolf's pelt.

'I'll wake a fire,' said Renn, 'you build a shelter around us.'

They worked in silence, Torak dragging fallen saplings, chipping off the ice, setting them against the boulder to close in the space; Renn rousing a smoky, reluctant blaze. In the warmth, Wolf's fur began to steam, but his eyes remained incurious, their amber light quenched.

Renn set a salmon cake by his muzzle. He ignored it. Alarmed, she tried to tempt him with a few dried lingonberries. He ignored them too. When Rip and Rek stalked in and stole the lot, he didn't turn a whisker.

'Thank the Spirit we found him in time,' said Torak, dragging the door shut behind him. 'He'll be all right once he's warmed up.'

Renn bit her lip. 'Give me your medicine horn. I'll try a healing rite.'

Feeling Torak watching her, she shook earthblood into her palm and daubed some on Wolf's forehead, muttering a charm.

'He'll get better now,' said Torak. 'Won't he? Renn?'

She did not reply. Wolf was sick to his souls with grief. And from that you can die.

As the moon rose, they got into their sleeping-sacks. Torak lay with one arm over Wolf, trying to comfort by his nearness, as in the past, Wolf had comforted him. At times, Wolf's tail stirred listlessly, but Renn could see that he was giving up.

Next day dawned icily clear, with no sign of a thaw. As light stole into the shelter, Renn saw with a clutch of terror that Wolf was no better.

Torak saw it too, but said nothing. Renn guessed that he was staring into the abyss of a future without Wolf.

Worried about their supplies, she said she would set some snares. Torak would not leave Wolf, so she went alone, not going far for fear of tokoroths. When she got back, she tried every healing rite she knew. Wolf submitted without so much as a twitch of his ears. He didn't care.

'I've done all I can,' Renn said at last.

'There must be something more,' said Torak.

'If there is, I don't know it.'

'But he's better than when we found him. He could barely move, he's stronger now.'

'Torak. You know what's happening as well as I do.'

She saw the terror in his face.

'But he's still got us,' he insisted. 'We're part of the pack, too.'

He was right. But whether that was enough to keep Wolf alive, Renn didn't know.

As dusk came on, she went to check the snares. Her hunting luck had held; one held a frozen hare. She told herself this was a good sign, but on her way back, she saw tracks. Small. Human. With claws.

At camp, she found Torak standing outside. His lips moved in silent prayer, and for one terrible moment, she thought Wolf had died. Then she saw the lock of dark hair tied to a branch. Torak was offering part of himself to the Forest in return for Wolf's life.

'Torak,' she said gently. 'You can't do this.' She reached out to untie the offering, but Torak pushed her hand away.

'What are you doing?' he cried. 'It's for Wolf!'

'I know, but *think*! Your hair contains part of your world-soul. There are tokoroths about. If they got hold of it, there's no knowing what they might do.'

In furious silence he watched her untie the hair and stow it in her medicine pouch. 'You think Wolf's going to die, don't you?' he said. He made it sound like a betrayal.

'If he doesn't want to live,' she said in a low voice, 'then no spells, or prayers, or offerings can make him.'

Angrily, Torak turned his back on her.

Feeling shaky and sick, she stowed her catch in the

shelter, and fed the fire, and stroked Wolf, and asked Rip and Rek to watch over him. Then she went to draw lines of power around the camp. To keep the tokoroths away.

山

Renn was right about Wolf, and Torak came close to hating her for it.

But what he really hated was what was happening to his pack-brother. He hated that he couldn't stop it. He hated the eagle owl. Most of all, he hated Eostra.

He slept fitfully, waking often, and always finding Wolf gazing at the fire. *I'm here, pack-brother,* Torak told him.

I miss them, Wolf replied.

I know. I'm here.

Torak sank his fingers into the warm fur of his pack-brother's chest, and felt the beat of his heart. He willed it to carry on.

Next time Torak wakes, it is to utter blackness. Wolf is gone. Renn is gone. He is alone.

He walks, but he can't feel the ground beneath his feet. He is cold, but he can't feel the wind in his face, or hear the creak of the trees. It is so dark that he can't see his hand when he holds it before him.

This is not spirit walking: he feels no wrenching pain. This is worse. He is still himself, Torak, but something is missing. Inside him there is a terrible, yawning emptiness.

'Renn? Wolf?' he calls, but his voice stays trapped inside his head. There is nowhere for it to go. He is alone in nothingness.

'Renn!' he screams as he spins in endless dark. '*Wolf!*'

Wolf woke with a start.

He heard the growls of the Bright Beast-that-Bites-Hot, and the pack-sister whiffling in her sleep. Tall Tailless was gone.

Worry gripped Wolf from nose to tail. Tall Tailless was clever, but he could hardly smell or hear, and in the Dark he was as helpless as a cub.

Swivelling his ears, Wolf caught sounds outside the Den. He heard trees shivering beneath the Bright Hard Cold, and voles scrabbling to break out of their burrows. He couldn't hear his pack-brother, but he sensed that Tall Tailless needed him.

Stepping silently over the pack-sister, Wolf left the Den. Hunger made him weak, but his senses prickled.

Lifting his muzzle, he snuffed the scents. His hackles rose as he caught the smell of demon.

Placing each paw with stalking care, Wolf moved noiselessly over the brittle ground.

Tall Tailless stood a few lopes away, beneath a spruce tree. He was swaying. His eyes were open, but he did not see, and Wolf knew that he slept.

In the tree above Tall Tailless' head, a shadow moved.

In a snap, Wolf took in everything. He saw the tailless cub-demon crouched on the branch above his pack-brother. He sensed its hunger and hatred, he saw the great stone claw in its forepaw, ready to strike.

With a snarl, Wolf sped across the Bright Hard Cold.

Something smashed into Torak and felled him.

He caught the glitter of demon eyes, the glint of a knife – then Wolf – *Wolf* – was leaping at the tokoroth, and it was scrambling up a tree and into the dark.

'Are you all right?' cried Renn, running towards him.

Dazed, he struggled to his feet. Branches cracked as the tokoroth escaped from tree to tree, and Wolf – a silver arrow in the moonlight – raced after it.

Torak tried to go after him, but his knees buckled.

'Come back inside,' urged Renn.

'I've got to help Wolf.'

'You're not wearing your parka. Inside before you freeze!'

Once they were in the shelter, Torak found that he was shaking, but not with cold. 'Wh-at happened to me?'

'You were sleepwalking.' In the firelight, Renn's face was ashen. 'I woke up, you were gone. I went out, saw you standing beyond the lines of power. You looked right through me. It was horrible. I saw the tokoroth in the tree, it was aiming at your head. Then Wolf came out of nowhere. He saved you.'

Torak thought of Wolf chasing the demon.

'I think Eostra made you sleepwalk,' said Renn, wrenching him back.

'How?'

'I don't know. But I think she tried it once before, in the Deep Forest. Remember?'

Torak shut his eyes. That brought the blackness back, so he opened them again. 'Why would she?' he mumbled.

'I think,' said Renn, 'she wanted to make you go beyond the earthblood I'd laid down, so that her tokoroth could get you. But *why?*' she said to herself. 'It wouldn't make sense to kill you, then your power would be lost. It doesn't fit. None of it fits.'

Torak rested his forehead on his knees. Renn touched his cheek with the back of her hand and asked how he was feeling, and he said all right. She asked how he'd felt when he was sleepwalking, and he said, 'Empty. I was in nothingness. I was lost.'

Renn sucked in her breath. Torak asked her what it meant, but she wouldn't say. He knew she was keeping things from him. He didn't care. Wolf had saved him, and now he was out there alone. Against the tokoroth.

出

The demon disappeared into a thicket, and Wolf lost the scent. Shaking himself in disgust, he turned and trotted back to the Den.

The Bright Hard Cold bit his pads, and he was extremely hungry and weak; but he felt better than he had since the owl attacked, and he held his tail high. He had saved his pack-brother from the demon. This was what he was for.

As he neared the Den, the ravens swooped and croaked at him, and he made a feeble play-leap to chase them away. The ravens were *with* the pack, but not *of* it; they had to be kept in their place.

The pack-sister came out of the Den and said something surprised in tailless talk. Then she ducked inside and came out again, with her forepaws full of those small, flat salmon that didn't have any eyes. Wolf gulped the lot, and felt much better. He was licking the last bits off her paws when Tall Tailless came out of the Den. Tall Tailless saw Wolf, and went still. Wolf gave a whimper and threw himself at his pack-brother, and they rolled, whining and rubbing their noses in each other's delicious scent.

The Hot Bright Eye rose in the Up, splashing the Forest

with light, and Wolf felt that this was good. Darkfur and the cubs were gone, and he would miss them always; but he understood now that he couldn't be with them. Tall Tailless and the pack-sister were part of the pack, too, and they needed him.

A wolf does not abandon his pack.

THIRTEEN

The wolf cub did not *at all* understand what was going on.

How had he got to this empty hillside so far from the resting place? *And where was the pack?*

He remembered the ravens cawing, and the terrible owl attacking his mother. He'd watched them fighting from under the juniper bush: his mother leaping and snapping, the great owl lashing out with its claws. Then his mother wasn't there any more, and his father was fighting the owl, and Tall Tailless was barking at the cub to *stay*, but he couldn't. He fled, and suddenly claws were biting his flanks and he couldn't feel the ground, he was *flying*.

He'd wriggled and whined, but nobody heard him. His father and Tall Tailless shrank to dots as the terrible owl carried him higher. Even the ravens dropped behind. Then there was no more Forest, only empty whiteness speckled with sticks that looked like trees.

The cub had whimpered in terror.

The owl flew for an endless time. Next thing, the cub woke to angry caws, and the ravens were diving out of the Up. They were mobbing the owl, who was twisting and swerving. The cub tried to bite its legs, but he couldn't reach. Again and again the ravens attacked. Suddenly the owl let go and the cub was falling.

He plopped into the Bright Soft Cold and lay shaking, too frightened to move.

When nothing happened, he struggled upright and poked out his head.

The terrible owl was gone.

So was everything else. No ravens. No Forest. No wolves. Only the wind and the white.

Digging himself out of the Bright Soft Cold, the cub floundered uphill to sniff the smells, as he'd seen his father do. His flanks hurt and his legs shook. He was hungry and very, very scared. He put up his muzzle and howled.

Nobody came.

The cub had eaten some of the Bright Soft Cold, but though it filled him up a bit, it didn't chase away the hunger.

Wearily, he padded along the hillside. The wind had dropped and the Dark was coming. His claws felt strangely tight, and he sensed that everything – the hill, the Bright Soft Cold, even the Up – was waiting: for something bad.

He came to a clump of small, twisted willows that clung

to the slope. They reminded him of the resting place, so
he decided to stay close.

Nosing around, he found what seemed to be a Den.
From it came an interesting smell that he couldn't
remember.

Just then, something hit him on the nose. With a yelp,
he sprang back – and something hit him on the rump.
Now it was pelting him all over, hitting his back, ears,
paws. It was coming from the Up. He raised his head. It
hit him in the eye. He shot under a willow.

The pattering grew to a thunder. The Bright Hard Cold
was roaring from the Up, snapping branches, pummelling
the cub.

The Den. Get inside the Den.

Seizing his courage in his jaws, he made a dash for it.

Ha! The Bright Hard Cold couldn't get him in here! He
heard it snarling, furious at not being able to reach him.

The Den was only a bit bigger than he was, but at the
back, that interesting smell was much stronger. The cub
remembered it now. *Wolverine.*

Wolverines are extremely fierce, but luckily, this one
wasn't moving. The cub sniffed. He extended a wary paw.
The wolverine was Not-Breath.

The cub was used to eating soft, chewable meat which
his mother and father sicked up; he had to struggle to get
his jaws around a part of the wolverine. The meat was so
tough it was like chewing a log, but after much gnawing,
he tore off a chunk and gulped it down.

He ate till his jaws ached and his belly felt full. Then he
rolled in the rotten smell and went to sleep.

When he woke up, the Bright Hard Cold was still
pounding the hillside, so he ate some more wolverine and
slept. And woke. Ate. Slept . . .

When he woke again, all was quiet.

In the Now that he'd gone to in his sleep, he and his pack-sister had been clambering over his mother, play-biting her tail while she nuzzled their bellies.

In *this* Now, he was alone.

He whimpered. The noise he made in the stillness frightened him, so he stopped, and gnawed some more wolverine. Then he padded to the mouth of the Den.

The glare hurt his eyes. No smells. The only sounds were a strange crackling, and the hissing of the wind.

Blinking, he saw that the willows lay broken beneath the Bright Hard Cold. The whole world lay beneath the Bright Hard Cold.

He ventured out. His paws shot from under him and he fell. He scrambled upright, digging in his claws.

Above him rose the white hill. Below him it swooped down, then up again. The cub didn't dare move. There was nowhere to move *to*. He lifted his muzzle and howled.

It was the strongest, least wobbly howl he'd ever managed – but no wolf answered.

Instead, a raven flew down, landing a few lopes away from him. Then another.

The cub lashed his tail and yowled with joy. These were *his* ravens, they belonged to the pack! Sleeking back his ears, he bounded towards them, slithering about on the Bright Hard Cold.

The ravens flew off, laughing. The cub didn't care, he was used to their tricks: they often pecked his tail and stole his meat. He raced after them – forgot about digging in his claws – and slid down the hill.

Still cawing with laughter, the ravens flew after him.

Crossly, the cub got up and shook himself.

The ravens lifted into the sky and flew away.

He barked. *Come back!*

The ravens circled over him, then flew off again, waggling their tails as they disappeared over the hill. Quork! *Follow!*

The cub laboured after them. When he reached the top of the hill, what he saw made him whimper in terror.

Above him rose the biggest rocks he'd ever seen, far bigger than even the boulder beyond the resting place.

Quork! croaked the ravens.

The cub was terrified. But he didn't want to get left behind.

Narrowing his eyes against the wind, he started after the ravens, towards the Mountains.

FOURTEEN

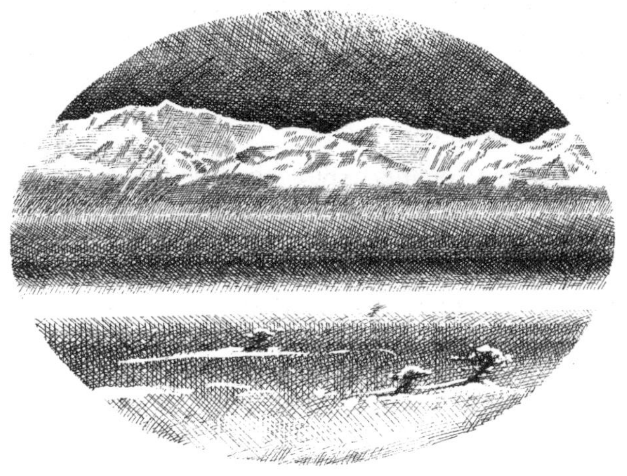

'How many daywalks to the Mountains?' said Torak.

Renn shook her head.

They stood with the Forest at their back, staring over the rolling, snowbound fells. Far in the distance – yet dreadfully present – rose the shining peaks of the High Mountains.

Torak's spirit quailed. From where he stood, he made out thousands of tiny pinnacles. Any one could be the Mountain of Ghosts. And his only hope of finding it lay with the Mountain clans.

Renn seemed to hear his thoughts. 'The reindeer will be heading for the shelter of the Forest. Fin-Kedinn says the Mountain clans always follow the reindeer. If we're lucky, we'll meet them.'

Torak didn't reply. He wanted to crawl into the Forest and hide.

Wolf came to lean against him. Torak slipped off his mitten and sank his fingers into his scruff. Wolf licked his wrist: a brief flash of warmth, snatched away by the wind.

'And remember,' said Renn, 'she *wants* you to find her.'

'But not you,' said Torak. 'And not Wolf, or Rip and Rek.'

'She tried to separate us. She failed.'

'She'll try again.'

Together they stared across the fells. A howling wind sent spears of snow streaming towards them. *Go back, go back!*

The ravens *loved* it. They swooped and soared in the fierce, cold, empty sky. Rek spun somersaults, while Rip folded his wings and plummeted onto a rise, landing in a puff of snow, flipping onto his back, and rolling down the slope. At the bottom he shook his wings, flew to the top, and started all over again.

Wolf gave a wuff! and bounded after him, but Rip hopped onto the wind and lifted out of reach. Wolf stood on the rise lashing his tail, gazing down at Torak. His fluffy pelt was spangled with snow, and his eyes were bright. *Let's go!* he yipped.

Their eagerness gave Torak courage. He turned to Renn. 'I think we can do this.'

She opened her mouth to protest.

'All we've got to do,' he said, 'is find the reindeer.'

She pointed at the fells. 'How?'

'We've got a wolf, two ravens, your Magecraft, and my tracking skills. We'll find them.'

They didn't.

For three days they laboured over the fells without seeing a single hoof-print. The flat white light made it impossible to judge distances, and the Mountains got no closer, while the fells proved even more formidable than they'd looked. They were seamed with gullies, frozen lakes, and iced-up thickets, some chest-high, others only ankle-deep, but always forcing them into a zigzag course. In places, they floundered through snowdrifts, while on ridges, the wind had blown away the snow to the pebbly ice beneath.

They tried to keep east, steering by the sun and the stars, but clouds defeated them, and they were led astray by what looked like reindeer, and turned out to be boulders.

They survived because of what they'd learnt in the Far North. They wore masks against the glare, and rubbed their faces with Renn's marrowfat salve to prevent windburn. They dug snow holes for shelter, and snared a ptarmigan and ate it raw, saving whatever twiggy firewood they could gather for melting ice. They kept their gear inside the snow hole so it wouldn't get lost in a drift, and their waterskins in their sleeping-sacks, to stop them freezing. Nights were cold. They dreamt of stacks of beautiful, dry wood.

On the third day, they spotted people in the distance, and hurried to meet them — only to find a man made of turf. He was bearded with icicles and his outstretched arms were antlers, supported by a spear in either hand. He didn't feel threatening, just oddly welcoming.

'Some kind of guardian?' said Renn. 'Maybe the Rowan Clan's, they build their shelters out of turf.'

'Then they made him last autumn,' said Torak. 'There's

moss on those antlers.' He scanned the fells. The Forest was long gone. All he could see were white hills. Beneath his boots, snow hid the ice which sealed off the land. Eostra had not relaxed her grip. And she was watching him.

'Dusk soon,' said Renn. 'We need to stop.'

They camped under the gaze of the turf man, in the lee of a hill by a frozen lake ringed with scrub. Renn said she would dig a snow hole, then try a finding charm for the Mountain clans. Torak went to set fishing lines and snares. Their supplies were down to a handful of hazelnuts, and so far they'd only caught a single ptarmigan.

Wolf trotted off to hunt, followed by Rip and Rek, who clearly thought he had a better chance than Torak.

On the lake, Torak hacked holes with his axe, then fed in juniper hooks on pine-root twine he'd brought from the Forest. To stop the holes re-freezing in the night, he plugged them with twigs and covered them with snow. Then he planted his knife beside them to deter Rip and Rek, who were quite capable of hauling in the lines with their beaks, and stealing the catch.

Back on shore, he circled the lake. The land felt empty, but his hunter's eye told him it was not. He spotted splayed wing-prints where a grey owl had punched into the snow after a lemming. Further on, a cluster of shallow hollows, each with a tiny pile of frozen droppings, where willow grouse had huddled together for company. And a web of ptarmigan prints, although no sign of their beds; ptarmigan like to fly high, then dive into soft snow to make a snug, invisible burrow.

They also love birch twigs, so Torak broke off some ankle-high branches of dwarf birch, rubbed off the ice, and stuck them in a patch of snow to make a tempting cluster, in which he hid snares of looped twine. He did the same with willow for the grouse.

Further up the slope, he found a hare trail. Following it to a windy ridge, he set his snare just before the point where the hare would have to leave the safety of the scrub and cross open ground. It would be preoccupied, and so less likely to notice a snare.

By now, Torak was giddy with hunger. All that awaited him at camp was his share of the hazelnuts. The sky was a deep, cold blue, strewn with stars. The moon was not yet up, but he made out the fanged blackness of the Mountains – and above them, faint and far, the red star of winter. The eye of the Great Auroch.

When the red eye is highest, Fa had said as he lay dying, *the demons are strongest.*

The Eagle Owl Mage and her minions were vivid in Torak's mind; but Fa's face was a blur. With a shock, Torak realized that he'd become a different person since his father had died. Maybe Fa wouldn't even recognize him. Maybe that was why his spirit had fled from him at the Raven camp.

'Fa,' he said into the dark. 'It's me. Torak. Where are you? How do I find you?'

The only answer was the hiss of windblown snow.

Huddled in her sleeping-sack, Renn listened to the whispering snow.

She was hungry and tired, but she knew she wouldn't sleep. The finding charm had been worse than a failure. A wall of ice had slammed shut in her mind. *Turn back,* commanded the Eagle Owl Mage. *None can hinder Eostra.*

Renn had been left dazed, clutching her pounding head. She felt so bad that when Torak returned, she had to ask him to sprinkle the earthblood around their snow hole. It wasn't a line of power, only a Mage could do that, but it was better than nothing. And maybe the turf man would help keep the tokoroths away.

Curled on her side, Renn watched the sky through the slit in the snow hole, and tried to work out Eostra's purpose.

The Eagle Owl Mage wanted Torak's spirit walking power, that much was clear. But how did she mean to take it? And when?

Torak crawled into the shelter, and Renn heard him take off his boots, pat them down for a pillow, and get into his sleeping-sack. He asked if she felt better, and she said no, and he said he was sorry. A few moments later, his breathing changed. Like a wolf, he had the knack of falling asleep in an instant.

Around middle-night, the half-eaten moon rose, and Renn asked it for help. She'd always felt close to the moon. She was sorry when the sky bear ate it, and she took strength from the fact that it always came back.

The moon.

Renn started awake. Why didn't I see it before? *I've been ignoring the moon!*

In several days, it would be the dark of the moon. And this moon was special: Souls' Night, when the World Spirit turns from a stag-headed man to a woman with red willow hair. A dangerous time, when ghosts are abroad, seeking the clans they have lost. When the dead get closest to the living.

Souls' Night.

This was what Eostra was waiting for. With a clutch of

dread, Renn saw how it fitted with what she and Saeunn had foreseen. The Listener shall die . . .

Until now, she had pushed that to the back of her mind. But soon, Torak would have to be told.

Sitting up, she saw that he was deeply asleep, frowning in his dreams. These days, he slept as if he didn't want to wake up.

It isn't fair, thought Renn. Why does he have to be the Listener? Why does he have to be different?

Turning on his side, Torak burrowed into his sleeping-sack, his hair falling over his face.

I'll tell him soon, Renn decided. But not yet.

Besides. A dark night on the fells was a bad time to talk of prophesies; and that line of earthblood around the camp was fragile. There was no knowing what might be listening.

FIFTEEN

Fin-Kedinn watched the pine marten dart up the tree. Then he moved on, careful and silent. The one he sought might be listening.

For days he had searched the places where his quarry used to hunt long ago. On the fringes of the Deep Forest, the Lynx Clan had heard rumours; the Bat Clan had found traces which had brought him south again, to this gully. And all the time, Torak and Renn were out there alone against the might of Eostra.

In the gully, nothing stirred. A while ago, these rocks would have echoed with the chatter of water, but the ice storm had silenced the stream with a blast of freezing breath. Now each ripple would last the whole winter. That wave cresting the boulder must wait till spring to fall.

Fin-Kedinn reached a fork in the trail. One path wound west, the other east, deeper into the hills. There were no tracks. He had to rely on the Forest to guide him, and on what he knew of the one he sought.

He took a few paces up the first trail. A woodpecker alighted on a pine trunk, cocked its scarlet head, and peered at him. Kik! Kik! Then it flew away.

He heard a distant clicking as a squirrel scampered from branch to branch. Further along, he found a small pile of droppings on a tree stump: twisted, musky smelling. Pine marten, perhaps the one he'd just seen.

Too many inhabitants on this trail. It probably wasn't the one.

Retracing his steps, he started up the other trail. Around him, spruce trees were frozen white cones. Under one, an auroch had cracked the ice with its hoof to get at a clump of willowherb.

In itself, this told Fin-Kedinn little, but among the remains of the willowherb, he found an exposed pine root which had been only partly stripped of bark. On it lay a brittle brown hair. He guessed that after the auroch had left, a red deer had come along and nibbled the bark; but it hadn't had the chance to eat it all. Its tracks were deep and splayed as it fled up the trail. Something had frightened it.

Not a bear; they were asleep for the winter. Lynx? Wolf? Fin-Kedinn didn't think so. He'd seen no yellow scent-markings in the snow, no claw-marks on trees. Perhaps, he thought, a lone hunter had caused the deer to flee.

Dusk was falling. Soon the first early stars would appear, although the half-eaten moon would not rise until middle-night. Fin-Kedinn hadn't gone far when he paused to listen. In the distance, a jay's warning call. A moment later, the dry swish of wings as it flew overhead, saw him, and gave another rattling kshaach!

It had been higher up the ridge when it uttered its first cry; Fin-Kedinn guessed that whatever it had spotted was near the top. He knew these hills. Ahead lay a rocky overhang: a good place to hide and keep an eye on what approached. And if he was wrong, he could shelter there for the night.

As he climbed, he caught a whiff of woodsmoke.

He heard the crack of a branch. Or was it the crackle of a fire?

Moving behind a holly tree, he scanned his surroundings.

Ah. Clever. Nowhere near the overhang, but down in that dell, thirty paces off the trail. The fire was hidden behind a boulder, and cast only the faintest glow. Fin-Kedinn hadn't expected less. The one he sought knew how to hide.

Quietly, he descended into the dell.

In the gloom, he made out a shadow that wasn't a rock. It sat hunched over the remains of a small deer, with an axe to hand.

Fin-Kedinn loosened his knife in its sheath and took a step closer. Stopped. Went on again.

The shadow rose, snatched the axe, and swung at him.

Fin-Kedinn gripped the axe-arm by the wrist.

Face to face, they strained against each other.

Abruptly, the tension went out of the axe-arm.

Fin-Kedinn relaxed his hold. 'Time to make amends, old friend.'

SIXTEEN

The fish-hooks came up empty, and a wolverine had raided the snares in the night.

'So no daymeal,' said Torak, flinging down the lines.

Renn blinked at the empty hooks. 'We'll have to eat lichen.'

He threw her a doubtful look. 'Can people eat that?'

'I think so.' But she didn't sound too sure.

Torak helped her scrape a few handfuls from under the ice, and they put them to soak in her waterskin. While she fed the fire, he went foraging. After a long, cold search, all he'd managed were a few crowberries and some frost-bitten sorrel.

Renn added them to the cooking-skin, where the lichen had stewed to a dark, slimy sludge.

'Are you sure people can eat this?' said Torak after the first mouthful.

'The Mountain clans do. If times are bad.'

'They'd have to be bad. Very bad.'

'Maybe Wolf will have better luck. We could share some of his.'

Torak didn't relish the idea of scavenging one of Wolf's kills, but Renn was right. It had been two days since their last ptarmigan. It was now vital to find the reindeer: not only to find the Mountain clans, but to eat.

By mid-morning, they reached a river which, surprisingly, was still awake. It rushed noisily between stony hills crowned with three more of the strange turf men. Its shallows were free of ice. Torak and Renn grubbed up clumps of brilliant green horsetails, and munched the swollen root-buds raw.

As he straightened up, Torak's head whirled. The horsetails had done little to assuage his hunger. His belly was beginning to hurt.

Renn slumped on a rock and took off her mask. Her eyes were ringed with blue shadows. 'You'd think there'd be fish in it,' she said. 'But I haven't seen any.'

They glanced at each other. How long could they carry on?

'When we find the reindeer,' said Torak, 'I'm going to eat a whole one. Starting at the neck and working my way down. I'll kill another one for you.'

She smiled wanly.

He squatted to refill his waterskin. 'What river is this, anyway?'

'I don't know and I don't care. If I don't get meat soon, I'll eat my medicine pouch.'

But Torak had stopped listening. Whipping off his

mitten, he plucked something from the water.

'What is it?' said Renn.

He showed her: a light-brown hair, as long as his thumb.

Reindeer.

'They must be upstream,' said Renn.

They listened. The river was too loud.

Its banks were boulder-strewn and impassable. They'd have to make a lengthy detour around the hills, or climb them. They decided to climb. It would be quicker, and give them a better view of whatever lay on the other side.

Climbing proved harder than they expected. Torak was appalled at how weak he'd become. Black spots swam before his eyes, and every step was an effort. Beside him, Renn's breath came in gasps.

Wolf appeared above them, pausing beside a turf man before racing down to Torak. His fur was fluffed up with excitement. *Reindeer! Hurry! We hunt!*

Torak translated for Renn.

Behind her snow mask, her eyes gleamed. 'Let's go.'

Swiftly, Torak told his pack-brother in wolf talk that he must hunt without them, as he'd have a better chance of making a kill. Wolf didn't argue, and disappeared over the hill.

The thrill of the hunt gave Torak and Renn new strength. As they neared the top of the hill, they dropped to the ground and belly-crawled. Reindeer have keen senses. If there were any on the other side, it was vital not to spook them.

Slipping his bow from his shoulder, Torak took an arrow from his quiver. Renn had already done so. She'd also tied back her red hair and tucked it inside her hood, so the prey wouldn't see. Catching his eye, she touched her clan-creature feathers and gave him her familiar, sharp-toothed grin.

The wind chilled Torak's face. Good. It was blowing his scent away from the prey.

Stealthily, he crawled forwards. He crested the ridge. He caught his breath.

Below him the hill fell away to the glittering sweep of the river. *Another* river flowed across it: a river of reindeer. Clouds of frosty breath hazed golden in the sun from thousands of muzzles. The air rang with the bleating of calves and the grunts of their mothers; the nasal hoots of rutting bucks. And beneath it all, like the beating of a great heart, the steady drumming of thousands of hooves.

Torak had only ever seen small groups of reindeer in the Forest. Awestruck, he watched the herd flowing slowly, purposefully, endlessly across the river. The hill where he lay dropped steeply through a thicket of willows to a flat expanse of gravelly riverbank, then rose again to another hill, also thick with willows. He guessed that the gap in between was one of the reindeers' ancient crossing places. Fin-Kedinn had once told him that the herds have followed the trails of their ancestors for thousands of winters.

He saw how they converged in a dense press of bodies as they passed through the gap. He saw the lifted heads and jostling antlers of swimming reindeer, the quick heave as they climbed the banks and scattered on the other side. He knew that this river of life would be trailed by many hunters: eagles, wolves, ravens, wolverines, people.

But where *were* the people?

He spotted Rip and Rek flying high, turning their heads from side to side as they searched for carcasses. He saw a buck rise on its hind legs and run a few paces to warn the others of danger, then thud to earth and charge a wolverine, who bounded away. And there in the distance was Wolf, a grey shadow at the edge of the herd, seeking an abandoned calf, or a reindeer too sick or injured to put up a fight.

But no people. Just three more turf men on the hill opposite, standing with antler arms outstretched.

Renn whispered in his ear. 'We're out of arrowshot. We've got to get downhill, into the thicket.'

She was right. Forget about people. The only thing that mattered now was meat.

And they'd have to get close. Success in a reindeer hunt depends on making a swift kill which fells the prey quietly, without alerting the herd. If you miss, they'll be off, and you'll have lost your chance.

Renn muttered a prayer to her guardian, and Torak asked the Forest to bring him luck. They began to edge down the slope towards the willows.

Torak glimpsed Wolf weaving among the reindeer. In his head, he wished him good hunting.

Wolf ran through the rich, swirling scent that made his pelt tighten with hunger.

He smelt the bloody tatters that swung from the reindeers' head-branches, and snuffed the delicious scent of calves. To his relief, he smelt no other wolves: no stranger pack which would attack a lone wolf who dared enter its range.

To make the prey run, he let them see him.

A big bull put down his head and thundered towards him: *Get away from my females!* Wolf dodged the lunging head-branches and bounded away.

In the din, he caught an anguished bleating. He loped towards it.

The calf stood shivering on a small, pebbly island in the middle of the Fast Wet. Wolf smelt its fear. It was unprotected. Its mother lay dead, her carcass already picked clean.

Wolf lowered his head and moved down the bank and into the Wet. He swam with the reindeer, and they ignored him, sensing that he wasn't after them.

The calf smelt him. Its bleating turned shrill. Wolf saw it move behind its mother's ribcage, ducking its head so that it couldn't see him, but sticking out its pale, fluffy rump.

Wolf's paws touched pebbles. He'd reached the island.

But as he emerged, a big cow reindeer surged onto the other side of the island and charged at him. Wolf scrambled to avoid her. She threw down her head and lashed out with her head-branches. Wolf leapt. The head-branches missed by a whisker, spraying him with pebbles. He'd made a mistake. That carcass wasn't the mother. *This* was. Wolf shot past her and jumped into the Wet.

As he reached the safety of the bank, he glanced back. The calf had ducked under its mother's belly to suckle, but the mother was still glaring at Wolf: *Stay away!*

Shaking the Wet from his fur, he scanned the herd for easier prey.

He caught a distant bleat of pain. There. A young buck struggling to climb the bank. Its head-branches looked sharp as fangs: one swipe would gut an unwary wolf.

But there was something wrong with its leg.

SEVENTEEN

Torak spotted Wolf among the reindeer, then lost him again.

Renn whispered in his ear: 'These willows are too thick, I can't get a clean shot.'

He nodded. 'If we can get down to those rocks by the river . . .'

Silently, they threaded their way between the man-high trees on the slope. Through the branches, Torak glimpsed reindeer trotting over open ground towards the water. They ran as reindeer do, with muzzles raised and hind legs splayed, white rumps swaying from side to side.

Beside him, Renn had taken off her snow mask. Her eyes shone. He knew she was thinking of marrowfat, and baked haunch so succulent that when you bite it, the blood squelches between your teeth and runs down your chin . . .

Stop it, Torak. You haven't got one yet.

As it was still the rut, bulls kept turning aside to clash antlers, scattering cows and calves as they raced after each other. The biggest bulls had swollen necks and heavy manes from throat to knees; some bore bloody tatters on their tines, where the hide hadn't finished peeling. Torak saw shreds of it fluttering from branches at the edges of the thickets on either side of the gap. The reindeer shied from these, as they did from the turf men who stood with open arms on the hills and banks.

Almost, thought Torak, as if they were herding the prey.

He noticed that the reindeer weren't as plump as they should be. After grazing all summer, they should have had thick pads of fat on their backs, but these didn't. Torak saw a young cow drop to one side and make a pitiful attempt to feed, pawing the ice with her front hooves, before trotting wearily on.

At last, he and Renn made it down the slope to an outcrop of boulders on the riverbank, surrounded by straggling willows. Torak saw reindeer jostling to get into the water. He saw moist pink tongues sliding over yellow teeth. He smelt musk, and heard the clicking of tendons as hooves struck icy ground. He nocked an arrow to his bow.

Renn pushed back her hood, fixed her eyes on her target, and took aim.

Wolf bit hard and the buck with the broken leg went limp.

In a frenzy of hunger, Wolf sank his teeth into its belly

and loosed a flood of delicious, slithery guts. He gulped them fast, leaving only the pouch that smelt of moss. When the buck's belly was empty and Wolf's nearly full, he started on the haunches, biting off chunks of hot, juicy meat.

The ravens alighted and hopped towards the kill. Wolf growled them away without lifting his muzzle. They stalked off to wait their turn.

The hunger was gone: Wolf couldn't eat any more. He was thirsty. His muzzle and chest fur were sticky. Trotting down the bank, he snapped up the Wet, leaving the kill to the ravens.

As he raised his head from the Wet, he caught the scent of taillesses. He sniffed.

Not *his* taillesses.

Other.

Renn was about to shoot when her quarry stumbled in the shallows, and fell with a spear quivering in its ribs.

A spear.

Torak met her startled glance and lowered his bow. Where had that come from?

The spear had dropped the reindeer so cleanly that the others splashed past it, unconcerned. Crouching among the willows, Torak and Renn peered down the bank. Those spears had come from the river . . .

There. Midstream, in the thick of the herd: a hide canoe. Torak saw a wooden reindeer head at the front, a stubby tail at the back. The craft sat low in the water, manned by hunters he could barely see. He made out four, cunningly disguised: antlers strapped to their heads, faces painted dark-brown, with patches of white around eyes and mouth, like reindeer. He saw another canoe downstream. Renn pointed to two more upstream.

Torak glanced at the shreds of antler hide fluttering at the edges of the thicket; at the turf men with open arms. They were there to herd the reindeer towards the river, where the hunters lay in wait, ready to pick them off while they were swimming, and least able to escape.

Renn had grasped it too. 'Now we've done it,' she breathed. 'We've blundered into someone else's hunt!'

Torak saw a hunter in one of the boats taking aim at a white reindeer in the water. Just as his spear drew back, a raven swooped out of nowhere.

'Oh, no,' muttered Renn.

Rip had eaten well, and was in the mood for fun. Flying low, he barked like a dog. The startled hunter cast his weapon, but missed his quarry's ribs and struck the rump instead. The white reindeer scrambled out of the river and galloped off, trailing the spear.

In an instant, the herd smelt the pain of its wounded sister and panicked. Torak saw white-rimmed eyes and flaring nostrils. Panic became a stampede. Reindeer reared, clambering over each other, churning water. The canoes rocked wildly, Torak saw hunters clinging on. Then he forgot about them as branches snapped behind him and reindeer crashed towards them through the thicket.

'Climb the boulders!' cried Renn.

They fled the willows and Torak boosted her onto the nearest rock, then swung himself up. The herd thundered around them, a torrent of antlers and hooves and powerful, crushing bodies. Renn wasn't high enough, the tine of a rearing bull snagged her hair. She screamed, struggling one-handed to pull free. Torak whipped out his knife and slashed her hair loose. The terrified bull thrashed its head and flailed its hooves, catching him on the shoulder. He fell, rolling sideways as a hoof struck the ground near his face. Renn leaned down and grabbed his arm. The reindeer blundered down the bank.

'You all right?' Renn shouted above the din.

'Yes! You?' yelled Torak.

She nodded grimly. But the back of her scalp was bleeding, where a lock of hair had been torn out by the roots.

Suddenly it was all over. The last reindeer cantered down the bank. The hoofbeats faded. The herd was gone.

Renn slid off the boulder, clutching her head. Torak jumped down beside her.

Below them, the hunters were splashing into the shallows, dragging their canoes. Already, some were running into the thicket, jabbing their spears as they sought those who'd ruined their hunt. Torak saw scowls on painted faces, heard voices buzzing like angry wasps. They had a right to be angry. One reindeer down and another wounded – which would mean tracking it, maybe for days, to finish it off. Not much of a catch for such a big clan.

Renn yanked him back behind the boulders. 'We need to get away before they see us,' she hissed.

'But they're our only chance of finding the Mountain.'

'Yes, but right now, they're furious, and in no mood to give us directions!'

The hunter who'd been the victim of Rip's prank was the angriest. 'Did you see it?' he shouted. 'A demon like a raven! Spoilt my aim, then vanished into thin air!'

Torak was about to call out, but Renn clapped her hand over his mouth. 'Are you mad?' she whispered.

Torak studied the hunters. Then he took Renn's hand from his mouth, rose to his feet, and stepped out from behind the rocks.

EIGHTEEN

Renn saw a big man turn and narrow his eyes.

'Krukoslik!' shouted Torak, tearing off his snow mask and running down the bank.

The painted face split into a grin. *'Torak!'* Striding forwards, the Leader of the Mountain Hare Clan put both fists to his chest in friendship. 'You've grown tall! Is that Renn over there? Come down, come down!'

Embarassed at not having recognized him, Renn did as he said, and everyone crowded round. Most were Mountain Hare, but Renn also saw a few rowanbark necklets and swan feathers tied to hoods. All had broad faces and welcoming smiles. Their anger seemed to have burnt off like mist.

Torak tried to apologize for spoiling the hunt; but Krukoslik waved that away. 'There's another crossing place at the next river, more hunters waiting. Come! You look hungry.'

Someone had already woken a fire. Krukoslik thanked the fallen reindeer for its body, and wished its spirit a safe journey to the Mountain. Then three men swiftly skinned it. After emptying the stomachs, they swilled one clean and drained the blood into it, piling the innards and stomach contents on the hide, and quartering the carcass. Nothing was wasted, and the snow was barely reddened.

Their deft work reminded Renn of Fin-Kedinn, and she felt a pang of homesickness. She was also shaky from her encounter with the reindeer, and her scalp throbbed. A Rowan woman saw her touching it, and quietly helped her bind on a sorrel poultice, which slightly numbed the pain.

Krukoslik handed Renn and Torak beakers and urged them to drink. The blood was turning stringy as it cooled, and Renn coughed when she gulped it down; but the reindeer's strength quickly became hers, and she felt a bit steadier.

Krukoslik's son Chelko – the young hunter who'd missed his aim – passed them chunks of raw liver: warm and unbelievably delicious. Now Renn felt *much* better. She mumbled a belated thanks to her guardian, as she'd forgotten before.

Krukoslik sat with them, but ate nothing. He'd scrubbed off his paint, revealing a round face that looked permanently flushed, as if by a good fire. Like the rest of his clan, he wore a calf-length tunic of reindeer fur, tied at the waist with a wide scarlet belt. His brown hair was cut short across the brow to reveal his red zigzag clan-tattoo, and his hare-fur cape was also stained red, although it had been turned inside-out for the hunt.

His eyes were shrewd, yet kind. When Renn unknowingly flouted the custom of his clan by turning her back on the fire, he gently corrected her. 'We don't do that, the fire doesn't like it.'

But he was also Clan Leader, used to doing things his way. When Torak asked about the Mountain of Ghosts, he stopped him. 'This isn't the place. You will come to our camp, while Chelko tracks the wounded one. Then we'll talk of sacred things.'

Torak nodded, and turned to Chelko. 'I'm sorry the raven startled you. You should know that he's – sort of our friend.'

Chelko blinked. 'Your friend?'

'He didn't mean any harm,' said Renn. 'He's young, he likes tricks.'

Chelko scratched his chin and grinned. 'And I thought it was a demon.'

'So it's really our fault,' said Torak, 'that your hunt was spoilt. I'd better help you track the wounded one.'

Chelko looked pleased.

'Good,' said Krukoslik. 'This is good.'

'I'll go with you,' said Renn.

But to her surprise, Torak shook his head. 'You're still shaken, you should go with Krukoslik.'

'I'm fine!' she protested.

'I'll see you at camp,' said Torak.

Krukoslik's small eyes darted from one to the other. 'Good,' he said again. 'Torak goes with Chelko, Renn with me. When we're together again and everyone's eaten, you can tell me why you've come.'

Renn wasn't looking forward to a long walk to camp, but she needn't have worried. The hunters had kept their dog sleds away from the reindeer, but at a whistle they arrived, driven by the children entrusted to mind them.

The sleds were of antlers lashed with willow withes, the runners coated in frozen mud rubbed smooth. They were smaller than those of the Far North, with just enough room for one person to sit, while the driver stood behind. First, Krukoslik introduced Renn to each of his dogs. He clearly thought they merited the same courtesies as people, which made her like him even more.

They started north, rattling over the icy ground. Krukoslik didn't use a whip; he called commands to his lead dog, who did the rest. While he drove, he made Renn tell him the news from the Forest. He frowned and touched his clan-creature skin when she spoke of the moths and the shadow sickness, and he was troubled that Fin-Kedinn had gone off on his own; but he seemed glad that Wolf had come with them, although he asked Renn not to name him out loud.

'We who live in the eye of the Mountain are careful with names. The grey one who is your pack-brother, we call his kind ghost hunter, because they stalk with such skill. And we don't name the prey aloud, either, as they have keen ears, and might hear our hunting plans. We call them the antlered ones.'

His face creased with worry. 'It's good that you've brought the ghost hunter. For three moons, none of his kind have been seen or heard on the fells – except for a dead one, which some Rowan hunters found in the west. They put food by its muzzle to feed its souls, then left it in peace. We fear the others have fled because . . .' he lowered his voice, 'because of the evil one.'

Renn glanced over her shoulder. The jagged peaks were suddenly much nearer.

Krukoslik did not speak again, and they went on in silence.

The shadows were darkening to violet as they reached camp. From a distance, it looked tiny, nestled beside a grey lake in the immensity of the fells. As they drew closer, Renn saw many shelters honeycombed with golden light: the huge hide tent of the Mountain Hares, the turf domes of the Rowans, and long mounds banked with snow, which Krukoslik said were Swan.

'These are terrible times,' he said. 'The Mountain clans must stay together. It's our only chance.'

The dogs barked as the sleds slewed to a halt, and shafts of gold speared the snow as hunters emerged to greet them. Krukoslik handed Renn a bone blade for brushing the snow from her clothes. Stiff with cold, she followed him inside.

She was greeted by a blast of heat and a wonderful, smoky smell of hot food and people. A large peat fire glowed in a ring of stones. Around it, on reindeer pelts flung over layers of springy birch, men and women sat sewing or grinding spearheads. Steam wafted from cooking-skins. Renn's hunger came back in a rush.

Taking off her outer clothes and hanging them to dry on a cross-beam, she followed Krukoslik round the fire, careful not to turn her back on it. Those she passed nodded to her with wary friendliness, but she felt conspicuous, and wished Torak were here.

Krukoslik settled himself at one end of the shelter. 'Nearest the Mountain,' he said as she sat beside him. He thanked the fire and the antlered ones for the food, and everyone did the same, while Renn mumbled a prayer to her guardian. Then the eating began.

A woman handed Renn a bowl, and explained that the stew was mostly fat: crushed marrow and back fat, tongue, and the fattiest innards.

'Meat is good,' said the woman, 'but fat's better when you live on the fells.'

Renn found the stew strengthening, but the fat stuck to the roof of her mouth, and she had to wash it down with heather tea. After that there was reindeer paunch stuffed with chewed lichen – this she politely declined – and platters of ribs and chewy, roasted ears. The toddlers had bowls of reindeer-foot jelly, and a mother gave her teething baby a stick of frozen marrow to gnaw. The elders got the reindeers' eyeballs, and nibbled the fat off them before popping them in their mouths and munching them whole.

Krukoslik apologized that there were no berries. 'Because of the ice,' he said. It was the only time he mentioned it.

When Renn was full, she curled up and lay listening to the sound of the fire and the murmur of voices. She was exhausted – she could still feel the movement of the sled bumping over the ice – but for the first time in days, she felt safe. Outside, the fells lay in Eostra's grip. In here, it was almost possible to forget.

Drowsily, she heard the creak of the tent-poles, and the snow blowing against the shelter. In the smoky half-darkness, she watched naked toddlers clamber over their elders, who steered them clear of the fire without glancing up from their work. The Mountain clans lived with more uncertainty than most; maybe that was why they took such pleasure in the good things.

And yet, Renn saw the hardships they endured. Some

were missing an eye from encounters with antlers. Others had lost fingers to frostbite. Krukoslik had said that his people didn't name their children till they reached their eighth summer, in case they fell sick and had to be left to die.

Thinking of that, Renn fell asleep.

She woke to shouting and laughter. Torak and Chelko were back.

Chelko beamed as he told everyone how Torak had summoned the ghost hunter, who'd helped them track the wounded reindeer. 'I killed it with a single spear-cast. Then some Rowans came by with their sleds and helped us.'

The clan looked at Torak with cautious respect, and a woman took a reindeer head outside as a present for Wolf.

Torak spotted Renn and came to sit beside her, bringing with him the clean, cold smell of the night. As he gulped a bowl of stew, he asked if she was feeling better.

'Of course I am,' she said tartly.

He warded off an imaginary blow.

Around them, talk sank to a murmur, and children snuggled into their sleeping-sacks. The Mages of all three clans came in and began to circle, mouthing spells.

'To keep us safe,' murmured one of them to Renn. She wore a necklet of white feathers, and her clan-tattoo was a ring of thirteen red dots on her forehead, for the thirteen moons of every cycle. Her eyes were pale, as if bleached by staring into great distances, and with a swan's thighbone she blew earthblood on the walls, breathing life into images of the guardians. A hare sat up on its hind legs and scanned for danger. A swan glided on wide wings. A tree spread protecting arms. There were spirals, too, and reindeer, and bison-like creatures with downward-curving horns.

Renn shivered. The Swan Mage had reminded her that only the thickness of a reindeer hide stood between them and the dark.

Torak sat with his arms about his knees, watching sparks shooting up the smoke-hole.

Suddenly, Renn felt the distance between them of things unsaid. She knew he had secrets from her. When he'd emptied his medicine pouch during the ice storm, she'd seen a scrap of the black root that made him spirit walk. He must have got it from Saeunn. And he hadn't told her.

But that paled beside what she hadn't told him.

'Renn,' he said quietly. 'Do you remember your dreams?'

'What?' she said, startled.

'Your dreams. When you wake up. Can you remember them?'

'Mostly. Why?'

'Since we left the Forest, I can't. It's all just black. What does that mean?'

She swallowed. Tell him, tell him.

At that moment, a strange, booming groan echoed through the night.

Krukoslik saw them jump. 'It's the lake. It's freezing. Crying to the Mountain to send more snow to keep it warm. We need this too. An end to this accursed ice that's starving the antlered ones.'

Firelight leapt in Torak's eyes. 'The Mountain,' he said. 'It's time for you to tell us what you know.'

NINETEEN

Krukoslik laid more peat on the fire, releasing a bitter tang of earth.

Renn glanced from him to Torak. In the red gloom, their faces were shadowed and unfamiliar.

'We who live at the edge of the world,' said Krukoslik, 'call two mountains sacred. The Mountain of the North, which is home to the World Spirit, and the Mountain of the South: the Mountain of Ghosts. But no matter how far we hunt from the Mountain of Ghosts, it's mother and father to us. It makes the rivers and the snow. It holds up the sky. It sends the sun, the bringer of all life. It takes the spirits of the antlered ones and gives them new bodies. And it shelters our ghosts, the souls of the dead who have lost their way.'

Renn said softly, 'Souls' Night. What happens on Souls' Night?'

'Souls' Night?' Torak turned to her. 'You think that's what she's waiting for?'

She signed him to silence.

'On Souls' Night,' said Krukoslik, 'the Mountain gives up its dead. When the wind howls, we hear them: the thundering hooves of the antlered spirits, and the lonely cries of the hungry ghosts.' His face softened. 'We comfort them. We put out piles of lichen for the antlered spirits, and for our ghosts we build a shelter. We fill it with warm clothes, their favourite foods, toys for the young ones. And a fire to banish the dark.'

He smiled. 'Oh, it's a good time! For a day and a night we keep them company, singing songs, telling stories. Then it ends, as it must, and we send them from us. Many of them find their way to peace,' he pointed to the smoke-hole, 'and join the ancestors, hunting the great herds which trek across the sky. Others don't, and go back to the Mountain. But they'll try again next winter, and we'll help them. We'll never let them down.'

Torak said what Renn was thinking. 'But this winter . . .'

Krukoslik's face darkened. He reached out and touched one of the painted guardians. 'It began the spring before last. We lost children. They vanished without trace. Dog sleds went missing. The wreckage turned up far away. Then the moths came, and the shadow sickness. Yes, Renn, we've had them too. Now ice starves the antlered ones. And yet it was less than a moon ago that our Mages began to suspect where the evil one had made her lair.'

'But what does she *want*?' said Renn. 'What will happen on Souls' Night?'

'No-one knows,' said Krukoslik. 'Terrible cries have been

heard in the foothills. Small, owl-eyed demons have been glimpsed flitting among the stones. Our Mages see visions: the grey terror gnawing the innards of the Mountain.' He swallowed. 'We fear that she has taken it for her own. This – this was always her way.'

'You *knew* her?' said Torak.

'Even the evil one was young once. When I was a boy, some of the Eagle Owl Clan still lived. Good people, we used to see them at clan meets. Eostra was different. Hungry for the secrets of the dead.' He glanced about him. The Mages had moved on to another shelter; everyone else was asleep. 'It's said,' he went on, 'that when she became a Mage, she carried out the forbidden rite.'

Renn gasped. 'She did that?'

'What?' said Torak. 'What did she do?'

Krukoslik leant forwards. 'One of her clan had been killed in a rockfall: a boy of ten summers. They say that on Souls' Night, in the moon's dark, she went to the cairn where the body lay. To raise the dead ...'

Renn put her hand to her clan-creature feathers. She shut her eyes. She saw a windswept hillside, a tall woman with long dark hair standing before a cairn.

The cairn heaves. Rocks fall away. Eostra peels back her sleeve and draws her knife across her forearm, anointing the lifeless flesh with blood. The dead boy sits up. His head turns. His clouded eyes meet hers. From his mouth bubbles the froth of decay. Like a lover, Eostra stoops. Her long hair caresses his face as she brings her head close, close – as she licks the corpse-froth from his mouldering lips ...

With a start, Renn opened her eyes. Torak's hand was on her shoulder. 'Renn,' he whispered.

She wiped her mouth with her hand.

Krukoslik was scowling at the fire. 'She'd got what she wanted,' he said. 'Henceforth, she could talk to them. Soon after, sickness took the rest of her clan. And Eostra disappeared.'

'And joined the Soul-Eaters,' said Torak.

'She *became* a Soul-Eater,' said Krukoslik with peculiar intensity. 'This is what you must understand, Torak. People say the Soul-Eaters took that name merely to frighten, but with Eostra, it's true.'

'What do you mean?' said Renn.

'The Swan Clan frequents the high passes. Sometimes they venture near the Gorge of the Hidden People. They've seen her. They say she walks with a three-pronged spear for snaring souls. They say that if you hear her cry, you're lost.'

Lost … Renn's fingers tightened on her clan-creature feathers.

'That cry,' said Krukoslik, 'rips the souls from your marrow. With her spear she snares them. She *devours* them. Eostra truly is an eater of souls.'

Torak placed his hands on his knees. 'But I have to find her,' he said.

Renn shot him a glance. 'You said "I". Not "we".'

He didn't reply.

Krukoslik was shaking his head. 'They say this is your destiny, Torak. But after what I've told you—'

'Krukoslik. Three winters ago, in the time of the bear, you helped me find a Mountain. Will you help me now?'

'This is no small thing you ask,' said Krukoslik. 'Our Mages used to go into the Mountain, but not any more. There's only one way to reach it, and that's secret.'

'You have to tell me.'

They faced each other, while the wind moaned and the lake cried out to the Mountain.

Krukoslik sat straighter. Once again, he was the Clan Leader who must be obeyed. 'We'll sleep now. I'll give you my answer in the morning.'

山

Renn woke to an unnatural silence that made her skin crawl.

The fire burned, but it made no sound. The walls of the shelter heaved in and out, but she couldn't hear them, or the moaning of the wind. Torak turned his head and muttered in his sleep. His lips moved noiselessly.

Slowly, Renn sat up.

At the far end of the shelter, in the dark of the doorway, someone stood.

Renn's heart began to pound.

The figure was tall. Its back was turned towards her. She saw ashen hair hanging in lank coils. From the shadowy head rose the spiked ears of an eagle owl.

Renn wanted to wake Torak, but she couldn't move. Her hands lay in her lap like stones.

The figure in the doorway must *not* turn round. If it did – if it faced her – her heart would stop.

Slowly, the figure turned.

TWENTY

E ostra the Masked One, whom even the other Soul-Eaters had feared. Her carved mouth gaped on darkness. Her unblinking glare froze Renn's souls with dread.

A dead chill settled on the shelter. The fire sank to ash. Ice crusted the reindeer hides and the faces of the sleepers. Renn's breath smoked.

Beside her, Torak slept with one arm flung above his head. Frost spiked his eyelashes and glittered on his skin. His lips were white.

Renn spoke his name. He didn't stir. She cried it aloud. Only a wisp of frosty breath showed that he was still alive.

'They hear nothing,' said a voice like the rattle of bones. 'They know nothing. Eostra wills it so.'

'You're not real,' said Renn.

'What Eostra wills shall be. Eostra commands the unquiet dead. Eostra rules Mountain and Forest, Ice and Sea.' Her voice was barren of emotion. The Eagle Owl Mage was dead to all feeling save the hunger for power.

Renn told herself that she, too, was a Mage. She started to speak a charm of sending, to banish this evil from the shelter.

The Masked One never moved, but Renn felt icy fingers on her throat, choking off the spell.

'None may hinder Eostra.'

'You're not real!' gasped Renn. 'I'm not afraid of you!'

'All fear Eostra.' Slowly, the feathered arms rose, and their shadows took wing. In an instant, the Masked One stood by the dead fire, looming over Renn.

Torak lay between them. Renn saw the unclean robe pooling about him. She saw the pulse beating in his throat. Exposed. Vulnerable.

'You can't have him,' she said.

The terrible mask leaned towards her, unbearably close. Ashen hair slithered across her cheek. She caught the stench of rottenness.

The spirit walker,' said Eostra, *'is already lost.*'

Renn stared into the pitiless, painted glare. Horror tightened its coils. Hope fled.

With a cry, she tore her gaze away. She saw the Soul-Eater's hand clenched on the head of a mace. Her flesh had the grainy density of granite; her talons were tinged blue, like those of a corpse. Between the fingers bled a fiery glow. The fire-opal.

'His time draws near,' said the Masked One.

Terror hooked Renn's heart and jerked it like a fish. 'You can't know that for sure.'

'Eostra knows all. He cannot escape.' One feathered arm

reached out and she raked the ruins of the fire. She opened her talons. Ash fine as crumbled bones hissed down onto Torak's unprotected face: filling his mouth, covering his eyes.

'No,' said Renn.

'Eostra shall suck the power from his marrow. She shall devour his world-soul and spew what remains into endless night.'

'No!'

'From host to host her souls shall spirit walk down the ages. Eostra shall conquer death. All shall cower before the undying one. *Eostra shall live for ever!*'

'No!' screamed Renn. '*No no no no no!*'

Men shouted. Dogs barked. The shelter was in uproar.

'Renn!' Torak was bending over her. 'Wake up!'

She went on screaming. 'No! You can't have him!'

The eagle owl glared down at her from the rim of the smoke-hole. Then it spread its wings and lifted into the dark.

ﰗ

'Was it a vision?' said Torak. 'Renn? Was it one of your visions?'

'She was real.'

'But she wasn't here, in the shelter.'

'She was.'

They sat with their backs against the peat-pile: Renn rigidly clutching her knees, Torak with one arm around her shoulders. Krukoslik had gone to the Swan Clan shelter to talk with their Leader. Most of the men were outside, calming the dogs. On the other side of the fire, women soothed children and cast fearful glances at Renn.

She'd stopped shaking, but she felt drained, as she always did after a vision. This had been the strongest and the worst ever. Dully, she stared at the glowing embers. No trace of the ash which Eostra had poured over Torak like a death rite.

'Tell me what you saw,' he said in a voice so low no-one else could hear.

Haltingly, she told him: about Eostra planning to rule the unquiet dead, and become the spirit walker. 'She means to eat your world-soul. That's where your power lies. She will eat it and – and spit out the rest. Then she'll be the spirit walker. She'll move from body to body. She'll live for ever.'

'And I'll be dead.'

She turned to him. 'No. That's the worst of it. You wouldn't die. You'd be Lost.'

'Lost? What's that?'

She sucked in her breath. 'It's when you lose your world-soul. You're still you – name-soul and clan-soul – but you've snapped your link with the rest of the world. You're adrift in the dark beyond the stars, in the night that has no end. Eternally alive. Eternally alone.'

In the fire, peat smoked and spat.

Torak withdrew his arm and leant forwards so that she couldn't see his face. 'When I was sleepwalking, I felt lost in nothingness. You were shaken when I told you. That's why, isn't it?'

She nodded.

'But why did I feel it then?'

'I don't know. Maybe she was trying out a spell. I don't know.'

He pushed the hair from his face, and she saw his hand shake. 'Can it happen to anyone? Or am I more at risk?'

'I think – you're more at risk. Because you're the spirit walker. And ...' she hesitated. 'Because you broke your oath.'

He waited for her to go on.

'When you swore to avenge the Seal Clan boy, you took your oath on your knife, your medicine horn, and your three souls. When you broke that oath, it may have weakened the link between them.'

He was silent, staring at the fire.

'But Torak,' Renn said fiercely. 'All this is only what Eostra *wants*, not what has to be! We won't let it happen. We can fight it together!'

Torak gave her a look she couldn't read.

Then daylight was flooding the doorway, and Krukoslik was stamping snow off his boots and letting in the dawn.

'It's decided,' he said. 'We'll take you to the Gorge of the Hidden People, but no further. You'll have to find your own way in.'

TWENTY-ONE

Torak had no time to take in what Renn had told him. The camp sprang into action, people running to harness dogs and prepare the sleds.

He and Renn were hustled off and given clothes 'fit for the Mountain'. When Torak got outside, the sky was overcast, and the peaks were hidden from sight. But he felt them as a tightness in his chest.

Renn emerged, looking ill at ease in her new clothes. They both now wore an inner jerkin and leggings of diverbird hide, the plumage warm against their skin, and a calf-length tunic of supple reindeer fur, cinched at the waist with a broad buckskin belt; socks and under-mittens of soft, light woven stuff which the Swans said was musk-ox wool; and long boots and over-mittens of tough reindeer forehead skin.

Such clothes must have taken days to make. When Torak remarked on this, Renn gave him an odd look. 'Can't you guess? These were made for Souls' Night. They've given us clothes for ghosts.'

Krukoslik came over to them. His face was grim – his camp had been menaced by a Soul-Eater – and he would not be going with them. A party of Swans would take them as far as they dared.

Krukoslik introduced their Leader, Juksakai, a slight man with disconcerting pale-blue eyes and a permanent frown. With a jerk of his head, he indicated that Renn would go on his son's sled, Torak on his. Torak thanked him for helping them, but Juksakai only scowled and shook his head.

As Torak got on the sled, Krukoslik said, 'I wish you'd change your mind, Torak.'

'You think I'm going to fail,' Torak replied.

'I think you're brave. But foolish. Such people don't live long in the Mountains. I hope I'm wrong.' Touching his clan-creature skin, he stepped back from the sled. 'Goodbye, Torak. And may your guardian run with you.'

Juksakai shouted a command to his dogs, and they were off.

All day they rattled over the ice, climbing first into the foothills and then the Mountains themselves, which remained shrouded in cloud. For a while, Rip and Rek flew alongside Torak, but they were soon off again, as if summoned away. Torak saw no sign of Wolf. He wondered if his pack-brother had caught the scent of the eagle owl, and given chase.

The wind was bitter. The lowering clouds weighed on Torak's spirits. He thought of being Lost in the dark beyond the stars. 'Eternally alive,' Renn had said. 'Eternally alone.'

They camped in a stony hollow where the invisible Mountains loomed over them. This was as far as the sleds could go. Tomorrow they would continue on foot.

The Swans built shelters by propping the sleds together and draping them with hides weighted with rocks. There were no trees, but fires were swiftly woken. Torak asked how, and Juksakai showed him a heathery plant which burned even when wet. He also showed Torak the cloven tracks of musk-ox, and clots of fine wool snagged on scrub. 'Be warned. They're faster than bison and can scale slopes you can't. And they're the prey of the Hidden People; we only ever gather the wool.'

The Swans were good at ice fishing, and a frozen lake yielded a pile of burbot and char. Over nightmeal, Juksakai thawed a little. He told Torak and Renn how his clan hunted in the Mountains with slingshots, and he showed them his clan-creature skin, a plaited wristband of swan hide, dyed red. The Swans, he said, used their clan-creature sparingly: children wore the claws, men the skin, women the feathers, the Leader the beak.

After they'd eaten, he insisted that Torak and Renn take what he called a steam bath, sitting with hides draped over their heads, dripping water onto hot stones and breathing in the steam. The Swans took no part in this, but watched in unnerving silence.

When it was over, Torak asked Juksakai why his clan was helping them.

'We're not,' he said. 'We're helping us.'

'What do you mean?' Renn said uneasily.

The Swan Leader regarded Torak. 'You seek the Soul-Eater in the Mountain. Maybe when she has you, she will send a thaw, and the antlered ones can eat.'

Torak grasped the significance of the steam bath: a ritual purification. He gave a wry smile. 'So I'm a sacrifice.'

Juksakai did not reply.

Renn looked stricken.

The dogs were restless in the night, and Torak slept badly. Renn, too, appeared tired, and she wouldn't meet his eyes. Torak felt the tension between them. He'd known for a while that she was keeping something from him. He wondered when she would have the courage to tell him.

Another overcast day, and the Mountains stayed hidden. The Swans led them through a snowy pass that followed a rushing river upstream. The ground rose so steeply that Torak and Renn had to use their hands to climb. Breathless, they lagged behind.

The Swans pitched camp by the river, at the mouth of a deep ravine. Two shelters were swiftly built by stretching hides over existing walls of stone and peat: the remains of Mages' shelters, said Juksakai.

Renn slumped on a rock and put her head on her knees.

Torak took deep breaths, but still felt breathless. 'What's wrong with us?' he panted.

'We're getting near the sky,' said Juksakai. 'Less air. Spirits don't need to breathe.' Nervously, he fingered his wristband. 'This is as far as we go. Tomorrow you're on your own.'

Renn sat up. 'You mean . . .'

Juksakai nodded. 'The Gorge of the Hidden People.'

Torak took a few steps towards the ravine. Precipitous cliffs reared above him, overhung by strange, twisted crags like enormous creatures peering down. A rocky trail wound inwards, following the river. Cloud seeped from the Gorge, shielding the Mountain from view – but Torak felt its icy breath. He saw the Swans muttering prayers; Renn touching the clan-creature feathers tied round her waist.

After a silent nightmeal, Juksakai took a portion of fish, made a reverent bow to the river, and cast the fish in the water. 'This is one of the veins of the Mountain,' he explained.

Torak asked its name, and Juksakai replied sternly that it was never spoken aloud. 'But I think you in the Forest call it the Redwater.'

'The Redwater?' Torak was startled.

'You know it?'

'I – yes. It was near the Redwater that my father died.'

Leaving Juksakai, he climbed down the bank and stared at the foaming water. This felt like an omen: the past thrusting into the present, like old bones emerging after a thaw.

An eerie twilight bathed the camp. As Torak turned to face the Gorge, the clouds parted – and at last there it was: the Mountain of Ghosts. Distant still, yet it towered above him. Snow streamed from its single, perfect peak which held up the sky. Its white flanks seemed lit from within by its own sacred light.

For three summers, Torak had pursued his quest against the Soul-Eaters over Sea and Ice, Forest and Lake – and it had brought him here. In a flash, he perceived that on those far-off slopes, he would meet his destiny. And for him, nothing lay beyond. On the Mountain, he would die.

This was what Renn had been keeping from him. This was the dread which had been growing inside him.

Panic flared. Run. Let someone else fight Eostra. You never asked for this.

But what about Fa?

The thought dropped into his mind like a pebble in a

pool. In some way that he couldn't yet fathom, his father's spirit was linked to this: his final quest against the last of the Soul-Eaters. He couldn't turn his back on Fa.

As he stood craning his neck at the Mountain, a great loneliness opened up inside him. He needed Wolf.

Putting his hands to his lips, he howled for his pack-brother.

The echoes wound into the Gorge of the Hidden People: fainter and fainter, dying to silence.

After a time, something howled back.

It wasn't Wolf.

Juksakai ran to him, his pale eyes bulging with fear. 'What was that?'

'I don't know,' said Torak. He scanned the darkening campsite. 'Juksakai,' he said sharply. 'Where's Renn?'

TWENTY-TWO

What was *that?* thought Renn.

Not Wolf. Not even *a* wolf. A dog? No dog sounded like that. Thank the Spirit it was so far off.

Hurriedly, she pulled up her leggings.

It had been dusk when she'd left, but now she could hardly see the sides of the gully. Night comes fast in the Blackthorn Moon. She should've remembered that.

With a flicker of irritation, she realized that she was going the wrong way. Those huge slabs of rock aslant each other: she hadn't seen them before.

Scowling, she retraced her steps. Stupid to have gone such a distance from camp, she'd only needed to get downstream and out of sight. The Swans had warned her to mark her trail if she went off on her own. 'Easy to get lost in the Mountains, especially for a girl from the Forest.'

She hadn't thought it necessary. Now it looked like she was going to prove them right.

She wasn't frightened. It wasn't completely dark, and camp had to be close. It was just that Torak would tease her, and she'd rather not give him the chance.

Hurrying out of the gully, she slipped on a patch of black ice and nearly fell. She decided to give him the chance. 'Torak!' she called.

No reply.

'Come on, Torak, this isn't funny! I need to know where you are!'

No answer. Only the stealthy hiss of wind. The brooding watchfulness of stones.

Uneasily, Renn remembered that the Swans had pitched camp by the noisy river. Torak wouldn't be able to hear her.

And like a fool, she hadn't told anyone where she was going.

Another howl shattered the stillness. Much closer than before.

The hairs on her arms stood up. She listened to the echoes die.

An answering howl, ending in two short barks. A signal.

She ran, scrambling over mounds of loose scree. This had to be the way back.

Dead end.

Stumbling, she headed out. Her mittens slipped off her hands and flapped on their strings like trapped birds. Her breath sounded panicky and loud.

Darkness closed in. She halted to listen.

No howls, no terse, signalling barks. That was worse.

Whatever hunted her was coming on in silence, as hunters do.

She ran into a wall of rock. Craning her neck, she saw the glitter of stars. She felt the red glare of the Great Auroch. Horror washed over her. What had Eostra created?

A trickle of pebbles.

Straining to pierce the blackness, she made out sheer slopes on either side. She was back in the gully. Around her, shadow shapes shifted and came together.

High above, something detached itself from the dark. Renn sensed rather than saw it raise its head and snuff the air.

She fled, leaping over rocks, careening off boulders. The stones watched her go.

Her foot jammed in a crack and she fell, pain exploding in her ankle. She couldn't run, couldn't put weight on it.

Behind her, she heard the click of claws.

Hide. It's your only chance.

She groped, found a gap and crawled in, dragging her injured foot. She scrabbled for something to block the hole. She couldn't find anything bigger than her fist.

She'd have to leave her hiding-place. She couldn't. *She could not do it.*

Pebbles rattled as the creature raced down the gully.

Crawling out, Renn fumbled for a rock. Found one, too heavy to lift; half-rolled, half-dragged it towards the hiding-place.

The creature was so close she heard its sawing breath.

One mitten on its string snagged under the rock. Sobbing with terror, she yanked it free, squeezed into the hole, hauled the rock after her, pulling it *tight*, shutting herself in.

Something smashed against it. The force shuddered through her. She clung to the rock, her only defence. She felt a gap where it didn't fit. Three fingers wide. It felt like a ravine.

Outside, silence.

Sweat poured down her spine.

Through the gap, breath scorched her fingers. Whimpering, she withdrew her hands as far as she dared.

A growl reverberated through the rocks. Renn screwed her eyes shut. The growl subsided to panting breath.

Now came the scratching of powerful claws. The creature was digging her out.

She smelt its stink. She sensed its limitless hunger to destroy. It would drag her screaming from the hole. It would sink in its fangs and rip out her throat as she lay twitching, still alive.

She couldn't breathe. But she would rather suffocate than face what was outside.

As she pressed deeper into the hole, her knife jutted against her hip. Awkwardly, she drew it from its sheath. When the creature came for her, she might be able to ram the blade into its jaws. She might make a brave death, even if there was no-one to see it.

Abruptly, the digging ceased.

Renn opened her eyes.

She heard a wet smack of jaws, as if the creature had jerked up its head. Then the whisper of pads on stone, receding fast.

Could it really be moving away?

Renn bit down on her lower lip. Stay here. It's a feint. It's got to be.

It wasn't. The creature was gone.

Renn was still cowering in her hiding-place when she heard voices, and Torak calling her name.

TWENTY-THREE

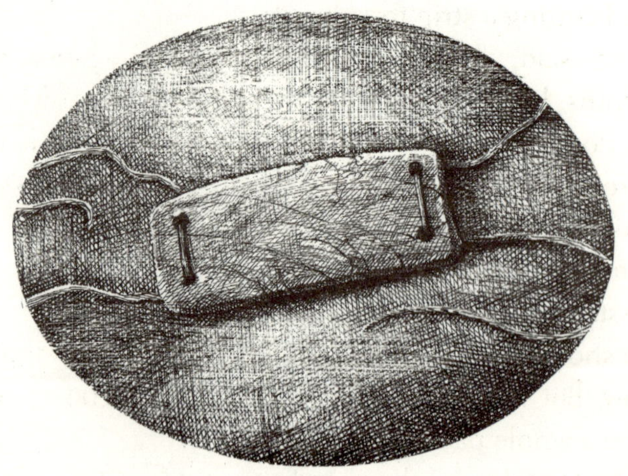

'I can't say for sure what it was,' said Renn as they helped her into the shelter, 'but I think . . .' she winced as her injured foot touched the ground.

'I saw a shadow like a huge dog,' said Torak. 'Then it was gone. As if someone had summoned it.'

'I didn't hear anyone calling,' said Juksakai.

'You wouldn't,' said Torak. He described the grouse-bone whistle he'd once made for summoning Wolf. 'It didn't make any noise, but Wolf could hear it. If what attacked Renn is anything like a dog, then it can hear what we can't.'

Renn sat shivering by the fire. The other Swan hunters were staring. Juksakai told them to go to the other shelter, and they gathered their things, avoiding her eyes. Maybe they could smell the creature on her.

When only Juksakai remained, Torak helped Renn out of her boots and gently rolled back her legging. She tried not to flinch, but the pain made her eyes water.

'But what *was* it?' said Juksakai again.

Torak didn't answer. He found his old Forest jerkin, and started cutting a strip for a bandage.

Renn said, 'Eostra has the fire-opal. She's made tokoroths. I don't know what she's done to that owl, or to those dogs – if that's what they are – but she's made them her creatures. They seem to feel only the will to destroy.'

Juksakai looked appalled.

Renn turned to Torak. 'Those howls. Could you understand them?'

He shook his head. 'It wasn't wolf talk, or any dog that I know. But it sounded as if there were several of them. Maybe a whole pack.'

Renn stared into the fire. She could still hear those growls; that hungry, sawing breath. Eostra had reared a brood of killers. She had taken the Mountain for her own.

Shakily, Juksakai poured ice water into a rawhide bowl, added dried willow bark, and mashed it with a stub of antler. He set the bowl beside Renn.

'Let me,' said Torak.

'I can manage,' she muttered. From her medicine pouch she took slices of horsehoof mushroom and put them in the bowl. When the strips were soaked, she gritted her teeth and laid the freezing poultice on her ankle.

She could feel Torak watching her. They both knew what this meant. Five moons ago in the Deep Forest, she'd twisted her knee. It had been two days before she could walk without help.

Stupid, *stupid*! she berated herself. Out loud, she told Torak to pass the bandage, then bound her ankle firmly, without wincing, to show him it didn't hurt.

He wasn't fooled. 'You won't be able to walk for days,' he said quietly.

Juksakai nodded. 'Tomorrow we'll carry her down to the sleds. She'll be all right with us.'

'A day's rest here and I'll be fine,' snapped Renn.

'No you won't,' said Torak.

She glared at him.

Juksakai glanced from her to Torak, and muttered about rejoining the others.

'*One day*,' said Renn after he'd gone. 'Then we can head into the Gorge together.'

Torak rubbed the scar on his forearm. 'Juksakai tells me it's two daywalks to the Mountain. Souls' Night is only four days away.'

'So there's time.'

'No, Renn. Not for you.'

'You can't decide that for me.'

'I don't need to.' He pulled on his boots. 'I'll say goodbye now. I'm leaving at first light.'

There was a ringing in her ears. This wasn't happening. 'But – you can't go all by yourself.'

'I won't. I'll have Wolf.'

'He isn't here.'

'He'll come.'

'How do you know? You'll be alone. That's just what Eostra wants!'

He did not reply.

Something in his manner made her look at him, really look. What she saw in his face made her catch her breath. There would be no need to tell him of Saeunn's prophecy.

'You know,' she said.

He nodded.

'How?'

'When I saw the Mountain.' He touched his breastbone. 'I felt it. Here.'

Renn was silent for a moment. Then she said, 'Prophecies can be wrong. We can prove it wrong.'

'Not this time.' He paused. 'Many winters ago, on Souls' Night, my father woke the great fire and broke the power of the Soul-Eaters. I have to finish what he began.'

'I know. But—'

'And maybe I can do it, even against Eostra. But the thing is, Renn ...' He broke off. 'The thing is, when I try to think about afterwards – about going back to the Forest and being with you and Wolf and Fin-Kedinn – I can't see it. It's all just dark.'

Renn stared at him, aghast.

She watched him roll up his sleeping-sack and gather his gear. 'Where are you going?' she said.

'I'll sleep in the other shelter, head off at dawn. You stay here. Get some rest.'

He wore his stubborn look, and she saw that it was hopeless. 'As soon as I'm better,' she said fiercely, 'I'll catch up with you.'

'No.'

'I will. And I'll prove it. Here. Take my wrist-guard. That's a pledge.' Somehow, she managed to untie the thongs and grab his wrist. She pushed back his sleeve and fastened the thin oblong of polished greenstone on his forearm. 'There. You can give it back when I find you.'

'You mustn't try to find me.'

'You can't stop me.'

'Renn, *listen!* That creature ignored me and went after you. Because Eostra wants me alive, at least until Souls' Night – but she doesn't care about you. Well, I do.' He slung his bow over his shoulder. 'Stay with the Swan Clan. Get better. Go back to the Forest.'

'No!'

'Goodbye, Renn. Whatever happens, you know – you must know how much I . . . ' His throat worked. 'May the guardian fly with you.' Stooping, he kissed her mouth. Then he turned and ran out into the dark.

TWENTY-FOUR

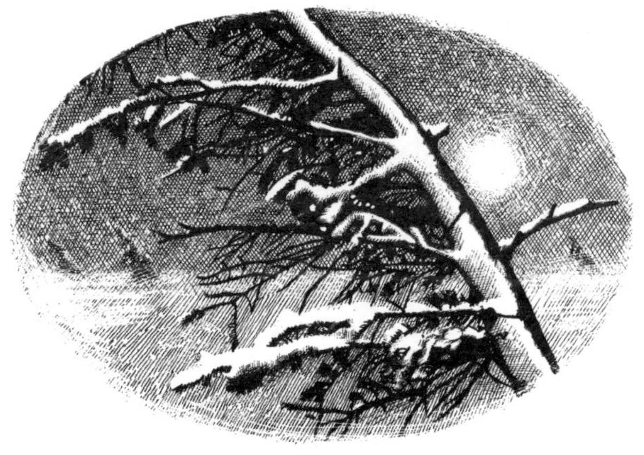

The wind howled around the Mountains and swept across the fells. It stirred a thicket fringing a frozen lake, where men crouched around a fire.

A group of Rowan Clan had arrived on dog sleds, bringing three hunters from the Forest. They'd nearly missed Fin-Kedinn's camp, as he'd concealed it well, but in the end, their dogs had found him.

Etan of the Raven Clan spoke urgently to his leader. 'Fin-Kedinn, we beg you, come back with us! Thull wouldn't have sent us if he wasn't desperate. The shadow sickness has spread throughout the clans. There aren't many people who are well enough to hunt. Those who are don't dare venture far, for fear of tokoroths. They're beginning to fight over food.'

Fin-Kedinn took this in silence. Then he said, 'Thull

isn't the only leader among them. What about the others?'

'The Willow Clan Leader helped keep order for a while, and Durrain of the Red Deer. Then the sickness attacked them too. They've had to be confined to their shelters. And now Saeunn is dying.'

'Saeunn has the shadow sickness?' Fin-Kedinn said sharply.

'No. She wore herself out tending her people. When we left, she was sinking fast. Thull says he can't lead without her. He's right. The clans won't listen to him alone.'

'They'll have to,' said Fin-Kedinn. 'I must reach the Mountain.'

'But *why*?' Uneasily, Etan peered into the thicket, where a shadowy figure hid beyond reach of the light.

'Who is that with you?' asked one of the Rowan hunters. 'Why won't they come out and speak their name?'

Fin-Kedinn did not reply. The shadow in the thicket edged deeper into the dark.

'What do you hope to gain out here?' said Etan. 'What can even Fin-Kedinn achieve against the evil one?'

'If we're to have a chance against Eostra,' said the Raven Leader, speaking the name distinctly, 'it won't be by might, but by Magecraft. I journey with one who knows these things; who knows how to find Eostra in the Mountain of Ghosts, and how to remain hidden from her and her creatures. That's all I can tell you.'

Etan met his eyes. 'Maybe this will change your mind. Saeunn herself sends word. She says only you can steady the clans.'

'Saeunn was against my leaving,' said Fin-Kedinn. 'Of course she wants me back.'

'She bids you remember what she saw in the embers. She says, the spirit walker will die. Not even you can alter that. She says the place of the Raven Leader is with the living. She says you must return.'

The fire sputtered. The hunters waited for Fin-Kedinn's answer. The figure in the thicket watched and listened.

Fin-Kedinn rose and strode to the edge of the trees, where a lone boulder stood guard over the lake. In the distance, the Mountains were black against the stars. They were still a long way off. If he returned to the Forest now, could he be sure that his companion would make the journey alone?

He stared at the sky. It gave him no answers. The World Spirit was far away, battling the Great Auroch. The troubles of men were not its concern.

And somewhere out there were Torak and Renn: isolated, vulnerable, like two tiny sparks about to be snuffed out by the night.

Fin-Kedinn ground his fist against the boulder. Duty called him to the Forest. His heart pulled him towards the Mountains.

The wind sank to a whisper. The granite was hard beneath his hand.

Fin-Kedinn turned from the darkness and walked back towards the fire.

TWENTY-FIVE

As Wolf slewed to a halt in the windy Dark, he sensed that his pack-brother was many lopes away. He'd made a mistake. He should never have run off into the Mountains.

He'd been gnawing the reindeer head near the great Den of the Taillesses when the eagle owl had swooped over him. He had known it was a trick, but he couldn't *not* follow. It had taken his cub.

Through Darks and Lights he had chased it, but now it was gone, and he didn't know where he was. His paws sank into the Bright Soft Cold, and the Mountains loomed over him. The wind carried the smell of ptarmigan and hare – but no Tall Tailless.

Lifting his muzzle, Wolf uttered sharp, seeking barks. *Where are you?*

No beloved answering howl.

The wind veered and Wolf turned into it – and caught a smell he'd never smelt before. Dogs; but something was wrong with them. Wolf smelt that they were big and strong, cunning and full of hate. His claws tightened. Against such as these, Tall Tailless had no more chance than a newborn cub.

It was a blustery day, and the wind moaned through the Gorge of the Hidden People. Torak had heard no strange howls, but whenever a pebble fell, he started.

From time to time, he came across a boulder on which a spiral had been hammer-etched. Juksakai had said that his ancestors had made them to mark the trail to the Mountain; but no-one had ventured in for many winters.

Who, then, had scraped the spirals clean of ice?

And where was Wolf?

Torak tried not to think of what Eostra's dogs could do to his pack-brother. And he couldn't even howl for him, except in his head.

In places, the snow lay thigh-deep; in others, Torak had to scramble over rocks scoured bare by the wind. He was soon sweating, but thanks to his Mountain clothes, he didn't get chilled. His jerkin had dense diverbird plumage at front and back, but looser-feathered ptarmigan under the arms to let out the sweat. His musk-ox wool socks were light as gossamer, yet incredibly warm. Pads of dried moss in his boots prevented blisters, and rawhide coils on the soles gave a good grip.

But nothing could protect him from the thinning air. His head ached. He felt constantly breathless. Worst of all was the knowledge that he was where he should not be.

The Gorge of the Hidden People was a bewildering maze of gullies and spurs and twisting valleys. Looming cliffs shut out the sky. The Redwater had fled underground. This was a world of stone.

And the Hidden People didn't want him here.

'They make you see things,' Juksakai had said. 'Once near the mouth of the Gorge, I found a snow-vole turned to stone. Another time I saw a great white bird vanish into the cliff.'

'But what *are* the Hidden People?' Torak had asked. He knew they lived in lakes and streams and rocks; he'd even sensed them at times, and the memory was very bad. But he'd never paused to consider what they were, or where they came from.

'They used to be clans, like us,' Juksakai had told him. 'But long ago in the Great Hunger, they took to killing and eating people. The World Spirit punished them by decreeing that they must hide for ever, only coming out when no-one is near. That's why you never see them. If ever you get close, all you find is stones.'

Torak sensed them peering at him from clefts in the rockface. He passed a ring of standing stones that leant towards each other. Glancing back, he caught a blur of movement. As he walked, he heard a furtive rustling. It stopped when he did, but when he went on, it started again.

Around mid-afternoon, he paused for breath. 'I mean you no harm,' he told the dwellers in the rocks. 'I seek the Soul-Eater. I have no quarrel with you.'

A whirring overhead. He threw himself sideways. The boulder exploded on impact, pelting him with fragments.

Later, he heard the gurgle of water, and traced it to a spring in a gully. He found clumps of the heathery scrub Juksakai had used for waking fire; and an overhang that he could wall in with rocks, for a shelter.

No stones whistled down in the night, and he heard no strange howls. But there was no sign of Wolf, either.

Next morning the wind was gone. The stillness felt unnatural. Intentional.

Torak wasn't long out of the gully when he found tracks in the snow. Some time before, a pack of dogs had raced through the Gorge. Torak made out seven sets of prints, all bigger than any he'd ever seen.

Dry-mouthed, he drew his knife, and followed the trail round a spur.

The young hare had been torn apart. Dark-red entrails were flung across the snow like discarded rope. Ice-rimed eyes stared from its mangled skull.

Torak pictured the hare's desperate zigzag as the dogs ran it down. They had ripped it apart, spattering flesh and brains over thirty paces, but eating nothing. They had done it because they could.

Pity and disgust churned inside him as he muttered a prayer for the hare's souls. But as he headed off, it was for himself that he prayed. He had told Renn that Eostra wanted him alive. But alive, he reflected, did not necessarily mean whole.

The smell of sweat wafted from the neck of his robe. A dog would scent that from a daywalk away. *I'm frightened*, it said.

A thud behind him.

He spun round.

And sagged with relief.

Rek raised her head from the hare's skull and gave a

preocuppied croak, then went back to pecking out an eye.

As Torak sheathed his knife, Wolf came bounding towards him over the snow.

Did you follow the owl? asked Torak when their first delirious greeting was over.

Yes, said Wolf. *But I didn't find the cub.*

I'm sorry.

Where is the pack-sister?

Safe, said Torak, *but she hurt her paw.*

You miss her.

Yes.

Me too.

Wolf snuffed the air. *Dogs. Far away.*

They're strong, and many, said Torak. *Much danger.*

Wolf leant against him and wagged his tail.

They hadn't gone far when the Redwater reappeared, in an echoing channel under the cliffs. Rip and Rek flew to the top of a spur that cut across the Gorge, then back to Torak, calling impatiently. *Come on, it's easy!*

'No it's not,' panted Torak as he and Wolf started to climb. The spur was made of knives. Some malign force had shivered its rocks into thousands of blades standing on edge. Even through his boots, Torak's feet were soon bruised. He hadn't gone far when he noticed that Wolf was limping. His pads were criss-crossed with cuts.

'I'm sorry,' said Torak.

Wolf licked his ear.

In the Far North, Torak had seen sled dogs with paw-boots. The best he could do for Wolf was to bind his paws with strips of buckskin from his old jerkin. Wolf kept butting in to see what he was doing, and when the bindings were securely tied, Torak had to tell him sternly not to eat them.

He was so intent on watching Wolf that he didn't realize when they reached the top of the spur. Straightening up, he caught his breath. The Gorge of the Hidden People lay behind him. Above him loomed the Mountain of Ghosts.

Its summit pierced the clouds. Its glaring white flanks warded him back. *Sacred, sacred. A place of spirits, not of men.*

Sinking to his knees, he sprinkled earthblood as an offering. In hushed tones, he begged the Mountain to forgive him for trespassing.

Clouds closed in, hiding it from view. Torak didn't know if that was a good sign, or bad.

To his right, a scree slope fell steeply to a shadowy valley. Ahead, glimpsed through the swirling whitenenss, a huge boulder-field led onto the Mountain. The Redwater cascaded from a small black cave mouth nestled in its midst.

Torak made out a spiral marker on one of the boulders. Filled with apprehension, he started towards it. Wolf padded after him, his tail down.

The boulders were treacherous with ice, and in places the snow was deep enough to make the going hard. They struggled past another marker, and another. They were now on the very Mountain itself.

And Torak had to find somewhere to camp.

They came to a spur where snow had drifted deep. Torak was relieved. He preferred hacking out a snow hole to rearranging so much as a rock in this sacred place.

He didn't dare wake a fire. Huddled in his snow hole, he shared a scrap of smoked reindeer with Rip and Rek, while Wolf chewed the paw-boots – which, as his pads were already healing, Torak had given him for nightmeal.

As night deepened, Torak listened to the distant voice of the stream and the silence of the Mountain. It had allowed him to camp, but it could crush him in a heartbeat.

And Eostra ... What of the Soul-Eater who waited within?

With the assurance of absolute power, she had let him venture through the Gorge; but she could send her pack to take him whenever she wanted. And the day after tomorrow was Souls' Night.

On his forearm, Torak felt the weight of Renn's wrist-guard. She had never seemed so far away.

He dreams it is summer, and he is playing with Wolf in a lake strewn with yellow water lilies. Wolf leaps clear of the water and lands with a splash. Torak dives, trailing silver bubbles of underwater laughter. Still laughing, he bursts into the sun. Everything feels *right*. His world-soul is a golden thread stretching out to all living things. And there is Fa, standing smiling in the shallows. 'Look behind you, Torak!'

Torak jolted awake. He heard the boom of falling rocks. The ravens' stony alarm calls.

Yanking on his boots and grabbing his axe, he scrambled out of the snow hole – and into a wall of fog.

Rip and Rek were invisible, he couldn't see two paces ahead. He glimpsed Wolf, a grey blur racing over the stones.

Stumbling towards him, Torak saw that part of the spur had collapsed; a few boulders were still rolling to rest.

Wolf halted, his black lips peeled back in a snarl.

Torak followed his stare. In the fog, all he could make out were the rolling boulders.

Wolf's growls shook his whole body.

Torak narrowed his eyes.

Not boulders.

Dogs.

TWENTY-SIX

Relentless as a tide, Eostra's pack surged towards them through the fog.

They were bigger than any wolf or dog Torak had ever seen. He took in shaggy manes clotted with filth. Bloodshot eyes empty of feeling.

Slipping off his mittens, he tucked them in his sleeves. He gripped his axe. Beside him, Wolf wrinkled his muzzle and bared his fangs.

Torak uttered a deep grunt-growl. *Stay together.*

Wolf edged closer to him without taking his eyes off the pack.

Silently, the dogs came on, utterly concentrated on their prey.

Defiance surged in Torak. All right, then. Let's see you fight.

One huge black beast lunged at him.

He swung his axe. Wolf leapt. The creature drew back, melting into the fog.

Another tried, then two together: harrying, disappearing, but always spreading out to surround them.

Torak knew what they were doing. With wolves and dogs, most hunts begin like this. Make the prey fight, make it run. Find the weakest. Go after that.

The weakest was Torak. He knew it. Wolf knew it. The dogs knew it.

Grabbing a stone, he threw it as hard as he could, hitting a brindled monster on the shoulder. The dog twitched an ear, as if at an importunate wasp.

The ravens dropped out of the sky with furious caws, their talons skimming the marauders' backs. The pack ignored them. Cowed, Rip and Rek flew higher – as if, thought Torak, they were already circling a carcass.

He threw more stones, and the dogs withdrew into the swirling white. But he could feel the ring closing in.

His grip on his axe was slippery with sweat. An axe wouldn't be much use except in close combat, and if it came to that, he wouldn't stand a chance. The only weapon that would've been any good was his bow, and that was in the snow hole, five paces away. It might as well be five hundred.

With the speed of a striking snake, a huge grey beast went for Wolf. Wolf whirled, sank his teeth into its rump. With a yowl it ripped free and fled, spattering blood.

The pack went on circling.

Wolf shook himself, unhurt.

At the corner of his vision, Torak glimpsed a black blur leaping towards him. He swung his axe, struck a glancing blow on the skull. The creature fell with a thud, then sprang to its feet as if nothing had happened.

As the pack prowled around them, the brindled beast – the leader – walked stiffly forwards and halted three paces from Torak. Torak felt Wolf tense for the attack. Urgently, he told him to stand his ground.

The leader's small, dull eyes fixed Torak's, and for an instant, he knew its mind. What it saw before it was not a boy, but a sack of meat, to be savaged till it moved no more. What kept that black heart beating was rage at all these running, howling sacks of *life* – this *life* which must be destroyed.

By an act of will, Torak tore his gaze away.

He had an image of himself lying dead. Then he realized that that was wrong, it wouldn't be *his* body; Eostra wanted him alive. This was about getting Wolf away from him: about slaughtering his pack-brother.

Two dogs sprang at him. Wolf darted to intercept in a flurry of fur and fangs. The brindled leader attacked Torak from behind. His axe caught it flat on the ribs. With a yowl it slunk back – but only a pace.

As Torak ran to help Wolf, the leader sprang again, seizing the hem of his tunic in its jaws, dragging him down. He lashed out. It dodged, hauling him after it, strong as a bear. Torak slipped, nearly lost his footing. He pretended to weaken, let the creature drag him closer – then brought down his boot, heel-stamping between the eyes. For a moment the great jaws loosened. Torak wrenched his tunic free and staggered back to Wolf.

With a wet slapping of jowls, the leader shook itself, then lowered its head for the next attack.

Three dogs sprang at Torak, four at Wolf. But in mid-air the marauders yelped and twisted, as if struck from behind. Stones came hurtling through the fog. The pack faltered, casting about for the unseen attacker.

Torak thought he glimpsed a pale figure vanish into the fog.

Who's that? he asked Wolf.

Tailless, Wolf told him.

More stones smacked into the dogs: now from one side, now from another. Confused, the pack turned from Torak and Wolf and sought its mysterious assailant.

Shakily, Torak touched his pack-brother's scruff. Wolf's rump was bleeding, his left ear torn, but his eyes were bright; he wasn't even panting.

Torak was. He couldn't get enough air into his lungs.

He thought fast. Whoever was distracting the dogs wouldn't be able to do so for long. They would be back. And although Wolf could keep up the defence all day, he, Torak, could not. Soon he would go down. And they would kill Wolf.

Behind him, Torak saw a narrow cleft on the other side of the spur: a crack in the Mountain. He backed towards it.

Wolf threw him a warning look. *No!*

Torak kept moving. Reluctantly, Wolf came too. The dogs, battling a hail of stones, didn't notice.

The snow was knee-deep, but at last Torak reached the end of the cleft. The relief when he felt solid rock against his shoulders! Now he *could* last all day: eating snow, warding off attacks which could come only from the front.

Abruptly, the hail of stones ceased. The invisible guardian was gone. For an instant, Torak wondered who it had been; then he forgot about that. Once again, the pack was moving in.

Beside him, Wolf bristled with dismay. He'd followed Torak out of loyalty, but this went against everything he knew: no wolf backs into a place from which there is only one way out.

And Torak couldn't explain why he'd done it, because Wolf wasn't able to think like prey. Torak, though, found it all too easy; and he'd seen enough encounters between wolves and reindeer to know how it works. Wolves – and dogs – hunt those who run. If you're prey, your best chance is to stand and fight.

He was right, but he'd underestimated Wolf.

For an instant, the amber gaze grazed his. In that moment, Torak sensed what he meant to do. No, Wolf, no, it's just what they want! Too late. A gap opened in the pack – and Wolf shot through it. The dogs sped after him.

It all happened in the blink of an eye, but Torak knew that he must seize the chance Wolf had given him.

Jamming his axe in his belt, he reached for the rocks and began to climb.

The last thing he saw before he boosted himself up the cleft was Wolf racing down the slope with Eostra's pack on his tail.

TWENTY-SEVEN

Wolf flew over the rocks and the dogs flew after him. Wolf *hated* running away – but he had to save Tall Tailless.

Wolf was heading for a great slope of Bright Soft Cold. From the voice of the wind coming off it, he knew it was deep, maybe wolf-high. So. The pack meant to chase him where even a wolf must flounder. But he *knew* this trick, he used it himself when he hunted deer. Did they think they could fool *him*?

Slowing his pace, he let the lead dog lope closer, till he caught the stony thud of its dark heart. It was snapping its chops, as if already tasting his flesh.

Too soon. As Wolf reached the edge of the Bright Soft Cold, he spun on one forepaw and leapt sideways onto solid rock. The dog behind him was too heavy, it couldn't turn in time. As Wolf sped off, he heard it thrashing and snarling in the Bright Soft Cold. Wolf threw up his tail. They might be bigger than him, but he was *faster*!

Although not by much. Already they were gaining on him again.

Over the pebbles he went, flicking his torn ear back to listen, the other ear forwards, for danger ahead.

He smelt darkness rushing towards him. The wind that blew from it made a booming sound, it was coming from underground. Suddenly there was no more stone in front and the Mountain opened to swallow him. Skittering to a halt, he saw that the crack was many paces across. From deep within came a howling cold.

In a snap, Wolf decided. Tensing his haunches, he sprang. His forepaws clawed the other side. Throwing his tail round and scrabbling with his hindpaws, he gave a tremendous heave . . . He was up.

Baying in fury, the pack ran along the other side of the crack. Wolf lifted his muzzle in scorn. No dog – not even these – can jump as far as a wolf!

And yet – something was wrong. There weren't as many of them as before.

Where was the leader?

The lead dog stood at the bottom of the cleft and watched Torak climb. Its stare never wavered.

As his fingers sought the next handhold, Torak pictured Wolf racing over the snow with the pack at his heels. Wolf stumbled. A dog sank its fangs into his flank. They were on him, tearing him apart . . .

Torak's axe-handle banged against his hip, wrenching him back.

They haven't got Wolf, he told himself. It's what Eostra *wants* you to believe.

The cleft was the height of four tall men, but narrow enough for him to climb by bracing one foot on either side. The fissured granite provided many hand and footholds, and on a summer's day, Torak would have scrambled up it like a squirrel. But the rock was running wet and veined with black ice. His fingers were clumsy with cold. His mittens had come untucked from his sleeves and swung loose on their strings, but he dared not slip them on.

Pausing for breath, he craned his neck. The Mountain was lost in fog, but he glimpsed the top of the cleft. He was halfway there.

'Don't rush, Torak.' In his head he seemed to hear the calm, steady voice of his kinsman, Bale. The summer before last, the Seal Clan boy had taught him rock-climbing. Bale had been patient, never imparting more than Torak could take in. 'Try to keep your arms no higher than about shoulder height; that way, your weight will stay mostly on your feet … And heels down, Torak. Standing on your toes only gives you leg-shake.'

Torak's heels *were* down, but his legs were still shaking.

Below him, the brindled creature growled.

Torak glanced down.

Cold, cold, that stony gaze; waiting for this sack of meat to drop into its jaws. Its hunger sucked at his souls.

He screwed his eyes shut. Don't look, he told himself. Don't think about it. Put something else in its place. Think about Wolf and Renn and Fin-Kedinn.

The darkness in his head blew away like smoke dispersed by a cleansing wind.

Opening his eyes, Torak forced his numb fingers to seek another handhold.

He found his rhythm again, moving a hand, then a foot, then the other hand, the other foot. Smooth and fluid, like a dance. Nearly there.

The axe in his belt snagged on an outcrop and yanked him back.

He clung on with both hands, his right leg raised to find the next crack. But the next crack was too high, his foot couldn't reach it because the axe was wedged, holding him down.

Lowering his right leg, he tried to find the foothold he'd just relinquished. His boot brushed solid rock, he couldn't find it. Now his left leg, bearing his whole weight, began to shake. He couldn't keep this up much longer, he would have to reach down with one hand and free his axe. But then he would have only one hand and one foot on the rock; and that wasn't enough to hold him there. Again he seemed to hear Bale's voice. 'If you remember nothing else, Torak, remember this. Always keep *three limbs* in contact with the rock. Move either an arm, or a leg, but never both at the same time.'

His left leg was trembling violently. Nothing for it: he'd have to *pull* himself clear.

The knuckles of both hands whitened as he strove with all his might to haul himself free. The axe made a terrible grinding noise. His belt tightened about his waist as the axe-handle twisted downwards. His arms shook with strain. With a jolt that nearly threw him off, the axe jerked free. He boosted himself up, and his free foot finally found the next crack.

Shuddering with relief, he braced both legs against either side of the cleft. When he'd stopped shaking, he made one last effort and hauled himself over the top.

Like a landed salmon he lay gasping, his cheek against icy stone. Before him stretched a plateau some fifty paces wide. It was shadowed by crags wreathed in fog, and littered with broken boulders which the Mountain had sent crashing down.

Torak got to his feet, and the freezing wind buffeted him, so cold it made his temples ache. He untangled his axe from his belt. It slipped from his hands and tumbled into the cleft. Aghast, he watched it clatter to the bottom.

The dog was nowhere to be seen.

Torak peered down, unable to take in the loss of his axe.

He felt eyes on him.

He turned.

Twenty paces away, on the rocks beneath the cliffs, stood the Eagle Owl Mage.

Her deathless, death-like mask was the livid white of shattered bone. The slit of her mouth gaped in a soundless scream. One hand clutched a mace topped by a glowing red stone; the other a three-pronged spear for snaring souls.

Torak fumbled for his knife. He knew it would be useless against the Soul-Eater, but it had belonged to Fa, and it lent him the courage to stay standing.

The evil of the Eagle Owl Mage crackled like lightning, blasted him back.

He thought of Wolf, hunted by the pack. 'Call them off,' he panted.

The painted owl eyes glared. No sound issued from the slitted mouth.

'Call off your dogs from my pack-brother!' shouted

Torak. 'You've got what you want! Here I am!'

The Masked One never stirred, but behind her, Torak saw shadows spread like wings. He felt her malice battering his mind.

Then from the nightmare mask came a cry that pierced his skull. Echoing from rock to rock, it grew; louder and louder, slivers of bone skewering his brain . . .

Look behind you, Torak.

Torak glanced over his shoulder – and ducked too late. The eagle owl struck him on the side of the head. He staggered, swaying on the edge. Above him the owl veered for another attack.

At that moment, a great white bird came swooping out of the fog, its talons outstretched to strike the owl. The owl swerved to evade it, and flew round to come at Torak again.

He tottered backwards and fell.

TWENTY-EIGHT

Torak woke up floating in a cloud. It was soft and light, and deliciously warm.

With an effort, he lifted his eyelids. Through a mist, he glimpsed white reindeer leaping over him. White wolverines ambled peacefully among white lemmings and willow grouse. A snowy musk-ox grazed near a raven bright as frost.

'Am I dead?' he mumbled.

'I don't think so,' said a voice that seemed to come from a great distance.

Torak sighed.

Later, it occurred to him that the voice had been right, as he was still in his body. His outer clothes were gone, but he wore his jerkin and under-leggings. The cloud tickled his bare feet.

'Where am I?' he murmured.

'Here,' the voice said quietly.

Torak tried to make sense of that. 'Are you the Hidden People?'

A pause. 'I hide. But I'm not one of them.'

The mist began to clear. Torak smelt woodsmoke. He heard water dripping; the spitting of a fire. He felt the tightness in his chest that he only got when he was in a cave.

His eyes snapped open.

He was lying on a mat of hare skins beneath a covering of musk-ox wool. The cave was so narrow he could have spanned it with his arms, but he guessed it must be deep. Beyond his feet, daylight rimmed a patchwork of hides that shut off the cave mouth. Nearer, a fire cast a ruddy glimmer. Torak saw piles of heather and dried musk-ox dung; and strings of herbs, mushrooms and trout, hanging to smoke.

White reindeer and musk-ox had been painted on the walls in gypsum. Lemmings, wolverines and grouse, cramming every ledge, had been carved in slate and dusted with chalk. The white raven was real. It perched on a rock, peering at Torak. Feathers, legs, claws, even its beak were white. But its eyes were dark, and raven-keen.

Shakily, Torak sat up. He felt giddy and bruised, but he could move all his limbs, so he guessed that the snow and his bulky clothes had broken his fall. His head throbbed. The eagle owl had reopened his scalp wound, which someone had bandaged.

The eagle owl.

Everything returned in a rush.

'Who's there?' he said. 'Where's my knife! Where's Wolf?'

No answer.

Torak staggered towards the cave mouth.

'Stop!' cried the voice.

Torak heard running feet and clattering claws. He pushed past the hides into an icy blast. Hands yanked him back from a dizzying drop. He sat down hard, and Wolf pounced on him, snuffle-licking his face and whimpering with joy. *You're awake! I hate these long sleeps! I'm here!*

Torak reached for Wolf's scruff. He stared up at the boy who had saved his life.

He appeared to be about Torak's own age. Grimy and thin, he was blinking and shielding his eyes from the light. He wore a shaggy robe of musk-ox wool, and had no visible clan-tattoos. But it wasn't any of these which made him extraordinary.

He looked as if someone had stolen all his colour. His long, tangled hair was white as cobwebs. His brows and lashes had the hue of dead grass, his face the pallor of fresh-cut chalk. His pale-grey eyes made Torak think of a sky full of snow.

'Who are you?' said the boy with an odd blend of fear and longing.

'*What* are you?' cried Torak, struggling to his feet. 'You took my clothes and my knife. Give them back!'

The boy stretched his lips in a gap-toothed smile that looked as if he hadn't used it in a while. 'Your knife is safe.' He pointed to a ledge. 'You're dizzy. I made you sleep. You talked a lot.'

'You're one of her creatures!' snarled Torak.

'Whose?'

'Eostra!'

'The one who has taken the Mountain?'

'Don't pretend you don't know!'

'Oh, I know. I've seen her.'

Torak saw the shadows under his eyes. This boy had endured days and nights of fear.

Or else he was a good liar.

'You must be helping her!' Torak insisted. 'Why else would you be here?'

'I was here before. I . . .' He broke off, turning his head to listen. 'I'm coming soon,' he called.

'Who's there?' said Torak suspiciously.

'You should rest,' urged the boy. 'You're dizzy.'

As he said it, the giddiness got worse. 'Are you a Mage?' Torak said. 'Making me feel whatever you want?'

'A Mage? I don't think so.'

Wolf was licking Torak's hand. Muzzily, Torak saw that his pack-brother's wounds had been cleaned and smeared with salve, and that he seemed quite at ease with the stranger.

'At first he wouldn't let me near you,' said the boy, holding out his fingers for Wolf to sniff.

'Why did you make me sleep?' said Torak, fighting to stay upright.

'I had to go and check my snares. I couldn't let you get away.'

Torak blundered past him and grabbed his knife. 'Give me my clothes. Let me out.'

The cave was whirling. Gently, the boy took his knife and made him lie down on the hare skins.

When Torak woke again, he was back under the musk-ox covering.

And he was bound hand and foot.

'Let me go.'

'No.'

'Why?'

'You'd get away.'

'But I can't stay here!'

'Why?'

Torak gave up struggling and stared at his captor.

The boy's hare-skin boots had been clumsily patched with bits of lemming, and his robe had been made by someone who'd never learnt to sew. He sat with his hands between his knees, gazing wistfully at Torak.

'Who *are* you?' said Torak.

The pale lashes flickered. 'I'm Dark.'

Torak snorted. 'Why'd they call you that?'

'They didn't. They threw me out before I got a name, so I chose Dark. I thought it might help.'

Torak felt a flicker of pity, which he swiftly suppressed. 'If you're nothing to do with Eostra, how come she hasn't killed you?'

'I keep off her dogs and the child-demon things with my slingshot. That's how I helped you when the dogs attacked. And Ark guards me when I sleep.'

'Who's Ark?'

On its perch, the white raven fluffed its head-feathers.

'If Eostra wanted you dead,' said Torak, 'she'd have found a way.'

'Yes. I think she likes the power. For her, I'm a game.' He gave Torak his odd, stretched smile. 'But now I've got you. I'm not alone any more.'

Torak couldn't make him out. He was scrawny, but he'd managed to get Torak into his cave, and he'd done a good job of tying him up. Wolf sniffed the bindings, but when

Torak told him in a furtive grunt-whine to chew the ones at his wrists, Wolf simply licked his fingers.

'Are you hungry?' said Dark.

'No,' lied Torak. 'Who *are* you? How come you're here?'

Dark took half a dried trout from inside his robe and began to gnaw. 'When my mother carried me in her belly, a white hare ran in front of her, so I was born like this.' He touched his cobweb hair. 'My mother said I was Swan Clan like her, but when I got older I began to see things, and they said I brought bad luck. My mother protected me, but when I was eight summers old, she died. Next day, Fa took me into the Gorge. I thought he was going to give me my clan-tattoos, but he left me. I kept the trail-markers clear so he could find me again. But he never came back.'

'Didn't you try to make your own way out?'

'Oh, no. I knew I had to stay.'

Torak thought about that. 'So you've been here ever since?'

Dark indicated the stone creatures thronging the ledges. 'One for each moon.'

'But – that must be seven winters. How did you survive?'

'It was hard,' said Dark, picking a fish bone from between his teeth. 'The first three winters, someone left food. After that, nothing. I was cold till I gathered the musk-ox wool. Once, my teeth went bad. They hurt till I knocked some out with a rock.' He paused. 'I was alone. Then I found Ark. Some crows were pecking her because she was white. I named her Ark, it was the first thing she said to me.' He grinned. 'She likes her name, she says it a lot!'

'So all this time, it's been just you and the raven?'

'And the ghosts.'

Wolf got up and trotted deeper into the cave. Dark turned his head to listen.

'You – can see ghosts,' said Torak.

Dark nodded calmly.

It was very still in the cave. Torak said, 'Was that a ghost you were talking to before?'

'My sister, yes. But as she's a ghost, she doesn't remember she *is* my sister.'

Torak peered into the shadows, but all he could see was Wolf, who sat sweeping the floor with his tail. He said, 'Have you seen the ghost of a man who looks like me? Long dark hair? Wolf Clan tattoos?'

'No. Who's that?'

Torak did not reply. 'But we are inside the Mountain? The Mountain of Ghosts?'

'Yes.'

'Are there other caves?'

'Lots. I like the whispering cave, because of the ghosts. But I haven't gone there since she took it. She brought demons and the cold red stone.'

Torak's heart began to pound. 'How do you get there? To the whispering cave?'

'Many ways.'

'Take me there.'

'No.'

'You've got to. How long have I been asleep?'

'Um – nearly two days.'

'*Two days?*' shouted Torak. 'But that means tonight is Souls' Night!'

His shouts brought Wolf racing to his side.

Now Torak understood why Eostra had let him escape:

because he hadn't. It suited her to leave him cocooned like a fly in a spider's web, until such time as she had a use for him.

'Dark, listen to me,' he said, forcing himself to keep calm. 'Tonight the Soul-Eater will do something terrible. I don't know exactly what, but I know she means to conquer the dead, and use them to rule the living. You have to let me go!'

'But in your sleep you said she wants to kill you. You must stay with me. You're safe here.'

'After tonight, nowhere will be safe, she'll be too strong! With the dead at her command, she'll rule the Mountains, the Forest, the Sea!'

'What's the Sea?' said Dark.

Torak let out a roar that shook the cave.

Wolf set back his ears and yowled.

Ark flapped her wings.

With a huge effort, Torak mastered his temper. 'Maybe this will persuade you. In some way I don't understand, my father's spirit is tangled up with her. If I can stop her, maybe I'll help him, too. Now do you see why you *have* to let me go?'

A shadow crossed Dark's extraordinary face, and he seemed suddenly older. 'My father left me. He never came back.'

Torak set his teeth. 'What if it was Ark who needed help? You'd do anything to save her, wouldn't you?'

Dark wrung his chalk-white hands till the knuckles cracked. Torak could see that he was torn. 'Winters and winters I've been here,' he said. 'You're the first person, the first living person.'

Sensing his turmoil, Ark flew onto his shoulder.

Wolf glanced anxiously from Torak to Dark and back again.

Torak waited.

Dark shook his head. 'No. I can't let you go.'

TWENTY-NINE

'*One day*,' said Renn as she limped over the boulders. 'That's all I asked. One day!'

A stone whizzed down and smashed behind her.

'Sorry,' she muttered to the Hidden People.

They didn't like it when she spoke too loudly. They didn't much like *her*. But so far they'd tolerated her; maybe because of the little bundles of rowan twigs she'd left at every trail marker.

It had been two days since Torak left. The Swans had wanted to leave at once, but Renn had insisted that they remain at the mouth of the Gorge. She'd spent a desperate day in camp, grinding her teeth as she waited for her ankle to get better. Next morning she'd lied to the Swans that it was, and headed after Torak. They hadn't tried to stop her. They'd simply given her provisions and watched her go.

At first, things had gone well. Torak's trail had been easy to follow, and though her ankle ached, she could walk on it. She'd jumped at every sound, but her Mage's sense had told her that Eostra's creatures were far away. And in the afternoon she'd made a heartening discovery: a rocky shelter that was unmistakeably Torak's. She'd spent the night in it, and fallen asleep planning what she would say when she caught up with him.

She'd woken stiff, cold and scared. A pallid sliver of moon hung in the morning sky. Tomorrow night was Souls' Night.

She hadn't gone far when she'd found the bones of a hare, picked clean by ravens. Nothing odd about that; and yet her hand had crept to her clan-creature feathers. Malice hung in the air. Bad things had happened here. Evil had soaked into the rocks.

That had been a while ago, but she was still shaken. Her boots crunched noisily over frozen scrub and black lichen brittle as cinders. The glug of her waterskin sounded like footsteps. She stopped, to make sure that they weren't.

'They're not real,' she said out loud. 'There's nothing here.'

The stones tensed. She felt the Hidden People watching.

Eostra was watching too.

Clouds began pouring over the edge of the cliffs. Stealthily, they swallowed the Gorge, folding Renn in a clammy embrace. Eostra hadn't sent her dogs to drive her back. She didn't need to.

Like a winged shadow at the corner of her vision, Renn felt the presence of the Eagle Owl Mage. Fog stole down her throat and took her breath. Her ankle throbbed. Her courage slunk away. Why go on, when she was doomed to fail?

She had an odd sensation of watching herself from above. There she was, a lame girl cowering in a ravine. She would never find Torak. He had left because he wanted to face Eostra alone: because he wanted to die, and be with his father. And soon that wish would be fulfilled.

In the distance, a raven croaked.

Renn raised her head. That was Rip.

Moments later, even further off, she heard Rek answer him.

As Renn listened to their cries slowly fading, she clenched her fists. Rip and Rek didn't sound defeated. They sounded intent on some mysterious raven matter of their own, probably concerning food.

As if in sympathy, her belly growled. Fog or no fog, she was hungry.

Opening her food pouch, she took out two strips of smoked reindeer tongue stuck together with marrowfat. Then she sat on a boulder and began to eat. It was the best thing she'd ever tasted.

She decided that her bow could do with some food, too. Juksakai had given her a bladder of oil from reindeer foot joints, which he'd said was better than anything for keeping wood and sinew supple, even in the coldest weather. Renn lavished some on her bow. Then she checked her arrows: a gift from Krukoslik, with fine quartz heads and white owl-feather fletching. '*Good* owls,' she muttered under her breath.

The fog swirled about her angrily.

The food, the oil, the arrows: these had been prepared by kind people. The clothes they'd given her were meant to confer courage as well as warmth. The Mountain Hares had said that they always made the front of their robes from reindeer chest fur, 'For in the breast of the antlered one, there beats a great heart.'

A great heart. Renn's thoughts went to Fin-Kedinn. She sat straighter. 'I'm bone kin to the Raven Leader,' she told the fog – and it writhed at the resolution in her voice. 'I'm Renn. I am a Mage.'

As she headed off, the fog no longer seemed quite so thick.

Feeling more equal to the struggle than she had all day, Renn turned over what she knew of Eostra's plans.

The Eagle Owl Mage meant to live for ever. She meant to eat Torak's world-soul and take his power.

Renn halted.

Until now, she'd never asked herself *how* Eostra meant to do that. But if she could work out how, then she might have some chance of stopping her.

The best Renn could come up with was a rite for *holding* souls which Saeunn had once told her about. This was carried out when a mother or father was grieving so fiercely for their dead child that they risked going mad. Their Mage would catch the newly disembodied spirit in a rowanbark box and tie it shut with a lock of the dead one's hair. The mourner must then live apart from the clan for six moons, with only the souls in the box for company. Then the souls were freed by opening the box and burning the hair on a hilltop, so that the smoke would waft up to the First Tree in the sky.

Slipping off her mitten, Renn scratched her head. What did this have to do with Eostra?

Her fingers stilled.

Hair.

Your hair holds part of your Nanuak. That's why the

Death Mark for the world-soul is daubed on the forehead.

And that, thought Renn in a flash of insight, is what the tokoroth was after on the night after the ice storm. Torak's hair. If Eostra could get some of his hair by Souls' Night, she could take his world-soul and his power.

It was horribly simple. And maybe it was also why Eostra had sent her tokoroth. She'd been taunting them, telling them that she could get Torak's hair whenever she wanted.

Renn began to run. She floundered through snowdrifts and slithered over icy scree. She ran past patches of bearberry, crimson as spilt blood.

A large bird swooped overhead, skimming her hood.

Its wingbeats faded. Renn hid behind a rock. The wingbeats were coming back. Too noisy for an owl, she thought.

Rip lit onto the rock and rattled an excited kek-kek-kek!

Renn gave an edgy laugh. Rip hitched himself into the air and flew off. Quork!

When Renn didn't follow, he flew back.

Renn chewed her lip. Torak's trail led straight ahead, but Rip wanted her to follow him down a gully.

Quork! he cawed impatiently.

Renn followed.

She hadn't gone far when the fog thinned, and she made out something lying on the rocks. Rip and Rek wheeled above it, as if circling a carcass.

Renn's belly turned over. It *was* a carcass.

Sound cut away as she stumbled towards it.

THIRTY

D arkfur's breath came in rasping coughs that made her flanks heave.

As Renn knelt beside her, the she-wolf raised her head and attempted one of her little greeting snaps. The effort was too much. She slumped back.

Slipping off her mitten, Renn laid her hand on Darkfur's side. She could feel each rib. The she-wolf hadn't eaten for days.

How had she managed to get all this way?

Renn pictured Darkfur hauling herself from the river after the owl's attack, and setting off: battered, longing for her cubs, determined to find her mate. Perhaps she'd been drawn by Wolf's howls; perhaps by the strength of the bond between them.

With the resilience of wolves which surpasses that of

the toughest man, she had survived the ice storm and made it across the fells. Renn remembered Krukoslik speaking of hunters finding a dead wolf, and leaving food for its spirit. Maybe that had been Darkfur. Maybe the kindness of strangers had saved her life.

Wrenching open her food pouch, Renn placed a slip of meat by the she-wolf's muzzle. Darkfur ignored it.

Rip flew down and sidled closer.

'No,' scolded Renn. 'She needs it more.'

The raven gave her a reproachful look, and stalked off to sulk.

Renn nudged the meat closer. Still no response.

Puzzled, Renn touched one large black forepaw.

Darkfur tensed, and uttered a low growl.

Renn's alarm deepened. That pad was burning hot. Then she noticed that Darkfur's nose looked dull. Her tongue was tinged grey.

Renn leant nearer – and recoiled at the stink. It wasn't hunger which had felled the she-wolf. The owl's claws had gashed her foreleg from shoulder to shin, and the wound was festering. Renn saw foul, oozing green pus.

Her thoughts raced. Darkfur lay in a hollow under a rock. It shouldn't take long to turn it into a shelter. Further back in the gully, she'd passed a clump of the heathery plant which Juksakai used for waking fires. She had herbs in her medicine pouch – she'd refilled it before leaving the Swans – and she knew a healing charm.

It flashed through her mind that all this would lessen her chances of finding Torak, but she told herself the delay would be slight. Dress the wound, coax Darkfur to eat, then leave her to get better. How long could that take?

Sure of herself now, Renn worked fast. Soon the shelter was built and a small fire woken. At the foot of a boulder where a hawk had perched to eat its prey, she found the tiny skull of a snow-vole: strong medicine against fevers. Best of all, the purple droppings on the boulder led her to a nearby stand of juniper. That would be a powerful aid to the healing charm.

Back with Darkfur, she heated water and made a brew of crushed sorrel root, vole bones and juniper berries. Cooling this with snow, she started cleaning the wound by trickling a few drops onto the injured shoulder.

Darkfur's growls shook her whole body.

Renn swallowed. She tried again. Same result.

She wished she was Torak, and could speak wolf. If only she could tell Darkfur that this would do her good. 'Darkfur, *please*,' she said. 'I'm trying to help you.'

Darkfur swivelled one ear.

'You have to let me clean your wound.'

The green-amber gaze touched hers, then slid away.

Maybe that's it, thought Renn. Just talk.

'I'm – I'm sorry about the cubs,' she stammered. 'And that the owl hurt you. But Wolf is alive. You will see him again. Only you have to let me help you.'

Darkfur remained tense, the sinews on her long legs standing out like cords. But she was listening.

Renn went on talking: softly, continuously. Praying that the she-wolf would hear from her voice that she meant no harm.

The next time she dribbled medicine onto the wound, Darkfur lay quiet.

Washing the injured leg was agonisingly slow. Renn did as much as she dared, then prepared the poultice. She chewed juniper berries, then ground sorrel root with earthblood and juniper bast, and mashed the whole into a warm pulp.

Muttering the charm under her breath, she leant closer, hiding the poultice behind her back.

Darfkur bared her fearsome white teeth.

Renn froze. Sweat broke out between her shoulder blades.

When the she-wolf's muzzle relaxed, Renn slowly brought out the poultice.

Darkfur swung her head close to Renn's face. Renn felt her hot breath. She stared into the open jaws. 'It – it's all right,' she faltered. 'Let me do this.'

The jaws slackened. The she-wolf lay back and shut her eyes.

Trembling, Renn laid the poultice on the wound. Darkfur didn't stir.

The ravens edged in and made off with the meat. Renn was too drained to care. She heard them squabbling, then a sleepy rustle of feathers as they settled down to roost.

To roost?

She crawled out of the shelter.

While she'd been tending Darkfur, the rest of the day had slipped away. By now, Torak might already have reached the Mountain of Ghosts. Tomorrow night, when the sun went down, it would be Souls' Night.

Too late, Renn perceived Eostra's cunning. The Soul-Eater had allowed Darkfur to get this far for a reason: to keep Renn away from Torak. And it wasn't hard to work out why the dogs hadn't menaced them. They had other prey to hunt. Somewhere, in some lonely place, they were cornering Torak and Wolf. Renn saw their evil heads sunk between their shoulders as they closed in for the kill . . .

Angrily, she pushed that away, and crawled back inside, where she found Darkfur twitching in her sleep.

Renn bit her lip. She knew she would have to spend the

night here – but what then? Should she stay and look after Darfkur? Or let the she-wolf take her chances, and catch up with Torak?

Wolves heal much faster than people, but even so, the wound would need bathing and dressing. Perhaps another whole day would be lost.

Renn didn't know what to do. She felt pulled in different directions by ropes of loyalty and love.

Beside her, Darkfur's tail thumped in her sleep. Her muzzle quivered. She was smiling. She gave an eager, keening whine.

Renn's heart twisted with pity. In her dreams, Darkfur was calling her dead cubs.

Moments later, the she-wolf awoke. For an instant, her eyes glowed. Then the dream faded, and she gave a defeated sigh.

Gently, Renn stroked her forepaw. If she followed Torak and Darkfur died, how would she ever face Wolf? How would she face herself?

Her doubts fled. If she broke faith with Darkfur now, then whatever happened on the Mountain of Ghosts, Eostra would have won. The she-wolf had come through grief and hardship. Although Renn's spirit cried out to follow Torak, her mind was made up.

She would stay.

THIRTY-ONE

Torak had lapsed into furious silence. Dark was going through his things, asking questions. What's this green thing? A wrist-guard? Who made it? What's a foster father? Does he love you? Why is this pouch made of swans' feet? What's this horn for? Who made it? Your mother? Does she love you?

'Yes!' shouted Torak. Souls' Night was looming, and here he was, trussed like a ptarmigan, while this extraordinary boy examined his gear.

'There's a red hair round the top of the horn,' observed Dark. 'Is that your mother's?'

'No. It's a girl called Renn's. Don't touch.'

Dark glanced at him. 'Is she your mate?'

'No.'

'But you like her.'

'Of course.'

'And she likes you.'

'Yes!' he snapped.

Dark's pale face closed. His white eyelashes trembled. Suddenly he flung down the medicine horn and ran off into the shadows. Moments later he reappeared with Torak's clothes in his arms. 'There.' He threw them on the floor.

Ark croaked and flapped her wings. Wolf sniffed the hides. Torak watched Dark.

Brusquely, the boy drew his knife and cut Torak's bonds. 'You're free. You can go.'

Torak lost no time in getting dressed. As he was tying his belt, he said, 'What changed your mind?'

Dark took a slate wolverine from a ledge and glowered at it. 'All those people would miss you. Nobody misses me.'

Torak paused. 'I'm sorry.'

Dark set down the carving. 'I'll let you out.'

The cave was deeper than Torak had thought. With Wolf padding behind him, he followed the glimmer of Dark's cobweb hair. The walls closed in. Snowy reindeer and musk-oxen peered at him. Mindful of what else dwelt in the shadows, he said, 'Your sister. Is she . . .'

'It's Souls' Night. She's gone with the others.'

Torak felt icy air, and guessed that they'd reached the way out.

Dark jammed a slingshot in his belt and tied a birdskin snow mask around his eyes. Torak cut the thongs on his mittens, so they wouldn't get in the way. Dark kicked aside a granite wedge and rolled away a boulder; but as he knelt to crawl out, Torak said, 'Wait. I need you to do something.'

The last time he'd worn Death Marks had been three

winters ago, when he'd prepared to hunt the demon bear. Then, Renn had helped him. Now it was Dark who must daub the earthblood circles on his breastbone, heels and brow.

As Dark stirred the ochre with thin fingers, he said, 'I remember this. It's for dead people.'

Torak didn't reply.

Dark's touch was light and skilled, and somehow reassuring. 'There's some left,' he said when he'd finished. 'You must put it in your hair. There will be ghosts. You don't want them to come too close.'

The red paste chilled Torak's scalp, but felt oddly comforting: maybe because his mother, who had been Red Deer, would also have worn ochre in her hair.

He rubbed the last of it between Wolf's ears. Soon his pack-brother would be alone on the Mountain. This might keep him safe.

The thought of leaving Wolf was unbearable; but so was the thought of taking him into the Whispering Cave and seeing him die.

With an irritable growl, Wolf wriggled free and shot out of the cave, followed by Ark and Dark. Torak crawled after them into the blistering cold.

He found himself on a precipitous, snow-covered slope. The fog was gone. The sky was an ominous yellow. Soon the Mountain would release its ghosts.

As his eyes accustomed to the light, Torak realized that they were on its eastern face. The cleft he'd climbed lay somewhere to the west. Above him, the Mountain of Ghosts pierced the sky, its peak blazing in the last rays of the setting sun. The demon time was close.

Ark flew overhead, her white wings flashing. Wolf raced about, sniffing furiously, and stopping now and then to watch something move down the slope: something Torak couldn't see.

Dark sealed the entrance to his cave with a clever arrangement of rocks which hid it from view. 'That's the way to the Cave,' he said, pointing. 'But it's steep, so first we have to head east, then loop back.'

The hard-packed snow was treacherous, and Dark showed Torak how to kick into the snow with his toes. 'You have to kick in *straight*, or your foot will slide out.' A slab of snow broke off and exploded far below, demonstrating what would happen if Torak got it wrong. 'Follow me,' Dark called over his shoulder.

His voice rang out, and Torak was about to hush him when he thought, But what does it matter? Eostra knows we're here. This is what she wants.

The madness of what he was about to do struck him. He had no axe, no bow and no plan, other than to find his way to the Whispering Cave and then – what? How did he imagine he could break the power of the Eagle Owl Mage? He would be as helpless as that young hare in the teeth of the pack.

Am I mad? he wondered. Is it because I've got too close to the sky?

Renn would have told him exactly what she thought with a roll of her dark eyes. Torak missed her so much he felt sick.

'Here's where we turn,' said Dark, waiting for him to catch up.

Wolf stood beside Dark, panting and swinging his tail. Sensing Torak's misery, he trotted back to him, his paws kicking up sparkling flakes of snow. *I am with you,* he told Torak.

'Not far now,' said Dark.

They tramped on with the sun in their eyes. Glancing down, Torak saw that shadows were creeping up the Mountain. Soon it would be Souls' Night.

'There,' Dark said quietly. 'That's the way in. The Scar.'

Shading his eyes, Torak saw a slash in the face of the Mountain. On either side, a hand had been hammer-etched in the stone. Lines of power emanated from the middle fingers, warding off evil.

In vain. Claw-marks had gouged the hands, annihilating their power so that Eostra might enter.

Torak felt the breath of the Scar chilling his face, stiffening the earthblood on his skin. Inside, death waited to claim him. Or worse: the unimaginable horror of being Lost.

Every shred of his spirit rebelled. I won't do it! Let someone else fight Eostra! It doesn't have to be me!

He fled, scrambling blindly up the slope. He tripped and fell to his knees.

When he raised his head, he saw that his flight had taken him much higher. He saw what until now had been hidden from view. The Mountain was indeed the easternmost peak, but what lay beyond it was not the edge of the world. Far below, marching away to the horizon, was another Forest.

In awe, Torak made out rowan and birch, oak and beech; pine and spruce standing guard over their slumbering sisters. And he, whose spirit had walked in the most ancient trees of the Forest of the west, now heard the call of the Forest of the east. *I am endless and enduring*, it murmured in his mind. *I give life to all who dwell in me. I am worth fighting for.*

Defiance kindled in Torak's souls. If he gave up now, then Eostra had won, and nowhere would be safe. The Soul-Eater would rip aside the skin between the living and the dead, and the balance of the world would be destroyed.

The sun sank. Brightness faded from the Forest. The demon time was come.

Torak trudged down the slope to where Wolf and Dark were waiting. He walked towards the Scar.

Two paces from it, he stopped. 'Look after Wolf,' he told Dark. 'I've got to leave him behind.'

Dark was horrified. 'But – we're coming with you! You need me to show you the way.'

'Dark, I don't think I'm going to live through this. No point you getting killed, too. As for finding the way …' He swallowed. 'I think there are those inside who will lead me.'

He knelt to say his last goodbye to Wolf. *Goodbye to Wolf.* It wasn't possible.

Don't think about Wolf left behind on the Mountain: bewildered, unable to grasp why his pack-brother has forsaken him.

Wolf snuffled his cheek, and Torak felt the tickle of his whiskers and the warmth of his breath. *Pack-brother*, said the golden eyes, as clear as sunlight in honey.

Wolf knew nothing of prophecies, or of Eostra's mad designs; but he would follow his pack-brother even into the terror of the Scar.

With a strangled sob, Torak buried his face in Wolf's scruff. Wolf whined softly and licked his neck. *I am with you.*

To leave Wolf behind would be a betrayal he would never understand; from which he would never recover.

'I can't,' Torak said in a cracked voice. 'Where I go, he goes.'

As he rose to his feet, he caught a flicker of movement inside the Scar.

Wolf lowered his head and growled.

'Do you see it?' whispered Dark.

Deep within, on a shadowy pillar of stone, crouched a tokoroth.

Through a tangle of filthy hair, demon eyes glittered with malice. In silence the creature pointed one yellow claw at Torak, then swung its skeletal arm to the darkness within.

Torak glanced over his shoulder at the world he was about to leave. Then, with Wolf at his side, he entered the Scar.

'I'm coming with you!' cried Dark.

Unseen hands rolled a boulder across the entrance, shutting him out.

And the Mountain swallowed Torak and Wolf.

THIRTY-TWO

R enn fell to her knees before the sacred Mountain.

Souls' Night. She felt the presence of the ghosts to whom it belonged.

With trembling hands, she made an offering of earthblood and meat. In a hushed murmur she begged the Mountain to let her pass. Then she shook what was left of the ochre over her hair, to protect her from the ghosts.

Above her the sky was a deep, twilit blue. The cold was savage. Her breath crackled in her nostrils. Her ankle ached, and her feet were bruised from the hill of vicious slate blades.

A few paces away, a shadow moved. It gave a low bark. Darkfur bounded towards her. Her tail was high, her fur fluffed up with excitement. Her starlit eyes glowed silver.

Renn's courage rallied. 'Come on then,' she said under her breath. 'Let's check your paws.'

To protect them from the hill of knives, Renn had cut up her food pouch and made paw-boots. They'd worked. The she-wolf's pads were barely scratched.

A good sleep and the poultice had done wonders for her, and after licking her wound clean and gulping most of Renn's supplies, she'd been a new wolf. By midday she was circling the shelter, limping, but snuffing eagerly at the scent trail of her mate.

Renn, however, had been apprehensive after terrible dreams of ghosts who'd whispered with Torak's voice. And when she'd crawled from the shelter, the ravens were gone.

She and Darkfur had made good speed as they'd found their way up the Gorge of the Hidden People, the she-wolf trotting ahead, then doubling back for Renn. She didn't need to know wolf talk to interpret those impatient yips. *Hurry up! Can't you go any faster?*

At times, though, Darkfur would halt, and turn her head to watch something Renn couldn't see. Sometimes she wagged her tail. Sometimes her hackles rose.

A white bird flashed across the stars. Renn thought of the white guardian in her vision, and rose to her feet.

To her right, a scree slope fell away sharply. Ahead, a boulder-field led onto the sacred Mountain. The sky was immense and pitiless. No moon to give her courage. Only the cold stars and the red glare of the Great Auroch – and beyond, the endless dark.

Renn thought, perhaps Eostra has already won. Perhaps Torak is already a Lost One.

The stillness as she laboured over the boulder-field was

terrible. The only sounds were the rasp of her breath and the creak of her clothes. Silent as a spirit, Darkfur raced ahead. A black wolf in blackness is hard to spot, and Renn had to follow the she-wolf's breath: little puffs of life in the desolation.

Suddenly, she saw Darkfur streak over a stretch of snow to a shadowy spur, where she raced about, sniffing excitedly. She vanished into a cleft. Renn heard echoing growls. Then she emerged and loped back to the spur, lashing her tail.

Renn hurried to investigate. As she drew closer, the hairs on her forearms rose. Someone had dug a snow hole. Around it was a mess of paw-marks. Huge. Not Wolf's.

Prickling with fear, she crawled into the shelter.

Her breath was loud in the cramped space. Her hands found a quiver of arrows. A food pouch. A waterskin. A sleeping-sack, rumpled and frozen stiff.

A bow.

Slipping off a mitten, she ran her fingers over the icy wood. There: the spiky Forest mark which Torak had notched in it last summer, matching the one his mother had carved on his medicine horn long ago.

Feeling sick, Renn set down the bow. The truth lay before her, crusted with frost. Some time before, Torak had scrambled from his shelter, leaving his gear behind. He had never returned.

Renn backed out and began to retch.

Darkfur gave a whine and shot to the edge of the scree slope, where she stood, listening intently.

Shakily, Renn straightened up.

Darkfur ignored her. Mewing, she ran in circles, as if

she didn't know what to do. Then she leapt down the slope.

'Darkfur!' called Renn in a horrified whisper. 'Come back!'

The clatter of pebbles died away. Darkfur was gone.

Renn's hand crept to her clan-creature feathers. She was alone on the Mountain of Ghosts.

Dimly, in the starlight, she made out the trail that led into the cleft, then out again; the swathe of churned snow heading east.

As she entered the cleft, she tripped over something. It was frozen to the ground: she had to wrench it free.

Torak's axe.

Renn knew at once what had happened. He had climbed the cleft to escape Eostra's pack. He had fallen. The churned snow was the drag-mark where someone had hauled away his body.

Renn dropped the axe and stood swaying in the gloom. 'Torak!' The cry burst from her. 'Torak! Torak!' The name echoed back and forth. *Torak! Torak!* Slowly it faded into the Mountain.

At the top of the cleft, a face peered at her.

Renn whipped out an arrow and nocked it to her bow.

'Don't shoot!' called a voice.

Renn tightened her draw arm and got ready to do just that.

Supple as a pine marten, a figure let itself over the edge and started climbing down.

Holding her aim, Renn took a step back.

With startling speed, the creature made its descent and leapt to the ground, spinning to face her. In one astonished heartbeat she took in a bone-pale face and a shock of white hair.

'Are you Renn?' panted the boy.

Her jaw dropped.

'Quick!' He grabbed her wrist. 'We've got to save Torak!'

THIRTY-THREE

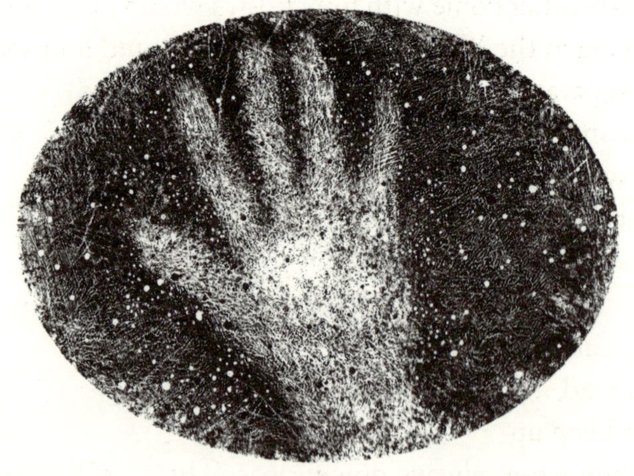

Flames leapt. Shadows reared. On its pillar, the tokoroth clutched a sputtering torch and glared at Torak.

He glimpsed glistening fangs and hair heaving with lice. He saw unblinking eyes ringed with chalk to give them the stare of an owl. Then the creature sprang away, plunging him in darkness.

Slipping off his mittens, he drew his knife and followed.

The tunnel was cold; he felt his way through a dank cloud of breath. Shadows scuttled. His hand moved over rock as ridged and slimy as guts. In a crack, something scaly withdrew from his touch.

Around him he felt the awesome weight of the Mountain. He was inside it: this vast, ancient creature which had only to twitch, to crush him to pulp.

Behind him came the subdued click of Wolf's claws.

He'd stopped growling, and hadn't tried to attack the tokoroth, perhaps sensing it would stay out of reach. But what alarmed Torak was that the tokoroth ignored Wolf, as if it knew that he posed no threat.

As they went deeper, Torak began to regret having let his pack-brother come with him. Eostra would never allow Wolf to reach the Whispering Cave. She would find some way to separate them – and Wolf would be killed.

He wondered how many more tokoroths lay in wait. Where was Eostra's pack? Her owl?

Crouching, he asked Wolf if this cub-demon was the only one.

More, replied Wolf, his whiskers brushing Torak's eyelids. *Can't smell where.*

Up ahead, the tokoroth bared its fangs and snarled at them to keep up.

On they went, always downwards. The cold lessened. Torak felt an uprush of warmer air. Strange signs loomed at him from the dark. A chalk zigzag. A yellow handprint. An alarming charcoal creature with many limbs. Were they a warning? Or had they been put here to keep the demons behind the rocks?

His groping fingers found a nest of pebbles, smooth and rounded as eyes. A memory surfaced from three summers ago: the riddle of the Nanuak. *Deepest of all, the drowned sight.*

Behind him, Wolf gave a low uff!

The tokoroth disappeared round a corner.

Torak felt his way past – and jolted to a halt.

Firelight glimmered beyond an arch of white rock; around it, a chaos of red handprints: *Go back, go back!*

Then everything happened at once. Torak saw the tokoroth douse the torch in a pool and scramble up the arch. Something came crashing down behind him: a wall of rawhide, barring his way. On the other side, Wolf was yowling and scrabbling to reach him. Torak tried to cut through, but the rawhide was tough, his knife bounced off. The tokoroth dropped on him like a spider, gouging at his face. As he sank to his knees, it yanked back his hood to throttle him. He slashed with his knife. The tokoroth shrieked, let go of his hood. Torak grabbed its arm and twisted. It squirmed out of his grip and vanished through the arch.

Panting, sick with the demon stench, Torak hauled himself upright. He stumbled, took a step back.

Into nothingness.

41

Wolf lunged and snapped at the cub-demons, and they fought back with their great stone claws.

Wolf pretended to spring one way, they leapt after him; he turned the other way, sinking his teeth into a scaly leg. The cub-demon howled and dropped its stone claw. Another bit Wolf's shoulder. He went for it, missing by a whisker. Both demons fled up the rocks where he couldn't reach.

It was too dark to see, but he sensed them. He heard their breath; the lice crawling on their flesh. Why didn't they attack?

In a snap, he knew. They might be demons, but they were in tailless bodies, so they had only feeble tailless ears and noses. If Wolf didn't move, they didn't know where he was.

Quietly, he closed his muzzle and took a silent sniff.

The stink of blood and hate was all around; but it was strongest above.

He heard Tall Tailless yowl on the other side of the hide. Wolf couldn't bear it, he leapt at the hide – and the cub-demons were on him.

They were quick, but Wolf was quicker. Whipping round, he sank his fangs in a bony neck. It snapped. The demon went limp. Wolf smelt the other and gave chase. It disappeared over the hide.

Wolf went to sniff the fallen tailless cub to make sure it was really Not-Breath. Yes. The meat was cooling. But Wolf saw the demon which had hidden inside the carcass slip out and scurry off to find a new body. He raced after it, cornered it in a Den where it couldn't escape, and chased it into the rocks. There. Now it couldn't get out again.

When he got back to the hide, he found the Breath-that-Walks of the tailless cub shivering beside its carcass. It was bewildered. After so long trapped with the demon, it didn't know what to do.

Wolf felt a lick of pity. It was only a cub. He nosed it up the tunnel towards the others. Go on, up there. You won't be lonely, we passed lots of your kind on the way down.

Whimpering, the Breath-that-Walks wandered off to find its pack.

From the other side of the hide came many noises. Wolf caught the growls of dogs and the click of cub-demon claws; the sly hiss of owl wings, and the distant whisper of a Fast Wet, all coming from far below.

He smelt his pack-brother, and another tailless he'd once known, but couldn't remember. Then the air shifted and he caught a smell that made his fur stand on end: the Stone-Faced One with the terrible, stiff muzzle.

Wild to reach his pack-brother, Wolf made a desperate

leap at the hide. It was too high, he couldn't get over. He tried to tear it with his fangs, but it was too flat, he couldn't get his jaws around it. He had to find another way.

Turning tail, he hurtled up the Den. Through the twisting tunnels he loped, bumping his nose and stubbing his paws. He burst into a bigger Den, where air from many smaller ones swirled around him.

Faint and far, he caught a scent that gave him hope. It was the scent of the new tailless with the white head-fur, and with him – Wolf could hardly believe his nose – *with him was the pack-sister.*

THIRTY-FOUR

'Who *are* you?' demanded Renn.

'Dark,' the boy replied.

'*What?*' Twisting out of his grip, she drew her knife.

'My name. It's Dark!'

Renn tossed her head. 'Whoever you are, you say you know Torak, but how do I know that's true?'

'I knew your name, didn't I?'

'You could've made him tell.'

'You've got red hair. He's got a strand of it round his medicine horn. There! Now d'you believe me?'

Renn hesitated. 'Where is he?'

'I *told* you, in the Mountain! I tried to go in too but they shut me out. But there's another way in. You coming or not?'

Still she hung back.

A white bird swooped onto his shoulder.

A raven. A white guardian.

Renn threw off her waterskin and sleeping-sack. 'Let's go,' she said.

Grabbing her wrist again, he set off at a run, the white raven flying ahead. The boy called Dark must have the eyes of a bat to see in this murk – Renn could hardly make out the ground in front of her – and he was sure-footed. 'I won't let you fall,' he told her, as if he'd heard her thoughts. And somehow, she believed him.

After a stiff, winding climb her ankle was hurting, and she was relieved when he halted at the foot of a rockface.

At least, she thought it was a rockface. Clouds blotted out the stars; the night was black as basalt. She watched the raven fly off, a white glimmer swallowed by the dark.

'Light,' muttered the boy, dropping to his knees. A birchbark torch flickered awake, lighting his strange, pale face. 'In there,' he said.

Renn's belly clenched. It was a jagged fissure, like a mouth with broken teeth, and hardly big enough for a badger. They would have to crawl in on their bellies.

'I can't go in there,' she said.

'You won't get stuck. I'll go first, you push your axe and bow in front, I'll take them. It'll be all right, you'll see.'

As Renn crawled in after him, she felt the stone jaws clamp shut, squeezing the breath from her chest. She wriggled forwards, trying not to think of the Mountain on top of her. Panic surged. Her arms were squashed against her chest. She couldn't move. She was stuck, as she'd been stuck in the Far North. But this time she wasn't getting out.

'We're through,' said the boy, grasping her hood and hauling her into an echoing space.

She bumped her head, and gave a jittery laugh.

'Hush! Some of these stones are loose, you could start a rockfall. And watch out for holes.'

It was frightening, seeing only a pace ahead. Beyond the jolting torchlight, the dark was so intense that it pressed on her eyeballs.

With an arrow she probed the ground ahead. She tripped. Her groping hand found something smooth and domed. A skull. Her whimper brought the boy running back. The light revealed the skull of a bear: huge, drowned in stone.

'Yes, lots of bones,' said Dark. 'From the old times, when the Mountain was more awake. It drowned many creatures.'

As they went deeper, Renn heard water trickling. She felt cold air from unseen tunnels. She glimpsed wet grey pillars clustered together. As she passed, shadows darted. She averted her eyes from the Hidden People of the Mountain.

'Careful, that's deep,' warned the boy.

She stepped over a crevice, and caught a whisper of water far below.

Dark stopped so abruptly that she walked into him.

'What is it?' she said.

'It's shut,' he said blankly.

A boulder blocked the tunnel. On it, an image had been daubed in gypsum, so that it glowed sickly white. An enormous owl. Its body was turned away – Renn saw its wings folded over its back – but its head was twisted round to glare at them. The meaning was plain. *Eostra sees all.*

'She knows we're here,' said Renn.

'Of course she knows,' said Dark.

He moved aside, taking the light with him, and the owl sank into shadow. Renn still felt its glare.

'I think there's another tunnel,' murmured Dark, trailing his long pale fingers over the rocks, as if feeling their message. 'Ah. That's it!'

He led her over a rockpile, then down into a clammy hole. This tunnel was narrower – they squeezed sideways – but to Renn's relief, it soon opened out.

Again Dark halted. 'I don't remember this.'

Raising the torch, he showed Renn a cavern roofed with folds of yellowish rock. Three tunnels yawned. The left one was low, fringed with dripping stone teeth. The middle one opened above a reddish stump like a severed limb. The third was the biggest, cut in two by a spear of stone jutting from the floor.

'Which one?' said Renn.

'I don't know. They all feel wrong. I think—'

'*You don't know?*' Pushing past him, Renn ran to the first tunnel and placed her hands on the edge, avoiding the stone teeth. The rock throbbed beneath her palms with the unclean heat of the Otherworld.

She ran to the tunnel with the stone spear. She felt the same pulsing demon heat.

Desperate, she scrambled up the stump and groped for the third opening. For a moment, the rock seemed to buckle under her fingers as demons jaws gaped to bite.

She pulled back. 'All three have demons behind them.'

'That's what I was going to tell you,' said Dark.

'So which one do we take?'

'Don't move,' he said in an altered voice.

'What?'

'Sh!' He jerked the torch upwards.

In a crack above her head, Renn made out another stone

owl. Its eyes were shut, its tufted ears erect.

'Climb down as quietly as you can,' said Dark.

The owl opened its eyes and hissed at her.

With a cry Renn fell, knocking Dark backwards. The torch went flying. Just before the blackness came down, Renn saw the eagle owl spread its wings and glide away.

Silence. A distant splash.

'That's the torch,' said Dark.

'Have you got another?'

'No.'

Panting, Renn got to her feet. 'What do we do now?'

'I don't know.'

Renn jammed her knuckles in her mouth. Somewhere in this terrible Mountain, Torak was facing Eostra alone.

A cold hand touched her wrist.

'Is that you?' she whispered.

'What?' said Dark, some paces away.

A chill finger touched her cheek.

'Stop it!' she cried.

'I didn't do anything!'

Renn screwed her eyes shut. She opened them. She saw. It wasn't possible in this darkness, and yet – she *saw*. 'Do you see it too?' she breathed.

'I see it,' Dark said softly. 'But I don't know who it is.'

Renn did. It was indistinct, as if in a mist, yet it seemed to hold its own light, as spirits do. Renn's fear drained away, leaving only a distant sense of loss.

Before her stood the wizened figure against whom she had rebelled all her life. For the last time she took in the flinty gaze, the lipless mouth which had never been known to smile.

Noiselessly, it extended one frail arm and pointed at the tunnel of the stone spear.

'Thank you,' murmured Renn. 'Thank you … And may the guardian fly with you.' With both hands on her clan-creature feathers, she bowed to the spirit of the Raven Mage.

When she straightened up, it was gone.

Renn hoisted her quiver and bow higher on her shoulder. Then she reached out and took Dark's hand. 'Come,' she told him. 'We know the way now.'

THIRTY-FIVE

Torak was tumbling down a waterfall of stone. The ground rushed to meet him. Pain exploded in his shoulder and skull.

He lay still. His cheekbone hurt savagely, but he could move his arms and legs. Somehow, he'd kept hold of his knife.

Above him the stone waterfall disappeared into the dark. Unclimbable. No getting back. He thought, at least Wolf isn't here. At least he's got a chance of getting out.

He had a sense of a vast, shadowy cavern. Stone had once flowed like honey: dripping, pooling, then freezing hard. Twisted fangs of rock hung down; others jutted from the floor to meet them. Like teeth, thought Torak. *Oldest of all, the stone bite.* I'm in the jaws of the Mountain.

Firelight glimmered. He caught the whisper of water far

below. Closer, he heard the rhythmic clink of bones. A voice chanted.

By power of bone
By power of stone
By power of demon eye
Eostra summons the Unquiet Dead
Eostra binds them to her!

Torak stumbled towards the light. No point trying to hide. She knew he was there.

Then he saw it.

In some ancient catastrophe, rocks had fallen in a pile as tall as two tall men. On the pile rested a slab of black stone, where a fire burned. Behind this altar, flanked by a pair of tokoroths rattling bones, stood the Eagle Owl Mage.

Her feathered robe seemed to gather the darkness to it, but her mask glowed ghastly white. In one corpse hand she grasped the mace which bore the fire-opal; in the other, the three-pronged spear for snaring souls.

By power of bone
By power of stone
By power of demon eye . . .

Torak tried to speak, but his mouth was too dry.

The arms of the Masked One rose, and her winged shadow engulfed the cavern. The tokoroths grovelled, their evil child-faces alight with terror and adoration.

'You know I'm here,' panted Torak. 'You know I'll stop you.'

The Masked One never faltered in her chant, but her

spear swung round and pointed at him. At the foot of the rockpile, seven pairs of eyes lit up. Dark shapes sped towards him.

Jamming his knife in its sheath, Torak kicked off his boots and scrambled up the nearest fang of rock. The pack was almost upon him. Heaving himself onto a ledge a few fingers wide, he drew up his legs. The dogs swarmed about his refuge, leaping, snapping. Their breath scorched his bare feet, their jaws clashed empty air. Snarling, they fell back and sprang again, their hatred sucking at his souls.

An arm's length above him, his rock fused unevenly with a hanging tooth. He could climb higher. But then, a tokoroth could climb down. A shadow swept towards him. He lashed out with his knife. The owl veered and flew back to its mistress.

Streaming sweat, Torak clung on. The fire's bitter smoke was making his head spin. Through it he saw the Soul-Eater set aside her spear and begin to wind a cord around the fire-opal. A sigh broke from the tokoroths. With frenzied lust they rattled their bones.

Firelight struck glints of russet and gold in Eostra's cord, which was braided, like hair. As Torak watched her wind it about the stone, he felt himself drawn deep into the heart of the fire-opal.

It was the terrible scarlet of a lethal wound. It was beauty and suffering and mad desire. It was the glare of the Great Auroch in the winter sky, and it blazed with all the pain it had ever created.

Suddenly, the Soul-Eater ceased her chant. In a grating whisper, she uttered, one by one, the names of the Unquiet Dead.

The shock was so great that Torak nearly fell. At last he

understood what she meant to do. And he couldn't stop her. He could only huddle on his perch like a pigeon about to be snatched by a hawk.

His medicine pouch dug into his hip. The horn was empty, it couldn't help him now.

And yet.

At the cost of her life, his mother had made a pact with the World Spirit. The World Spirit had made him the spirit walker. He owed it to her to use his gift one final time.

Dashing the sweat from his eyes, he called to the Soul-Eater. 'You think you've got me! You think I can't reach you! You're wrong!' His voice sounded reedy and frightened.

Climbing to where the upward and downward fangs fused, Torak straddled the join. Now, though his legs hung down, the pack couldn't reach. Swiftly, he lashed himself to the stone with his belt. Then he took Saeunn's black root from his pouch and crammed it in his mouth.

Pain clawed his innards. He cried out . . .

. . . and his voice was the rasp of the Soul-Eater, summoning the Unquiet Dead.

Through her eyes and her slitted mask, Torak peered at the senseless body of the spirit walker. His flesh was grey; and grey the flames that leapt on the altar. All was grey, save the cold red heart of the fire-opal.

Deep in her freezing marrow, Torak's spirit strove to make her grasp a rock and shatter it, but her will was the strongest he'd ever known. Her will turned his to stone. This was her strength: that she felt no pleasure, no pain, *nothing* save the hunger for eternal life. Her tokoroths were not tortured children possessed by demons, but creatures created to do her will. Her dogs were merely weapons to be used and flung aside like broken flints. The boy on the rock was the husk of the power she craved; tear away that husk and the power became hers. *This* was evil and it was cold, cold. Torak's spirit drowned in it.

Abruptly, Eostra's voice ceased. The tokoroths' rattles stilled.

In the silence, the Masked One cast a rawhide shield across the fire, and its light was quenched. In the darkness, she spoke.

Sleek as the seal . . . the cunning one,
Tenris . . . Come forth!

Almost imperceptibly, the cavern filled with the lapping of waves. Behind the altar, smoke thickened – coalesced – and formed the figure of a man. Through the eyes of the Soul-Eater, Torak perceived a handsome, ruined face; he heard a voice as smooth and strong as the Sea.

Tenris is come.

Chanting, the Masked One raised the rawhide from the altar. Smoke billowed, flames leapt. She quenched them again.

Mighty as oak, the strongest one,
Thiazzi . . . Come forth!

A rustling of leaves. A hulking shadow loomed.

Thiazzi is come.

Again Eostra chanted. Again she quenched and revived the fire.

Swift as the bat, the twisted one,
Nef . . . Come forth!

The leathery rustle of bat wings. Swirling motes came together and made the limping one.

Nef is come.

Cowering in Eostra's marrow, Torak could only witness her summoning the Unquiet Dead; and they were hers to command, bound by the power of the fire-opal.

In the darkness of her mind, Torak saw her vision of what was to be. *On Mountain and Ice, in Forest and Lake and Sea, the clans cower in dread before Eostra, who rules the living and the dead . . . Eostra, who lives for ever.*

Eostra was invincible. Everything Torak had fought for over three long winters had been for nothing.

The Soul-Eaters were back.

THIRTY-SIX

Deep in the Mountain, Wolf heard the rustling of leaves.

Leaves?

He slewed to a halt. That didn't fit.

Was this another trick of the Hidden Ones? They hated him being here, they hated *anyone* in the Mountain, they kept scattering sounds and smells, so that he couldn't tell where they were coming from.

Wolf raced on, though he didn't know where he was going. He'd been running for ever through this terrible, winding Den. He'd lost the scent of the pack-sister; all he could smell was wet rock and frightened Wolf. He was thirsty, his flanks hurt from the cub-demons' claws, and he *still* couldn't find Tall Tailless.

He reached a place where the Den widened and the

breath of the Mountain ruffled his fur. He found some Wet in a dip and snapped it up, ignoring the stone bones lying nearby. They were just another trick; he'd tried one before, and nearly broken a fang.

Suddenly, he jerked up his head. A faint scent brushed his nose. Trembling with eagerness, he took deep sniffs to make sure. *Yes!* His pack-brother!

The scent was trickling from above. Rising on his hind legs, Wolf placed his forepaws on the rock. Too dark to see, but he felt the breath of a tiny Den. He leapt – scrabbled – he was in.

The Den was so small he had to flatten his ears and crawl on his belly. It scraped his sides and squeezed till he couldn't breathe. Then it spat him out and he fell, bashing his nose on a rock.

A torrent of smells whirled around him. The demon stink; the Not-Breath smell of the Stone-Faced One; the rich scent of the tailless whom Wolf now remembered from long ago. *And the scent of his pack-brother.*

Wolf flew through the dark. The tunnel was narrow and twisty as guts, but he caught the snarls of the pack. They had a hollow sound which told Wolf he was heading for a very big Den indeed.

He heard the familiar whine of the pack-sister's Long-Claw-that-Flies, and the swish of owl wings. He quickened his pace.

Hunting demons was what he was for.

Ψ

The mouth of the tunnel was drawing nearer, and Renn quickened her pace.

'Not so fast!' warned Dark.

She ignored him. She could hear the clink of bones and the death-rattle chant of the Soul-Eater.

By power of bone
By power of stone
By power of demon eye
Eostra summons the Unquiet Dead
Eostra binds them to her!

Renn tried to remember a severing charm to counter the spell, but Eostra's icy will froze her thoughts. *None can hinder the Masked One.*

Renn reached the mouth of the tunnel.

Dark yanked her back.

The tunnel opened dizzyingly high, near the roof of the cave. There was no way down.

Biting back a cry, Renn sank to her knees and peered over the edge. Through a thicket of huge stone teeth, she saw that the cave was split by a chasm that zigzagged across it like black lightning. On the near side, a fire burned on an altar wreathed in smoke. Below this, shadows prowled at the base of a pillar whose top she couldn't see. Even from far away, she felt their hatred, and knew that this was Eostra's pack. There was no sign of Torak.

Eostra summons the Unquiet Dead . . .

Renn flung down her weapons. Her axe and bow were unhurt, but her quiver had been squashed when she'd squeezed through a gap, and only three arrows remained intact.

Eostra binds them to her!

The smoke parted, and Renn caught a fleeting glimpse of the Masked One. She saw a livid hand pass over the mace that held the fire-opal. She saw its scarlet light bleeding through a shadowy network of cords criss-crossing the crimson stone. She grabbed an arrow. Eostra sensed the threat and cloaked herself in smoke.

'Can you feel them?' whispered Dark, kneeling beside her.

'Feel what?'

'Down there in the smoke. Something terrible.'

'I can't see anything.'

'Neither can I. But I feel them.'

Renn felt them too. There was more in the Whispering Cave than Eostra and her minions.

'It's the smoke,' she breathed. 'It's part of the spell. Don't look.'

But Dark couldn't tear his eyes away. Neither could she.

The Soul-Eater broke off her chant. Blackness descended on the cave. In the silence, she spoke.

Subtle as snake, the seducer . . .
Seshru . . . Come forth!

Renn's flesh crawled.

The cave seemed to fill with a thin, echoing *hissss*.

This can't be, Renn told herself. It cannot be.

As she watched, the smoke swirled to form a sinuous shape . . .

No. Seshru is dead. Your mother is dead. You put the Death Marks on her. You watched them lay her body to rest.

The chanting resumed. After an endless time, it broke off again. Once more, the fire dimmed.

... Narrander ... Come forth!

From the far side of the cavern, a man's voice rang out. 'Narrander comes.'

Renn caught her breath. She knew that voice.

'Your spell is flawed,' it declared. 'It holds the hair of a living man.'

No answer from Eostra.

'Who *is* he?' said Dark.

Renn didn't reply. The past was coming together like pack ice as she watched the man emerge from the shadows.

The eagle owl swooped towards him. He warded it off with his axe. His gait was unsteady. Tattered hides flapped about his scrawny limbs. Renn knew that if she were closer, she would see a tangled beard glistening with slime. A filthy, one-eyed face as rough as bark.

The seventh Soul-Eater. He had hinted as much at their first encounter. *Before the flint bit him, he was a wise man ...*

'Narrander died,' rasped Eostra from the smoke. 'He died in the great fire.'

'Another died!' bellowed the Walker. 'He should have *lived*! The Walker ends it now!'

'None can hinder the Masked One.'

The Walker roared and threw himself at the rockpile – but before he could reach it, he lurched to a halt. The chasm was too wide. He couldn't get across. 'He should have *lived*!' His howl filled the cave with pain.

Suddenly, Renn saw the small, hunched figures clinging to the rocks above his head. Desperately, she took aim. Dark loaded his slingshot.

They lowered their weapons. The tokoroths were way out of range.

'Above you!' shouted Renn and Dark together.

The Walker glanced up as the first rock struck. He sank to his knees. Another rock hit. He fell to the ground at the edge of the chasm. His axe dropped from his hand, and a moment later there came a distant splash. The Walker lay without moving. Renn had never hated Eostra as much as she did then.

'I see Torak!' hissed Dark. Pulling her sideways, he pointed – and at last she saw him.

Torak was halfway up the pillar round which the pack prowled. He was tied by the waist, his head sunk on his chest. He wasn't moving.

'Torak!' screamed Renn.

No response.

He must be either stunned or spirit walking. She refused to believe that he was dead. Clenching her jaw, she got ready to shoot. How many dogs? Six? Seven? And only three arrows.

A brindled beast leapt at Torak's bare foot. Renn's bow sang. The dog fell with a gurgling yowl and an arrow through its throat.

Beside her, Dark let fly with his slingshot. A grey brute fell and did not stir again. Dark killed another with a stone that split its skull; Renn shot one in the chest. It staggered backwards into the chasm, its yowls dying to nothing.

Two dogs streaked across the cavern, disappearing into a tunnel as if they'd scented prey. The remaining dog circled Torak's perch. A tokoroth appeared at its base and began to climb, a knife clamped between its teeth. Renn nocked her final arrow and took aim. Her hands shook. The creature was a demon, but it had the body of a child.

A stone whistled through the air. The tokoroth fell with a shriek, clutching a broken shin. Grimly, Dark reloaded his slingshot, but the tokoroth dragged itself into the shadows.

Peering into the haze, Renn sought another target. The smoke was too thick. Its fumes reached into her mind. She pictured the Masked One gloating over the fire-opal. *None can hinder Eostra.*

Renn set down her bow. So. This was not to be won with arrows.

Something of Saeunn's uncompromising will stiffened her resolve. You are a Mage, she told herself. Think like one.

Your spell is flawed, the Walker had said. *It holds the hair of a living man.*

Renn went still. She peered at the cord which netted the fire-opal. It seemed to be braided with different-coloured threads. She caught glints of black, russet, gold . . .

Hair. Eostra had snared the spirits of the Soul-Eaters with their own hair. She had woven it into this cord which now bound the fire-opal, this cord which bound the dead Soul-Eaters to her – just as, with Torak's hair, she meant to bind his world-soul and take his power.

'Torak!' shouted Renn. '*Cut the cord!*'

ЦІ

Trapped in the Soul-Eater's marrow, Torak struggled to break free. His spirit was tiring. Eostra was too strong.

From a great distance, he heard someone shouting. It sounded like Renn. It couldn't be.

For an instant, the shouting distracted Eostra. Torak felt her will waver. It was enough. He seized his chance.

His eyes snapped open. He was back in his body. Someone was still shouting.

'Cut the cord that binds the fire-opal! Torak! Cut it and you'll break the spell! You'll send them away for ever!'

It *was* Renn. He couldn't see her, but he saw one of her arrows, jutting from the throat of the brindled dog.

The cord. Strength coursed through him. He knew what to do.

Swiftly, he untied himself and slid down the pillar. A dog sprang from the murk. He thrust his knife in its belly and ripped. Kicking the carcass aside, he jabbed at the dark. No tokoroths, no dogs; though he heard the snarls of a savage fight. With his free hand he grabbed a stone and staggered towards the rockpile. Renn was right, there *was* a way. The spell could be broken, the Soul-Eaters banished for ever. Why, then, was Eostra undeterred?

Once again, the fire was quenched and her chanting ceased. Through the drifting smoke, she spread her wings and summoned the last of the Unquiet Dead.

Wise as the wolf, the wilful one . . .

No! Torak tried to shout, but his tongue stuck to the roof of his mouth. Helpless, he heard the Soul-Eater call the beloved name he hadn't spoken out loud for three summers.

For a moment there was silence.

The cave seemed to echo with the howls of unseen wolves. Behind the altar, smoke danced and drew together. A tall figure began to take shape.

Torak dropped his knife with a clatter. 'Fa.'

THIRTY-SEVEN

The figure in the smoke was as faint as moon-shadow on a cloudy night – but Torak knew. He knew as he stood gazing up at his father.

'Fa – it's me. Torak.'

The dead white eyes stared down at him without recognition. His father's spirit belonged to Eostra.

Somewhere, Renn was shouting. 'Cut the cord! Send them away for ever!'

Send Fa away? Away for ever?

He couldn't do it. He was twelve summers old: bewildered, terrified, watching his father bleed. Fa, don't die. *Please* don't die.

Tears slid down his cheeks as he stumbled towards the rockpile.

'Cut the cord!' shouted Renn.

'I can't,' Torak whispered. 'Fa . . . I can't lose you all over again.'

He began to climb.

He heard the rattle of bones and the chant of the Soul-Eater. He felt a sudden sharp pain at the back of his scalp, and saw the owl fly off with a lock of his hair in its talons. It didn't matter. Nothing mattered except reaching Fa.

He stood in the bitter haze before the altar. Behind it the Masked One chanted, surrounded by the shadowy throng of the Unquiet Dead. He stretched out his hand towards his father. The figure in the smoke did not respond.

A vision flashed across Torak's mind of what might have been if Fa had lived: if they were still together, and the fire-opal had never existed. Grief twisted in his heart like a knife.

But the fire-opal *did* exist. There it was in the mace, throbbing like an open wound.

With a cry, Torak reached across the altar, seized the mace, and dragged it towards the flames.

The Soul-Eater's grip was stone. He couldn't do it. With her other hand she raised her spear to strike. Torak lashed out with his rock. The spear clattered to the floor. A tokoroth fastened its jaws on his forearm. Renn's wrist-guard protected him. Again he brought down the rock, crushing the creature's skull like an eggshell. Still gripping the mace, he fought the Soul-Eater across the flames. He caught the glitter of her eyes behind the mask. He gave a desperate wrench and dashed the mace into the fire. Choking on the stink of burning hair, he raised the rock – and shattered the fire-opal to bloody shards.

With a shriek, Eostra plunged both hands into the

flames, clawing out the fragments and holding them up. The last shreds of burning hair curled and shrivelled to nothing.

The Unquiet Dead began to disintegrate. Through a mist of tears, Torak watched his father fade.

But in the final moment, the smoke face changed. It became Fa as he had been when he was alive, and it lit up as he saw his son. '*Torak* ...' he murmured, as quiet as a sleeping breath.

Then he was gone.

Torak stood shaking before the altar. Some part of him knew that Eostra still held the fragments of the fire-opal. Some part of him heard her beginning to chant.

Eostra summons the spirit walker
Eostra binds him to her!

Far away, Renn was screaming a warning. 'Torak! *Behind you!*'

THIRTY-EIGHT

'**B**ehind you!' screamed Renn. She was ready to shoot, but the tokoroth kept slipping into shadow, dragging its broken leg.

Torak appeared to come to himself at last. He saw the tokoroth crawling up the rockpile. He saw Eostra brandishing the fragments of the fire-opal and lifting her free hand to the owl which swooped towards her with the lock of his hair in its talons.

In the blink of an eye, the tokoroth sprang. Torak seized its arms and flung it bodily over his head. It came on again, relentless. They grappled, moving too fast, Renn couldn't get a clear shot. Beside her, Dark gripped his slingshot. Torak threw the tokoroth upon the altar. It twitched as its spine snapped – and slid off, dead.

Two black shapes came racing from the shadows, up the

rockpile towards Torak. Renn and Dark let fly at the dogs. They hit the same target. The stricken creature scrabbled at the edge of the chasm, and fell with a howl. Torak turned and seemed to see the chasm for the first time. The other dog sprang.

Renn had no more arrows. Frantically, she searched for stones.

'None left,' panted Dark. Grabbing her axe, he flung it with all his might. It struck short of the rockpile.

Torak was on his knees fighting the dog, his hands in its scruff, battling to keep its jaws from his face.

Renn beat the stones with her fists.

A silver arrow streaked across the cavern: Wolf racing to save his pack-brother. His sides were bloody, his white fangs gleamed, and his glare was more ferocious than Renn had ever seen. In a flying leap he was on them, sinking his teeth in the dog's throat, tearing it off Torak. Wolf and dog tumbled down the rocks, a snarling tangle of black and grey. Wolf sprang to his feet and stood panting, his pelt matted with blood. The dog lay still. Wolf had torn open its belly, spilling its guts.

The eagle owl swooped across the cavern, flying low to decoy him from Torak. Too low. As they disappeared into the dark, Renn saw Wolf snap at its wing and bring it down, savaging it to pieces.

Torak was leaning on the altar, utterly spent. Behind it, the Soul-Eater brandished the lock of his hair in triumph.

'*Eostra binds him to her!*' she shrieked. '*Eostra lives for ever!*' Feeding the hair between her wooden lips, she snatched up her spear and thrust it at his chest.

He stumbled sideways. They circled the altar: Eostra jabbing, Torak staggering out of reach.

On the far side of the cavern, a shadow moved.

Renn caught her breath. In disbelief, she saw the Walker on all fours, shaking his head.

'Hidden Ones,' he croaked.

Torak and the Soul-Eater went on circling the altar.

'Hidden People of the Mountain! The Walker calls on you! Rid the world of this canker!'

At first, Renn felt nothing.

Then: a faint tremor beneath her hands.

The Walker lifted his scrawny arms, his voice gathering strength. 'The Walker calls on you! Let the jaws of the Mountain snap shut!'

In the cavern, the stone teeth shuddered. Renn saw a great, jutting pillar topple and fall with a crash.

'Rid us of the Soul-Eater for ever!'

A hanging column thundered down upon the altar, splitting it in two. Still clutching the fragments of the fire-opal, Eostra staggered back from the ruins. She teetered on the brink of the chasm. With a terrible, unearthly cry, she lost her balance and fell.

But as she fell, her spear caught the hem of Torak's tunic.

In horror, Renn saw him pull back. The weight was too great. He had no knife to cut himself free.

'*Torak!*' Renn screamed.

Torak dropped to his knees.

The Soul-Eater dragged him with her into the chasm.

THIRTY-NINE

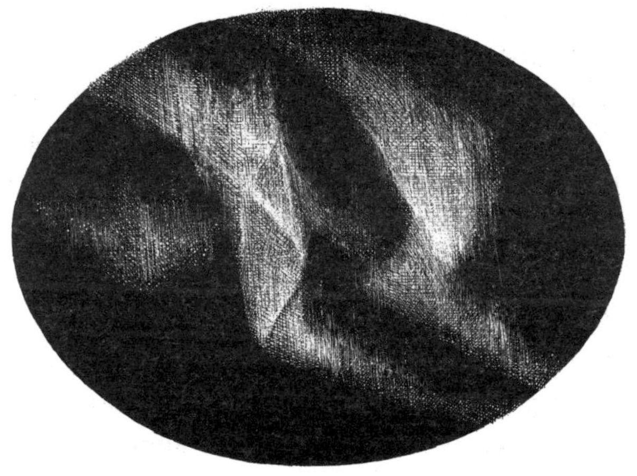

He is deep in the earth. It is cold and dark, and there is a roaring in his ears and a smell of rottenness in his nostrils. Is he already dead?

Someone is carrying him. They must be taking him to the bone-grounds.

Now they're laying him down, passing hands over his face, muttering a death chant. Leaving him alone.

The stars wheel above him. Moons rise and set and rise again. All that has been, and is, and will be, flows through him. He is a baby in the Den, suckling his wolf mother. He is running from the clearing where Fa lies dying. He is falling into the chasm in the Mountain of Ghosts.

He is back beneath the stars. Small, shadowy people are bending over him. He gazes up into strange, grey, pointed faces and moon-bright eyes.

Where's Renn? he tries to ask. Where's Wolf?

The eyes blink out. Once again, he is alone.

Still the stars wheel above him. *Coldest of all, the darkest light.* The last light a man sees before he dies.

He feels no pain; only a great emptiness. He doesn't want to die alone.

But he is so tired.

He stands looking down at his body. He doesn't want to leave, but he has to, he is so tired. With a reluctant sigh, he turns and begins to climb towards the stars.

The First Tree was shining brighter than Renn had ever seen. The whole sky was alive with rippling, shimmering green, waiting to welcome Torak's spirit.

The white-haired boy drew the hanging across the mouth of his cave and made her sit by the fire, where he wrapped a woolly mantle around her shoulders and put a steaming beaker in her hands. She was shaking so hard that she spilt most of it. Torak and Wolf were gone. They had left her behind in the emptiness.

Numbly, she took in the white stone creatures peering from every crack. Nothing was real. Not this cave, not that nightmare rush through the tunnel, with the rocks falling and Dark dragging her to safety. Torak was dead. Not real.

On the other side of the fire, the ravens – the white and the black – awoke, and irritably snapped their wings.

'It was the ghosts that woke them,' said Dark, warming his hands at the fire. 'Most have gone to be with their clans, but a few always get left behind.' He went on talking – something about his sister not being here, so maybe this time she'd found peace in the sky – but Renn had stopped listening.

Souls' Night. She pictured the Mountain clans feasting with their dead; and her own clan, far away in the Forest. Perhaps already they'd sensed that the menace of Eostra was ended.

'Renn,' said Dark, wrenching her back. 'He'd put on the Death Marks. At least his souls will stay together.'

But he hasn't got a guardian, she thought bleakly. So who will come for him and guide him up to the First Tree?

Wolf watched the last of the Walking Breaths disappear down the gorge.

He'd followed them out of the Mountain, hoping they would lead him to Tall Tailless. They hadn't. Now he stood in the howling Dark, with the wind clawing his fur and snatching the scents away.

Wolf was frightened. This was different from the other times when he and his pack-brother had been parted. This was as if a great Fast Wet was rushing between them: one that couldn't be crossed.

Whimpering, Wolf raced over the Bright Soft Cold and back again.

Above the yowling of wind and Wet, he caught a whine so high that it was like hearing light. He knew that whine. It was the voice of the deer bone which Tall Tailless carried at his flank: the deer bone which held the dusty earth that he sometimes smeared on Wolf. The deer bone which, once before, in the Forest, Wolf had heard sing.

Eagerly, Wolf sped after the singing: down the slope,

past where they had fought the dogs, towards the Fast Wet which bubbled from the Mountain.

Tall Tailless lay beside it.

Wolf pounced on his chest and licked his nose. *Wake up!*

Tall Tailless didn't move.

Wolf barked in his ears. He scrabbled and pawed, he nipped the cold face. No response.

Wolf's world broke apart. *No. No. Tall Tailless was Not-Breath!*

But the horn was still singing.

The singing sank deep into Wolf and became the strange, clear certainty which came to him at times. At last he knew what to do.

Filled with new purpose, he cast about for the scent. There: faint, but very familiar. The scent of his pack-brother. Wolf loped after it.

He hadn't gone far up the Mountain when he saw it. It was the same size and shape as Tall Tailless, but a bit fuzzy at the edges: the Breath-that-Walks.

Wolf sensed that it was lost and confused. He slowed to a trot, so as not to startle it, and wagged his tail. It saw him and stood, swaying and blinking. Wolf leant against its legs and gave it a gentle push. The Breath-that-Walks staggered. Nudging it along, Wolf guided it down the slope. When at last they reached the body, he nosed it back inside.

Tall Tailless gave a shuddering gasp – and breathed.

Wolf licked his pack-brother's face to warm him up, then lay down on top of him, to make quite sure that this time, the Breath-that-Walks stayed in.

⋀⋁⋀

Dark said he was going to fetch Renn's gear that she'd left on the Mountain, and maybe she should come too, as seeing the sun come up might make her feel a bit better, it sometimes helped him.

It had snowed in the night. Eostra's dead cold was gone. The ravens chased each other through the shining sky, and the new snow sparkled gold in the rising sun.

Dark was wrong. This didn't help. It was her first dawn without Torak.

As she crunched along in Dark's trail, she thought of the long journey before her, back to the Forest. She would have to tell everyone what had happened. And with Saeunn dead, they would want her to be the Raven Mage. A life of aching loneliness stretched ahead. She couldn't bear it.

They neared Torak's old snow hole, and Dark went in search of her gear.

'Something odd,' he said when he came back.

Renn couldn't bring herself to care, but he was shyly insistent, so she let him show her what he'd found.

Big, blunt footprints in the snow.

She thought, so the Walker found a way out. That's good.

But she couldn't feel it.

The white raven gave a deafening croak, and veered west.

Dark hurried off in pursuit. Renn stayed where she was.

The raven's wings flashed like ice as it flew down to a stream bubbling from a small cave in the boulder-field. Settling on a snow-covered hillock, the raven fluffed up its chin-feathers and cawed, exhaling little puffs of frosty breath.

'Renn,' called Dark.

Renn kneaded her temples. What now?

The white raven lifted off sharply as the hillock heaved, and Wolf burst out, shook the snow off his pelt, and bounded towards her.

'*Wolf.*' Her voice cracked. She floundered down the slope. Wolf leapt at her, knocking her backwards and covering her in slobbery wolf kisses. She flung her arms around him, but he squirmed away and loped back to Dark.

The white raven was still cawing, and now Rip and Rek were joining in. Wolf was lashing his tail as he bounded in circles round the hillock, and Dark was sinking to his knees beside it, shouting, 'Renn! It's Torak! He's *alive!*'

FORTY

The cub woke with a start. Those were wolf howls!

No they weren't. It was only the ravens making wolf noises. They did that a lot. They laughed when the cub raced about, searching for his pack.

Crossly, he slumped down and flipped his tail over his nose.

But he couldn't get back to sleep. He was too hungry.

Crawling out from under the rock, he stood at the mouth of the Den and snuffed the air.

The Light had come, but not the ravens; so no chance of any meat. It was warmer, and the Bright Soft Cold was deeper. From where the cub stood, the white hill dropped steeply, then rose again to make the Mountain. Even that looked kinder. Once, the cub had tried to reach it, but the ravens had driven him back. He'd been annoyed. Then he'd heard the baying on the Mountain: dreadful, angry dogs who sounded as if they ate wolf cubs. He hadn't tried again.

Blinking in the glare, the cub padded out into the Bright Soft Cold – and sank to his belly. Anxiously, he scanned the Up for the terrible owl. Nothing. Maybe the big tailless had scared it away.

The big tailless had come in the Dark, when the cub – who'd been trying to hunt lemmings – had fallen into a hole and couldn't get out. The cub had been yowling for a long time when the big tailless had peered in. He had a rich, reassuring smell, so the cub had wagged his tail. The big tailless had scooped him out, tossed him a scrap of beautiful slimy meat, and shambled off.

It was very quiet on the hill. Even the wind was gone. The stillness was frightening.

The cub barked. *I'm here!*

Nothing replied. The cub began to whimper. He missed his pack so much that it hurt.

Suddenly, he stopped whimpering. In the distance he heard the deep, echoing croaks of ravens. He swivelled his ears. Those were *his* ravens!

He yowled.

They didn't come.

Well, then, he would go to them.

Eagerly, he bounded through the Bright Soft Cold. It broke beneath him and he tumbled down the hill.

At the bottom, he righted himself and sneezed. The Den was high above, unclimbably high. Now what to do?

Somewhere in the hills, a wolf howled.

The cub sprang alert. This wasn't a raven trick, this really was a wolf. *It was his mother!*

Frantically, the cub barked. *I'm here! I'm here!*

The howling stopped.

The cub barked and barked as he floundered through the Bright Soft Cold. *I'm here!*

He was beginning to tire when a dark shadow came rushing down the hill – and suddenly his mother was pouncing on him and they were rolling together and she was whining and nuzzling and he was mewing and burying himself in her wonderful warm fur, snuffling up her beloved, strong, meaty mother smell. Then she sicked up some food and he gulped it down, while she gave him a thorough licking all over. After that they leaned against each other and howled their happiness to the Up.

The cub was still howling when his mother gave a whine and shot away.

The cub stopped in mid-howl and opened his eyes.

And there was his father, racing towards them over the Bright Soft Cold.

FORTY-ONE

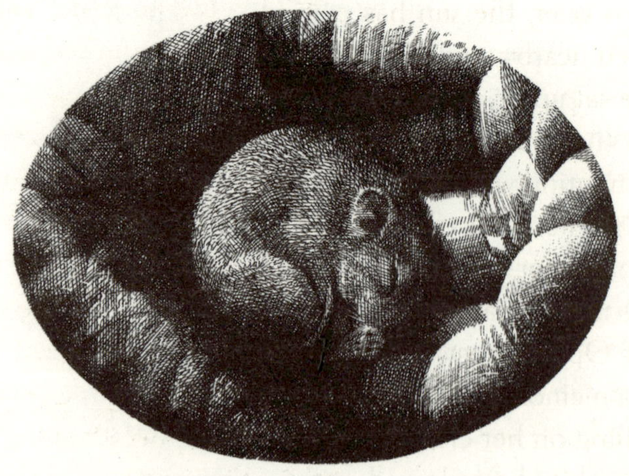

It's summer, and Renn walks with Torak under the murmuring trees.

'Don't go,' she says.

Torak turns to her and smiles, and she sees the little green flecks in his eyes. 'But Renn,' he says. 'The Forest goes on for ever. I saw it from the Mountain.'

'Please. I can't bear it.'

He touches her cheek and walks away.

Renn bit her knuckle and curled deeper in her sleeping-sack.

It might never happen, she told herself. Everything is fine.

Lying on her side, she watched the firelight rippling over the cross-beams. She was back in the Forest, in the big shelter where the Raven Clan lived together in midwinter. All was familiar: the tree-trunk walls plugged with moss, the reindeer-hide roof open to the stars above the fire. She smelt woodsmoke. She heard the crackle of flames and the low hum of voices.

You are safe with your clan, she told herself. The Dark Time is over, the sun has come back. The Red Deer are camped nearby, and Torak is . . .

She sat up. In the gloom, she couldn't see him.

But that wasn't unusual. With the days still very short, most hunting was done at night, by the light of the moon and the First Tree.

Around her, people sat calmly sewing or knapping flint. Three moons had passed since Souls' Night. To the clans of the Open Forest, Eostra and the shadow sickness were only a memory.

Pulling on her clothes, Renn went to find Dark.

His white hair glowed at the other end of the shelter, where he sat on the edge of the sleeping platform, intent on a carving. Durrain, the Red Deer Mage, was talking to him as she marked out a jerkin on a reindeer hide with a piece of charcoal.

Renn asked if they'd seen Torak. Dark said he thought he'd gone to find the wolves. Abruptly, Renn turned her back on him and pretended to warm her hands at the fire.

'What's wrong?' said Durrain.

'Nothing,' lied Renn.

She wouldn't have thought it possible that she could miss the Mountains, but she did. She missed those first days in Dark's cave; and later, with the Swans and the Mountain Hare Clan. Torak had healed slowly in body and spirit, but she had been with him. He'd told her how Wolf had brought him back from the dead, and about his father. She'd told him about the Walker, and Saeunn's last gift to her in the Mountain. They had discussed Eostra's Magecraft, and decided that it was the earthblood from his mother's medicine horn which had protected his world-soul. They had been together when he'd left his father's seal amulet as an offering for the Hidden People; and when she'd helped the Mountain Mages chase the demons back to the Otherworld – and then stayed to perform a rite for the souls of the tokoroth children; because if things had been different, she too would have been a tokoroth.

Through it all, they had been side by side. But since they'd got back to the Forest, that had changed.

'Renn?' said Dark.

'What?' she snapped.

'Shall we go and look for him?'

'Oh, leave me *alone*!'

Ignoring Dark's hurt smile and Durrain's reproachful glance, she stomped off to fetch her bow.

'Ah, Renn.' Fin-Kedinn sat on the other side of the fire, making arrows. 'Help me with these, will you?'

'I'm going hunting.'

'Do this first.'

Blowing out a long breath, she threw down her bow.

Her uncle had already smoothed the alderwood shafts and secured the flint heads with sinew. Piles of halved woodgrouse feathers lay beside him, sorted into left and right wing, and he was binding them in threes to the shafts. A large dog leaned companionably against his calf.

Fin-Kedinn asked why Renn was angry, and she said she wasn't.

Why, she thought, does he want me to say it? He knows what's wrong. Torak never seems to be around. And people keep bowing to me as if I was already the new Raven Mage – which I'm *not*, not till I say yes.

As if he'd guessed her thoughts, Fin-Kedinn said, 'You've been back some time, yet you've never asked how the ancient one died.'

Ignoring him, Renn trimmed an arrow with her knife, leaving just enough feather to make it fly straight.

'It was just after I'd returned from the fells,' began the Raven Leader. 'She'd waited till she knew I was back to keep the clans together. She chose a still, cold day; a grove of hollies half a daywalk from camp. We laid her in the snow in her sleeping-sack, and she drank the potion she'd prepared to make her drowsy. We sang to the ancestors to tell them she was coming, then she told us to leave. She made a good death.'

Renn set down her knife. 'I know why you're telling me this. The same reason you got Durrain to stay. To make sure I take her place.'

Fin-Kedinn regarded her steadily. 'Is that why you're scared?'

'I'm not scared!' she flung back.

The dog flattened his ears and pressed against Fin-Kedinn.

Renn glowered at the fire. 'It's not fair!' she blurted out. 'They bow to me and call me Mage, but they're frightened of him. Some even make the sign of the hand to ward him off.'

'He came back from the dead, Renn. Of course they're uneasy. But they do know what they owe him.'

'Oh, yes,' she said drily. 'They've even started telling stories about him: the Listener who talks with wolves and ravens. They just don't want him living with them.'

'And Torak. What does he want?'

As always, he'd sensed what really troubled her. 'I don't know,' she said miserably.

Fin-Kedinn ran his thumb along an arrowshaft. 'They say that in the Beginning, all people were like Torak, and knew the souls of other creatures. Now it's only him. Durrain thinks he may be the last. That in times to come, there will be no more spirit walkers; and all that remains will be the friendship between man and dog: a memory of what once was.' He paused. 'Torak is one apart, Renn. The clans know it. He knows it.'

Renn sprang to her feet. 'Even *you?* You want him gone?'

'*Want?*' Fin-Kedinn's blue eyes blazed. 'You think I *want* him to leave?'

'Then tell him to stay!'

'No,' said the Raven Leader. 'He has to find his own way.'

Fin-Kedinn caught Torak as he was heading off to find Wolf, and told him to come with him up-valley to check the snares. Torak was about to protest, but something in his foster father's voice made him think better of it.

Dawn was still far off, but the moon was bright, and the trees threw long blue shadows across the frozen river. Torak and Fin-Kedinn crunched over the ice in a haze of frosty breath. On the opposite bank, a reindeer stopped pawing the snow to watch them pass, then went back to munching lichen.

Belatedly, Torak noticed that Fin-Kedinn carried a food pouch and bedding roll; he asked if he should have brought his too. Fin-Kedinn said no. Some time later, he turned up a side-gully.

'But the snares are upriver,' said Torak.

Fin-Kedinn continued to climb.

The snow was deeper in the gully. Trees which had been snapped in the ice storm cast weird, humped shadows in the moonlight.

The Walker sat beneath a broken holly, retying his foot-bindings.

Torak halted. It seemed impossible that this ragged ruin of a man had once been a great Mage. Only Fin-Kedinn had seen deep into the Walker's heart, and perceived that he still possessed the skill and the spark of sanity which would drive him to cross the fells and find Eostra's lair. The Raven Leader's faith had not been misplaced.

Fin-Kedinn put his fists to his chest in sign of friendship. 'Narrander,' he said quietly.

The Walker ignored him.

Cautiously, Torak went to squat beside him. 'Walker,' he said. 'You saved my life. Thank you.'

'What? What?' snapped the old man.

'You carried me out of the Mountain. You covered my hands and feet so I wouldn't get frostbite.'

The Walker clawed a louse from his beard, squashed it between finger and thumb, and ate it. 'Hidden Ones saved the wolf boy. The Walker just pulled him out.' Munching another louse, he gave a spluttery laugh. 'A rock cut the Masked One in two, like a wasp! Now where's Narik?'

Fin-Kedinn approached. 'Come with us to camp, Narrander. You'll be warm. We'll look after you.'

The Walker drew his mouldering hides around him and waved the Raven Leader away. 'Narik and the Walker are off to their beautiful valley. They look after themselves.'

Fin-Kedinn sighed, and set down his bundles. 'Clothes. Food. They're yours, old friend.'

'Clothes, food,' mimicked the Walker. 'But where's Narik?'

Fin-Kedinn hesitated. 'Narik died in the great fire,' he said gently. 'You remember. Your son died.'

Torak stared at him.

'Ah, *here* is Narik!' cried the Walker, pulling a sleepy-looking snow-vole from his cape.

Torak said slowly, 'Walker. You told me once that you lost your eye in an accident, knapping flint. But did you lose it in the great fire, when my father shattered the fire-opal?'

The old man stroked the vole with a grimy finger. 'It popped right out,' he crooned, 'and a raven ate it. Ravens like eyes.'

Fin-Kedinn regarded him gravely. 'You've avenged Narik's death. You helped end the terror of the Eagle Owl Mage. Come with us. Be at peace.'

The old man went on crooning as if he hadn't heard.

Fin-Kedinn indicated to Torak that they should leave. To the Walker he said, 'Farewell, Narrander. May the guardian swim with you.'

As they rose to go, the Walker flashed out a claw and dragged Torak back. His grip was strong. Torak caught a blast of foul breath, and saw something flicker in the single eye, like a minnow in a murky pond. 'The wolf boy's troubled, eh? Bits of souls sticking to his spirit? The Great Wanderer, the Forest, the Masked One? He's like the Walker, yes, he got too close, so he has to keep moving!'

With a cry, Torak pulled free. The Walker gave a bubbling laugh which ended in a cough.

They left him in the moonlight among the broken trees, clutching the snow-vole to his breast.

Neither of them spoke on their way to the snares. When they got there, they found three willow grouse and two hares stiffening in the snow. Fin-Kedinn plucked one of the grouse, while Torak woke a fire and set a flat stone to heat. Fin-Kedinn split the grouse and laid it on the stone. When they'd eaten, he took an antler point from his belt and started sharpening his knife.

After a while, he said, 'I told you once that the seventh Soul-Eater had died in the fire. I told you that because I'd sworn to Narrander not to reveal that he'd survived.'

Torak took this in silence. Then he said, 'Narik. His *son?*'

Fin-Kedinn paused. Then he told the story which Torak's father had told him the night after it happened.

'Narik was eight summers old when Narrander joined the Healers. Narrander soon wanted to leave. They wouldn't let him. He was stubborn. To make him obey, the Eagle Owl Mage took Narik.' He shook his head. 'Souls' Night. Your father summoned them to what would become the Burnt Hill. He woke the great fire. Shattered the fire-opal. The Seal Mage was terribly burnt. The Walker lost an eye. All escaped with their lives ... except Narik. Bound, hidden by the Masked One. His father found the body. He went mad with grief.'

Embers spat. A grey owl swept past on its way to hunt.

Raising his head, Torak watched the lights of the First Tree fade as dawn approached. He thought of Narik and Narrander, and his father and mother; and of the brilliant, flawed Mages who had become the Soul-Eaters. So much suffering. And for what?

'It's over, Torak,' Fin-Kedinn said softly.

'I know. But I thought – I thought I'd feel better.'

'It takes time.'

'How long?'

The Raven Leader spread his hands. 'After your mother died, it took many winters for my spirit to heal.'

'What brought you back?'

'Caring for my clan. Looking after Renn.'

Her name hung between them in the frosty air.

Torak got up and walked away, then returned. 'I know she has to stay. And maybe the Walker's right, maybe I will always be a wanderer. But I can't . . . I don't want to lose her.'

He needed Fin-Kedinn to make things better; but the Raven Leader's face was hard as he sheathed his knife. 'I'll take the prey back to camp,' he said brusquely. 'You put the fire to sleep and see to the fishing lines on the river.'

Renn had forgotten to take any food with her, so by dawn she was hungry and bad-tempered. She hadn't found Torak, though she'd seen plenty of wolf tracks; and she felt awful about Dark.

The Mountain clans had only tolerated him because he was with Torak, and they'd made him sleep in a separate shelter at the edge of their camp. The Raven Clan, too, had been wary at first, though they'd changed when they'd seen Ark; a boy with a white raven deserved respect. Dark himself had taken instantly to the Forest, and adored being among people. But yesterday, Renn had found him anxiously fingering the small slate musk-ox he'd brought from his cave. She'd reminded him that Fin-Kedinn had said he could stay as long as he liked, and he'd nodded politely; but she could see that he didn't really believe it, and dreaded being told to leave.

And you were nasty to him, she berated herself as she plodded towards camp. Very clever, Renn. Just what he needs.

Torak was on the river, hacking open ice holes with an antler pick and drawing in the lines. A pile of whitefish lay beside him, rapidly freezing, and Rip and Rek were walking about, pretending they weren't interested.

Torak glanced at Renn as she approached, then resumed his work.

Unlike her, he still wore his Mountain Hare tunic, drawn in at the waist by the belt Krukoslik had given him as a parting gift: a broad band of buckskin, sewn with many rows of reindeer teeth. Renn thought he looked good, but unlike anyone in the Open Forest. She asked him if he didn't mind appearing so different from everyone else.

'Why should I?' he said with a shrug. 'It's what I am.'

She picked up the antler and scratched the ice. 'Don't you even care?'

'What's the point? I can't change it.'

For a moment, he truly seemed a stranger to her: a tall young man in outlandish furs, with an outcast tattoo on his forehead and unsettling light-grey eyes. She thought, Fin-Kedinn's right, he *is* apart. He always will be.

Out loud, she said, 'I need you to promise something.'

He threw her a wary look. 'What?'

She'd intended to ask him not to leave the clan, but instead she blurted out, 'Don't ever spirit walk in me.'

'*What?*' He flushed the colour of beechnuts. 'But – I'd never ... I mean, why would I? I already know what you think.'

Renn stared at him. 'You – *know* what I think?'

He swallowed. '... Yes. In a way.'

She flung down the antler and stalked off.

'Renn ...'

The snowball hit him full in the face.

'There!' she shouted. 'You didn't know I'd do that, did you?'

Torak was blinking and spitting out snow. His expression turned thoughtful. Renn decided she'd better run.

As she sped up the bank, she heard him coming after her. She ducked. His snowball missed her and hit Dark, who'd come to investigate the shouting.

Dark was astonished. 'Wh-at . . .'

'It's a game!' panted Renn as she raced past, yelping as Torak's next missile struck her hard on the shoulder.

Dark caught on fast, and soon the air was thick with snowballs. Renn's aim was good, Dark's was better. Torak's was the worst, but he made up for it by relentless firing. The ravens' excited caws brought the wolves bounding out of the Forest. Wolf made great twisting leaps and snapped snowballs in mid-air; Darkfur got spattered all over, as she was such an easy target; and Pebble raced about, barking and getting under everyone's feet. Eventually, Torak and Renn ganged up on Dark and pelted him until he laughed so much he fell over. Gasping and clutching their sides, Torak and Renn collapsed beside him, Wolf and Darkfur crashed into them, and Pebble climbed on top.

They lay gazing up at the sky, munching some hazel cakes Dark had brought with him, and tossing crumbs to the ravens. Then a cloud drifted over the sun, and it was suddenly cold.

Pebble wandered off and got entangled in a fishing line. Dark went to help him, followed by Wolf and his mate.

Renn flipped onto her belly and looked at Torak. 'If you're going to leave,' she said quickly, 'get it over with.'

Torak sat up. 'Renn . . .'

'Well?'

He frowned. 'Renn.'

She got to her feet and walked away.

The wolves went to hunt in the Forest, and the others returned to camp: bedraggled, covered in snow, and having forgotten the whitefish on the ice.

Fin-Kedinn glanced from Torak to Renn, then told Torak to go and fetch the fish, and Renn to find Durrain, who was asking for her. 'Dark, stay with me,' he said curtly. 'I need to talk to you.'

Oh, no, thought Renn. She saw Torak hanging back, worried for his friend.

'I'll fetch my gear,' said Dark in a defeated voice.

'Why?' Fin-Kedinn said sharply. 'Are you leaving?'

'Um. But I thought . . .'

'Do you want to leave?'

Dark shook his head.

'Then stay.'

'D-do you mean for good?'

'You belong with us. Yes?'

Shyly, Dark nodded.

'Well, then stay.' Without waiting for a response, Fin-Kedinn turned on his heel and walked off.

Stunned, Dark watched him go. Torak grinned and clapped him on the shoulder. Renn wondered why her uncle wasn't smiling.

That night, she woke to see him sitting hunched by the fire. Unusually for Fin-Kedinn, he wasn't doing anything; he was simply staring into the flames.

In the Forest, the wolves howled. Renn made out Wolf's

strong, happy song, and Darkfur's musical howls, and Pebble's ever-improving yowl.

She watched Fin-Kedinn turn his head to listen. His expression was sad: as if the wolves were telling him something he didn't want to hear.

After a while, he sat straighter, and squared his shoulders.

And nodded once.

FORTY-TWO

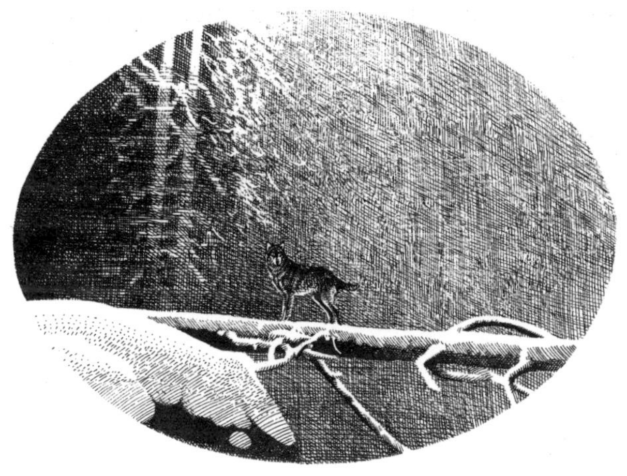

The Dark was gathering under the trees as Wolf trotted through the Bright Soft Cold to wait for his pack-brother.

He reached the hill above the great Den of the taillesses, and jumped on a log to catch the smells. He watched some of the raven-smelling pack emerge from the Forest with piles of branches in their forepaws. The white raven lit onto the top of the Den, and the kind tailless with the pale head-fur came out and called it down.

The black ravens flew past Wolf and greeted him with soft gro-gro's. As he was in a good mood, he acknowledged them with a lift of his muzzle. He'd brought down a roe buck, and his belly was full. When he'd left Darkfur and the cub, they'd been comfortably gnawing bones.

A loud crunching in the Bright Soft Cold told Wolf that

his pack-brother was coming. So noisy, thought Wolf affectionately.

To make sure that Tall Tailless saw him, he left the trees and stood in the open, swinging his tail. Tall Tailless' greeting was subdued. He sat on the log and stared at nothing, and Wolf sat beside him. Poor Tall Tailless. Still confused about what he should do.

They were silent for a while. Then Tall Tailless said, *Your Breath-that-Walks. I saw it on the Mountain. It shines very bright.*

At least, that was what Wolf thought he said. Sometimes it was hard to tell.

You are wise, Tall Tailless went on. *You always help. Help me now. Should I stay with the raven pack? Or leave?*

Wolf put his head on his pack-brother's knee, and met his gaze. And told him.

Next morning, Torak was tying his sleeping-sack roll when Dark appeared at the door of the shelter. They exchanged glances, and Torak saw with relief that he didn't have to explain to his friend.

'I'll miss you,' said Dark.

Torak tried to smile. 'My father used to say that the best thing in life is moving on to the next campsite.' He paused. 'Of course, that's a Wolf Clan saying, and I'm not Wolf Clan.'

'Well. I'm not Raven Clan. They don't seem to mind.'

'Do you know that some people are already calling you the White Raven?'

Dark smiled. Recently, he had gained a new assurance. Torak thought it suited him.

'What will you do?' said Dark.

'Oh … hunt. See parts of the Forest I've never seen before. Be with Wolf and Darkfur and Pebble.' He thought for a moment. 'I'm tired, Dark. I want to be at peace among trees.'

Dark nodded. 'Renn says that too much has happened to you, and not enough to me.'

Torak looked down at his sleeping-sack and thought, Trust Renn to understand. Scowling, he yanked the last knot tight.

'Here,' said Dark, holding out his palm. 'You haven't got an amulet, so I made you one.'

It was a small stone wolf on a thong: beautifully carved in grey slate, its eyes half-closed as it lifted its tiny muzzle to howl. 'I've scratched the Forest mark on his belly,' said Dark, 'and I reddened it with alder blood. That's quite important. The red is for fire and the Mountains, and friendship. You should renew it from time to time. The alder blood, I mean.'

Torak took the amulet and put it round his neck. 'Thanks,' he said. 'I will.'

He found Fin-Kedinn sitting by the river, mending fishing nets. The Raven Leader stopped working and watched him approach. 'I wish you didn't have to leave,' he said quietly.

'So do I. But my pack-brother reminded me of something. That a wolf cannot be of two packs.'

Fin-Kedinn nodded thoughtfully. 'You know, when you were small, and your father sought out the ancient one at the clan meet by the Sea, he said to her, *Although my son isn't Wolf Clan, I think he is truly wolf.* I finally understand what he meant.'

Torak's throat worked. 'Fin-Kedinn. I don't – I don't

know how to thank you for all you've done.'

The Raven Leader frowned. 'Don't thank me. Just remember, Torak. Wherever you go, you'll find friends among the clans. And I hope ... I hope some day you'll come back.'

'I will. I will see you again. I promise. My foster father.'

Fin-Kedinn rose to his feet. His blue eyes glittered as he put his hand on the back of Torak's neck. They touched foreheads. 'Goodbye, my son,' said the Raven Leader. 'May your guardian run with you.'

Torak left him and walked blindly out of camp.

It was a calm, sunny day in the Willow Grouse Moon, and although spring had not yet come, the Forest was beginning to stir. A woodpecker drummed in the distance. A tough little bullfinch perched in an ash tree, cracking seeds in its bill. A white hare sat on its hind legs to nibble frost-blackened haws.

Torak hadn't gone far when Wolf appeared and trotted beside him. His fur was spangled with snow, and his amber eyes were bright. Torak asked him where was the pack-sister, and Wolf led him halfway up the side of the valley.

Renn sat on a rock in a patch of sun, re-stringing her bow. Darkfur lay beside her, running her jaws over a bramble branch to clean them, while Rip and Rek perched in a tree, throwing pine cones at Pebble.

Darkfur and the cub came bounding over to greet them. Renn didn't even turn her head. Her hood was thrown back, and her red hair flamed. Torak paused to fix the image in his memory.

'I came to say goodbye,' he said at last.

She glanced at him, then went back to her bow. 'To whom?'

'Renn. I can't stay. And you can't leave.'

'And if I could, you'd want to spare me the choice.'

He did not reply.

Renn stood up and faced him, very pale and composed. 'It's not your choice to make. It's mine.'

Something in the way she said it made his heart skip a beat. 'But . . . you're going to be the Clan Mage.'

'No. That will be Dark.'

Dark.

'Fin-Kedinn saw it before anyone,' said Renn with a break in her voice. 'That's why he got Durrain to stay. Not for me, but for Dark. She says he has amazing skill. And he wants it, he really does.' Two spots of colour had appeared on her cheeks. 'Fin-Kedinn saw it all. He . . .' She swallowed. 'He gave me the choice.'

It was then that Torak saw the rest of her gear piled behind the rock.

'Torak,' Renn said sternly. 'You've tried to leave me behind before. This is *the last time.* Do you want me to come with you or not?'

Torak tried to speak, but he couldn't. He nodded.

'Say it,' commanded Renn.

'. . . Yes. Yes I want you to come with me.'

She began to smile.

'*Yes!*' he shouted, lifting her in his arms and swinging her round so that her red hair flew, while the ravens burst into the air in a flurry of wings, and the wolves lashed their tails and howled.

Down in the valley, Fin-Kedinn heard them, rose to his feet, and raised his staff in farewell.

Torak and Renn jumped onto the rock so that Fin-Kedinn could see them, and waved their bows above their heads.

Then they grabbed Renn's gear and headed off into the morning, with the wolves trotting behind them, and the ravens sky-dancing overhead.

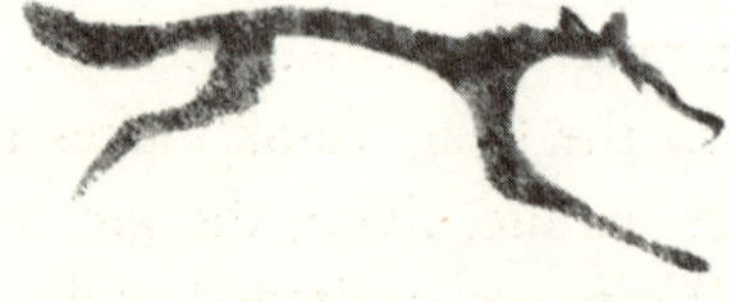

CHRONICLES OF ANCIENT DARKNESS

Six adventures. One quest.

There are six books in the Chronicles of Ancient Darkness, and all feature Torak, Renn and Wolf.

In *Wolf Brother*, Torak finds himself alone in the Forest, when his father is killed by a demon-haunted bear. In his attempts to vanquish the bear, Torak makes two friends who will change his life: Renn, the girl from the Raven Clan, and Wolf, the orphaned wolf cub who will soon become Torak's beloved pack-brother.

In *Spirit Walker*, a horrible sickness attacks the clans, and Torak has to find the cure. His search takes him across the Sea to the islands of the Seal Clan, where he encounters demons and killer whales, and gets closer to uncovering the truth behind his father's death, as well as learning of his own undreamed-of powers.

In *Soul Eater* Wolf is taken by the enemy. To rescue him, Torak and Renn must journey to the Far North in the depths of winter, where they brave blizzards and ice bears, and venture into the very stronghold of the Soul-Eaters.

Outcast takes place on and around Lake Axehead. Torak is cast out of the clans, and has to survive on his own, separated from Renn, and even from Wolf.

In *Oath Breaker* one of Torak's closest friends is killed, and he tracks the murderer into the mysterious heart of the Deep Forest. Here the clans are at war, and punish any outsider venturing in. In the Deep Forest, Torak learns more about his mother, and about just why he is the spirit walker.

Ghost Hunter is the final adventure. Set in the High Mountains, it tells of Torak's battle against the most fearsome of all the Soul-Eaters, Eostra the Eagle Owl Mage, who seeks to rule both the living and the dead.

A legend for all time.

AUTHOR'S NOTE

Torak's world is the world of six thousand years ago: after the Ice Age, but before farming spread to his part of northwest Europe. The mammoths and sabre-toothed tigers had gone, and the land was one vast Forest. Most of the trees, plants and animals were pretty much the same as they are now, although the forest horses were a little sturdier, and you might be astonished at your first sight of an auroch: an enormous wild ox with forward-pointing horns, which stood about six feet high at the shoulder.

The people of Torak's world looked like you or me, but their way of life was very different, as they lived by hunting and gathering what they wanted. They hadn't yet thought of farming, and they didn't have writing, metals, or the wheel. They didn't need them. They were superb survivors. They knew all about the animals, trees, plants and rocks around them. When they wanted something, they knew where to find it, or how to make it.

Hunter-gatherers lived in small clans, and they tended to move from place to place: sometimes only staying in a campsite for a few days, like the Wolf Clan, sometimes for a whole moon or a season, like the Raven and Boar Clans; while others stayed put all the year round, like the Seal Clan. (Thus the map of Torak's world on the endpapers of this book shows where the clans happen to be during the events in *Outcast*; thereafter, in *Oath Breaker* and *Ghost Hunter*, some of them have moved a bit.)

I've learned all this from archaeology: that is, from the study of the traces left behind of the clans' weapons, food, clothes and shelters. But how did they *think*? What did they believe about life and death, and where they came from? For that, I've looked at the lives of more recent hunter-gatherers, including many American Indian tribes, the Inuit (Eskimo), the San of southern Africa, and the Ainu of Japan.

This still leaves the question of how it *feels* to be a hunter-gatherer. What does it feel like to sit round a fire in a reindeer-hide tent in the middle of winter? Just how warm is musk-ox wool, and how easy is it to gather? I've tried to find out.

To research *Outcast*, I spent time around Lake Storsjön in northern Sweden. There I was lucky enough to hear elk bellowing as I wandered the springtime forest, and to find a whole clearing and dam system made by beavers. I also got muzzle to muzzle with some elk (called moose in north America) at an elk refuge, including some adorable five-day-old calves and a mournful yearling who'd just been abandoned by his truly enormous mother. The inspiration for the healing spring came from the hugely evocative rock carvings at Glösa, near Storsjön, which are believed to have been made by people who lived in Torak's time. While there, I was able to view some superb reproductions of Stone Age clothes, musical instruments, weapons, and an elkhide canoe. And to get the feel of snakes, I met some at Longleat, where I handled a very beautiful cornsnake and two regal, curious, and extremely strong royal pythons. I hadn't understood just how beautiful and fascinating snakes can be until I held one, and felt the flicker of her tongue on my face as she inspected me.

For *Oath Breaker*, I visited a number of the ancient trees

with which the UK is so richly endowed. I also spent time in the largest area of primeval lowland forest left in Europe, in the Białowieża National Park in eastern Poland. There I saw the *żubroń* (a hybrid of cattle and European bison), boar, tarpan (a kind of wild horse), a number of lighting-struck trees, and more species of woodpecker than I'd ever seen. In Białowieża I gained inspiration for the various parts of the Deep Forest and its inhabitants, particularly during my long hikes into the Strictly Protected Area of the Forest. I also got the chance to study two magnificent beaver dams and lodges, which gave me the inspiration for Torak's hiding place.

To research *Ghost Hunter*, I visited Finnish Lapland in midwinter. There, in the Urkho Kekkonen National Park (part of the Saariselkä Wilderness), I snow-shoed for miles, following the trail of an elk, and watched reindeer happily pawing the snow off lichen in temperatures of -18'C. I also spent time in the Dovrefjell highlands in Norway, where, on many solo hikes, I got the feel of the fells, and experienced that strange, haunting feeling of being alone in the mountains. On many occasions I observed musk-oxen, which resemble extremely shaggy bison, but are in fact related to sheep. I gathered scraps of their incredibly warm wool, which they'd left behind snagged on branches; and I often had to alter the course of my hikes when a herd of musk-oxen blocked my path. I also climbed the slopes of Mount Snøhetta (2286m). Its sudden fogs, eerie crags and treacherous boulder-field gave me much inspiration for the Mountain of Ghosts.

For all the books, a crucial part of my research has been getting close to wolves. I've gained many precious insights into how Wolf perceives his world from watching them as they investigate their surroundings, squabble over food and their position in the pack, and communicate with each other in ways that only Torak could truly understand. Watching the cubs at the UK Wolf Conservation Trust grow to adulthood, and talking to their devoted volunteer carers, has been a constant source of inspiration and encouragement. Above all, such times have allowed me to do justice to these intelligent, endearing, and endlessly fascinating creatures.

I'd like to thank all those who helped me when I was researching *Outcast*, including Sunne Häggmark of Orrviken for sharing his extensive knowledge of elk and for letting me get close to his rescued elk and elk calves; the friendly and enormously helpful people at the Tourist Information Centres at Krokom and Östersund, who made it possible for me to reach Glösa, then showed me round on a cold, rainy, but highly atmospheric day; and Darren Beasley and Kim Tucker of Longleat, for introducing me to some amazingly beautiful and fascinating snakes.

For *Oath Breaker*, my thanks go to The Woodland Trust for helping me gain access to some of the ancient trees featured in my research; the friendly and helpful people of the Authority of the Białowieża National Park and the Natural History and Forestry Museum at Białowieża; the guides of the Biuro Usług Przewodnickich Puszcza Białowieża and the PTTK Biuro Turistyczne, particularly the Rev. Mieczysław Piotrowski, Chief Guide of the PTTK, who – with the gracious permission of the Chief Forester of the Druszki district of the Białowieża National Forest – made it possible for me to see those beaver lodges.

For *Ghost Hunter*, my thanks to the friendly and helpful people of the district of Ivalo in Finland; Ellen and Knut Nyhus of the Kongsvold Fjeldstue, Dovrefjell, particularly for getting me across the army firing range to the foot of Snøhetta, thus enabling me to climb it (almost) to the top.

I also want to thank Mr Derrick Coyle, the Yeoman Ravenmaster of the Tower of London, whose extensive knowledge and experience of the ravens there has been a continual inspiration; and, of course, the UK Wolf Conservation Trust for generously giving me so many unforgettable times with their wonderful wolves.

Lastly, I need to thank those special people who have helped me throughout the series: the Orion Publishing Group for their whole-hearted support of these books from the start; Geoff Taylor for creating the gorgeous chapter illustrations and endpaper maps; John Fordham for capturing the essence of each story in his beautiful, and distinctive cover designs; my agent, Peter Cox, for encouraging the idea from the beginning and supporting it so tirelessly throughout; and my wonderful editor and publisher, Fiona Kennedy, who has encouraged me in the writing of these books with such boundless imagination, talent, patience, commitment and understanding.

Michelle Paver
2011

THE WAYS OF THE LAKE

'"Eat," she said, ladling a grey sludge over Renn's gruel.'

The Otter Clan make their grease from the stickleback, a small freshwater fish. The Tsimshian and other peoples of the Pacific Northwest made grease out of the eulachon or candlefish, a sardine-like fish, which is a species of smelt. Grease was highly prized, and people ate it with fish, roasted roots and berries; in fact, pretty much everything. They made beautifully carved containers to hold their grease, and traded it with others. They also lavished it on their guests, just as the Otters do with Renn and Bale. Many people believed that to eat berries *without* grease was a mark of poverty.

Methods for making grease varied, but a simple one was to fill a wooden canoe with whole fish and leave them to rot in the sun for several days, often adding hot stones, to speed things up. When the fish were nicely rotten, the oil was extracted by pouring it off, squeezing the carcasses, heating, and straining. As you can imagine, the grease was *extremely* smelly, and took some getting used to; so it's hardly surprising that Renn, who is new to it, thinks it's horrible. It's an acquired taste, and some American Indian peoples still relish eulachon grease today. They have a point. Eulachon grease is rich in iodine and vitamins: just the things that many of us buy as supplements from health food stores, to improve our diet.

'When the eating was over, the Otters collected all the fish bones which were too small to be useful and took them to the Lake, so that they could be born again as new fish.'

Uncertainty was an ever-present part of a hunter-gatherer's life, and it remains so today. Will there be many reindeer or lingonberries or grouse this year, or will they mysteriously disappear, as sometimes happens? Such uncertainty is particularly acute when, like the Otter Clan, you live mainly on fish. Why is it that in some years, lakes and rivers are teeming with fish, while in others, nets are empty? To deal with this uncertainty, fishing peoples had a whole range of customs, taboos and ceremonies that governed every aspect of catching, preparing and eating fish. These were designed to honour the fish and make sure that they would return.

Returning fishbones to the water was a widespread custom. Bones are the part of the body that last longest after death, so it was natural to think that they held the secret of life. Many fishing peoples, including the Kwakiutl of the Pacific Northwest, held a feast to honour the first salmon of the year's catch. This was because they regarded these first fish as scouts, whose spirits would swim back to the others and report on how well they'd been treated. If the scouts told the others that the people were disrespectful, the rest of the fish would stay away. An important part of this feast was to return the bones to the water. The Koyukon Athapaskans of north America dealt carefully with the bones of all water-going creatures, including beavers. In contrast, we tend to regard the meat and fish we eat simply as "food", perhaps because we believe we'll always have an unlimited supply.

'The fish had mysteriously returned to the Lake . . . although the Otters didn't dare remark on this out loud for fear of chasing away the good luck.'

The American Indians of the Pacific Northwest considered it unlucky to comment on a good catch, in case a demon or bad spirit overheard and made mischief. Simliar beliefs are extremely widespread. At the beginning of the 20th century, the fishermen of the Orkney islands north of Scotland never asked each other the size of their fishing catch, for fear of incurring bad luck. Today, many people all over the world don't like to boast too loudly about any good fortune which has come their way, in case they "tempt fate".

'Now they were coming through the mist: three reed boats curved at stem and prow, like water birds.'

Like the Otter Clan, the Paiutes of the American Southwest made many things out of reeds, using in particular the cat's tail or cattail (*Typha latifolia*), which the Otters simply call "reeds". The Paiutes and others like them, such as the Coast Salish people further north, were and are amazingly skilled at basketry and all forms of weaving. From reeds they fashioned boats, shelters, ropes, cooking utensils, sleeping-mats and clothes; and like the Otters, they ate the reed stems, shoots and pollen. Paiute weavers were so skilled that they made water jars of tight-woven reeds that contained the water without leaking, while allowing just enough to seep through so that the contents stayed cool: very useful at the height of summer.

'Twins, thought Renn. Dread stole through her.'

To lots of traditional peoples, twins have special powers, such as the ability to summon the weather, or prey. To the fishing peoples of the Pacific Northwest such as the Nuxalk, twins and their families were believed to cause the all-important salmon run to start. Nuxalk twins would help this along by casting small offerings of carved salmon into the water. Until the last century in some parts of England, a surviving twin, known as a "left twin", was believed to have special powers, particularly the ability to cure certain throat infections by breathing into the mouth of the sufferer.

'Now the girl withdrew a long loop of twisted sedge and wove it between her fingers. Renn saw patterns form: a fishing net, a boat, a tiny Death Platform.'

The weaving of patterns with a looped cord, known in England as "cat's cradle", has a long history. Some Inuit still pass long winter evenings by weaving figures with a loop of string, sometimes illustrating stories, for example, the tale of the lemming who fell through the smoke-hole. However, "cat's cradles" weren't always simply for entertainment. In parts of Canada and Alaska, they were woven in the autumn as a means of keeping the sun above the horizon for a little longer, while in the spring, the loops were cut to bits, to allow the sun to rise higher in the sky.

Weaving patterns in string could be dangerous, too. Until fairly recently, Inuit children in some parts of the Arctic were forbidden from playing cat's cradle when the men went hunting, for fear of causing the harpoon lines to get tangled up. And in the Orkney islands in the early 20th century, a fisherman's wife would never wind wool while her husband was out fishing, in case he got caught in the lines and thrown overboard.

'We will ride with the spirits on the voice of diverbird and reed.'

The English name for the Otter Clan's diverbird is the red-throated diver or loon (*Gavia stellata*), a bird revered throughout the northern world for its strange, haunting cry. This and the fact that it is equally at home in the sky, the water, or the forest, led many to believe it has supernatural powers. In the Pacific Northwest of America, some Kwakwaka'wakw shamans (Mages) thought loons were powerful spirit helpers who could help them contact the spirit world. To the Inuit, the diverbird is the bird of eloquence and song, and the Copper Inuit wore caps of loon skin for their ceremonial dances. To many Inuit, the skin, claws or beak of the diverbird were valuable amulets for health, happiness and skill at kayaking. So when the Otters give Bale a diverbird claw, they are giving him an amulet of great power, and one well suited to his talents.

Michelle Paver
2008

N
W E
S
THE SEA
CLAN MEET
SEA EAGLE CLAN
RAVEN CLAN
RAVEN CAMP
GREEN RIVER
BROKEN RIDGE
WHITEWATER
RAPIDS
TWIN RIVER
RIVER AXEHANDLE
SALMON CLAN
BOAR CLAN
WIDEWATER
WILLOW CLAN
THE OPEN FOREST
INCLUDES ROVING CLANS
SUCH AS WOLF
WINDRIVER
VIPER CLAN
TO THE SEAL ISLANDS
SEAL CLAN
WHALE CLAN
TUMBLERO
REDWATER
FA KI
TO WA PTA
TH F.